Summer
BLOCKBUSTER 2023

ANNIE WEST **KAREN BOOTH** **TRACI DOUGLASS** **SHARON SALA**

MILLS & BOON

CONTENTS

Contracted To Her Greek Enemy

Annie West

MODERN

Power and passion

Books by Annie West

Harlequin Modern

Inherited for the Royal Bed
Her Forgotten Lover's Heir
The Greek's Forbidden Innocent
Revelations of a Secret Princess

One Night With Consequences

Contracted for the Petrakis Heir

Secret Heirs of Billionaires

The Desert King's Secret Heir

Passion in Paradise

Wedding Night Reunion in Greece

Royal Brides for Desert Brothers

Sheikh's Royal Baby Revelation
Demanding His Desert Queen

Visit the Author Profile page
at millsandboon.com.au for more titles.

Growing up near the beach, **Annie West** spent lots of time observing tall, burnished lifeguards—early research! Now she spends her days fantasizing about gorgeous men and their love lives. Annie has been a reader all her life. She also loves travel, long walks, good company and great food. You can contact her at annie@annie-west.com or via PO Box 1041, Warners Bay, NSW 2282, Australia.

This is my fortieth book for Harlequin!

Celebrations are in order, and thanks:

To the readers who enjoy my stories. You've made my dream of writing romance come true.

To my terrific editor Carly Byrne.

To my writer friends, especially Anna Campbell, Abby Green, Michelle Douglas and Cathryn Hein.

To Efthalia Pegios for advice on Greek.

To my wonderful family.

This book is dedicated to my mum.

CHAPTER ONE

'I'VE HAD ENOUGH, DAMEN. I can't stand it any more. I feel like running away.'

Damen's eyebrows rose. Clio wasn't the sort to run from trouble. 'It can't be that bad.'

Wrong response, Nicolaides!

Even before she flashed him an outraged glare, Damen realised his mistake. With a mother and two younger sisters, he had a healthy respect for feminine temper. Clearly this was serious.

'Oh, can't it?' She shook her head and her diamond drop earrings swung. 'He's not just badgering me, but Mama too. It's his only topic of conversation. I don't dare show my face or call Mama because it sets him off again.'

She hefted a shuddery breath and Damen was horrified as he watched tears well. He'd never seen his cousin Clio cry. And though they were only second cousins, they were as close as siblings.

Clio's chin wobbled. 'It's Cassie's wedding soon but I'm not sure I can face going to it. My own little sister's wedding!'

Damen's gut churned. Clio was hurting and *he* was responsible. He should have realised—

'All my father does is rave about how *I* as the eldest should be marrying first. How you and I are a perfect match and how selfish I am not settling down with the man who's decent, honourable and suitable in every way.' She bit her lip and slanted him a glance. 'Of course, he never mentions how suitable your fortune is.'

That flash of humour didn't ease the dark cloud settling over Damen's conscience.

This was no joke. Manos was a difficult man at the best of times and he could make life hell for Clio and her whole family.

Damen grabbed her hand, felt it tremble and cursed himself for putting her in this situation. Once Manos got an idea it was almost impossible to shift it.

'I'm sorry, Clio. This is all down to me. I should never—'

'*Don't* go all macho and say it's your fault, Damen Nicolaides! I know you're used to shouldering responsibility for everyone, but you're not solely to blame.' She sighed. 'We both are. You think I haven't enjoyed going to all those A-list parties with you? You think I haven't been networking like mad, building up a list of potential clients for my business?'

'It was my idea.' Because he'd tired of fending off women who wanted more from him than a mutually satisfying fling. No matter how often he said he wasn't in the market for the long term, they thought they could change his mind.

With Clio as his semi-regular date things had been much easier. His occasional lovers were more accepting of the fact he wasn't shopping for a wife.

A cold shiver started at his nape and crawled down his spine at the word, chilling each vertebra as it went.

Gentle fingers squeezed his hand. 'You did nothing wrong, Damen.'

He focused on Clio's earnest face and wondered if she was talking about this issue with her father or the past, when clearly Damen *had* been to blame. Typical of Clio to try to absolve him.

She'd stood by him when he'd really needed it. She deserved better than this mess.

'Okay, let's agree neither of us were at fault.' They were adults, entitled to socialise together, even if they weren't and never would be lovers. 'That still leaves the problem of your father. We have to find a way to disabuse him of his expectations without him blaming you.'

Clio pulled her hand away, smoothing it down the silk dress she wore for today's celebration.

'I tell you, I'm running away. To Tierra del Fuego.'

Damen heard despair beneath that light-hearted tone.

'Do you even know where that is?'

'Okay, then, the Arctic Circle. I'll branch into interior design for igloos.'

Despite himself, Damen laughed. His cousin could do it too. She was a talented designer, up for any challenge.

Except getting herself out of this mess. It would take more than Clio's word to convince Manos she and Damen weren't an item. Especially with the prize of Damen's vast fortune in the equation. Which it always was.

That was one of the prime reasons he'd resorted to 'dates' with his cousin, to stave off the women angling to snare a rich husband. A Greek billionaire with no wife and a healthy cash flow despite the recent economic troubles was a catch. One in his early thirties with a full head of hair and all his own teeth was a rarity.

'Forget the igloos and leave this to me.'

'You have an idea?' No mistaking the hope in her tone.

Damen nodded. 'The beginnings of one. But give me time to sort out the details. Trust me, I'll sort Manos.'

Relief eased her tight expression. 'Thanks, Damen. I should have realised I could count on you.'

Twenty minutes later, Damen stood beside his best friend, Christo, who was to marry today. Christo was checking his phone, leaving Damen free to admire the panoramic view of

the sea off Corfu. But Damen ignored the vista, instead surveying the guests gathered in the villa's garden.

What he needed was a woman. And quickly.

A woman to play the part of his lover long enough to persuade Manos that Damen and Clio had no future together.

If he attended the upcoming wedding of Clio's sister, Cassie,
with a striking new girlfriend in tow, that would dent Manos's
hopes. If Damen kept that new girlfriend with him for a couple
of months, his very public companion...

But which woman?

Someone single. And attractive, for Manos was no fool.
There had to be a sizzle of desire between Damen and his new
companion.

But Damen needed someone who wouldn't see this as an
opportunity to angle for a real relationship. A woman who
wouldn't try to win his affections and carve out a place for
herself in his life.

'Relax.' Christo's voice interrupted his thoughts. 'I'm the
one getting married, not you.'

Damen flashed his old friend a smile. 'And marrying the
same woman twice. That's some sort of record.'

Christo shrugged and spread his hands. 'The first time I had
no idea how much she meant to me. This time everything is
perfect between us. I just hope you find a woman like Emma
one day. A woman who's the centre of your world, the love of
your life.'

Damen's smile solidified. As if he believed in that any more!
For others, if they were extraordinarily lucky, but not himself.
He'd lost his naivety a decade ago.

Ruthlessly he yanked his thoughts from the events that had
changed him, and his family, for ever. Today was a joyous day,
not one for dwelling on mistakes and tragedy.

Damen retrieved two glasses of champagne from a passing
waiter and passed one to his best friend. 'Here's to you and your

lovely Emma. And,' he added when they'd both sipped their wine, 'here's to me finding my own perfect woman.'

One who was attractive, intelligent, amenable and, above all, expendable.

'You look stunning, Emma.' Steph finished pinning the antique lace veil in place and stepped back. She'd never seen her best friend so happy. She positively glowed.

Emma grinned. 'You've seen the outfit before.'

It was the one she'd worn the first time she married Christo, before she deserted him on learning he didn't love her. So much had happened since, but miraculously, in that time Emma and her Greek billionaire husband had sorted out their differences. They were so much in love it almost hurt to look at such joy.

'Hey, Steph, what is it? Are you sure you're okay?'

Instantly guilt crowded in. Emma was too sharp. She'd taken one look at Steph when she stepped off the plane at Corfu Airport and asked what was wrong. Persuading Emma that she was fine, just tired after the trip from Melbourne, had taken all Steph's skill.

Steph refused to mar Emma's big day with her woes. She'd find a solution to the fix she was in, though every avenue she'd pursued so far had proved a dead end. She'd just have to try harder.

Because this trouble didn't affect her alone. She suppressed a shiver.

'Of course I'm okay! Can't I just be a little emotional, seeing you so radiant? You look like a fairy princess.'

For a second she read doubt in Emma's expression before it was ousted by another smile. 'I *feel* like one! Pinch me so I know this is real.'

Steph didn't pinch her, but she did hug her, hard. 'I'm so happy for you, Em. You deserve this after all you've been through.'

'If it's a matter of deserving...' Emma stepped back, shaking her head and clearly intending to say more, but Steph stopped her.

'Come on, Em, it's time to get this show on the road.'

Emma gasped when she saw the time and turned to the door in a flurry of long skirts. Steph twitched the veil into place and followed her out into the warm Greek sunshine.

It was a glorious day in a perfect setting. The garden of the gracious old villa made a wonderful wedding venue, with the stunning blue-green sea as a backdrop. But what made the event so special was the sight of her dear friend committing herself to the man she loved.

Yet now, as Steph mingled with the well-wishers after the ceremony, she couldn't concentrate fully on this wonderful occasion. Not because of her own worries. They'd still be there later, crowding close again soon enough.

No, the buzz of discomfort came from *him*. The man who, every time she turned, was watching her. Even as he chatted with, it seemed, every female under forty at the reception.

Steph could trace his progress through the crowd, since he left behind a trail of starry-eyed women.

But not her.

Because the dark-haired man standing head and superb shoulders above the throng was Damen Nicolaides.

Snake.

Lowlife.

The man who'd conned her into making a fool of herself.

She felt sick when she thought of it.

She couldn't believe how simple it had been for him. Steph might be impulsive but when it came to men she'd learned almost from the cradle not to trust easily.

So why had she forgotten her hard-won lessons the moment Damen Nicolaides crooked his finger? She who'd never allowed herself to be swayed before by masculine charm and a sexy body.

Because she'd made the mistake of believing Damen was different. That he was loyal and caring. Which it appeared he was, for those he genuinely valued. Anyone outside that charmed circle had to be wary. For he was also devious, calculating and utterly ruthless.

The memory of that evening in Melbourne still haunted her when she let her defences down or when she was tired. Which was often, these days, as worry kept her awake most nights.

And why, oh, why had she allowed herself to be wrong-footed by yet another plausible, smooth-talking male, even after her experience with demon Damen?

In her weaker moments Steph toyed with the idea that in succumbing to Damen's charm she'd somehow destroyed her defences and her judgement. Obviously it was now fatally flawed when it came to the opposite sex.

From now on she'd have nothing to do with them. It was safer that way.

At least with Damen it was only her feminine pride that had been bruised. Which led inevitably to thoughts of the catastrophe facing her back in Australia.

Anguish churned her insides. Suddenly she wasn't in the mood for celebrating.

Steph spied a path leading away from the villa. Picking up her long skirts, she followed it, only stopping when the sounds of celebration grew muted. She was at the top of a low cliff looking over a horseshoe beach of perfect white sand. The breeze brought the mingled scent of cypresses and the sea, and Steph drew a steadying breath.

She'd head back soon. Just take a few moments to recharge her batteries and overcome her maudlin thoughts. This was Emma's special day and Steph intended to be there for her.

'You're not enjoying the party?'

The voice slid through her like melted chocolate, smooth, rich and compelling. To her horror Steph felt something deep inside ease and loosen.

As if she'd been waiting for this.

She'd avoided speaking to Damen Nicolaides. Yet she'd know his voice anywhere. Not merely because she'd earlier heard the deep tone of his murmured conversation with Christo, but because she still heard him in her dreams.

Steph clenched her jaw and stood straighter. So he had a great voice, deep and luscious. She knew better than to be taken in by that.

'I wanted a breather. Some time alone.'

If she stared at the picture-postcard view long enough surely he'd get the message and leave.

Instead she heard the crunch of measured footsteps on gravel.

'Direct as ever, Stephanie.'

Steph bit her lip, hating the way that softening sensation spread, as if the man only had to speak and her female hormones got all fluttery and eager.

Just because no one else called her by her full name. Or made it sound like an invitation to sin.

Heat flared in her veins and shot to her cheeks.

'Then perhaps you'll take the hint and go back to the party.'

His only answer was a huff of amusement that rippled across her tight shoulders and nape. Instead of retreating, he stopped behind and to the side of her. She couldn't see him in her peripheral vision but sensed him. It was an awareness she couldn't explain and didn't want to.

'Here, I brought you a peace offering.'

A hand appeared before her, broad, olive-skinned, perfectly manicured. It held champagne in a crystal glass.

Steph was about to refuse when he continued. 'I thought we could toast the happy couple.'

It was the one thing that could persuade her to accept the drink. Did he know that?

Of course he did. He was smart, this man. Cunning. Steph recalled how easily he'd made her dance to his tune.

And you're only giving him more power now by letting him see that still bothers you.

Steph reached for the glass, careful not to touch those long fingers. She drew a deep breath, reluctantly inhaling that faint scent she remembered from before, a woodsy, warm, appealing aroma. Recognition skittered through her, a spurious sense of rightness. She ignored it and turned.

'To the bride and groom.' She lifted her glass and swallowed. Then took another long sip to ease the sudden dryness in her throat.

Up close he didn't look like a snake. He looked as handsome as ever. Honed cheekbones and a squared jaw that gave him an aura of determination. Long, straight nose, a sensual mouth and eyes of forest green that seemed to glint in the afternoon light. Dark hair that she knew to be soft to the touch.

Her fingers twitched and the glass jerked in her hold. Quickly she dipped her head and took another tiny sip.

'To Emma and Christo,' he murmured. 'May they be happy together for the rest of their lives.'

He drank and Steph found herself watching his throat work. As if there was something innately fascinating about the movement. When she lifted her gaze it meshed with his and awareness jolted through her.

No, no, no. Not awareness. This wasn't like last time. Dislike. Scorn. Disdain. Any of those would do.

'Thank you for the drink,' she said politely, as if to a complete stranger. There, that was better. Treat him like a stranger. 'Now, I'd better head back. Emma—'

'Is surrounded by excited friends and family. She can do without you a little longer.'

Steph's eyebrows rose. 'Nevertheless, it's time I returned.'

'I'd hoped we could talk.'

'Talk?' What could they possibly have to discuss? 'We have nothing to talk about.'

Was it her imagination or did that strong jaw clench? The

gleam in those remarkable eyes dimmed and Steph had the impression, suddenly, that something serious lurked behind his air of assurance.

'About Melbourne—'

'There's nothing to discuss. It's in the past.'

'It doesn't feel like it. You look at me with hostility, Stephanie.'

Her fingers curled around the stem of the champagne glass as she fought the impulse to throw the rest of her drink over his too-handsome face.

Except she wouldn't make a scene at Emma's wedding.

Her eyes rounded in disbelief. 'You're surprised by that?'

'I apologised.'

'Oh, and that makes it all right, does it?' Steph waved her hand and vintage champagne arced through the air, splashing onto the ground.

'I did what was necessary to help my friend.'

'You *kidnapped* me!' Steph jammed her finger into the centre of his chest.

'Only a very little kidnap. Christo was desperate, wondering where his bride had disappeared to on their wedding day.'

'That's no excuse. She sent a message saying she was safe. Besides, you can't blame Emma for leaving when she discovered the real reason he'd married her.'

Slowly Damen shook his head. 'They've made their peace now. But that week Christo was mad with worry. I had to help him locate her. And you,' suddenly he leaned towards her, his free hand covering hers and capturing it against his chest, 'you knew where she was.'

'You *assumed* I did.' Steph kept her eyes on his face, rather than that broad chest where his heart thudded strongly beneath her palm.

'It was more than an assumption, Stephanie. It didn't take a genius to work out she'd had help disappearing so completely and quickly. I could see you were uncomfortable keeping quiet about Emma's whereabouts. I knew if I could just get you alone and persuade you...'

The heat in Steph's cheeks turned scorching hot, exploding in fiery darts that shot through her whole body. She ripped her hand from his grasp and stepped back.

'Is *that* what you call it? Persuasion?' Her breath came in sawing gasps that didn't fill her lungs.

Dull colour scored his sculpted cheekbones but Steph felt no satisfaction that she'd actually dented his ego or his conscience.

She was too busy remembering that it wasn't Damen but she who'd made the first move that night.

Exhausted from a long week at work, she'd had no excuse to refuse Damen when he arrived saying he had a lead on Emma's location. He'd asked her to go with him to persuade her back to her husband. Steph had known Emma was in Corfu, since she'd made Emma's travel arrangements. But she couldn't admit that. So she'd gone with Damen, only to doze off on the long drive out of the city.

When she'd woken the car had stopped and Damen was leaning towards her, his breath warm on her face. Half-awake and unthinking, she'd reacted instinctively and lifted her hand to his face. He'd stilled and Steph could have sworn the atmosphere turned electric with mutual need. Then his arms were around her and she was arching into him as he kissed her with a thoroughness that unravelled everything she thought she knew about desire, and every defence she'd ever erected.

Her hands had ploughed through that thick, soft hair with a desperation that betrayed an attraction she'd tried and failed to suppress. All week she'd seen Damen, handsome, caring Damen, support his friend and Emma's family, checking on them all, leaving no stone unturned in the quest to find Emma.

It was only when they'd finally left the car for the deserted beach house that Steph discovered the truth. She'd been walking on air, her blood singing in her veins. Until Damen admitted why he'd brought her to that isolated place.

He'd hold her there till she told him where Emma was, for days if necessary. Even then she hadn't believed him. Thought he actually had a romantic rendezvous in mind. Till eventually she'd reached for her phone and he'd told her he'd taken it from her bag in the car and locked it away.

He hadn't been leaning towards her to wake her, or to steal a kiss. He'd been reaching into her handbag, palming her phone so she couldn't call for assistance.

And when she'd reached for him?

Well, why look a gift horse in the mouth? He must have decided that softening her up with a little seduction would make it easier to get to the truth.

Steph shut her eyes, trying to blot out the memory of that night. Of how she'd betrayed her yearning for a man who didn't care for her. Who'd callously used her attraction to him for his own ends. No doubt he'd silently laughed at her gullibility.

'Stephanie?' A firm hand gripped her elbow. 'Are you okay?'

'*Don't*. Touch. Me.'

One staggering step back and she came up against a cypress tree. Instead of sinking against it she stood straight and stared up into green eyes dark with concern.

He was a good actor. Last year in Australia she'd believed he was as attracted as she.

The worst of it was that to him it had merely been a *little* kidnap, since Christo had phoned soon after Damen's revelation with news he'd discovered Emma's whereabouts. Her abductor had then apologised for his 'drastic action' and driven her home, politely seeing her to her door in a painful parody of a date. All the time she'd squirmed at how she'd revealed her feelings for him. Feelings he didn't return. Feelings he'd callously used.

Steph had felt about an inch tall.

Like all those times when her dad had failed to show up, despite his promises. Because something had cropped up that was more important than spending time with his girl.

'I wanted to apologise.'

Damen's deep voice held a husky edge that might have sounded like guilt. Except Steph would rather trust a crocodile that claimed to be vegetarian than she would this man.

'You've done that before.'

Wide shoulders lifted. 'It obviously didn't work.'

'Work?' Her gaze slewed back to his face and she took in his serious expression.

'You haven't forgiven me.'

For a long time his eyes held hers, then she looked beyond him to the bluer than blue sky and the scented cypress trees. 'You can't have everything.'

She was *not* going to absolve his outrageous behaviour.

'Yet you haven't told Emma what happened.'

Unwillingly she turned back to him. 'Emma had enough to deal with. And later...' She shrugged. 'There was no reason to tell her. Especially as you're her husband's best friend. Why put her in the impossible position of disliking you when she'll have no choice but to see you regularly?'

'Is that how you feel? You dislike me?' Again that echo of something Steph couldn't identify in his tone.

Regret?

Probably more like curiosity. Steph was fairly certain most people approved of Damen Nicolaides, given his looks, charm and stonking great fortune.

She breathed deep, steadying herself. It was time to end this. 'I was brought up to be polite, Mr Nicolaides. But clearly you're too thick-skinned to get the message.' Steph wondered if anyone, particularly a woman, had ever said no to him. Had they all fallen victim to his charm? 'The answer is yes, I dislike you.'

To her chagrin he didn't react. Not even a flicker in that sharp green stare. Clearly her words had no impact on his monumental ego.

Her chin hiked higher. 'I'll be happy if I never have to see or speak with you again.'

That was when she saw it. A stiffening of muscles, drawing

the skin tight across the hard planes of his face. A flare of imperious nostrils. A twitch of the lips. And those eyes...despite their cool colour they burned for a second with shocking heat.

A moment later Steph was left wondering if she'd imagined his reaction. He looked as he always did, effortlessly urbane and totally at ease, as if his only worry was deciding whether to summon his jet for a jaunt to Acapulco or Monte Carlo.

His mouth stretched into a smile that made Steph's thudding heart skip. It was a crying shame that the man should be so formidably attractive when he was such a louse.

'That's unfortunate. I was hoping to get to know you better. Spend some time together.'

'Together?' Steph couldn't believe it. Did he really think she'd be sucked into falling for his macho charisma again? Couldn't he comprehend how thoroughly she detested him? 'You have to be joking. I wouldn't spend time with you if you offered me a million dollars.'

A heartbeat's silence, a tic of pulse at his temple, just time enough for Steph to wonder how far her strident words had carried. She was turning towards the path back to the wedding when his voice halted her.

'Then how about two million dollars?'

CHAPTER TWO

THE WORDS WERE out before Damen could think about them. But even as they sank in, he felt a surge of satisfaction.

Because finally Stephanie looked at him with something other than disdain?

Or because instinct told him the offer, despite being instinctive, was pure genius?

He'd wanted a woman who was single, attractive, clever and short-term. Stephanie met his requirements exactly. The fact she didn't like him only made her more perfect.

Except for that niggle deep in Damen's belly when she looked at him like he was something unsavoury.

Then he felt guilt. Regret.

And, he admitted, indignation.

He knew he deserved her anger, understood he'd hurt her. But how could he have stood by and watched his best friend go crazy with worry, knowing Stephanie Logan held the answers he needed?

He'd tried everything he could think of to get the truth out of her but she'd withstood all his appeals for help. When those failed he'd acted decisively to end the farce that she didn't know where Emma was. His motives had been laudable. He'd done it for the best, to give Christo a chance to find his bride and sort out their problems.

Yet it was true Damen had been too taken up with getting answers to consider his actions from Stephanie's perspective. Until she'd looked at him with those huge brown eyes full of hurt. Even her subsequent lashing temper hadn't erased the memory of her embarrassment and pain. That night Damen felt emotions he hadn't felt in a decade or more. Since he'd faced his father that fateful night.

Damen had intended to see her again, to make things right between them, except there'd been a business crisis that needed his personal attention and he'd had to leave.

Or maybe it was easier to walk away and not face what she made you feel.

'If that's your idea of a joke I don't appreciate it.'

Stephanie swung away, her loose, dark curls bouncing.

She'd had short hair in Melbourne. Short and severe, yet somehow the boyish style had emphasised the feminine allure of features that should be merely ordinary.

Watching those glossy curls swirl around her head, Damen recognised she was anything but ordinary. How could she be when she was so vibrant? The air around her crackled with energy and an inner force lit her features whether she was sad, happy or furious.

And when she kissed—

'It's no joke.'

That stopped her. She slammed to a stop and turned to face him. Her chin hiked up as if she had a chance of meeting his gaze on the same level. Yet, though she was far shorter, somehow she managed to look down that petite nose at him. One eyebrow arched and her velvety gaze turned piercing.

That was better.

Her anger he could handle. It was the shadow of hurt he'd seen before that discomfited him.

As if he, Damen Nicolaides, could be swayed by a tiny brunette's emotions! He regularly played hardball at the negotiating table with competitors, contractors, unions and regulators.

The idea was laughable. And yet...

'Obviously you're not serious. You'd never pay two million dollars to—'

'Spend time with you?' He stepped towards her, but cautiously, not wanting her to dash off in a temper before she heard him out. 'In fact I do mean it.'

She shook her head, her forehead wrinkling. 'How much have you had to drink?'

Damen felt his mouth stretch in a grin. 'Barely anything. I'm stone-cold sober.' Far from being insulted, he enjoyed her directness. Only his close family and Christo treated him like a real person these days. Most others were busy trying to get on his good side.

'It can't be a pick-up line because I know you have no interest in picking me up.'

Her voice was cool but the streaks of pink across her cheeks betrayed emotion. Instantly Damen was swept back to that night outside Melbourne. How delicious she'd been in his arms. How delectably flushed and aroused.

'So what's your game? Are you trying to make a fool of me again? Did you enjoy it so much you've developed a taste for it?'

She looked like she could spit fire, arms crossed, empty wine glass beating a tattoo against her bare arm. In her slinky green dress she looked like an angry sea sprite.

Damen felt a tug of desire. He had vivid recollections of how her initial, tentative caresses had grown demanding and surprisingly addictive.

He forced himself to concentrate.

'Come on, Stephanie. I'm not like that. You know why I did what I did.' Enough was enough. He'd inadvertently hurt her but she made him out to be some sort of sadistic manipulator. 'I've said I'm sorry. I'll do what I can to make amends for what I did.'

'Good.' She inclined her head regally. 'You can leave me alone. That will do nicely.'

With a flounce she spun away. The long dress flared out around her legs, drawing attention to her tiny waist. Damen's fingers twitched as he remembered the feel of her slim, restless body against his.

'Don't you want to hear about the two million dollars?' he said silkily, crossing his arms. One thing he knew. There were few people who'd spurn the chance to get their hands on that sort of money.

Naturally she paused. Money talked. Damen told himself he wasn't disappointed that she was like all the rest. He was pleased, because he needed her.

'I can't believe you're serious.'

'Oh, I'm serious.' He'd do whatever it took to bring peace to Clio and her family. Two million was nothing compared with their wellbeing.

'Okay, then.' Again that chin hitched high. Her eyes narrowed to suspicious slits. 'What do you want?'

'You.' He watched her stiffen and hurried on. 'Or, more precisely, your company in public.'

'In public?'

What had she thought? That he'd pay for her in his bed? His jaw tightened. He'd never paid for sex and he didn't intend to begin now. His voice was steely as he answered. 'Of course in public. This is a PR exercise, nothing else. I'm not proposing we become lovers.'

Inexplicably, though, his stomach clenched as her head jerked back and her cheeks turned pale.

As if he'd insulted her.

It reminded him of her bruised look that night in Australia after their kisses in the car. When she discovered he'd taken her there not for seduction but to demand the truth about Emma's location. He'd hurt her and clearly he wasn't forgiven.

The look in those liquid dark eyes when she'd woken to discover him leaning across her, slipping the phone from her bag, had been one of delight. Not surprise, but welcome. As if there was nothing more natural than the pair of them together.

For a few minutes Damen had forgotten why they were there and fallen under her sensual spell. It had been surprisingly potent and he'd been shocked at the depth of his response. The extent to which she distracted him from his purpose.

Ignoring a sharp pang that felt like guilt, Damen spoke. 'I need a woman to act as my companion, my girlfriend, for the next few months. And who'll keep the secret that it's a pretence. That's all.'

'That's all?' Her eyes rounded. 'What happened? You can't get a girlfriend? Have all the women in Greece finally seen past the smiles and the charm to the louse behind the mask?'

Now she tried his temper. A temper Damen was barely aware he had. For years everything in his world had gone the way he wanted it to. Except for the trying tendency of women to see him as a matrimonial prize.

Damen's chin lifted as he stood straighter. Stephanie's expression stilled, her eyes growing wary as she sensed his anger, yet she didn't retreat.

With enormous restraint Damen refused to take the bait. Stephanie's dislike of him meant she was perfect in this role. She'd never hanker for more from him than his money.

'We're not discussing my personal life, except to say that I don't have a lover at the moment. You wouldn't be stepping on anyone's toes.' She opened her mouth, no doubt to say something he didn't want to hear, so Damen kept talking. 'I need someone who can give the *appearance* of being my girlfriend.'

'Why?'

'Does it matter?'

'Of course it matters. No woman worth her salt would get involved in such a crazy scheme without knowing why. It sounds shonky. You're asking me to lie.'

'As I recall, it's not the first time you've done that.'

Her cheeks pinkened and despite his impatience Damen found himself intrigued as fire flashed in her eyes. He couldn't remember any other woman who telegraphed her emotions that way, or who regularly managed to get a reaction from him.

'That was different! I was protecting my friend.'

'As I was protecting mine.'

Her breath exhaled in a slow stream as she clearly fought for control.

'Okay, I'll bite, Mr Nicolaides. Tell me more.'

'Damen.' He stifled a sigh. He sensed he'd wait till Hades froze before she willingly used his name. That should please him, more proof that she had no scheme to become his girlfriend for real, yet he was chagrined. He wasn't used to being summarily rejected by a woman. Especially a woman who still... intrigued him.

He digested that. It could be a mistake, asking her to do this when he wasn't totally immune to the appeal of those big brown eyes or that trim figure.

Plus it would be problematic getting involved with Emma's best friend. He could do without the repercussions.

But if this scheme was to work he had to act now. Cassie's wedding was soon and this masquerade had to seem plausible. The earlier reports filtered to the press and to Manos that Damen had a live-in lover, the better. Anyone who knew him would understand how momentous that was, for in Damen's world the words 'live-in' and 'lover' never existed together.

'I want it to appear for the next month or two that I'm committed to a woman.'

She shook her head, curls swirling around her face. 'But why? As a decoy while you have an affair with a married woman? Am I supposed to keep her husband off the scent?' Her mouth pursed.

'No!' Where did she get these ideas? Did she think he had no honour? 'I'd never touch another man's woman!'

Stephanie's expression didn't change. It was a new thing to have his word doubted. Damen didn't like it.

He raked a hand through his hair, frustration rising. 'Someone has the idea, the completely wrong idea, that I'm planning to marry...a particular woman. I need a pretend lover to convince them they're wrong.'

'You led some poor female to believe you were serious about a relationship and now—'

'No!' Damen blinked as he realised his voice had risen to a roar.

He *never* shouted. Nor did he explain himself. His pride smarted and his chest felt tight with anger and frustration. Suddenly Stephanie Logan's suitability for this masquerade lessened. She had a knack for provoking him that no one else had.

'I haven't misled any woman. The woman in question has no interest in marrying me. It's her family that wants the marriage, primarily because of my fortune.'

'Now, that I can understand.'

Her tone implied no one would want Damen for himself, only for his money. That rankled. Especially as it cut too close to the truth.

The murky past raised its ugly head but he'd had years to practise avoiding painful memories. Ruthlessly he shoved thoughts of the past away.

And found his lips twitching.

A month with Stephanie Logan would whittle his ego down, that was for sure.

If he could get her to agree.

Had he ever met a woman so ready to think the worst of him?

'Listen, the woman and I are friends only. However, her father has other ideas and he's bullying her.'

'To marry you?'

Damen nodded. 'He's a determined man and he's making her life unbearable. He won't let it rest unless I show him my interests lie elsewhere.'

Did Stephanie's flush deepen or did he imagine it?

'So you *do* want camouflage.'

'Listen, Stephanie. No one will be hurt by this masquerade. On the contrary it will make life a whole lot easier for my friend and her family.'

For long moments Stephanie stared back at him. This time Damen found it impossible to read her thoughts. Was she leaning towards agreement? Wondering if she should ask for more money?

'No one would believe we were together.'

He frowned. 'Because we mix in different social circles?'

'You're saying you're out of my league?' She snapped out the words and he knew he'd offended her. 'Actually, my friends wouldn't believe it because I have better taste in men.'

Her bright eyes and angled chin signalled pure challenge. Strangely Damen found himself suppressing a smile. She was so determined to rile him. It made him wonder what it would be like if she put all that energy into something else. His thoughts strayed into scenarios that would make her blush if she knew.

'Why me?' she asked at last.

Damen shrugged. 'You're single. You've got some time free—Emma mentioned you were on holiday. And I know you wouldn't misinterpret this as a chance to establish yourself in my life permanently. The fact you dislike me is a point in your favour.'

Her eyes narrowed. 'Because any other woman would try to worm her way into your affections?'

He spread his hands wide. 'It's a possibility.'

She muttered something under her breath. The only word he heard was 'ego'.

Damen stiffened.

Did he truly want to tie himself for a couple of months to a woman who despised him? Would she even be able to play the part of besotted lover?

The answer was yes and yes.

Stephanie Logan was the ideal candidate for this masquerade. She was an outsider, unknown to friends or family in Greece. And he could trust her motives to be strictly short-term.

As for acting besotted...they said love was the opposite side of hate. Damen just had to harness all that emotional energy in a constructive direction. The way the atmosphere sparked and sizzled when they were together would convince even a sceptic that they were connected.

'And you don't want to settle down because you're busy being a carefree bachelor?' Her voice dripped disapproval.

'Something like that.'

Damen had no intention of explaining his plan to avoid marriage. He'd never have kids. Eventually he'd pass the family enterprise to his sisters' children. Damen had enough family without creating more. Especially as he'd always wonder if his wife had married him for himself or his money.

'I still don't understand why you asked me and not someone else, but the answer's no. I don't like deception and you're the last man I want to spend time with.'

Damen stared at Stephanie's flushed face, her clenched jaw and those high breasts rising and falling with each rapid breath.

He wanted to seal this deal here and now but he read the warning signs. Stephanie was a passionate woman in a temper, ready to lash out, even if it meant passing up an opportunity she'd later regret.

She needed time to consider the advantages of his proposition.

He had a little time. She was staying at the villa while Emma and Christo went on their honeymoon. And his yacht was moored offshore.

'Don't decide now, Stephanie. I'll come back for your final answer later.' Then, scooping the empty glass dangling from her hand, he strolled back to the party.

Take your time!

Because the man couldn't accept a simple no! He was so

arrogant, so stupendously sure of himself, he made Steph's blood boil.

Thinking about Damen made her pulse skitter and her breath came in hard, short bursts. She remembered him saying she was perfect for his plan because she wouldn't try to worm her way into his affections.

As if!

There was only one worm here and it wasn't her.

But, she remembered as she leaned back on the padded sun-lounger by the pool, he wasn't here, was he?

Typical of him to throw out such an outrageous proposition then not follow through. Obviously he was toying with her. She'd known he couldn't be serious. Even a shipping tycoon didn't squander two million dollars on such a farcical scheme.

He made her so *angry*. Angry enough to tell him to his face she had better taste in men than to stoop to him. There was a laugh. Her taste in men was abysmal. Nor had there really been men in her life, not the way he'd think.

Steph hadn't seen Damen Nicolaides since last night when they and the other wedding guests waved farewell to the new-lyweds.

From things Emma had let drop Steph suspected they were on their way to Iceland to see the Northern Lights. It was a place Steph longed to visit but now, like all those other places on her travel list, it was out of her reach. She'd make the most of these days on Corfu. It was likely to be her last holiday.

Steph picked up her pen and focused on her list of potential employers, but her heart wasn't in it. She'd already contacted the best agencies and there was no work.

Even when she got a new job, her troubles wouldn't be over. There was the matter of all the money she had to recoup. The wheels of justice turned slowly. By the time the authorities caught Jared, if they ever did, her money would have disappeared. And Gran's too.

Steph's belly clenched as she thought of Gran, so eager to

support her only granddaughter's first business venture that she'd put her life savings into it.

If Steph had known, she wouldn't have let her take the risk. She'd never have introduced her to Jared.

Steph shook her head. If-onlys were pointless. Jared, her one-time boss and almost business partner, had skipped the country, leaving Steph with nothing but a debt she couldn't service. And Gran with no way of funding the move to the retirement village she'd planned.

Steph ground her teeth and flung the notebook down.

A steady wage wouldn't rectify her financial problems. It was lucky she'd paid for her return flight to Australia months ago. She had barely enough for a week's rent in a hostel when she got back.

There was one obvious way out of her troubles.

Tell Emma. Her friend and her husband were wealthy. Emma wouldn't hesitate to help.

But the thought sickened Steph. She couldn't leech off Emma. This was *her* mistake. *She* had to fix it. She'd trusted Jared, believed him when he said he was moving the money to put a deposit on their new premises.

Besides, money issues could destroy friendships. Emma and Steph had been best mates since they started high school, when Steph had championed quiet Emma and in return been gifted with the truest friend she'd ever made. She'd never jeopardise that.

Nausea rose as she remembered earlier days when she'd still lived with her mother. Suddenly the kids next door weren't allowed to visit. They'd shunned her. Ugly words had been hurled and a shame she'd been too young to understand weighed her down. Because Steph's mother, battling to support them both on her cleaner's wage, had borrowed from her friend next door. Borrowed money she couldn't repay. The friendship died and they'd had to move again to a smaller flat.

Steph's mother had worked hard but she'd never been able to

hold on to money. They'd lived from hand to mouth until Steph had finally been packed off to live with Gran.

Steph grimaced. She'd been determined not to be like her mother. From the day she got her first paper round then worked several part-time jobs, she'd scrimped to save and contribute to Gran's housekeeping.

So proud of herself, she'd been. Confident about this exciting venture with Jared, a bespoke travel company, catering to those who wanted an individualised holiday experience.

It had all turned to dust.

Steph swung off the lounger and shot to her feet. She needed a plan. A way to salvage Gran's savings at least.

A way to get money quickly, not in twenty years.

Two million dollars.

The tantalising echo of that deep voice rippled through her. Damen made his crazy proposition sound almost reasonable.

With two million dollars she could buy Gran a home in the retirement village she had her eye on, with the lake view. There'd be money to start again. To avoid the trap her mother had fallen into, working low-paid jobs to get by.

Steph had loved her mother but vowed to learn from her mistakes. She'd be financially independent and never be taken in by a guy who'd let her down. Like Steph's feckless father, who'd never provided emotional or financial support and then disappeared for ever.

A bitter laugh clogged Steph's throat. Look at her now!

She'd fallen for the double whammy. Jared hadn't romanced her, but she'd believed his plausible talk about a new venture, put her money into it, and lost everything.

It was enough to make a woman crazy. She strode towards the beach path. She needed to work off this agitation then find a solution.

She turned the corner at the end of the villa and walked into a wall that shouldn't be there.

A wall a few inches over six feet tall, cushioned with muscle and smelling of the outdoors and hot male flesh.

Steph's middle turned inside out and a fluttering rose in her chest.

'Stephanie. I'd hoped to find you.'

His smile, a flash of perfect white teeth against olive-gold skin should have made her wonder how much Damen had spent on dental surgery. But she suspected it was all real. Just as every inch of that tall frame was the real deal, lean yet strongly muscled. Wearing cut-offs and a T-shirt that clung to that impressive chest, it was clear his masculine appearance owed nothing to his tailor.

Steph swallowed annoyance. Was anything about the man, apart from his morals, less than perfect?

Damen looked into those sparkling eyes and felt a punch to the solar plexus. Stronger even than yesterday, when the sight of Stephanie, alluring in her long gown, had dried his mouth. Only for a moment, because no woman had the power to unnerve him. He wouldn't allow it.

Yesterday it had been due to surprise. Stephanie had seemed so different with those dusky, clustering curls and formal dress. She'd been ultra-feminine and disturbingly sultry.

And today?

His hands closed on her bare arms as he took her in. The scarlet one-piece swimsuit should have looked demure, but on Stephanie's slender curves...

Damen yanked his gaze to her face. That was when he read something other than the scorn he'd seen yesterday.

Was that distress as well as anger?

He looked past her, searching for the person who'd upset her, but there was no one. Beneath his hold she was taut, almost vibrating, like a wire strung too tight.

'What's wrong?'

'Nothing's wrong.' Predictably her chin rose and she drew a

deep breath that tested Damen's determination not to ogle her trim body. 'Except you've intruded on my privacy.'

It felt like relief to have her snark at him, yet Damen wasn't convinced. There were shadows around her eyes, shadows he hadn't put there. She'd already been upset when she stormed towards him.

Bizarre to feel protective of a woman who despised him, yet...

He released his hold, surprised when, for a millisecond, she swayed towards him. Then she planted her feet as if to steady herself.

'I've come for an answer.' Damen folded his arms over his chest, surprised to discover his heart thudding fast.

'You were serious?'

He held her gaze. 'Absolutely. Two million dollars for a couple of months of your time.'

She swallowed and Damen repressed the impulse to lean closer, pushing his advantage.

'Think of all you could do with the money.' He was surprised she'd delayed. Any other woman would have leapt at the chance straight away.

Stephanie Logan had a contrary streak.

Surprising that didn't deter him.

Her eyelids flickered, veiling her eyes as she gnawed lips he knew to be soft and delicious. He was so focused on her mouth it took a moment to realise she'd turned that bright gaze on him again.

'Okay, you've got a deal. I'll be your fake girlfriend for two million dollars.'

CHAPTER THREE

TRIUMPH WAS A surge of adrenalin in Damen's arteries. A lifting of tension he hadn't been aware of till the weight across his shoulders eased.

Because the way was clear to scotch Manos's wedding expectations.

Because Damen hated the idea of people he cared for, like Clio and her mother, being hurt. Especially when it was his fault.

His thoughts strayed to that terrible time when he'd been the catalyst for the disaster that rocked his family. He yanked his mind from that and back on track.

Stephanie at his side, sexy, provoking, intriguing... Which of course was only important as it made her the perfect person to play his pretend lover.

Damen's thoughts slowed on the word 'lover'. Slowed and circled. Despite her animosity and her insults, she intrigued him as no woman had in years.

Another reason to remember this was purely business.

'But I have conditions.'

'Conditions?' He frowned. Was she going to try to negotiate for more money? She must guess he was desperate or he'd never have made the offer.

'Yes.' She folded her arms and her breasts burgeoned against the top of her swimsuit. Damen breathed deep and concentrated on her face. He refused to be distracted during negotiations. 'I want everything spelled out in a legal contract.'

He released his breath. 'Is that all?' Of course there'd be a contract, including a watertight non-disclosure clause so she couldn't sell her story or details of his life to the press.

'Not all.' She paused. 'I want half the money in advance when I sign.'

Damen saw colour rise up her chest and throat into her cheeks. She swallowed quickly and the pulse at the base of her neck beat a rapid tattoo. She expected an argument. Obviously it was important that she get the funds quickly.

Why? Was she in financial difficulty? Or couldn't she wait to get spending?

Damen was on the verge of asking but stopped himself. He didn't need to know her motivations, despite the urgent curiosity he refused to give in to. This was a deal. Her services for his money.

'Done.'

Her eyes widened and he fancied he read surprise there. And nerves. Why? Because she'd hoped he wouldn't agree? Was the offer of two million so alluring she'd been persuaded despite her better judgement?

Now he was being fanciful.

'One other thing.' Her gaze settled near his ear.

Now he was definitely intrigued. Despite the disparity between them, in wealth, power and physical size, Stephanie always met his gaze.

This condition she'd left till last was vitally important.

'No kissing.'

Finally her eyes locked on his and a sizzle pierced Damen's belly, driving down like a hammering pile driver. Then the connection was severed and she stared at his ear again.

'Sorry?'

'You heard me.' She dropped her arms to her sides then almost immediately refolded them. 'I'll play your girlfriend in public, but I won't kiss you, *and*,' she hurried on as if expecting him to interrupt, 'I won't have you kissing me. No lip locks. I want that spelled out in the contract.'

Damen lifted an eyebrow, intrigued. 'If we're lovers people will expect us to be intimate and show affection.'

Her flush intensified. Damen's curiosity deepened. Was she annoyed or embarrassed?

'Intimate in private. In public there are ways of showing affection without kissing.'

Damen shoved his hands into his pockets. 'I'm paying you an enormous sum. I expect you to be completely convincing.'

'And I will be. I just won't kiss you.'

'For religious reasons? Health reasons? I can assure you you're not going to catch some terrible illness.'

She unlocked tightly crossed arms and spread her hands. 'Because I don't care to, okay? Once was more than enough. I won't repeat that mistake.'

Damen was about to say it hadn't felt like a mistake. In fact their kiss had moved him in ways he wasn't used to.

That in itself was reason enough not to say it.

He frowned. 'Then how do you intend to persuade people we're lovers?'

She made a vague gesture. 'By hanging on your every word. Looking into your eyes. Snuggling up—'

'Snuggling? So we're allowed to touch?'

Stephanie's mouth thinned and Damen suspected she stifled the urge to swear.

'Don't be asinine. Sarcasm doesn't suit you.' She shook her head and those lush curls brushed her cheeks. 'There are ways of signalling attraction and intimacy without—'

'Putting my lips on yours.' He watched her blink and something inside him shifted.

Did this woman have any idea how provocative, how downright dangerous, it was to throw down an ultimatum like that? Especially to the man paying such a price for her company?

It was more than an ultimatum. It was a challenge.

Damen didn't back down from challenges. He won them.

'Prove you can be convincing as my lover or the deal is off.'

Damen saw dismay flicker in that bright gaze. Was she going to renege?

Disappointment stirred.

He'd imagined, after the way Stephanie Logan had once stood up for her friend Emma, defying both him and Christo to keep her secret, and the way she'd lambasted him after he'd abducted her, that nothing could daunt this woman. Now he read something in her expression that made him doubt. Maybe he'd misjudged—

She stepped towards him, so close he caught the scent of sun lotion and vanilla. That vanilla fragrance stirred memories of her in his arms, kissing him with a fervour that shredded his control.

Damen was still grappling with that when a small, firm hand closed around his bare forearm, curling loosely yet seeming to brand him. A shiver of something disturbingly like delight reverberated through him.

Stephanie leaned in, her eyes a golden brown that for a change looked soft and melting rather than distrustful.

He liked that look. Very much.

Just as he liked the way her lips parted as if being close to him affected her breathing.

Damen realised his own lungs were working harder. In anticipation, he told himself. If she couldn't convince as his girlfriend he'd have to find someone else.

He didn't want anyone else.

The unsettling notion stirred then was squashed as Stephanie moved nearer.

Sweetly rounded breasts jiggled a hair's breadth from his arm as she rose on tiptoe. She was so close he felt her warm breath on his face. It should have been a mere waft of air. It felt like a deliberate, sensuous stroke of her fingers. Her lips formed a pout that turned her mouth into an invitation to kiss.

Damen didn't bend his head. He stood, waiting.

He didn't have to wait long. She planted her other hand on his chest, over the spot where his heart accelerated to a quicker beat. Her fingers splayed, slid across the contours of muscle, then stopped.

She blinked and he had the impression she was as surprised by that caress as he was.

Damen expected her to pull away but she leaned still nearer. Delight surged as those brown eyes locked on his in clear invitation.

'Damen,' she murmured in a throaty voice that belonged in the bedroom. Her fingers walked up his chest. Soft fingertips flirted against his collarbone and his flesh tightened.

Something jolted through him. Delight? Anticipation? Both?

He reminded himself this was a game, a test. It wasn't real. But his body ignored logic. Heat trailed low in his groin.

Stephanie leaned still closer, her full breast warm and intoxicatingly inviting against his arm.

'You have no idea,' she whispered, so close that they breathed the same air, 'how very, very alluring I find...'

Damen inclined his head, drawn to those luminous eyes fringed with lush dark lashes. And more, by the conviction she'd finally put aside her dislike, giving in to the attraction that had connected them from the first.

Her fingers on his lips stopped him just as he heard '...your two million dollars.'

Abruptly she was gone.

Damen chilled. It felt like she'd cut him off at the knees.

He'd issued the challenge. He should have known Stephanie Logan would accept it and shouldn't have let himself get distracted. She wasn't the sort to back down.

Or, apparently, to give up the chance of a couple of million.

His lips twisted. He needed to remember that. No matter how sweet he'd once found her. How he'd respected her loyalty to her friend even as he'd cursed her obstinacy.

She was doing this for money and far more convincingly than he'd thought possible.

An undercurrent of doubt channelled through his belly. His hackles rose.

She'd only done what he'd demanded, prove she could play the convincing lover. Yet, looking into that pretty face flushed with satisfaction, he was irresistibly reminded of another woman who'd been all too convincing at feigning ardour and even love.

A woman who'd almost wrecked his life and who'd been the catalyst for his greatest regret.

'How'd I do?' Stephanie stuck her hands on her hips, looking up expectantly.

Did she expect applause?

Grudgingly Damen realised she probably deserved it. She didn't care for him but he'd insisted on a demonstration of fake affection. It was unreasonable to feel betrayed by how well she'd pretended.

'Well enough.'

She frowned but Damen wasn't going to heap praise on her ability to lie.

The muffled voice of his conscience said he was unreasonable. He'd be lying about this fake relationship too. At least Stephanie was upfront about her motives.

Yet it took an effort to shake off his dissatisfaction as he looked into her features, again wearing that familiar, guarded expression.

'So we have a deal?'

'I'll have the contract drawn up straight away. With the specifications you requested.'

Half the money in advance. And no kissing.

Maybe it was his unsettled mood. Maybe it was annoyance at how she'd dredged up negative memories. More probably it was the way she'd bruised his pride, being immune to him when just months ago she'd been eager for his touch.

Whatever the reason, Damen found himself adding a mental corollary to their deal. He'd stick to their bargain but he'd make Stephanie Logan regret her no-kissing rule. In fact, he'd make it his business to ensure she too felt this tingling dissatisfaction that their affair wasn't real.

He'd seduce her into wanting him again.

You're crazy. You hate deception. Yet you're going to lie for a man you don't even like.

Steph threaded her fingers together, willing the voice in her head to stop.

It's worse than that. You don't like him but you're still attracted, aren't you?

'Stephanie?'

'Sorry.' She turned her gaze back to the tall man whose presence filled the study of Emma's villa. Sunlight streamed through the windows, slanting across those high-cut cheekbones before pooling on the papers he'd brought.

'I said, I had the contract drawn up in English, so you don't need a translator.'

'Thank you.' Surprised at his thoughtfulness, she smiled, despite her nerves.

She should have guessed Damen would think of that. He was thorough. In Melbourne he'd been a pillar of strength for his friend, leaving no stone unturned to locate Christo's missing bride. Damen seemed to think of everything.

Suppressing a shiver, Steph crossed to the desk on reluctant feet. Now it came to the crunch she had doubts.

Except Damen would transfer cash to her account the moment she signed. Cash she'd use to buy a lovely, purpose-built home for her grandmother in the development she had her heart set on.

How could she refuse?

Yet her movements were slow as she took the chair he held out. The contract sat before her, a stylish fountain pen beside it.

She breathed deep but instead of settling her nerves, it had the opposite effect. For she inhaled an attractive woodsy scent that she identified as Damen's. Rich, warm and far too appealing.

Steph shut her eyes and suddenly she was back in the garden yesterday, when Damen had threatened to scrap this deal unless she could play the convincing lover.

She'd felt challenged, daunted and a little too excited at being up against all that magnificent manliness. Her heart had raced and she'd told herself it was because she refused to back down. The prize was too big.

Steph had felt a surge of recklessness and been buoyed up by it. It was a welcome change after so much recent self-blame and doubt. For a few moments she'd felt her old self, confident, decisive and practical. Able to handle anything. Sheer relief at that once familiar feeling of assurance had filled her.

Until she'd closed the gap between them to kissing distance. Then she'd felt like a mouse who'd unwittingly been lured between a cat's paws. The heat in Damen's eyes had slammed into her and she realised she played with fire.

She'd retreated from him and suddenly, it seemed, she'd been wrong. There was no fire in his eyes. No desire. Damen Nicolaides didn't want her. He'd never wanted her.

He'd made that embarrassingly clear in Melbourne.

She'd been relieved at the reminder. Truly relieved.

What she'd seen flash in those stunning eyes was pique. Anger that she could act the part so easily yet remain immune to him.

Well, not immune, but she'd do whatever it took to hide that from him!

'Have you finished reading?' His deep voice came from over her shoulder and her eyes popped open.

'I like to take my time with legal documents.'

Not that that had stopped Jared running off with her money.

Cold settled in Steph's bones and she set her teeth. This deal seemed the only way to recoup what she'd lost, not just the money but her control over her life.

Yet she couldn't ignore the feeling it was a mistake.

But she needed to take the risk to reverse the plight she'd put herself and her beloved Gran in. Playing safe wouldn't help now.

Even if it didn't feel safe, she wouldn't fall for Damen Nicolaides again. She was over him, or almost over him. A few weeks in his company would destroy any lingering weakness. He didn't want her, so what was the risk?

Steph concentrated on the contract, reading each sentence carefully, grateful it was set out in simple terms. Her eyes rounded at the penalties she'd incur if she sold her story, but as she had no intention of broadcasting her time with Damen, that was no problem. She had to decide what to tell Emma, but that could wait.

Her breath eased out. There it was, the payment. Half today and half in eight weeks.

And there was her other stipulation.

No kiss on the lips unless specifically verbally invited by Ms Logan.

What an ego this guy had! As if she'd *ever* invite him to kiss her.

Steph frowned. No kiss on the lips. Surely she'd stipulated no kissing at all? Then she recalled saying 'No lip locks'. She reached for the pen. Should she change it?

'Is there a problem?'

She looked up to see Damen, hands in his trouser pockets, wearing a bland expression she suspected hid boredom. There was nothing in his expression that hinted at attraction. All he cared about was convincing people he had a new lover. It was a business deal, nothing else.

Why quibble over terminology? Over a kiss on the lips as opposed to any kiss? Damen wasn't interested in her kisses.

With a determined smile Steph picked up the pen and signed the contract.

'Excellent.' Damen nodded and drew out his phone. 'I'll organise the transfer of funds.'

See? It was easy and straightforward.

Soon Gran would have the home she wanted and a comfortable nest egg too, and Steph would be free of debt.

So why did her neck tingle with a premonition that this wouldn't be safe or easy after all?

CHAPTER FOUR

DAMEN STEPPED ONTO the main deck of his yacht and paused. He'd searched for Stephanie through half the vessel till a crew member mentioned she was outside. Now he saw her, barefoot and compellingly attractive in cut-off white jeans and a red-and-white-striped top.

Usually his girlfriends wore designer labels and regularly checked their hair and make-up. Stephanie didn't bother with make-up and her clothes didn't come from exclusive boutiques. Yet too often he found himself watching her, unable to look away.

He couldn't put his finger on why she drew him. She was attractive rather than beautiful. Engaging. Appealing.

She leaned out, drinking in the view as they came into Athens, curls lifting in the breeze and every line of her body straining forward in excitement. A smile lit her face.

A smile she rarely turned on him.

A now familiar sensation stirred. It was a mix of appreciation, anticipation and annoyance. Though he'd given her time, choosing to sail rather than fly from Corfu to the capital, she was still guarded around him.

That wouldn't do if Manos was to believe they were lovers.

Besides, her cool distance rankled. He was used to fending off women, not exerting himself to draw them closer.

Maybe Stephanie Logan was good for him. Clio always said he had it easy with women.

Not this woman.

At least she wasn't trying to engage his interest, as so many other women had. Yet there had to be a happy medium.

There'd been a couple of memorable times when her defences had tumbled. Like when they'd stopped off the island of Kefalonia for some snorkelling and a sea turtle had swum by. Stephanie had been so delighted she'd grabbed Damen's arm, her face wreathed in smiles.

For the rest of that sojourn he'd basked in her warmth and enthusiasm, enjoying the camaraderie and, he admitted, her approval as he shared his knowledge about the species and efforts being made to protect them.

That was the way she needed to be with him if they were to seem like lovers. No more tiptoeing around each other.

Damen had given her time. He'd waited long enough.

He stepped into the sunshine and felt a fillip of anticipation as Stephanie swung towards him. As if she was as attuned to his presence as he was to hers.

Her eyes ate him up and answering arousal kick-started in his belly. Then, as usual, her expression smoothed out, turning bland. But Damen focused on that moment of unguarded awareness. Despite her disapproval there was still attraction.

That was what they needed to persuade Manos. Damen intended to tap into it, starting now.

'*Kopela mou!* There you are.' He strolled to her side and wrapped his arm around her, drawing her close.

Stephanie froze, her head swinging up. 'What are you doing?' Her whisper was fierce.

'Beginning our liaison, sweetheart. What else?' He settled his hand on her hip and bent closer, enjoying her little shiver of response. He'd been right. For all her disapproval, Stephanie felt this attraction too. His mouth curved in a lazy smile. 'We're in Athens, or almost, and any one of those vessels you're watching could have curious eyes turned this way.'

His gesture encompassed the traffic in and out of the busy port. 'The *Amphitrite* is well known and there's money in selling photos of an elusive billionaire and his new lover.'

'Photos?' Her eyes widened as she turned to stare at the harbour. 'You mean the paparazzi keep you under surveillance?' Her voice sounded brittle with shock.

Had he just destroyed an innocent's illusions? But it was better she was prepared for the inevitable media speculation. An unknown Australian, appearing at his side out of nowhere, would provoke interest.

Was that why he'd been so determined it should be Stephanie at his side? To get maximum coverage for this masquerade?

It was convenient to think so but Damen knew his motives were more complex. More personal.

'There's nothing to be scared of. I'll protect you. They won't invade our privacy.' Or they'd suffer the consequences. 'Especially if we provide some photo opportunities.'

He turned, curling his index finger under her chin and lifting her face towards his.

To her credit she didn't shy away, but nor did she look lover-like. If there was a photographer out there with a telephoto lens they would see his companion wary rather than enthusiastic. He needed to remedy that, quickly.

Steph told herself there was nothing to be nervous about in broad daylight on the open sea. Except the idea of hidden cameras trained on them sent tension darting through her. Plus Damen's expression did little to reassure.

He barely touched her, yet the warmth of the skin-to-skin touch felt intimate. It was a lover's caress.

No other man had touched her like this.

There'd been no lovers. Her early experiences, with a

stressed, distracted mother and an absent father who never kept his promises had made her wary of emotional intimacy. And from her teens on she'd put in long hours working while her peers partied. The closest she'd come to letting down her guard and giving in to passion had been with Damen Nicolaides.

How he'd gloat if he knew! It would feed his already enormous ego.

'What are you doing?' Was that reedy voice hers?

'Providing a photo opportunity.' His mouth kicked up at one side, driving a groove down his cheek that was ridiculously sexy. Or maybe it was his intense stare that was sexy, as if he was aware of nothing but her.

Steph breathed out slowly, finding calm. The notion of Damen unaware of anything but her was laughable. This was an act for the benefit of the public. The realisation eased her racing pulse.

'You really think there are paparazzi out there?'

He shrugged. 'Probably. It pays to be careful. From now on it's best we act in character.'

In character.

As lovers, he means.

Steph gulped and told herself she could do this. She had to. She'd accepted a great wad of his money and it was currently being used to purchase Gran's new home.

Yet now it came to the crunch, with his body a mere hand span away and his breath feathering her face, the warning voice Steph had ignored for days became strident.

'What is it, Stephanie?' Damen actually sounded concerned, which made her wonder what he read in her face.

She tried to smooth her expression. 'This is tougher than I expected.'

Because in his embrace she felt things she'd vowed she wouldn't. Even knowing this was a charade, it was hard not to respond to the evocative tenderness of his touch and the hint of blatant possessiveness.

That scared her. Steph didn't want to be possessed by any man. She was her own woman. She'd learned never to be reliant and had no intention of forgetting that lesson, especially after the way Damen had made a fool of her.

'You've got cold feet?' His fingers tightened on her waist and a crease was carved between those ebony eyebrows. 'It's too late. You signed a contract.'

His voice was terse, at odds with the lingering hint of a smile.

The disparity chilled her, sending a shiver scudding down her backbone. It was proof that appearances and embraces could lie. They had before with this man.

'Of course I've got cold feet. I'm not used to living a lie. But,' she said when he opened his mouth, 'I won't go back on my word.'

Especially since she no longer had the money he'd paid her.

'I knew I could count on you.' His voice dropped a notch, burring like rough suede across her bare neck and arms.

That, too, was a lie. That hint of desire in his voice. Yet some fatally feminine part of her responded, secretly thrilled.

Steph swallowed.

She was in trouble. Deep trouble.

But there was no escape.

His face tilted and his hand glided along to her jaw, her cheek, brushing her unruly hair back. She'd been too busy before she came to Greece and a hairdresser had been an unnecessary expense. She wished she'd had her hair cut short again, as strong fingers tunnelled through her curls, massaging her scalp in delicious circles that loosened her tense shoulders.

Her blood thickened and slowed and she found herself leaning into his touch.

Not to convince unseen eyes that they were lovers, but because Damen's touch was magic. Slow, sure and sensual, it mocked her determination to keep her distance.

He'd done this before, pretended attraction when there was none, yet even pride couldn't make her pull away.

If she did he'd realise his touch bothered her.

She was caught whatever she did.

Steph opened her mouth to say something, anything to divert him into conversation, when that arm at her waist tightened and his head lowered.

For a second shock held her still, then her hands went to his broad chest, flat against hot muscle and thin cotton as she tried to hold him at a distance.

She needn't have worried. He stopped a scant centimetre away, but his mouth was at her temple, lips scraping her skin as he spoke.

'Try not to look fazed. We're supposed to be lovers, remember?'

How could she forget?

With an effort that felt shockingly like no effort at all, Steph made her hands slide up his chest. Of their own volition they continued, curling around his neck. It felt hard and strong, the flesh there smooth and warm.

It was like the day he'd insisted she prove she could act the part of his lover. She'd made the first move, pleased with her boldness, until proximity to Damen made her body go soft and eager. As if it had been waiting to get close to him.

'Much better,' he purred against her forehead and to Steph's dismay she felt the words like an unfurling ribbon that trailed down through her body.

'You're not supposed to kiss me,' she protested, far too aware of the graze of his mouth.

The protest sounded limp, but she needed words to keep him at a distance when her body refused to obey her command not to melt against him.

'Hardly a kiss, *kopela mou.*' A pause and then he spoke again, his voice deeper than before. 'You'd know it if I kissed you.'

She would indeed. She had perfect recall of the last time. Of how she'd thrown caution to the wind as their mouths fused and desire had quaked through her.

It had been wonderful and cataclysmic at the same time, leaving the defences she'd spent a lifetime constructing in ruins.

'Not that I will, of course, given our contract.' He paused. 'Not without a specific, spoken invitation.'

Steph licked her lips. She was about to blurt out that she'd never give such an invitation, when instinct stopped the words. It would sound like a challenge and the last thing she needed was to provoke Damen Nicolaides into seeing this as a game of one-upmanship.

'How long do we have to stay like this?'

She hitched a breath, conscious of his torso so close she could almost feel it abrading her budding nipples. Heat drenched her. She told herself it was a hot day and Damen held her too close. But Steph wasn't that innocent. This heat came from deep inside. From the feminine core that gloried in being held by Damen. The part of her that had sprung to life once before in his arms.

That untamed, unthinking woman terrified her. She couldn't let her loose. She had to keep control.

'You make this sound like a chore, Stephanie.' Once more his voice drifted low on her name to a note that settled in her bones.

Steph drew a deep breath then stilled when it brought her breasts into contact with Damen. Did she imagine a change in the tempo of his breath tickling her forehead? A tightening in the clasp of that hand at her waist?

She didn't have time to be sure, for Damen stepped back, just enough to watch her with enigmatic eyes. For a moment she felt as if she were sinking out of her depth. Then his mouth crooked up in that slight smile she was coming to know and enjoy far too much.

'But practice makes perfect and in Athens we'll get plenty of practice.'

'We will?' Steph rubbed her palms together, trying to erase the tingling memory of his flesh against hers.

'Of course. I have business here but we'll go out too. Plenty of opportunities to be seen together.'

It was a timely reminder that this was for show. The closeness, his touch, the way his gaze lingered.

'Will she be in Athens? The woman you were involved with?'

That cleared her head like a shower of ice water. The thought of the woman who was the reason for this charade. No matter what Damen said, she was clearly important to him.

Steph reserved judgement on whether the mystery woman was really just Damen's friend or, more likely, his lover. Yet she felt something akin to dislike for the unknown woman.

Because Damen cared so much for her that he'd embark on this outrageous scheme?

It couldn't be that. Steph wasn't *jealous*.

'That needn't concern you.' His hand dropped and the remnants of that satisfied smile disintegrated.

So she was in Athens. Would Steph meet her? Would she even know her if she did?

She folded her arms and looked straight back at that narrowed green stare.

'This masquerade won't work if you're secretly meeting a lover on the side. Someone's bound to find out—'

Damen shook his head and said something sharp in Greek. Steph didn't need to understand the language to hear scorn and impatience.

'How many times do I have to tell you she's not my lover? I don't have a lover!' His voice rose as he made a dismissive gesture. 'The only girlfriend I have is you, Stephanie.'

This was the second time she'd provoked an unguarded response from Damen. Steph told herself she shouldn't be pleased at puncturing his formidable self-assurance. At seeing emotion flare in those heavy-lidded eyes. Yet she was. The sight made her feel less helpless, less a mere pawn caught in his machinations.

'Careful, Damen.' She wagged her finger. 'If there are paparazzi out there, they'll see you scowling at me. That would destroy the illusion you care about me before we start.'

Even if he did look dramatically sexy with those dark eyebrows scrunched and that strong jaw honed tight.

For a second he didn't react. Then Damen surprised her with a crack of laughter, his face creasing into a smile of rueful amusement that tugged at something deep inside her.

'What they'll think is that we've had a spat. But that's okay because it gives us the chance to make up, very publicly.'

His eyes danced and anticipation swirled through her at the thought of making up with Damen.

Till she realised what she was doing and slammed a brake on her thoughts.

She'd assumed a few days on his yacht would cement her dislike but her feelings for Damen were ambiguous. He got to her in a way no other man did. Even the way he insisted on using her full name, lingering on the syllables as if savouring them, unravelled her defences.

Steph leaned on the railing, needing to look at something other than this man who disturbed her so easily. She saw a marina filled with luxury yachts. Some almost as enormous and beautiful as the *Amphitrite*. Maybe there was some billionaire's convention in town.

'Are we staying on the yacht?'

Not that 'yacht' seemed the right word for a ship with its own helipad, cinema, glass-bottomed pool and umpteen guest suites.

Steph had been in awe, until Damen's insistence that she was free to use anything she wanted, and the genuine friendliness of the staff, put her at ease. She'd earmarked a cosy corner of the library as her own and grown used to the state-of-the-art gym equipment. Playing the doting girlfriend would be easier if she could retreat to her comfortable stateroom.

'No, we'll head to my apartment.'

'Just an apartment?' She turned to look at him as he joined her at the railing, trying to hide her nerves. Suddenly this masquerade felt uncomfortably real. 'You surprise me. I thought you'd have a posh town house.'

Actually, she hadn't thought about it. The opulence of his superyacht had been a revelation. She'd known Damen was rich, but this level of wealth was far beyond her experience.

'Sorry to disappoint.' The curve of his mouth told her that her jab didn't bother him. 'But in Athens I find an apartment convenient. I'm sure you'll find it comfortable.'

'I'm sure I will.' If his yacht was any indication it would be gorgeous and purpose built. He probably owned the rest of the building too.

'And it's convenient for shopping. I've had a list drawn up of the boutiques that might be best for you.'

'That's kind.' If a little strange. 'But I doubt I'll be shopping.'

If she had time in Athens she intended to use it to see the sights she'd read about. Besides, the money she'd got from Damen had already been sent to Australia for Gran and to put towards the business debt Jared had left her with. The business loan still needed servicing even though there was now no business.

Damen's eyebrows lifted. 'You'll need new clothes.'

Steph straightened, pushing her shoulders back. Her hackles rose. 'Are you saying I don't measure up to your exalted standards?'

Damen read the flash of heat in those wide brown eyes and felt a frisson of awareness.

It was like that each time he and Stephanie argued. Or touched.

Her pride and contrariness were a nuisance. Yet he relished each clash, revelled in the moments when Stephanie shared her feelings and thoughts instead of keeping her distance.

This was when he felt closest to the passionate woman who intrigued him despite his best intentions.

Logic said she could be trouble. But Damen had been careful and sensible for a long, long time. Would it be so wrong to give free rein to this attraction?

Damen shook his head. 'Charming as your casual clothes are, they won't do. You're my girlfriend now.'

Though if she really were he'd be happy for her to dress as she did.

His gaze dropped to the cropped red and white top that barely reached her waist. She looked feisty, fresh and sexy. He'd found it almost impossible to keep his hand firm on the waistband of her jeans and not let it slide under the loose-fitting top to her warm flesh. Not because he didn't want to but because he didn't want to spook her. She was already jittery.

As far as he personally was concerned, Stephanie didn't need couture clothes. She was alluring whatever she wore. But this was about image.

Predictably her hands jammed onto her hips and her chin tilted. 'Because your high-class friends wouldn't believe we're an item? Are you ashamed to be seen with me as I am?'

'I'm not ashamed, Stephanie.' It was something quite different he felt when he was with her.

Would she feel so confident surrounded by socialites wearing expensive fashions? This wasn't just about looking good for the press but protecting Stephanie from condescension. Not from his friends or family. They wouldn't care, but there'd be others who'd underrate her because of her simple clothing choices. Damen refused to put her in that position.

He sighed. Why must she make this tough? Pride he understood but surely she was eager to get spending.

'Do you have an outfit for a wedding?'

Her brow crinkled. He could almost see her reviewing the contents of the single suitcase she'd brought.

'Your bridesmaid's dress is very attractive—' that was a masterly understatement, given the effect the sight of her in it had on his libido '—but as my girlfriend you'd have something new for the wedding we're attending at the end of next week.'

'You didn't mention a wedding.'

'I'm mentioning it now. And there'll be social events in Athens. The women will wear designer originals, high heels, jewellery, that sort of thing.' He paused. 'Have you got something suitable in your luggage?'

'Of course not. I came for a relaxed holiday on Corfu.'

'Then you'll feel more comfortable with a new wardrobe.'

Her gaze drifted from his and colour rose in her cheeks. 'I can't afford designer clothes.'

Damen stared. He'd just deposited a million dollars in her account. Surely she could afford a couple of dresses?

The silence lengthened and his patience wore thin. Stephanie was playing this part for the money, he understood that, but was she intent on screwing every cent she could from him?

Memories stirred of another woman who'd milked him for cash. And he, young and besotted, hadn't seen her for what she was till it was almost too late.

Damen's jaw gritted, his nostrils flaring in disdain as the woman before him stood silent, her eyes not quite meeting his.

So much for believing her to be difficult but fundamentally honest. It seemed she too was grasping when it came to getting her hands on his money.

He bent in a mocking bow, hiding his disappointment with a grim smile. 'Then allow me, *kopela mou*. I'll buy the clothes you need. But I reserve a buyer's right to choose.' His smile widened. 'It will be a pleasure, dressing you.'

CHAPTER FIVE

STEPHANIE MET THAT glittering stare and wolfish smile and felt about an inch tall. Damen made her feel like a commodity he'd bought for his pleasure.

He talked about dressing her but the rapacious gleam in his eyes spoke of undressing.

She swallowed the knot of discomfort blocking her throat. He was aiming to unsettle her because she'd annoyed him. Fortunately she was wise to the fact his supposed attraction was a sham.

That didn't make her feel better.

It didn't take a genius to see Damen thought she angled to get whatever she could from this deal. He thought her a gold-digger.

She opened her mouth to explain then stopped. She had no intention of explaining the tangle of her financial affairs to this incredibly successful businessman. If she said she no longer had the money he'd pepper her with questions. The fiasco of her failed business venture, stolen funds and, above all, her grandmother's precarious financial position because she'd trusted Steph—no, she wasn't ready to share all that.

Pride rescued her.

'Thanks, Damen. I'm quite capable of choosing an outfit for a wedding. Though you have the right of veto, since this is your scheme and you know the people.' Anxiety shimmered through her at the thought of parading in unfamiliar finery amongst a crowd of sophisticates, pretending to be someone she wasn't. Steph wasn't and never would be a glamazon. She knew what she looked good in but her knowledge of designer originals was zero. 'Other than that, I'll get by with what I've brought.'

It wouldn't be pleasant. She knew cheap and cheerful would only go so far when surrounded by elegant and rich, but she'd get by. She'd never see these people again and if they were so hung up on her wardrobe they weren't people she wanted to know.

Damen's eyes narrowed as if her words puzzled him. 'You'll arouse suspicion if you don't dress like my lover.'

Steph raised her eyebrows. 'You expect me to wear a negligee in public?' She had no doubt his women wore silk and lace, enticing and scanty.

Instead of responding in anger, Damen smiled, a slow, heart-kicking smile that made her legs wobble.

How did he do that when she was annoyed with him?

'I prefer my women to be discreet in public. It's a different matter in private, of course.'

Steph searched for a crushing response but he spoke first.

'How about a compromise? Wear your clothes when you're alone but when you're out with me wear something new, which I'll buy. Yes?'

She wanted to say no. Agreeing would cement his belief that she grasped for every penny she could get. But reason prevailed. She'd look out of place if she stuck to her guns. That would only make her more uncomfortable.

Reluctantly she nodded. 'Okay. A couple of outfits.'

The shopping expedition didn't start well.

Steph's heart sank as the limousine stopped in a street that screamed wealth and exclusivity. Damen gestured to a boutique with a single dress in the window, a dress that even Steph with her limited knowledge knew was a couture original. She swallowed. It was so unlike the chain stores she frequented. Appallingly she felt nervous.

Worse, she felt like a complete fraud.

She *was* a fraud. She was embarking on a big, fat lie.

She just hoped no one would get hurt as a result. Despite Damen's assurances she wondered if his female friend truly had no hopes of a permanent relationship. How would she feel when she saw Steph with Damen?

Steph stepped onto the heat of the Athens pavement, telling herself not to be intimidated. Yet a lifetime of scrimping, determined to avoid the financial difficulties that had beset her mother, had its downside. Steph was used to searching for bargains, not dropping a wad of money on the latest fashions.

'Sorry, Stephanie. I have to take this call.' Damen looked at his phone. 'You start and I'll join you.'

Steph lifted her chin, intensely aware that her dusky pink cotton sundress and flat sandals were out of place here. Memories hovered, of early years when she'd been teased by schoolmates about her ill-fitting clothes, cast-offs her mother had found at a charity shop.

But only for a moment. It had been a long time since she let anyone make her feel uncomfortable because of what she could or couldn't afford.

Yet her heart sank as she entered the shop with its plush, pale carpet and hushed atmosphere. Even the air smelled different. Expensive. Two saleswomen turned, poised, elegant and wearing polite smiles that dimmed as they took her in.

Her *'Kalimera'* was greeted with a cool nod from the older woman and a stare from the younger. Stephanie made herself walk further into the store, towards a sparsely populated rack of clothes. She hadn't reached it when the older saleswoman stepped forward, planting herself before the clothes.

'Can I help you with something specific?' She spoke English, clearly pegging her as a foreigner.

Steph told herself she imagined the protective way the woman stood between her and the rack.

'Thanks. I want a dress, but I prefer to browse.'

After a moment the woman moved aside, hovering too close as Steph examined the clothes.

That was just the beginning. Every time she moved, one of the women shadowed her. When she paused near a display of handbags, all ostentatiously embellished with a well-known couturier's logo, the younger saleswoman deliberately blocked her path.

Steph's eyes widened. She'd told herself she was oversensitive but she didn't imagine this. They thought her a potential shoplifter. Heat filled her cheeks and she was torn between outrage and embarrassment. Outrage won.

She opened her mouth to speak when a deep voice made her turn.

'Stephanie? Is everything okay?'

Damen stood in the doorway, wide shoulders silhouetted against the sunshine. But there was enough light from the overhead chandelier to see he wasn't happy. That chiselled jaw was tight and a scowl marred his handsome face.

'What's going on here?' His tone was peremptory, but his ire wasn't directed at her. Steph watched the saleswomen stiffen and their eyes widen as he surveyed them. It was a look that could freeze at fifty paces.

'Nothing's going on,' Steph said, her voice a little over-loud. There was no way she'd buy clothing here. Her skin crawled at how they'd made her feel. 'I can't see anything I want to wear.'

Damen stalked across the room, his gaze now focused on her, and she felt a glow begin deep inside. Long fingers threaded through hers as he stood close and heat spread through her whole body.

'You're sure? If there's something you want...' He waved towards the handbags.

Instantly the younger saleswoman stepped aside, her smile

wide but lacking the smug confidence she'd shown before. 'This is a very exclusive range.' Her words tripped over themselves with eagerness. 'We're the only stockists in the country and I'm sure madam—'

Steph interrupted. She couldn't stand that fake friendliness. 'No, thanks. They're not my style.'

Damen looked from her to the other women and then to the leather goods. 'You're right. They're too gaudy. You don't need to wear someone else's name on your accessories to look good, *agapi mou*. Leave them for someone who feels the need to buy attention.'

Steph swallowed a gasp that was part giggle as she saw the other woman's eyes bulge. But it was true. The bags might be the latest must-have fashion but they were little more than advertisements for the designer whose logo was emblazoned on them so prominently.

Damen whisked her outside, not lowering his voice as he promised to take her somewhere with a better selection.

'You don't need to hold me so tight,' she murmured as they marched down the street.

'Sorry.' His grip on her arm eased and he slowed. 'That pair—'

'Forget them. They're not worth worrying about. I was about to leave when you arrived. There really was nothing there I wanted.' She refused to be treated that way.

Nevertheless, she admitted to herself at least, seeing Damen angry on her behalf made her feel good. She didn't need him to rescue her. She could fend for herself. But his protectiveness, for that was what it had been, warmed her.

Especially since Steph had seen their horror at Damen's scathing words and dismissive look. It was clear they'd recognised him or at least his air of authority, a man who expected and got the best.

Which set that nervous feeling going again in her stomach. She still had the ordeal of another high-end boutique to face.

But contrary to expectations she fared better in the next shop. It was just as exclusive with its white-on-white minimalism, stylish décor and vast arrangements of lilies scenting the air. But Steph was welcomed by a woman with a sincere smile. Even better, as well as clothes in the pale shades that had featured in the last place, the hangers also held bright colours.

Steph gravitated towards them, her hand lifting towards a fall of shimmering turquoise silk.

'How about this?' Damen picked up a dress in chic shades of cream and camel.

Steph's 'No, thanks,' coincided with the saleswoman declaring it was the wrong colour palette for her.

Damen suppressed a smile of satisfaction as Stephanie's expression lightened when the boutique owner insisted she should wear bold colours. Soon the pair were nodding, murmuring about cut and colour as they pored over the floor stock.

Clearly she'd got over her apparent unwillingness to get a new wardrobe. He'd thought she would.

Yet Damen was curious about their disagreement on the yacht. He'd sensed her protest about new clothes wasn't just so she didn't look too eager. As if he really had dented her pride.

He settled in a chair and drew out his phone, skimming messages. But he read none, his attention all on Stephanie.

He'd seen her frozen look of dismay in the last boutique and something inside him had given way. He'd wanted to savage the woman who'd put that expression on her face. As much as he'd wanted to hold and comfort Stephanie.

Except her rigid expression reminded him of the way she'd been with him in Melbourne. After they'd kissed. Her look had made him feel like he'd betrayed her. Despite the bigger picture and his need to help his best friend find his missing wife.

Now he felt like he'd done it again. Hurt her.

Why? Because he'd paid her to play a role? He hadn't forced

her hand. Or because he'd left her alone with those snobby witches down the street?

Stephanie could stand up for herself. She didn't need him as a champion. Damen remembered Emma saying her friend was strong and independent, that Stephanie had stuck up for her when they'd been kids together.

Yet his conscience prickled. And something else. Something more than guilt.

Whether he was responsible or not, Damen didn't want to see her look like that again, pale with distress. Her barbs he could cope with. He almost enjoyed them. Her rare smiles ditto. But that frozen look of stunned hurt pierced something behind his ribs.

Fortunately movement from the rear of the boutique distracted him from his churning thoughts. The saleswoman stepped back from the changing room, looking satisfied. She was followed by...

Damen breathed deep and told himself to ignore the strange little jitter that made his pulse uneven.

It was simply Stephanie dressed up. Not in a pretty bridesmaid's gown. In an outfit designed with one aim. To seduce.

He'd seen his share of seductive women. Had bedded them too. Yet the sight of Stephanie in that clinging outfit sent a blow to the solar plexus that hampered his breathing.

It was a jumpsuit. Was that what you called it? That sounded too prim and old-fashioned for this. She wore silky material that wasn't red and wasn't dark pink but somewhere in between. The neckline lifted to a high collar, but her shoulders were completely bare and there was a narrow slit down between her breasts that gave teasing glimpses of her cleavage. A cleavage that seemed unfettered by a bra. The fabric clung to her waist and hips before falling in loose folds to her feet. Feet encased in high-heeled sandals. She looked fabulous. Sophisticated and effortlessly sexy.

Except he knew the high tilt of that chin. He'd learned that pugnacious angle could signal anger or doubt.

Damen got to his feet, his phone falling. 'You don't like it?'

She swung around, drawing a breath that made her breasts rise against the thin fabric. Heat stirred low in his body. He kept his eyes on hers and read what looked like concern.

She bit her lip and lifted those slender bare shoulders.

It was ridiculous. Except for her arms and shoulders she was covered to her toes. Yet the sight of that flesh, looking velvety soft against the contrasting material, seemed more enticing than if she'd worn a bikini.

'I'm not sure.' Her gaze turned to the full-length mirrors at the back of the room and Damen caught an expression that hovered between wistful and worried.

'It might have been made for you, madam,' the saleswoman said. 'That colour is perfect.'

Still Stephanie looked uncomfortable.

Damen cleared his throat. 'I like it.' Too much. Far, far too much. He looked at her in that slinky, flirty outfit and imagined what she'd look like without it. Without anything. 'You don't?'

In the mirror Stephanie's gaze snared his and his throat dried.

'It's not me, is it? I mean, it's beautiful.' She smoothed her hands down the fabric. 'But it's designed for someone more...'

Damen wasn't used to Stephanie tentative or uncertain. She was forthright to the point of driving him crazy.

'More what?' His voice hit a gravelly note as he took in her slightly lost look. 'It's a perfect fit.' Too perfect but he couldn't complain, for that would be admitting the sight of her in it tied his libido in knots. 'You look classy and sexy.'

'I do?' Her eyes widened.

The saleswoman, after a look at Damen, excused herself and headed back to the changing room.

Damen stared at the sultry figure in the mirror. Two hours ago he'd been annoyed with Stephanie and the way she seemed bent on screwing him for every cent she could. What had happened to his anger?

She hadn't asked for sympathy. If anything she'd downplayed that scene in the other shop. Yet her nervous expression made him pause, and not just because she looked good enough to eat.

Was it possible Stephanie doubted herself in that outfit? Surely that was impossible. He strode across to stand behind her. 'What's the problem? Isn't it comfortable?'

She shook her head. 'It feels gorgeous to wear.' Was that longing in her tone?

Damen stepped in, so close the scent of warm vanilla teased his nostrils. 'Then we'll take it.'

'It's not too...?' She made a vague gesture.

'Too?' He was tempted to agree that she looked too disturbingly sexy. He didn't want other men to see her dressed like this. But Damen wasn't stupid enough to reveal that.

Fascinated, he saw a hint of colour at the base of her throat. Her gaze slid to a point in the mirror near his shoulder. When she spoke the words were clipped. 'I've never worn haute couture. You probably need a certain air to carry it off, to be glamorous and...' Her words petered out with a shrug. 'I'm afraid I look like someone playing dress-up, someone who doesn't belong in such clothes.'

Something tugged at Damen's chest. His eyes narrowed. Was she serious? Stephanie always seemed so confident.

He saw that flush rise higher. He doubted even the best actress could blush at will.

'What you look like, Stephanie, is an attractive, desirable woman. The clothes look great on you but that's window dressing. You looked fabulous in cut-off jeans and bare feet.' He paused as she swung to face him. Her velvety eyes rounded.

For a long moment she didn't say anything. Then a smile curled the corners of her mouth and her shadowed expression morphed into one of pleasure. For Damen, standing so close, the impact of her smile was palpable.

'You made me think my appearance didn't meet your exacting standards, Mr Nicolaides.'

Damen shook his head, entranced by the way she smiled with her whole face. He wondered what it would be like to have her look at him that way regularly. Damen liked it. Too much.

'I never said that. I just want you dressed appropriately for the occasion.'

She tilted her head as if trying to read more than his words. Then she nodded once, her manner turning businesslike, that warm glow quenched as if it had never been. 'Okay. How many outfits do I need?'

Steph was incredibly glad Damen had insisted on new clothes, though she hated the idea of him buying them.

There was something suggestive about a man paying for what she wore. As if he'd bought her too. The idea had made her feel grubby at first, until she saw he was right—she was more comfortable mixing with these well-dressed people wearing what she thought of as her camouflage.

At least she didn't look like a charity case.

Steph washed her hands and told herself he paid her to play a part but he hadn't bought *her*. Even if it felt like it on occasions like this, at his friend's party in a spectacular house looking over Athens and the coast.

Damen was as good as his promise, never kissing her, but whenever they were together in public each look, each touch, even the slightly deeper tone he adopted when speaking to her, gave the impression they were lovers.

He was so adept at it sometimes she found it hard to remember it was an act.

The first night, at the cocktail party opening of a new museum wing, Steph had been fazed by his faux intimacy, struggling to play her part and respond in kind.

What worried her now, after more than a week, was how easily she'd grown accustomed to it.

Looking away from her accusing eyes in the mirror of the guest bathroom, Steph busied herself reviving her lipstick.

She should be able to take this charade in her stride now. Damen stuck to their agreement and she was gradually getting used to the bustle of Athens as she explored the sights each day, chauffeured by his driver.

Instead her uneasiness grew. Oh, she was having a ball exploring this amazing city. That was an experience she'd carry for the rest of her days. But the more time she spent with Damen the more he undercut her prejudice against him. Yesterday he'd even come home early to drive her to Cape Sounion to watch the sunset. She knew he'd done it so they could be seen together, yet Steph hugged to herself a secret delight that he'd been prompted by her saying she wanted to see the famous temple ruins.

They spent every evening together and he was not only attentive but also considerate, charming and with a vein of dry humour that appealed too much. Just the sort of man she could imagine being attracted to.

He was too good an actor, she told herself, remembering how he'd feigned interest in her before. When he'd tried to milk her for information.

She put the lipstick away and surveyed herself. She wore the boldly coloured outfit she'd tried on that first day. Its fragile silk clung to her breasts and hips and swished around her legs like a caress.

Crazy how for a couple of minutes in the boutique she'd been racked by self-doubt. As if she were still the scrawny kid in second-hand clothes who never fitted in. She'd thought she'd got over that self-consciousness, the fear of being judged and found wanting. Steph had buried that sense of being second-best with years of hard work and achievement. She believed in her ability to build the future she wanted, to be the woman she wanted to be.

Yet as she'd stood there, wearing this stunning outfit only the rich could afford, she'd felt out of her depth. Suddenly it wasn't just her ability to play this masquerade that she doubted, but herself. Jared's betrayal, her gullibility in being sucked in by a fraud, losing everything she'd worked for, had smashed her confidence. She'd got the wobbles.

Till Damen's words and the look in his eyes reassured her. She remembered the swelling warmth unfurling through her at his male appreciation. He'd told her she was desirable and she'd seen proof in his body language and gleaming eyes.

Steph didn't need a man's opinion to feel good about herself. Nor did she care for people who'd judge her on how she looked.

Yet she was honest enough to admit that when Damen looked at her with that flare of heat, when she *felt* as much as saw his smile as he took in her appearance, it did wonderful things for her bruised ego.

That had to be why she didn't mind those admiring looks from him. Not because she wanted Damen to want her. That would be disastrous. But because it was balm to her wounded soul.

Steph squared her shoulders and opened the door. Music reached her ears, and the hum of voices. She walked down the corridor and into the vast sitting room that could have swallowed her flat several times over.

Knots of people stood chatting and laughing, all elegant, all beautifully dressed. A few, glimpsed through open doors to the next room, danced. Jewels sparkled and the air was rich with expensive scents. But she couldn't see Damen's dark head above the rest.

Her host, a pleasantly ordinary man for a billionaire, caught her eye. 'You're looking for Damen? He's on the terrace.' He smiled. 'Unless you'd care to dance?'

'Thank you but no.' Steph softened her rejection with a smile.

The idea of dancing in these teetering heels terrified her. She loved the way they looked, making her legs seem so much longer, but dancing in them? She'd probably break her ankle and that would be the end of her attempts to be poised and glamorous.

She threaded through the crowd to the huge space where floor-to-ceiling windows were folded back, opening the room to the terrace and gardens.

There were fewer people here but Damen was easy to locate. Steph told herself it was because of his height but she had the disquieting feeling it was more. Even at a crowded event, on the rare occasions they got separated, she always knew precisely where he was. She had the feeling it worked both ways. More than once she'd seen him look up from a conversation, his gaze unerringly catching hers. Steph wasn't sure whether to be flattered or worried by that.

This time, though, he didn't notice her. He stood at the far edge of the paved terrace, away from other guests, and his attention was on someone beside him, his head inclined as they spoke.

Steph started forward then paused, taking in the scene. There was something about their body language, how close they stood. They didn't touch yet it was obvious even from a distance that they shared an intimacy.

Even in the gloom, with her face averted, it was clear Damen's companion was incredibly beautiful.

She was everything Steph wasn't. Tall and effortlessly poised, as if she was used to holding her own at sophisticated parties full of celebrities and the ultra-wealthy. Her hair was blonde and straight, worn in one of those apparently casual styles that combined an elegant knot with sexy wisps around her neck. She wore a strapless gown that revealed endless legs. She was stunning.

Gazing at her, Steph was aware of the unfamiliarity of her high heels. Of the unruly mass of curls clustered around her head. She'd planned to get a haircut in Athens, thinking even a gamine cut was preferable to her natural look, but Damen had forestalled her, saying she looked charming.

Sophisticated and gorgeous beat charming hands down.

Steph hated the little corkscrew of hurt as memories surfaced, of being ridiculed about her appearance, because poverty *looked* different. But that was then and this was now. Steph hadn't been that girl for a long, long time.

Besides, this wasn't a competition.

Damen was merely talking to the woman.

Yet their ease together, the way their heads angled as if they were sharing secrets, made Steph wonder if *this* was the woman he went to so much trouble for. The woman he insisted wasn't his lover.

Steph began walking, swallowing a bitter taste in her mouth.

Damen's head turned, eyes fixing on her.

She felt that stare like the scrape of a blade over her bare arms and shoulders, like a hand sliding, slow and deliberate, over the flimsy silk that covered her body. He made her feel supremely aware of her body in a way no other man had. It was scary and exciting at the same time.

And it infuriated her that, even now, when she'd interrupted him with another woman, Steph was ultra-aware of him. Not out of self-defence, but with that trembling feminine awareness he'd stirred in her from the first. The awareness that had allowed him to make a fool of her.

Steph was mortified at how he could unsettle her. Her skin flushed and her insides rippled with nerves. She was like a silly sixteen-year-old facing the object of her first crush.

When she stopped it wasn't Damen who broke the silence, but the woman who stepped forward with a welcoming smile.

'Steph, it's great to see you again!'

Steph inhaled a scent of cinnamon and roses, felt the brush of soft skin and softer hair as the woman kissed her on the cheek.

Steph blinked. 'Clio?'

They'd met the previous week on Corfu. The Greek woman was a friend of Emma and Christo's and Steph had liked her.

Her heart dropped like a stone through water.

She'd told herself it didn't matter who the woman was that Damen cared about so much that he'd go to ridiculous lengths to protect her.

But it did matter.

Clio wasn't just gorgeous and sophisticated. From the little Steph had seen and heard, she knew Clio was kind-hearted, clever and nice. The sort of woman a man was drawn to not just for a fling but for life.

Even if Damen didn't want to marry yet, Clio was the sort of woman who'd fit into his world and make him happy.

She was perfect for him.

What Steph didn't understand was the pang of hurt that lanced from her chest to her stomach. A ripping pain that skewered her to the spot and caught her breath.

Almost as if she was envious.

CHAPTER SIX

STEPHANIE WAS QUIET on the drive home. Not relaxed, but humming with tension. Damen could read her more easily now, even when she tried to keep her feelings to herself. She was full of pent-up emotion. Had been ever since she'd seen Clio.

Silently he sighed. Things had been going so well before that.

Stephanie hadn't been brittle in his company any more. She relaxed with him, smiled, and it was easier for them to play the part of lovers. Except for the frustration that rode him as he looked at her pretty mouth, remembered its taste, and his promise not to kiss her.

Until she invited him.

That day couldn't come soon enough.

Looking at her tight features as they entered his penthouse, he saw it was clear today wasn't that day.

The front door hadn't even closed before Steph swung round, her breasts swaying, bright silk flaring around her legs.

'Is she the one? Clio?' Her words were bullet fast.

Damen shut the door and led the way into the sitting room.

'Would you like a drink?' He poured himself an ouzo, for once not bothering with water. He wanted the burn of aniseed fire, hoping it might sear away his annoyance at her probing and the feeling of being on the brink of doing something irreversible. Damen had spent the evening drinking sparkling water because it was increasingly difficult to hold Stephanie close, pretend they were lovers, and not plant his mouth on hers.

'What I'd like is an answer.'

She stood, arms akimbo, head and shoulders thrust back, breasts forward. In the lamplight the silk was like flame licking her body, turning her into a fierce, sexy Amazon.

Damen tipped back his head and swallowed the ouzo in one mouthful. Fire ripped from his mouth down his throat to his belly. But it didn't quench the need vibrating through him. He slammed the glass down and stepped away.

Why had he thought alcohol would help? Nothing would help, except Stephanie in his arms, in his bed.

'What was the question?'

Her eyebrows rose. 'Is Clio the lover you're protecting with this masquerade? Or are you deceiving her?'

'You don't need to know who it is. That's irrelevant. Two million dollars' worth of irrelevant.' Why must she pester him about this?

Dark curls danced as Stephanie shook her head, her mouth drawing into a straight line. 'I won't be party to a scheme that's going to hurt anyone. I *like* Clio.'

'I've told you, no one will be harmed.' Impatience rose. Hadn't he assured her of that, explained why this charade was necessary? 'Believe me.'

Again she shook her head, her expression implacable.

'I can't.' This time she spoke softly, not gently but as if her voice stretched thin. 'Don't you understand? How can I trust you? You're a liar.'

The accusation was a punch to Damen's gut. He stood straighter, words of outrage forming. No one accused a Nicolaides of dishonour.

'Don't give me that intimidating stare! You know it's true.

You don't get to be a multi-billionaire by playing nice. Who knows what sort of shady deals you do to make money?'

Damen stared, taken aback. Where had that come from? Simply because he was successful? Did she have something against businessmen?

'You made me leave Melbourne with you because of a lie that you knew where Emma was—'

'Only to get the truth from you.'

'And the next time I see you you offer me money to lie to your friends and family, to all the world for that matter.' Stephanie drew another, audible breath. 'How can I believe you? I need to *know* what's going on. All week I've wondered about every woman we meet. Is this the one? Or that one? Is she hurting seeing us together? I don't want to be party to a scheme to dupe someone. I should never have agreed to it.'

The wrathful words died on Damen's tongue. There was true distress in Stephanie's face and restlessly plaiting hands.

Everything inside him stilled as suspicion stirred.

'Because someone duped you? Hurt you?'

Stephanie's chin shot higher. Her hands clenched and her hunching shoulders pushed back again so she stood tall.

Yet it was there in her eyes. Acknowledgement. Though he guessed she'd die if she thought he could see it.

Damen's next breath was uneven, as if his lungs refused to work. The thought of someone betraying Stephanie, creating that wounded look, made him want to commit an act of violence.

But with that came the sober realisation that she spoke the truth. She had a right to know more. Especially as they were about to head into the lion's den, visiting Clio's family.

Damen was appalled that Stephanie believed him to be dishonest. It went against everything he stood for.

This had to be sorted.

Plus he wanted to find out about the person who'd harmed her.

Damen drew a slow breath. 'Take a seat, Stephanie.'

* * *

Steph sank onto a sofa. Her emotions were jumbled. She didn't understand why seeing Clio with Damen had disrupted her fragile equilibrium. Yet the suspicion they'd been, or perhaps still were, together changed everything.

'*Is* it Clio?'

He took a seat opposite, his arms on his thighs as he leaned forward. For a long time he regarded her enigmatically. Then, reluctantly, it seemed, he nodded.

Steph's heart sank.

'Don't look at me like that,' Damen growled. 'It's not what you think.'

He ploughed his fingers through glossy hair that fell perfectly back into place. Of course it did. Everything in this man's world worked the way he wanted. Business, money... Even women he barely knew agreed to put aside their principles to lie for him.

'Clio isn't and never has been my lover. She's like a sister. In fact, since she's nearer to my age, in some ways she's closer to me than they are.'

'You have sisters?' Steph could have done an internet search on his family but she'd felt that the less she knew about him the better. So far ignorance hadn't provided any protection. She was involved, more involved than was safe.

'Two sisters, one studying in the States and one working overseas.' He paused. 'But my mother's in Greece. You'll meet her at the wedding.'

'Not your father?'

Damen's eyebrows arrowed down. 'He died. A long time ago.'

Maybe that accounted for Damen's innate air of authority, as if he was long used to people jumping to do his bidding.

'I'm sorry.' It was an automatic response, yet that frown told her his father's death still evoked emotions.

'Clio and I are related. Her father is my mother's cousin. Manos is a decent man. He was even something of a mentor when I took over from my father.' Steph noted a twitch of the eyebrows as if the memory of that time wasn't easy. 'Perhaps that gave him expectations where there should be none, because of the bond between our families. He's also extremely obstinate. Once he gets an idea he's likely to steamroller people into agreeing with him.'

Not unlike Damen. But Steph kept the observation to herself.

'Now he believes Clio and I should marry. He's a traditionalist and Clio is his eldest, yet it's her younger sister, Cassie, marrying this weekend and that doesn't sit well. He wants Clio to marry and settle down soon. Plus,' Damen spread his hands, 'he'd like to see the Nicolaides money benefit his family. He thinks I've reached an age where I'm looking for a bride.'

Something shifted in Steph's middle. It wasn't a pain but there was definite discomfort. It had to be due to tension. It had nothing to do with the idea of Damen searching for a wife. That was none of her business.

'That doesn't explain why he thinks you and Clio might marry.'

Damen rolled his shoulders as if they were tight. 'Clio and I have an informal arrangement.'

Steph's stomach lurched as she imagined that agreement. Her own experience was limited but she could imagine Damen enjoying a casual sexual relationship with the lovely Clio. She sat further back on the seat, away from the man watching her so intently.

'Not what you're thinking.'

'You have no idea what I'm thinking!'

He shook his head. 'When you're annoyed or offended you purse your mouth and your nose scrunches up. Despite what I've already told you, despite the fact Clio wasn't in the least jealous, seeing you with me tonight, you've decided we're having an affair. We're not.'

His laser-sharp stare dared her to disagree. Steph said nothing, too concerned about his ability to read her so easily.

'Clio is establishing her interior-design business, and going out with me is a way to network with wealthy potential clients. Plus we like each other's company. I can relax and laugh with her.'

He couldn't relax with other women? It sounded odd, but perhaps wealthy men found it hard to make true friends. Maybe that was why Damen and Christo were close. Each knew the other wasn't angling to benefit financially from their friendship. It struck Steph that living with a fortune had downsides she'd never considered.

'Clio knows I'm just a pretend girlfriend?'

'I didn't tell her and she didn't ask. A party isn't the place for confidences, especially as the aim is to make the world believe you and I are an item. But, as she begged for help last week to get her father off her back, she probably guessed. You're my way of helping her.' He paused. 'I can give you her number if you want, though I suspect she'd prefer not to talk about her family troubles with someone she barely knows.'

Steph blinked, digesting that. It should sound ridiculous. Instead she found it...plausible.

'I see.' He didn't care if she contacted Clio and it was true Clio hadn't seemed disturbed to see them together. It must be a strong friendship for him to go to such lengths. 'But you have no qualms, lying to everyone else, including your mother?'

Damen folded his arms and surveyed her down that imperious nose like a judge examining a prisoner. Once more she felt she was pushing her luck, pursuing this. But she had to know. Despite how easy it was to feign intimacy with Damen, she hated being party to deception.

'I won't lie to my mother. Nor do I want her thinking I'll marry when I have no intention of ever taking a wife. I'll tell her what she needs to know.'

Steph was torn between wondering why Damen was anti-marriage and a prickling of hurt pride at the idea of his family viewing her as expendable. They'd believe he'd picked her up for a short fling. That she wasn't good enough to be considered for anything else.

But she'd been well paid to play that part. She couldn't afford to be offended or embarrassed.

'Satisfied?' His sensuous mouth curled up at one side.

Steph despised the way she noticed such things, responding to his allure. If she didn't, this would be much easier.

Reluctantly she nodded. She still had questions but she believed what he'd said. Why lie? Especially when she could get the truth from Clio.

'Good. Now tell me why you're so ready to believe the worst of me. I admit we got off to a rocky start in Melbourne. But it's more than that. You don't trust easily.'

Steph met that unblinking stare and wondered how many of her secrets this man had read. Most people saw her as bright and friendly and didn't realise how hard she found it to put her trust in others, especially men.

He turned the tables on her, putting her on the defensive.

'Was it a man?'

She couldn't prevent her flinch. Jared's deception was too recent, too raw. But she hid it, she hoped, with a shrug, horrified at how Damen had pinpointed her weak spot so easily. 'Just because I question your motives doesn't mean I have difficulty trusting people.'

He lifted his eyebrows.

'Besides, my past is my own business. It doesn't concern you.'

'So it was a man. What did he do? Leave you for another woman? Or was he married and you didn't know?'

Steph stifled her automatic response, that it was typical of a man to assume the betrayal was sexual. What would Damen say if he realised she'd never been with a man? She learned to be wary of trusting too much. Besides, instead of going out dating she'd spent almost every waking hour working so she could be totally independent.

'You've got it wrong.'

'Have I?' Again Damen leaned towards her and she had the crazy idea those narrowed eyes saw everything she kept hidden.

'Let's just say I've had my fill of unscrupulous people, ready to do anything to get ahead.'

Her words hit home, for Damen's expression turned dark.

Maybe she should apologise, explain that for once she didn't mean him. But that would lead to demands for explanations and she was exhausted. Steph didn't have the stamina for more.

Tonight had been an emotional minefield. She believed Damen's explanation about Clio but that didn't make their situation easier. It seemed more perilous with every hour they were together.

Steph shot to her feet, wobbling a little on her heels. 'I'm tired. I'll see you in the morning.'

Damen stood too. One long stride closed the gap between them.

There it was again, that shiver of awareness racking her body. To her horror Steph felt her nipples bud against gossamer-fine silk.

Did he notice? His eyes held hers but she saw heat flicker in his expression. His gaze dropped to her mouth and it felt like a caress, there on her lips. All night he'd looked at her mouth in a way that made her tremble with expectation. Made her want him to kiss her.

Did he move closer or did she sway towards him?

Abruptly she stepped away, turning for the door, heart pounding in her throat. 'Goodnight, Damen.'

Would he follow? Reach for her? Forget the contract he'd signed and kiss her?

She wanted him to. Wanted it with a self-destructive force that scared her. Her breath snagged as she waited, pulse thundering, for his touch.

But he made no move. She was almost at the corridor to the bedrooms when he spoke.

'Don't forget we leave early tomorrow.'

'I won't forget.'

How could she? She'd barely got through ten days pretending to be his lover and she was about to head to an island wedding where she'd have to play the part to perfection.

The worrying thing was that part of her wished it were true. That they were lovers. She was tying herself in knots trying to quell this attraction.

Steph no longer hated Damen, could no longer rely on negativity to keep her safe. Tonight he'd taken her into his confidence, naming names and explaining facts about his personal life that she sensed he hated revealing.

Yet he'd done it because he accepted she needed to know. He'd heard her qualms and put her needs above his own desire for privacy. That meant a lot. It also changed the dynamic between them.

This attraction she'd tried to conquer was burrowing deeper than doubt or conscience. Alarmingly, it grew stronger rather than weaker the more she discovered about him.

'You're kidding, right? The whole idea of bringing your megayacht was so you could stay on it, surely?' They reached the end of the path and Stephanie swung to face him, her eyes sparking.

Damen knew he should be focused on other things, like handling Manos, who, while ostensibly welcoming, was suspicious and far from happy. Or his own mother, who, despite being told the truth about Stephanie, had regarded the pair of them through today's pre-wedding party with a speculative twinkle that spelled trouble. Or even solving the puzzle of who'd hurt Stephanie so badly, creating that deep-running vein of distrust that she used to keep him at a distance.

But he couldn't concentrate on those things. The late-afternoon breeze teased Stephanie's summery dress and played with those dark curls in a way that made him wish he were free to touch her. Not for the benefit of an audience, but for mutual pleasure.

His belly tightened as he imagined her lifting her pouting lips to his.

Her skin was sun-kissed and, he knew, silky soft. The dress, a floaty thing in white, decorated with cornflowers, accentuated her tiny waist and delectable figure. The cornflower-blue sandal straps tied around her delicate ankles kept drawing his attention to her legs.

'Damen? Are you listening?'

'I am.' And looking. And smelling too. For, as well as the salt scent borne off the water a few hundred metres away, he inhaled Stephanie's warm, vanilla perfume. It was wholesome yet sexy and had a direct line to his libido.

Damen shoved his hands in his pockets and looked at the guest house behind her. Set away from the mansion that was Clio's family home, it perched on a low cliff above the beach.

'I'm sure it's comfortable. Clio refurbished it.'

'It's not the comfort I'm worried about. It's the size. It looks small.'

It was. Bright white like most traditional houses in the Cyclades Islands and surely no bigger than a few rooms. The door gleamed blue, matching the pair of chairs on a tiny terrace positioned to take in the view. Pink geraniums frothed from matching blue pots.

It was charming.

And small, very small.

Damen looked away to his yacht moored in the bay. That was where they should be spending the next two nights. In separate staterooms. Instead...

Damen suppressed a frisson of anticipation.

'It's generous of Manos to offer us the guest house during the wedding celebrations. I couldn't refuse.'

'Of course you could refuse. You're Damen Nicolaides! You run a shipping empire. You make billion-dollar decisions.'

He bit back a laugh. 'Thanks for the pep talk. But this isn't business, this is family, and consequently far more complicated and important.'

He thought of Manos's almost bullish attitude as he'd hosted today's pre-wedding lunch for extended family. Of Clio's set jaw and brittle air and her mother's drawn face. Only Cassie, the bride-to-be, had looked happy.

To refuse Manos's hospitality on such an occasion would have been to insult him. Manos had given him helpful guidance in the turbulent time when Damen had unexpectedly inherited Nicolaides Shipping. His family had supported Damen's in that time of terrible grief. Manos's company and personal wealth hadn't fared as well in the last decade as Damen's, not that he'd reveal that on the occasion of his daughter's wedding. But to have Damen, younger, far wealthier and more successful, the relative he'd once helped in a time of crisis, reject his personal invitation...

Damen refused to do it. Besides, a suspicion had grown today that Clio had arranged the invitation to ram home to her stubborn father that Stephanie was Damen's lover, not a casual friend. One thing was certain—this secluded guest house was designed for intimacy.

Stephanie tilted her head as if seeing him for the first time.

'I'd rather stay on the *Amphitrite* too, but I can't insult Manos by refusing his hospitality.'

If it *had* been Manos's idea originally, he'd probably hoped having Damen stay on the premises would be a chance to pressure him into an engagement with Clio.

'Because it would hurt his pride?'

'Something like that.' Damen wondered how he'd let things get so far. How he hadn't realised his relatives had unrealistic expectations of a match.

'Come on.' He opened the door. 'Let's see what it's like.'

It was worse than he'd thought.

Or, depending on your perspective, he realised, better.

Clio had made the place a sumptuous escape. Wide floorboards gleamed beneath their feet, extending to a wall of windows. From here you could see only sky and the sea, from aquamarine shallows through shades of turquoise to sapphire depths. A soaring ceiling and simple but luxurious furnishings added to the sense of space. As did the lack of internal walls.

The living space swept around the curve of the cliff. Set in a semi-circular alcove to the left, in front of more windows, was a large bath designed for two, a platform beside it holding towels and an ice bucket. On the other side, in a large alcove with its own set of panoramic windows, was a wide bed, dressed in shades of cream, turquoise and blue.

Damen heard Stephanie's breath hitch. She marched past, surveying first the open bathing area then the bedroom that wasn't a room. The stupendous view she ignored. She opened a door, but it revealed only a fridge and a benchtop with a state-of-the-art coffee machine. Another door opened into a walk-in wardrobe. A third led to a bathroom containing only a toilet and a pair of washbasins.

'Two sinks but they can't afford a wall around the bath!'

Damen's lips twitched. 'The open feel is very popular. I'm told it maximises space.'

'And minimises privacy.' Stephanie strode past him, investigating the sofa and chairs placed to make the most of the view. 'There's not even a pull-out mattress.'

Damen's smile vanished as he registered her distress. 'It will be fine. It's just two nights.'

She spun to face him, hands on hips.

'This isn't a joke. If you think for one minute I'm going to share a bed with you—'

'Of course not.' Damen raised his hands. He was too sensible to admit that his first thought on seeing that massive bed and luxurious bath was to imagine sharing both with Stephanie. Stephanie in his arms, warm, willing and eager for his loving.

He repressed a shiver of arousal that arrowed straight to his groin, and kept his expression bland.

'This isn't a trick to compromise you.'

For a taut second she held his stare, then nodded once and turned away. Damen was surprised at the pleasure he felt knowing she believed him. It was a start, a small one, but important. He'd been stunned in Athens to discover how deep her distrust ran.

And the fact that he wanted her in his bed?

He had every intention of achieving that but not by trickery.

'I could sleep on the sofa,' she said.

Over his dead body. What sort of man did she think him? Actually, it was probably best not to go there.

'You have the bed and I'll take the sofa.' Earnest brown eyes met his. 'Don't even think of arguing, Stephanie.' His pride wouldn't let him sleep in comfort while she bunked down there.

Finally she nodded and turned to the bed. 'They've brought our bags from the yacht. I suppose we should freshen up before this restaurant dinner.'

Damen saw her wistful glance at the massive bath.

She'd done marvellously all day, fielding questions from his extended family, playing his devoted girlfriend and doing it well. Stephanie had been attentive and friendly but not gushing. She'd coped with meeting not only his mother and Clio's family but also dozens of distant relatives, all excited and curious to meet his companion, for Damen was notorious for never bringing a woman to any family celebration.

But, while he'd grown more relaxed as the day wore on, Stephanie had become more tense. Her shoulders were set high and her breathing was shallow, as if she was on high alert.

'Why don't you relax and have a bath? We've got plenty of time and I have calls I need to make. I'll go down to the beach to make them and stretch my legs.'

'If you don't mind, that would be great.' Her smile was tentative but genuine and he felt as if he'd won a victory.

She turned and opened the case that his staff had packed and brought from the yacht.

A second later she was scrabbling to pick up the item on top, moving it from his view. But not before Damen saw a black, lacy bra that looked almost see-through in her hands. Next was a skimpy pair of matching knickers, which left him imagining Stephanie wearing sexy underwear and nothing else, posing for his approval as she had at that Athens boutique.

He sucked in his breath so sharply, pain jabbed his ribs. Heat drenched him.

Damen's ease disintegrated. And so did his amusement at her disapproval of this beautiful retreat.

It struck him that she wasn't the only one who'd be grateful for a barrier between them tonight. A convenient wall so he didn't have to watch her sleeping or lie awake calculating how many steps between the sofa and the bed.

Staying here together would be a special form of torture. Not because he couldn't cope with a sofa, but because, much as he wanted to seduce Stephanie, he refused to take advantage of a situation that made her nervous.

He had a long, frustrating night ahead.

CHAPTER SEVEN

THE MUSIC WOUND to a halt but Steph's heart kept pounding a matching rhythm. The traditional music had initially sounded slow, almost ponderous, but it had altered as the dance went on. Or maybe once she'd been tugged into the line of women holding hands, following the bride, she'd begun to notice extra nuances.

She'd been happy to sit at the outdoor table with its flickering candles and watch. She'd been fascinated by the beauty of what seemed simultaneously a simple dance yet at the same time intriguingly intricate. Women of all ages joined the growing line. There was one, iron-haired and sturdy-framed, who danced with the grace of a professional. There was the little girl in plaits, eyes round with excitement as she watched the bride.

Suddenly, without giving her time to think, there was Clio, pulling Steph from her seat, dragging her to join the throng. Steph had stumbled, protested, but the smiles and nods had drawn her in till she found the beat and then, heart swelling with delight, she hadn't wanted to stop. She'd felt not only welcome but also included, a real part of this joyous event.

She'd barely been aware of the men at the tables. This didn't feel like a dance performed to attract their attention, but something done for the participants, especially the bride. She met the smiling faces of the other women and grinned back. They'd all been so kind and friendly.

It had been the same all day. Except for a few women who'd looked at her when she arrived with Damen as if they'd like to claw her eyes out. But she'd received jealous glares like that in Athens. It came with the territory.

Damen's woman. That was how everyone saw her.

The knowledge set up a familiar thud in her chest. A thud that echoed the erratic pulse beat that had kept her from sleep last night.

She must have snatched some rest, for she'd woken scratchy-eyed to find Damen gone, for an early swim, she discovered later. But it felt as if she'd spent most of the night awake, listening to her drumming pulse, thinking how close he lay, how she wanted to go to him.

Would it have been the bravest thing she'd ever done or the stupidest?

All this flirting, the fleeting caresses and searing looks, was undermining her resistance. Logic said it was all for show. Something else, deep-buried and needy, declared those looks, that tension, the sparking heat when they touched, were more than playacting.

If only she had enough experience to know for sure.

The events of the last months had damaged her self-esteem but Steph wasn't by nature a shrinking violet.

She wanted Damen.

She'd given up trying to avoid that truth. The wanting drove her crazy. If the desire was mutual...

Her breath shuddered out. If it was *mutual* she'd be tempted to do what she'd never done and invite physical intimacy. Because surely that would be a way of getting rid of it. Like an itch that needed to be scratched. Because so far it was simply compounding, growing stronger and more distracting almost by the hour.

Except Steph recalled how easily Damen had feigned attraction. She refused to make that mistake twice. It was one of the reasons she'd been horrified to discover they had to share that sybaritically luxurious and far too small guest house.

She was caught, unable to be sure what he felt but unable to escape this increasingly urgent physical attraction.

She swung round to look for Damen. He was still where she'd left him, but instead of watching her he was in conversation with a group of men.

Steph's heart sank. What had she expected? That he'd be transfixed by the sight of her stumbling through a traditional Greek dance?

He'd spent the afternoon glued to her side. He'd been the one to pick up her filmy shawl when it slid off on the way to the church. She recalled the warmth of his hands as he'd placed it around her shoulders and the whisper of his breath tickling her face as he stood close and explained the wedding ceremony. He'd spent the day playing the attentive lover, showing Manos and everyone else that he was devoted to his new girlfriend. Was it any surprise his attention wandered now he was alone?

'May I?'

Steph swung around to meet melting dark eyes. The guy's smile was wide and friendly and Steph felt none of that jangling hyper-awareness that taunted her with Damen.

What was more, he looked at her with an avid appreciation she knew was real. Today, when Damen had seen her in her stunning new dress, ready for the wedding, he'd smiled and said she looked perfect. But his gaze hadn't lingered the way this guy's did. Damen had seemed distracted, as if he had something else on his mind. Inevitably Steph decided she looked 'perfect' for her role as pretend girlfriend but the sight left him unmoved.

'You'd like to dance? Yes? My name is Vassili. Come.' He held out his hand, his smile widening. 'Let's have some fun.'

Fun. How long since she'd had that? Always at the back of her mind were worries.

Suppressing the need to check on Damen again—she didn't

need his approval—she smiled and put her hand in Vassili's. 'My name is Steph.'

'I know. Stephanie. The most beautiful woman here.'

That smile became a beaming grin and suddenly Steph felt lighter than she had in ages. Laughter trailed behind her as he drew her close.

Damen's eyes narrowed as he watched Stephanie dance. Not traditional dancing now. The music was modern, the moves unchoreographed, and it was hard to see her for the other dancers thronging the outdoor dance space. But he glimpsed turquoise silk, that collar of crystals around her throat, bouncing curls and her glorious, uninhibited smile. A smile she never turned his way. Not since what had happened in Melbourne.

His throat dried to sandpaper roughness. He'd returned to the guest house to find her dressed for the wedding. She wore a dress once more in a style that left her arms and shoulders bare, the fabric attached around the neck only by that glinting collar. And when she turned the upper half of her back was tantalisingly bare.

Damen's palms had prickled with the urge to touch that expanse of skin. Or trace the gleaming fabric as it clung and dipped across her curves before flirting out around her legs. It was a dress made to drive a man to distraction.

She was made to drive him to distraction.

After a sleepless night he wasn't putting up much of a fight. All day he'd been on edge, his body hyper-alert as they acted the loving couple. As he leaned close to explain customs or conversations for her. As he endured the torture of Stephanie turning and murmuring to him, her breath an intimate caress.

Even entering the church and placing that gauzy wrap over her bare shoulders out of respect for tradition, only part of Damen's mind had been on the wedding or Manos or curious onlookers. Most of his brain had been cataloguing how very much he wanted Stephanie.

He'd held back, hadn't tried to seduce her in Manos's home. Now he couldn't remember why that had seemed a point of honour.

She wanted him. He felt it in those tiny hitched sighs of hers, her dazed look when he touched her and the fluttering pulse that betrayed her time and again.

Damen leaned back in his chair, half listening to the conversation about global markets, financial recovery and bad debts. He couldn't stalk across and claim Stephanie. No one would believe he was so besotted with his new woman that he needed to be with her all the time. It would only make Manos suspicious.

Then the dancers parted and there she was, smiling up at her partner, who'd closed the space between them. He leaned in, whispering something, and she laughed.

Damen sat up, catching the rich yet breathless sound as the music faded.

His jaw clenched. He knew the guy dancing with her. He fancied himself irresistible with his ingratiating smile and practised charm. Let him work his charm on someone else!

'Don't you think, Damen—?'

'Sorry, Manos. Let's talk about this later. Stephanie needs me.' He was already out of his seat, stalking towards the dance floor.

She needed him all right, to keep her safe from suave seducers. From men who looked at her in that sexy dress and wanted her out of it. As he did.

Damen kept his eyes on her as he detoured past the DJ, throwing out not a request but a terse command. A loud pop song, just starting, stopped abruptly, making heads turn.

Stephanie turned too, her gaze colliding with Damen's, as he paced towards her. Her mouth, those lips that drove him again and again to the edge of control, opened as if she couldn't catch her breath.

The first bars of a new tune poured through the evening air, soft, slow, resonant with longing.

Damen saw her swallow, the wide circlet of exquisite crystals around her throat catching the glow from fairy lights strung all about.

Then he was there, looking down at her.

'My dance.'

In his peripheral vision her partner shifted his weight, huffed as if to say something, then faded away.

Damen reached out and did what he'd wanted to do all day. He slid his arm right round her back, low across her waist, feeling the exquisite softness of naked flesh against his palm. He pulled her close, snug against his thighs, and took her hand. His breath eased out in satisfaction. Better. Much better.

'What's the matter? You think Manos won't believe in us if we spend half an hour apart?' Her voice was a hoarse croak that lacerated his control. He wanted to hear more of it, throaty and out of breath, calling his name, crying out for release.

'I'm rescuing you from a playboy who thinks he can seduce my woman.' Damen registered the growl roughening his voice and didn't care. He'd had enough.

The familiar ballad swelled around them and they began dancing, circling, barely moving from the spot.

'Was that necessary? You know I'm not going to be seduced.'

Oh, yes, you are.

For sitting there, watching Stephanie with another man, something inside Damen had snapped. Not his patience. Something more fundamental. He didn't want to think about it or give it a name. He was a pragmatist and he knew the time for resisting was over. That was all he'd let himself consider.

Damen hauled her closer, pleased when her body melted against his despite the stunned expression in those wide golden-brown eyes.

Oh, yes. There'd definitely be a seduction tonight. And it would be he, Damen Nicolaides, orchestrating it. Beginning now.

* * *

Steph felt as if she was floating as they strolled down the secluded path. The faint sound of music reached her. Damen said the revellers would continue partying into the early hours, but the bride and groom had left and there was no need to linger.

Steph would have liked to linger, swaying in Damen's arms under the canopy of vines and tiny lights. For the first time since their charade began she hadn't given a thought to the lie they lived, for there, in his arms, it hadn't felt like a lie.

She was no fool. She knew it was the romantic setting, the handsome partner, Damen's proprietorial manner, which should have annoyed her and instead made her insides turn stupidly mushy, that created the strange ambience. Plus her own heightened desire.

She sighed. It was time to shake off the romantic illusion. When they entered their guest suite and were away from prying eyes, the masquerade would end. She was nothing more to Damen than the woman he'd paid a fortune to pretend to be his girlfriend. And he...well, he'd still be too potently alluring for her peace of mind but he needn't know that.

There it was, coming into view at last. The retreat they'd share for one more night. Would she lie awake again, wondering how it would be to indulge in a fling? Imagining being with Damen, the only man who'd broken through her wall of caution, awakening her body to desire?

A large moon hung low over the sea and silvery light bathed the scene in magic, making it impossibly beautiful. Something caught in her chest.

'It's been a wonderful day. Thank you.' Steph made to withdraw her hand from Damen's but he kept hold of her fingers as they stopped on the terrace.

'Thank *you*, Stephanie.' His low voice skated across her skin, drawing it tight. 'I hadn't expected to enjoy today as much as I did.'

She shrugged. It had been a lovely celebration with friendly people. Even Manos, whose fierce, dark eyes had glittered dangerously at first, had mellowed as the evening progressed. Last seen, he'd been laughing with a group of men who'd shed their jackets, rolled up their sleeves and huddled around a table, drinking brandy and talking earnestly.

Steph moved towards the door but Damen blocked her way.

'Damen?' His arm came round her, drawing her close, his other hand still holding hers.

Delight shivered through her and she stiffened. It was one thing to enjoy the illicit pleasure of being in his arms, knowing it was for show, but they were alone here.

'What is it? Can you see someone?' Were they being watched?

His head lowered and for a snatched moment she imagined his mouth covering hers, those wide shoulders curving around her.

But he didn't do that. He'd promised not to kiss her. He'd signed a contract.

That memory stiffened her spine, a reminder that this wasn't real, as his mouth settled near her ear. Yet her eyes fluttered shut as his breath feathered her skin.

'I can't see anyone. That doesn't mean we can't be seen.' He paused. 'Hold me, Stephanie.'

Steph blinked her eyes open, trying to decipher the curious note in his voice. It wasn't an order so much as a request. There was a yearning in that deep voice that—

She pressed her lips together. There was no yearning, just a man speaking softly so anyone near by wouldn't hear. Reluctantly, enjoying every centimetre of sensation and knowing she shouldn't, Steph slid her hands up his chest to clasp the back of his neck.

He felt so good. That warm, woodsy scent tickled her nostrils and she ran her fingers through his thick hair, scraping along his scalp, telling herself she was making this look real for a potential onlooker, ignoring the fierce hunger drilling down through her middle.

A sigh shuddered through him, and then she was trembling too as his mouth moved along her jaw and down her neck. They weren't kisses exactly. Just the brush of his lips as he whispered something in gravelly Greek beneath his breath. The sound carved a channel of need through her, leaving her wide open and gently aching.

'Damen, I think we should go inside.' Because she couldn't play pretend lovers any more. Not tonight. Not when she felt so...

'Excellent idea, *kopela mou*.'

Yet instead of stepping back, Damen took her by surprise, bending to scoop her into his arms. The world tilted. Steph had never been held like this. Her arms went round his neck, hanging tight lest he drop her.

But it wasn't falling she feared. Not really. It was the riot going on inside her body. The jumble of excitement and anticipation, even knowing this was for the benefit of some unseen watcher.

'Do you really think this is necess—?'

'I do. Absolutely necessary.' His voice was as taut as her stretched nerves.

He opened the door, holding her in his arms, and stepped inside. All the while Steph was bombarded with new sensations. The feeling of being in his arms, surrounded by him. The heat where their bodies pressed together. The fact she could hear his heartbeat if she let herself rest her head against him. The awareness of how close his mouth was. Above all the almost wonderful, almost scary, sense of being totally reliant on his strength.

Steph waited but Damen didn't release her.

'Damen? I can stand. No one can see us.' The massive windows on the sea side spilled moonlight into the large space, but they were private from prying eyes.

Instead of putting her down, Damen firmed his hold.

'Maybe I don't want to,' he murmured. 'Maybe I've been wanting to hold you like this all night.'

Steph's heart jumped. 'Stop it. We're not playing parts now. You can drop the besotted act.'

'And if it's not an act?' Above her his mouth twisted into a hard smile that looked like a grimace.

'What are you saying, Damen? That you've spent the last few hours longing to hold me like this?' It was preposterous, yet Steph heard the wobble in her voice, as if she wanted to believe it.

'That too. But what I really long for is your mouth on mine.' She felt as well as heard his voice rumble up from his chest. 'Your kisses. Your lips have been driving me crazy. *You've* been driving me crazy. Not just today. For weeks.'

Suddenly she was shoving at his shoulders, wiggling her legs, trying to sit up, get down, till eventually he relented and lowered her to the floor.

She felt her shawl slip to the floor but didn't pick it up. Steph backed up a step, far enough to meet Damen's dark eyes. In the gloom they should have been impossible to read. Instead she felt a punch to the solar plexus when she deciphered his expression.

Yearning, that was what she saw, or imagined she saw. A yearning such as she felt.

Except that couldn't be.

'Stop it. We don't have an audience here. There's no need to keep up the act.'

Slowly he turned his head from side to side. 'It's no act. That part hasn't ever been an act with you, Stephanie.'

Her nape tightened and her hands anchored at her hips. 'It was in Melbourne. That time in the car—'

'When we kissed?' His mouth curled at one side into something too taut to be a smile. 'I didn't plan that, you know. But how could I resist when you were so lush and inviting and I'd been trying to keep my distance all week? When we kissed it was like spring after the longest winter. Like sunshine after frost.' He shook his head. 'No, that's not right. It was more like a volcano erupting out of the blue. As if the caldera at Santorini exploded again, turning everything lava-hot. Burning away the world.'

The image branded her, deep inside, in that place where she tried to hide her feelings. He was right. It had been just like that. For her. Not for him. He'd merely been using her weakness against her.

'What's wrong, Damen?' She turned her voice to steel. 'Are you bored? Is it so difficult to go a few weeks without a woman in your bed that you'd even turn to *me*?'

Pain blanketed her chest but she made herself face him. If he knew how she really felt about him she'd be lost.

If she'd expected her lashing accusation to provoke him she was disappointed. 'Actually, I'm very discerning about who I take to bed. I learned the hard way to be very, very choosy.'

The hard way? Steph frowned, wondering what he meant.

'So what am I? A challenge? The one woman who refuses to be seduced by your charm?'

He folded his arms and she wished she didn't notice the way the gesture accentuated the power of his upper body. 'Definitely a challenge, Stephanie. But that's a separate issue. I've wanted you since I met you. The only reason I didn't seduce you that night in Australia was because I had an obligation to find your friend Emma for Christo. And after that,' he lifted his arms wide, 'I'd hurt you. It wasn't the time.'

To her surprise Steph thought she saw shame or at least regret flicker across his face.

'And you think things are different now? Because you're paying me?'

'They're absolutely different, and not because I'm paying you.' He shook his head. 'I never have and never will pay for a woman in my bed. This, what's between us, has nothing to do with money.'

Steph folded her arms across her chest, holding in her madly pounding heart.

'Then what's changed?'

'*You've* changed.' His night-dark eyes pinioned her. 'You've lost that wounded look as if I'm the big, bad wolf. Instead you look at me the way a woman does when she wants a man.'

Steph's chest rose hard on a shocked intake of air.

'You don't deny it.' His voice was soft as a summer breeze, warm as seduction.

'I don't need to deny it. You're paying me a fortune to pretend to be your lover. Of course I look at you…fondly. I have to be convincing.'

'Fondly?' Slowly he shook his head. 'It's more than that. You're not that good an actress.'

Steph's chin shot high. 'You've got an ego the size of the Aegean, Damen Nicolaides.'

'It's not ego, Stephanie. It's facing the truth. The same truth I faced ages ago. I *want* you, Stephanie, and I've given up pretending not to. You want me too.'

'In your dreams.'

'At least in my dreams I get to have you, Stephanie. There you're always willing and eager in my arms.'

Heat saturated her from the crown of her head to the soles of her feet. He dreamt of her? Just as she dreamt of him? Had he lain awake last night too, imagining what it would be like if they shared that big bed looking out over the sea?

'Nothing to say, Stephanie?'

She opened her mouth then shut it. Bandying words with him was too dangerous. Every word he spoke tapped into the secret channel of desire within her that she'd tried and failed to dam.

Damen stepped closer and her chin rose as she held his stare.

'You don't get anything in this life playing safe, Stephanie.'

'But you don't get burned either.' She hadn't planned to answer but then the words were out, revealing things she'd tried to hide. The yearning. The combustible heat within. The weakness.

Yet, instead of triumph, Damen's expression held understanding.

'Sometimes,' he murmured, 'playing with fire has compensations.'

He paused, watching her. Stephanie almost wished he'd reach for her, touch her and make the doubts disappear. Make it simple by stripping away her defences. But he didn't. He met her gaze gravely, not trying to hide his hunger. Not trying to hide anything. The silvery moonlight revealed features stark with longing but not a man who'd try to force her.

'If you're brave enough to take the risk.'

Steph tried to summon outrage, to be annoyed that he thought her a coward, just for being sensible. It didn't work because the pressure didn't come from Damen. It came from inside herself.

All her life Steph had played safe. Working, saving, planning for the future. Keeping herself to herself rather than venture into the wild realms of passion as so many of her peers had done. There'd been no boyfriends, no lovers. Just a man who'd duped her into trusting him, only to steal from her. And now Damen, who turned her inside out so she hardly recognised herself or what she felt.

She'd tried safety and it hadn't worked.

What did she have to lose?

As the thought surfaced the voice of reason screeched inside her brain, listing all the reasons this was dangerous.

For once Steph ignored the voice of reason.

'There's something I want.' Her voice held a strange, flat note, as if her heart weren't racing or her breaths coming in short gasps.

'Anything I can help with?' He didn't move but somehow he seemed nearer, the air thickening between them.

Steph unfolded her arms and let them hang by her sides. 'I'd like you to kiss me. On the lips.'

CHAPTER EIGHT

DAMEN'S BREATH SEARED IN, leaving his lungs overfull yet somehow without enough air to sustain him.

This was what he wanted. What he'd planned to get for so long. Yet, as he looked into Stephanie's serious face with that tiny frown on her brow and lips parted as if she too couldn't get enough oxygen, it wasn't triumph he felt. Or not entirely.

The hammer beat in his blood revealed the depth of his need. He wasn't besting her. This wasn't a contest. He felt almost scared to touch her, as if she'd melt away or change her mind and he'd be left alone, the craving for her eating him up.

Damen didn't let himself hesitate. He stepped in to stand toe to toe with her. Her nipples grazed him and a spiral of hot metal coiled down from his chest to his groin, screwing his body tighter and hotter.

He palmed her bare back. Her flesh was velvety. His other hand ploughed through her curls, tilting her head. She looked up at him with wide, wary eyes. It was too dark to see their golden depths but even in the gloom he felt her scrutiny. As if she didn't trust him to make this worth her while. As if expecting him to let her down.

That spurred him to take his time, though he wanted to plunder her lips till she stopped thinking and gave him everything.

He pressed his lips to the corner of her mouth, teasing them both, telling himself he could withstand a few more moments' waiting. She trembled and something hard inside softened.

Damen gentled his hand on her scalp, slid his mouth along her cheek, peppering tiny kisses along flesh that tasted like vanilla and something far more precious. To the edge of her jawline, to her ear. Slender fingers grabbed his upper arms. He felt rather than heard her sigh.

That was when his patience disintegrated, even as he told himself to go slow. Now he was back at her mouth, tugging her bottom lip between his teeth, hearing her gasp, feeling her fingers dig into his flesh through his jacket. Damen licked that delicate lower lip, savouring a taste of paradise.

He was telling himself to move on, press more teasing kisses along her jawline, when Stephanie slicked her tongue along the seam of his mouth. A second later she fastened her teeth on his bottom lip and nipped hard.

Sensations, raw and hot, shot through him. All thought of slow seduction faded as he gathered her in, hauling her against a body forged hard as steel.

No coaxing now, just a driving hunger that melded their lips, their tongues tangling in a wild dance of eager ecstasy.

Stephanie quivered against him, but not with nerves. Not with her hands clutching so tight it was as if she wanted to climb up him, all the better to devour him. And even though he, from his superior height, bowed her back over his arm, this wasn't about dominance and submission.

Submission! She was anything but submissive. She didn't just kiss with her lips but with her whole, glorious body. She undulated against him, a symphony of female sensuality as her tongue danced in his mouth, eager and erotic.

Still it wasn't enough. The kiss was deep and druggingly arousing, yet he needed more. With a grunt Damen tugged her closer against his arousal. His arm at her waist shifted till he grasped her bottom and lifted her.

Shards of heat shot through him. It wasn't enough. Not with the taste of Stephanie like sweet, wild honey in his mouth and the feel of her eager body against him.

Damen heard a hum of sound, a low, vibrating growl. It took a moment to realise it came from him. A gruff sound of encouragement and demand so primal it startled him.

Nothing about this kiss was ordinary. He'd expected pleasure, anticipated arousal. He'd even spoken to her of volcanic heat, yet till their mouths touched he'd forgotten how devastating it was, kissing Stephanie Logan.

This was elemental. Like a combustible chemical reaction and as inevitable as the sun rising tomorrow.

Damen gave himself up to it, letting the relentless driving force take him, knowing that to resist, even to think, was pointless.

Some time later, he had no idea how much later, he lifted his head enough to allow them both to breathe. His lungs worked like bellows and his brain had ceased functioning beyond *mine, mine, mine*.

He blinked, trying to ground himself, stunned at his loss of control. At his inability to think. As if he were the one out of his depth.

Damen looked into slumberous eyes slowly opening to look up at him, at a kiss-ravaged mouth, those lips plump and pouting, and self-knowledge smote him. He *was* reeling. For the first time he wasn't in command of himself.

He didn't give a damn.

He wanted more. He wanted everything.

Her hand on his chest stopped him when he made to kiss her again.

'Wait. Stop.'

Chest heaving, Damen paused.

'Yes?'

'This feels dangerous.'

Damen suppressed a smile. 'Not dangerous, *agapi mou*. Just a little on the edge.'

Who was he kidding? They were combustible. It was like saying a summer wildfire, scorching all before it, was just a little dangerous.

'I can't think when we kiss.' Her voice was breathless, wondering, and Damen wanted to reassure her everything was okay. That she could rely on him to put the brakes on. But he couldn't. Kissing Stephanie was like being on a runaway train and never wanting to get off.

He shook his head and straightened. 'You're right. When we kiss...'

He paused, cleared his throat. The man he'd become didn't admit to weakness. He'd forced himself to learn from his past, catastrophic mistake. He didn't hand anyone, especially a woman, the power of holding the truth about him.

It would be easy to step back, murmur something about respecting her desire for caution. Well, not easy, but more acceptable than admitting the truth, that she threatened to undo him.

'When we kiss?' Her eyes searched his, her hands still clutching his arms as if she needed his support to stay upright.

Damen could lie, brush off the truth and walk away. But if he did, would he ever hold her in his arms again? The thought of never kissing her again left him bereft.

'When we kiss,' he growled, 'I don't want to stop. I want you, Stephanie. Completely. Unreservedly. I want you wild, wanton and abandoned. I want to worship you with my body till you scream in ecstasy and barely have the energy to give yourself to me again. And I want to keep loving you till we're both wrung-out wrecks, unable to move.'

Damen's lips twisted into a grimace. So much for keeping the truth to himself. To not handing her power on a plate.

* * *

Steph felt the thrill of excitement start in her belly and spread in radiating waves. She trembled so hard surely Damen saw. Yet he scowled down at her as if she'd done something wrong.

He looked so *fierce*. As if he wanted to fight rather than kiss. As if this were some battle between them.

Slowly she processed his words. Not just the shiver-inducing promise of sexual satisfaction but that revealing comment. *I don't want to stop.*

Steph didn't pretend to be an expert about Damen but she knew some things about him. One was that he guarded himself. He thought before he acted, each action planned and scrutinised. He didn't rush headlong into things but considered them, then worked out the strategy that would best suit his needs, like hiring a faux-girlfriend.

He'd even taken a pragmatic approach to his love life, guarding against importunate lovers via his arrangement with Clio.

Yet there was nothing pragmatic about his expression now.

He looked different, his features stripped back as if passion had scoured any softness from his face. Yet Steph felt no fear, just fellow feeling. It was the same for her. As if their kiss had stolen away the comfortable platitudes she surrounded herself with and left only a single truth.

She wanted Damen, and no amount of prevaricating or pretending could change that.

Beneath her palm his heart thundered.

They were equals in this. He'd admitted as much. It wouldn't be safe. It would be wild and ecstatic. But maybe just once in her life she should discover what that felt like. Step off the straight and narrow and let herself go.

It wasn't as if Damen would be around long term, interfering with her life or trying to turn a moment's wildness into something more significant.

The choice was hers.

Steph moistened her lips, aware of Damen's eyes following the movement. It sent a corkscrew of heat twisting through her.

'I'm not experienced.'

His head reared back as if he needed to distance himself and Steph felt a jerk of dismay at that tiny withdrawal. Damen blinked, his eyes narrowing as if wondering if he'd heard right.

'Not *very* experienced?'

Was this a deal-breaker for him? Pride told her if her virginity was a problem, then tough, he'd be the one to miss out. But she wanted him so badly. Couldn't imagine turning back now.

Her chin rose and she focused on a point beyond his shoulder. 'It doesn't matter. Forget I spoke.'

Warm fingers cupped her chin and turned her face to his. 'It matters, *kopela mou.*' He breathed deep, his chest a living wall before her. 'Thank you for telling me.' He paused. 'It's an unexpected...responsibility.'

She opened her mouth to say it wasn't a responsibility, just a physical fact she thought he should know about. But before she could speak his mouth covered hers.

This kiss was different. Not desperate or wild. It was light, gentle, but with no less purpose and no less pleasure. It was a kiss that tasted sweet with promise, heady with longing and as it went on something vital melted inside her. Steph could almost swear she heard music somewhere, beautiful music. But that was impossible.

Heat rose, weaving through her blood, softening her bones. Steph leaned into him, needing his strength to support her, and once more Damen scooped her close.

This time when he lifted his head, breathing hard through his nostrils, there was no looking away, no pretending. He stared down at her and it felt as though he saw her in a way no one else ever had. It should have been scary but it felt right. Steph wanted him to see her, the real her, to be as wholly caught up in this moment as she was.

Damen lifted his fingers to her forehead, smoothing a line

above her eyebrows. 'There's nothing to worry about, Stephanie. I promise you.'

She wasn't worried. Well, not much. But there was no need for words as Damen led her to the bed.

'Undress me.' His voice, low as a caress, wound through her as he shrugged out of his jacket and tossed it over a chair. His shoulders looked so broad in that white shirt, gleaming in the moonlight. Her fingers twitched and she swallowed hard, knowing she'd fumble her way through undressing him, revealing her ineptitude and nervous excitement.

What did it matter?

Steph reached for his bow tie, the silk soft to the touch as he undid his cufflinks. Tugging the tie free, she undid the top of his shirt then got distracted by the dark, silky skin she revealed. The pads of her fingers slid across his collarbone, discovering dips and notches, then down to where a smattering of crisp hair dusted his chest. It tickled her fingers and palms when she spread them across that wall of hot muscle.

One brown nipple budded under her palm and Damen's skin tightened as muscles jumped then eased.

Steph looked up to find his gaze fixed, dark and glowing on her as he reefed off his shirt. His hands went to his belt and the thrumming beat of her heart rose to her throat.

Her hands drifted lower, discovering flesh that was surprisingly soft, taut over muscle and bone. Her gaze followed her hands and she discovered he'd shucked his trousers and underwear down to his ankles, standing before her proudly erect.

Steph's throat tightened. He looked impossibly beautiful, impossibly huge. A flutter of nerves butterflied through her middle to settle between her legs, turning into a hot, achy sensation that made her shift restlessly.

Damen said nothing, just stood with his arms at his sides, waiting.

Steph anchored one palm on that flat abdomen and dragged her other down, fingertips touching the thatch of dark hair then reaching his heavy arousal. To her surprise it felt like silk over solid heat. Tentatively she curled her hand around him, sliding gently right to the tip.

A sound like the wind soughing through trees penetrated the silence. It took a moment to realise it was Damen, sighing in pleasure, his eyes glittering through narrowed slits. She repeated the movement, feeling a rising power, and this time he moved, thrusting into her hand, his hips tilting to follow her caress.

'You like that.' It should have sounded stupid. It probably did sound naïve. Yet Damen didn't laugh. The tendons in his neck stood proud and the muscles in his arms and chest bunched as if he forced himself into immobility.

'I do. When you touch me I feel...' He shook his head, his mouth a grimace as Steph let her other hand dance, feather light across his abdomen, grazing one hip, then down, then up again.

She saw what it cost him to stand while she looked her fill, exploring. She watched his pulse judder, saw the sheen at his throat as if he was burning up. Damen was a strong man, used to wielding authority, making things happen. Yet he held himself still, giving her time to adjust. Giving her power.

Because she'd told him she was inexperienced. Because he knew she was nervous as well as excited. Suddenly she wasn't nervous any more. Not enough to wait, at any rate.

She dropped to her knees before him, scrabbling to find first one gleaming shoe then another, helping him out of them and his socks till he could step free of his clothes and stand naked before her. She lifted her eyes, drawn once more by the uncompromising shape of his erection. Would he—?

Damen's hand closed around hers, drawing her up.

He didn't say anything, simply reached around to the back of the halter-neck collar of her dress and flicked it undone. Steph blinked, her arm automatically lifting to hold the bodice up while Damen dragged the side zipper open. Then his arms dropped and he stood, waiting.

Steph's heart thundered as she released the fabric, felt it slide free, down her breasts, stomach and thighs, to land with a plop around her feet.

Damen's chest rose mightily then sank again before he lifted one hand, brushing across her breasts. He teased her nipples with a barely there touch that sent shocking jolts of heat shooting to that needy place between her legs.

'And your shoes.' His voice was a whisper of sound, barely audible over her pulse.

Steph reached for his arm, clutched as she lifted one foot and fumbled at the buckle, drawing off the high heel. Then the other. Now she stood before him, naked but for panties of skimpy lace.

She drew a deep breath, registering a new scent in the air, not the evocative scent she associated with Damen but something headier, slightly musky.

Arousal. That was what she smelt in the air thickening between them. It was what she felt pounding through her blood, heating her body till she glowed.

Eyes on Damen's, she hooked her thumbs under the lace at her hips and dragged it down, letting it pool at her feet.

His gaze tracked down, zeroing in on the dark V between her legs, and his mouth crooked up at one side as if in approval. He lifted his hand, palm up, and Steph put hers in it, feeling relief and excitement as his fingers folded around hers. Fire skated from their linked hands all the way up her arm then down, down, deep inside. He led her to the bed, drawing her down beside him so they sat side by side.

It wasn't what she'd expected. She'd supposed that once naked they'd be in each other's arms, kissing, letting nature take its course in a flurry of urgent excitement.

Instead the line of Damen's jaw looked almost grim in the spill of moonlight.

'I want to make this good for you, Stephanie. You'll need to tell me what you like and what you don't.'

'I don't know.' Steph swallowed, feeling suddenly gauche.

Damen shook his head. 'You will soon enough. Promise me,'

he paused, 'if you feel uncomfortable, tell me and I'll stop. At any point. Agreed?'

She nodded, suddenly alarmed at the possibility he might expect more than she knew how to give. She thought of stories she'd heard about sexual kinks and—

'Don't worry, *koritsi mou*. All you have to do is enjoy yourself. Okay?'

Steph nodded. She hated feeling like this, with no clue. So she lifted her palm to his shoulder, feeling a frisson of response in the shiver that passed through his big frame.

'What I'd really like,' she said, her voice hoarse, 'is to kiss you. To lie against you naked and kiss you.'

The serious expression around his eyes eased and the smile he sent her was pure devilry. 'Since you insist.'

Then, before she had a chance to register movement, she was flat on her back on the mattress, with Damen lying half above, half beside her, his shoulders wide against the streaming moonlight.

Steph sucked in an urgent breath, full of that heady scent of Damen and sex. It lifted her breasts against his chest and everything inside stopped for a second in sheer wonder at how good that felt. But there was more, far more. The scratchy friction of his hairy leg, hot as it slid over hers. Hard fingers pushing through her hair, holding her still as his mouth lowered to hers.

This time his kiss stole her breath instantly. For they were together as never before. So close, touching everywhere. The furnace-like heat of his tall frame, even the way his arms caged her as he propped himself above her, taking some of his weight, all added to the amazing intimacy.

Soon that expectant stillness vanished, obliterated by the need for more of what Damen gave her. His hard body against hers, his hands moving knowingly, his mouth... Oh, his mouth. That earlier kiss had been a mere prelude to what he did now, drawing her to the edge of ecstasy with his mouth on hers till she writhed, eager for more.

Strong hands clamped hers, lifting her arms above her head. 'What—?'

'It's okay. We just need to slow things a little. I don't have many condoms with me and they need to last the night.' He nipped the sensitive place between her neck and shoulder, making her gasp.

'That's not slowing things. That's...' Her words ended with a sigh as Damen worked his way up to her ear, kissing, nipping, turning her to jelly. Yet before she could catch her breath he moved down her body, settling between her thighs as if he belonged there and capturing her breasts in his hands. His breath was hot on first one nipple then the other as he blew across them, watching them rise to aching points.

'Please, Damen.'

He lifted his head. 'You don't like this?'

Steph shook her head. 'I do. Too much.'

'Then relax, and I'll show you how much better it can be.'

That was the start of what she thought of later as exquisite torture. Damen worked his way around her body, drawing wild responses from the tiniest caresses. And all the time she heard his voice, deep enough to shudder through her bones, asking if she liked this, or this. When the truth was she liked it all. Too much. Each new caress, each press of his lips or stroke of his hand drew the tension in her tighter.

Till finally, with a gleam in his dark eyes, he sank once more between her thighs. It took just the touch of his tongue, a single, sliding stroke, and Steph shattered in a piercing explosion of pleasure. Light burst in a rainbow of colour behind her eyelids, the breath seized in her lungs and her body stretched taut, racked by aftershocks that gradually diminished, leaving her dazed and boneless.

Finally she opened her eyes. There was Damen, his gaze fixed on her, his face intent, as if there was nothing more important than her pleasure.

Steph's mouth curled up in a breathless smile. 'Before you ask, I *did* like that.'

His answering grin was the sexiest thing she'd seen, perhaps because of where he lay, his broad shoulders between the V of her legs.

'Good. Let's do it again.'

Steph lifted herself on one elbow, a protest forming on her lips because of course she couldn't possibly climax like that again, not now she was totally sated.

Except it seemed Damen knew her better than she did. This time he used tongue, lips and teeth to ease her back into that state of frantic need, while his long fingers explored and delved, making her arch off the bed as that tightness gathered again, sensitive nerve endings singing with excitement.

All through it, Damen held her gaze.

That, his knowing look, the dark, hungry gleam that caressed as surely as his hand and mouth, was what turned her to mush. Stopped the protest that had formed in her mouth. Why would she want to stop anything that felt so wonderful?

That time when she came Steph screamed, her fingers clutching the thick hair on Damen's head, her eyes locked with his. Her cries took ages to die, morphing into something like a sob as finally he prowled his way up her body and she could put her arms around him, clutching him close.

She squeezed him tight, wrapping her leaden legs around him, burrowing her face into his shoulder, drawing the spicy hot scent of him deep inside. In the pulsing quiet everything seemed to slow and centre. Steph felt as if she'd discovered a new world, a place she'd never known existed. Because of Damen.

Eventually there was movement as he rolled over, taking her with him so she lay straddled and boneless across his tall frame.

For a long time they lay like that, unmoving, till finally Damen stroked his hand down Steph's spine and, to her surprise, she felt herself arch into him.

'Are you ready for more, Stephanie?'

'More?' Blearily she lifted her head but his meaning was clear as he shifted and she felt the slide of his arousal against her core.

Of course there was more. He'd given her orgasms and it was only fair he should claim his own. Yet as his hips tilted and Steph felt the press of that iron and silk shaft between her legs, she didn't feel as exhausted as she had before. Instead she was...excited. Her breath caught deep in her chest as Damen's hands brushed her breasts, then sank to her hips.

Experimentally Steph slid against him and was shocked by the white-hot bolt of heat that shot through her.

'I like that,' he growled, his voice barely recognisable. The sound of it, rough and hungry, made something dance inside, some feminine part of her that revelled in the idea of Damen on the edge. 'Do you?'

For answer Steph moved again, more deliberately, bracing her hands on his shoulders, concentrating on his flesh gliding against hers. 'I do.'

In the gloom she caught his grin, or was it a grimace? 'Good. Then take me.'

It took Steph a moment to digest his meaning. It wasn't what she'd expected. She'd imagined him propped over her, powering into her, setting their rhythm.

But this was the man who'd taken an age pleasuring her, leashing his own desires to make her first time good. More than good. The wetness between her legs, the melting sensation there, told its own story. Now he let her set the pace. How much easier could he have made it? If there was going to be pain, she sensed it would be fleeting.

Besides, she decided as she wriggled back a little, despite her climaxes, Damen had left her with an aching emptiness inside. An emptiness she wanted him to fill.

She rose onto her knees then gingerly reached for him, finding him already sheathed. His fingers clamped tighter around her hips.

'Like this?' She centred herself over him, watching him nod, seeing his mouth pull back into a flat line as she slowly sank. It was the weirdest feeling, a stretching sensation that made her pause, panting.

Steph waited for him to tell her to keep going, to pull her down with those large hands, but he simply waited, watching, till the slight discomfort faded. She tilted her hips and, as if in response, Damen lifted up from beneath in a long, slow glide that stole her breath.

'More,' he urged in a voice of gravel.

Steph blinked. There was more? How was that possible?

She longed to find out. Steadying herself on his shoulders, she bore down till they were locked together with him buried deep inside.

She blinked, astonished at how easy it had been and how remarkable it felt. Except Damen's hands on her hips were urging her up. She followed the prompting, then blinked as he tugged her back down while he tilted his pelvis and thrust.

The sensation was amazing. It felt…

Steph gasped a shocked breath and repeated the movement, more smoothly this time, meeting the angle of his thrust with her own, then feeling the aftershock ripple through her like the shadow of an earthquake.

'Damen. Please, I…'

Her body began to shake, those worn-out muscles trembling as pleasure rose. Not like before. This was bigger, deeper, tugging at her soul as well as her body. She felt them moving as one, then moving in counterpoint, making the most remarkable magic between them.

That was how it felt. Magic.

Like the most profound magic in the world. Steph felt bigger than herself, part of something wondrous.

Maybe it was the way Damen held her eyes as they made the magic together, or the press of his hands so possessive at her hips. The thrusting caress of his body within hers, circling in a way that shot showers of flaming sparks through the darkness at the edge of her vision.

Then she heard it, Damen's voice, but not his voice. A low growl of triumph and wonder as he called her name and thrust high. Suddenly she was falling to meet him, the whole world bursting into flames around her, consuming her, cradling her in a fiery embrace that became Damen's embrace, his arms tight round her, his breath caressing her cheek, holding her to him as ecstasy took them both.

CHAPTER NINE

DAMEN WATCHED HER SLEEPING. It had been late when finally they'd collapsed, sated, in a tangle on the sheets. For hours after that he'd lain there, unable to sleep, his brain racing as he surveyed the woman curled so trustingly in his arms.

He didn't do post-coital cuddles. He didn't invite lovers to spend the night. Not in ten years. Not since Ingrid.

He waited for the familiar shudder of revulsion at the name but for once it didn't come. Probably because he held Stephanie warm and limp in his embrace.

Last night had felt like a turning point and he'd spent the last couple of hours inventing plausible reasons for that.

Because she'd been a virgin.

Because he'd wanted her for so long, longer than he'd ever wanted and gone without a woman.

Because, although he'd paid for her presence in his world, she'd made it clear that she gave her body as a gift that had nothing to do with the contract they'd negotiated or the masquerade they played.

Because her innocence and forthrightness were a combination so heady it made her different to any other woman he'd let into his life.

Because he'd *let* her into his life. He'd explained the reasons for their masquerade, explained his relationship with Manos and Clio, he who never explained himself to any woman.

He sensed that last came closest to the truth.

Damen had let Stephanie in, not just to his bed, but under his guard in ways that hadn't been apparent till too late.

Now, watching the sun rise over the Aegean, the pink and apricot dawn light changing to a clear blue sky, Damen wasn't concentrating on the work he'd do later from his yacht, or the discussions he'd have with Manos. He was thinking about how and when he'd have Stephanie again. Whether she'd be sore from making love and whether he should back off for a day and whether he had the resolve to do that if she needed space. Whether she'd enjoy it if he took her from behind, and how she'd feel about spending the whole day naked in his bed.

He scrubbed his palm over his face, trying to erase the erotic fantasies that crowded his brain.

Every time he tried to think about the next few weeks, even the next couple of days, he circled back to Stephanie naked beneath him, above him, before him. Stephanie caressing him. How would she feel about using her mouth on him?

She sighed and stretched voluptuously, her lips soft against his chest, her legs sliding around his, sending his temperature soaring and his libido into overdrive.

Damen waited, breathless, for her to wake. Instead she sank more deeply against him as if he were her own private pillow. Her even breathing was a caress against sensitised flesh. The sight of her pink nipple, trembling invitingly with each rise of her chest, was designed, surely, to taunt him.

Carefully Damen slid from the bed, propping a pillow under her arm and cheek, telling himself he didn't really want her to wake. Because Stephanie would wake full of questions.

Questions he had no desire to answer.

Questions about how their relationship would change now they were lovers.

Loping to the wardrobe, Damen gritted his teeth. The answer was simple. There was no change. Not in any material way. They'd go on as before except—here he allowed himself a satisfied smile—that when they were alone they could indulge their taste for passion. He was pretty sure after last night that Stephanie, so sensual and passionate, would be eager for that.

But that would be only in the privacy of their bed. Nothing else was different. She wasn't his girlfriend. There'd be no long-term relationship, no matter how phenomenal the sex.

Damen grabbed swim shorts and a towel. He'd take an early dip and give her some privacy when she woke. She'd appreciate that.

And it would signal that nothing significant had altered. She was smart. She'd understand he wouldn't make promises he had no intention of keeping. Promises that might lead a woman to believe in happy endings.

No fear of that with Stephanie, despite the surprise of her virginity. She was here solely for the money. She'd made no bones about that. She wouldn't start dreaming of a wedding ring just because they'd enjoyed sex.

Which meant, he realised as he dragged the shorts on, that she really was the perfect woman. Sexy, passionate and short-term.

Damen smiled and let himself out into the sunshine. It was going to be a glorious day.

Where was she?

Damen stalked along the path to the main house, his brow knotted as he scanned the terrace where last night guests had danced till late. It was empty and tidy too, as if an army of helpers had cleared away last night's detritus.

She must be here. There was no other possibility.

When he'd returned to the guest house it had been empty, the bed tidy, Stephanie's bag packed beside it. But there'd been no sign of her. Only the lingering aroma of coffee in the air, making his nostrils twitch.

Damen had returned warily. He'd enjoyed his morning swim, then, since it was early, had swum to the *Amphitrite* to put in an hour's work on the computer. An hour had become two but he'd known Stephanie would be exhausted after last night. *He'd* been exhausted, but so energised with his brain on overload, rest had been out of the question.

Besides, he admitted to a lingering doubt about whether she'd see their situation with quite the same clarity he did. Women could be emotional and it would be no surprise if, the morning after losing her virginity, Stephanie was a little clingy.

He should never have had sex with her, not after discovering she was still innocent, sexually at least. But abstinence had been impossible by the time he'd tasted her lips.

He'd returned to the guest house wondering if he approached an emotional battleground.

Only to find that, far from clinging unbearably, Stephanie had deserted him!

Pain arced through his jaw and he realised he was grinding his teeth.

He didn't want her clinging but he didn't expect her to disappear. What if he'd wanted to discuss this development in their relationship? What about laying out new ground rules? Had she no consideration?

He pushed open the door to Manos's home and followed the sound of voices.

Steph looked up from the laptop as Clio offered another plate of goodies. Baklava this time, dripping with sweet syrup. 'Truly, I couldn't eat any more.'

'Nonsense. You worked hard helping out, which you shouldn't have done, being a visitor.'

'I was glad to help. It was nice to be involved.'

She'd arrived at the big house to find Clio, her mother and Damen's mother putting things to rights after the caterers had finished the heavy work of clearing up.

It had been a relief to see Clio's warm smile, and accept her offer of breakfast with the three women in the massive kitchen.

Steph had felt so very alone this morning.

She'd told herself she was being overly emotional. Of course she hadn't expected Damen to be there, waiting to share breakfast with her.

Or hold her in his arms as he'd done last night.

She'd woken to unaccustomed aches in places she'd never ached. Not badly, just a gentle throb that reminded her of how they'd spent the night.

It was stupid to want those strong arms holding her close to the comforting thud of Damen's heart. Stupid to long for his hoarse endearments in Greek that melted her insides, for that sense of oneness that had transformed a physical act into something wondrous.

Steph should be grateful he'd left early and she'd had the guest house to herself. There'd been no stilted morning-after conversation. She'd been able to take a leisurely bath and make strong, sweet coffee to help banish the lingering wisps of fantasy.

Because it had been fantasy. A night of glorious passion in the arms of her perfect lover.

But now it was a new day. The passion was gone and so was her lover. Damen wasn't perfect and nor was she. She'd made the massive mistake of giving in to desire, telling herself she could enjoy simple sex then walk away.

Now she realised there was no such thing as simple sex. Not for her, and not with Damen.

'Try it at least,' Clio urged. 'Mama made it to a family recipe.'

Steph took a spoonful and glorious flavours exploded in her mouth. 'This is stunning.'

From the other side of the kitchen Clio's mother beamed. 'I'm glad you like it. It's the least I can do, especially as you're doing me this big favour.' She nodded to the laptop in front of Steph on the marble island bench. 'If I can get away for a little while, maybe even persuade Manos…' She shrugged. 'You have no idea how much that would mean.'

Steph looked at the worry lines marking the older woman's face and remembered Manos's dark eyes flashing with suppressed temper yesterday. Damen had said Manos would make his whole family's life miserable if he didn't get his way. It seemed he'd been doing just that. Even beautiful Clio looked tired and drawn.

Suddenly Steph was glad she'd agreed to Damen's scheme to rescue Clio from her father's machinations.

But she could do more. 'I think I've got the perfect place for the quiet holiday you wanted. It's in a scenic part of Italy, not crowded with tourists yet gorgeous and utterly peaceful. I found it for clients recently and they loved it.' She turned the laptop.

'Is that a convent?' The women crowded close.

'Yes, but the accommodation is luxurious. It's a guest house in the grounds and no tourists are allowed, only the nuns and their guests. There are views to the lake and mountains plus a walled courtyard full of roses.' Steph scrolled through photos, pleased to see her audience's excitement. 'It's a short walk to town, where there are restaurants and a supermarket if you want to self-cater.' Manos might be wealthy but his wife enjoyed cooking.

'The comforts of home,' Clio murmured, 'without the stresses.'

Her mother nodded. 'It looks amazing. How did you know about it?'

'It's what I do. I'm a travel advisor and I specialise…specialised in tailoring unique holiday experiences. Mainly at the luxury end of the market.'

'Specialised, past tense?' Clio asked as the two older women focused on the photos. 'What happened?'

Steph shrugged. 'It's a tough time in the travel industry. Lots of people don't think they need professional help when they can trawl the internet themselves.'

Clio tilted her head, as if considering. 'But if you were work-ing at the luxury end of the market...?'

Steph met her questioning gaze and finally nodded. It wasn't a secret really, even if she didn't usually like discussing it. 'I came unstuck in a business venture.'

'Oh, rotten luck. The business model wasn't sound?'

Steph knew Clio was running her own start-up company and didn't take offence at her direct question. 'Oh, it was sound. Sadly my partner wasn't.'

She turned as Manos and Damen entered the kitchen, Manos speaking Greek and gesturing emphatically.

Steph's skin prickled as she met Damen's unblinking green stare.

Last time he'd seen her they'd been naked in bed.

She sat straighter, wishing she had more than palazzo pants and a slinky top to keep her safe from that heated gaze. He only had to look at her and her skin heated to a fiery blush.

Could everyone tell? Did they all know that she and he...?

Belatedly she stopped her runaway thoughts. Of course no one else knew she'd given Damen her virginity last night. Or that she'd spent hours learning how dangerous a patient, gen-erous, potently desirable man could be to her equilibrium. As far as the world was concerned, she and Damen were already lovers, even if Clio suspected otherwise.

Steph drew a breath and tried to tame her racing pulse. She nodded to both men. 'Good morning. Have you come to join us for coffee?'

The morning tested Damen's patience.

He wanted, desperately, to get Stephanie alone. He'd told himself he needed to clarify with her that nothing had changed, that she had no expectations beyond their contract. Yet to his chagrin it seemed there was no need. She treated him with a ca-sual friendliness that should have pleased him, yet instead irked.

Or maybe he wanted to get her alone so they could revisit

some of last night's more spectacular moments. Since waking he'd been unable to concentrate fully on anything but the memory of her satiny skin, her sighs of pleasure and the exquisite delight she'd offered him.

But every attempt to be alone with her was thwarted. By Clio and her mother offering food and coffee. By Manos, eager to talk business. By the interested gleam in his own mother's eyes as she looked from Damen to Stephanie and back again, clearly wondering if there was more to their relationship than he'd let on.

Obviously he wasn't the only one to notice Stephanie's delightful blush when their eyes met. It was the only hint that anything had changed between them.

Such as him taking her virginity in the night.

That knowledge throbbed through him every time he saw her looking cool and exasperatingly sexy in jade-green silk and those wide, floaty trousers that made him think of veils and beds and sex.

Damen considered himself a modern man, not hung up on old traditions. Yet to his surprise, the knowledge he'd been Stephanie's first lover branded itself on his psyche. He felt…engaged. Protective. Possessive.

He wanted to haul her away to somewhere private where he could keep her for himself.

Which didn't make sense when he'd already told himself nothing had altered between them.

By the time they finally finished their goodbyes, late in the afternoon, and headed for the yacht, Damen's patience hung by a thread.

He should have been pleased that Stephanie didn't attempt to talk on the walk to the beach, or the short trip to the yacht. There were no fluttering eyelashes, no hand on his arm as she leaned close to whisper in his ear. None of the tactics previous lovers had used to manufacture an illusion of emotional intimacy. Instead she seemed interested in everything but him. The colour of the water. The view of the island. The silver flash as a school of fish passed them. Even her phone, as if she had urgent business to conduct.

Which reminded him. Her partner. Who was that? He'd caught the phrase as he walked into the kitchen. He'd been listening to Manos but, as usual, when Stephanie was near, Damen's attention veered straight to her.

Who was this partner? He couldn't have been a lover, since only Damen could claim that role. Yet dissatisfaction niggled. He needed to know more.

When they stepped onto the deck Damen took Stephanie's arm and guided her into the privacy of a sitting room. For an instant she looked as if she'd protest, but only for an instant. She must realise there was no point trying to avoid this discussion.

He waited till the door was closed and Stephanie stood by the window, as if drawn to the view of the island.

Damen was drawn to the view of her. Utterly alluring despite the tight set of her shoulders. Was she going to make trouble after all?

'Are you okay?'

It wasn't what he'd planned to say. It surprised her too, for she swung to face him, eyes wide.

'Of course. Don't I look it?'

What she looked was sumptuously inviting. Her slender curves showed to advantage in that outfit and her skin had a healthy glow.

Was she embarrassed? Nervous under his scrutiny?

Her chin lifted and her eyebrows too, as if challenging him.

'You look fine.' Her eyes narrowed and he hurried on. 'More than fine.' Damen cursed his sudden inability to articulate. 'We need to talk.'

Did he imagine that Stephanie tensed? Her mouth drew into a flat line, as if she didn't want to hear what he had to say.

'Go on.'

Damen stuck his hands in the pockets of his jeans. Did he

start by finding out how she felt physically after last night? Or come straight to the point and reiterate that their agreement hadn't changed?

He opened his mouth and heard himself say, 'Tell me about your partner.'

'Sorry?' She definitely stood straighter this time, arms curving around her waist in a defensive gesture.

So the guy *was* important to her. Damen had sensed it. 'Earlier today you said something about a partner. I want to know about him.'

'Why? He has nothing to do with this…us…' She made a wide, arcing gesture.

'I don't want any loose ends that might complicate things. We've still got six weeks together and I don't want any murky surprises.'

Steph bit her lip. Murky surprises. That was one way to describe Jared. He'd wrecked her life and even now she couldn't be rid of him. Not with Damen standing there like the lord of all he surveyed, demanding she lift the lid on her private life.

Disappointment was a swirling, bitter pool in her stomach.

What did she expect? That after last night Damen would turn to her with affection in his eyes? Or at least softness?

That he'd want to be alone with her to make love again? Because, like her, he felt bound together by this spell, even when they were surrounded by others?

Except it wasn't making love, it was sex.

Yet every time she'd met his eyes today she'd felt a great whump of emotion slam into her, like the roar of a bonfire igniting in a rush of flame. Heat trickled through her at the connection they shared, the connection no one else seemed to have noticed.

She was deluded. There was no connection. Last night meant nothing to him. She wouldn't allow herself to be so pathetic as to reveal how much it had meant to her.

'You needn't worry. He's out of my life. I'll never see him again.'

'Nevertheless, I need to know.' He paused, expectant. Finally he added, 'I'll treat what you tell me in confidence. I just need to know nothing from your past will derail our…arrangement.'

Clearly her word wasn't good enough.

Steph bit back the words of hurt cramming onto her tongue.

But a look at Damen's set jaw and hard eyes told her he wouldn't back down. Besides, what did it matter? She was past the stage of caring what he thought of her gullibility. She'd laid herself wide open to him last night, not just physically, but emotionally too, and he didn't give a damn. There'd been no tenderness today, no acknowledgement. Nothing.

It left her feeling hollow. Which was good, because the alternative, to feel upset that he took what had happened last night for granted, would put her in an untenable position.

Suddenly Damen's lack of sensitivity felt like a blessing in disguise. If he didn't care then she didn't have to either.

'What do you want to know?'

He blinked and for a moment she could almost believe she'd discomfited him. Only for a moment.

'Everything. Who he is, what he is to you. What he did.'

Steph swallowed, her throat gritty. 'Not much, then.'

Yet had locking the past away like a shameful secret helped her deal with it? It wasn't as if she'd done anything wrong. Besides, with the money she was earning from Damen she had the power to undo the damage, financially if not personally. It would take a long time to trust again.

She swung away towards the bank of windows. Already the island was slipping away, the big yacht gathering speed as it headed for open water.

'His name's Jared and he was my boss. He managed a travel agency in Melbourne, though he didn't own it.'

'Just your boss?'

Steph frowned at the terse question but didn't bother turning. She kept her eyes on the creamy arc of sand that fringed the bay and the bright sparkle of sunlight on water. A couple of seabirds wheeled, pale against the brilliant blue sky.

'I looked on him as a mentor. Later he was my business partner.' She swallowed a bitter tang.

'You went into business together?'

Did he have to sound so surprised? 'I'm excellent at what I do. I brought in more business than anyone else in the team. Travel is my passion.' She paused, 'Well, other people's travel. I haven't done much myself.'

'You're a travel agent who hasn't travelled? I thought that was a perk of the job, trying out fabulous holiday destinations.'

Steph shrugged. 'I've travelled in Australia but not overseas. There was never time. I was always working.' Putting money aside for a secure future. 'Exploring the world was my dream. I almost went to South America but Gran got sick and...'

She stopped. He didn't need to know about Gran's cancer scare.

'So you became partners. In a new agency?'

Steph nodded. 'It was to specialise in bespoke, luxury travel. That's what I'm good at.' What she'd *been* good at. Who knew if she'd work in that field again?

Damen didn't say anything, just waited, and suddenly Steph wanted this over. 'We signed an agreement, pooled our resources, secured a loan and...' She stepped closer to the windows, putting out her hand to the wall of glass. 'He was going to put a deposit down on our new premises but instead he disappeared.'

'He had an accident?' Damen's voice came from just over her shoulder and she turned to meet his stare. It was steady and unemotional.

'No accident. He simply took off. He cleared out the money we'd borrowed, the money I'd put up, even...' She stopped then shrugged. It was strangely cathartic telling the tale. Why not continue? 'I'd introduced him to my gran. What I didn't know was that he persuaded her to invest a chunk of her savings.' Steph dragged in a deep breath. 'The police are looking for him.'

Dark green eyes bored into her. 'That's why you wanted cash up front.'

He didn't sound happy. He sounded disapproving, as if she'd done something wrong, instead of being left high and dry by a fraudster.

Steph folded her arms again. 'It is. You have a problem with that?'

His brow furrowed. 'You should have told me.'

'Why? So you could lecture me on financial risk?' A flicker of familiar flame shot through her. 'I did everything right, everything by the book. How was I to know Jared would run when he got the cash?'

She shook her head. 'No, don't answer that. I'm sure you'd tell me I should have checked his background better, should have somehow divined he was a crook. Even though he had no criminal history.'

Steph swung away and stared at the fast-receding island. Would they return to Athens now? To days spent alone then evenings where Damen showed her off like a trophy? She shivered and rubbed her hands up her arms.

'Is there anything else? If not I'd like to go and lie down. It's been a…tiring couple of days.'

She felt him behind her, so close his warmth seeped into her. Even now, with her nerves jangling, she had a fantasy that he'd lean forward, put his arms around her and hold her close. Tell her he was sorry about what had happened with Jared. Tell her he was sorry they hadn't spent the day together because what he'd wanted, more than anything, was to be alone with her.

Because last night had been special.

She was special.

'Stephanie, I—'

'No!' Those couple of syllables didn't reveal any of the tenderness she'd come to crave last night. 'Not now. I need to rest.'

She spun on her heel and marched to the door. She'd had enough of men, and of Damen Nicolaides. She needed time alone.

CHAPTER TEN

DAMEN JABBED THE PUNCHBAG. Left, left, right. The quick blows should relieve the tension grabbing his shoulders and chest.

Not tonight. He'd been in the gym for forty minutes and was still wound too tight.

He turned away, unlacing the boxing gloves and scrubbing his face with a towel.

The problem was Stephanie and the nagging feeling he'd done the wrong thing.

He should have trusted his instincts. Not the familiar voice of caution that urged him to keep his distance, but the one that wanted to sweep her into his arms and his bed and keep her there.

He'd made a tactical error keeping his distance. It was clear she didn't want anything to do with him. He'd missed his chance for more intimacy. Strangely though, that wasn't the worst. The worst was knowing she was hurting and he was part of that hurt because he'd let her down.

Clio would say he felt this way because of his managing personality, because he'd shouldered responsibility for his family and the vast empire that was Nicolaides Shipping at a young age. Damen wasn't so sure. This felt different.

Stephanie wasn't family, yet he felt…

Damen shook his head. Better to stick to facts than feelings. Fact one. Last night had been phenomenal, and instead of thanking Stephanie, and looking after her when he guessed she was physically sore and possibly feeling out of her depth, he'd left her at first light then found excuses to keep away.

Fact two. She'd more than fulfilled her part of their bargain. Not only had she played her part in public but today she'd gone beyond what was necessary, helping Clio and her mother with this idea of a luxury retreat in Italy and even charming Manos. He hadn't seen his aunt look so relaxed in ages.

Fact three. Stephanie wasn't a gold-digger, eager for his money. She'd needed cash to make good money stolen from her and her grandmother.

Pain tore through Damen's belly as he imagined how she'd felt, discovering her business partner was a thief. That everything she'd worked towards was gone, and her grandmother's savings too.

Damen remembered his annoyance at having to pay for Stephanie's wardrobe in Athens and felt his skin crawl. He was so used to assuming people were avaricious he hadn't considered any other option.

That was one thing, at least, he'd rectified. He'd transferred the other million dollars into her account and discreet enquiries were being made in Melbourne to ensure that would cover the business loan she'd mentioned. Technically it wasn't Damen's debt and yet he felt he owed her.

He wasn't used to feeling guilty, as if he'd done the wrong thing. There must be something he could do to make it up to Stephanie.

Damen raked the towel around his neck then stopped, an idea forming.

She wanted to travel. It was her dream. He recalled all her outings in Athens to museums and ancient ruins, to markets and landmarks. She'd spent every moment of her free time exploring the city. No doubt she'd spend the next six weeks doing the same. Unless Damen changed his plans.

A smile eased across his face as he reached for the ship's phone.

Next morning Steph woke alone.

Of course she didn't miss Damen!

Yesterday she'd hoped for even a shadow of the intimacy they'd shared. Instead Damen had interrogated her about her past as if he was more interested in Jared than their lovemaking.

Even so, her thoughts were all of Damen.

Till she opened her curtains.

Steph stared, dumbfounded, at the view. She recognised it, of course, though the iconic vista, known the world over, was usually from above, looking down to where she was.

Beyond the window the sea was the rich blue of lapis lazuli. Rising from it were cliffs of deep ochre red and dark grey, frosted along the top with a canopy of white buildings, bright in the sun.

Santorini.

She breathed deep and blinked. From here she could make out a zigzag track up the slope that she knew was popular with tourists who paid to ride donkeys along the steep, cobblestoned road. She thought of the honeymoons she'd booked here for clients, the luxury hotels with terraces that seemed to hang out over the cliffs, the perfect venue for cocktails as the sun sank into the sea. The marvellous frescoes that had been discovered at the other end of the island, remnants of an ancient civilisation that had been shattered by a massive volcanic eruption. The fabled Atlantis, some said.

Steph almost danced with excitement as she dressed and hurried from her room.

Only to skid to a stop when she found Damen emerging from his stateroom at the same time.

'You look well,' he said. 'You had a good rest?'

It was crazy to feel a flicker of exultation at the sound of his voice. The man was just making polite conversation. Yet the impact of that deep tone and his penetrating forest-green stare was real.

'I did, thank you.'

He nodded but didn't move. His brows twitched together and Steph had the curious idea that he hesitated, as if he wasn't sure how to proceed.

Damen Nicolaides, hesitating? Not possible. Yet, instead of turning away in search of breakfast, Steph waited, heart thudding high in her throat.

He reached a hand towards her then dropped it, the furrow deepening on his brow.

'I owe you an apology, for yesterday.'

Steph felt her eyebrows lift.

His gaze drifted away then slewed back, pinning her to the spot. 'I should have been there in the morning. When you woke. What we shared was...'

Steph held herself completely still, waiting.

'... Phenomenal. And I didn't even thank you.' Again his hand rose, this time to the back of his neck, as if the muscles there were tight.

They couldn't be as tight as Steph's. She didn't want a post mortem of that night, not if it entailed this stilted conversation. Two nights ago intimacy had seemed right, perfect. But now...

'I don't need your thanks.' She turned away, preferring not to meet that searching stare. 'You're not obligated to me.'

'Stephanie.' This time his voice was urgent. He stepped close, hemming her in. 'Please listen.'

Reluctantly she turned back. Damen met her gaze steadily. 'I'm trying, very badly, to apologise.' He spread his hands. 'What we shared was special. So special it threw me. Yesterday I didn't behave well. I should have checked you were okay and—'

'Of course I was okay. It was just sex.' Her voice was too strident, as if she tried to convince herself as well as him.

'Nevertheless, I apologise for deserting you. I went off to do some work but that's no excuse for poor behaviour.'

Stephanie wished the carpeted floor would open up and swallow her. Which was worse, Damen thinking she was so fragile she needed him by her side because she'd surrendered her virginity, as if she were some Victorian maiden? Or the decadent thrill of excitement stirring inside, hearing him admit what they'd shared was special?

Because that would mean she felt the same. That she wanted more of what she'd tasted that night in Damen's arms. The idea terrified her.

'Apology accepted.'

For a long moment Damen said nothing, his stare far too unsettling.

'Why are we at Santorini?' she said quickly. 'I thought we were returning to Athens.'

Damen drew her arm through his, leading her away from the staterooms. Steph tried not to react, though the feel of his arm on hers made her nerve endings jitter and heat pool low inside. 'I changed my mind. I can work from the *Amphitrite* a bit longer. You might as well see some of the islands while you're in Greece.'

Steph rocked to a halt. 'You came here for me?'

She frowned, trying to fathom what was going on. Damen didn't change his schedule for her. *She* fitted into his world.

'What do you want, Damen?' Carefully she slipped free of his hold. 'Why are you doing this?'

Because he wants more sex.

And that's good because you do too.

Ruthlessly Steph stifled the voice in her head. She had more self-respect than to give herself to him just because he'd arranged a treat. Even if it was a wonderful treat. Even if she wanted him as much now as she had two nights ago.

Damen tilted his head as if to get a clearer view of her face. 'You're helping me enormously, performing this charade, and you went further than you needed to yesterday, helping Clio and her mother. They really do need to get away and you've got them excited at the prospect.'

Steph shrugged. 'It wasn't difficult. It's what I do.'

'But you didn't *need* to. You did it because you're a nice person.'

Strange how those simple words resonated like the most lavish praise.

'I wanted to do something for you. You said you'd never had the chance to travel and here we are on the Aegean. It seemed selfish to sail back to Athens before you'd seen more of the islands.'

Dazed, Steph stared up into that handsome face. Every time she felt she understood Damen Nicolaides he pulled the rug out from under her feet.

'Come on.' He reached for her elbow and led her down the wide passage. 'The sooner we eat, the sooner you can explore.'

They stayed at Santorini for two days and to Steph's surprise Damen took several hours off from his work each day to accompany her ashore. Steph thought he'd be bored doing tourist things, seeing ancient frescoes, clambering up and down meandering streets and stopping every few metres as she found yet another spectacular view. But never once did he reveal impatience, though he admitted he preferred visiting when the crowds were thinner.

From Santorini they cruised east, calling at Astypalaia, Kos and Symi. Steph explored quaint towns, museums and ancient ruins, and swam in crystal waters. She'd never felt more relaxed and enthralled. Each day brought new discoveries, stunning vistas, friendly people and fascinating places.

It also brought hours with Damen, not at some exclusive party, but hand in hand as he led her through narrow streets, drank thick Greek coffee in the shade of vine-covered pergolas and told her about his country.

What surprised her most was that Damen seemed at home in such simple surroundings, far from the trappings of enormous wealth. And the fact that she enjoyed being with him. Enjoyed it too much to maintain a proud distance.

Back on the yacht they dined on deck, eating sumptuous meals perfectly prepared, and watching the sun set in a glow of tangerine over the dark sea. Each night, as they sat in the candlelight, it became harder for Steph to recall why she was angry with Damen.

Especially when she discovered he'd paid the second instalment of her contracted fee. Because, he said, he trusted her to make good on her contract and act the part of his lover for another six weeks. And because he didn't want her to suffer any more because of Jared's theft. He'd been concerned to learn about the joint loan they'd taken out and her ability to service the repayments.

It was amazing how wonderful it felt to have the burden of the lost money completely lifted from her shoulders.

His gesture rocked Steph. She'd thought Damen a man who'd stick to the letter of their agreement. She'd never expected such generosity, or trust.

No one in her life had shown such faith in her. With two exceptions: Gran and Emma. Steph understood how rare it was.

That action by Damen, extravagant and unexpected, confused her. It was too big a gesture. It evoked a raft of emotions she struggled to contain. Emotions she didn't know what to do with.

It would have been simpler if Damen had made a move on her, assuming that she'd agree to have sex again, partly because, as he said, it had been phenomenal, and partly out of gratitude.

Instead she was flummoxed to find he treated her like an honoured guest. He was charming and attentive but didn't press for intimacy. When they were ashore he played the part of lover in public with his arm around her waist, or feeding her delicacies from his plate, or whispering in her ear.

Steph got almost used to it. What she couldn't get used to was the way Damen's arm would drop from around her once they boarded his yacht and there was no need for a public display of affection.

What did that say about her?

It had been a week since they'd shared a bed. A week during which she'd gone to sleep each night recalling how magical that night had been. Her mind tortured her with steamy erotic dreams that left her wide awake in the early hours, heart pumping and body aching for fulfilment.

Damen had done that to her.

Except Steph knew that wasn't right.

She'd done it. She'd opened the Pandora's Box that was sexual desire. She'd chosen to seek physical release with Damen and now she bore the consequences. The fact that he was an amazing, generous lover only compounded the problem. If he'd been selfish in bed, a total disappointment, it would have made things so much easier.

Instead the memory of him, them, drove her crazy.

She wanted him. Badly. It was worse now she knew what she was missing. Especially spending this time with Damen, seeing the best of him, enjoying every day to the full. Even the casual brush of his arm against hers sent a thrill of wanting through her.

They emerged from deep shadow and walked out into the heat bouncing off the cobblestoned square. Automatically Steph turned around and stared back up at the thick, crenellated towers soaring up against the blue sky.

'My first visit to a castle.'

'I guessed.' Damen's voice was soft in her ear.

She turned to find those deep green eyes crinkling in amusement.

'There wasn't a centimetre of it you didn't examine. Especially the mosaics.'

He was right. She'd taken hundreds of photos. The Palace

of the Grand Master of the Knights of Rhodes was a stunning building. It mightn't be filled to the brim with antiques but she'd strung out their visit, poring over every detail.

Steph's lips twitched. 'You're right and you've been so patient. I owe you. What would you like in return?'

Just like that the amusement faded from his eyes, banished by a hot glitter that sent fire curling through her blood. Steph's breath snagged and her heart pounded high and hard as if it tried to leap out of her chest.

Steph knew that look. She'd seen it the night they'd gone to bed together. And every night since in her lonely bed as she relived the thrill of being naked with Damen.

She licked dry lips, his gaze following the movement. The way he watched her was so…intimate, she felt it as if he reached out to trail his fingers across her mouth.

Abruptly he looked away, surveying the streets leading from the palace into the old town of Rhodes. It was a reminder that they were in public. She noticed some phones and cameras turned their way.

Had that look on Damen's face been for show?

She couldn't believe it. When they were out together Damen smiled at her but never once had she glimpsed that hot, hungry stare that turned her insides molten.

'I'm ready for a cool drink.' His hand closed around hers, sending a quiver of excitement through her. Steph curled her fingers into his and let him lead her, not down the main street but into a picturesque alley that was blessedly cool, with high stone buildings on either side. Beaten copper pots hung outside an artisan's workshop, gleaming even in the shadows.

Damen led her down the lane, taking a side turning and then another, till they were in a street so narrow Steph could almost touch the walls on each side. Then on their left was an open door, a small, shaded courtyard with rush-bottomed chairs and tiny tables.

Minutes later she was sipping gratefully from an iced glass. But the cold drink didn't quench the heat that had erupted at Damen's blatantly possessive stare outside the palace.

It was a warm day, even in the trellised shade, even with the icy drink. But not that hot. The fiery heat came from within. She put her glass down and turned to Damen. Predictably he was already regarding her, his gaze steady but unreadable.

'What's wrong? You're not enjoying yourself now.'

The man was too perceptive. He saw things she preferred he didn't.

No, that wasn't right. Steph couldn't lie to herself any longer. She liked it when they were both on the same page. When it took just a look and they were in agreement. It happened increasingly as they spent time together and she discovered Damen was far more than a bossy tycoon. He was a man with a sense of humour, with patience and much more.

'It's not that. Visiting Rhodes is the best. I've wanted to come here for so long. And it's every bit as wonderful as I thought.'

'But?'

Steph's pulse thudded as she held his eyes.

She could prevaricate.

Or she could trust her instinct.

'Perhaps there's something else you'd like even more than exploring a medieval city.' He paused, his eyes glittering like shards of precious gems. 'I know there's something else *I* want.'

'What do you want, Damen?'

He leaned close. 'To kiss you on the lips. To take you in my arms. To make love to you.'

Steph's breath escaped in a sigh that felt like relief. 'I want that too.'

The words were barely out when he stood, drawing her up beside him, tossing some money onto the table.

His mouth curved into a smile that threatened to unstring her knees. 'Then what are we waiting for, *agapi mou*?'

* * *

If he'd cared about such things Damen would have been annoyed at his total lack of cool as he strode through the winding streets of old Rhodes, back to the harbour. A couple of times Stephanie almost had to trot to keep up, but she didn't complain. Far from it. Her eyes glowed in anticipation, and whenever he glanced at her beside him it was all he could do not to scoop her up in his arms and break into a run.

She was so deliciously alluring. Damen couldn't believe how lucky he was.

They made it back onto the yacht in a breathless rush that made him feel like a reckless teenager. Except that wasn't quite right. Oh, the rampant lust was there, but beneath it was something else. Caring, admiration, something deeper than he'd felt in his youthful testosterone-fuelled amours.

Damen didn't release her hand as they marched through the yacht to his stateroom. The door swung shut and he turned to face Stephanie.

Her breasts rose rapidly as if, like he, she had trouble capturing enough air. Her eyes were wide with a saucy excitement that drilled heat straight to his loins.

'You wanted to kiss me.'

'Yes.' His voice emerged as a rasp.

'I wish you'd hurry up. It's been so long.'

Beneath her bodice Stephanie's nipples peaked in invitation. His body tightened.

'I want more than that.' Why he held back he didn't fully understand. To be sure she needed this as much as he did? He couldn't be the only one to feel this desperation. 'I want everything. Once I touch you...' He spread his hands.

Stephanie smiled. A sultry smile that lifted the corners of her mouth and shimmered in her gold-toned eyes. It was bewitching. So must Circe have smiled on Odysseus, luring him. It was hard to believe that a week ago Stephanie had been a virgin.

Damen's hands cupped her cheeks as he took her mouth, plundering deep into her sweetness, sealing her lips with his.

It was everything he remembered and more. He was only dimly aware of their surroundings as he backed her across the room till her legs touched the bed and he tumbled them both onto it.

Stephanie was all satiny limbs, ardent mouth and soft, eager body. Her fingers ripped at his shirt as he shoved her skirt up.

The next moments were a blur of building excitement. His shirt came off, and then his belt. Stephanie's lacy underwear came away in his hand with one forceful tug. The sound of it ripping fed a frenzy for completion that he only just managed to leash.

'Condom,' he gasped, forcing himself to move away.

Stephanie's hands were busy with his trousers as he reached for the bedside table, tearing a packet open with his teeth. Seconds later, sheathed, he settled between her bare legs, her skirt rucked up beneath his bare torso, her eyes heavy-lidded in anticipation.

She was glorious.

Damen made himself pause, hefted a breath that felt like agony as his lungs heaved.

A hand between her legs confirmed she was ready. He palmed her thigh, smooth and supple, and lifted it high. She lifted the other one too, hooking it over his bare hip, and something dived deep in his belly. It was a swooping sensation that heralded the end of his control.

Damen lowered his head and took her mouth again, glorying in the way she opened for him, like a flower to sunshine. He tilted his hips, finding the spot he needed and moving slowly, inexorably, alert to any sign of discomfort. Stephanie gasped against his mouth, lifted her pelvis and wrapped her legs tight around his hips, locking him to her.

He had a moment to glory in the perfection that was their

joining. But only a moment. For he needed to move, withdraw and glide back again, harder this time and faster.

Stephanie's breath expelled in a soft *oof* of air against his lips as her hands clawed his bare shoulders.

Another thrust, this time met by a perfectly timed lift of her hips that sent flickering sensation from his groin to his spine and up to the back of his skull where his skin pulled tight. Everything pulled tight.

'Stephanie,' he growled, turned on even by the sound of her name on his tongue.

Her palms lifted to his cheeks as she put her mouth to his and bit his lower lip.

Liquid heat seared him, incinerating control.

He gathered her close, angling till he felt Stephanie's giveaway judder of response, then thrusting home again and again until she broke apart in his arms and he fell with her into the vast, consuming wave of ecstasy.

Damen held her tight, thoughts disintegrating under that powerful onslaught.

As he slowly came back to himself, Damen had enough sense to roll onto his back so as not to crush her. He took Stephanie with him, cradling her.

It took a long time for his brain to crank into gear. When it did he was torn between satisfaction and consternation.

Because he was certain of one thing. He wanted more than six weeks with Stephanie. Their allotted time wouldn't be nearly enough to make the most of this explosive attraction.

Inevitably his mind went to Ingrid, who'd seduced his younger self with sex and a display of affection that had been as false as her promises.

Ingrid, who'd made him dance to her tune, all the way, almost, to the altar.

As ever, his thoughts slewed away from that. There'd be no altar, no marriage in Damen's future. That was the one thing of which he was absolutely sure. The very thought made him break into a cold sweat. Because tangled with that thought was the memory of the tragedy he'd created, which affected his family to this day.

Damen wasn't certain what this connection to Stephanie meant for his well-ordered life, but he wasn't stupid enough to ignore something so profound. So pleasurable.

His lips curved in a lazy smile as he smoothed his hand over her damp, flushed skin and she arched beneath his touch, her sated body responsive even now.

So it was settled. He'd keep Stephanie with him beyond the term of their contract. He'd talk to her about it later. As soon as he worked out the terms of a new arrangement that would satisfy them both.

CHAPTER ELEVEN

STEPHANIE'S PULSE THROBBED so fast and hard she put a hand out to the door jamb, steadying herself. She was light-headed, but only, she assured herself, because she was nervous. More nervous than she'd ever been in her life.

One slow breath. Another.

They didn't help much.

Nothing would help, till she could dismiss the suspicion that had gnawed at her the last few days.

She'd left Rhodes in a rosy haze of delight. Stephanie had barely been aware of their surroundings, so wrapped up was she in Damen. Even his apology about returning to Athens for necessary meetings hadn't punctured her happiness.

They took several days sailing to the capital and spent most of the time together. When Damen worked, Steph caught up on her sleep. Which was just as well, since Damen usually woke her with the devil in his eyes and seduction in those clever hands.

Increasingly Steph wondered where this relationship might lead. For, great as the sex was, it *was* a relationship. That, more than anything, was what had taken her unawares. Sexual compatibility she'd been prepared for, but this...this was more.

They talked, sharing information about themselves, often small things, it was true, but it felt as if she was finally coming to understand this complex man and he her. He even told her about his sisters, clearly proud of their achievements. They laughed and found pleasure in each other's company, even when they were too exhausted to make love. Or when she was. Damen had a stamina that astounded her, but he tempered it with concern for her wellbeing, as if she were still an untried innocent.

Innocent! Her mouth tightened as she surveyed the sitting room of his penthouse. It was designer-elegant with sculptures and other artworks that could have graced a museum. The morning view over Athens was stupendous and even the floral arrangements cost more than she'd spend in a week on food in Melbourne.

What she and Damen shared felt wonderful, so wonderful she didn't want to question too closely where it might lead. As if by doing so she'd tempt fate to end it. Yet in the cold, hard light of day some might look at this arrangement and say he'd bought her company.

Steph's stomach clenched and nausea stirred.

No! That wasn't what this was.

This relationship was about mutual attraction and respect. Despite the money he'd paid her for the charade, in their *real* relationship they were equals. Each giving freely of themselves. Neither expecting nor demanding anything long term.

Long term…

Another unsettling swirl of nausea.

Steph straightened. It was time to scotch the anxiety that had been nibbling away at her since she realised her period was late.

She looked at the pregnancy kit she'd bought from the chemist down the road as soon as it opened. It was just a precaution. The chances of pregnancy were ninety-nine point something per cent against, since Damen had used a condom every time.

Of course it would be a false alarm.

'I gather congratulations are in order.' Christo's voice on the end of the line didn't sound congratulatory. It sounded terse.

'Sorry?' Damen turned his back on the now empty conference table and strode to the windows looking out on the sea, darkening as the sun set. The headquarters of Nicolaides Shipping faced the harbour of Piraeus, a reminder of the company's focus and the source of its vast wealth. 'Are you back from your honeymoon already?'

'No. But Emma will be concerned when she reads the reports so I thought I'd get the story from you first.'

Damen frowned. 'You've lost me. What story?'

'You don't know?'

'Christo, I don't have time for guessing games. I've got my hands full with major negotiations.'

He rolled his shoulders. That last meeting had been long and trying, but his plans to re-establish his firm's shipbuilding capacity in Greece might finally come to fruition. In his father's day all that had moved offshore to places where costs were cheaper. Damen was determined that at least some of that work would return to his own country, his contribution to the local economy.

'You and Stephanie. You're in the press.'

'Is that all?' Damen smiled as he thought of Stephanie. Persuading her to be his companion was surely his most brilliant idea.

Manos had backed off. Clio was ecstatic. But most important of all was Stephanie herself. He couldn't recall the last time a woman had made him feel so good. So full of anticipation just at the thought of seeing her at the end of the day.

He'd known she was special from the start. The attraction between them was explosive and showed no signs of diminishing. He liked spending time with her out of bed too. She was bright and fun and genuine and he wanted her to stay in Greece past the end of their contract. He wasn't foolish enough to expect what they had to last. Damen knew not to expect permanency. But for the foreseeable future...

'All? You don't sound fazed.'

'Of course not.' He made himself focus on Christo. 'Stephanie...' He paused. He preferred not to mention the money she'd accepted from him. Christo might get the wrong idea about her. 'She agreed to stay with me for a couple of months. To play the part of my girlfriend. I was getting heat from another quarter to marry and you know that's impossible.'

'Is it?'

Damen frowned. Christo was one of the few who knew the details of his past. Though even he didn't know it all. 'Of course. You know I'll never marry.'

Christo muttered something that sounded like a curse. 'You're saying the latest reports aren't true? I can tell Emma the gossip online is wrong?'

Damen hesitated. Their relationship might have begun as a charade but it was more now. Damen planned to ask Stephanie to stay with him, past the expiry of their agreement, until their passion died a natural death. Something that burned so brightly must destroy itself eventually. But there was no reason they shouldn't make the most of it while it lasted.

'Stephanie and I...enjoy each other's company.'

'And?'

'Isn't that enough?' No doubt gossip was ramping up because Damen didn't have live-in lovers. He valued his privacy too much and didn't trust women not to get the idea they could worm their way into his life permanently. But Stephanie was different.

'So you're sharing a bed. All the world knows that, except Emma, so far. She'll get her hopes up about the pair of you when she finds out. But this new rumour...'

'What new rumour?' Damen frowned. Why were they wasting time discussing paparazzi gossip?

'You really don't know?' There was a strange note in his friend's voice. 'Then it's unfounded gossip. I knew you'd never—'

'Never what?' Damen spoke through gritted teeth.

There was a pause, long enough to hear his pulse beat once, twice, three times.

'Get her pregnant. A story broke today that you're expecting a child together.'

Shock jabbed Damen, before reason took over. He laughed, assuring his friend that the gossip-mongers were inventing a story where there was none.

His good humour lasted until, trawling through so-called news reports, he saw a photo of Stephanie on the street outside his apartment, smiling directly into the camera. Below it, the article said:

An excited Stephanie Logan, Damen Nicolaides' girlfriend, confided it was early days, with the pregnancy only a few weeks along.

Stephanie felt trapped. She didn't want to go out after what had happened on the street this morning, when a man had shoved a camera in her face. But nor did she feel like asking if Damen's driver could take her sightseeing.

Not when her world had just turned upside down.

Pregnant. She was pregnant with Damen's child.

Even now, hours after seeing the pregnancy test results, she couldn't process it.

How could she be pregnant? Yet she'd heard stories about people who'd conceived despite protection.

Her hand crept to her abdomen. Was it true? Was a new life forming there? She told herself she wouldn't be certain till she'd had the test confirmed by a doctor, yet she *felt* different. When she crossed her arms her breasts were sensitive. That, combined with her late period, had sent her scurrying to the chemist.

It had been embarrassing, explaining to a stranger what she wanted, but she'd needed help to find the kit and translate the instructions.

Maybe she'd done it wrong? Maybe it was a false positive? She was clutching at straws.

Steph planted her hands on the railing of the penthouse terrace and tried to still her whirling thoughts. She had no plan for the future. All she felt was shock.

And a tiny seed of what might be excitement.

Because, no matter how unexpected, there was something thrilling as well as terrifying about the prospect of a baby.

She narrowed her eyes against the glare of late sun on the pale city.

All her life she'd told herself she wouldn't make her mother's mistakes. She'd be independent financially and emotionally. No struggling as a single mum to make ends meet. It was true that, thanks to Damen's money, she was able to repay the money she owed, and her gran's money, and have some left for herself.

But she'd still be a single mother.

An unemployed single mother. Despite the cushion of cash in her account, she'd have to find a job eventually.

Steph dragged in a deep breath, filled with fear.

It wasn't simply fear about the burdens of bringing up a child. Selfishly it was as much about herself and Damen. About what this news meant for them. She hadn't let herself hope for permanency with him. But the prospect of losing him now made her feel hollow with pain.

This news would end their idyll.

She wrapped her arms around herself. Was it selfish to worry about that when she should be worrying about the new life inside her?

The undeniable truth was that Damen *mattered* to her, far more than she'd let herself believe. *They* mattered as a couple. What they had was so fragile, so new, yet it felt profound. Not like a fling at all.

For her.

But for him?

'Enjoying the sunset?' Damen's voice reached out from the shadows, curling like a lasso around her middle and drawing tight.

Steph swung round, a relieved smile tugging at her lips. Despite her nerves, despite everything, she felt better now Damen was here.

What did that say about how far she'd come from the fiercely independent, fiercely distrustful woman who'd arrived in Greece last month?

Steph feared it said everything.

The way she felt about Damen—

'Nothing to say, Stephanie?' He stepped further onto the terrace, the sunset burnishing his face to stark bronze. He looked like an ancient warrior, proud and relentless. A shiver scuttled down her spine.

This wasn't the lover she'd known the last few weeks.

It wasn't even the managing billionaire who'd expected her to fall in with his outrageous plans.

Steph looked into blazing eyes that nevertheless made her bones frost. This was a stranger. A man she didn't know. Something almost like fear stirred at the base of her spine.

'Damen. I didn't expect you yet.' He'd mentioned late meetings.

'I found I couldn't keep away.' His lips curled at the corners, but instead of forming a smile his expression looked more like a grimace.

'What's wrong? Has something happened?' She walked towards him, thinking of his mother, of Clio and the others she'd met at the wedding. Or maybe he'd had bad news about one of his sisters.

'I thought you could tell me.' He paused, his brow drawing down in the middle. 'Have you got news for me?'

'How did you know?' She goggled up at him, stunned.

'Call it a hunch.'

Steph frowned. She'd told nobody. Even without the time difference from Greece, she couldn't talk to Gran about this yet, or Emma, who was still on her honeymoon. First she had to come to grips with the news. And talk to Damen. She hadn't looked at her phone all day, worried that if she started searching for information on pregnancy she'd scare herself silly.

'A hunch?' She shook her head. 'How——?'

'What's your news, Stephanie?'

Dubiously she stared at him. Every sense told her something was wrong. He couldn't know about the baby. Yet...

'You might want to sit down.'

Instead he simply folded his arms over his chest. His body language worried her. She told herself she was upset, misreading his non-verbal cues.

'Okay, then.' She drew a slow breath. 'I took a pregnancy test this morning. And it appears I'm pregnant.'

Nothing. Not a word for two whole beats of her heart.

'Appears?'

Steph frowned. He didn't look surprised.

'I *am* pregnant.' Now it came to the crunch she was sure of it. 'Though I'd like to check with a doctor.'

'How very convenient.'

She blinked and it was as if the movement dragged the scales from her eyes. For now she read Damen's expression. Anger laced with disdain.

At *her*!

Her head reared back. 'It's not my fault. You can't think I engineered this. There were two of us having sex.'

Making love, that was how it had felt, but she couldn't say that, not when he looked at her with fury in those glittering eyes.

A chill iced her to the marrow. Steph stepped back till she came up against the railing. Horrified, she told herself not to cringe. She'd done nothing wrong!

'You were the one to handle protection.'

If anything the reminder only stoked his anger. His eyes

narrowed and his jaw tightened. It was a wonder steam didn't come out of his ears.

'You really think I'm so gullible?' His words were soft but tinged with menace.

Sternly Steph reminded herself Damen might be furious but he wasn't dangerous.

'You might not want to believe it, Damen, but it's true.' She stared up at him, refusing to be cowed by that pulsing anger. 'You might not like the surprise but I'd thought you a better man than to react like this.'

His hand sliced the air dismissively. 'Stop now. I know this is a con.'

'Sorry?' She'd expected surprise, but nothing like this.

'I know you've contrived this. You should stop while you're ahead.'

Abruptly, gloriously, it was Steph seeing red. Contrived, indeed! Did he think she'd engineered a lie to—what? Trap him into a long-term relationship?

Steph gasped as the pieces clicked into place and she realised that was exactly what he thought. The monstrous ego of the man!

It didn't matter that mere minutes ago she'd realised she... cared for him much more than she should. That the idea of ending their affair tore at her heart. She'd like to slap him for his egotistical arrogance.

Steph swung away and marched inside.

'Don't walk away from me! We haven't finished.'

Too bad. Steph refused to stand there, an unwilling target for his poisonous barbs.

She strode to the bathroom off the master bedroom, swiping the test result off the marble counter. When she turned it was to find Damen filling the doorway. He was a tall man, broad-shouldered and well-built, but anger seemed to make him even bigger. Steph didn't care. She crossed the space and shoved the plastic into his hand.

'What's this?' But his eyes were rounding as he spoke. His olive-gold skin paled a couple of shades.

'Proof.' Steph folded her arms tight across her heaving chest. 'I went to the chemist and bought a kit.'

But Damen was already shaking his head. 'Of course you've somehow got hold of a positive result. The bluff wouldn't work otherwise.'

'Bluff? I don't understand.'

His steely gaze captured hers. 'You really are a good actress, Stephanie. First class. But I know this is a lie. Otherwise why leak the news to the press? You're trying to force my hand.'

She shook her head. 'You're not making sense.' Had he had an accident? A blow to the head? But no, he looked pulsing with vibrant energy.

For answer he pulled a phone from his pocket, thumbed the screen and held it out to her.

Shock Baby Revelation for Nicolaides CEO!

That was as far as Steph got, as the words began to run together. But that was enough. That and the photo of her taken this morning.

A trembling began in her knees, turning into racking shudders. Her stomach, empty because she'd been too agitated to eat lunch, lurched. The room swayed, or maybe it was her.

Big hands grabbed her arms, half hauling, half lifting her across the room and onto the deeply cushioned seat beside the sunken bath. Damen forced her head down between her knees and slowly the awful sick feeling receded.

'Let me go.' She shook him off. 'I'm not going to be sick.'

Yet horror lingered at the back of her mouth. Steph took her time, breathing slowly, confronting the fact that her precious secret had become fodder for a sleazy press story. Eventually she realised that must be why Damen had come back looking like some merciless god seeking vengeance.

But how…?

'How did they get the story if you didn't tell them? Why did you smile for that photo if you weren't colluding with them?' His voice was hard but she saw something like concern in his assessing eyes, as if the sight of her weak and upset bothered him.

'I didn't. I smiled at the doorman to your building. He's always so friendly and today he helped me, directing me to a chemist. But as I came back to the apartment some guy with a big camera got in my way just as I was saying hi.'

She lifted the phone still clutched in her hand. Yes. It made sense. That was when the photo had been taken. By the man in the T-shirt of bilious green.

Steph frowned. 'It was him!'

'What is it? What did he do?'

Damen hunkered before her. He didn't touch her but he was so close his body heat blanketed her. She shivered, suddenly aware of how cold she felt.

'Stephanie?'

Muzzily she looked up into those brilliant eyes. If she didn't know better she'd say he looked worried. Except that would mean Damen cared when instead he thought she'd constructed a hoax and sold her story to the press.

'You think I went to the media with a story that I was pregnant? Why? For the cash they'd give for a scoop? Or to force your hand into a long-term commitment? Because you wouldn't kick me out if I was pregnant?'

Her voice was a shallow rasp but he heard her and his expression told her everything she needed to know.

Wearily she held out the phone to him then leaned back in the chair, closing her eyes. She didn't want to deal with the media stories or Damen.

'Tell me about the man, Stephanie.' His voice was soft, persuasive yet still compelling.

She wanted to yell at him, demand he leave her alone, that he go and take his massive ego with him. But she didn't have the energy. All day she'd been wound so tight and now she felt totally undone.

'Stephanie, talk to me.'

He palmed her cheek with a warm hand just as he'd done when they made love. It sent pain arrowing through her, a jab to the heart. She wrenched her head away, snapping her eyes open to glare at him.

'Don't. Touch. Me.'

Something ripped across Damen's expression, something she couldn't name and didn't want to.

'Please, Stephanie. Tell me about the man.'

She sighed. She was tempted to let him work it out himself but what was the point?

'The man with the camera, who took the photo. He wore a distinctive green T-shirt. He was there in the chemist when I was.'

'Did you talk to him?'

'No. I just spoke to the pharmacist. I needed help finding a pregnancy kit and getting instructions on how to use it.' She paused, frowning. The other guy had browsed for something in the next aisle.

'Did you tell the pharmacist anything else?'

'I didn't give him my name or yours, if that's what you're thinking.' She paused. 'I did ask if it would work in the very early stages of pregnancy because I couldn't be more than a few weeks along.'

Damen's expression changed, hard lines marking his features. 'What?'

'That's what they wrote in the press, that the...pregnancy was in the early stages.'

'So maybe they got that from the pharmacist or the man with the camera.' She sat straighter. 'They certainly didn't get it from me. I was hoping it was a false alarm, that I wasn't really pregnant.' Her voice dipped on the word as the enormity of the situation hit her. 'If I was going to tell someone it wouldn't be the press, no matter what you think.'

'I believe you.'

'Sorry?'

Sombre eyes met hers. Damen held his phone out to her. 'Is this the man you saw?'

She peered at a grainy photo. 'Different clothes but that's him.'

'He's paparazzi. He's been hanging around since we got back to Athens. Security moved him on but not effectively enough. He probably followed you from the apartment building.' Damen drew a slow breath. 'I owe you an apology.'

'You do.'

'I'm sorry, Stephanie. I shouldn't have doubted you. I should have known better.'

'You should.' It had hurt terribly that he'd jumped to such a vile conclusion about her. 'I thought we were beginning to know each other.' That had been the worst part. That he knew her now, or should, yet still he'd thought the worst.

Damen's mouth flattened, but then he nodded. 'You're right.' He drew a deep breath. 'I've spent a long time learning to be suspicious, especially of women. It's a hard habit to break. I can't tell you how sorry I am.'

Steph wanted to know why he was suspicious of women. But this wasn't the time to pursue it. She felt appallingly light-headed. Shock, she supposed.

It was as if he read her mind. 'Would you feel better lying down?'

She nodded but before she could stand Damen slid his arms around her and lifted her high against his chest. Steph didn't need to be carried. But her legs felt like overcooked pasta and, despite everything, it was comforting to rest her head against his shoulder. She didn't even protest when he took her to the master suite. She'd fight that out with him later, when she had more energy.

Damen laid her on the bed and took her shoes off, pulling a light blanket over her. It was like when she was a child and Gran had taken care of her when she got ill. Except she wasn't a child and Damen was nothing like Gran.

Then he confounded her by pressing a kiss to her brow.

'Rest now. The doctor will be here soon.'

'Doctor?' She scrambled up onto one elbow.

'You said you'd like to see a doctor. I'll feel better too. You're as white as a sheet.'

Steph lay back and watched him march out of the room. He meant it. There was concern on that wide brow and in his clenched jaw.

For her wellbeing?

Or because he needed to know for sure if she was pregnant?

To her dismay Steph discovered she wanted it to be for her. Because that would mean Damen cared.

It was dangerous, wishful thinking, the sort that could get her into trouble.

Except she was already in as deep as it went. For though she smarted at Damen's suspicions and wasn't in a forgiving mood, she'd realised something today that changed everything.

She'd fallen in love with Damen Nicolaides.

CHAPTER TWELVE

DAMEN STARED INTO the darkness. It was well past midnight and he needed sleep. Tomorrow there'd be vital negotiations and decisions. Yet sleep eluded him.

His brain raced, sifting the day's events. Confirmation from the doctor that Stephanie was pregnant, and, despite his fears at seeing her so weak, essentially well. And the unholy mess he'd made of things, shattering the trust he'd built with Stephanie.

Distrust came naturally to a man who'd been pursued all his life by those wanting a piece of his wealth. It became his default mode after Ingrid and her scheme to marry him, not for love, as she'd made him believe, but for money. The fact that fiasco—his fault for being gullible—had resulted in his father's death…

Damen's chest cramped as memories rose. But he didn't allow them to tug him into that black vortex of regret. He couldn't afford to, not with Stephanie's news. He needed to focus on the future.

His arms tightened around her, soft and trusting in his embrace. She was burrowed against him, head under his chin, her arm around his waist. It was all he could do not to wake her and lose himself in her sweet, welcoming body.

That moment this evening when she'd shied from his touch as if it were poisoned, when she'd looked at him with hurt branded in that shimmering stare...

That had pierced him to the core.

He deserved her disdain. Yet he hadn't been able to keep away. There'd be hell to pay tomorrow when she realised they'd shared a bed.

She'd been asleep when he'd entered, curled in a ball as if to protect herself from forces beyond her control. Damen had tasted guilt, like chilled metal on his tongue, knowing he was responsible for her distress.

He'd come to check on her, concerned despite the doctor's reassurances. But he'd been unable to walk away when she looked so vulnerable.

It had felt natural to strip off and get into bed, purely so he could be sure she was okay in the night. When she'd turned to him in her sleep...as she had every other night recently... of course he'd cuddled her, doing his best to assuage the hurt he'd caused.

But their closeness brought no relief.

Instead it magnified the size of their problem.

He grimaced. How skewed were his priorities to see a child as a problem?

It wasn't that he didn't like kids. It was that, after Ingrid and his fatal error in judgement, he'd known he'd never have children.

Now he would. He tried to imagine a child with his nose or the trademark Nicolaides stubbornness. Instead he saw a little girl with curls and golden-brown eyes. Stephanie holding her.

His breath snagged. Excitement stirred. A thrill of delight. And possessiveness.

He knew without a moment's doubt that he wanted this baby. Would do everything to care for and protect it.

Did Stephanie even want the child? The thought of her terminating the pregnancy made him break into a cold sweat.

Surely that wasn't likely. He couldn't imagine Stephanie taking that step.

What, then? The child was his too. He wanted to be part of its life. No. More. He wanted to be a full-time father. His family was close-knit and family ties were an ingrained part of him.

Damen had to persuade Stephanie to stay in Greece and raise the child together. Or, if that wouldn't work, let him raise it without her.

His mind darted from one possibility to another. He could offer her money to relinquish the baby.

Right. As if that would work.

Stephanie had taken his money once but only because of her financial distress. Offering money now would set her against him. She wasn't avaricious. She was grounded, honest, honourable. She'd make a great mother.

He doubted she could be bought.

Did he even want to try?

Pain rayed through his jaw from grinding his teeth.

He needed Stephanie here, with him. Their baby deserved to have both parents.

But there was nothing to bind Stephanie here, to guarantee he'd have his child permanently.

Another contract? Without the lure of money, what could he offer to persuade her to stay?

What would cement his role as a full-time father?

He refused to consider being in his child's life for half of each year or just for holidays.

Could he appeal to Stephanie's maternal instincts? Persuade her two parents were better than one?

Stephanie shifted and Damen relaxed his hold, all the time searching for something that would bind her and their child to him.

There had to be something. If not money, then…

He grimaced as he tasted a familiar sour tang.

There was one way to secure a permanent role in his child's life.

The one thing he'd vowed on his father's grave to avoid.

Marriage.

Damen's breath whistled from his lungs and his heart set up a rough, catapulting rhythm. Nausea churned and his skin prickled as a decade of self-disgust and regret scoured him.

He couldn't do it.

There had to be another way. He had all night to find an alternative. Anything but that.

'Ochi, Baba. Ochi!'

This time Steph caught Damen's husky words. Before they'd been just a hoarse mumble of Greek. His head turned and he flung an arm across the bed.

She'd woken as the mattress moved beneath her, only to discover it wasn't the mattress but Damen. She'd been lying across him, cosily curled up in his big bed.

The room was dark and she blearily wondered how they had come to be sharing when she realised Damen was in the throes of a nightmare. He was scorching hot, as if with fever, his legs shifting restlessly as if trying to run.

She sat up and he instantly rolled away, clawing the bedding, his voice urgent, shoulders heaving.

Steph knew distress. This was real, and, despite her earlier anger, seeing him like this made her heart turn over.

Damen was controlled and strong. Even in anger he was composed. Only when they made love—

No, she wasn't going there.

'Damen.' She grabbed his shoulder, slippery with damp heat. 'Wake up.'

He turned, flinging out an arm that caught her on the elbow. He mumbled, and in the gloom she saw his ferocious scowl.

'Wake up. You're having a nightmare.' She put her other hand on his cheek, feeling bristles scratch her palm. It reminded her of the nights they'd slept together after hours of…no, not love-making, but sex.

She knew this man intimately, or so she'd thought. Till he'd stalked in tonight like an avenging angel.

Yet his fury hadn't lasted, had it? Only a few minutes into their argument and he'd been hunkering down before her, con-cerned and gentle.

Steph shook him harder. She refused to make excuses for appalling behaviour. How dared he accuse her of selling sto-ries to the press?

Except she remembered goggling at Clio as she recounted the lengths women had gone to to snare Damen Nicolaides. Bribing hotel staff so they could wait, naked, in his bed. The short-lived paternity suit by a woman who, it was soon proved, had never even met him.

She leaned closer. 'Quick, Damen. You need to wake up!'

His eyes started open. For a long moment he stared blindly up at her. Then his hands curled around her shoulders.

'Stephanie? What is it? Are you all right?'

He sat up in a rush, his gaze darting around the room as if searching for a threat, then coming to rest on her. Those strong hands stroked down her arms.

'What is it? Are you ill? What can I do?'

And just like that, Steph's righteous indignation faded. He'd done wrong but he did care. Really care.

'Stephanie, tell me!' His urgency tugged at her heartstrings. Ridiculously she found herself blinking tears.

'I'm okay. It's you. You were having a nightmare.'

His grip tightened around her wrists. His chest rose on an audible, uneven breath.

'A nightmare.'

'You were thrashing around. It must have been a bad one.'

'Was I?' His voice sounded flat. He dropped his hands and

she felt suddenly bereft. 'I apologise. I didn't mean to wake you. You need rest.'

This wasn't about her. He'd been so tortured. 'Do you have nightmares often?'

'Never.' He dragged a hand across his scalp in a gesture she knew signalled he wasn't as in control as he wanted her to believe.

'And this time?'

Damen's voice hadn't merely been agitated. He'd sounded as if his heart were being torn out.

'I don't recall.' He turned and retrieved the pillow that he'd pushed off the bed, leaving her staring at bare shoulders and the streamlined curve of his spine.

So very strong and yet, it seemed, vulnerable.

Curiosity rose. What did he dream that distressed him so? Something to do with their baby?

'I apologise for waking you, Stephanie. Shall we try to sleep?'

He had the decency at least not to lie down and assume she'd spend the rest of the night with him. He sat, hair tousled, big frame tense, watching her.

She should move to another room. Or demand he go.

She had a right to privacy.

Except she craved the comfort of Damen cradling her as much as ever.

She wanted to bridge the gulf between them, not widen it.

Silently she nodded and lay down. Damen drew a light cover over them both and sank onto the pillow beside her.

'I promise not to disturb you again.'

How could he promise that? The only way to prevent another nightmare was to stay awake all night.

She opened her mouth to ask him about it, then stopped. He wouldn't answer her questions. He'd made that clear.

But he had revealed something. She knew very little Greek but she knew *ne* was yes and *ochi* was no. She'd also heard Clio's sister calling her father *Baba*, which Steph assumed meant Dad.

Damen had been dreaming of his father, shouting, 'No, Dad, no!'

Something about his father stressed him unbearably. Something one of them had done or not done?

Was the nightmare triggered by today's news?

Steph wrapped her arms around her middle and rolled away to stare, wide-eyed, into the dark.

'I keep telling you, I'm perfectly fine. Yesterday was an aberration.' Steph saw a pulse tick at Damen's jaw but eventually he nodded.

Damen's concern was pleasant but she didn't need cosseting, or being told to rest when what she wanted was exercise. A walk or maybe a swim. After yesterday's fiasco with the paparazzi she'd content herself with a swim in the rooftop pool.

'Aren't you going to work?' They'd slept late and now lingered over breakfast on the terrace. Usually Damen had left for the office by now.

'Not today. We need to talk.'

Looking into that handsome face, tight with tension, Steph felt her stomach dip.

'I'm having the baby,' she blurted. She'd spent yesterday examining every option and knew that was non-negotiable.

'Good.' His mouth eased into a smile. 'I'm glad.'

'You are?'

Crazy that her heart thumped at his approval, or maybe just at the sight of his smile. Surely loving someone didn't make you so completely vulnerable to them? Steph was still her own woman. That wouldn't alter.

'Absolutely. Family is important. Of course I want this child.'

His starkly possessive tone simultaneously thrilled her and made her skin prickle with apprehension.

'*Our* child.' This baby wasn't his alone.

'Exactly. Our child, our responsibility.' He nodded and offered her more fresh orange juice. 'It's early, I know,' he said, 'but have you thought about the future?'

'Of course.' She'd peppered the doctor with questions about pregnancy, about diet and vitamins. Beyond that loomed the scary prospect of childbirth and motherhood. Steph didn't have much experience with babies. She had a lot to learn.

'So have I.' He paused. 'I have a proposition.'

Steph looked up from her bowl of yoghurt drizzled with honey and nuts to find him watching her closely. His smile had gone and he looked as serious as she'd ever seen him. More than serious. Grim.

Something inside plunged. Her defences rose. After yesterday she'd thought her trust in Damen had hit rock bottom. Surely he wasn't going to disappoint her again. She didn't think her bruised heart could bear it.

'A proposition?' She sat straighter, breathing carefully to slow her racing heart. 'You're not going to propose buying my child from me, are you?'

Damen inhabited a world far removed from hers. He had incredible power and money.

Damen's hand closed around her fist. '*Our* child needs both of us, Stephanie. You and me together. As its mother, you hold a very special place no one else can fill.'

Steph sank back in her chair, relief filling her. She'd got him so wrong.

Excitement rippled through her. He'd called her special, said their baby needed them both.

Tendrils of hope wound through her. She loved this man and she knew he...liked her. He was attracted. Now he spoke with respect in his voice about her being special.

Was he beginning to feel a little of what she did? Not love, but perhaps one day he'd assess his feelings and realise—

'What's your proposition?' She needed to hear, not try to guess.

Steph told herself to be calm, not to expect too much. Yet she couldn't stifle a jitter of excitement.

'That you stay in Greece, with me.' He halted, surveying her closely.

Had he registered her suddenly indrawn breath? At least he couldn't feel her fluttering pulse.

'You want me to live in Greece?'

'With me, Stephanie.' His thumb stroked the tender flesh at her wrist. Maybe, after all, he was aware of her runaway heartbeat. 'I want to marry you.'

She froze, unable to speak or even, it seemed, breathe. Her chest tightened from lack of oxygen as she stared across at Damen.

He meant it. She'd never seen him look so serious. In fact, he was frowning. New lines bracketed his mouth and his jaw was a study in tension.

Steph swallowed but couldn't dislodge the blockage in her throat.

This was when he'd tell her he didn't want to lose her. That she'd come to mean so much to him. That together, with time and a common cause in bringing up their child, they might find love.

Steph waited.

Damen's eyes met hers but there was a curious blankness in them, so different from the heat she was used to, or the charming devilry. The lines around his mouth became grooves, carving deeper as she watched.

Was he nervous? No. This wasn't the expression of a man holding his breath as he waited his beloved's response.

'You don't look happy at the idea.'

His shoulders lifted. 'This is a serious matter. It's not about happiness but doing right.' Then, as if reading her expression, he added, 'Happiness will come through our child.' He curved his lips into a smile but it didn't reassure. His face looked tight, painfully so, as if the stretched lips made his face ache.

Disappointment tasted bitter on her tongue. Disappointment and dismay.

She'd imagined that a proposal of marriage would be a happy event.

Not this one. Not with the would-be groom looking as if he tasted poison. Even his golden tan had paled. He looked almost unwell.

A proposition, he'd called it. Not a proposal.

As if this was a business deal.

'Why marry?' she eventually croaked.

Damen looked down to their joined hands. 'Many reasons. Above all, to do what's best for our baby. Children thrive in a stable home, loved by their family. We can give the baby that. I will love our child with all that I am, and I believe you feel the same.'

Piercing green eyes snared hers and Steph nodded. Already she felt protective of this new life. Soon, she guessed, it would become love.

'If we marry we can give it the support and stability it needs. We can support each other, and our families will too. Your grandmother, my mother and sisters. I'll fly your grandmother to Greece as often as she likes. Who knows, she may even settle here once you're living in the country.'

Steph tried to imagine Gran in Greece. It was generous of Damen to think of her, to realise Steph would want her support.

'I want the best for our child, Stephanie. Sharing the burdens and joys of parenthood is not only fair but also the best outcome for all of us.'

It sounded as if he was speaking about a commercial merger, not a family.

'I know it's a big thing to move to a new country. But we'll visit Australia often. If you want to pursue your business here, I'll back you, give you every support. Plus we'll travel.' His hand squeezed hers. 'That's your dream. I can make that happen. We'll go wherever you want.' He stopped and she saw calculation in his expression. 'That's the benefit of marrying a wealthy man. I can provide whatever you want.'

Except love.

Except being wanted for myself, not because of my baby.

A great hollow formed in her middle, expanding wider and deeper till it felt as if she was nothing but a narrow layer of flesh over gaping emptiness.

Questions crowded. Why did he want marriage so badly when he must know he'd already have rights as a father? What if it didn't work? What if Damen fell in love with someone else? For as sure as her name was Logan, he wasn't in love with her.

Soon, she knew, the hurt would start.

It was starting now as she stared into a face set with determination yet almost gaunt with...what? Damen looked ill.

His proposition sounded like a company merger.

A merger he doesn't really want.

As soon as the thought rose Steph knew it was right.

He offered marriage to stake a claim for complete access to the baby.

'You really want this child,' she murmured and had immediate confirmation from the flash of excitement in his eyes.

'Absolutely!'

Steph's insides churned in distress.

He wants the child but not you.

He doesn't want marriage but he'll go through with it to secure his baby.

'I'm sorry, Damen, I—'

'Don't make up your mind now!'

'I was about to say I need time to think.'

'Fine. Excellent.'

But it wasn't fine and it certainly wasn't excellent. Steph's heart had cracked and she feared that soon it might just shatter.

CHAPTER THIRTEEN

DAMEN HAD LEARNED to rein in impatience. Even as a CEO he occasionally had to bide his time, wait for the right moment to seal a deal.

This was one of those times. Stephanie was coming to terms with her pregnancy. She wasn't her usual bright, forthright self. Even allowing for shock and the life changes she faced, he worried at her lacklustre mood.

His own mood was best not examined. He got through each day focusing on what needed to be done.

He'd begun searching for a family home. An island within commuting distance. Somewhere with a private beach and large garden. Stephanie might like overseeing the renovations. Or perhaps they'd build. That could be the project to drag her out of the doldrums.

Damen devoted himself to persuading her to accept him by showing her how good life would be for her here.

He spirited her away for an overnight stay on picturesque Hydra. In Athens he took her not to crowded social events, but to his favourite restaurants where the food was exquisite and the ambience delightful.

Knowing her interest in his country's culture, he organised a special night visit to the Benaki Museum, a jewel in the crown of Athens' attractions, where the curator led them on a private tour. For the first time in days Stephanie was animated, inspecting exquisite ancient gold jewellery, hand-stitched traditional clothes and embroideries, art works and other treasures.

He thought about buying her lavish gifts, jewellery and clothes, a car, but decided to wait. He sensed gifts wouldn't sway her.

But what would?

What would make her say yes?

After days of Stephanie avoiding meaningful discussions, the time had come. Damen needed an answer. He was strung so tight at the looming prospect of marriage that it felt as if he might just snap. He barely slept and when he did he was haunted by dreams.

He found her burrowed into the corner of a sofa, a magazine on her lap.

'We need to talk, Stephanie.'

Her head came up as he took a seat opposite, and that was when Damen saw the phone at her ear.

'I have to go, Emma,' she said into the phone. 'I'll call later. I'm fine, truly.' She ended the call, eyes wary. 'What is it, Damen?'

Her eyes were shadowed. She didn't appear like a woman excited to spend her life with him.

His gut clenched. He didn't want marriage either, yet he *needed* it. He *had* to persuade her.

'You haven't given me an answer.' Damen made his voice gentle. He even managed an encouraging smile.

She stared back with unwavering eyes. Her gaze drilled right through him.

'You don't really want to marry me.'

Damen sat taller. 'Of course I do! I proposed, didn't I?'

The words were less than persuasive but she'd caught him off guard. He felt himself floundering.

'That wasn't a marriage proposal, it was a business proposition.'

Was that where he'd gone wrong? Did she want flowers and candles? The trappings of romance? He delved into his pocket and brought out the ring box that had weighed him down for days. He should have produced it earlier.

He was extending his hand when she shook her head and jumped up from the sofa.

'No! Don't.'

Damen frowned. She sounded distressed, as if he'd offered her an insult instead of an honourable proposal.

He shot to his feet.

'Stephanie. *Koritsi mou*. I *do* want to marry you. To make a family for our child.'

Vehemently she shook her head 'That's just it, Damen. You're only interested in the baby. You're not even interested in sex, just fussing over me because I'm carrying your precious heir.'

He stepped forward, the ache in his chest easing. Is that what worried her? 'I've been putting your needs ahead of my own. I—'

'It's more than that.' She heaved a deep breath. 'For days I've watched you. Just as I watched you when you made your... proposition. And one thing is absolutely clear. You don't want to marry me. You looked sick to the stomach when you proposed. Even now you're unhappy. You're not an eager bridegroom.'

That was what made her hesitate?

For the first time ever Damen wished he could lie with ease. Over the years he'd become adept at hiding his feelings, but when it came to marriage the very thought scraped him raw.

'I do want to marry you, Stephanie.' Couldn't she hear the urgency in his voice?

'No, you want control over our baby. You don't want me to leave with it.'

Damen's breath snared. If she knew that, then why hadn't

she walked away? She wasn't happy but she hadn't left. Which meant he had a chance to get what he wanted.

His brow corrugated. He was fumbling in the dark, missing the clue that would unlock this situation.

'This isn't about control, Stephanie. This is about caring, building a future.'

She folded her arms, the gesture both protective and defiant. 'But you don't really want marriage, or me.'

Damen's jaw jammed. They were going in circles. Of course he didn't want marriage. The very word was associated in his mind with tragedy and guilt. But he'd do what was right.

'Stephanie...' his voice sounded stretched too thin '...you're wrong. That's exactly what I want.'

'Prove it. Explain why you never intended to marry. Tell me what happened to make you look sick whenever you mention marriage.'

'I don't—'

'I need the truth, Damen. Don't you see?' Her mouth crumpled, her distress stabbing him. 'How can I trust you when there's a problem but you won't acknowledge it? How can I spend my life with you? Be honest and I can decide what to do. Tell me what happened to you.'

Her words shook him to the core.

It was one thing, an appallingly difficult thing, to speak of marriage. It was another, he discovered, to share the secret that darkened his soul.

Yet if he didn't she might leave and never come back.

He dragged air into constricted lungs and gestured to the sofa. 'You should sit.' He waited till she was settled then forced himself to follow suit. What he really wanted was to walk away and not have this conversation.

'I almost married once.' His tone was clipped. 'I was twenty-two and in love. Ingrid was...' he paused '...perfect.' He breathed out the word.

'Or so I thought.' He caught Stephanie's sombre stare. 'She

was beautiful and engaging. Clever, great company.' Great in bed.

At least he'd thought so. Now he had trouble remembering sexual pleasure with her. His mind was too full of Stephanie.

'What went wrong?'

'My father advised me to wait but I was young and impatient, so sure of myself.' His next breath felt like millstones grinding in his chest.

'You ignored him?'

'I listened but I wasn't convinced. Then, a week before the wedding, I found her phone. Not her usual phone but a spare I knew nothing about. I picked it up thinking to leave a surprise message but I was the one to get the surprise.'

Damen looked away, his thoughts a decade in the past.

'I found messages between her and her boyfriend.'

He heard a gasp.

'I thought it was a joke but I couldn't let it go. I dug deeper. It turned out she had a boyfriend when she met me. Our great romantic love was a calculated scheme to get their hands on my money. Even with a prenup there was a sizeable profit to be had if she left me after a year. Plus anything she'd managed to siphon off in the meantime.'

Ingrid had been good at that, convincing him to splash the cash on her. On things with a solid resale value, like jewellery.

'She was going to marry you then take your money to her lover?' Stephanie's tone was breathless.

'Exactly.' He darted a look her way.

'But she didn't get it...you.'

'I dumped her five days before the wedding.'

'Good! You were well rid of her.' The spark in Stephanie's eyes might have cheered him in other circumstances.

'That's not all.' Damen looked at the doors to the terrace. The impulse to escape was almost unstoppable. But she needed to hear this. 'My father called me into his office. He was... severely disappointed.' Damen's mouth twisted, remembering his normally placid father's tirade about staining the family honour and what a disappointment his only son was.

Damen looked down at his linked hands, the movement pulling the muscles in his neck too tight.

'He wouldn't let me explain, just launched into a diatribe about how I wasn't fit to bear the Nicolaides name. How close he was to disowning me for dishonouring my fiancée and creating a scandal. I, being young and proud and hating that I hadn't taken his original advice, just stood there, getting angrier and more outraged. How dared he berate *me* when Ingrid was a liar? How could he take her part without asking my side of things? I didn't rush to disabuse him. I let him rant, knowing he'd have to eat his words when he learned the truth.'

'But he calmed down when you told him.'

Damen lifted his head. His body felt leaden, each movement ponderous. Even sucking air into his chest was an effort.

'No.' Damen swallowed. The knot of terrible emotion rose from his chest to his throat, threatening to choke him. 'Before I'd even started explaining he collapsed. The scene brought on a massive heart attack. He died before the medics arrived. I tried CPR but...'

Damen looked into Stephanie's pale face but it wasn't hers he saw.

'He died because of me. I'm to blame for my father's death.'

He sucked in a breath that didn't ease the cramping pain in his chest.

'Of course I feel sick when I think of marriage. It makes me remember a death that could have been avoided. My actions destroyed my father and my whole family paid the price.'

Stephanie reeled. Damen's anguish shattered her lingering anger and disappointment. He looked like a man crushed under an impossible weight, his features stark with pain, his voice unrecognisable.

She stumbled up, her instinct to comfort him. She couldn't

bear to see him so tortured. But she'd only taken one step when Damen flung out an arm to ward her off.

She stopped, heart contracting. That gesture said so much. About his hurt. And his ability to hurt her, more, it seemed, every day.

'Damen, you can't take responsibility for your father's death. There must have been an underlying condition—'

'Didn't you hear what I said?' He shot to his feet but turned away, not towards her. His shoulders hunched as he shoved his hands in his pockets. 'It happened because of my actions. There's no changing that.' He paused. 'So now you know. Are you satisfied?'

Steph stared at that proud, handsome profile set in obdurate lines. Her heart bled for him. Yet the taut way he held himself confirmed his mind was closed.

For one heartbeat, then another, she stood poised to go to him. Comfort him.

Till he turned his back as if to stare at the city view. The discussion was over.

Finally Steph stumbled from the room. With each step she ached for Damen's touch on her arm, the sound of him calling her back.

There was nothing.

Hours later she sat in the shade of a spreading tree in the ruins of the city's ancient marketplace. Before her was a marble temple but she didn't see its beautiful symmetry. Instead she saw the anguish in Damen's eyes, heard the rasp of guilt and regret in his voice.

He believed he'd killed his father. It seemed the terrible events of that time, his fiancée's betrayal and guilt over his father's death, had melded in his mind. He saw his marriage plans as a catalyst for disaster. No wonder he'd planned never to marry.

That explained his nightmares, calling out to his father.

Sympathy knotted Steph's insides. She'd hung on to disappointment because she sensed his proposal was reluctant. Now indignation and anger transformed into pity. What a burden Damen carried!

She wanted to wrap her arms around him and comfort him. She wanted the right to be at his side.

She loved him.

Instead of happiness the knowledge brought pain.

At least now she understood it was the idea of marriage itself that sickened him.

It wasn't anything personal.

That was the problem. None of Damen's plans for her was personal. He didn't want *her*. He wanted their baby. Tying her to him in marriage guaranteed that.

She doubled up in distress. It would be cruel to abandon him, knowing the past tortured him. But how much crueller to her child to stay, living a lie that might end in heartache for everyone?

Could she accept his proposal and hope marriage might lead Damen to love rather than to boredom or dislike?

Or should she make a clean break?

'And so,' she paused to twist her goblet of sparkling water, 'I've decided to go home, to Australia.'

The words pounded into Damen like sledgehammer blows.

He wished he hadn't eaten his delicious dinner. It curdled in his stomach.

'But I'll stay till the end of our two months.' Her lips formed something approximating a smile. 'I'll honour our contract.'

Damen shoved his chair back from the table, the legs screeching on the flagstones of the rooftop terrace. But instead of shooting to his feet he reached for Stephanie's hand.

Touching her silky skin eased his rackety heartbeat.

It had been an emotional day. He'd plumbed the depths with his admission. Yet in the face of this the burden he'd carried for a decade faded towards insignificance. He'd learned to cope with guilt. He sensed he wouldn't cope with Stephanie leaving.

The world blurred as his heart beat too fast and the edges of his vision blackened. He saw her eyes widen.

Damen focused on keeping his hand gentle on hers while the rest of his body went rigid.

All except for that bit of him deep within that crumbled at her words.

Stephanie leaving him.

The thought was unbearable.

Stephanie living on the other side of the world. Taking their baby.

He'd be reduced to seeing his child for, at best, six months a year. As for Stephanie... He imagined cursory conversations as the child passed from one to the other. They'd be strangers, living separate lives.

That odd feeling intensified. As if bits of his organs, his bones, broke away. Roaring white noise filled his head. Reality reduced to the racing thrum of his heart and the hand so soft and unresponsive beneath his.

Arguments to make her stay formed in his head. Inducements that only extreme wealth could buy.

Yet, as he looked into those earnest eyes, read the downward turn of her mouth and the fluttering pulse beneath his hand, Damen knew he was beaten.

Nothing he could offer, neither money nor privilege, would buy her company.

Devastation filled him.

Yet he had to ask. 'Is there anything I can do to change your mind?'

Her mouth crimped at the corners as if she bit back an instinctive response. For a second her eyes blazed more gold than brown. Then they shuttered.

'Nothing.'

CHAPTER FOURTEEN

DAYS LATER, DAMEN stood before his mother in the comfortable sitting room of her Athens home.

His world had tilted on its axis since Stephanie had forced him to reveal his dreadful secret, then declared she was going back to Australia.

Her decision had left him, for the second time in his life, feeling utterly powerless.

Who could blame her for choosing to go? Why would she tie herself to a man who'd killed his own father?

The pain wrapping around his chest worsened daily, as if unseen bonds tightened with each passing hour.

Now Damen had one more trial to face. He couldn't make things right for his father or for Stephanie, couldn't convince her to stay. Yet the unquiet past still haunted him. He'd been a coward in not speaking the truth before. It was a truth he owed his mother.

Yet speaking the words, watching comprehension dawn on her beloved face, made his heart break.

'Damen, no! It's not true!' Her voice shook.

Damen stood his ground, hands clasped behind his back.

'I'm sorry, Mama. But it is. Ten years ago I told you a sanitised version of what happened.'

He moved towards her as she scrambled from her seat, taking her trembling hands.

'You were distraught. I didn't think you'd cope with the whole truth. That *I* was responsible for *Baba's* death. Later...' he sighed. 'Later I was a coward. I couldn't bear to hurt you even more.'

'Foolish, foolish boy.' To his amazement she leaned against him, letting him embrace her. His heart catapulted against his ribs. He'd feared her reaction. Yet still he was gripped by a terrible tension.

His mother leaned back in his arms, her eyes locking on his. 'You're wrong. You didn't kill your father.' Her voice cracked and she squeezed his arm.

Damen shook his head, pain shafting through his soul. Of course his mother didn't want to believe it.

'I'm sorry, Mama.' His breath lifted his chest. 'I didn't listen to him earlier when I should have. Then, that final day, I let him rant because I was too proud, too hurt that he blamed me.'

'He wasn't himself,' she answered. 'He was stressed about the business—'

'That doesn't excuse me.'

His mother shook her head, her expression wistful. 'Your father was a good man but he wasn't himself. He was...scared.'

'Scared?' Damen's head reared back. He couldn't believe such a thing of his father.

'I wanted to tell you but he was adamant. He was scared for the business. Times were tough and you were relatively inexperienced. He had faith in you,' she said quickly, 'but he feared you had a lot to learn if you had to take over.'

'But—' He stopped when she raised her hand.

'He was moody, seeing disaster everywhere, which wasn't your father.' Her expression was wistful. 'You know how positive he usually was. But the doctors warned his health was bad and told him to step back from work. He'd already had two heart attacks.'

'Two heart attacks?' Damen goggled. How had he not known?

'I'm sorry. I wanted him to tell you and your sisters but he refused. They were mild attacks but he was told to work less and get more exercise. He promised he would but instead he put in extra hours, wanting to fix some problems before he handed over to you.'

'He never mentioned me taking over. Never mentioned being ill.'

'He was going to talk to you after the wedding.' She dabbed her eyes. 'He wanted to hand Nicolaides Shipping to you in good shape, but with the economic troubles...' She shrugged. 'You weren't responsible. He'd promised to reduce his hours but he was obsessed with fixing the business first. I tried to persuade him—'

'It's not your fault, Mama.'

'And it's not yours. You said he was ranting. You know how out of character that was. The stress got to him, the worry he wouldn't be around to support you and your sisters.' She bit her lip. 'If anyone caused the attack, it was him. Ignoring medical advice.'

His mother blinked back tears and Damen pulled her close, murmuring words of comfort.

His head spun. If what his mother said was true...

Of course it was. She'd never invent something like that.

It didn't excuse his stupid behaviour, putting his pride first, but it changed so much. Gave a new perspective. The revelation of his father's physical and mental state suddenly made sense, explaining his unusual behaviour. It didn't absolve Damen but already the dread weight of guilt eased.

Maybe now he'd learn to cope better with the past.

Was it possible he might even move on from it?

Steph smoothed her hands down the red dress, avoiding her eyes in the mirror. She was afraid her reflection would reveal her pain. Damen had said they were going ashore for a special party.

Hopefully this bright colour would divert attention from the smudges beneath her eyes that concealer hadn't quite covered.

She put on the wide silver bangle Damen had given her in Rhodes. The piece was funky and pretty. She'd seen it in an artisan's shop and when Damen bought it for her she'd felt trembling excitement as if she was on the brink of a thrilling new part of her life.

Her breath shuddered. Thrilling, yes, with single motherhood and a broken heart. Not what she'd hoped for.

She'd fallen for a man so damaged by his first love that he was incapable of loving. Or at least loving her. Maybe one day he'd love again, but she'd be gone. She couldn't live with the little he offered. Duty. Responsibility. Never love.

Two weeks ago in Athens she'd announced she was leaving and for a few moments she'd thought there was hope. That he *did* care for her and would fight to keep her. Instead Damen accepted her announcement with soul-destroying equanimity.

All she could do was hope to get through their contracted time with dignity.

Fifteen minutes later she and Damen were on a small island. It was beautiful. Even the water in the bay was jewel-toned. Ahead was a gracious old house. Pale yellow walls, terracotta tiles, long windows with white shutters. It looked charming.

Steph drew a deep breath scented by the sea and wild herbs.

'Who lives here?' She looked for evidence of a party but all was silent.

'It was built a long time ago by a famous admiral.' It was the first time Damen had spoken since they left the yacht and his deep voice trawled through her like honey-dipped silk. 'He was a pirate too, according to the stories. You like it?'

'It's gorgeous.' Easier to concentrate on her surroundings than Damen, close beside her but distant in every way that mattered.

How was she to get through the next weeks? She couldn't

leave. They had a deal. It wasn't his fault she'd made the error of falling in love.

Steph's heart squeezed.

They reached the front door and Damen opened it. 'After you.'

Steph stepped into the hallway, blinking after the dazzling sunshine. They were in a square foyer with an elegant curving staircase.

'This way.' Damen ushered her into a sitting room, the furnishings beautiful but worn.

More silence. There were no voices. No clink of china or glass. She looked out to Damen's yacht, moored in the bay. There were no other boats.

Her spine prickled with belated warning.

Steph swung around to find Damen close. His distinctive scent wafted into her nostrils. Her yearning grew. How was she to pretend not to care?

'What is this, Damen?'

'It's the house I've bought. I'll use it as my base and commute to Athens when I need to.' He looked around. 'It needs renovation and a sympathetic extension, but when it's done it will be special.'

Steph agreed but didn't want to discuss renovations.

'There's no party, is there? Why are we here?'

To her surprise Damen smiled. It was the first genuine smile she'd seen from him in two weeks and it unravelled her defences.

'This is a kidnap.'

'Sorry?' She must have misheard.

'I'm kidnapping you. I botched my first effort but this time I'm determined to do it right.' The smile faded and suddenly he was standing so close the heat from his body washed through her. 'I'm keeping you on the island till you agree to my terms.'

Steph tottered backwards, her hand at her throat. 'You can't!'

'Watch me.' He looked more sombre than she'd ever known him.

Tears of fury and hurt pricked her eyes. 'You're utterly ruthless. What do you want, Damen? Another contract? I can tell you now I'll never sign over my baby to you. I'll swim to the next island if I have to.'

'It's not like that.'

'Of course it's like that. If you think holding me here will convince me to—'

'It's not the baby I want.'

Steph's mouth sagged open.

'Not the baby?'

He was so close she had to tilt her chin to meet his eyes. Awareness zinged through her. She tried to stifle it and focus on anger.

'No, I want *you*.'

'You're not making sense.'

'On the contrary, for the first time since we met I'm talking perfect sense.' His glittering eyes held a promise of something that made her heart turn over. 'I've wanted you since the day we met.'

'You had me, remember?'

He shook his head. 'I've never had you, *agapi mou*, not really. Oh, we had sex, and it was amazing. But I want more than your body.'

'Yes. You want my baby.' She couldn't let herself forget that.

'Of course I want our child. Or, I should say I want to share our child. But there's something I want more.'

Steph frowned, not daring to hope.

'I want *you*, Stephanie. Not just sleeping in my bed or sharing responsibility for our child.' He paused and she saw his nostrils flare as if he fought for breath. 'I want you with me because you care for me. Because I care for you.' Another pause. Another deep breath.

'I love you, Stephanie. If you give us a chance, I believe I can make you happy. You might even come to love me too.'

Steph shuffled back till she came up against a sofa. 'You're lying. You don't…love me.' Her heart dipped on the word and she wrapped her arms around her middle to keep the hurt at bay. 'You're cruel pretending to.'

'You accused me of lying before, *agapi mou*, and I regret you had cause ever to doubt my honesty. But I tell you now, on my oath as a Nicolaides, I've never been more genuine. I love you.' He said it again slowly, his gaze pinioning her so she couldn't look away.

'No!' She put out a hand to ward him off, though he hadn't moved. Her palm landed on his chest, her fingers splaying on familiar hard contours. 'You're saying this so I'll marry you and so the baby—'

'Actually, I do want to marry you. I want that more than anything.' Damen's hand closed on hers, holding it against his staccato-beating heart. His eyes gleamed as if lit by an inner fire. 'The thought of losing you has cured me of my horror of marriage. Because I've realised life is too short to waste a moment of being with the woman I love.'

His words slammed the breath back into her lungs. Her head swam.

'I had a long talk with my mother too. I told her about the day my father died. What I hadn't known was that he'd already had a couple of heart attacks. That doesn't excuse my behaviour, but you were right. I was too ready to blame myself. And stupidly I let that stand in the way of *us*.'

Could there really be an *us*? Steph watched him in amazement, trying to process the change in him.

'I want to be your husband, Stephanie. But if you don't want to marry, I'll accept that. Whatever you like, as long as you stay. Give me a chance to show you how good our life can be together.'

Steph blinked, overwhelmed. She wanted so much to believe but she couldn't let herself.

'I was attracted to you from the first. I only left because I thought I'd wrecked my chances with you. Then in Corfu...' He paused and she felt his heart quicken beneath her palm. 'You have no idea how much I wanted you. Even if I hadn't needed a pretend lover I'd have tried to seduce you. Everything about you attracted me. Your looks, your feisty attitude, your sense of humour. Even the way you refused to be impressed by me. You sizzle with energy and passion and I wanted that for myself. I still do. Especially now I've learned what a warm and honest heart you have.'

Steph's breath came in short bursts, warring emotions filling her. His words meant so much, and she desperately wanted to believe them.

'You didn't love me a fortnight ago. You didn't want to marry me.' His unwilling proposal had hurt so badly.

Damen lifted his other hand to her cheek, and to her shame she didn't have the strength to shy away. If anything she nestled closer.

Damen's pupils dilated. His fingers moved in a tender caress.

'That's just it. I *did* love you, though I hadn't let myself think in those terms. Because I'd loved Ingrid and that led to heartache and tragedy.'

'It wasn't your fault!' She'd felt helpless, watching Damen grapple with his demons. 'Stop blaming yourself.'

'That's what my mother says.'

'She's right.' Steph hoped never to see such anguish as she'd seen in Damen's eyes that day.

'I'm glad you think so. She also told me I was a fool if I let you go without telling you how I feel.'

Steph's eyes widened, hope rising.

'But I was going to tell you anyway. I can't let you go because I love you. Not as I thought I loved Ingrid, with a boy's infatuation, but deeply, with all I am and all I hope to be.' His voice deepened on the words. They sounded like a pledge. '*S'agapo*, Stephanie *mou*.'

'Oh, Damen.' She blinked back tears. 'How am I supposed to stay strong and resist you when you say that?'

'I want you to be strong, *asteri mou*. To be the independent, gorgeous woman you already are. I just don't want you to resist *me*.' His voice cracked and her eyes widened. 'Stay with me. Things were good between us and they can be even better. Look in your heart and give us a chance. Maybe you'll come to love me too.'

The last of Steph's resistance crumbled. She'd taken chances and made mistakes. But this wasn't a mistake.

This was the man she wanted to build a life with. A man who'd wrestled his demons and emerged wanting her. A decent, caring, wonderful man who deserved a second chance.

In the end the words slipped out easily.

'I already love you, Damen. That's why I've been miserable, thinking all you cared about was our baby.'

She felt the crash of his heart at her words.

He must have seen the truth in her face, for he smiled. That soul-lifting smile that made her heart beat double time.

'You love me.' His voice held wonder and satisfaction.

His arm looped around her waist, pulling her to him.

Steph went willingly.

'And you love me.' It was there in his eyes, his embrace, in the very air they breathed.

'Let me show you how much.' His arms were strong yet gentle as he scooped her up and headed for the staircase and the bedrooms above. 'I'll never tire of saying the words, *agapi mou*, but I want you to be absolutely sure of my feelings, and actions speak louder than words.'

In the end he convinced Stephanie both with words and potently persuasive actions.

EPILOGUE

A COOL BREEZE ruffled the cypresses but the sky was cloudless and the day perfect.

Damen's gaze traversed the garden from the villa, across the terrace where friends and family clustered. The steps to this garden by the sea were bright with potted roses and other flowers in shades of red, Stephanie's favourite colour. Red ribbons decorated the arbour where he stood with Christo.

Damen didn't care about decorations. Nor witnesses, though he was glad his family was here. His sisters gossiped with Clio. Manos and his wife chatted with friends and kids raced in circles, laughing as parents herded them to seats. His mother sat with Stephanie's grandmother and the friend she'd brought from Australia, a tall, white-haired man. From the older man's expression when he looked at Mrs Logan, Damen guessed there'd be another wedding soon.

'Emma's done a fantastic job preparing for today.' Damen mightn't care about decorations but he wanted today perfect for Stephanie.

'I'll tell her you said so,' Christo responded. 'She'll be thrilled. Even more thrilled than when you said you wanted to be married on Corfu.'

'It's a special place for us.' Where he and Stephanie had met again, argued and struck sparks off each other, and agreed to become pretend lovers. Now they were so much more. 'Besides, the renovations aren't finished at our villa.'

'You can have the christening party there.'

Damen met his friend's grin just as the string quartet began playing a familiar tune. His heart shot straight to his throat, beating hard and fast.

He turned and his breath stopped.

She was even more beautiful than he remembered. He hadn't seen her since yesterday, having stayed aboard the yacht while she spent the night with Emma.

Damen's throat dried.

Stephanie's hair shone like ebony and she carried red flowers before her small baby bump. Her gown was deep cream, wide across the shoulders but fitted across the breasts and falling in folds to her feet. The pearl and ruby necklace he'd given her glowed against her skin. She looked as elegant as a princess, as delicate as a fairy. She was his dream of heaven.

Then she was there, before him. Her eyes shone golden brown, her smile turned him inside out.

Damen took her hand, lifting it to his mouth. The scent of vanilla and Stephanie, of happiness, filled him.

He whispered in her ear, 'You're absolutely sure?' He'd suggested that they marry after the baby was born, a gesture to prove he wanted marriage because he loved her, not to secure their child.

'I'm sure.' Her eyes flashed. 'I can't wait to be your wife. I love you, Damen Nicolaides, and I mean to have you.'

Damen grinned as his heart filled. 'Have I mentioned I adore a woman who knows what she wants?'

Ignoring custom, he swooped down to kiss her lips. Instantly she melted, his fiery, adorable love.

The sound of Christo clearing his throat finally penetrated and reluctantly Damen straightened. Stephanie's eyes shone and a tantalising smile curved her sweet lips. Damen took her arm and turned to the celebrant.

Could any day be more perfect?

And this was just the beginning.

* * * * *

Forbidden Lust

Karen Booth

DESIRE

Scandalous world of the elite.

Karen Booth is a Midwestern girl transplanted in the South, raised on '80s music and repeated readings of *Forever* by Judy Blume. When she takes a break from the art of romance, she's listening to music with her college-aged kids or sweet-talking her husband into making her a cocktail. Learn more about Karen at karenbooth.net.

Books by Karen Booth

Harlequin Desire

The Eden Empire

A Christmas Temptation
A Cinderella Seduction
A Bet with Benefits
A Christmas Seduction
A Christmas Rendezvous

Dynasties: Secrets of the A-List

Tempted by Scandal

Dynasties: Seven Sins

Forbidden Lust

Visit her Author Profile page at
millsandboon.com.au,
or karenbooth.net, for more titles.

You can find Karen Booth on Facebook,
along with other Harlequin Desire authors,
at Facebook.com/harlequindesireauthors!

Dear Reader,

Thanks for picking up *Forbidden Lust*! I loved writing this book because it was yet another chance for me to explore two of my favorite romance tropes—unrequited love and the best friend's younger sister. Both themes are so much fun!

Zane and Allison have known each other since Zane's life fell apart in the aftermath of the Black Crescent scandal. Allison was a few years younger and developed a massive crush on Zane that never quite went away. Even all these years later, her lust for him is still bubbling under the surface. He's just too sexy and brooding for her to stay away. Zane never dared to think about Allison that way when they were in high school, but now that they're both grown up, it's impossible to ignore the beautiful, vibrant woman she has become.

Enter Allison's brother, Scott. Zane is indebted to Scott for standing by him during the most difficult time of his life. Scott is incredibly protective of Allison, who went through a scary illness when she was a young girl. Scott doesn't want Zane and Allison within fifty feet of each other, let alone stuck on a remote Bahamian island together...but sometimes a hurricane rolls in and there's nothing to do but ride out the storm! I think it made for a sexy, emotional story with lots of ups and downs.

I sincerely hope you enjoy Dynasties: Seven Sins and continue to read through the series. There are so many fabulous authors to discover. In the meantime, drop me a line anytime at karen@karenbooth.net. I love hearing from readers!

Karen

For the members of the Backstage Antics with Karen crew on Facebook. You guys are the absolute best!

CHAPTER ONE

ZANE PATTERSON'S HEART was hammering. His T-shirt was soaked with sweat, clinging to his shoulders. "I need to get out of this town. That's all there is to it." He dribbled the basketball with his right hand. *Thump. Thump. Thump.* Switching to his left, Zane waited for his opening—his chance to drive past his best friend, Scott Randall. Their weekly game of one-on-one was tied. One more point and victory was Zane's. So very close. He did not like to lose. He hated it.

"Dude. You've been saying that since high school. It's been fifteen years." Laser-focused on Zane's every move, Scott shuffled from side to side, hands high, low and anywhere Zane dared to even think about looking. Scott didn't allow himself to get distracted by the perspiration raining down from the top of his shiny bald head. He only cared about not giving up the final point. "You either need to leave or get over it."

The reason for leaving—Joshua Lowell—popped into Zane's head. Zane despised him. He had the smuggest smile, like he was perfectly comfortable with the silver spoon firmly lodged in his mouth at birth. The entirety of Falling Brook, New Jersey, put that jerk on a pedestal, even when his father had destroyed lives and families, including Zane's. Deep down, Zane loved his hometown, but being here was pushing him closer and closer to the edge. *Get over it? No way.*

Thump. He palmed the ball. *Thump.* Left. *Thump.* Right. *Thump.* Back left. He dropped his shoulder, slipped around Scott and beelined for the basket. With Scott in hot pursuit but several strides behind him, Zane finger-rolled the ball for a layup. It circled the rim. And popped back out. Scott grabbed the rebound, spun away from Zane and hoisted up a perfect jumper. Nothing but net.

Dammit.

"Yes!" Scott darted under the basket and snatched the ball. "Rematch? Best two out of three?"

Zane bent over, clutching the hem of his basketball shorts and planting the heels of his hands on his knees. "No." The competitive part of him wanted the win. Needed it. Playing basketball was one of the only activities that had ever made him happy. He'd been at it since he could walk, precisely the reason he had an indoor court installed when his company, Patterson Marketing, took off and they built their own state-of-the-art office building. But he was too exhausted to compete. Or fight. Mentally, more than anything. "I'm done."

"This Joshua Lowell thing is really getting to you, isn't it?" Scott rested the ball on his hip, letting the weight of his forearm hold it in place.

"I can't get away from it. The anniversary article was supposed to remind everyone what crooks the Lowells are, how they destroyed lives, how they can never be trusted. Instead, Josh's engagement to Sophie Armstrong is all anyone is talking about. It's everywhere. Facebook. Twitter. The Java Hut. My own freaking staff meeting."

"It's a big deal. He's stepping away from BC. Nobody saw that coming."

BC. The initials for Black Crescent were enough to make Zane cringe. The hedge fund, founded by Joshua Lowell's father, Vernon, had been an ultraexclusive avenue of investment for the superrich. Zane's family had once breathed the rarefied air of those on the limited client list, and for a time, the world was sunshine and roses. There was no shortage of money, and Zane's life was golden—king of the school at Falling Brook Prep, captain of the basketball team, parents happily married. Then Vernon disappeared with millions, Zane's family was left penniless and his parents' marriage was destroyed.

Losing their family fortune meant that Zane had been moved from Prep to the public high school at the age of sixteen. It was another brutal adjustment, especially since the kids at Falling Brook High treated Zane like the rich kid who needed to be taken down a notch or two. They had no idea Zane was already at rock bottom. The only consolation was that he'd met Scott there, and they'd been best friends ever since.

Scott saved Zane, mostly from himself. Scott didn't give a damn about the money; he only wanted to help, and he only wanted to be friends. They were solid from day one. When Zane's mom and dad fought, which was often, Scott's parents allowed Zane to seek refuge at their house. It was an oasis of calm—the one place happiness seemed possible. One of the best parts of those stays was spending time with Scott's younger sister, Allison. She was the coolest, smartest and most creative person Zane had ever met. She was supercute, too, but Zane had always looked past that. She was Scott's sister, and Zane would never, ever go there. Never.

"Did you see Josh's press conference? Did you hear what he said? 'She brought me out of the dark with her love'? 'Because she loves me, I am worthy'? What a load of crap." Zane didn't enjoy being so bitter, but the fifteen years since Vernon Lowell disappeared had done nothing to assuage his pain over his entire life crumbling to dust. As far as Zane was concerned, all Lowells—Vernon; his wife, Eve; and his kids, Joshua, Jake and Oliver—were pure poison. He didn't want to see any of them happy.

"You know what they say. Love makes everything better."

Zane shot Scott a look. Romantic love was a farce. It rarely, if ever, lasted. Zane's parents were a classic example. Yes, they'd been tested when Vernon Lowell stole every penny they had, but wasn't love supposed to conquer all? Not from where Zane was sitting. "Said like a very married man."

"Don't get salty because I'm happy. Last time I checked, there wasn't a law against it."

Zane grumbled under his breath. He didn't want to continue this part of their conversation.

The two men wandered over to the corner of the gym to grab the six-pack of microbrew Scott had stashed in the fully stocked beverage fridge. Zane was more of a tequila or mescal guy, but after a game, there was nothing better than knocking back a cold beer. They took it outside to the patio, where employees often enjoyed their lunch or an afternoon meeting if the weather was nice. A warm June night, the air was sweet and a bit heavy with humidity, but there was a pleasant breeze. Zane and Scott sat at a table, and Scott popped open the first two bottles. They clinked them to toast.

Zane took in a deep breath, washing down his resentment with that first sip of beer, trying to remind himself that he really did love it here. "I never should have gone to Joshua Lowell at the bar and told him I knew about the DNA report because I was the one who gave it to Sophie for the article about Black Crescent. I should have let him wonder who her sources were. I should have let him stew in his own juices. That's what he deserves." He took another long draw of his drink. That had been a difficult confrontation. Just seeing Joshua Lowell face-to-face was enough to make him physically ill. "I wanted him to know that he wasn't as high and mighty as everyone thought. That I knew who he really was."

Zane remembered the odd jolt that went through his body when he received the DNA report in the mail, saying that Josh had a daughter and was refusing to take responsibility. It hadn't occurred to Zane just how peculiar it was for someone to have sent that to him. He hadn't even thought too hard about why the anonymous sender would pick him as the recipient. He'd only known that it was ammunition to take down a Lowell, and that had been more than enough. "The whole point of talking to Sophie was to finally tell the world that Josh Lowell is not the savior everyone thinks he is. I even gave her personal photos to use, to show her I was a legit source. Somehow that all backfired. The DNA bombshell never made it into the anniversary article, because I picked a reporter with scruples. Now everyone seems to adore him even more than before. Just in time for him to fall in love with a beautiful woman, decide to get married and conveniently step away from Black Crescent, which is the main reason to hate him. He's getting off without a scratch, just like his dad."

Scott shook his head, the corner of his mouth turned up in a pitying smirk. "Maybe you do need a break. Get away."

"Or move."

Scott set his elbow on the table, pointing at Zane with his beer bottle. "You cannot move. I need you."

"You're drunk."

"Half a beer in? I don't think so. It's the truth. You're like a brother to me. And honestly, I think you need me. Who else is going to listen to you bitch about this?"

Scott wasn't wrong. He grounded Zane and helped him stay away from his inevitable downward spiral. "Okay. So where do I go? I need a beach, preferably with lots of women."

"It does not surprise me that you would say that."

Zane let a quiet laugh leave his lips. Yes, he had been with a lot of women over the years. That was his escape. No strings attached, no messy feelings getting in the way. In high school, it had been to numb the effects of his fall from grace. The poor former rich kid proved an easy target for other guys, but the girls didn't see it that way. His money and status might have been gone, but the body he'd spent hours working on in the gym and his face were still enough to turn a few heads. So he'd taken what he could get.

"If it's the beach you want," Scott said, "you should go down to the Bahamas. My aunt and uncle's resort off the coast of Eleuthera. I can hook you up."

Scott and Zane had talked many times about making that trip. Scott's mom was Bahamian, but had moved to the US permanently after attending college stateside and meeting Scott's dad. "Yes. Dudes' trip. We've talked about it a hundred times. It's perfect."

"Sorry, man. You're on your own. Brittney just got a promotion at work, and her schedule is crazy. It's June, so the kids are out of school. I can't just take off. Plus, if you're picking up women, I think we can both agree that my days of being your wingman are over."

Zane didn't let the disappointment get to him too much. Everything was a downer of one sort or another. He was used to it. "Okay. I guess I'm flying solo. Can you text me the info? I'll call first thing tomorrow morning."

Scott shook his head. "Just give me the dates and I'll take care of it. It's on me."

"I do not need your charity. This isn't high school."

"Will you just shut up and let me do something nice for you? Plus, I gotta keep you happy. I would be ridiculously bummed out if you moved out of Falling Brook."

Zane glanced over at Scott. He didn't know what he would do without him. He was the thing tethering him to earth. Keeping him from going off the deep end. "I'm not leaving. I might desperately need a few days on that beach to clear my head, but I'm not going anywhere." He knocked back the last of his beer. "I have to at least stick around long enough to avenge this loss."

"Black Crescent?" Scott asked.

"No. Tonight's game."

* * *

When Allison Randall saw her ex-boyfriend's name on the caller ID, she flipped off her phone. Juvenile, but incredibly satisfying.

"Let me guess. Neil?" Allison's best friend and business partner, Kianna Lewis, was perched in a chair opposite Allison's desk, flicking a pen back and forth between her thumb and forefinger. They'd been discussing the state of their corporate recruiting business, which frankly, wasn't that great.

"I really don't want to talk to him. Ever."

"Aren't the movers at his house right now? What if there's a problem?"

Kianna was so levelheaded. Allison needed that. She could get tunnel vision. And a little spiteful. "You're right. I'm just ready for one of these conversations to be our last." Allison plucked her phone from her desk and spun her chair around to peer out the window of her office, which overlooked nothing more scenic than a sea of expensive cars in a parking lot. Such was LA—asphalt and BMWs. "What's wrong now?" she asked Neil.

"You could have hired a normal moving company, Allison. Hunks with Trucks? Seriously?" Her ex-boyfriend was not taking her departure from his life well. That was perfectly okay with her.

Allison snickered under her breath. Neil was in ridiculously good shape, and he loved to flaunt it. He took any excuse to whip off his shirt in public. Allison had figured he might as well spend the afternoon with a bunch of guys who were even more buff and cut than him. Served him right for cheating on her. "They hire college students, Neil. These guys need the work. For tuition and books. Just forget the name, okay?"

"That's a little difficult when their ten-foot-high logo is emblazoned on the truck outside my house. The neighbors can all see it."

What a drama queen. She should have known better than

to date a movie producer. "Sounds like good marketing on their part."

"There's a crowd gathering. A bunch of women from my street are outside taking selfies with these guys."

This had gone far better than Allison could have anticipated. She nearly wished she'd been there to witness it, except that would have meant seeing Neil, and she couldn't guarantee she wouldn't strangle him. "If you hadn't cheated on me, you wouldn't have to suffer this supposed embarrassment."

"I made a mistake, okay? It happens. You need to get off that high horse of yours. Not everyone can be perfect like you."

She choked back a grumble. "Not cheating does not make me perfect. It makes me a decent human being, which is more than I can say for you."

"I've told you one hundred times that she meant nothing to me. It was just a few months of hookups. I was stupid for doing it, and I'm sorry."

Allison clamped her eyes shut. She was not going to let him manipulate her anymore. "I'm done with this conversation, Neil. Unless there's a real problem you need me to address, I'm going to hang up now."

"I want my key back, Alli."

"Change the locks. And don't call me Alli." She hit the red button on the screen and tossed her phone onto a pile of papers on her desk. The desire to scream was so intense she dug her fingernails into her palms.

"You okay?" Kianna asked, arching her perfectly groomed eyebrows.

"I'm fine." Allison was a firm believer in fake it 'til you make it. She would keep saying she was fine until she was actually fine. Still, the Neil situation had her shaken. How had she not seen that Neil was an arrogant jerk? How had she managed to miss the signs? As an executive recruiter, it was Allison's job to read people, but she'd clearly been all wrong about Neil.

"It's okay to have a human moment. Your boyfriend cheated on you. No one would blame you for crying or throwing things."

No, no one would fault her, but Allison refused to let this drag her down. Neil would move on with his life in his perfect house, with his suspiciously white teeth and 3 percent body fat. Allison was not going to let him be the only one to find happiness. "I'm fine. Let's get back to work. We need to finish this up so I can head over to my new place and meet the movers."

"Okay. If that's what you want." Kianna launched into a summary of their bottom line. It didn't take long. The upshot was too many expenses, not enough income. "All of this makes the Black Crescent account that much more important. If we nail this first assignment for them, we should be able to go on retainer. That will put us safely in the black."

Having a new client in her hometown of Falling Brook, New Jersey, was a real boon. Allison had pulled in a favor to make it happen, but she was sure it could translate into big things. "We can do it. I can do it. I will knock their socks off. I promise." The best part was that it would not only bring in money, she could see her brother, Scott. Allison had been there for his birthday last month, but she always looked forward to their time together.

"How soon are you planning to go out there and meet with them?"

Allison flipped through her calendar. "I haven't booked my travel yet, but I'm thinking next week. My plan is to walk into that meeting with the three amazing candidates we've been talking to for the position."

"Can I make a suggestion?"

"You think I should go sooner?"

"I think you should *leave* sooner, as in go somewhere for a few days. Relax. Unwind. Meet a hot guy and let him rock your world. Get Neil out of your system."

"But we have so much work to do."

"And we need you on top of your game when you meet with Black Crescent. You're wound way too tight right now."

Allison had to laugh. "Have you been talking to my mom?"

"Please tell me your mom didn't tell you to hook up with some guy."

"She didn't. But she did tell my aunt Angelique about Neil, and Angelique called last night begging me to come and stay with her and my uncle for a few days at their resort in the Bahamas. Bad news travels fast among the women in my family." Allison was incredibly close to her mom, so much so that she felt suffocated sometimes. So of course, they'd had many phone conversations about the Neil situation, and it was only a matter of time before her aunt found out.

"That sounds perfect. I say you do it. As long as there are men available, of course." Kianna got up from her chair, gathered her notes in her arms and headed for the door.

"A man is the last thing I need."

Kianna turned and cast Allison a stern look. "I'm not talking marriage. I'm talking sex. A few mind-blowing orgasms and Neil will be a distant memory."

"I'm not much for random hookups. I'm not even sure I can do that."

"Have you looked at yourself? Any sane guy would be psyched to take you to bed." Kianna turned on her heel and headed down the hall.

Allison wasn't sure about that, but maybe it was time to do something nice for herself—book a bungalow on the beach and fall asleep in the sun with a good book. She fumbled for her phone and dialed the number for her aunt.

"Tell me you're on the plane," Angelique said when she answered.

Allison smiled. She couldn't help it. She loved her entire family deeply. "Not yet."

"But you're coming?"

"As long as you have room for me."

"I have one bungalow open, so we have room. It's all yours. I hope it's okay if I put you next to one of your brother's friends, though. Zane Patterson?"

That name started a long-forgotten hum in Allison's body. Zane was the guy Allison had crushed on for every waking minute of her adolescence. "He's not coming with Scott, is he?"

"Oh, no. By himself. Just for a few days. He gets here tomorrow."

Allison's heart was jackhammering in her chest. Visions of unbelievably sexy Zane rushed into her consciousness—thick dark hair with a hint of curl, piercing blue eyes that made her melt and a long, lean body she'd wanted to touch forever. She had a good dozen or so Zane fantasies she'd concocted over the years. Why had she never thought up the one where they both ended up on a secluded Bahamian island at the same time? "Oh. Funny. I was thinking I'd fly in tomorrow, too."

"Do you know him?"

"I do. He's a great guy. It's always nice to see him." Allison couldn't ignore the way her voice had suddenly pitched to a higher octave. "Nice to see him" didn't begin to cover it.

But there'd always been a massive obstacle with Zane—Scott. The only time she'd had any real physical contact with Zane was three weeks ago, when they were at her brother's house for his birthday dinner. This was right after Allison had first found out Neil was cheating. Feeling hurt, reckless and pleasantly tipsy, she'd spent most of the evening testing the waters of flirtation with Zane. She knocked her knee into his under the table, brushed his hand with her fingertips when reaching for the butter and made a point of making eye contact when she laughed at his jokes. There was a palpable connection between them, a very real spark, and she could only play with fire for so long before jumping in headfirst. So as soon as Scott and his wife left the table to put their kids to bed, Allison had grabbed her chance. She gripped Zane's muscled forearm, leaned in and kissed him. For a blissful instant, Zane was into it.

So into it.

He'd cupped her jaw with his hand like he was drinking her in. The years of wanting him day after day had been building for that moment, and she was overwhelmed by a deluge of heat and a rush of something she hadn't experienced in too long— pure hope. She arched into him, and he followed her cue, wrapping his arm around her and pressing his chest against hers. It was really happening, and her mind had leaped ahead to what came next…a quick escape, a race back to his place, clothes coming off before they were even inside, lips and hands exploring the landscape of each other's bodies until they were both exhausted. It was going to happen. Finally.

Then he froze. And everything else became a blur. He pushed her away, ashamed to look her in the eye. He blurted something about betraying Scott. He said he was sorry. He shook his head and muttered that it had been a mistake. He pushed back from the table and rushed out the door, leaving Allison shell-shocked. How could she have been so close and have it all taken away? It felt like a cruel joke life was playing on her. It hurt like hell.

For weeks, that painful scene played in her head. But once she got beyond the hurt, she realized that the real problem had been Scott. If they'd been truly alone that night, her fantasies would've come true. She and Zane would've been naked and sweaty in no time.

But hopefully, Zane wouldn't be so worried about her hyperprotective brother if he was a thousand miles away. With close proximity to Zane and some privacy, she could finally go for what she'd always wanted—a night of pure abandon with Zane. She knew better than to hope for more than that. He was the ultimate ladies' man, and she was okay with that. He was who he was, and she still wanted him more than any man she'd ever laid eyes on. If she played her cards right, she'd at least get to fulfill this fantasy, even if it was only a onetime thing.

"Do you want me to tell him you're coming?"

If Allison had been talking to Kianna, she might have made a joke about orgasms, but that was not appropriate with her aunt. "No. Don't. I'll surprise him."

"I'm so happy you're coming to stay, Alli. It's been too long."

"I'm excited to spend some time unwinding."

"Text me your flight details. I'll have someone pick you up at the marina."

"Sounds perfect. See you tomorrow."

Allison gathered her things, closed up her office, said good-bye to Kianna and hurried out to the parking lot, feeling a new purpose in every step. She hopped into her Mercedes, cranked the stereo and headed toward her new apartment, where the guys from Hunks with Trucks would soon be waiting to move her into her new place. She wasn't even going to bother to unpack. She was going to let them in to do their work while she turned around to go shopping for a hat, a sarong and the skimpiest bikini she could find. Then she was going to get a good night's beauty sleep and get her butt on a plane tomorrow morning.

Next stop, paradise. Next stop, Zane.

CHAPTER TWO

THE FLIGHT FROM Miami to Eleuthera Island was not for the faint of heart. Scott's aunt and uncle Angelique and Hubert had booked a charter for Zane on the tiniest of Learjets. Still, Zane loved the freedom of hanging by an invisible thread over the jaw-dropping blue of the Atlantic.

Zane's pulse skipped a beat as the aircraft floated down to the tiny landing strip and bounced its way to an abrupt stop. Another five hundred yards and they would've been in the ocean. Engines whirring, the plane taxied around to a modest outbuilding—yellow with a rust-red roof. The crew quickly opened the cabin door, and Zane whipped off his seat belt, sucking in his first sweet breath of Bahamian air. Sunglasses on, he surveyed the landscape from his vantage point at the top of the plane stairs. Palm trees rustled in the wind, and gauzy white clouds rolled across the seemingly endless stretch of azure sky. This was exactly what he'd needed. He knew it already.

A driver from Rose Cove, the boutique resort owned by Scott's aunt and uncle, met him outside the airport building, and after a quick zip through customs, Zane was on his way to the marina in a golf cart. From there, a speedboat captain named Marcus took Zane for the two-mile trip to Rose Cove Island, off the southernmost tip of Eleuthera. The water was tranquil and clear, the wind buzzing through Zane's ears as the boat sliced through the water and the sun blanketed him in warmth. He pulled his phone out of his pocket and powered it down. He had zero plans to look at it while he was in paradise. He not only needed to unwind, he wanted to disappear. Falling Brook, the Lowell family and Black Crescent weren't even a distant thought—they'd evaporated from his mind.

Pulling up to the dock at Rose Cove, Zane was struck by the beauty of the pink sand beaches from which the tiny private island got its name. Marcus directed him down a crushed-seashell path through a tropical forest so shaded by palm trees that it was a good ten degrees cooler. Colorful birds chirped and flitted from tree to tree, while the occasional lizard skittered across the sandy ground to hide behind a rock. He eventually reached a clearing with a white single-story building of colonial architecture, with a porch that wrapped around the entire structure. Inside, Zane finally got to meet Scott's aunt Angelique.

"Welcome to Rose Cove!" she exclaimed, rushing out from behind the check-in desk, wearing a beautiful turquoise sundress, flat sandals and her braided hair pulled up in a twist. Despite her enthusiasm, Angelique's peaceful voice suggested that she lived her life at a pace far different from the rest of the world's. "My nephew has told me so much about you." She gave him a hug, showing the same warmth Zane had found in Scott's entire family. He already felt at home here. He wasn't sure he ever wanted to leave.

"You can't believe everything Scott says," Zane joked.

Angelique smiled wide. "He had nothing but great things to say." She bustled back behind the counter and unfolded what appeared to be a map. "Here's all you need to know about the island. This is the main building, where my husband, Hubert, and I live." She circled a picture of the building where they were. "The ten cottages spoke out from here and are a good distance from each other for privacy. You're in cottage number eight. You have a quiet stretch of beach, a hammock and a private plunge pool. There's a beautiful king-size bed, a luxury bath and a fully stocked kitchen. Or our staff will bring you breakfast, lunch and dinner every day. Simply fill out the card waiting for you in your room. Until then, I invite you to relax and enjoy the island. Perhaps say hello to your neighbor in cottage nine. She's been waiting for you to arrive."

"A neighbor?" *A she, no less?* Perhaps this was Zane's lucky day, although there was a part of him that knew his tendency to get lost in women was not his best trait. Really, he should be focusing on fishing and swimming while detoxing from social media and the internet.

"My niece, Allison. She arrived a few hours ago."

Zane's jaw dropped so far he had to make a conscious decision to close his mouth. He was flabbergasted. What were the chances that he and Allison would end up on the island at the same time? "Allison is here. On this island. Right now."

"Is there a problem?"

He shook his head so fast he nearly lost his sunglasses, which were resting on top of his head. "Absolutely not. I love Allison. I'm just surprised. I'll have to stop over and say hi." He hadn't seen Allison much in the years since he graduated from high school. He'd gone to college in North Carolina on a basketball scholarship, and when he returned to Falling Brook after four years, she was off to school in Los Angeles, where she stayed to start a business. She returned every Christmas, but Zane always seemed to be visiting his mom in Boston at the same time. But three weeks ago Scott's wife, Brittney, invited both Allison and Zane to a surprise birthday dinner she was having for Scott. Allison flew in for the weekend. The instant Zane saw her, he knew exactly how good the years had been to Allison— almost too good. She'd taken a straight line from cute to drop-dead gorgeous. Her long and wavy black hair was pulled back in a ponytail, showing off the incredible depth and warmth of her brown eyes. The chemistry of the entire room shifted when she smiled or laughed. He'd always found her interesting and a bit otherworldly, with a style and vibe all her own, but that night he was transfixed.

She'd surprised him many times when they were younger, like the day she got her nose pierced, but she'd flat-out shocked him that night at Scott's house. She kissed him—soft and sensuous and so packed with sexy intent that he'd felt the earth shift beneath him. He was so conditioned to think of Allison only as his best friend's little sister that he'd been wholly unprepared for Allison, the fully formed woman. And with Scott in the other room, a man to whom there would be no explaining, Zane had done the unthinkable that night. He'd pushed beautiful, beguiling Allison away.

"Well, she has the cottage next to yours, so I'm sure you'll see her," Angelique said.

Now Zane was wondering how in the hell he was going to navigate these difficult waters. He didn't want to relive the awkward aftermath of that kiss. Their conversation from that night was permanently emblazoned on his psyche.

This is wrong, Allison. Your brother.

Don't talk about Scott.

But he's right in the other room. He will never forgive me.

Women had been Zane's escape many times, but not like that. Never before had he risked one of the most important things in his life for a kiss.

It had been such a blur, Zane had left without saying so much as goodbye to Scott, asking Allison to tell him that he had a headache. She told him he was getting freaked out for nothing, but Zane knew his weakness when it came to women, and Allison was the one woman he absolutely could never have.

"Mr. Patterson? Are you sure everything is okay? Scott mentioned that you've been under a lot of stress." Angelique looked at him quizzically, knocking her head to one side.

"Oh, yes. Sorry." He shook his head in an effort to get it straight. He needed to get a grip. He and Allison had shared a kiss. It was no big deal. Scott would never know about it, and it would never happen again—end of story.

"Is there anything else you need?"

"My room key, I guess."

"There are no keys on Rose Cove. You will enjoy more seclusion and privacy than you ever imagined. But I'm happy to have someone show you to your cottage."

Zane picked up the map from the registration counter. "Not necessary. I think I've got it from here."

"You can't get too lost. Just stop when you reach the ocean." Angelique winked and grinned, then waved goodbye.

Zane followed the path and the small wood signs to cottages eight and nine. As he walked under the canopy of trees, he had to remind himself that Allison was not fair game. He would be friendly and cordial. He might even spend a small bit of time with her while they were both there, but there would be no replay of that kiss. Scott was too important to him. He would not betray the bro code. Never.

Ahead, Zane could see the water and two cottages set several hundred yards away from each other, one a shade of sky blue and the other pure turquoise, each with painted white trim and a bright red roof. All around them, the powdery pink sand was a bright and summery accent, while the sun glinted off the calm crystalline sea. It could not have been a more stunning setting, and despite his worries over how he would handle the situation with Allison, Zane could feel himself unwinding, his spine loosening and his shoulders relaxing.

He opened the door to his cottage and stepped inside, his eyes immediately drawn to the stunning vista of ocean at the far end of the house. He set down the map and strolled through the open living room, which had a vaulted wood-beamed ceiling and entire wall of windows, all open and letting in the sea breezes. At center was a set of oversize French doors, which led out to Zane's patio, covered in terra-cotta tile with an arbor above it for shade. Beyond that was his private plunge pool, surrounded by lush tropical plantings.

Not wanting to wait another minute for his vacation to start, Zane found the bedroom, which, as advertised, had an intricately carved wood bed with another beautiful view of the sea. His suitcase had been delivered by staff, and he wasted no time getting into his swim trunks, grabbing a towel from the beautifully appointed bathroom and making one more stop in the kitchen to grab a beer. He poured it into a shatterproof tumbler, and, sunglasses on, he strolled out onto the terrace and jumped into the pool.

The water was cool and exhilarating, the perfect counterpoint to the strong Bahamian sun. He slicked his hair back from his face and swam over to the edge of the pool, folding his arms up on the edge and drinking in the beautiful ocean view. As difficult as the last few weeks had been—hell, the last several years—Zane could feel that all fading away. Scott had been so right. Maybe he just needed some time to clear his head and stop thinking about Josh Lowell and Black Crescent.

Zane dropped his chin down onto the back of his hand and something caught his eye. More specifically, someone—a woman sauntering down to the water in front of the other cabin. *Allison.* It had to be her. She was turned away from him, but he'd have to be dead to not admire the view—her hair down the middle of her back, tawny skin set against a colorful sarong, lithe legs and bare feet. She stopped where the pink sand met the water and turned, ambling in his direction while gently swishing her feet in beautiful blue.

He wasn't sure what to do. Call out to her? Submerge himself in icy water and try to hide for the next five days? This never, ever would have been a question if she hadn't kissed him on Scott's birthday. She was permanently off-limits, fruit so forbidden that he would be blowing up his entire life if he dared to go there.

Before he had a chance to formulate any sort of plan, Allison looked up and spotted him. His heart instantly began pulsing, jumping to double time when she raised her sunglasses up onto her forehead for a moment, smiled and waved. Good God, she was unfairly beautiful. And she was coming his way. He had no means of stopping this. He had to go with it and try to have a casual conversation with the sister of his best friend.

So he did what he would have done if they'd never kissed— he waved back and called her name. "Allison!"

As Allison walked up the beach toward Zane's cottage, she could hardly believe this was really happening. How many times had she concocted some dream scenario in her head where she and Zane were alone? Too many to count. And what was unfolding before her was exactly the kind of fantasy she loved to weave—a perfect sunny day, not another human in sight, the breeze brushing her skin and the air so sweet.

Her pulse raced. Every nerve ending in her body was firing. Her breaths were deep, and yet she still felt as though she couldn't get enough oxygen. If she wasn't careful, she was going to hyperventilate or pass out. This was Zane's effect on her. It was as if the real Allison was no longer in control and some other version of her was pulling the strings. It had been like this since she was thirteen and he was sixteen.

But Zane wasn't a teenager anymore. And she wasn't, either. She was twenty-eight years old, and she knew what she wanted. She also knew that the world didn't go around handing out opportunities. Life didn't work like that. You had to take what was yours when you had the chance. And as she got closer to Zane's cottage and watched him climb out of his plunge pool, water dripping from his magnificent, lean and athletic form, she didn't even have to ask herself what her goal was—she knew it in her heart and in her gut. She wanted Zane's naked body pressed against hers. She needed his mouth on every inch of her. She had to have him, if only for a few days in paradise. Zane was not "for keeps," but he could absolutely be "for right now."

"Hey there," she said, stepping up onto his patio. She studied him as he toweled off his chest. She'd only seen him with this shirt off a few times, but his shoulders were just as amazing as she'd remembered. Firm and contoured from thousands of hours playing basketball. His chest was even more glorious, with a tiny patch of dark hair right at the center. She wanted to tangle her fingers in that hair. She wanted to kiss him there. She hungered to skim her lips over every inch of his pecs, rake her fingernails across the warm skin of his abs and tease open the drawstring of his swim trunks.

"How weird is this?" Zane rattled her back to the present with the question. In her fantasies, he would have opened with something far more seductive. Maybe something like, *Hello, beautiful. Can I help you with your sarong?* "We live on opposite ends of the country but we both end up at your aunt and uncle's resort at the same time?"

"What are the chances, huh? Small world, I suppose." She couldn't help but notice his body language—shoulders tight and hands clutching the towel to his chest, as if he was hiding from her. This was all wrong, and she was desperate to change the dynamic. "Can I have a hug?"

"Uh, sure. Of course." He grabbed his T-shirt from one of the chaise longues by the pool and put it on. He was definitely trying to keep his distance. She might need to take things slow. She didn't want to scare him off or freak him out. The last thing her already-bruised ego needed was another interaction like the one at Scott's birthday party. She couldn't endure it if he pushed her away again. She spread out her arms and gave him the sort of embrace only friends exchange. It was quick and to the point, and not at all what she wanted. Just that one little taste of his body heat left her longing. Her chest ached for more.

"So what are you doing here?" he asked.

"I needed a break, and my aunt is always begging me to visit."

"Things stressful at work?"

She looked around for a place to sit. "Do you mind?" She gestured to one of two chaises under an umbrella.

"Yeah. Of course. Do you want a beer?"

"I'm good for now, but thanks." She did want one, but she wasn't sure it was a good idea. She needed to keep her wits about her while she was trying to suss out where his head was at. They hadn't talked once since the kiss a few weeks ago. For all she knew, he thought she was a lunatic. "I just broke up with my boyfriend. We were living together, so it was a pretty big ordeal, moving out and all of that."

Zane sat in the chair next to her and reclined, crossing his legs at the ankle. He had incredibly sexy legs, a mile long but still pure muscle, with just the right amount of dark hair. "I'm sorry to hear that. If you need a shoulder to cry on, I'm a pretty good listener. Plus, I figure I'm forever in debt to the Randall family."

"For what?"

"Where do I start? Turning around my entire life when I was at my lowest point?"

Allison waved it off. He still clung to a debt of gratitude for her family, but the truth was that Zane had given them a lot, too. He'd never been anything less than a positive presence. For Scott and Allison, who'd had a mostly stable childhood, watching Zane battle through his family's reversal of fortune had taught them a lot about humility. "Are you kidding me? My parents love you. And obviously Scott is obsessed with you." Her phone, which she had tucked into her bathing suit top, rang. Things at work were so tenuous right now that she couldn't afford to turn off her ringer, as much as she wanted uninterrupted time with Zane. "I'm sorry. I should look to see who it is." She glanced at the caller ID. It was Scott. Did he have some sort of psychic ability to interrupt her at the most inopportune time? For an instant, she considered sending the call to voice mail, but she knew that he would just keep calling her back.

"Speak of the devil," she said to Zane. "It's my brother."

"Oh. Wow."

"I know." She answered the call to speak to Scott. "Were your ears ringing? We were just talking about you."

"What the hell, Allison? You're down at Rose Cove by yourself and Zane is there, too?"

Of course he's not only calling, he's taken issue with the fact that I'm with Zane. "Yes. I'm doing this thing where you travel to a place where you don't live and you relax. It's called vacation. You should try it." She glanced over at Zane, who she hoped would at least be smiling after her wisecrack at her brother. But no. Zane's handsome face was painted with entirely too much concern. She'd seen that look before, and she didn't like it.

"Is there something funny going on between you two?" Scott asked. "Don't think I didn't notice how weird you were being at my party."

Being under Scott's thumb had grown so tiresome. In many ways, Allison felt as though she'd been born under it. "We're hanging out. He's my friend, too."

Zane cleared his throat. "Hand me the phone."

Allison shook her head and held the receiver to her chest. "No. I've got this. He's being ridiculous, and you and I are sitting by the pool, talking. He needs to get over himself." She raised the phone back to her ear. "Unless you have something nice to say to me, I'm going to say goodbye now and get back to my vacation."

"He went on this trip to hook up with women," Scott blurted. "He told me as much. And I do not want you to fall for his charms. Nothing good comes of it, and you just came off a bad breakup."

Allison grumbled under her breath. As if she needed another reminder that Zane had a zillion other women waiting in the wings. Her brother was ruining her fantasy, and she wasn't going to sit around for any more of it. "Okay. Sounds great."

"You aren't listening to me. You're just saying that so Zane won't know what I'm saying about him."

"Yep. You're right. Anything else? I need to get going."

"Are you watching the forecast? There's a system forming in the Atlantic. The weather channel says it could dip down into the Caribbean. It could be upgraded to a tropical storm by late today. It could easily become a hurricane."

Allison looked overhead. There wasn't a cloud in the sky. "You are such a weather nerd. I'm not worried about something an ocean away, okay? Plus, it's June. The hurricane season just started. I'm sure Angelique and Hubert will let us know if it's anything of concern. Now, go back to your life so I can try to unwind. Kiss the kids for me."

"I'm calling you tomorrow. And just punch Zane if he tries anything. Or remind him I will kill him if he touches you."

Allison didn't want to tell Scott that if there was any smacking going on, it would be only of the playful variety, and only if she was very lucky. "Got it. Love you." She pushed the red button on her phone and tucked it back inside her swimsuit top. "Sorry about that. I think he's paranoid that there's something going on between us."

Zane got up from his seat and ran his hand through his hair. His forehead creases were deep with worry. "Then you need to call him back and tell him that absolutely nothing is going on. Or I'll do it. Give me your phone."

Allison sat back on the chaise and didn't bother to cover up when her sarong slipped open, revealing the full stretch of her bare leg and a good bit of her stomach, as well. She loved seeing the way Zane tried not to look…and failed. Did he want her the way she wanted him? Did he crave her touch? Her kiss? The thought of unleashing all of her pent-up desire on him, especially in paradise, where they could be blissfully alone, was so tempting it made her entire body tingle. It would be so easy to undo the knot of her cover-up and let it fall away. Give Zane an eyeful. Run her fingers along the edge of her bikini top, right where the swell of her breasts could draw the most attention. She wanted to do it so badly that her hand twitched. But she had to play this slowly. "Don't be threatened by my brother. He's just watching out for me. It's a bad habit of his. He needs to cut it out."

"You know why he's so protective of you. There's a good reason for it."

Allison did know there was a good reason, but she'd been a little girl when she got sick. She hardly remembered any of it—it was practically a lifetime ago. Most important, she was perfectly healthy now and had been cancer-free for more than twenty years. Her entire family needed to stop hovering over her like she was made of porcelain. "And because my family is always around, I think we should take this chance to hang out on our own terms. Talk. Like friends. We are friends, aren't we?"

"I don't know."

"What? You don't know if we're friends?"

He shook his head, seeming frustrated, which was not what she was going for. She wanted him relaxed. At ease. "I don't know if it's a good idea for us to spend time together."

"What are you afraid of, Zane? That I'm going to kiss you again?" She had a sliver of regret at putting things on the line like this at the outset, but perhaps it was for the best. If he was going to reject her, best to get it out of the way.

"For starters, yes."

Allison pressed her lips together tightly. She decided then and there that if any moves were going to be made, the first would have to be his. If he wanted her the way she wanted him, he was going to have to show her. She wasn't putting her heart and pride on the line a second time, especially not when he was so willing to say out loud that he was worried about what she might do. "I promise I won't kiss you, okay? Just stop acting like you're afraid of me, because I know you aren't."

"Of course I'm not afraid."

"Then prove it. Let me make you dinner."

Zane ran his tongue across his lower lip tentatively. It was one of his most adorable quirks and he always did it when he couldn't make up his mind about something. Allison didn't like that her offer required any deliberation at all, but she certainly appreciated the vision of his mouth. "Dinner? Nothing else?"

Allison closed up her sarong and rose from her seat. "Fair warning. You might go home incredibly satisfied." She patted him on the shoulder. "From my cooking. It's really good."

CHAPTER THREE

ZANE'S ENTIRE BODY was humming when Allison left, which left his brain running at a clip to catch up. If Scott knew what was going through Zane's head right now and how that all centered on his little sister, he would end him. It wouldn't be a quick death. It would be a long, painful one, during which Scott would drive home a single point—Allison was off-limits. Always had been. Always would be.

But here on a dot of an island, more than a thousand miles away from his best friend, Zane couldn't deny his churning thoughts or the insistent pulse of electricity in his body. The second Allison's sarong fell open to reveal the tops of her luscious thighs, the soft plane of her stomach and that little spot on her hip where the tie of her bikini bottoms sat, all bets were off. Or most of them, at least. He'd withstood an unholy rush of blood to the center of his body, so fierce that it nearly knocked him off his feet. Thinking about it was only providing an opportunity to put a finer point on the things he'd wanted to do to her—drop to his knees, start at her ankle and kiss every inch of her lovely leg, moving north until he reached the bow at her hip. The only thing that would make sense if he ever got that far would be to tug at the string, quite possibly with his teeth, slowly untie it and use his mouth to leave her curling her fingers into his scalp and calling out his name.

Thoughts like that were going to ruin Zane and everything he held dear.

He stalked into his cottage and opened the fridge, if nothing but for the blast of cold air against his overheated skin. It didn't help. It somehow made everything worse—another bodily conflict to endure as the shot of coolness mixed with the balmy salt air—everything on this island felt good. Too good. He popped open another beer and took a swig, but dammit, it was only a pleasing jolt of sweet and bitter, a shock of frothy cold followed by a wave of warmth that made him pleasantly dizzy. The erection he'd tried so desperately to fight off was now at a full salute, begging for attention and hungry for release.

There was only one way to get past this, and it didn't involve an icy shower. He couldn't wash away Allison's effect on him. He had to get past it. He stormed off to his bedroom, shucked his clothes and stretched out on the magnificent bed. The linens were smooth and impossibly soft against his skin, another pleasure he didn't relish, but this was the only way to keep himself from doing something foolish later tonight when he saw Allison. It was time to take matters—namely, his erection—into his own hands.

He didn't bother with seduction, reaching down and wrapping his fingers around his length. He closed his eyes and allowed himself the luxury of visions of Allison—glossy hair framing those deep, soulful eyes, plump lips and a smile that could turn ice to a puddle. Her shapely legs and curvy hips. Her luscious breasts. He took long strokes with his hand, imagining kissing her again, except there was no stopping this time. He started things, and she turned up the volume, their tongues winding, mouths hot and wet and hungry for more.

The tension in his body built, but coiled tighter, a push and pull he wouldn't be able to take for long. To edge himself closer, he conjured an illusion of Allison naked and the feeling of her body on top of him, holding him down with her warmth and softness. He imagined being inside her—the closeness, the heat—and her heady sweetness perfuming the air as he brought her to her peak. With that thought, the pressure was released and he arched his back, riding out the waves of pleasure. His breath hitched in a sharp inhale, then came out in a long rush of relief. He settled back on the pillow and slowly pried his eyes open, not to the sight of Allison but to the white painted ceiling and whirring fan overhead. He turned and glanced at the clock on the nightstand. He had four hours until dinner. Hopefully this solo rendezvous had prepared him. Now to shower, read a few chapters of a book, take a nap and hope that he could keep his libido in check.

Five minutes before six, Zane headed to Allison's cottage, dressed in jeans and a dress shirt with the sleeves rolled up to the elbows. He carried his flip-flops and walked barefoot through the sand, which was still warm from the day's rays. Over the water, the sun was dipping lower, painting the sky in vibrant shades of pink and orange. It was so obvious and easy to say, but Rose Cove really was paradise. He didn't want to leave anytime soon. Having distance from his past and from Joshua Lowell? Amazing. If it weren't for Scott, and Zane's company, he might never go back to Falling Brook.

He found himself taking his time as he strolled across the beach, now approaching Allison's. She had every window and door flung open, allowing him to watch her in the kitchen, milling about. He really hoped she wasn't going to put the full-court press on him tonight, and that her only intention was for the two of them to spend a few hours together. It was time to leave The Kiss where it belonged—in the past. Their circumstances did not allow for him to ever go there again. One thing he'd learned when his parents lost every penny of the family's money to Black Crescent and Joshua Lowell's father was that the sooner you learned to accept your personal situation and deal with what you had in front of you, the better.

"Knock, knock," Zane said, standing at the French doors to Allison's cottage. "I brought a bottle of wine, but I can't really take credit for it. Your aunt stocked my fridge."

Allison turned and smiled, looking fresh-faced and sun kissed, wearing a swishy black skirt and a royal blue tank top. Her feet were again bare and her hair was up in a high ponytail. There wasn't a single made-up thing about her, and that made her perfect, however much he wished he hadn't noticed. *She's your best friend's little sister. Don't be an idiot.* It was his new mantra. He committed himself to repeating it over and over until it became part of his psyche.

"I'm glad you came." She took the wine from him and carried it straight to the kitchen counter. No kiss on the cheek hello. No hug.

Zane was relieved, even if there was something in his body that was registering as disappointment. "Well, you know, I had so many invitations, I wasn't sure what to do." He took a seat at the kitchen island, with a view of the cooktop, where something delicious-smelling was simmering away.

Allison laughed, then handed him the corkscrew. "Here. Make yourself useful."

"Yes, ma'am." He got up and opened the bottle, then took the liberty of finding the wineglasses, which was easily done since this kitchen had the exact layout of his own. "To friends." He offered her a glass and held up his own for the toast.

"Yes. To friends." She took a sip, hardly looking at him at all.

He wondered if he'd been too standoffish earlier. He only wanted to keep things in a place where nobody got hurt. He didn't want to lose *all* of the warmth between them. Just some of it. Keep things friendly, but not too friendly. "Have you seen any of the other guests on the island at all?" he asked.

She shook her head and lifted the lid off a pot. "I haven't. Angelique stopped by and told me that a few people canceled their reservations because there's talk of a hurricane."

"That's what you were talking about with Scott, isn't it?"

This didn't sit well with Zane. It would be just his luck that the weather would go bad and ruin his idyllic vacation. Worse than that, they were sitting ducks if a bad storm came through.

"Don't worry. Both Angelique and Hubert said this happens all the time. The forecasts are often wildly inaccurate, and the models have the storm going any number of directions." Allison gestured outside with a nod. "Look at that sunset. There's no way a storm is coming."

He stole a glance, even though he'd been admiring it minutes earlier. "You're probably right."

"You need to relax, Zane. The whole point of being here is to unwind. Dinner is just about ready."

Zane had thought he was relaxed. Apparently not. "What are we having?"

"A conch ceviche with lime and fresh chilies to start, then baked crab with rice and pigeon peas. All my mom's family recipes."

"That's why it smells so amazing. It makes me think of your mom and being at your house."

"Of course. She must have made this for you one of the times you stayed with us." Allison spooned the ceviche into two small dishes and sprinkled fresh herbs on top.

"That seems like forever ago." Being with Allison while memories of time with her family surfaced had Zane wedged between nostalgia and the pain of that period of his life. It was about so much more than the financial struggle. The real misery had come from watching his parents' marriage fall apart before his very eyes. Allison was a reminder of both things he cherished and things he wished had never happened, which he knew was part of the reason every sense was heightened around her. "You were just a girl then. How old were you when we met? Thirteen?"

She cast him a disapproving look. "I'm all for memory lane, but can we not talk about me as an awkward teenager?"

"Why? You were the coolest kid I ever met. You had the best

taste in music. You were always reading all of these books I'd never heard of. You totally had your own fashion sense. You'd wear those flowery dresses and black Doc Martens boots. Or T-shirts with bands I'd never heard of."

Allison blushed and tried to hide a smile. "Will you please shut up? It's embarrassing."

Zane couldn't help but love that they had this history and that he could have playfully tease her because of it. She'd always had a tough outer shell, carrying herself with an air of disaffection. She wanted the world to think that she didn't care what anyone thought of her, but Zane had long suspected that wasn't quite the case. "It's the truth. That was the first thing that struck me about you. You always had an amazing sense of self. I'm not sure I ever did."

"I think you've always known exactly who you are. The problem is that you weren't always happy about it."

For a moment, the air in the room seemed to stand still. Was that his problem? Or was it that the wounds inflicted by the Lowell family had been so slow to heal? "Well, if that's the case, it's only because I'm pretty easy to figure out. Feed me and I'm happy." He smiled, hoping to lighten the mood. He'd never intended to steer them down such a serious path.

"Then I'm your girl." She held up the two dishes of ceviche.

Zane swallowed hard, and not because the food was so mouthwatering. He was reading too much into everything Allison did and said. And it was going to be his undoing if he wasn't careful. Again, he reminded himself to relax. He was more than capable of enjoying a beautiful home-cooked meal with an old friend. "Should we eat out on the patio?"

"Whatever and wherever you want."

Allison had to hand it to herself—dinner was incredible. Her mom and Aunt Angelique would be proud.

Zane sat back in one of the lounge chairs out on the patio,

rubbing his belly and gazing up at the stars. "That was unbeliev-able. I don't think I'm going to need to eat again anytime soon."

"You went back for seconds. I'm impressed."

He turned and smiled at her, and, even in the darkness, with only the faint light from inside the house, she was struck by just how damn handsome he was—kissable lips, stormy eyes and the smile of a heartbreaker. The sight of him made her breath catch in her throat in a painfully familiar way. It was exactly like every other time she'd tormented herself with the conscious thought of how perfect he was. "Like I said, feed me and I'm happy. You fed me so well, I'd have to say I'm euphoric."

It was reassuring to know she could do this much right, but this entire evening had too many echoes of the past—the friendship was there between them, but she wanted more. She would always want more. The itch to be with him would never go away unless she had the chance to scratch it. "Any interest in working off that meal tomorrow?" She knew that there was a little too much innuendo in the wording of her question, but it was meant to be a test.

"What'd you have in mind?" He returned his sights to the night sky, not taking the chance to flirt with her.

Any other woman might be deterred or discouraged, but Al-lison hadn't come this close to give up now. She would forge ahead with her suggestion and keep the ball in his court. "Snor-keling. If we hike around to the north side of the island, the water and fish are unbelievable. If we're lucky, we'll see sea turtles, too. We can swim out right from the beach."

He was doing that thing with his tongue and his lower lip again, driving her crazy in the process. "Yeah. Cool. That sounds fun. What time?"

Allison wanted to spend the entire day with him, and the sun would be too strong by midday to spend too much time in the water. "Morning is best if you can haul your butt out of bed. Nine o'clock?" Just then, her phone rang. Out of habit, she'd brought it with her out onto the patio. She glanced at the caller

ID and knew she had to take it. She didn't want to interrupt her evening with Zane, but this was one of her Black Crescent candidates, someone she'd been trading phone calls with for a few days. "I'm so sorry. I need to get this. You can go if you want to. I'll see you tomorrow morning." She scrambled up out of her seat and pressed the button to answer the call. "Hello? Ryan?"

"Hi, Ms. Randall. I'm so glad I reached you," Ryan Hathaway answered.

"Me, too. I've been waiting to talk to you." Allison shuffled off into the house, but something stopped her from going too far—Zane's hand on her bare shoulder. She froze, but only because that one touch was making her head swim. The power he had over her was immense. If anything ever did happen between them, she might burst into flames.

"Hey. I thought we were having a nice night." Zane glanced at the phone. "Now I feel like you're blowing me off for someone else."

Allison raised the receiver back to her ear. "Ryan, can you hold on for one minute? I need to take care of something."

"Sure thing," Ryan replied.

"Thank you. I promise it'll only be a minute." She pressed the mute button on the screen. "We were having a nice night, but all good things must come to an end, right?" She didn't want to brush off Zane, but this call was incredibly important. Not just for her, either. Kianna was counting on her.

"Well, yeah, but you're also the one who was talking a big game to your brother about relaxing and unwinding while you're here. I turned off my phone completely. It's back at my place."

"This is work, okay?" The realization hit her hard. It wasn't merely work. This was Black Crescent, and Zane might never forgive her if he found out she was working for them. The decision to pursue business with BC had been easy enough to rationalize when Zane was living on the opposite side of the country. After all, it had been fifteen years since Vernon Lowell took off with all that money, and the current powers that be at BC were not like him. But now that she and Zane were inches away from each other, and her mind had been flooded with memories since seeing him, she understood just how betrayed he might feel if he discovered the truth.

"It's nine thirty at night."

"I know. My work calls happen at odd times sometimes. I'm sorry, but I really need to take this. So you can either stay or go, but I need a few minutes."

Zane nodded, but seemed entirely suspicious. "Cool. I'll clean the kitchen while you talk."

Dammit. Allison knew there was no way she could talk to Ryan with Zane in the same room, and she ran the risk of him joining her if she went back out to the patio. "Great. I'll take the call in my bedroom." Without further explanation, she ducked into her bedroom and closed the door. "Ryan. I'm so sorry."

"No problem, Ms. Randall."

"Please. Call me Allison."

"Okay, Allison. I've rearranged my schedule so I can be back in Falling Brook for the interview next week. I'll get in the night before."

Allison loved how prepared and thorough Ryan was. "Perfect. And you're sure you're okay with the idea of working for this company in particular?" She highly doubted that Zane might be listening at her door, but she still hoped hard that he wasn't. It hadn't been her intention to hurt Zane when she'd taken the BC gig. She was trying to save her company.

"I am. I know the history. It's pretty crazy all of the stuff that happened with the Lowell family, and of course I hate that Vernon Lowell ruined so many families. But maybe that's why they need somebody like me at the helm."

"That's a great attitude to have. They've really put that past behind them and are focused on the future. This job is the chance of a lifetime. No one ever imagined the CEO position could go to someone outside the family." Allison sucked in a deep breath, amazed she'd managed to keep herself from uttering the name Joshua Lowell.

"I agree. It's an excellent opportunity. I'm excited to interview and I'm excited to finally meet you in person, too."

"Sounds great. I'm in the Bahamas right now visiting family, but I'll see you in Falling Brook next week. Good night, Ryan."

"Have a wonderful vacation. Good night."

Allison ended the call and for a moment, stared at the back of her bedroom door. She felt as though she were teetering on the edge of a cliff. The Black Crescent account was crucial to the success of her company, and she'd promised Kianna she would nail this first assignment BC had given them. But she also knew firsthand the damage inflicted by BC, and exactly how Zane would feel if and when he found out that she was working for them. This absolutely put a wrench in her romantic hopes, but she reminded herself that Zane would never be a long-term thing. He wanted the physical parts and none of the emotional entanglements. Yes, she was risking their friendship, but, in her experience, those things could be mended. If needed, she could get Scott to talk Zane off the ledge, tell him that the Black Crescent thing was just business. Surely a friend could understand that.

She opened her door and walked back into the main room. Zane was drying one of the hand-painted platters she'd used. "Hey. I'm so sorry."

"Don't apologize. I shouldn't have given you a hard time. You have things you have to do. I get it."

"Thank you. I appreciate that."

Zane set down the clean dish and leaned against the kitchen counter. "Nice guy?"

"What?"

"The guy you were talking to. You seemed pretty chummy. I thought it was just you and your partner in that office."

For a moment, Allison struggled to figure out what he was asking, but then she realized there was the slightest chance that

Zane was jealous. That was so incongruous with his personality that it didn't really compute. He could have any woman he wanted. And he'd pushed her away the one time they'd kissed. "Great guy, actually. Supersmart. Handsome, too."

"Yeah? Could there be something brewing between you two?"

He might not be jealous, but he was curious, which made her both nervous and a bit exhilarated. "I hate to disappoint you, but no. He's a recruit. Nothing else."

Zane nodded. "Oh. Okay."

She scanned his face, and he returned the look. Good God, she had the most urgent desire to show him the reason why a guy like Ryan Hathaway was not what she wanted. If only she could press Zane against that kitchen counter and kiss him into oblivion, thread her hands into his hair and show him just how badly she longed for him. She wanted to tell him everything— that she'd fantasized about him hundreds of times, how she needed to finally get him out of her system. Being this close to him and knowing she couldn't do any of that was testing what little resolve she had left. But she had to hold strong. She would not make the first move.

"I should probably get going," Zane said, finally breaking their eye contact. "Get out of your hair."

"You aren't in my hair, Zane. This is fun. I could talk to you all night." She did her best to hide the soft rumble in her voice, the way she secretly wanted to beckon him to her bedroom with her tone.

"I need to get a good night's sleep if we're going to go snorkeling tomorrow."

Tomorrow. Allison could wait until then. Tomorrow was another chance to show Zane that she was a woman. He'd been with so many over the years, why not her? Why couldn't she have at least one taste of him? "Right. Snorkeling."

He pushed off from the kitchen counter and walked to the door leading out to her patio. Allison followed, tormented and enticed by everything about him. "Thanks for dinner. It was amazing." He ran his hands through his thick hair, seeming at least a little conflicted. She took solace in that. She was at war with herself, too.

"You're more than welcome."

He leaned in and pecked her on the cheek. It happened so fast, she had no time to grip his arms or pull him closer or even simply wish for a real kiss. It only left her once again hungry for everything she couldn't have.

"See you tomorrow morning."

"Yep. Got it." She watched as he disappeared down the beach, into the darkness. It hurt to see him go without leaving her more, but she'd felt this way about Zane forever. The yearning might never go away. It might always be an unanswered question. Still, she really wished he would finally get up enough nerve to be the one to break their never-ending standoff. Her heart couldn't take much more.

CHAPTER FOUR

ZANE WOKE WITH the sun and too many thoughts rolling around in his head. He was excited by the prospect of spending the day with Allison. Snorkeling with a friend sounded fun, and "fun" was something he so rarely had. But last night had been a close call from his side of things. He'd wanted to kiss Allison so badly that he'd volunteered to clean her kitchen—not his favorite activity.

What was keeping him from going for what he wanted? He'd never felt shy about it in the past. His greatest fear was Scott finding out, even though in all likelihood, Zane and Allison could do whatever they wanted without fear of repercussions. But guilt would crush him alive. Betrayal was at the top of Zane's to-not-do list. He needed trust in his life. He'd learned that the hard way when he was a teenager and his life fell apart. Everything he'd ever counted on—the stability of his family and, more important, his parents' marriage—was upended. He realized then just how badly he needed to be able to trust in something or someone. But that was a two-way street—if he couldn't be trustworthy in return, what was he doing with his life? Giving in to his desire for Allison would give Scott every reason in the world to feel betrayed. He'd never breached their friendship like that and he didn't want to start now.

He was assuming a lot, though. Just because Allison had once kissed him didn't mean she still wanted that from him. She'd taken that phone call last night and seemed eager to distance herself. She'd said it was about work, but Zane wasn't convinced. Why duck into the other room and close the door behind her? She was an executive recruiter, not an undercover FBI agent. She obviously had some new guy after her, which should come as absolutely no surprise. Or perhaps she was doing the pursuing. He could imagine that, too.

Get a grip, Zane. Get a damn grip. Allison was his friend. Last night, they'd had a friendly dinner. Today, they were going on an adventure. This was meant to be fun. It was meant to be platonic. Nothing more.

He slathered on sunscreen, got dressed in his swim trunks and headed over to Allison's cottage. She was hanging out on her patio, again on the phone. He waved at her and, although she returned the gesture, she quickly shot up out of her chaise, plugging a finger in her free ear and hustling back into the house. Perhaps it was work again. He hadn't realized Allison was quite so driven, but it would certainly be in line with her personality. Then again, there was the chance that it was a guy. Definitely a plausible explanation. He hung out next to her pool while she finished her call, taking deep breaths and admiring the gentle lap of the water on the sand.

"Hey. Sorry," Allison said, reappearing from inside the house. She was wearing her sarong again and through the thin fabric, it was apparent she was wearing that same maddening bikini.

He prayed for strength. So much strength. "Everything okay? It wasn't Scott giving you a hard time again, was it?"

She unleashed her electric smile, which calmed him, but sent a noticeable thrill through him, as well. "No. Although, he did call again last night. He keeps telling me to watch the forecast. And to watch out for you."

Zane directed his sights skyward. "It's another beautiful day in paradise. And I think we demonstrated last night that there's no need to worry about anything else."

She nodded. "Right? He needs to get a hobby."

"I could call him and tell him to get to work, but I promised myself I wouldn't turn on my phone once while I'm here." Zane deliberately delivered a pointed glance. "Maybe you should try the same thing."

She looked at her phone and hesitated. "You know, I think that's a great idea. I will do that. I've already talked to my partner today, and honestly, I think it'll be good for Scott to not be able to reach either of us for a few days. Let him wonder what's going on." She bounced her eyebrows playfully.

Zane felt a distinct tug from his stomach. He didn't want Scott worrying, but there was likely no avoiding that, with or without phone contact with his sister. "We ready to head out?"

"Yes. My uncle had someone drop off the snorkel gear for us about an hour ago." She grabbed two mesh drawstring bags that were sitting on the patio tile next to the French doors. "I just need help getting sunscreen on my back before we get in the water. And I'm guessing you do, too."

Indeed, that had been the one place Zane hadn't been able to reach on his own. He considered accepting the reality of a sunburn, but skin cancer was no joke. "Yep."

He followed Allison into her cottage, where she had a bottle of SPF 50 on the kitchen counter. "I'll do you first. Turn around."

Zane swallowed hard at the notion of either of them *doing* the other, but followed Allison's directive. He heard the squishy sounds as she rubbed the lotion between her hands, and even though he knew it was coming, he winced when she touched him.

"Still cold?" she asked as she began to spread the silky liquid over his back and shoulders.

"No. No. It feels great." He closed his eyes to attempt to ward off how damn good it felt to have her touch him. This was

what he'd wanted, if only for an instant, that night that she'd
kissed him. They'd been fully clothed then. Not now. Instead,
they not only had too much bare skin between them, they also
had privacy, solitude and an entire sunny day stretching out
in front of them. He tried to quiet his mind, but that only put
the physical sensations at center stage. Her hands were pure
magic as she worked the lotion into his shoulders, then down
his spine until she reached his waist. He heard her pour more
into her hands, then she swiped the velvety cream in circles at
the small of his back.

"You're good to go," she said, handing him the bottle. "Now
me."

He turned, only to see that she'd taken off her sarong and
tossed it aside. And now he was confronted with her in that
tiny black bikini. She did a one-eighty, putting her back to him,
gathering her hair with both hands and holding it atop her head.
He tried to think of a chaste and asexual way to go about this,
but it was impossible. Every fiber of his being wanted to untie
her top, kiss her neck, take her hand and lead her into the bedroom. Hopefully this would be as trying as today got, so he
went ahead and got to work.

The first touch on her shoulders felt innocent enough. Sure,
her skin was impossibly soft and even more shimmery with the
lotion on it, but he could take it. The second touch across the
center of her back prompted a definite ratcheting of tension in
his body. The tie of her bathing suit was right there, millimeters
from his fingertips, and everything about her was so damn inviting. The third touch, however, against her lower back, all the
way down to the top of her bathing suit bottoms… Well, that
felt as sexual as anything Zane had done since yesterday when
he'd had to pleasure himself in search of some relief.

"Don't miss a spot," she said, looking back over her shoulder.

If only she knew that was not the danger. He wasn't about
to miss even a fraction of an inch. Wanting to get on with their

hike and swim, and get himself out of this situation, he finished up as quickly but as thoroughly as possible. "All set."

"Thanks. Let me just grab my sun hat." She flitted off and was back a few seconds later.

They headed outside, up the beachline away from both of their cottages. At first, their walk was nothing more than a leisurely stroll along the sand, but then the coast got rocky in patches, and they would wade through knee- to waist-high water to get past the tougher terrain. A few times, they hiked inland and made their way on footpaths that wound through the forest.

"You sure you know where you're going?" Zane trailed behind Allison as they walked down a narrow trail under dense tree cover. It was a welcome break from the sun and the heat of the day. "We haven't seen a single person or even another cottage this whole time."

"Yep. I know this trip like the back of my hand. I promise. Scott and I did this a hundred times when we were kids."

"The resort has been in your family that long?"

"Yes. It originally belonged to my grandparents, but it was a little more rustic when we were growing up. The bungalows weren't quite so fancy. They didn't have all of the amenities they do now. My aunt and uncle made it into what it is today."

Ahead, Zane saw the bright sun breaking through the trees. "Is that where we're going?"

She turned back and flashed her smile at him, the one that made it hard to think straight. "Yep."

"Awesome." Zane took stock of their surroundings as soon they were out of the wooded area and back on the beach. To his right, the coast was again rocky, with a steep and densely overgrown hillside racing up from it. He then looked out over the water, spotting a tiny island. It appeared to be about the length of four or five football fields away. It had three palm trees on it but no other signs of life. "What's that?"

"That's where we're going if you're up for the swim. Scott and I named it Mako Island."

"As in the shark? Because I was more in the mood for colorful tropical fish today. Not so much into man-eating aquatic specimens."

Allison laughed. "Scott was really into sharks when we named it, but don't worry. I've never seen anything too scary in these waters."

"Oh. Okay."

"It'll take about twenty minutes to get over there, but it's an easy swim and you'll get a beautiful view the whole way. Just follow me."

Zane nodded in agreement, declining to say that if he was following her, it wasn't the ocean that would be providing the beauty. That was all on Allison.

Zane and Allison put on their fins and snorkel masks, then she grabbed the inflatable swim buoy her uncle had left for her. With a belt that went around her waist, it would float behind her, hold a few bottles of water and could double as a flotation device if either she or Zane got into trouble during their swim.

"Your aunt and uncle think of everything, don't they?" Zane asked.

"They love to be protective." Always. But she wasn't going to let things like her family come between her and a good day with Zane. "Come on."

Allison waded into the sea, feeling so blissfully at home the instant she was floating in the water. They swam at a leisurely pace, buoyed by the saline. Below, the ocean floor was dotted with clusters of starfish, while schools of fish in bright shades of yellow and blue darted between the sea plants. One thing Allison loved more than anything about snorkeling was that the only thing she could hear was her own breath. She purposely made it deep and even, forcing every stress in her life from her body. Today was for her and Zane. She'd waited fifteen years for it to happen.

As they approached Mako Island, the water became quite

shallow—only two or three feet deep. That allowed them to walk the final fifty yards to dry land, or in this case, what was really a very large sandbar with a few rocks, trees and plants.

They both collapsed when they reached a shady spot on the beach, sitting down and taking off their fins. "That was incredible," Zane said, a bit breathless. She tried not to watch the rise and fall of his enticing chest. She tried not to think about how badly she wanted to touch him there. "Thank you so much for sharing it with me."

"Of course. I'll give you the quick tour of the island. It won't take long." Indeed, it was only about the size of the combined footprint of five or six Rose Cove cottages. Mostly sand and rocks, some low brush and a half dozen palms. Unfit for human life, it wasn't completely uninhabited. Plenty of birds were busy up in the trees, and there were even a few iguanas, who could make the swim from Rose Cove or other nearby islands.

They found their way back to that shady, cool spot on the beach and took a breather. "You know, half of the fun of this is getting to show it off to someone I care about."

Zane sat forward, resting his forearms on his knees and looking down at the sand, and nodded. "That's a nice thing to say." His voice was so burdened it made her heart heavy. Why did he have to be so deeply conflicted about every nice thing she chose to say? "I care about you, too."

She had too many words on the tip of her tongue—things about her brother or other women or why in the hell he couldn't just give in to the attraction that she had to believe he felt. There was no way that the electricity between them only went one way. But she didn't want their conversation to get too serious, so she kept these nagging, negative thoughts to herself. Instead, she fished the bottles of water out of the small pouch attached to the swim buoy and handed one to Zane. "Here. Drink. I need to keep you safe out here. Scott will never forgive me if you die of dehydration."

Zane laughed. It was deep and throaty and sexy as ever.

"Same for you. I think we're equally responsible for each other at this point." He took a long drink of his water, then replaced the cap and reclined back in the sand, resting on his elbows. "It's so amazing to think about, isn't it?"

"What? How my brother has an ironclad hold on both of us?"

"Well, that, sure, but that's a long conversation. I was talking more about the here and now. When we met, did you ever think that you and I would end up together on this tiny uninhabited island in the Caribbean?"

Allison hugged her knees to her chest and ran her hands through the sand, too embarrassed to tell Zane that she'd spent more than a decade crafting fantasies about him. Of the many times she'd felt like a naive schoolgirl around him, this moment might have been the most striking. It felt as though there was an invisible force between them, keeping them apart, and she didn't know how to get rid of it. "Hard to believe, huh?"

"We're so far away from it all. From everyone. From responsibility and expectations. From family and our jobs. I had no idea it would be so freeing."

Freeing. This scenario they'd found themselves in should've felt freeing, but they didn't have true freedom, and they wouldn't unless she finally shook loose the words buzzing in her head and forced the conversation. "We could do whatever we want, you know. Nobody can say a thing."

Zane was quiet for a few heartbeats, and Allison braced for a reprimand about being suggestive. "So true. We are the extent of the society on this island." Just then, an iguana jumped up onto a rock a few dozen feet away. "Well, us and that guy."

"He won't care what we do. We could scream at the top of our lungs if we wanted to and nobody could say a thing."

"Or you could sing too loud. It might drive out the wildlife, but you could do it."

She smacked him on the arm. "Hey. I'm not that bad a singer."

"Let's just say that fifty percent of the people on this island disagree with that statement."

Allison swiped at him again, but this time, Zane ducked away before her hand could connect with his arm. He popped up onto his feet. Allison did the same. He ran into the water up to his knees and she followed in close pursuit. Before she knew what was happening, he turned and, with both hands, delivered a tidal wave of a splash, dousing her.

"Hey!" Allison protested, but she loved the playful turn Zane was taking. "That's not fair." She ran into the surf up to her waist, furiously broadcasting water back at him. He joined in and they splashed each other like crazy for a good minute, laughing and trying to outdo each other. "Okay. Okay. Truce." Allison sucked in frantic, deep breaths.

Zane relented and straightened to his full height. He was like a god standing there in the crystal clear sea, tanned and glistening with water. "I'm officially soaked." He walked several steps into the shade of a palm tree over the water, still standing in it up to his knees.

"Me, too." Allison was determined to not make the first move, even when ideas of what do with wet bathing suits were whizzing around in her head. Still, she wasn't going to avoid him. She inched closer, stepping out of the sunlight. Their gazes connected, and she reckoned with how apparent his inner conflict was. It was all over his face. It hurt to see it—he had good and valid reasons for not wanting anything physical with her. She admired those reasons. She also wished they didn't exist, or at the very least, that they could set them aside for a while.

"You're pretty when you're wet."

Something in her chest fluttered—the physical manifestation of years of wanting to hear words like the ones he'd just uttered. "Thank you. You don't look bad yourself."

He cleared his throat, and a blush crossed his face. He looked down at the water. "Your brother would kill me for what I'm thinking right now."

Her heart galloped to a full sprint. "And he's not here."

Zane returned his sights to her and tapped his finger against his temple. "Unfortunately, he's here." He then pointed to the vicinity of his heart. "And in here."

"That's so sweet. And I get it. I do." She shuffled her feet ahead on the sandy bottom.

"Do you? Really?"

"I do. You love my brother. He loves you. I admire the hell out of your friendship." She sucked in a deep breath, hoping that she could summon the courage to say what she would always regret if she didn't let it out. "But I also know that I'm incredibly attracted to you, Zane. And judging by what you just said about the thoughts going through your head, I'm reasonably sure you're attracted to me. If I'm wrong, you could save us both a lot of time by saying it. Then we can go on with the rest of our vacation as nothing more than friends."

"I'm attracted to you. A lot."

She was thankful for the forward progress, but she wanted more. She needed to seize this moment. "I'm glad. Relieved, actually."

"You had to know that."

She shrugged. "A girl likes to hear that she's pretty. That a guy is attracted to her. It's not rocket science, Zane. I'm glad you confessed what you're thinking."

"Do you want to know what I'm really thinking?"

Words seemed impossible. All she could do was nod enthusiastically.

Zane then did the thing she'd been waiting a decade for. He gave her a sign that he wanted this, too, by taking a single step closer. "You're so beautiful. I just want to see you. All of you."

Goose bumps blanketed her arms and chest, even in the warm breeze. She swallowed hard. Without a word, she reached back and pulled the string on her bikini top. As the knot fell loose, she lifted the garment over her head and tossed it up onto the sand. "Like this?"

It was his turn to move closer again, his eyes first scanning her face, then shifting to travel all over her body, looking hungry, but he would likely never know that whatever lust he was feeling for her wasn't even a fraction of what she felt for him. "Yes. Like that."

She took another step. Mere inches separated their feet. Their legs and stomachs. Her breasts were only a whisper away from his unbelievable chest. "Do you want to know what's going through *my* head?" She loved the way his lips twitched at the question.

"It would make my life so much easier if you told me."

A tiny laugh escaped her lips, but there was no mistaking the gravity of this moment. "I want you to touch me." The words came out with little effort. She'd been practicing them in her head for eons.

He raised his hand slowly, his palm facing her breast. Her nipples gathered tight in anticipation. He breached the sliver of space between them, his warm and slightly rough hand covering her breast. This was not sex, not even close, but it caused such a rush of heat in her body that she gasped.

"Like this?" he asked, gently squeezing.

"Yes." Allison's need for Zane made her breasts full and heavy. Electricity was buzzing between her legs. Now that the floodgates had been opened, she didn't merely want him anymore.

She needed him.

CHAPTER FIVE

WHAT IN THE world was he doing? Zane's hands were on both of Allison's magnificent breasts, and he knew the logical next steps—kissing, trunks off, bikini bottoms gone and what he could only imagine would be the hottest sex of his life. Up against a palm tree. Rolling around in the warm sand. As amazing as that sounded, there was part of him that was terrified to go there. The temptation of forbidden fruit was no joke—he already had an erection that was not going to go away without some effort on somebody's part. He never should've started this by touching her, but the look on Allison's face right now, eyes half-closed in absolute pleasure, was such a turn-on, he wanted to get lost in it.

"Allison, I want to kiss you."

"I want you to kiss me." Her reply was swift and resolute.

He sucked in a deep breath as the ocean breezes blew his hair from his forehead. He dipped his head lower and closed his eyes, not thinking about anything other than doing what felt good. His lips met hers, and it was like tossing a match on a pile of tinder—her mouth was so soft and sexy. So giving and perfect. It was everything he could ever want from a kiss as her tongue swept along his lower lip. She popped up onto her tiptoes and leaned into him, telling him with a simple shifting of weight how badly she wanted him. But to punctuate the gesture, she reached around and grabbed his backside with both hands, pulling his hips sharply into hers. His body responded with a tightening between his legs that left him dizzy.

Allison flattened both hands on his pecs and spread her fingers wide, curling the tips into his muscles while peering up at him. "I want you, Zane. I want every inch of you."

"Here? Now?"

She slid her hands across his chest away from each other and turned her attention to points south. His swim trunks were fully tented. "I hate to make either of us wait, but I don't want to do this in the sand. The beach is beautiful, but one of our beds would be even better."

Zane didn't want to put anything on pause now that he'd made his decision. Everything between his legs was screaming at him to argue her point. But it might be wise to hold off until they could get back. It would give Allison a chance to change her mind. Zane could endure his inner tug-of-war some more. Then, if he and Allison still ended up in bed, he'd know in his heart that it hadn't been a rash decision.

She grabbed his hand. "Come on. We can get back to my cottage in a half hour if we hurry."

Disappointingly, while Zane collected their gear, Allison put her bikini top back on. They sat together in the shallow water, donning their fins. As he stood, something in the view of Rose Cove caught his eye—a sprawling white house atop the big hill rising from the beach where they'd embarked on their snorkeling trip. "Who stays up there?" he asked as they walked through the shallower depths. "I thought Hubert and Angelique lived in the main house, where the office is."

"That's the honeymoon cottage. It's undergoing renovations. They're giving it a serious face-lift. It'll probably run five grand a night when they're done."

"Wow."

"I know. I'm hoping to see the progress before we leave."

"I'd like to see it, too."

"For now, you and I need to swim." Allison pulled down her mask, adjusted the straps, plugged the snorkel end into her mouth and, like a frogman, dived into the deeper waters.

Zane followed, and this time they swam at a far less leisurely pace. Now the fish were dots of color as they zoomed past. Zane was focused on their destination until Allison came to a stop, treading water and pointing ahead. Zane scanned the depths, only to see a sea turtle come into his frame of vision. They floated in place, masks in the water as the massive creature glided toward them, then turned when it got too close, graceful, beautiful and all alone. Zane had never spent any time at all thinking about what it might be like to be a sea turtle, but he was struck by how apt the phrase "just keep swimming" was. To survive, all one could do was keep moving forward. His breaths came slow and even as he realized that he might be better served to get out of his own head every now and then and actually enjoy his life.

He and Allison watched as the turtle skated away, waiting until he was well out of sight before resuming their trek. It took very little time before they reached the beach and scooped up the rest of their belongings, including Allison's hat. She urged him ahead with a wave. "Come on. I know a shortcut through the forest."

He hustled behind her. It wasn't long before he saw her cottage through the trees. "Why didn't we go this way before? This is so much shorter."

"I wasn't in a hurry then."

When they arrived at Allison's cottage and they stepped through the door, Allison wasted no time, rising up on her tiptoes and kissing him deeply, digging her fingers into the hair at his nape. That kiss swept aside the doubts and questions he had about whether or not this was a good idea. That erection from before? It sprang to life in seconds flat as he returned the kiss and wrapped his arms around her naked waist. It felt impetuous. And dangerous. And for once in his life, he was ready to take caution and run it into the ground. Nobody had to know. This moment was all about Allison and him.

She wrenched her mouth from his, gazing up at him, her eyes wild and scanning. She probably thought he was about to bail on her like he had at Scott's birthday, but he would not do that. Not this time. He scooped her up in his arms and carried her off to the bedroom.

"How chivalrous of you," she said.

"I try," he quipped back.

He set her on her feet, and she turned her back to him, lifting her hair and letting him do what he'd wanted to do so badly before—tug on the strings of her top. With the garment gone, he reached around and cupped her breasts, which fit so perfectly in his hands. A breathless sigh left her lips, and he knew he was on the right track. He wanted to please her so much that she had no choice but to make that sound over and over again. Allison pressed her bottom against his groin, wagging her hips back and forth, cranking up the pressure already raging in his hips and belly. She craned her neck to kiss him. Their tongues teased each other, wet lips skimming and playing.

"You're so damn sexy," he whispered, moving to her glorious neck. It wasn't merely a nice thing to say. It was the truth. Every soft curve of her body had him turned on.

She hummed her approval, dropping her head to one side. He ran his lips over every available inch, exploring the delicate skin beneath her ear and the graceful slope down to her shoulder. Her unbelievable smell, sweet jasmine and citrus, mixed with the salt of sea air, filling his nose and leaving him a little drunk, although everything about Allison was intoxicating. Her voice, her words, her touch…

He shifted his hands to her hips and with a single tug at both strings, undid her bikini bottoms. She wriggled a bit and they dropped to the floor. He pressed his hand against her silky smooth belly, inching lower until he reached her center. She was slick with heat, and Allison gasped when he touched her, reaching up and back to wrap her fingers around his neck. With his other hand he caressed her breast lightly, loving the velvety texture of her skin against his palm, teasing her pert nipple, as he returned his lips to her neck. Her breaths were labored and short and, judging by the sound, she was close to her peak, but he wanted to savor this time with her. He didn't want to rush. There had been so much buildup to this moment, and he was certain it could never happen again. He wanted to appreciate this time with sweet and sinfully sexy Allison.

As if she knew what he was thinking, she turned in his arms and grabbed both sides of his head, pulling him closer in a kiss that put every other one to shame. Mouths open and hungry, wet and hurried, it was as if she was acknowledging that they could only travel this path once, and they had to make it count. She let go of her grip on him and moved to the drawstring of his trunks, making quick work and pushing them to the floor. As soon as she wrapped her hand around his length, he knew there was a good chance he wouldn't last long. He clamped his eyes shut and walked that delicate line between relishing every firm stroke she took and trying to think about anything other than how damn hot she was. Unfortunately, his best friend popped into his mind, but he quickly banished the thought. He would not disappoint her. Not today.

Again he scooped her up in his arms, but this time, he laid her out on the bed. The vision of her soft and sumptuous naked body, his for the taking, reminded him that he was a fool for wanting anything less than hours of getting lost in her. One time didn't have to mean a short time. They could make memories in this room.

She grinned as he allowed himself the luxury of her beauty. "Coming to bed?" She swished her hands across the crisp white sheets.

All he could think about was that this was the exact fantasy he'd had the other day. And now he got to live it. He was a ridiculously lucky man right now. "Just try to stop me."

Allison could hardly believe this was happening, except that it was. Her body was buzzing with appreciation for Zane and the glee of finally having a taste of what she'd wanted for so long. Judging by his opening act, she was in for an unbelievable afternoon...and, hopefully, evening. She wondered if she could convince him to never get out of bed, or if they did, to switch to the sofa in the living room. Or the kitchen counter. Or the plunge pool. *Ooh, yes.* She wanted Zane everywhere.

But she couldn't let her silly brain get so far ahead. *Go with it. Enjoy him.*

"Scoot back, darling." Zane gestured for her to move, then set his knee on the bed. Even now, when they still hadn't done the actual deed, she knew that this had been so worth the wait. All those years of pining were about to pay off. It made her heart swell, her lips tingle and her entire body reverberate.

She did as he asked and slid herself back until her head was on the pillow. Zane was now on both knees at her feet, dragging his fingers along the insides of her calves and down to the arches of her feet. Being totally naked and exposed to him like this was so exhilarating that the goose bumps came back. She liked being vulnerable with him. It made her realize exactly how much she trusted him. Not knowing what he would do next added another level of thrill. It would be so easy to chalk all of these feelings up to this being the first time, except that this was the first time with Zane, the one guy she'd always wanted.

He gripped her ankles with both hands and spread her legs wider. His eyelids were heavy, like he was drunk on appreciation for her body, and that was such a boost to her ego she could hardly wrap her head around it. She lapped up every nanosecond of the image. He leaned down and kissed the inside of her knee, then began to move his way up her thigh, in absolutely no rush, holding his lips against her skin for a heartbeat or two each time. She arched her back in anticipation of where he was going. She had not banked on him wanting to take on the oral exam, but she should've known all along that he would not only want to please her, but that he would know exactly how to do it.

She squirmed when his fingers grazed her center again and he urged her thighs apart with his forearms. She watched for a moment in awe as he used his mouth, but the pleasure became too much. She had to shut her eyes. Her head drifted back onto the pillow, and all she could do was express her appreciation with moans and single-syllable words like *yes* and *more*. She'd never imagined he had such an artistic side, but the man was playing her perfectly, with firm pressure from his lips and steady circles from his tongue. The tension had already been building when he drove a finger inside her and curled it against her most sensitive spot. Three or four passes and she felt the dam break, and warm contentment washed over her. She combed her fingers into his hair, massaging his scalp to show her appreciation.

"That was unbelievable," she said, knowing that the words didn't come close to telling him how she truly felt. She would need time to process what had just happened. For now, her brain was in frothy, happy disarray.

He raised his head and smiled with smug satisfaction, then kissed her upper thigh. "I enjoyed it, too."

"Hopefully you'll enjoy the next part even more. I need you, Zane. I need you inside me."

He planted both hands on the bed and raised himself above her, dipping his head down and kissing her softly. She wrapped her legs around his hips, waiting for the moment when he would finally drive inside. He was hesitating, and she could sense it. She truly admired the thoughtful side of him that felt that hesitation, but she needed him to know that it was okay. They could do this together, and it would be nothing short of amazing.

"All these years I've known you and I had no idea what talents you were hiding," she said. "You've been holding out on me, haven't you?"

He laughed quietly, but it felt forced. He nuzzled her cheek with his nose. She lowered her legs a bit and stroked the back of his thighs with her ankles. *Come on, Zane. Don't let me down.*

"I, uh…" His voice faltered.

"What is it?" She was careful to keep her voice warm and soothing. She did not want to witness another of his panics.

"I don't know."

"Don't know what?"

"I'm so sorry. So incredibly sorry." He turned away, avoiding eye contact. "I can't do this." Seeming defeated, he climbed off the bed and plucked his swim trunks from the floor.

Meanwhile, Allison was knee-deep in confusion. "Zane. What's wrong? I thought we were good."

"I thought we were, too. But I can't do it. I can't betray my best friend."

Naked on the bed and reeling from the pleasure Zane had just given her, the rejection still landed on Allison like the proverbial ton of bricks. Zane, the man she'd dreamed of for years, had just told her no. Logic said she should be incredibly hurt. Devastated. But right now, with this beautiful man still standing in her bedroom with an obvious erection, she was nothing but flat-out mad. It didn't have to be this way. And he knew it.

"Please don't do this," she said. "Don't leave."

"I have to. I'm sorry, but I do. I shouldn't be here in the first place."

His apology didn't do much to quiet her anger. "You're doing this. You're seriously putting on the brakes." She rolled onto her stomach, head and arms dangling off the side of the bed, and grabbed her sarong from the floor, where she'd tossed it earlier. Let him have a perfect view of her backside. Let him see what he was missing.

"I don't know why you're mad. From where I'm sitting, I just gave you a pretty mind-blowing orgasm."

"It *was* amazing. And not the point. I want you, Zane. All of you."

"I can't give you that. Not now."

A deep grumble was forming at the base of her throat. "Then when? Later tonight? Tomorrow morning? Please don't tell me we're going to leave this island without having sex." She wanted to applaud herself for truly putting it all out there.

"I've thought about it, and it's not a good idea. We've already gone too far."

She knew what that really meant. "You're going to let my brother come between us here? Nobody needs to know about this, Zane. Nobody. I don't kiss and tell. And I certainly wouldn't kiss and tell about you to him."

Zane turned away from her and stalked over to the French doors. His heavy steps were born of frustration, which seemed like an awfully good argument for him getting back in bed with her. But apparently not. "*I* would know it had happened. That's all that matters. I can't violate that trust."

"I would like to know where in your friendship agreement it says that you can't sleep with your friend's sister, when she's a consenting adult and so are you."

He whipped around, his eyes full of an emotion she couldn't put a label on—it wasn't anger and it wasn't hurt. It was something in between. "It's a guy thing. Plus, you and I both know that this would be nothing more than a hookup. Is that really what you want?"

"Are you saying that because it's all you're capable of? Hookups? Why is that, Zane? Why do you seek out one-night stands with women, but never actually commit?"

"Now is not the time for us to discuss the rest of my personal life."

"Oh. Right. Because you're always beyond reproach." She was so angry, it felt as though her blood was boiling. She hated that this was her reaction, but it was the only thing that made sense right now.

"That's not what I was saying. You just came off a breakup, Allison. You told me yourself that it was bad. I'm not the cure for that. The cure for that is time."

Allison jumped off the bed and wrapped her sarong around herself, tying it at the shoulder. Her breakup had been a distant thought until then, and she didn't appreciate him bringing it up or, worse, using it against her. "I don't need to be cured. I need the chance to move on." She stormed past him into the living room. Out of habit, she picked up her phone from where she'd left it on a side table. She had a text from Kianna. Nothing of paramount importance, but she replied. She watched as the bar moved across the screen, then she got an error message. *Not delivered.* That was when she saw she had no bars. "Service is out."

"You said you were going to turn off your phone."

"Well, I didn't."

Zane's eyes went wide with disapproval, and Allison was struck with a horrible realization. This really was all a mistake. Zane still saw her as a kid. He'd always see her as Scott's little sister. He'd never think of her as an actual woman.

"I love how you just come out with it," he quipped.

"I'm being honest. I told you I'd turn it off because I knew that it would be the sensible thing to do on a vacation where you're supposed to truly relax, but the reality is that Kianna and I are just barely keeping our heads above water with our business and we have an important new client that could turn into a long-term retainer. I need to be able to work."

"Oh, give me a break. That guy you were talking to yesterday? That was not work. If it was, you wouldn't have sneaked off into your bedroom and closed the door. It's not like I know a single thing about your company or what you're doing."

Allison's heart was hammering in her chest. She'd thought it would seem reasonable that she'd want some privacy during a work call, but she had to admit to herself that it was solely because she was working for the one person on the planet Zane would hate forever. "It actually was business. I owe it to my recruits to exercise discretion. I'm sometimes going after very high-level people who already have important positions with big companies. I'm sorry if it's my regular practice to conduct those phone calls out of earshot of anyone. It's nothing personal." Except that it was, because the conversation was about Black Crescent. She regretted tacking on that last comment. Everything before it had been nothing less than the truth.

Zane reared his head back and held up his hands in surrender. "You don't have to get so angry, Allison. I'm sorry. If it really was work, I'm sorry I said anything, okay?"

She knew then that she'd overreacted, but it was only because she was so deeply frustrated. "Do you want to know why I'm so mad?" She felt her entire body vibrate from head to toe. Could she really come out with it? Tell him about the feelings that were tucked deep down inside her? These were things she'd never told anyone. Not her mom or Kianna. The pages of the diary she'd kept in high school were the only place where she'd ever come clean about Zane. And maybe that was part of her problem. She felt as though Zane needed to let go of his feelings about his past. Maybe she needed to set loose the things that kept haunting her, too. "I'm angry because over on Mako Island, and back there in my bedroom, I was so close to what I've wanted for fifteen years, and you decided to yank it all away."

Zane stood there, frozen, blinking like he had far more than a speck of dust in his eye. "Hold on a minute. What did you say?"

She couldn't suffer any more humiliation today. She'd had more than her fill. "You heard me. And you can feel free to go now. I just want to be left alone for the rest of my trip." She stormed off into the kitchen. That was when she saw a note on the counter. Even from across the room, she could tell it was Angelique's handwriting. She beelined for it.

Dear Allison,

I'm not sure where on the island you are, and I couldn't get a text to go through, so I'm leaving a note. Hubert was having chest pains, so I've taken him to the doctor in Nassau. Don't worry. This has happened before. I think it's stress. I considered staying on Rose Cove, but I wanted to be with him, and our remaining guests have opted to leave because of the weather. I don't think the storm will hit the island, but we will feel some of its effects. I would not leave if I didn't think it was safe for you and Zane to be here. You have lived through many storms at Rose Cove and know what to do. Stay safe and hunker down if necessary. I'm sure Hubert and I will be back on the island tomorrow.
Love, Angelique

Zane hadn't left her cottage as Allison had asked. In fact, he was standing right behind her. "Have you looked outside? The sky is getting menacing. I guess we didn't notice it since we walked back inland in the shade."

"The weather can turn on a dime here." Allison handed him the note from her aunt. "And we were busy for a little while after that, too." She watched as Zane scanned the note.

"Whoa. I hope your uncle is okay."

"Yeah. Me, too." Everything about this day had gone so wrong. Right now, she just wanted to go to bed and try to sleep it off. "Not much we can do right now but wait."

"But the storm. Don't you think we should figure out what's going on?"

She'd been through dozens of false alarms with storms on this island. The weather was the least of her worries. "You do whatever you want, Zane. For me, I'm going to get some sleep and try to forget that you don't want to have sex with me."

CHAPTER SIX

BY LATE THE NEXT MORNING, the rain was coming down in torrential sheets, and Zane was deeply concerned about what might be in store for Allison and him on Rose Cove. He couldn't get a signal on his phone. The other resort guests were all gone. Zane had been to the dock several times, hoping there would be a boat there, but he'd had no luck. Either they'd missed them all or no one was coming to get them. Angelique had told Allison to hunker down, but Zane wanted to make one more attempt to look for a way off this island. And he wasn't going without Allison. He had to keep her safe. Even if she hated him, he was going to drag her along.

He trudged down the beach to her cottage, rain pelting his entire body while the wind pushed against him, forcing Zane to dig his feet deeper into the sand with each step. His thighs burned from the effort; his skin stung from the sheets of rain. He squinted through the drops but could see up on Allison's patio. Her doors and windows were closed. Once he arrived at her back door, Allison was nowhere in sight, so he had to knock. As he waited for an answer, he turned back to the ocean. The waves that had been so lovely and calm a day or two ago were now starting to rage. The water was at a full-on churn like a washing machine. Best-case scenario as far as Zane could guess would be that the storm would only skirt the Bahamas and they wouldn't sustain a direct hit. But with no access to a forecast, it was impossible to know what they were waiting for, whether this was as bad as things would get or if this was only the beginning.

He turned back to the door and pounded again. "Come on, Allison. Answer the damn door." Impatient, he turned the knob and stepped inside just as she stumbled out of her bedroom.

"Zane. What the hell? You just walk in here? I was taking a nap. There's nothing else to do with this weather."

Zane hated how beautiful she looked. He especially hated the way his entire body had gone warm and his face had flushed. He might have been struck by a sudden case of best-friend guilt yesterday, but that didn't change the fact that he wanted her badly. "It's getting worse out there, and I have no cell service, so I don't know what's going on. Are you able to get any bars?"

"Oh, this from the guy who criticized me for using my phone." She turned on her heel and retreated to her bedroom.

He had no choice but to follow her. "Don't be mad about yesterday. This is important."

She was standing in front of her dresser, staring at her phone. The bed was disheveled, and good God he wanted to scoop her up and lay her down on it. But this was no time for that. "I'm planning on being mad about yesterday for as long as I feel like it." She held her phone up over her head at a different angle, then off to the side. "And no. I'm not getting any bars, either."

Zane still wasn't sure he'd heard her correctly yesterday afternoon when she'd said that thing about him taking away the thing she'd wanted for fifteen years. Was it really possible that she'd had some sort of crush on him all that time? And if so, what in the world was he supposed to do about that?

"I think we should grab our stuff and camp out by the marina in the hopes that somebody shows up."

She cast a look at him that said she thought he was an idiot.

"There's no shelter out by the dock. We'd literally be standing there in the rain. Quite possibly forever."

"Do you have a better idea? I have to think that your aunt and uncle are worried about you. That they would try to send someone to get you."

"Angelique and Hubert have a lot on their plates right now, and they know the weather here better than anyone." She closed her eyes tightly and shook her head. "Now, the rest of my family is another case. I don't even want to think about Scott right now. He's probably losing it."

There was that name again—the reason for this state of torture he was in with Allison. "They're probably all worried sick. I'm also thinking there's no way they'll let you stay here if there's a way to safely get you back. Which is why I think we need to stay as close to the dock as possible."

"Okay. Fine. Let's go. It'll just take me a minute to pack up."

"Perfect. I'll be back in five." Zane ran over to his place as fast as the rain and wind would allow, and chucked everything into his backpack. By the time he returned, Allison was waiting for him.

"This is a terrible end to what should have been a perfect vacation," she said.

Somehow, Zane sensed that she wasn't merely talking about the weather. "I know. But I'm not going to die out here, and I'm not going to let anything happen to you, either." Not thinking, he took her hand and led them around to the path that would eventually take them to the main office. When they arrived up at the clearing, the ground was littered with palm fronds. The trees were bowing with every new gale. "The wind is only going to get worse," he called out, still pulling her along.

"I'm not worried about wind so much as I'm worried about the water. If there's a big storm surge, the sea level will rise considerably. Ten feet. Maybe more. I don't know how smart it is to wait by the dock."

She had a point. When Falling Brook was hit by Hurricane

Sandy, the storm surge had been overwhelming, flooding countless homes and businesses. People had died. It had been a disaster in every sense of the word. "We have to find a way to leave a message at the dock to let someone know we're still here, but then we need to find the high point of the island."

"That's going to be the honeymoon cottage up on the hill. The one they're renovating."

"Won't we be sitting ducks up there? If there are tornadoes, it could pluck the building off the top of the cliff and toss it out into the sea." It seemed that no matter what they did, they were in deep trouble.

"It's somewhat protected, because the back side of the building is built into the rocks. And it's on the western side of the island, where the winds won't be quite as strong."

"You really know a lot about hurricanes."

"My brother is a weather nerd."

"Okay, well, let's focus on the message first. Any ideas?" Zane asked, setting his backpack on the ground for a moment.

Allison let go of her small overnight bag and started untying her sarong. She was wearing the same bikini top, but this time with shorts.

"I'm not sure what kind of message you're trying to send," he blurted. This was not the time for him to have another moral crisis prompted by Allison disrobing.

"Everyone who works on this island has seen me wearing this. I'll tear it into strips and we'll tie those onto trees to lead someone up to the honeymoon cottage. We'll start with one of the metal pilings on the dock. Hopefully that will be enough of a signal that we're still here."

"Do you really want to rip that up? You love it."

Allison pulled at the fabric until it gave way and she was able to get a strip of it free. "I don't love this thing more than I love being alive." She waved him ahead as she made off in the direction of the small marina. "Come on."

Zane's mind raced as he struggled to keep up and surveyed

the island landscape—the wild rustle of the palms above them and the constant sideways pelting of the rain making it seem like they were on another planet right now. It certainly felt like a different place than it had been twenty-four hours ago. This was paradise upended. Gone was the calm serenity he had sought.

They jogged ahead, breaking out from under the canopy of shade only to learn how much the trees had been blocking the wind. Allison's hair whipped like crazy. Ahead, the ocean's churn was an endless sloshing of unfathomable amounts of water. Gone was the crystalline blue. This sea was coal gray and angry. The whitecaps and foam were of no consolation; they only served as a reminder that things were not as they should be. And against that tumultuous backdrop was Allison, looking tiny and defenseless running toward the dock, even when Zane knew very well that she was as tough as nails. If anyone was well suited to survive, it was her. Zane felt as though he was still honing the skill, but he would be damned if this storm was going to hurt her. Not on his watch. Not while he had anything to say about it.

He hustled to catch up. They arrived at the dock, which was now nothing more than a series of gray wood planks nearly submerged in the water. There was no boat, nor were there any other people. Zane now doubted that anyone would be coming for them despite Allison's family's concern for her safety. The seas were too rough. It was all too dangerous.

Allison carefully started down the dock and Zane followed right behind her, just in case she slipped. They both pitched to the side with every wave that threatened to swallow up the slick wood planks beneath their feet. Zane again told himself that he would not let anything happen to her. He had to keep Allison safe. Still, he knew that fighting Mother Nature was a losing proposition. If she decided she was going to win, there was not much to be done.

About halfway down the dock, the water was getting even deeper and Allison smartly came to a stop. She took the strip of sarong and wrapped it around the metal pole that moored the structure to the seafloor. On a calm day, this would have been a simple task, but it was pure chaos outside right now. With her hands occupied and the wind threatening to topple her, even while she used her strong legs to brace herself, Zane had no choice but to wrap one arm around her waist, steadying her while pressing his body into hers. She felt too good against him. Too right. And maybe it was the adrenaline coursing through his veins that made him think that if ever there was a time to throw caution to the wind, it was now, when life was hanging in the balance and they had no idea if they were going to survive.

Allison couldn't take any more of Zane's hands around her waist. It was too great a reminder of everything she couldn't have. She pried herself away from him now that the fabric was tied to the dock piling. She ran along the planks, but lost her footing at the very end. With a definitive *thud*, she landed on her butt. Pain crackled through her hip and down her thigh.

"Dammit!" She scrambled to her knees, embarrassed, frustrated and several other unpleasant emotions. She attempted to stand, but the dock was like a skating rink, and the ocean wasn't playing nice, either, sloshing water in her face.

"Let me help you." Zane threaded his hands under her armpits and lifted her to her feet with what seemed like zero effort.

"I can take care of myself." She twisted her torso and leaped up onto the sand.

"I'm well aware of that. It doesn't mean I can't still help you. If anything ever happened to you, Scott would never forgive me."

Allison was so tired of this. She turned to Zane, planting a single finger in the center of his chest to put him on notice. "I don't want to hear one more word about what my brother will or will not forgive you for. If I die in this storm—which, for the record, I know I will not—I will take all of the blame. You are officially recused of your bro duties."

He grabbed her hand with both of his. "But you'll be dead, so I will definitely get blamed."

"Then my ghost will haunt you and Scott and make sure you both know it was all me. Now, come on, let's finish leaving our trail of fabric." Allison didn't wait for him to respond and trekked up to the spot where they'd dropped their bags next to the trail that led to the clearing. She tore off another piece of the sarong and handed it to Zane, pointing to a tree branch she couldn't reach.

He tied it off. "We should go get whatever food we can and bring it up the hill with us."

She didn't want to give him any credit at all right now, but that was an excellent call. She hadn't thought twice about food since yesterday, too miserable over his rejection. "Good idea."

"Thanks." He smiled, which seemed like more of an apology than anything.

Allison wasn't quite ready to accept that from Zane, spoken or otherwise. So she started walking.

They split up back at their cottages, each scavenging for supplies. Allison took a moment to use a pair of scissors she found in her kitchen to cut up the rest of her sarong, but she still managed to return to their meetup spot first with bananas, bread, a flashlight and a blanket.

Zane emerged from his place second. "I brought a bottle of champagne."

Allison just shook her head. "I'd say you were a numbskull if I didn't need a drink so badly right now."

"For what it's worth, I also brought cheese and crackers, apples and a deck of cards."

"Great. It'll be just like summer camp." Chances were that it might be just as rustic up the hill. She had no idea what they were walking into, whether the solar was connected up there and whether they'd have furniture to sit or sleep on.

They retraced the inland path they had taken yesterday, stopping periodically to tie another piece of her sarong to a tree.

Having some protection from the rain and wind made the trip much easier than it would have been near the raging ocean, but it was still slow going. The ground seemed to shake with every gust of wind, rain was still coming down in sheets and they were both completely soaked. Allison didn't necessarily fear for her life, but she was scared of the unknown right now. She was reasonably certain that she and Zane could work together as a team to survive, but what toll would it take on her heart when this was all over? A huge one, she feared. She was going to need a vacation from her vacation.

When they reached the base of the hill, it looked like an almost insurmountable climb. She was already exhausted and dreading what it was going to be like, holed up inside a shell of a house while riding out the storm. Even worse, the spot on her hip where she'd fallen was throbbing. "I'm really not excited about doing this," she said.

"Seriously? You? The woman who marched me all over this island and had me snorkeling long distances?"

"Seriously. Me." Deep down, the real reason she wasn't looking forward to getting herself up the hill had nothing to do with exhaustion. Yesterday, she could stay away from Zane in her own space. How was she supposed to do that when they were about to be living in tight quarters and having to rely on each other to survive?

"It's okay. We can do it. We just need to get to shelter." He peered down at her, and all she could think was that this was such a damn shame. He was perfect. The two of them together for a night or two could have been magical. But no.

"Yeah. Okay. Let's do this." She led him down a narrow path at the foot of the hill, which eventually brought them to a wider trail that zigzagged its way up the incline. The terrain was mostly low scrub, giving them zero protection from the wind and rain. They both walked with heads down, watching the trail, slogging through what was quickly becoming a muddy mess.

"Is it just me or is the weather getting worse?" Zane asked as they made the final turn on the trail. They were close.

"It is. I wish we had access to an actual forecast. It would be nice to know if this was going to be the worst of it or if it's only the beginning. I hope this hike won't end up being for nothing."

"Better safe than sorry, right?"

She shrugged. "You can't spend your whole life staying out of trouble."

"Why do I have the feeling we aren't talking about the storm anymore?"

She came to a stop at the end of the trail, turned and confronted him. Water was running down her nose and cheeks. She felt like a drowned rat. "We aren't."

Zane's shoulders dropped in defeat. "Allison, come on. I don't want to argue."

"I don't, either, Zane. I shouldn't have to." Allison trudged her way around to the front of the house via a crushed-shell path with manicured hedges on either side. Bright pink bougainvillea was trailing from planters situated between the windows of the house. It had been years since she'd been up here, and she had no idea what state the house would be in, but the exterior already looked much nicer than she'd ever remembered, even in the pouring rain.

When they rounded to the front of the house, they both froze, even though they were standing in a complete downpour.

"Holy crap, Allison."

She didn't have a great response. It was beyond words. "I know." There was so much to take in, it was difficult to figure out where to start. First, either she hadn't appreciated the view when she was younger or it had somehow gotten better over the years. From this vantage point, you could see for miles, even with the disastrous weather. The glassy azure ocean was gone, replaced by a tumultuous cobalt sea, but it was still a sight to behold, and somehow seemed less menacing all the way up here.

And then there was the house. From the outside, everything

was definitely upgraded from the last time she'd been up here. The old tiny plunge pool had been replaced with a sprawling one, complete with an infinity edge and surrounded by a gorgeous patio. If she wasn't already as wet as she could possibly be, Allison would've jumped right in.

They ducked under the sizable porch roof. "I'm confused," Zane said. "I thought you said they were renovating. I don't know what the exterior used to look like, but it seems pretty damn perfect to me. The pool's full of water."

"They *were* renovating. Or at least that's what I thought, although I didn't actually speak to Angelique about it before I came down. It wasn't like I was going to be staying in the honeymoon villa." Nor would she be staying here again anytime soon. Her romantic future looked as bleak as could be, hot on the heels of rejection by not one, but two men. First Neil and his cheating ways, and then she attempted to distract herself with Zane, which didn't work at all. Maybe she needed to just give up on men entirely. Focus on her career. The financial and professional upside with Black Crescent was potentially huge, and now that she wasn't quite as concerned with hurting Zane's feelings, she could really put her foot on the gas when they finally got out of this mess of a storm.

Zane turned and cupped his hands at his temples, peering into one of the windows. "Uh. Allison. It looks pretty spectacular inside, too."

She strode over to one of the French doors and turned the knob, then stepped inside. "Wow. Gorgeous."

The space was light and airy, twice the size of either of their cottages, but with one noticeable difference—the bed was right in the main living space. Situated on a platform that spanned the long back wall of the building, it had a soaring canopy overhead and sumptuous white linens. Allison walked across the room and took the two steps up onto the raised area, still several feet from the bed.

Zane was right by her side. "I guess if you're on your honeymoon, there's no reason to think about being anywhere other than in the sack."

"Yeah. I guess." She had to wonder what that would be like, to be so enamored of someone that you wouldn't even bother to get out of bed. The only person she'd ever imagined that with was Zane, and she already knew that wasn't going to happen.

"That bed looks so damn good," she muttered. "I just want to take a nap."

"You can do whatever you want, you know."

"My clothes are still wet."

"We should both change. You can have the bathroom, of course."

Of course. Allison snatched up her bag and poked her head into a doorway she assumed was the bathroom. Out of habit, she flipped the light switch. To her great surprise, the fixture over the vanity came on. "The light works," she shouted out to Zane.

"Thank God for solar," Zane called back.

This room would be gorgeous eventually, but was definitely still under construction, with the tile of the two-person walk-in shower not yet complete. It had the other creature comforts, though—running water at the sink and toilet. Allison was happy for the little things.

As soon as she pushed down her shorts, the pain in her hip flared. She took a look in the mirror. Her upper thigh was turning a deep shade of purple. "No wonder it was hurting." The thought of putting on more clothes that might bind against her injury was too unpleasant, so she put on a black sundress and skipped panties.

"Better?" Zane asked, wearing a dry pair of gray shorts and no shirt. He was currently toweling his hair and making it look like a seduction move. He was clearly oblivious to his effect on her.

She decided to save them both the lecture about how he should really be wearing more clothes. "My hip is all messed up." She lifted the hem of her dress to show the edge of her deepening bruise.

"We need to get some ice on that, stat." He made off for the kitchen.

"I doubt the fridge is working," she said, gingerly sitting at the foot of the mattress.

"Got it," Zane said, rattling a white plastic bin presumably filled with ice.

"Wow. A second round of applause for the solar."

Zane dug around in a drawer, eventually finding a towel and placing a handful of ice in it. He brought it to her. "Scoot back on the bed."

She raised both eyebrows at him. This was way too much like yesterday's invitation, and she already knew this wasn't going to end well, either. "Maybe I should sit on the floor."

"Don't be ridiculous. You're hurt. You should be resting. Scoot back and lie on your side."

She didn't have the strength to argue. Zane sat next to her on the mattress, placing the ice pack on her hip. She winced at the pain.

"Just relax," he said, grabbing a pillow for her.

She took a deep breath, extended her arm and rested her head. "Thanks."

"Looks like the rain and wind aren't letting up anytime soon."

Indeed, there were sheets of sideways drops again. They pelleted the surface of the pool, creating ripples and waves. It was oddly soothing, which was nice because not much else could make her happy right now. It felt as though life was playing a cruel trick on her, sticking her in the honeymoon cottage with Zane.

"So, I wanted to ask you something," he said.

"Go for it. It's not like I have anything better to do."

"Were you serious when you said you'd been waiting fifteen years to have sex with me?"

CHAPTER SEVEN

ZANE DIDN'T ENJOY putting anyone on the spot, but he'd been wondering about this since the minute Allison said it. Between that and the storm, his mind had been occupied with nothing else. Had she really had a thing for him all these years and he'd somehow managed to be oblivious? When she'd kissed him at Scott's birthday he'd assumed it was nothing more than the impetuous move of a woman who'd had a few glasses of wine with dinner. Now he was eager to find out if he'd been wrong.

Allison stared at him, shaking her head. Her talent for making him feel like an idiot was unparalleled, but she somehow managed to make it charming. "You know, I've been thinking about it, and there's no way you're this clueless. You had to know I had a crush on you back in school. So if this is just some exercise to stroke your ego, I'm going to skip it." She snatched the ice pack from his hand, climbed off the bed and tossed the cold bundle into the freezer.

"I swear I had no idea." Of course, all those years ago, his brain had been occupied elsewhere. Women seemed to be the only thing that distracted him from the misery of his family's abrupt and complete falling apart. Plus, Allison had been totally off-limits. Scott's friendship and support had saved Zane. There was no breaking that trust, but it had been especially true at that time. "But I was pretty stuck in my own head when we were younger."

"I think you're still stuck in it." She walked back to the bedside and planted her hands on her hips.

Zane was sitting on the edge of the mattress, looking up at her, mystified. "Excuse me?"

"Your loyalty to Scott all stems from this time in your life that you aren't willing to let go of, Zane. It's not healthy. Being a good friend is one thing, but it's not like you're forever indebted to my family because we were kind to you. Because we welcomed you when things were rough. That's just what people do."

"You didn't go through what I did, Allison. You have no idea what it felt like."

She closed her eyes and pinched the bridge of her nose, as if she couldn't possibly be more frustrated with him. She chose to sit next to him on the bed, which was of some consolation. "You know what? I don't know, exactly. But I do know what it's like to struggle or to get knocked down or to have a hard time. You don't have a lock on that. You need to find a way to let go of what happened. Or at least move past it."

"That's why I came to this island. To clear my head. To try to let go of my animosity toward Black Crescent and the Lowell family. Or at least some of it. I don't know that I can ever let all of it go."

"Why not? Why can't you just forgive everyone at Black Crescent for what Vernon Lowell did? It's not their fault." Allison's eyes were wild and pleading. Meanwhile, the storm outside was starting to rage like never before. The windows rattled, and rain made a thunderous chorus on the roof.

"The Lowells destroy everything. Families most of all. They ruined my family. My parents got divorced because of the things they did. And for what? So somebody who was already making way too much money as far as I'm concerned could make *more* money? I just can't forgive them for that. It's the worst kind of greed." As if Mother Nature was on his side, a massive gust of wind whipped up, smacking a massive palm frond against the French doors. He and Allison both jumped.

"Whoa," Allison said, holding a hand to her chest, breathing hard.

"It's getting scary out there." The sky blackened. It was as if the sun had been extinguished.

"I'm tired of this, Zane. So tired."

"The weather?"

She inched closer to him on the bed. "No. This. Us. We could die up here. This is serious. And I have waited for you for years."

He was still having a hard time understanding this. Years? He really had been oblivious to her feelings, and that made him feel worse. "But I didn't know. I swear."

She pressed her finger against his lips. "No. I know that now. And it makes me feel like a loser, but I don't care. I don't want to die not knowing what it's like to make love to the one guy I have always wanted."

Zane felt as though his heart was going to beat its way out of his chest. In some ways, it still felt impossible that she was talking about him. There hadn't been enough time to riffle through the memories they shared to look for hints of this crush she'd supposedly had on him. "Don't say that. Don't hold me up on a pedestal and put yourself down at the same time. You're beautiful. You're smart and amazing. You could have any guy you want."

"Any guy?"

He didn't understand the question. Had she not looked in the mirror? Did she not realize that she was not only beautiful on the outside, but on the inside, as well? "Yes. No question."

She shook her head, not taking her sights from his face. "If you think that's really true, I want you to prove it, Zane. Show me that I can have *you*."

Damn, she was clever. "I see what you did there."

"Look, I know what you're like. You don't like to feel tied down or obligated. I know you're not a forever kind of guy, but will you be mine for right now? Nobody ever has to know. Not my brother. Not anyone. I just don't want to live with this regret. I know I'm not going to get another chance."

His breaths felt as though they were being dragged from his body as Allison's warm eyes pleaded for an answer. How could he ever be good enough for her? She was everything any guy with half a brain would want. Gorgeous. Exceptionally smart. Sweet, while still standing for what she wanted. She was quite possibly the most complex and unpredictable woman he'd ever met. He cared about her. And she cared about him. These were not the circumstances under which he normally pursued sex. It was so much easier when there was nothing but physical pleasure on the line. There was more at stake here. So much more. But how could he say no to her again?

He pressed the palm of his hand against her cheek. The house shook with another gale. He watched as her eyes drifted shut and she leaned into his touch. The world was threatening to rip the rug out from under them, and she didn't care. He could see it on her stunning face as she drew in a deep breath through her nose. Warmth radiated to his hand from her silky soft cheek, and he knew then that he could not let her down. He would give in to every carnal inclination he had when it came to Allison. And he would do it because she wanted him just as badly as he wanted her.

He cupped her face with his other hand and pressed his lips against hers. They stumbled into the kiss like it was the only way forward for either of them. Her tongue swept along his lower lip, sending need right through him, like a shot to the heart. His pulse picked up, and she dug her fingers into his hair, craving, needing, curling her nails into his scalp and raking his skin. He pulled her against him and lay back on the bed, tugging her along with him. She straddled his hips and ground against his crotch with her center.

Everything in his groin went tight. His mind went blank. Need slipped into the driver's seat when she countered his weight by lifting her hips and bucking against him. He felt her smile against his lips before she got serious again, kissing him deeply and squeezing his rib cage with her knees. Zane's hands went to the hem of her dress, slipping underneath it and skimming the sides of her thighs. He sucked in a sharp breath when he realized she wasn't wearing any panties. All that time he'd spent holding the ice to her hip...he'd been so close to touching her and hadn't realized it. No wonder she'd finally put him on notice. She'd had enough.

He gripped one of her hips, but touched the other one lightly. "Does it hurt?"

She shook her head, then began to kiss his neck. "No. I don't really care about pain right now anyway. Hurt me if you need to, Zane. It's okay."

"I really don't want to."

She pressed another kiss to his lips. "I know. And I love you for it. But it's okay. I won't break."

"Promise?"

"I do." She trailed her mouth to his ear, then down his jaw and his neck, leaving a blazing white trail of heat behind as each kiss evaporated on his skin. Down the center of his chest she continued to drive him wild, her hands spreading across his pecs. Squeezing. Caressing. Exploring. He'd never had a woman show so much appreciation for every inch of him.

One leg at a time, she shifted herself between his knees. She sat back and ran one hand over the front of his shorts. That one brush of her fingers nearly drove him insane. His legs felt like they were made of rubber while his entire crotch strained with urgency. His balls drew tight. With a single finger, still through the fabric of his clothes, she drew a line from the base of his length all the way to a tip. He managed to pry open his eyes halfway for an instant—he loved the look on her face. The one that said she had him at her mercy and she was going to enjoy the hell out of this.

And he expected nothing less.

* * *

Allison didn't bother with thoughts of what might happen tomorrow or the next day. It wasn't hyperbole to say they might not ever come. The storm would take what it wanted, and so would she. So she kept her senses, her thoughts and her heart in the present—this precious moment with Zane, the one she'd waited on for so long.

She unbuttoned his shorts and shimmied them, along with his boxers, down his hips. She wrapped her fingers around his length, in awe of the tension his skin could hold. He moaned his approval as she stroked him firmly, but she knew she could do better. So much better. She could make him immensely happy.

She lowered her head and took him into her mouth, leaving her lips a little slack and letting the gentle glide of her tongue deliver the pleasure she was so eager for him to have. A deep groan left his throat, just as another mighty gust of wind made the rafters quake above them. If this was how she died, she could be happy with that. She would have had everything she'd ever wanted.

Sealing her lips around him, she built some suction, appreciating the tightness it created in his body. It radiated off him in waves. He dug his fingers into her mess of hair, but he was more encouraging with his touch than anything. He wanted her to keep going, and she did, not thinking about time, the passes of her lips slow and methodical. As his skin grew more taut, she knew that he was close to his peak. There was a temptation to drive him over the cliff, but this degree of intimacy wasn't what she'd waited for. And she wasn't about to let him get there without her.

She gently released him from her lips and sat back on her haunches. She crossed her arms in front of her and lifted the sundress over her head. The soft fabric brushed against the skin of her belly and breasts. Her nipples went tight and hard from the rush of air. She flung the garment aside, not wanting to put it back on ever.

The slyest grin crossed Zane's face as his eyes scanned her naked body. She loved feeling like his reward. It was all she'd wanted to be for so long. "Get over here."

She climbed back on top of him, straddling his hips and resting her hands on his abs. His hard erection was right between her legs, and she rocked her body forward and back, letting his tip ride over her apex. Meanwhile, she dropped her head and kissed him. She loved this all-new level of getting to know him, of being able to correctly guess when he might nip at her lower lip or tangle his tongue with hers. Even more, she loved it when he surprised her with a squeeze or lick.

Or at the moment, by rolling her to her back. He pushed her hair away from her face and kissed her deeply, full of passion she'd never seen from him. It was as if he was putting all of the intensity of his personality into a kiss. She soaked up every minute of it while trying to match it, wrapping her legs around his waist and muscling him closer. Every inch of her body felt like it was on fire right now, burning with urgency. "I need you, Zane. I want you inside me."

"Let me get a condom." He hopped off the bed and traipsed across the room to pick up his backpack.

Allison propped herself up on her elbows, in part to watch his beautiful naked form in motion, and in part to take a peek outside. The sky was so dark it looked like midnight, but it was still afternoon. Wind rasped against the windows. The wood structure of the house creaked. But fear was nowhere in sight. She had Zane, and that was all that mattered.

He returned to the bed, tearing open the packet and rolling the condom onto his erection. He positioned himself between her legs, and she raised her hips, waiting for him. He was taking things slow. Too slow. How she disliked being treated as though she were fragile. She closed her eyes, reminding herself to stay in the moment. It was then that he came inside. Inch by inch, she felt herself mold around him. She had to look at him to keep herself locked on what was really happening, and she was gladly greeted by his incredibly handsome face.

She ran her hand over his cheek and strong jaw, loving the feel of stubble against her palm as they moved together. "You feel so good. So much better than I ever imagined."

"You actually imagined this before?"

She might die of embarrassment, but she also didn't want to lie about it. "Yes. Many times."

He grinned and kissed her softly. "Were we doing it like this?"

"Sometimes."

He lowered his head and nestled his face in the crook of her neck, resting his body weight against her center, applying the right pressure. "Tell me, Alli. Tell me more."

The tension in her body was building so fast, she was a little appalled that he expected her to answer, let alone weave together the many stories she kept in her head. "In my imagination, you're perfect. You know exactly how I like it. How deep." She bit down on her lip as he punctuated her own statement with a forceful thrust. "You know that I love feeling your mouth all over my body. My neck. My breasts."

He raised his head, kissing his way from her collarbone to her nipple, swirling his tongue around the tight and sensitive bud. "Like this?"

He switched to the other side, giving it a gentle tug with his teeth and sending a verifiable wave of electricity right between her legs.

"Yes." *Yes yes yes yes yes.* Her breaths became sharp and short. The peak was chasing her down the way a lion seeks its prey. It wasn't just physical right now. Knowing she could say something, and that Zane would follow her cues, was almost too much. She was drunk on power and craving the release.

He took her nipple between his lips and sucked harder while taking more deep strokes. That was enough to push her over the edge, and her head thrashed back on the pillow, the delicious reward spreading through her body, wave after wave. Zane drove deeper and more deliberately, and she was still knee-deep in the pleasure when he came, burying his face in her neck and arching his back. His entire body froze for a moment before he collapsed on top of her and rolled to her side.

"That was amazing," she said, her chest still heaving. She was pretty proud of herself for putting together so many words. Her brain could hardly function right now.

"It was unbelievable. Just knowing that you thought those things about me. I had no idea it would be such a turn-on."

She immediately rolled to her side, planting her hand in the dead center of his chest. "Don't you dare make fun of me for it."

"Are you kidding? I would never do that. What guy doesn't want a sexy woman to tell him the things she's fantasized about, especially when she's imagined doing those things with him?"

She was filled with a surprising amount of pride. "Okay. Good. I was a little worried."

His adorable smile crossed his face. He reached out and tucked a tendril of her hair behind her ear. "Don't worry. I'm just in awe of you, I swear."

She knew she was grinning like a fool. She could see the tops of her own cheeks. Her face hurt. In fact, she was so giddy, she couldn't think of a thing to say.

"What are you thinking?" He smoothed his hand over her bare belly. Even in the warm afterglow, she wanted more of him.

"That I hope we don't get rescued anytime soon. Or ever." It was the truth. She could stay here forever and be happy. She didn't need another thing in the world right now. It was a scary admission to make to herself. She knew what it meant—she'd been fooling herself when she'd decided that one time with Zane would be enough.

He smiled and laid another devastating kiss on her. "I don't want to get rescued, either."

CHAPTER EIGHT

Zane woke to the sound of her name.

"Allison!"

It had to be part of a dream, he guessed, but then she curled into him, snuggling her face against his chest, and he didn't question it. He stroked her hair and pulled her closer, inhaling her sweetness. He wanted to bottle up her smell and carry it with him everywhere.

"How do you do that?" she asked.

"Do what?" He was still drifting in and out of sleep.

"Make it sound like you're shouting at me from far away when you're actually right here."

"Huh?"

"Allison Randall! If you can hear me, say something!"

That was when Zane realized it was a man's voice calling Allison's name, and it was coming from outside the house.

Allison shook his arm. "I think someone has come to rescue us."

Still half-asleep and bleary-eyed, Zane could see that the sun was peeking between the clouds. The storm had passed. They were alive. "What? Where?" Zane sat up and shook his head to rid himself of the mental cobwebs. "Hurry. They're probably wondering where in the hell we are."

Both naked, they scrambled for their clothes. As much as Zane had hoped for a sexy morning with Allison, it appeared that was not going to happen. They raced to get dressed, Zane finishing first. He stumbled for the patio door and flung it open, rushing outside. Allison was right behind him. They rounded the house on the crushed-shell path. Several hundred yards away, Marcus, the man who had piloted the boat he took onto the island, was on his way up the hill.

Allison waved. "Marcus! Up here! We're here!"

Marcus's vision fell on her. His shoulders dropped in relief. "Your family has been worried sick!" he shouted back through cupped hands before resuming his climb.

Zane could only imagine. He'd witnessed the way Allison's family fretted over her. Scott was probably beside himself. "I'm sorry you had to come all the way up here," Zane said when Marcus reached them. "We decided the highest point was the safest. We were worried about the storm surge and the water more than I was worried about the wind."

"Smart. You probably saved yourselves. The cottages you two were staying in both had significant flooding."

Allison's sights darted to Zane, and it was as if he could see her heart plummeting to her stomach. Her aunt and uncle would be devastated to learn of the fate of their resort, especially on the heels of her uncle's health issues. "Do you know how my uncle Hubert is doing?" she asked.

"He had a heart bypass, but he's doing well. They ended up transporting him to a hospital in Atlanta. It was too dangerous with the storm to try the surgery in Nassau or even in Miami. They didn't want to risk the power going out. But he's recovering well. Your aunt, on the other hand, has been so worried. She said she would never forgive herself if you got hurt while staying on the island. She wanted to send me back for you earlier, but the waters were too rough."

"I was very lucky to have Zane with me. He knew exactly what to do."

Zane emphatically shook his head. He wasn't about to take credit for their safety. In truth, he'd been hoping that they wouldn't be found. He and Allison had such an amazing night. Unforgettable. Most likely a once-in-a-lifetime event, which struck him with a sense of melancholy he hadn't thought to prepare himself for. "It was a joint effort. Allison came up with the idea to leave the scraps of her sarong to send a message about where we were."

"It was smart. That's exactly how I found you." Marcus tugged the final strip of sarong fabric off a nearby shrub. "Come on. Let's get your things and get you to Eleuthera and on the plane to Miami. Your brother is waiting there."

Oh, crap. This was not a good development. Zane wasn't even close to being ready to see his best friend. If Scott was worried enough to fly to Miami, he would be that much more likely to pick up on any romantic vibes between Allison and Zane. For that reason, Zane was going to have to shut it all down way before they went near Scott. The thought pained him, but it was for the best.

"Scott flew down to Miami? Was that really necessary?" Allison asked.

"Like I said. Your whole family has been extremely worried about you," Marcus said.

Zane patted Allison's arm as platonically as possible. They needed to get back to being friends *without* benefits. "It'll be okay. We're safe. That's all that matters."

Allison, Zane and Marcus forged their way back to the honeymoon villa and collected what few belongings they still had. Zane was the first inside and found himself rushing inside to make up the bed, which was pretty much a disaster. The things he and Allison had done to each other there felt like a dream. They'd been amazing in the moment, but Zane needed to get his head out of the clouds and hop back on the straight and narrow. He desperately hoped that Marcus did not have a relationship with Scott. Loose lips could sink ships, or in this case, a deeply important friendship.

It took about an hour to make it back down the hillside and across the island to the dock. There, flapping in the bright early-morning sun, was the first piece of Allison's sarong, still tied to the metal piling. She'd been collecting the strips of fabric along the way. Zane got to it first and rescued it for her.

"Maybe you can have it sewn back together," Zane said, thinking that if he could have anything right now, it would be one more chance to see her wearing it. But he needed to stop thinking of Allison that way. Their fling was over.

"It'd be nice to keep it as a remembrance of our time together, but we're headed back to reality and my brother right now. I'd like to know where things stand." Her face was colored with a seriousness he hated to see, but he understood why it was there. This was no joke. Zane had crossed a line, and he needed to return to the other side of it.

"I can't betray him, Allison. You know that. Nothing about that has changed." Zane could see the frustration bubbling up inside her. He knew that she was tired of this argument, but it was the truth.

"But the betrayal is done. It happened, and you can't unring that bell. So now the question is what are you going to do about it?"

"You're the one who said we would keep it all between the two of us. I think we stick to the plan. It was amazing, Allison. But it's over." If only the words didn't sound so wrong coming out of his mouth. They certainly weren't enough to convince him. If only they'd had a little more time…to talk all of this through, to share one last mind-melting kiss.

"We're ready to leave," Marcus called for them both from the boat.

Allison stepped past Zane. "Let's just get out of here."

Her tone told him all he needed to know. So that's what last night had been—he'd been an itch that Allison had needed to scratch. Nothing more. He couldn't allow his feelings to be hurt by this revelation. He'd felt that way about many women in the past, and he was certain that women had felt that way about him, as well. Still, it didn't sit entirely right with Zane. Allison had never seemed like the type to love 'em and leave 'em, but her words and her posture were saying exactly that right now.

Between the persistent roar of the wind and the engine noise, Allison and Zane were unable to talk at all on the ride to Eleuthera. As soon as they arrived, a woman who said she was a friend of her aunt Angelique's descended upon them. She was a physician's assistant and insisted on joining them on the Learjet for the flight to Miami. She checked their vital signs and made sure they both ate and drank plenty of water. It was nice to feel taken care of, but at this point, Zane was just ready to get home. Between having weathered the storm, enduring the current cold shoulder from Allison and preparing himself for seeing Scott, Zane was completely and utterly exhausted.

As soon as they landed in Miami and walked into the private terminal, Scott rushed forward and scooped Allison up in her arms. "Thank God you're okay," he said over and over, squeezing her tight.

Zane watched the exchange, remembering the many times Scott had recounted the stories about Allison's cancer as a young girl and the havoc it had wreaked on their entire family. Scott had said many times that he'd never been through anything more difficult than that—life and death, wondering if his sweet and innocent sister would live or die. To hear Scott tell it, every day since then with Allison was regarded as a gift by their entire family.

"I'm fine," she said when he'd finally put her back down on the ground. "Really. Zane took care of me. He made sure nothing happened."

Scott clapped Zane on the shoulder, nodding in appreciation. "I owe you one for keeping her safe."

The guilt Zane had feared was slowly starting to crush him.

He'd only done what a good friend would do. But then he'd also done what a good friend *wouldn't* do—he'd slept with his sister. "Honestly, I think she saved me more than the other way around. She would've been just fine on her own. She's too resourceful and smart to get herself into too much trouble." Zane shot her a sideways glance to let her know he had her back. He'd paid attention when they'd talked about this on the island. He understood that she was fighting for Scott to see her in a different light.

"You need to stop worrying so much," Allison said to her brother.

"Plenty of smart people die in natural disasters," Scott said. "Especially when there's flooding."

"She's an unbelievable swimmer. You should have seen her the day we snorkeled over to Mako Island. I could hardly keep up with her. And she wasn't tired at all."

"You two went to Makeout Island?" Scott asked.

Zane wasn't sure he'd heard that right. "Wait? What?"

Scott narrowed his sights on his sister and twisted his lips. "Didn't Allison tell you? That's where teenagers go if they want to hook up with someone and want privacy."

Zane would've laughed if it didn't make the two of them look incredibly guilty. "You told me it was called Mako Island," Zane said to Allison.

"It *is* called that. Scott's being childish." Just then, Allison's phone rang, and she answered it right away. "Hello?" Her face lit up as she listened to what the caller was saying. "Ryan, you are so sweet," she said, distancing herself from her brother and Zane. "I'm totally fine. Just got back to the States. We're in Miami, safe and sound."

Allison's words reverberated in Zane's ears like a bass drum. *Ryan, you are so sweet.* No wonder she'd agreed that anything between them was to stay on the island. There were other men in her orbit, and she didn't want to mess with that. She'd given him an awfully hard time about his unwillingness to get serious with any woman, but she seemed to be playing the field just as hard.

"Hey. Can we talk?" Scott asked Zane.

Zane was not ready to fall under the purview of Scott's eagle eye, especially not when he was so distracted by Allison and her phone call with Ryan. She kept smiling and laughing, which was driving Zane nuts. He was back to not buying the story about working together. "Yeah. Of course."

The pair walked off to a corner of the gate area. Scott stuffed his hands in his pockets and looked down at the floor, seeming tormented. "Is there anything I need to know about? Anything with my sister?"

Zane's brain shifted into overdrive. He did not want to couch things with his best friend, so he was immensely thankful for the phrasing of the question. "There's nothing you need to know about." That much was true. What had happened between Allison and him was entirely private. Nobody's business. She was a grown woman, he was a grown man and they were two adults who had given their enthusiastic consent. End of story.

"You sure?"

"Well, it's been kind of a whirlwind, if that's what you're asking. Not quite the relaxing vacation I'd been hoping for."

"You know that's not what I'm wondering about. I know you. I love you, but there's a damn revolving door in your pants."

Funny, but last night, Zane had been thinking about that very thing, wondering if maybe it wasn't time to set aside his ridiculous bachelor ways. It wasn't making him happy, that was for sure. Those few days he'd spent with Allison were the closest he'd ever felt to having an actual relationship. They'd formed a partnership, they'd worked together and they'd done it well. Plus, being able to act on their incredible chemistry had been a transformative experience. But as Allison hung up her phone and fought a smile, Zane knew that they were back to being nothing more than friends.

* * *

"Sorry about that," Allison said, approaching Zane and her brother. The call had been from Ryan Hathaway, who was clearly a great guy. He'd heard about the storm on the news and wanted to make sure she was okay. How sweet was that? She was very excited about the prospect of him interviewing for Black Crescent. "I had to take a work call."

"Yeah. Right," Zane said, his voice clipped. "How's Ryan?"

Oh, hell no. Allison was not going to play this game with Zane, especially when he'd been the one to declare that things were "over" back on the island. "He's wonderful. Thanks for asking. He was really concerned about me and the storm. He wanted to make sure I was safe and sound."

"How nice. He sounds like a great guy." Everything in Zane's tone suggested he did not truly hold this opinion.

Scott looked back and forth between Zane and Allison, seeming perplexed by the conversation. "Uh, okay. I was able to snag the last three first-class seats on the next flight to New Jersey. We'd better get ourselves to the gate. It's boarding in less than an hour."

"What about Allison?" Zane asked, turning his attention to her. "Are you coming with us? I figured you were flying back to LA."

She'd been so nervous about accidentally revealing the Black Crescent information that she hadn't mentioned this detail to Zane. "Didn't I tell you? I'm actually coming back to Falling Brook for a week or so. I have some work I need to do."

"No, you didn't tell me. Do you have a client in town?" Again, his voice was nothing short of perturbed, but Allison was pretty determined to let him stew in his own juices.

"Yes."

"Who is it?"

"I can't say. It's confidential."

"How long is that supposed to last? Falling Brook is not a

big place, and I have lived there my entire life. I'm going to find out sooner or later."

Allison's pulse raced. She felt queasy at the thought of Zane figuring this out. She knew exactly how he would react—badly. "If you were my client, I wouldn't talk about you to anyone else. It's just the right thing to do."

He rolled his damn eyes, not bothering to say that of course it made sense for her to keep things to herself for the sake of her business interests. She could hardly believe how things between her and Zane had changed in the last few hours. So much for fantasies brought to life—she wondered now if it wouldn't have been better to keep Zane in her dreams, rather than begging him to become a reality. *Careful what you wish for.* It hurt too much to have him be such a jerk to her. And to think that she'd been mulling over some ridiculous confessions last night when she couldn't fall asleep. She'd wanted to tell him that she wanted more of him. So much more. And if he'd given her any indication that he might feel the same way, she would have been all in. She would have even called Kianna and told her that they had to drop Black Crescent.

The Allison of last night was clearly an idiot. It didn't matter that she and Zane had had an amazing time on the island together, and not just in bed. It didn't matter that he'd made her happy. Made her laugh. Made her feel sexy and desired. Zane would always choose his friendship with Scott over her, and she couldn't entirely blame him. That relationship had longevity. It had never faltered. He could count on it, and Allison understood how anyone would want to stick to the things in life that were reliable, especially if you were Zane, a man who'd been through the wringer.

That still didn't keep her from wanting him.

The three of them took a shuttle over to the commercial terminal and waited to board, standing on the concourse outside the busy gate area. Scott and Zane had been knee-deep in conversation, leaving Allison to feel like the third wheel until Zane wandered off to find a bathroom and Scott pulled Allison aside.

"You didn't tell him why you were coming back to Falling Brook?" Scott asked her pointedly.

"Wow. You really don't waste any time, don't you?"

"It's a valid question, and he's going to be back any minute now. You two just rode out the storm together and the topic of you coming back to Falling Brook never came up? Not once? It makes me wonder what in the heck you two did talk about."

"I don't want him to know about Black Crescent, okay? And I don't want you to tell him, either. You know how he feels about it. You know it hurts him to talk or hear about it, and you also know he has a blind spot when it comes to the Lowells. I don't want it to mess with our friendship."

"Since when have you two been close?"

If Allison could've shot laser beams from her eyes at her brother, she would have. Why did he have to think that only he could be close to Zane? "We've always been friends, Scott. You know that. I can't compete with your friendship, okay? So don't try to compare the two." She saw down the concourse that Zane was on his way back already. Even in rumpled clothes, with two days of scruff on his face and with an attitude that was decidedly cooler than the one she'd experienced during their last day on the island, he was irresistible. She was going to have to learn to resist. "He and I just went through a life-and-death situation, and I don't want to hurt his feelings unnecessarily. He's tired. I'm tired. Plus, there's a good chance that I won't get hired by BC long term. So if it's only a one-off, I really don't see the point in telling him and hurting his feelings for no good reason."

Scott nodded. "Okay. That's probably the right call then. Your intentions are good."

Zane smiled as he approached them. It still made Allison's heart melt. She was going to have to figure out a way to get over him. She had no idea how that would work. "You guys talking about me?" he asked.

"Always," Scott said.

"Never," Allison countered.

"Ladies and gentlemen," the gate agent announced over the intercom. "We're ready to begin the boarding process for Flight 1506 with nonstop service to Newark International Airport. We'll begin by inviting our first-class passengers to board."

"That's us," Scott said.

"Good. I can't wait to get home to a hot shower and a good night's sleep," Zane said.

Allison felt the same way. She also wished she could do those things with Zane. She was going to need to work up to this whole business of forgetting her attraction to him.

The three boarded the plane, but as soon as Allison figured out the seating arrangement, she realized just how much she would always be the odd man out when it came to her brother and Zane. The two guys were seated together, across the aisle from her. That had been Scott's decision, since he'd booked the flights, and Zane was obviously perfectly happy with it. Allison flagged the flight attendant and asked for a gin and tonic before takeoff. She needed something to soothe her ragged edges. Maybe she could catch some sleep after they were in the air.

But for now, since Zane and Scott were immersed in conversation, and the plane was still boarding, Allison took this chance to give Kianna a quick call.

"Tell me you're okay," she blurted without even saying hello.

"I'm fine. In one piece. On the plane to New Jersey."

"I can't believe that storm hit the island. It all happened so fast. I kept watching the forecast, hoping it would change for you. I can't help but feel responsible. It was my idea for you to go down there in the first place."

"No. No. It's not your fault. I wanted to go. And believe it or not, it was still a good trip. Despite the storm. Despite everything." She was trying to put the best possible spin on this, not merely for Kianna's sake, but also for her own. She didn't want to regret her time with Zane. She didn't want to believe that it might have been a big mistake. But what do you do when you get what you've always wanted and then it's snatched away by timing and circumstance? What do you do when the guy you've wanted for years tells you that it's over before it's had a chance to really start? Right now, it felt like nothing would ever sting as much as this rejection.

"Did you at least find a hot guy? Please say yes."

Allison couldn't suppress the smile that crossed her face. "I did. But I'll have to tell you about it later. We take off soon, and I have to turn off my phone."

"Okay, hon. Did you postpone your meeting with Black Crescent?"

"Nope. Still going in tomorrow. As planned."

"Did you talk to Joshua Lowell?"

"I texted his assistant. We're all good."

"You're a badass, you know that, right?"

Allison laughed. Her friendship and partnership with Kianna meant the world to her. She really hoped she wouldn't end up letting her down. This Black Crescent meeting had to go well. "I'm trying."

"Call me after the meeting tomorrow?"

"You know it. Talk to you then."

Allison hung up the phone, switched it to airplane mode and tucked it into the seat-back pocket. She swirled her gin and tonic, took a long sip and glanced over at Zane and Scott. Zane, who was sitting at the window, made eye contact with her. That instant seemed to speak volumes—there was a connection between them that hadn't been there before they got to the island. Zane knew it. She did, too. But he seemed resigned to setting it aside. Keeping it in the past. No matter how hot and passionate that connection was, it didn't seem to be enough for Zane.

He dropped his gaze and returned his attention to her brother. Allison's heart plummeted to her stomach, but she was used to the disappointment now. It was the story of her life with Zane. And exactly the reason why this visit to Falling Brook would be all about her role as businessperson supreme, not the woman who couldn't stop pining for a man she couldn't have.

Scott leaned across the aisle to talk to her. "Do you have plans tomorrow night?"

"Hanging out at your house. Not sure what else I would possibly be doing."

"I wasn't sure if you had work obligations."

Allison wanted to strangle her brother for bringing up Black Crescent while Zane was sitting right next to him. "Nope. I should be done by midafternoon. Why?"

Zane peered around Scott. "He invited me over for dinner."

"I wanted to thank him for taking such good care of my little sister," Scott added.

What in the world was her brother up to? "Okay. Sounds great."

CHAPTER NINE

RIGHT ON TIME, Allison pulled her rental car into the Black Crescent parking lot the following afternoon, shortly before two o'clock. She'd arrived back in Falling Brook in the nick of time—less than twenty-four hours before her scheduled meeting with Haley Shaw and Joshua Lowell. Anyone else might have used the fact that she'd been stranded on an island in the middle of a hurricane as an excuse to postpone the meeting, but that detail was a dramatic selling point. She could tell Josh Lowell that not even a natural disaster would keep her from doing her job, and doing it well. In the end, she and Kianna needed the Black Crescent contract. It was their best shot at keeping their company alive.

Of course, the only trouble with that was Zane. If she got the contract, she would have to tell him that she was working for the company that he considered the enemy. Even though there were no more remnants of romance between them, she couldn't keep the secret from him forever. As she walked up to the sleek and modern building that had always stuck out in the otherwise traditional Falling Brook landscape, she was well aware that if Zane knew what she was doing right now, he would tell her she was not only a terrible friend, she was foolish. The things he'd said while they were riding out the storm in the Bahamas echoed in her head. *The Lowells destroy everything. Families most of all.* He'd been deeply hurt by the things the Lowell family had done to him and his parents, and it was clear that for Zane, it was about far more than the money. His entire world was turned upside down the day that Vernon Lowell made off with his family's fortune. As far as Zane was concerned, his old charmed life ended that day and his new, far less shiny life began.

Allison had a somewhat different perspective. Oddly enough, she felt a debt of gratitude to the Lowells. If Vernon hadn't disappeared with all that money, she might have never met Zane. That thinking might be employing some pretty messed-up logic, but that was truly the way she felt. Not having Zane in her life was an incredibly depressing thought, almost as sad as the other thought that had been winding through her head since the Bahamas—that Zane would ultimately be a thirst unquenched. She'd thought that making love with him would get him out of her system. But that had been a horrible miscalculation on her part.

The flight had given her entirely too much time to mull over Zane's latest rejection. She wanted to shrug it off and move ahead, but her heart just wouldn't let her go there. Her heart wanted to drag her down to the bottom of this murky sea in which she was adrift and remind her of the reasons why it was such a shattering disappointment to have him choose his friendship with her brother over a chance with her. She was in deep, and she had no idea how to swim her way out. Scott would never buy into the idea of her with Zane. He would always think of Allison as that little girl with cancer, even when she was strong and healthy and a grown woman. And if anyone knew Zane forward, backward and every other way imaginable, it was her brother. He was convinced that Zane wasn't capable of commitment. The allure of other women was too great, although Allison also suspected that there was more to it than that. Zane might have been unbelievably brave in the face of that storm, but he was afraid of commitment and was possibly even more terrified of love. That put Allison in the category of a good time, right where every other woman he'd ever met also resided. Allison didn't want to be just another girl, but it sure felt that way.

With the Black Crescent building looming before her, Allison couldn't afford to think about that. She had a job to do and a business to keep afloat. Her first allegiance had to be to herself and Kianna now. She straightened her designer jacket and shrugged her laptop bag up onto her shoulder, then marched into Black Crescent.

She approached the main-floor reception desk. "Allison Randall for Joshua Lowell. We have a two o'clock."

The receptionist picked up the phone. "One moment, please."

Before she could dial an extension number, another woman emerged from a side door in the reception area. "Ms. Randall?" The woman was willowy with wavy blond hair. She offered her hand. "I'm Haley Shaw, Mr. Lowell's assistant. We're so glad you're here. Especially considering everything you've been through. I still can't believe you were able to keep this appointment."

Allison shook hands with Haley. "It would've taken more than some bad weather to keep me away from this opportunity."

"Come on. I'll give you the lay of the land and show you where we'll be conducting the interviews."

Haley led Allison upstairs to the second floor and a conference room right outside Joshua Lowell's office. The one thing that struck Allison about Black Crescent was that no expense had been spared. Every detail was of the finest quality. It did make Allison wonder if the rumors about Vernon Lowell were true, that he'd never actually left Falling Brook and had merely been in hiding this whole time. If that was ever proved to be the case, she could imagine Zane blowing his top. Another lie from Vernon Lowell would only reopen Zane's deep wounds. Plus, Zane was the sort of the man who wanted to get even. Knowing he could have hunted down Vernon all these years would at the very least eat at him.

"Please, make yourself at home," Haley said, gesturing to the gleaming mahogany meeting table. "Mr. Lowell should be here in a few minutes. He's just finishing up a phone call."

Allison set down her Louis Vuitton bag and pulled out her laptop. "Great. We're seeing three candidates today. Ryan Hathaway, Chase Hargrove and Matteo Velez."

Haley pursed her lips in a particularly odd way. "Chase Hargrove, huh?" Her voice was dripping with doubt, something Allison wanted to get to the bottom of before Joshua arrived.

"Yes. He's highly qualified for the position. And I was impressed with him when we spoke on the phone."

Haley nodded, but seemed unconvinced. "I'm sure he has the right credentials. I just don't know if he's a good fit for the office."

This was an interesting development. Allison had never had an assistant offer her opinion of a candidate, and especially not before the interview had even taken place. But in her experience assistants seemed to always know more about everyone and everything than the majority of their bosses. "Can you tell me why?"

Just then, a young man poked his head into the meeting room. "Ms. Shaw. Chase Hargrove is here for his interview."

"Can you let Mr. Lowell know? And can you ask Chase to hold on a minute?" Haley asked.

"Sure thing, Ms. Shaw." The man darted back into the hall.

"If there's something I need to know, now would be a great time to mention it," Allison said. She couldn't afford to mess up when it came to Black Crescent. She had to nail this job. On paper, Chase was a highly qualified candidate, and Allison had found him charming and affable during their one phone conversation.

Haley seemed deep in thought for a moment, as if she was

calculating her response. "I'm afraid I don't have a specific reason for feeling that way about Chase. It's more of a hunch."

The meeting door opened again and in walked Joshua Lowell. Allison had never met him in person, but she'd seen his pictures all over the papers and in business magazines, especially the last few years. "Mr. Lowell, I'm Allison Randall." She offered her hand.

"Please. Call me Joshua. It won't be long before I'm not the boss around here anymore."

"That's why I'm here, right?" Allison wondered if that aspect of her job might help her smooth things over with Zane whenever he discovered she was working for Black Crescent. So much of his hatred seemed aimed at Joshua, and she was in charge of finding his replacement. She tucked the idea away in her head. The idea of needing to explain herself to Zane, all in the name of making a case for them as a couple, was a stretch. She was sure he didn't see her as anything more than a fling.

"Absolutely," Joshua answered. "So, please, let's bring in these candidates."

Allison asked Haley to go ahead and bring Chase in for his interview. The instant he walked through the door, the energy in the room changed dramatically. Tall, handsome and completely self-assured, Chase was a formidable presence. With Joshua also in the room, it was no easy task to take center stage, but Chase seemed to do it at will. Was this the reason for Haley's hesitancy when it came to Chase? Was he simply too much to deal with?

Chase sat opposite the three of them at the conference table and Allison wasted no time conducting the interview. This was not about putting the candidate on the spot—she'd already gone over these exact questions with them over the phone. They'd also already been fully vetted by Allison and Kianna. This process was all for the client. This was Chase's chance to put his well-honed answers on full display for Joshua.

When Allison was finished, she was fairly certain Chase could not only land the job, but could perform the duties with aplomb. But she wasn't done with showing off the product of her hard work—Ryan Hathaway and Matteo Velez were up next.

"Thank you so much, Chase, for coming in today. We'll be in touch," Allison said.

All four of them stood and Chase began to round the table.

"I'll fetch Mr. Hathaway," Haley blurted, darting out the door before Chase had a chance to shake her hand and say goodbye.

Chase took notice, watching as she disappeared. "Ms. Shaw sure is on the case, isn't she?"

Joshua extended his hand to Chase. "She's the best. No matter who comes in as CEO, Haley needs to stay. She makes this office run."

"Believe me, if I get this job, Ms. Shaw is the last person I'd dream of replacing," Chase said. Allison couldn't ignore the glimmer in his eyes.

Just then, Haley walked in with Ryan Hathaway, who Allison recognized from his headshot. Typically, Allison did not want the candidates for a position to encounter each other in the interview room, but what was done was done. She made the introductions, and Ryan seemed immediately suspicious of Chase.

"I suppose this is my cue to make way for your interview," Chase said to Ryan before turning to Haley. "And, Ms. Shaw, I hope to see you again very soon."

Haley's face flushed with a brilliant shade of pink. She was noticeably conflicted as they shook hands. "I wish you the best of luck."

Ryan seemed to take notice of the sparks between Haley and Chase, arching both eyebrows and pressing his lips together firmly as he witnessed their goodbye. He pulled Allison aside as Haley and Joshua talked privately.

"Is there something I need to know about that guy? Did he already get the job? I don't want to interview for a taken position," he said.

Allison shook her head, but she could tell that Ryan was seriously concerned. Given their earlier conversations, she was eager to put him at ease. "Everything's fine. I think he's just a little heavy-handed with the charm. If I had to place a bet on it, I'd say he has a bit of a crush on Ms. Shaw."

Ryan glanced over his shoulder. Joshua and Haley were still conferring. "Okay. Good."

Allison gently placed her hand on Ryan's shoulder. "You sure you're okay?"

He nodded enthusiastically. "Yes. Definitely. I'm just used to guys like that being rewarded for their bad behavior. You know what they say. Nice guys finish last."

Allison took a moment to consider Ryan's words. Had he been burned? Was that where that was coming from? If so, she felt his pain. She'd gone for what she wanted, and it had been a miserable fail. "Nice guys finish first with me. As long as they're qualified and nail the interview, of course."

Ryan grinned. "I'm glad you recruited me. I really enjoyed our conversation while you were on your trip. I'm so relieved you weren't hurt in the storm. Everything I saw on the news looked terrifying."

"It wasn't fun, that's for sure." Except that it had been. It had been amazing. She'd never felt more alive when the sea seemed determined to carry them away, but Zane was resolute about keeping her safe. She'd let herself be vulnerable with him, something she rarely ever did, and in the moment, it had been so richly rewarding. Even with Zane behaving like an ass since then, and trying to discount everything that had happened between them, she knew in her heart that it had all been worth it. Kissing him, touching him, having his hands all over her body. She'd wanted him for so long. How could she have ever said no? Even if she'd known all along what would happen? She couldn't have.

Allison shook her head and brought herself back to the present. She couldn't daydream about Zane right now. Not with work on the line. "I have to ask if you're looking at other positions right now," she said to Ryan.

"I have a few more interviews over the next several weeks. But I'll be honest. This is the job I really want."

There was no greater satisfaction than finding the right candidate for the job, and Allison had a good feeling about Ryan. "Music to my ears. Now, let's see if Mr. Lowell and Ms. Shaw are ready to get this show on the road."

Ryan hit it out of the park during his interview, as did Matteo after him. When it was time to say goodbye to Josh and Haley, Allison knew she'd done an amazing job.

"Very impressive, Ms. Randall," Joshua said, sitting back in his chair. "Thank you for going the extra mile in making today happen."

"Literally," Haley added. "She just flew back from the Bahamas last night."

"I'll do whatever it takes to make my clients happy." Allison collected her papers into a neat stack. "Do you have a sense of the timeline for the hire?"

"I'm eager to get the new CEO in as soon as possible. What are your thoughts as far as the timing for second interviews?"

"It'll depend on the candidates' schedules and yours, of course, but Haley and I can coordinate. I do recommend you think about it for at least a week. Spend some time with the files and background info I provided. In my experience, it's best to not rush with a decision like this."

Joshua nodded, seeming to consider all she said. "I suppose you're right. I'm just ready to move forward."

Allison couldn't help but think of the subtext—he was eager to move on with his life. He had love and happiness ahead, and he didn't want to wait. "Of course. I understand."

"Will you be able to stay in Falling Brook for a few weeks? It would be great if I knew I could call on you to walk us through this process. The phone is one thing, but there's no substitute for having someone on hand."

Allison knew this was her opening for driving home the deal she wanted to make. "It depends on whether or not I'm on retainer. I have a partner out in Los Angeles and other clients who also expect my time."

"I'll pay triple your normal retainer for the next month." Joshua hadn't hesitated to up the ante. "That should give us enough time to make a hire for this position."

Allison swallowed hard. Three times her normal rate was certainly a great starting point. "And beyond that?"

"The new CEO will ultimately make the call as to whether we put you on permanent retainer. But I will certainly have a say in it, and, as far as I'm concerned, you have the job."

Goose bumps raced over the surface of Allison's skin. Any sliver of victory in business felt good, and Kianna was going to flip out when she got the good news. Even so, there was a downside. A month in Falling Brook would make it impossible to stay away from Zane. And that meant she had to come clean with him about working with Black Crescent. "Fantastic. I'm staying with my brother here in Falling Brook, working out of his house. I can be on-site anytime you need me. Just call."

"You can expect to hear from me."

Allison strode out of the meeting, feeling as though she was walking on a cloud. She'd nailed it, in every sense of the term. She called Kianna and told her everything as soon as she got in the car.

"You are not only a badass, you're a rock star," Kianna said.

"It's only a month. It's not the long-term retainer we wanted."

"It'll come. I know you'll get it done."

"I'll do my best."

"So, can you tell me about the guy in the Bahamas?"

Allison hesitated, not sure she wanted to dive into the topic. This wasn't a quick conversation, and there was so much about this situation that she was still trying to mentally unpack. "His name is Zane. I've known him for fifteen years. He's a friend of my brother's, and we just happened to end up at Rose Cove at the same time." She decided to skip the heavier part of the story, the details about how she'd been longing for him all those years and that the idea of letting go was a miserable one.

"Did he at least rock your world?"

"Oh, yes. Several times."

"And now?"

"I don't know. I think we're back to just being friends."

"Are you happy with that arrangement?"

Allison sighed. She wasn't happy with it, but she also didn't see a way past it. Maybe it really was easier if she and Zane stayed friends. "I'm not sure, but I'll figure out at least some of it tonight. He's coming over to my brother's for dinner."

CHAPTER TEN

ZANE'S FIRST DAY back at the office after the Bahamas trip was less than productive. Between a million phone calls from concerned friends and clients, and his pervasive thoughts of Allison, he got very little work done. For some ridiculous reason, he kept seeing flashes of Allison flitting around the island in her sarong. It was so bad that he'd referred to one of his marketing managers as Allison when her name was in fact Maria. He hadn't even been close. A mistake easily swept aside when he blamed it on the exhaustion from the storm, but it was a sign that he was going to have deal with this. It had been shortsighted to think that he and Allison could sleep together, shrug it off and return to their old dynamic. So where would they land? He had no idea.

By the time he'd hopped in his BMW to head to Scott's house for dinner, he was still catching up. He'd left a voice mail for his mom, but she was just now calling him back. He pressed the button to put her on speaker.

"Hi, Mom. I take it you got my message?"

"I didn't even know you'd left the country. Shows you how out of the loop I am."

"Would it have been better if I'd told you I was down there? Wouldn't you have worried? I know you don't like to worry."

"Well, of course, I would've been concerned, but you're a survivor, Zane. I never doubt your ability to figure out how to find your way through a tough situation."

The undertone of her comment was that he'd managed just fine in his teenage years when everything had gone south. It was nice to get that stamp of approval, although he knew that it was just his mother being a mom. "Thanks."

"What took you down there? New marketing client in the Bahamas?"

"I went on vacation."

"No!" His mother gasped, which turned into her musical laugh. "My son? Went away for fun?"

Zane had to chuckle, too. "Believe it or not, yes. I've been stressed, and I needed to get out of Falling Brook to clear my head."

"Are things at work not going well?"

Zane took the turn onto Scott's street. Scott and his wife lived in one of the original Falling Brook neighborhoods, which was seeing a revival. Older, stately homes were being remodeled and updated, with young families moving in. Zane saw it as a move in the right direction. This town needed some freshening up. "Actually, things at work are amazing. We're too busy, but in a good way. We've reached the point where we're turning away potential clients. That's something I never even imagined six or seven years ago."

"Then what's bothering you?"

Zane pulled up in front of Scott's house, a recently restored five-bedroom Tudor with a pristine putting green of a front yard that was Scott's pride and joy. Zane put the car in Park and killed the engine, sitting back in the driver's seat and running his hand through his hair.

"You're being quiet," his mom said. "Just come out with it. You know you can tell me anything."

He knew that. It didn't make his embarrassment over what he was about to say any less real. "It's Joshua Lowell. I got sucked into some drama with him. Someone anonymously sent me a paternity test saying that he had a child he wasn't willing to claim responsibility for. I talked to a local reporter who was working on a piece about him."

"Have you lost your mind? Why would you get involved in that?"

"I don't know. Revenge? Or as close as I'll ever get to it? It doesn't really matter now. It all backfired. The story ran, without that bombshell, and Josh Lowell ended up smelling like a rose, he and the reporter fell in love and now he's getting married. He's even leaving Black Crescent."

She sighed heavily.

"I know," Zane said. "The guy is golden. Everything he does turns out perfectly, and it makes me nuts. I know it shouldn't, but it does. Just thinking about it is making my shoulders lock up." He cranked his head from side to side, hoping to loosen the tension.

"You realize that people think the same thing about you. That you're golden. That you can do no wrong."

"*You* might say that about me, but other people do not. Plus, that isn't the point."

"But it *is* the point. It's not just me who says it, either. Your father thinks the same thing. Your grandparents. Aunts and uncles. Your colleagues and employees. Remember when you invited me to your company Christmas party two years ago? All night long, all I heard about was how great you are and it's not just because you're the boss. I heard it from your clients, as well. I'm your mom, and even I got a little sick of it."

Zane laughed, but he was astonished to be hearing this from her. He'd never seen himself as anything more than the guy who was still striving to get back on top.

"Look at your life," she continued. "You have an immensely successful business. You own a beautiful home in one of the most exclusive towns in the country. You're handsome, and people love you. Whatever it is that you think the Lowells stole from us or from you, it doesn't matter. It hasn't kept you from having it all, and it never will keep you from it. You need to find a way to move forward."

"This isn't just about what they did to me. It's about what they did to our family. The Lowells are the reason you and dad split up."

"You know, your dad and I had a drink a few weeks ago. We talked about it."

"You did?" His parents' divorce had been as acrimonious as they came. To Zane's knowledge, his parents had only been in the same place twice since their split fourteen years ago, at Zane's high school and college graduations, and they'd barely spoken to each other. "You didn't tell me this."

"He came to Boston for work, and he called me. It was nice. We had a chance to say a lot of things that should've been said a long time ago. The truth is that your dad and I were never going to make it. Of course, losing everything put a massive strain on the marriage, but the underlying problems were already there. We weren't in love. I'm not sure we ever were. We would have split up eventually."

Zane was struggling to keep up, but he couldn't help but notice that it felt as if a weight was being lifted. A burden from his past was evaporating before his eyes. "Wow, Mom. You are kind of blowing my mind right now."

"Does that help you see that you need to let Joshua Lowell do his own thing and maybe get out there and keep looking for your own happiness? You know, I'd like to have a daughter-in-law, maybe become a grandmother at some point."

"Mom…"

"No pressure."

"Oh, right. No pressure." Zane glanced at the clock on his dashboard. It was seven o'clock and he didn't want to be late. "Mom, I need to run. Scott invited me over for dinner and I'm sitting outside his house. His sister, Allison, is in town."

"Oh, how nice. Say hi to them both for me. I've always adored those two, especially Allison. She's always been such a sweet-heart to me."

And just like that, Zane felt like the universe might be telling him to salvage the romance that had started at Rose Cove. It was at least worth trying. "Love you, Mom."

"Love you, too."

Zane grabbed the bottle of Chateau Musar he'd brought, which was Scott's favorite wine, and hopped out of the car. He strode up the long driveway and couldn't ignore the way his pulse picked up at the thought of seeing Allison again. Maybe this could actually work. Of course, there was a lot standing in his way. He'd have to find a way to sort things out with Scott. And he'd have to hope that there weren't other guys in the mix. He'd also have to smooth Allison's ruffled feathers. He'd been a jerk when they left the island. Allison deserved so much better than that. As to how difficult it would be to convince her to accept his apology, he wasn't sure. He was prepared to grovel. It was difficult for him to set aside his pride, but he'd overcome worse.

He rang the doorbell, and Scott quickly answered, waving him in. When Zane handed over the wine, Scott unleashed a mile-wide grin. "You're the best friend a guy can have. Let's get this decanted."

Zane followed him inside. He was looking forward to spending an evening with these people he cared about so deeply, but coming to dinner at Scott's house felt a bit like returning to the scene of the crime, given the kiss with Allison at his birthday party. He wished he could find a way to rewind the clock to that moment when her luscious lips first met his. If only he'd known then that she hadn't done it on a lark. She'd spent years building up to it.

They wound their way down the wide central entry and into the newly remodeled gourmet kitchen. Scott's wife, Brittney, was cutting up vegetables at the center island. "Look who's here," she said, taking a kiss on the cheek from Zane. "I'm glad you could come over on such short notice. Scott was eager to express his thanks."

"He keeps saying that, but Allison would've been fine without me. Seriously. She's tough as nails."

She swept the contents of the cutting board into a large bowl. "I agree. But you know how he is. Super protective. Is there such a thing as a helicopter brother?"

"Hey. I'm standing right here." Scott sniffed the wine cork, then emptied the bottle into a decanter.

"Well, the kids and I are thankful if nothing else," Brittney said. "I swear the only thing that kept Scott from freaking out about Allison was knowing that you were down there with her."

"Did I hear my name?" Allison poked her head into the kitchen.

Zane's heart did a veritable flip when he saw her. There had been countless moments on the island when he'd been taken aback by her beauty, but right now, with her sun-kissed skin glowing and the stress of their life-and-death situation during the storm no longer showing its effects, she absolutely stole his breath away. "There she is."

Allison grabbed at the kitchen counter and dragged one leg into the kitchen, followed by the other. Zane peeked around the island and saw what was slowing her down—Scott's five-year-old daughter, Lily, had wrapped herself around Allison's ankle. "Sorry. I'm having some trouble walking today," Allison said. She gave her eyebrows a conspiratorial bounce.

"I noticed there's a large growth on your leg. I'd better take a look at it and make sure it's not anything contagious." He crouched down and looked Lily in the eye. The little girl was already giggling. "I might need to administer the tickle test."

"Noooo!" Lily unspooled herself from Allison's leg, rolled across the floor and scrambled off behind her mother.

"Miss Thing," Brittney said. "You and Franklin need to go get washed up for dinner."

"Can we eat in front of the TV?" Lily asked, warily peering at Zane.

"Yes. I think the grown-ups would enjoy some adult conversation anyway."

Scott scooped up Lily into his arms. "Come on. Let's go hunt down your brother."

Brittney nodded to two empty wineglasses on the kitchen counter. "Why don't you two grab a drink for yourselves? We'll be ready to eat in a little bit."

"You sure we can't help?" Allison asked.

"I'm sure. Cooking is one of the only things that relax me," Brittney said.

"Wine?" Zane glanced at Allison, wondering how she was feeling about being around him. She had every reason in the world to give him some steely attitude. And he was going to have to find a way to work through it. "We can go out on the balcony and catch up."

"About what? Not much has happened since yesterday."

He knew then that he was going to have to try a little harder. "You can tell me how your meeting with your client went."

Allison found it impossible to swallow and not much easier to breathe. Zane had picked the one topic of conversation she did not want to explore, especially not when he was looking good enough to eat. Damn him. It was one thing when he was wearing a pair of board shorts, but there was something about Zane in a pair of perfectly tailored flat-front trousers and a dress shirt, with the sleeves rolled up to the elbows, that absolutely slayed her. He would always have her number. Even when he'd been a jerk to her. Even when he was going around picking uncomfortable things to discuss. "Wine sounds great, but I'd rather skip work talk. It's been a long day."

"Whatever you want."

He poured them each a glass of wine, and she tried to ignore the pull he had on her. It came from the vicinity of her belly button, although just being around him made the more feminine parts of her body quake and yearn, as well. They stepped out onto the patio overlooking the back of Scott and Brittney's beautiful wooded lot. The early-evening air was warm and breezy, hearkening back to their time on the island. Part of her wanted to go back so badly and relive every unbelievable minute, but she knew that wasn't reality, and one thing she prided herself on, aside from her predilection for fantasies about Zane, was her ability to stay grounded.

"Did you sleep well last night?" He took a sip of his wine after he posed the question, regarding her with a look that took no effort from him and still felt like pure seduction.

"Like the proverbial rock."

"We didn't get much sleep during that last day or so on the island, did we?" He leaned against the balcony railing, inexplicably turning her on by leaving his firm forearms on display.

She smiled. Heat rushed to her face. "No, we did not. That damn storm kept us up."

A subtle blush colored his cheeks, and he hung his head, nodding. "Right. It was the storm that kept us awake. The weather was nothing if not distracting."

She sucked in a deep breath. She loved this glimmer of normalcy between them, their ability to fall into a fun back-and-forth, but it only made her crave more. Was there a way to get beyond the things standing between them? Even if Scott was ever able to get over himself, the Black Crescent problem was inescapable. Her meeting had gone exceptionally well today. She wasn't about to turn her back on hard-earned success, no matter how much she knew it would anger Zane. Yes, she would come clean, but everything else was on Zane. It was his choice. Not hers.

She glanced over her shoulder to make sure Scott or Brittney wasn't looking. "No matter what, I will never regret what happened, Zane. I need you to know that. It was amazing."

He straightened to his full height, leaving her in the shadow of his towering frame, and touched her arm gently. How could he bring her entire body to life with only an instant of caring contact? "Yes. Of course. I feel the same way."

Her heart began to gallop in her chest, beating an uneven rhythm.

"Dinner's ready." Scott was standing at the door to the balcony. His vision noticeably landed on Zane's hand touching Allison's arm.

Allison reflexively pulled back from Zane, and he did the same. The instant it happened, a wave of guilt blanketed her. Resentment followed. These games were so stupid. And idiotic. She had to put an end to them. Part of that was finding the right time to tell Zane about Black Crescent. "On our way."

Allison and Zane joined Scott and Brittney in the dining room. On the front of the house, it had a splendid view of the front yard, and was appointed with all of the elegant trappings of a comfortable life. Allison didn't like to get too wrapped up in material things. There was plenty of that going on in LA. Still, she could admit that she wanted this for herself. She wanted a husband and a house and children. More to the point, she wanted love and a life partner. She wanted it all.

The spread Brittney put out was truly spectacular—filet mignon cooked to an ideal medium-rare, with rosemary roasted baby potatoes and green beans. The wine Zane had brought was a sublime complement to the meal, and Scott seemed nothing if not relaxed and content because of it. The conversation was fun and light, full of laughs and interesting stories. Zane and Scott told tales—a few from high school, but most from recent years, stories about pickup basketball, epic golf tournaments and even a few nights out drinking. All Allison could think as she watched Zane and Scott together was that she didn't merely appreciate that they had such a solid friendship, but that she also loved being witness to it. It was a real shame that Zane was a no-go because he was her brother's best friend. In a lot of ways, it was also what made him perfect.

There were a few moments when Zane delivered a knowing glance with his piercing gaze, leaving Allison to grapple with the resulting hum in her body. Did he know that he could affect her like that without so much as a brush of a finger against the back of her hand? Did he know how much it made her want him, and how frustrating it made the knowledge that she'd never likely experience his touch again?

At the end of the meal, the conversation continued in the kitchen as the four of them cleaned up. They were just about finished when Lily walked in, complaining of a stomachache.

"Come on, sweetheart," Brittney said. "It's probably time for you to go to bed anyway. Why don't you say good-night to Aunt Allison and Uncle Zane?"

Lily merely waved at them, curling into her mom's hip. "Good night."

Allison crouched down to give Lily a kiss on the forehead. "Sweet dreams, Lils."

"Good night."

"I'm going to help Brittney with bedtime. I'll be back in a few minutes," Scott said.

The quiet in the kitchen when her brother left was deafening. She and Zane had just been presented with the same scenario they'd been in last month. Except this time, the playing field had definitely changed. Gone were many of Allison's old reservations, replaced by newer and more intense ones. She didn't have to wonder how badly it hurt to be rejected by Zane. She'd experienced it firsthand.

"I forgot you were staying here." Zane took a step closer to her.

"Yes. I always do. The guest room is beautiful. Very comfortable." She leaned back against the kitchen island, gripping the cool marble counter with both hands.

"Good bed?" he asked.

She laughed and shook her head. "Smooth, Zane. Real smooth."

He shrugged and inched even closer. "I had an opening, I had to take it." His hand was inches from hers. He reached out with his thumb and lightly caressed her fingers.

A zip of electricity wound its way down her spine. "Zane…"

"Yes? That is my name." He slipped his fingers under her hand and lifted it to his lips. It made her dizzy.

"My brother."

"His name is Scott. And he's in the other room. And we're here. And I've missed you." He kissed her hand again, except this time, he closed his eyes and seemed to savor it.

She nearly passed out, but she had to keep her head straight. "You're being so goofy. You missed me? I just saw you yesterday."

He opened his eyes. "I know. And I was an ass by the dock."

Hard to believe that had only been thirty-six hours ago. It felt like a lifetime. "Yes, you were. I get it, but it doesn't change the fact that I wasn't a fan."

Scott's voice came from the hall.

"Come on. Let's get out of here." Zane tugged on her hand.

"What? Now? Where?" Her vision darted to the kitchen entry, then back to Zane.

He rolled his eyes. "So many questions." He pulled her back into the dining room, where they could buy a few more seconds of privacy. "Come to my place, Allison. I want to be alone with you. I need to be alone with you."

Her pulse went to thundering in her body the way it had during the storm. "What about what you said to me at the dock?"

"I was an idiot. I'm sorry."

"There's more to it, and you know that. What about Scott?"

"Now you sound like me." He again raised her hand to his lips and delivered a soul-bending kiss. "No more excuses. Let's get out of here, spend some time together and we'll deal with him later. I need to be alone with you, Allison."

How in the hell could she say no to that? She couldn't, even when there was a small part of her that wanted to press him for more. For an explanation. For clarification about everything. But the reality was that she'd been waiting forever to hear him saying something so desperate, especially unprompted. So she'd take Zane's offer. Even if it ended up being only sex. One more time. "What do we tell Scott?"

Zane pulled his phone out of his pocket and tapped away at the screen. He showed it to her. Taking your sister for a drive. Thanks for dinner.

"That's it?" she asked.

"That's it." He tapped at his screen one more time, took her hand and out the door they went.

Just like Allison had always wanted.

CHAPTER ELEVEN

THIS WAS CRAZY. Absolutely certifiable. But something about the impetuousness of stealing away from her brother's house with Zane, like a couple of brazen teenagers, made it so thrilling. Perhaps it was because at this time yesterday, when they'd been on the plane back to New Jersey, she'd been convinced this was never going to happen again. It might be foolish and stupid, but she had a glimmer of optimism. She hoped like hell Zane wouldn't end up quashing it again. If he did, the disappointment would be of her making. She'd said yes to this. She'd gone with him because her heart had convinced her to take another chance.

Zane was showing off with the car, taking turns a little too fast, changing lanes when he had a whisper-thin margin of error and generally acting as though he didn't care about repercussions. Allison sat back in the seat and allowed him his macho moment while she studied his grip on the steering wheel and counted the seconds until they would be at his place and those glorious hands of his could be all over her naked body.

The trip probably clocked in at under twenty minutes, but all of that anticipation made it feel as though it had been a cross-country trek. She'd never been to Zane's place before, which was in one of the newest and most exclusive neighborhoods in town. The street was lined with stately houses, but Allison found Zane's to be the most beautiful. Tucked away on top of a hill, a long stone driveway leading to it, the sprawling home was an oasis in this bustling town. She couldn't help but think about how it was so much like Zane—on its own, standing apart, quietly magnificent.

He opened one of three garage bays and pulled the car inside. Two other gleaming sports cars and a motorcycle were already parked there. Zane had done well for himself with his business. That much was clear. He turned off the ignition, and they were both noticeably rushing to get inside. He opened the door for her, shut off his security system via a keypad and took her hand, marching through the mostly dark house. They traveled through an unbelievable kitchen, nearly three times the size of Allison's back in LA, then down a central hall toward the back of the house. Allison was busy trying to look at everything—she wanted to soak up every bit of Zane's tastes. She wanted to scrutinize the artwork and try to speculate about what had drawn him to the pieces he'd chosen. She wanted to do the same with furniture and paint colors. She wanted to know him inside and out.

"A tour would be nice," she said when they'd reached a set of tall double doors at the end of the hall.

Zane pushed them open and flipped a light switch. "I know. Let's start here."

Allison stepped into the most stunning, jaw-dropping bedroom she'd ever seen, which was saying a lot since Zane was adjusting the dimmer to a level fit for seduction. The space was like something out of a magazine, with a soaring cathedral ceiling, a spacious seating area to one side with a modern charcoal-gray sectional sofa and a TV, and at the very center of the room, a gorgeously appointed bed. She took her chance to run her hand over the crisp white duvet, the threads silky beneath her touch. This room was nothing short of sheer perfection.

Zane came up behind her, gripping her shoulders and pressing his long frame against her back. He kissed her neck softly, bringing her body to a gentle boil. "Do you approve?"

Allison's eyes drifted shut, luxuriating in the action of his lips as he skimmed them over the delicate spot beneath her ear. "Which part? The room or your amazing mouth?"

He spun her around and wrapped her up in his arms, drawing her flat against his chest and kissing her deeply. His tongue wasn't playing—he was determined, consumed by a drive she could not see, but could certainly feel. "You were all I could think about last night. And this morning. And all day at work."

"Really?" she asked, grinning to herself in the dark.

"Yes, really."

"What were you thinking?" She'd shared her fantasy with him…if he'd taken the time to think up one about her, she wanted to hear it. Every last word.

"About you and the sarong." He dug his fingers into her hair, gently tugging at her nape to encourage her to drop her head to one side.

"I'm listening. What else?"

His mouth, hot and wet, skated down the length of her neck, settling in the slope where it met her shoulder. One hand went to the zipper on her dress, slowly drawing it down while the other grabbed her backside. "I'm not as good at this as you are."

"Something tells me you could be great at this if you just applied yourself." She untucked his shirt and threaded her hands underneath it, exploring the landscape of his muscled back. "Don't think too much about it. Just tell me what happens with me and you and the sarong." To encourage him, she placed one hand flat on his crotch and rubbed his erection through his dress pants.

A raspy groan escaped his throat. "I untie it. I take it off."

She unhooked his belt, unbuttoned his trousers and unzipped them. Slipping her hand down the front of his boxer briefs, she caressed his solid length with her fingers. "Good. What else?"

"In my fantasy, you're already naked. No bathing suit." With a pop, he undid the clasp of her bra, then pulled the dress and the rest of the ensemble forward, leaving her chest bare to him. "I love your breasts. They're so perfect. Silky and velvety. I love the way they fit in my hands. So I do this." He lowered his head, cupped both breasts with his hands and swirled his tongue around her nipple. Teasing. Flicking. Then sucking.

Allison's eyes fluttered shut as white flames of lust seemed to envelop her thighs. She was so hot for him already. Having him tell her what he liked about her body was only heightening the experience. "That feels so good, Zane. You have no idea."

He dropped to his knees, pulling her dress down to the floor. She kicked her heels off, and he sat back on his haunches, gazing up at her like she was a goddess. "You didn't have these panties on in my fantasy, but I like them. They're sexy." He hooked his finger under the waistband of her lacy black undies, traveling from one hip to the other, just gently grazing her most delicate area at the center. "But they need to go." He tugged them past her hips, leaving her to step out of them. Then he stood back up. "In my fantasy, you're so wet for me."

Allison thought she might melt into a puddle. She also knew she couldn't take so little nakedness from him. Her fingers flew through the buttons of his shirt as he reached down between her legs, separating her delicate folds with his fingers.

"Yes. Exactly like this." He rubbed her apex firmly in a circle, kissing her neck again, using his tongue to drive her wild. With every rotation of his hand, he was sending her toward her peak. Pushing her closer to the edge.

"I want you. There's no hiding it." It took every ounce of strength she had to push his pants to the floor, but she had to have him in her hand. She needed to even the score between them. She stroked firmly, from base to tip, and kissed his chest. "What comes next?"

"Then I make love to you in several gravity-defying positions." He laughed against his lips. "I turned myself into quite the performer in this fantasy."

She smiled, but she wanted to explore this idea. She wanted to know his steamiest thoughts and act on them. "Show me."

"Really?" He ran his tongue along his lower lip, showing her his trepidation.

"Yes." She nodded and looked him right in the eye, wanting him to know how serious she was.

"Okay, then." He took her hand and led her over to the bedside table, where he opened a drawer and pulled out a box of condoms. He handed her the foil packet. "In my fantasy, you put it on for me."

"Accuracy is very important in a fantasy." She took her time, tearing it open, then carefully rolling it on, eliciting a groan of pleasure from Zane as she did it.

"Up against the wall." She stepped to the side of the table, where there was an expanse of open space. She placed her back to the wall, and he reached down for one of her legs and hitched it over his hip.

Allison wrapped her calf around him and watched as he took his erection in his hand and positioned himself at her entrance. He drove about halfway inside, taking her breath away, then pulled her other leg up around him. Her body weight rested against the wall, but his hands cradled her backside. This angle was incredibly gratifying from the start—it let her sink deep down onto him, centering the pressure in the ideal spot. She rocked her hips forward and back, her entire body buzzing with pleasure. She was close. So close.

"Was it like this?" She dug her fingers into his hair and kissed him, relishing the tension in his body right now—the flex of his biceps and forearms as he held her up and the tautness of his abs with every stroke.

"This is better," he said. "You're better in real life. The stuff that's in my head doesn't come close to the real you." The kiss he laid on her then was one for the ages, intense and raw. Honest and sincere. It sent her body over the edge, the peak rattling her to her very core, shaking her physically and mentally. Zane followed right after, pressing her harder against the wall as he rode out the waves of pleasure.

For a moment, neither said a thing, breaths coming fast and heavy as they coiled themselves around each other tighter. A thought flashed in her head, and she dared to utter it. "The fantasy just isn't enough anymore, Zane. I need this. So much more of this."

Zane's mind and body were reeling in the best possible way. It took every ounce of energy he had left to carry her over to the bed and set her down without dropping her. He was wonderfully spent.

He tossed aside the throw pillows littering the bed, then pulled back the duvet. Both a bit delirious, they found their way under the covers, immediately drawn to each other. Allison curled into his body and kissed his chest. He loved having her in his bed. As amazing as things had been on the island, this was different. The fantasy world had fallen away, but even framed by his everyday reality, being with Allison felt like a dream. Was he falling for her? The perpetual bachelor? His mom had certainly made a compelling case for his finally jettisoning those ways.

"You're so amazing," she muttered.

"You're the amazing one." The words came so fast. He didn't even have to think about them. That was it—he really had fallen. He'd gone through life telling himself that he wouldn't let it happen. He'd seen what it did to his parents when love fell apart. There was no way that risking that much pain could ever be worth it. But being here with Allison and knowing that his heart wanted nothing else made him realize that there was no way to build up an immunity to love. It had taken the right woman to show him that. The perfect woman. Allison. He caressed her naked back with his hand. "No argument?" He'd half expected her to dispute his claim that she was the amazing one. Instead, she was being incredibly still and quiet. He must have really sent her to the moon and back. She'd certainly done that for him.

"I'm thinking."

"About what?"

"Everything."

He smiled in the dark. "Me, too." So many thoughts were swirling around in his head, all of them surprisingly good. When had things ever been like that? No time in recent history, that was for sure.

"I need to tell you something."

He'd been about to say the exact same thing, but she'd gotten to it first. "What is it?"

She drew in a breath so deep her entire body rose and fell in the cradle of his arm. "What I'm about to say... I just... I don't want you to get upset. But I would understand if you did." She rolled away from him and switched on the lamp on her side of the bed.

He squinted at the bright light. It got Zane's attention, and not just because he was enjoying the view of her naked backside while she was turned away. He sat up in bed. "Okay." Whatever she was about to say, he wanted to just get past it. He was tired of bad news and dire circumstances keeping him from happiness. Whatever it was, they would find a way around it. "Please. Just tell me. I can take it."

She grabbed a corner of the comforter and covered herself up. "First off, the job I'm working on here in Falling Brook is going really well. They've put me on retainer for the next month, and if things go the way I think they will, it will become permanent. They would be a big enough client for me to move back to Falling Brook. To stay here in town."

The relief Zane felt was immense. It was like someone had been standing on his chest and they'd finally stepped off. "That's amazing. I'm so happy for you." In truth, he was happy for *them*. Long distance would have been terrible and certainly no way for them to truly move forward together. Now he had one less thing to worry about.

"Thanks. I'm really happy about it, too. I've worked really hard for this."

Now that he'd had a minute for this news to sink in, his brain was starting to catch up. Falling Brook was a small town. Most businesspeople who lived here were CEOs or senior management for big corporations in the city, not local operations like Zane's. But who could it be? "And this company is based right here in town?"

"Yes, but hold on a minute. Before I get to that, I need to tell you that I realized tonight that I can't make the decision to stay here in Falling Brook until we have a discussion about us. And I don't want to hit you with some big heavy talk right now, especially after we just had totally mind-blowing sex, but I can't move back here and see you on the street or at the Java Hut and not be able to walk up to you and hug you. Kiss you and hold your hand. I've done that before and it nearly killed me."

Now he was starting to see where she was coming from, and he was totally on board. In fact, he couldn't ignore the happy feeling in his heart. She wanted him and he wanted her, for more than just sex. "So we need to come clean with Scott. I completely agree. We can either do it together or if you want, I can tell him on my own and then you guys can have your own talk. But no matter what, I think we need to make it clear that this isn't us asking him for permission. In the end, we're our own people. We make our own decisions. We have to do what's right for us."

She dropped her shoulders, seeming frustrated. "Yes. I completely agree. That is all true and that does need to happen. Right away. But first, there's one more thing I have to tell you."

An unsettling quiet filled the room. "Is this the thing that might upset me?"

"Yes."

His heart hammered. "Please tell me. Say it and get it over with."

"The client is Black Crescent."

The blood drained from Zane's face so fast that it made him sick. This couldn't possibly be happening. No. Absolutely not. How could what was starting to work out perfectly take such a nightmarish turn? "You're working for Black Crescent." He sat up a little straighter in bed. "You, quite possibly the most decent and upstanding person I know, are working for the most evil and vile company imaginable. You're working for the devil. Why would you do that?" With every word out of his mouth, his disgust grew. "Why would you even entertain the idea?"

"Zane, come on. Isn't that all a little overdramatic?"

Zane had been trying to keep himself in check, but that word pissed him off. He'd had it lobbed at him before, and he disliked it greatly. He threw back the covers and scrambled out of bed, plucking his underwear from the floor and putting them back on. He was so full of anger right now it felt like it might bubble up out the top of his head. He had to move to keep his mind straight. And he couldn't be naked in bed with Allison anymore. "Is that why you said all of that stuff to me on the island about letting it go? Is that why you were being so secretive about your work calls?" He ran his hand through his hair, pacing back and forth across his bedroom floor. "Does that Ryan guy work for BC? No wonder I had a bad feeling about him."

"Ryan is a candidate to take Joshua Lowell's place."

Zane's stomach turned. "So the guy you were talking to while we were on the island is going to be the new Josh Lowell? That's just awesome." He sincerely hoped the sarcasm was hitting home for her. He didn't want to be a jerk again, but he needed her to understand how hurt he was right now.

"Maybe. He's just interviewing right now. Actually, you should meet him. He's a really nice guy. I think you would like him. I think you would like all of the people who are interviewing for the job."

Zane made a point of looking at her as though she'd lost her mind. He didn't want to ask the question out loud, but he wasn't afraid to suggest it by other means. This entire line of think-ing was so off base.

"Honestly," she continued. "I think you would really like Josh if you got to know him. In a lot of ways, he's just as much a victim of his dad as you are. None of what happened was your fault, but it wasn't his fault, either."

And to think, Zane had been so sure that Allison understood him. Now he knew that he was wrong. So very wrong. "That's okay. I think I'll skip the part of this scenario where you whip up some dream of Josh Lowell and me becoming best friends. I realize that it's your special talent to come up with fantasies."

"That's really mean. And completely uncalled for."

"It's the truth."

Allison grumbled under her breath. "You know what, Zane? Screw you. That's not what I was suggesting. All I'm saying is that I think you need to take a deep breath, try to take a step back and look at this from my perspective. You can't undo what happened, okay? You need to let it go. I'm sorry, but you do. At some point, you're going to have to get over this or you're just going to be stuck forever."

Zane disliked a lot of things, but he despised it when anyone told him to get over Black Crescent. His entire life had been ground into the dirt by the greed of the Lowell family. He and his parents had been treated like they were nothing, taken for their family fortune and cast aside, with absolutely zero reper-cussions for those who committed the crime. That injustice sat in the depths of his belly every day. He couldn't "just get over it." It was impossible. "I'm not talking about this anymore. You were there for the fallout. You know how badly I was hurt. You saw it firsthand. I not only shouldn't have to explain it to you, I won't."

"I'm sure you're going to say this is just a cliché, but every black cloud has a silver lining. If Vernon Lowell hadn't taken off with that money, you and I never would have met. You and Scott wouldn't have the friendship you have today. Black Cres-cent isn't all bad. I wish that you could see that."

"And I wish you could see why that is beside the point." He scanned her face, desperate for some sign of the Allison he so adored. Right now, it was hard to imagine he'd dared to think about the future with her. How could he have been so stupid? "I think you should go home."

"Seriously?"

"Seriously."

Allison whipped back the comforter and grabbed her dress from the floor where it had landed earlier. She threaded her arms through it, wrapped it around her body and zipped it. "You drove me here. I'm not using a ride app this time of night. I've heard too many scary stories about women ending up with creepy drivers."

Zane plucked his pants from the floor and fished his car keys out of the pocket. "Take my car. I'll get it back from you later." He tossed them to her.

She caught them, staring down at her hand for a moment. "Oh, right. Zane Patterson, the golden boy, the super successful entrepreneur, has an entire garage full of cars. He has them to spare."

"That's right. That's me. Mr. Perfect." Right now, he felt as far from that as he'd quite possibly ever felt. If that was what Allison truly thought, she'd lost it. So had his mom, for that matter.

"Goodbye, Zane. I'll let myself out." She pivoted on her heel and headed for the bedroom door.

"You *knew* this was going to happen, Allison. You knew this would be my reaction. Nothing about the conversation we just had should come as any surprise. And you knew it the whole time we were on the island, didn't you?"

She stopped in the doorway and turned back to him. "I'd foolishly hoped for a better outcome."

"You don't understand what this is like for me."

She shook her head with a pitying look in her eyes. "I do understand it, Zane. And I don't know what I have to do to convince you of that."

CHAPTER TWELVE

SCOTT BELLOWED AT the guest room door. "Zane Patterson, I know you're in there. Get out here. You have some explaining to do."

Allison pried open one eye and looked at the alarm clock on the bedside table. The numbers were a bit blurry, probably because she'd taken a sleeping pill last night after her big knockdown, drag-out fight with Zane. She was only half-awake.

Boom boom boom. Scott pounded on the door. "Up and at 'em, you two."

Allison scrambled out of bed. She wanted to shut her brother up before he woke up the entire house. She did *not* want her niece and nephew thinking the worst of her. She opened the door, leaving a space just wide enough to talk to him. "He's not here. Will you please be quiet? It's freaking six thirty in the morning."

"You know I get up early to work out."

"Good for you. I'm going back to bed." She left the door ajar and shuffled across the room, flopping down on the mattress. Her motivation was gone. In a lot of ways, it felt like her whole life was gone. She didn't want to work today. She didn't want to talk to anyone or go anywhere. She wanted to call in sick to life.

Unfortunately, Scott had followed her into the room and was standing at the foot of the bed. "Why is his car outside?"

"He gave it to me to drive home last night. He has several cars, you know. He gave me an extra." Last night was still a blur. It had started so amazingly and gone so incredibly wrong. She'd worried that Zane would take the Black Crescent news badly, but she'd underestimated the scope. She'd certainly never imagined he'd toss her out of his house.

"What in the world is going on, Alli?"

Allison sat up in bed and scooted back until she was leaning against the headboard. She blew out a breath of frustration and crossed her arms over her chest. Was she really ready to spill the beans to Scott? This was not going to be a fun conversation. But she had to take what had been handed to her, fun or not. She patted the mattress. "Come. Sit."

Scott joined her, but she sensed that he was deeply uncomfortable. He was sitting like he had a board strapped to his back. His shoulders were tight, as was his whole face. He had to know what was coming next.

"Zane and I slept together when we were in the Bahamas."

"I knew it." He practically pounced on her with his words. "I knew that was going to happen. I warned you, and you just couldn't listen to me, could you? I'm just the lame older brother who's too heavy-handed with advice."

"I didn't listen because I didn't want to, okay? Scott, you need to know that I have had a thing for Zane since I was a teenager. We're talking fifteen years. I always hoped that it would go away, but it just didn't."

"What? No way. I would've seen it."

She pressed her lips together tightly. The years of longing for Zane would always bring a sting to her eyes, but they especially did now. "I'm serious. I'm just really good at hiding it. I can always put on a good face."

"So when you guys were acting so odd at my party, was that part of it?"

"We kissed that night."

"Ugh." His voice was rife with disgust. "Did you guys make a plan to meet up at Rose Cove? Has this been in the works the whole time?"

She shook her head. "No. It was just dumb luck, believe it or not." Now it felt like tragic luck. If it hadn't happened, her heart wouldn't be in tatters.

Scott got up from the bed and began pacing. "I love him, but I'm going to kill him. I told him you were off-limits, and he completely disrespected my wishes."

She pinched the bridge of her nose and made an inward plea for strength. "Will you stop jumping to conclusions and let me talk, please?"

He turned back to her with a distinct scowl on his face. "So talk."

"When I kissed him, he freaked out. He said he could never betray you. That's why he left that night. And it was a big topic of conversation on the island. He refused to let it go. Believe me, Zane put your wishes first."

"Until he didn't."

"Until *we* didn't. It was both of us. We both wanted to do it, and we both knew exactly what we were doing."

Scott grimaced. "Please. Spare me the details."

Allison rolled her eyes. "I'm only saying that it was two adults doing what adults do. We were in a very intense situation with the storm and I guess that just made everything that much more heightened. As soon as we were rescued, he wanted things to go back to the way they were before."

"Really?"

"Really."

"So then what happened last night?"

She shrugged. "He had second thoughts, I guess. So we went back to his place."

Scott held up a hand to keep her from saying more. "Okay.

I got it. But I don't understand. He made you drive yourself home?"

She shook her head. "Unfortunately, I had to tell him about Black Crescent. Things went really well there yesterday and I don't think it's going to be a onetime job. Joshua Lowell is putting in a good word for me, and he's put me on retainer for the next month. I was going to tell you yesterday, but I never had the chance."

Scott drew in a deep breath through his nose, the gears in his head clearly turning. "What did Zane say? Did he hit the roof?"

"He did. But then it snowballed from there and he just sort of shut down. That's when he asked me to leave. That's why I have his car."

"So what now? Is it over?"

Allison froze as a single tear rolled down her cheek. As upset as she'd been last night, she hadn't cried. But something about those three words—*is it over?*—made the dam break. "I don't know. I don't want to think that last night was the end, but I just don't know. He has such a grudge when it comes to Black Crescent and the Lowells. It's so frustrating."

"Well, of course it is, but it's not like there isn't a good reason for it. The scars you get as a young person are always the ones that feel the deepest. It's just the way life is."

Allison had never thought of it that way. She'd never seen a parallel between her life and Zane's. Until now. Her brother was right. The pain she had from years of Zane being her unrequited love was very real. And there was something about it that had always felt especially raw. She hadn't been able to start exploring it until the kiss at Scott's party, but it hit her hardest at Rose Cove. A single "no" from Zane was far more devastating than any rejection she'd ever experienced. "Yeah. I suppose you're right."

"And as the person with a front-row seat when his family fell apart, I can tell you that it was incredibly difficult for him. The number of nights we sat up with him talking and me listening? I couldn't begin to count. I don't really know that I was equipped to help him through it. All I could do was listen and be his friend. I'm guessing the guy needs some therapy."

"You're probably right, but that doesn't help at the moment. I don't know what to do to make any of this better, and I hate feeling so helpless. I feel like screaming. Isn't love more important than any of this? Isn't it supposed to conquer all?"

Now it was Scott's turn to remain perfectly still. "Do you love him?"

She nodded, her sadness morphing into conviction to put it all out there with her brother. She had to make this declaration to somebody, even if nothing ever came of it. "I do. The big dumb jerk. I love him. And I don't know what to say or do to help him get past this."

Scott sat back down on the bed and took her hands. "This is why I didn't want you to get involved with him. I never want to see you get hurt."

Allison saw her chance to finally sort this out with brother, hopefully once and for all. "Scott, life hurts. Love hurts. I don't want to sit on the sidelines and be an observer. I can take care of myself, and if I get hurt, I'll be okay. Even now, with my heart in twenty pieces, I know that I'll be okay. I have a good career and great friends and an amazing family I love more than anything. I know you still look at me and see that sick little girl in the hospital bed, but that isn't me anymore, and it hasn't been me for a long time."

Scott's eyes misted. He was a tough-as-nails guy, but this got to him. "I realize that I was just a kid when it happened, but I've never been as scared as I was when you were sick. Never."

Allison felt like her heart was going to break every time she listened to Scott or one of her parents talk about this. She hated that it was still so raw for them, but they'd all understood that it was a matter of life and death. She'd been too young to understand, but she wanted to believe that she did now. "I know, honey. But I'm fine. I'm here. And you need to let it go."

He cleared his throat and collected himself. "Just like Zane needs to let Black Crescent go?"

Apparently they all had things they needed to let go of. "Yes. If you can figure out how to make him do that, I'd love to hear your suggestions." From the bedside table, her phone beeped with a text. Her brain flew to the thought that it might be Zane, but when she consulted the screen, her heart sank with disappointment. It wasn't him. "Speak of the devil. It's Joshua Lowell. He wants me to come in to the BC offices this morning."

"A little early for a work text, isn't it?"

"Apparently he's like you. He doesn't like to sleep in, either."

Zane hadn't slept at all. Not a damn minute. And he couldn't begin to process what he was feeling. Every time he followed one line of thought, he got distracted by another. He'd start to think about Black Crescent, familiar anger and pain welling up inside him. The fact that his feelings about BC were now tied to Allison made it even more difficult to sort any of it out. Her betrayal ran deep, registering in the center of his chest and causing him physical pain. Allison knew how he felt about Black Crescent. She'd not only witnessed the initial fallout all those years ago, he'd told her everything he was still feeling when they were in the Bahamas. And she hadn't said a thing. Not a peep. That hurt most of all. They'd made love, and she'd known that what she was doing would hurt him. She'd known it all along.

There was no telling how any of this would work out. When he tried to see his future—the days and weeks beyond now— he still saw Allison there. He'd seen her there last night before everything fell apart, and now in the light of day, she was still there. He didn't want to imagine tomorrow, the next day or the day after that without her. She'd opened something up in him on the island. She'd done it again last night. It didn't feel as though he could shut the door on that, even if he wanted to. So how was he going to get past this?

One thing Allison had said last night kept bubbling to the

surface—how every black cloud had a silver lining. How BC had ruined one thing, but it had brought them together. It wasn't all bad, as much as he'd always seen it as such. And Allison in particular was easily the best thing that had happened to him ever. He couldn't fathom walking away from that. From her. It made no sense.

The realization made his end of the conversation from last night sting. He'd said some horrible things. He'd stupidly let his anger take control, as was so often the case with BC. If he was ever going to move forward in his life, he had to force himself to stop allowing what had happened with BC to define him. He was stronger than that. He knew that. He'd simply let his anger get the best of him.

He had to talk this out with Allison. He had to explain himself to Scott. He had to open himself up to the fact that he'd been wrong about more than a few things. His own mother had proved him wrong yesterday. Allison had done the same with everything she'd said about silver linings. And now he had to talk to her. To find a way through the mess he'd created from years of clinging to anger and resentment. This was about more than making amends. This was about making a future. He had to find Allison. Luckily, he knew exactly where to look.

He jumped in the shower, hoping a little hot water and soap might help to reset his head. He couldn't begin to figure out where to start with Allison. There was a part of him that wanted to confess his feelings and hope that would be enough to make her step away from Black Crescent. There was another part of him that wanted an apology. There was yet another piece of his soul that knew he should be the one to say he was sorry. He hated that his feelings were so jumbled out of control. He hated that he couldn't let everything go after all these years.

Freshly shaven and dressed for work, he drove his Porsche over to Scott's house. When he arrived, his BMW was parked out front, but Allison's zippy silver rental was noticeably absent from the driveway. Hopefully Scott had let her put it in the garage. He wasn't worried that she'd left town. Black Crescent was keeping her here for the foreseeable future. But he was concerned that she might not be home. He wasn't eager to chase her all over Falling Brook, but he would if that was his only option. He had to sort this out, and the only logical path started and ended with Allison.

He rang the doorbell, then stuffed his hands in his pockets. He'd never before been nervous to arrive at his best friend's house, and the feeling was unsettling.

Scott flung the door open, sweating profusely and wiping it from his forehead with a towel. "Looking for your car keys, I take it?" Scott's voice had a cutting edge. His best friend had never before taken that tone with him. He disliked it greatly.

"I'm actually looking for Allison. Is she here?" Zane peered around his best friend. "Can I come in?"

"I don't know, Zane. Right now, I'm trying to keep from punching you in the face."

At least Zane now knew that the cat was out of the bag. Clearly, Scott had been briefed on the state of his relationship with Allison. "You know I'll hit you right back, and then where will we be? Fighting in the middle of your front lawn for all of your fine and upstanding neighbors to see."

Scott stepped back and opened the front door wider. "Fine. Come in." He closed it as soon as Zane walked past him. "I could literally kill you for sleeping with Allison. How could you treat her like one of your hookups? She's my damn sister. You're my best friend, for God's sake."

Zane turned back to Scott. The guilt he bore from his own actions was eclipsed by his best friend's misguided characterization of what had happened. "I did *not* treat her like a hookup. I care about her. Deeply." He felt the wobble in his own voice before he heard it. As if he needed any more confirmation that he was in deep with Allison. "That's why I'm here. I need to talk to her."

"She left about ten minutes ago."

"It's not even eight o'clock. Where did she go?"

"I'm not sure I should tell you."

Zane swallowed the bile that rose in his throat. His best friend still felt the need to protect his sister from Zane. He had to put an end to that. "Look, man, you and I have got to get past this. I know I crossed a line, but you need to know that I did not do it without thinking about it hard, and for a very long time. I fought our attraction as long as I could, but in the end, Allison made a compelling case. I'm drawn to her, and she's drawn to me. We work well together, and we care a lot about each other." Zane directed his gaze down at his feet, knowing he wasn't 100 percent certain about her side of that assertion. "Well, I care deeply about her. I think she cares about me."

"Yeah?" Scott asked, seeming unimpressed.

"Yes, Scott. I care about her. I want to see where that can go."

"You. The guy with the revolving door in his pants."

"Hey. Am I not entitled to want more? Do I not get to change the direction of my life because I've found the right girl and I want to be with her? You found that with Brittney, and you're happy. In fact, you love to remind me of it. All the time." Zane again looked Scott square in the eye. "Please don't torpedo our friendship because I'm looking for the same thing that you have. It's not fair."

Scott drew a deep breath through his nose and leaned against the doorway into the dining room. "You have to swear to me that you will not intentionally hurt her."

"Of course."

"You promise?"

"Yes."

Scott clapped his hand on Zane's shoulder. "Okay then. You have my blessing."

"Now tell me where she is."

"She's at Black Crescent."

Just when Zane thought he couldn't take another shock to the system, he got another. Black Crescent was the exact last place on the planet he wanted to visit. Was this the universe's way of forcing him to deal with every sticking point in his life all on one day? If that was the case, bring it on. He was done letting BC define him. He certainly wasn't going to let it stand in the way of what he really wanted—Allison. "Got it. Thanks." Zane reached for the doorknob.

"Don't make a fool of yourself, okay?"

Zane opened the door. "I won't embarrass Allison, if that's what you're trying to say. I would never put her job in jeopardy."

"Good."

"As for me, I've already made myself look like an idiot. Things can't get any worse." With that, Zane rushed down the driveway to his car. He knew that his conversation with Scott was as close as they would ever come to working things out in regard to Allison. If this next part went well, he and Scott would hopefully return to their affable, hypercompetitive dynamic. Another outcome to wish for.

"I can't believe I'm doing this," he muttered to himself when he pulled into the Black Crescent parking lot. He'd come here a few short weeks ago to come clean to Joshua Lowell about the anonymous DNA report he'd received and shared. Unfortunately, Josh had left the office. It took several hours, but Zane had been able to track him down in a bar in the neighboring town. Zane wished he could erase that entire chapter of his personal story with BC. He never should have gotten involved. He never should have let Josh get under his skin.

He pulled into a space with a decent view of the entrance, rolled down the windows and sent a text to his assistant letting her know that at best, he'd be late getting in the office. In truth, he hoped against hope that he and Allison could work everything out and he wouldn't feel driven to go to work at all.

An hour passed. Then another. He knew better than to waltz into that office and ask for her, but damn he was tempted. He didn't want to wait. Impatience was gnawing at him. But he stayed put, running through the words he wanted to say, pray-

ing that somehow it all worked out. Even with all that prepara-
tion, he wasn't truly ready when Allison walked out of the BC
building, looking like a million bucks in a sleek black skirt,
white blouse and heels. She was smiling. A big, wide grin.
And it stole more than a breath. It knocked the wind out of him.

The Zane of old would've allowed her facial expression to
send him into a downward spiral. How could anyone walk out
of that building and be happy? But he knew that his old thinking had gotten him nowhere. It had left him running in circles.
Allison's business was important to her. It must have been a
good meeting. He had to believe that whatever had happened
in that building had made her happy. And that made *him* happy,
which was yet another reason to see BC in a different light. Yes,
his old life had been ended by forces within that company. But
his new life, the one that left him with a sliver of a chance with
Allison Randall, had started at the same time.

He jumped out of his car and called her name. "Allison!"

She startled, then swiped off her sunglasses. "Zane? You
came to Black Crescent? Are you insane?"

"Maybe a little," he muttered to himself.

"What in the world are you doing here?" she asked, incredu-
lous, marching toward him.

He rushed over to her and didn't wait another minute to just
come out with it. "I'm sorry. So sorry about last night. I was
wrong."

She shook her head. "No, Zane. I was wrong. I should've told
you back on the island. Before anything happened. That was
wrong of me, and I'm sorry that I did it."

Relief washed over him in a deluge. All was not lost. He
took her hand, loving the feel of her silky skin against his. "It's
okay. I forgive you."

"If anything, it should tell you how much I was worried
about messing things up with you. I had to have my chance,
and I couldn't bring myself to jeopardize it by coming clean."

He brought her hand to his lips and kissed it. He wanted to be able to do that every day. Forever and ever. "That's the sweetest thing anyone has ever said to me."

She turned for an instant and glanced back at the building. "I hope you know it's just a job. I mean, I will kick some serious butt for them, but it's what I do. It's not out of some grand allegiance to the company or the Lowell family. It's out of a commitment to being a professional, working hard and supporting myself and Kianna. That's all it is."

He nodded. "I know. And I get it. You weren't afraid to do the thing no one would've expected you to do. You're great at taking chances. It's something I need to get better at."

"I took a chance when I kissed you that first time."

"That's the perfect example. I need to stop playing it safe." He swallowed back the emotion of the moment, of how much she meant to him and how grateful he was that she'd stuck around and kept pushing when he'd been doing nothing but putting up walls. He was so lucky to have her in his life. "When you've lost everything, it's just easier to play it safe. Don't risk a thing. Don't put anything of importance on the line. Friendship. Your heart. But then you came along and took my heart from me. You have it, Alli."

She cocked her head to one side. "I do?"

"Yes. And I don't want it back." He took her hand and pressed it flat against the center of his chest. It had hurt so badly that morning, and now it was nothing but impossibly warm. A single touch from her and he was healed. "I want you to keep it forever. Promise me that you'll hold on to it. I love you, Allison Randall, and I don't want you to ever forget that."

Her eyes lit up, bright and brilliant. "Oh, God, Zane. I love you, too." She gripped his elbows and leaned into him. "I think I've loved you since the moment I met you."

His heart felt as though it had swelled to twice its normal size. He hadn't realized how little hope he had that she'd return the sentiment until the words crossed her lovely lips. They fell into the most memorable kiss yet—it was an unspoken promise, wrapped up in years of friendship, tied with a wish for forever.

They came up for air, and he rested his forehead against hers, holding her close, not wanting to let her go ever. "I want it all with you, Allison. I realize it hasn't even been a week since we first slept together, but I know that the foundation is there between us. I don't want to wait to build our life together. The two of us. Forever and ever. Husband and wife. Best friends. Platinum bands and wedding bells."

She bit down on her lower lip. "A Rose Cove honeymoon in a cottage up on the hill?"

"Will it make you say yes?"

"I don't need a trip to an island to know that I'll love you forever, Zane. Of course I'm saying yes. A million times yes."

EPILOGUE

One month later

ANGELIQUE AND ALLISON'S mom walked into Angelique's bedroom at the exact right moment—Kianna was putting the finishing touches on Allison's bridal hair.

"So beautiful," her mom said, smiling, then kissing Allison on the cheek.

"The most beautiful," Angelique added.

Allison's heart was already so full of love, she wasn't sure how she'd survive the wedding. She knew she'd better prepare. There was only a half hour until they'd walk from Angelique and Hubert's house for the dock at Rose Cove. From there, Marcus would be taking everyone via boat to Mako Island. Zane had decided it was only fitting that they get married there. He liked the idea that no one else would ever be able to say that their wedding had taken place on that particular patch of sand in the Caribbean.

As for Allison, she was simply glad that they'd decided to have the ceremony be a small and informal affair. Only so many people could fit on Mako Island, so they'd kept the guest list small—Scott, Brittney and the kids, Zane's mom and dad, Allison's parents, Angelique and Hubert, and Kianna. The dress code was decidedly casual—bare feet and flip-flops, shorts and sundresses, hats and sunglasses. Allison had gone with a new white bathing suit—a simple one-piece for modesty since her parents were in attendance, but with a plunging back for Zane's required sexy factor. A white sarong embroidered with silver threads wrapped at her waist completed the look. Zane had once said that he loved her flair for fashion, and she was happy her bridal ensemble perfectly reflected her individual style. She could not have gotten away with this getup in Falling Brook. All the more reason to be glad to be far away from that.

"It's so amazing that you were able to get the guest cottages fixed up in time for the wedding," Kianna said to Angelique. "From everything Allison said, things were pretty messy."

"My husband was highly motivated. He had a crew out here as soon as Alli called to tell us the news. He didn't want her second visit this year to Rose Cove to be anything less than perfect," Angelique said. "It was mostly water damage. Luckily, all of the building structures rode out the storm just fine."

"I'm so glad," Allison said. "It could've been so much worse." Although that scary weather event had caused so much heartache, she was still oddly thankful for it. It forced her and Zane to get past their other issues. It brought them together. If it hadn't happened, she might have spent the rest of her vacation holed up in her cottage, mad at Zane. And the rest of her life feeling as though something big was missing.

"How is your husband doing?" Kianna asked Angelique.

"Hubert is a new man. The doctor gave him a clean bill of health, so it looks like we're in the clear, which is a huge relief."

A knock came at the door and Brittney poked her head inside. "I think they're ready for you. It's only forty-five minutes until sunset."

"Angelique, we'd better get the flowers," Allison's mom said. "We'll meet you on the boat, sweetheart." She cupped Allison's face. "I love you. Always."

Moments like that reminded Allison how precious her family's love was. It wasn't a burden as she'd sometimes felt. "I love you, too, Mom."

Angelique and her mom left, while Kianna made one final adjustment to the tropical flowers in Allison's hair.

"Thank you for being here for this," Allison said. "I know it's a pain to fly across the country to spend time in Falling Brook, then all the way down here."

She shook her head. "Do not thank me. I'm over the moon to be here. I couldn't feel more honored. Plus, I'd better get used to flying great distances to see you."

"You're sure you're okay with us running a bicoastal operation?"

"I don't want to do it forever, if that's what you're asking, but I'm cool with it for the next several years. You got a one-month extension on the Black Crescent retainer, and we'll see how that plays out. Sounds like your future hubby wants us to do some recruiting for his company, and I figure it's just another selling point for potential clients that we can say we have offices in New Jersey and LA."

"Yes. I think so, too. We can cover the entire country. No problem."

"I will say, however, that if you decide to find a wealthy CEO in Falling Brook to set me up with, I could be very happy becoming an East Coast company, too."

"Really? You liked Falling Brook?"

Kianna shrugged. "I did. I can also admit to being a bit jealous. You have it all, girl. A beautiful place to live and the best man ever. Zane is a dream come true. If I can find a guy half that good, I'll be happy."

"You'll find him." She thought about it for a minute. "Although if it might get you to move to New Jersey, I might have to start looking for him myself. In earnest."

"Executive recruiter and matchmaker. I like it." Kianna unleashed her megawatt smile, her cheeks plumping up. "That could end up being your ultimate calling."

"I'm on it. As soon as I get married."

They walked down the crushed-shell path toward the dock, where the rest of the guests would be waiting on the boat. Zane and Scott had gone out to Mako Island an hour earlier so they could spend some time talking and Allison could still make her traditional bride's entrance. Scott and Zane's friendship had not only withstood the test of the romance between Allison and Zane, it had come out on the other side much stronger. Both Zane and Scott had admitted as much to Allison—not voluntarily; she'd had to drag it out of each of them separately. She was glad they had each other. She was relieved that hadn't gone away.

When Allison and Kianna approached the boat, the gathered family all stood and clapped. Allison felt a rush of pleasant warmth to her face. She didn't relish being the center of attention, but on this day, she lapped it up. They were soon on their way, the warm sea breezes brushing against her skin while the sky turned the most brilliant shades of pink and orange as the sun began to make its descent. Her heart picked up in anticipation when she caught sight of tiny Mako Island and could see those two tall figures standing on the beach—Scott and Zane. Her two favorite guys.

Marcus carefully motored the boat into the shallowest navigable water, then set anchor, instructed Allison's dad to roll up his pant legs and helped to guide everyone through the knee-high depths to shore. They all gathered under the shade of the largest palm with Scott standing at the center. He'd been ordained via the internet for the occasion, and was quite proud of his job as officiant, although Zane and Allison had designed the ceremony to be ultrashort and sweet. Zane was to his left, and even from this far away, with Allison still standing on the boat in the bobbing water, she could see how happy and relaxed he was. She hoped he could spend as many days of his life as possible looking and feeling that way. He deserved it. They both did.

Finally, it was Allison's turn to be helped off the boat. Her dad was standing only a few feet away, ready to walk her down the aisle, or, more specifically, across the sandy bottom. She kissed his cheek, then hooked her arm in his and snugged him closer.

"I love you, Alli," he said as they began their father-daughter ocean stroll.

"I love you, too, Dad. So much."

Ahead, all Allison could see was Zane, the man of her dreams. His heartbreaking smile seemed like a permanent fixture on his handsome face, which was exactly the way she liked him. Off in the distance, the sun was slowly sinking toward the horizon, coloring the sky with more deep and mesmerizing shades of summery pink, warm beachy orange and beautiful blue. At Allison's feet, tiny tropical fish darted through the water, and all felt right with the world. Everyone she loved was here. And she was ready to start her new life.

When she reached Zane, she gave her dad one more kiss before letting him join her mom. Then it was time to take the hand of the man who was her whole future.

"Hey there, beautiful," he whispered into her ear.

"You're not half-bad yourself." Dressed in a white shirt and pants, with the legs rolled up to midcalf, he was an absolute vision. She'd purposely asked him not to shave—she loved his late-day scruff. It was so sexy.

"Family and friends," Scott began. "We're gathered here today to witness the joining of Scott and Allison in matrimony. They will now share their vows."

Zane went first as they joined both hands and faced each other. She peered up at him, allowing herself to get lost in his eyes as he spoke. "Allison, you are my everything. You are my reason for getting up in the morning and the thing I am most thankful for when I lay my head down at night. I promise to always hold you in my heart, to support you in all your endeavors, and most of all, I promise to always love you."

"Allison, do you take this man to be your husband?" Scott asked.

"I do." She sucked in a deep breath and embarked on her own pledge. She'd practiced it one hundred times or more, but she'd wanted to get it just right. "Zane, you were once only a dream to me. And now you are my reality. When we're together, I feel nothing less than loved and cherished. When we're apart, I'm sad, but you're still there with me, in my head and in my heart. I promise to always keep you there, to support you in all your endeavors, and most of all, I promise to always love you."

"Zane, do you take this woman to be your wife?" Scott asked.

"Do I ever." Zane didn't wait for Scott to make the final proclamation. He gathered Allison in his arms, picked her up to her tiptoes and laid an incredibly hot kiss on her. It might not have been totally appropriate for a family gathering, but she was glad it was a taste of things to come. Their guests all clapped, hooted and hollered.

"Well, then," Scott said. "That makes you husband and wife."

After a few minutes of hugs and congratulations, everyone gathered to board the boat, with Zane and Allison last in line. They were actually hanging back a bit, taking their chance to wade through these warm waters, hand in hand, husband and wife. Zane pointed to the honeymoon cottage up on the hill. "I can't wait to spend the next few days with you up there."

"No storm this time."

"Not unless I manage to brew one up on my own."

Allison laughed and swatted Zane on the arm. "It's going to be perfect."

"It's where we fell in love," he said, pressing another soft kiss to her lips.

Allison knew then that all those years she'd lusted after Zane, it hadn't been love. Now it was nothing less. In fact, it was everything she'd ever wanted. "It absolutely is."

* * * * *

Their Hot Hawaiian Fling

Traci Douglass

MEDICAL
Pulse-racing passion

Traci Douglass is a *USA TODAY* bestselling author of contemporary and paranormal romance. Her stories feature sizzling heroes full of dark humor, quick wit and major attitude, and heroines who are smart, tenacious and always give as good as they get. She holds an MFA in Writing Popular Fiction from Seton Hill University, and she loves animals, chocolate, coffee, hot British actors and sarcasm—not necessarily in that order.

Books by Traci Douglass

Harlequin Medical

One Night with the Army Doc
Finding Her Forever Family
A Mistletoe Kiss for the Single Dad
A Weekend with Her Fake Fiancé

Visit the Author Profile page at
millsandboon.com.au.

Dear Reader,

Hard to believe this is my fifth book for the Harlequin Medical Romance line already! Seems like just yesterday I was dreaming of achieving my goal of becoming a Harlequin author. I still pinch myself every day to make sure it's all true! And thanks to each and every one of you who make all this possible. I'm eternally grateful to you! <3

Holden and Leilani's story is dear to my heart for several reasons. First, Hawaii is a fantasy destination of mine, Oahu in particular. Researching the settings for this book was a true pleasure and gave me all sorts of fun ideas to check out once I do eventually get to travel to this beautiful tropical paradise.

Second are the past traumas my characters need to overcome to find their HEA. For Holden, it means surrendering his survivor's guilt and PTSD and letting down his guard. For Leilani, it's risking her heart after losing those closest to her.

Both must learn to trust again in order to move forward into their future together. But can they?

You'll have to read the book to find out!

Until next time, happy reading! <3

Traci :)

May there always be warmth in your hale,
fish in your net,
and aloha in your heart.

—Traditional Hawaiian Blessing

Praise for
Traci Douglass

"Ms. Douglass has delivered an absolutely engaging and unputdownable read…. It was from the moment the hero and heroine come face-to-face for the first time where things get really interesting."

— Harlequin Junkie on
One Night with the Army Doc

CHAPTER ONE

"SIR, CAN YOU tell me your name?" Dr. Leilani Kim asked as she shone a penlight to check her newest patient's eyes. "Pupils equal and reactive. Sir, do you remember what happened? Can you tell me where you are?"

"Get that thing outta my face," the man said, squinting, his words slightly slurred from whatever substance currently flooded his system. "I ain't telling you my name. I know my rights."

"How many fingers am I holding up?" she asked.

"Four." He scowled. "How many am I holding up?"

She ignored his rude gesture and grabbed the stethoscope around her neck to check his vitals. "Pulse 110. Breathing normal. Blood pressure?"

"One-thirty over 96, Doc," one of the nurses said from the other side of the bed.

"Find any ID at the accident scene?" Leilani asked over her shoulder to the EMTs standing near the door of the trauma bay. "Any idea what he's on?"

"Cops got his license," one of the EMTs said, a young woman name Janet. "His name's Greg Chambers. According to the officer who ran his plates, he has a history of DUIs and a couple arrests for meth too."

"Great." It wasn't, in fact, great. It was exhausting and brought up a lot of memories Leilani would just as soon forget, but that wouldn't be professional, and she couldn't afford to seem anything but perfect these days with the Emergency Medicine directorship up for grabs.

A quick check for signs of distress on the guy—airway, breathing, circulation—all seemed intact and normal. Next, she moved to palpate the patient's torso and extremities. "Do you have pain anywhere other than your head, Mr. Chambers? Can you feel your arms and legs?"

"I feel you poking and prodding me, if that's what you mean." The guy groaned and raised a hand to the bandages covering his scalp. "My head hurts."

"Smashing it into a windshield will do that," Leilani said, finding no evidence of broken bones or internal bleeding on exam. She returned to his head wound. He was lucky. If only the people Leilani had loved most in the world had been so fortunate.

She blinked hard against the unwanted prickle of tears. Must be the exhaustion. Had to be. She never let her personal feelings interfere with her duties.

"Everything okay, Doc?" Pam, the nurse, asked while adjusting the patient's heart monitor.

"Fine. Thanks." Leilani gave her a curt nod, then turned to the paramedics again. "Any other casualties from the accident?"

"Other than the palm tree he hit at forty miles per hour?" Peter, the other EMT, said. "No. No other passengers or vehicles involved, thank goodness. When we arrived, the patient was standing outside his vehicle, texting on his phone. He took one look at us and complained of neck pain before collapsing on the ground claiming he couldn't stand."

"Where's my truck?" Mr. Chambers grumbled.

"Your vehicle is a total loss, sir," Leilani said, hackles rising. People died because idiots like this guy drove under the influence. She checked the laceration on his head.

"No!" He wrenched his arm away from the phlebotomist who'd arrived to take his blood. "You can't take it without my consent. I know my rights."

Energy and patience running low, Leilani fixed the man with a pointed stare. "You keep complaining about your rights, Mr. Chambers, but what about the rights of the other people on the road who just wanted to get home to their family and friends? You put innocent lives at risk driving while intoxicated. What about *their* rights?"

His chin jutted out. "Not my problem."

It will be, if your test results come back positive, she thought, but didn't say it out loud.

Leilani had dealt with her share of belligerent patients during her ten years working at Honolulu's Ohana Medical Center, but this guy took the cake. She turned to Pam. "Call radiology and see if they can get him in for a stat skull X-ray, please. Also, we need a Chem Seven, tox screen and blood alcohol level." Then, to the phlebotomist, "Strap his arm down if needed."

"I'm no addict," the guy yelled, trying to get up and setting off the alarms on the monitors. "Let me out of here."

Several orderlies stepped forward to hold the guy down as Leilani recorded her findings in the patient's file on her tablet.

"How much have you had to drink tonight, sir?" she asked, glancing up.

"Few beers," the patient said, shrugging.

The scent of booze had been heavy on his breath, and Leilani raised a skeptical brow. Based on his delayed reaction times during her exam and his uncoordinated movements, he'd had way more than he was letting on. "And?"

"A couple shots of whiskey."

"And?"

His lips went thin.

Right. Her simmering anger notched higher. The fact someone could be so reckless as to get behind the wheel when they

were obviously impaired sent a fresh wave of furious adrenaline through her.

Movements stiff with tension, she set her tablet aside and
returned to the bandages on the guy's forehead, peeling them
back to reveal a large bruise and several small cuts. She dictated her findings as she went. "On exam there are no obvious
skull fractures. Several small lacerations to the forehead and
a golf-ball-sized hematoma over the left eye. No obvious foreign bodies seen in the wounds, though we'll need the X-rays
to confirm. Sutures aren't necessary, but Pam, can you please
clean and dress this again." She glanced over at the EMTs once
more. "You said he hit the windshield?"

"Glass starred from the impact."

"Okay. Let's examine your spine next, Mr. Chambers."

"No." He attempted to climb off the bed again. "I want to
go home."

"You're not going anywhere until I sign the discharge papers
and the police release you from custody," Leilani said, leverag-
ing her weight to hold her uncooperative patient down. People
always assumed because she was petite she couldn't handle it if
things got rough. What those same folks didn't know was that
she was an excellent kickboxer and had already survived way
more hardship than most people faced in a lifetime. She was
more than capable of fighting her own battles.

"Cops? Aw. Hell. No." The patient gave Leilani a quick once-
over. "What are you, ten?"

"Thirty-four, actually." She opened his brace with one hand
and carefully palpated his neck with the other, moving her fingers along his spine before cupping his head and turning it
slowly from side to side. "No step-offs. Pam please order a stat
spinal series as well, since he complained of difficulty walking at the accident scene. Mr. Chambers, were you wearing a
seat belt at the time of the accident?"

"Nah. Don't like them. Too confining."

That was kind of the point. Seat belts saved lives. She was proof.

The phlebotomist finished drawing her last vial of blood, then placed a bandage on the patient's arm. "I'll get this right up to the lab, Dr. Kim."

"Thanks." Leilani picked up her tablet once more. "Patient has a possible concussion and will need observation for the next twenty-four hours. Pam, make sure the jail can accommodate that order."

"Will do, Doc," Pam said.

"I ain't going to jail," Mr. Chambers snarled.

"The police might think differently. You caused quite a bit of property damage, from what I've been told, and this isn't your first offense." Leilani rubbed the nape of her neck, her fingers brushing over the scar there. Twenty years since the accident that had changed her life forever, but the memories still brought a fresh wave of pain.

"Police are ready to question the patient whenever you're finished, Dr. Kim," Pam said, hiking her head toward the two uniformed officers standing just outside the door.

"Okay." Leilani turned back to the patient. "Almost done, Mr. Chambers. Just a few more questions."

"Not saying another word," the man said, his scowl dark. "Told you I know my rights."

"Anything I can help with, Dr. Kim?" a new voice said, deep and distracting as hell.

Leilani turned to see Dr. Holden Ross wedging his way between the cops and into the room as Pam was leaving to call in her orders. Ugh. Just what she didn't need. The ER's new locum tenens trauma surgeon barging into her case uninvited. He'd only been here a month, so perhaps he didn't know any better, but it still irked her. She didn't do well with people overstepping her boundaries. She'd worked hard to put up those walls over the years, both professionally and personally. Letting people too close only meant a world of hurt and trouble when they left.

And in Leilani's experience, everyone left eventually. Sometimes with no warning at all.

The fact his gorgeous smile filled her stomach with anxious butterflies had nothing to do with it.

She straightened and smoothed her hand down the front of her white lab coat, giving him a polite smile to cover her annoyance. "No. I've got it, thank you, Dr. Ross. Just finishing up."

"Got something you can finish up right here, darlin'." The patient shot her a lewd look and grabbed his crotch.

How charming. Not.

Holden's expression quickly sharpened as he moved to the patient's bedside, his limp drawing her attention once more. She wondered what had caused it before she could stop herself, though it was none of her business. His metal cane clinked against the bedside rails as he glared down into the drunken man's face, his stern frown brimming with warning. "Show Dr. Kim some respect. She's here to save your life."

"I appreciate your concern, Dr. Ross," Leilani said, clearing her throat. "But I've got this. I'm sure there are other patients for you to deal with."

"Actually, I'm just coming on shift." He leaned back, his gaze still locked on the patient. "Fill me in on this guy, so I can take over after you leave."

Darn. He was right. Her shift was over soon, and she needed to get home and rest. Leilani looked over at her colleague again. Holden looked as fresh and bright as a new penny, while she probably looked as ragged as she felt. Add in the fact she seemed irrationally aware of his presence today—not just as a colleague, but as a man—and her stress levels skyrocketed.

The last thing she needed right now was an ill-advised attraction to her coworker.

Distracted, Leilani turned away to futz with her tablet. "What time is it now?"

"Quarter past six," Holden said, moving around the bed to stand next to her. He propped a hip against the edge of the counter, using his cane to take the weight off his right leg. "Your shift ended fifteen minutes ago."

The low hum of the automatic blood pressure cuff inflating on the patient's arm filled the silence. Gossip was already flying amongst the staff about how handsome, intriguing Dr. Ross had ended up at Ohana. Everything from a bad breakup to a good recommendation from some powerful donors. There was one rumor, however, that concerned Leilani the most—that he'd come to their facility at the request of the hospital's chief administrator, Dr. Helen King, and that he was in line for the same directorship she wanted.

Ugh. She shook off the thoughts. None of that mattered at present. She had a patient to deal with. Plus, it was silly to operate off rumor and conjecture. She was a woman of science; she dealt with facts and figures, concrete ideas. Nothing silly or scary like gossip or emotions. Acting on "what-if's" and messy feelings could bring a person to their knees if they weren't careful. Leilani should know.

Pam poked her head into the room again. "Sorry to interrupt, but Dr. Ross, there's a new arrival for you. Female with abdominal pain for the last six hours."

"Duty calls." Holden held Leilani's gaze a moment longer before pushing away from the counter to scan the tablet computer Pam handed him. Leilani found herself unable to stop watching him, darn it. Her curiosity about him was a mystery. Sure, he was charming and would've been just her type, with those dark good looks and soulful hazel eyes. Not to mention he was more than competent at his job, according to the residents on staff. Neither of those reasons was good enough to go poking around into things that were better left unexplored though. Besides, Dr. Ross would hopefully be gone once a suitable replacement for his position was found. Leilani's life was here, in her native Hawaii, and right now her attention was on her career.

There'd be plenty of time for a personal life later.

Maybe.

Shaking off the odd pang of loneliness pinching her chest, she continued to complete her documentation while Holden rattled off his orders for Pam.

"Okay. Let's start by running an HCG to make sure the new patient's not pregnant, since she's not had a hysterectomy," Holden said, tapping his tablet screen several more times. "I've added a couple of additional tests as well to get things rolling."

"Thanks, Dr. Ross." Pam took the tablet and disappeared around the corner once more, leaving just the two of them and the patient in the trauma bay again.

Leilani stayed determined to power on through because that's what she did. She was a survivor, in more ways than one. She swallowed hard and rubbed her neck again. The scars reminded her how life could change in a second. There was no time to waste.

Her patient's snores filled the air and she shook the man gently awake. "Mr. Chambers? Can you tell me where you are?"

He squinted his eyes open and scrunched his nose. "Why are you asking me this crap?"

"Because you could have a concussion." She glanced over at Holden and gave a resigned sigh. He obviously wasn't going to leave until she shared the case details with him. Seemed he was as stubborn as she was. Not a good sign. After another resigned sigh, she ran through the details for him. "Single car MVA. Male, twenty-six years old, drove his pickup truck into a tree. Head struck windshield. Denies lack of consciousness. He's alert and—"

"Let me go, dammit!" The patient flailed on the bed and clawed at the neck brace. "Get this thing off me!"

"Combative," Leilani finished, giving Holden a look before returning her attention to Mr. Chambers. "Sir, tell me where you are, and I'll get you something for the pain."

He rattled off the hospital's name, then held out his hand. "Where's my OxyContin?"

"Acetaminophen on the way," she countered, typing the order into her tablet and hitting Send.

"Hell no." The patient struggled to sit up again. "Opioids. That's what I want."

Holden stepped nearer to the patient's bedside again, his face pale. "Calm down, sir."

"Go to hell!" The patient kicked hard, his foot making hard contact with Holden's right thigh.

Holden cursed under his breath and grabbed his leg, "What's he on?"

"Not sure yet. Definitely alcohol, but probably drugs too. Waiting on the tox screen results," Leilani said, scanning her chart notes for an update and finding none yet. "Patient has a hematoma on his forehead and a few lacerations, as you can see. No palpable fractures to the neck or spine, no internal bleeding or injuries upon exam, though I've ordered X-rays to confirm. According to the EMTs, his head starred the windshield, so no air bags either. I'd guess the vehicle was too old."

"Before 1999, then," Holden murmured as he rubbed his thigh and winced.

"Before 1998," Leilani corrected him. "Air bags were required in 1998."

"Sorry to disagree, Dr. Kim, but I researched this during my time in Chicago. Air bags became mandatory in 1999 in the United States."

"Then your research was wrong." Leilani battled a rising tide of annoyance as her grip on her tablet tightened. She of all people should know when air bags became mandatory. The date was seared in her mind for eternity. "It was 1998. Trust me."

"Why are we even arguing about this?" he asked, the irritation in his voice matching her own.

"I'm not arguing. I'm correcting you."

"That would be fine if I was mistaken. Which I'm not."

"I beg to differ. The date was September 1, 1998, to be exact."

She squared her shoulders and held her ground, feeling a

strange rush of both energy and attraction. No. Not attraction. She didn't want to be attracted to this bullheaded man. Period. Still, her heart raced and her stomach fluttered despite her wishes. Must be the exhaustion. Had to be. She turned away, incensed, both at herself and Dr. Ross.

"The Intermodal Surface Transportation Efficiency Act of 1991 went into effect on September 1, 1998."

Her words emerged in staccato fashion. Rude? Maybe, but then he'd been the one to insinuate himself into her case without asking. She did a quick internet search to prove her point, then held the evidence on screen before his face.

"See? Every truck and car sold in the US had to have air bags for the driver and front seat passenger."

Holden scanned the information, then crossed his arms, the movement causing his toned biceps to bunch. Not that she was looking. Nope. He narrowed his gaze and studied her, far too perceptively for her comfort. "And you know all that verbatim why?"

Because they would've saved the lives of my family.

She swallowed hard and turned away, not about to share the most painful secrets of her past with a virtual stranger, even though some odd little niggle inside of her wanted to.

Gah! She must be way more tired than she'd originally thought. Sleep. That was what she needed. Sleep and food, because perhaps her blood sugar was low. That could explain her stumbling heart rate. Perhaps could even explain how she seemed hypersensitive to the heat and nearness of him now as they faced off over the span of a few feet. Might also explain her weird sensory hallucinations, like how the scent of his skin—soap and musk—seemed to surround her. Or the way her fingertips itched to touch the shadow of dark stubble just beneath the surface of his taut jaw.

Ugh. Leilani clenched her fists on the countertop, the weight of his stare still heavy behind her. He was waiting on her reply and didn't appear to want to leave until he got it. Fine. No way would she tell him the truth, so she went with a half lie instead. "I watch a lot of documentaries."

"Hmm." He sounded thoroughly unconvinced. "I like those shows too, but that's a lot of random facts to remember for no rea—"

"Radiology's ready for your patient, Dr. Kim," Pam said from the doorway, giving Leilani a much-needed reprieve.

"Thank you," Leilani said as two techs wheeled Mr. Chambers out the door.

Holden still stood there though, watching her closely. "I'll handle him when he's done, Dr. Kim. Go home."

"I'm fine, Dr. Ross." Keeping her gaze averted, Leilani headed for the hallway, thankful to escape. "I've got plenty of paperwork to catch up on before I leave, so I'll still be here to wrap up his case."

Holden couldn't understand the enigma that was Dr. Leilani Kim and it bothered him.

Figuring people out was kind of his thing these days. Or at least attempting to understand what made them work, before they did something completely unexpected, like shoot up a room full of innocent people.

Frustrated, he ran a hand through his hair before heading down the hall to check on his abdominal pain patient. Each step sent a fresh jolt of pain through his nerve endings, thanks to that kick from Dr. Kim's patient.

He stopped at the nurses' station to grab his tablet and give his right leg a rest. Honestly, he shouldn't complain about the pain, since he was lucky to still be breathing, let alone walking, after an attacker's bullet had shattered his right femur and nicked his femoral artery. He could have just as easily bled out on the floor of that Chicago ER, same as David…

No.

Thinking about that now would only take away his edge and he needed to stay sharp, with a twenty-four-hour shift looming ahead of him. Bad enough he still had that argument with Dr. Kim looping through his head. There was something about her excuse for knowing all those obscure facts about air bags that didn't ring true. And sure, he loved documentaries as much as the next person—in fact, those things were like crack to an analytical nerd like himself—but even he couldn't recite back all the information he'd learned in those films word for word like she had. It was odd. And intriguing. He'd had a good reason for discovering all that information, namely for an article he'd written for a medical journal. But her?

Not that he should care why she knew. And yet, he did. Way more than he should.

Irritated as much with himself as with her, he shook his head and pulled up his new patient's file. The last thing he needed in his life was more puzzles. He already had more than enough to figure out. Like where he planned to live after his stint here in Hawaii was done. Like if he'd ever walk without a cane again. Like when the next attack might occur and if he'd be ready this time or if he'd become just another statistic on the news.

The area around the nurses' station grew more crowded and Holden moved down the hall toward his patient's room and open space. He didn't do well with crowds these days. Preferred to keep to himself mostly, do his work, handle his cases, stay safe, stay out of the way and out of trouble. That was what he focused on most of the time. Which is what made his choice to charge into Dr. Kim's trauma bay so strange. Usually, he wouldn't intrude in another colleague's case unless he'd been called for a consult, but then he'd overheard her arguing with her obviously intoxicated patient and something had smacked him hard in the chest, spurring him into that room before he'd even realized what he was doing.

Holden exhaled slowly and dug the tip of his cane into the shiny linoleum floor. His therapist back in Chicago probably would've said it was related to his anxiety from the shooting. After all, the gunman back in Chicago had been intoxicated too.

He'd wanted opioids, just like Dr. Kim's patient was demanding. There was a major difference this time though. No firearm.

He took another deep breath. Yes. That had to be it. Had to explain his weird fascination with finding out more about Dr. Leilani Kim too. The fact she was beautiful, all dark hair and dark eyes and curves for days on end—exactly his type, if he'd been looking—had nothing to do with it.

He definitely wasn't looking.

It was simply the stress of being in a new place, and his post-trauma hypersensitivity to his surroundings. He'd only been here a month, after all. Yep. That was it. Never mind his instincts told him otherwise. Holden didn't trust his instincts. Hadn't for a year now.

Twelve months had passed since the attack on his ER in Chicago. Twelve months since he'd lost his best friend in a senseless act of violence. Twelve months since he'd failed to keep the people closest to him safe.

And why risk getting closer to anyone again when they could be lost so easily?

The tablet pinged with his patient's results and he pulled them up, scrolling through the data. Pregnancy test negative. White blood cell count normal, though that didn't necessarily rule out appendicitis. Amylase and lipase measurements within normal limits. Next steps—an ultrasound and manual exam.

"Hey, Pam?" he called down the hall. "Can you join me in Trauma Three for a pelvic?"

"Yep, just give me a sec to finish up calling the lab for Dr. Kim," she said, holding her hand over the phone receiver.

He nodded, then leaned a shoulder against the wall to wait. Ohana Medical Center was relatively quiet, compared to the busy downtown ER he'd come from in Chicago. Back then he'd loved the constant hustle, but after the shooting, going back to work there had been too painful. So, he'd chosen the locum tenens route instead. And it was that choice that had eventually reunited him with his old friend, Dr. Helen King. In fact, she was the reason he'd ended up at Ohana. He owed her a debt he could never repay, but he'd wanted to try.

Which explained why he was here, in the middle of paradise, wondering how soon he could leave. Staying in one place too long didn't suit him anymore. Staying put meant risking entanglements. Staying put too long made you vulnerable.

And if there was one thing Holden never wanted to be again, it was vulnerable.

A loud metal clang sounded down the hall and his senses immediately went on high alert, his mind throwing up reminders of a different ER, a different, dangerous situation. His best friend lying on the floor, bleeding out and Holden unable to stop it because of his own injuries. His chest squeezed tight and darkness crept into his peripheral vision as the anxiety took over.

No. Not here. Not now. Can't do this. Won't do this.

Pulse jackhammering and skin prickling, Holden turned toward the corner, trying to look busy so no one questioned why he was just standing there alone in the hall. He'd spent weeks after the attack learning how to cope with the flashbacks, the PTSD. Sometimes the shadows still won though, usually when he was tired or anxious. Considering he'd slept like crap the night before, he was both at the moment.

"Sorry for the holdup," Pam said, near his side and breaking through his jumbled thoughts. "Things are a bit crazy right now, with tourist season and all."

He nodded and hazarded a glance in her direction.

Her smile quickly dissolved into a frown at whatever she saw in his face. "You okay, Doc?"

It took him a moment to recover his voice, his response emerging more like a croak past his dry vocal cords. "Fine." He cleared his throat and tried again, forcing a smile he didn't quite feel. "Isn't it always tourist season in Hawaii?"

"It is," said another voice from the staff break room across the hall. Leilani. Crap. He'd been so distracted he'd not even seen her go in there. Adrenaline pounded through his blood. Had she seen his panic attack?

When she came out of the room though, she thankfully gave no indication she'd seen him acting strangely. She just walked past him and headed for the elevators as radiology wheeled out her inebriated patient.

The lingering tension inside Holden ratcheted higher as the patient continued to shout at the staff while they wheeled him back toward the trauma bay. "Pain meds! Now!"

Leilani headed behind the desk at the nurses' station once more. "Let me check the images."

Holden followed behind her, the pain in his leg taking a back seat to his need to prevent a possible calamity if her patient got out of hand again. He reached the nurses' station just as Dr. Kim pulled up the patient's images on the computer. "No embedded glass in his scalp, cervical vertebra appear normal. No damage to the spinal cord or—"

"I'm getting the hell out of here!" A jarring rip of Velcro sounded, followed by a resounding crack of plastic hitting the floor. "And I will take everyone down if I don't get my meds!"

The cops still waiting near the doorway tensed and Holden's heart lodged in his throat.

Oh God. Not again.

Undeterred, Leilani took off for the patient's room. "Time to get this guy discharged."

"Wait!" Holden grabbed her arm. "Don't go in there."

"That's my patient, Dr. Ross." She frowned, shaking off his hold. "Don't tell me how to do my work. We need that bed and he's cleared for discharge. He's the cops' problem now. Excuse me."

She continued on down the hall, signaling to the officers to follow her into the room.

"I want my OxyContin!" Mr. Chambers yelled, followed by a string of curses.

Holden breathed deeply, forcing himself to stay calm, stay present, stay in control.

This isn't Chicago. This patient doesn't have a gun. There are police officers present. No one will get hurt.

From his vantage point, Holden saw the patient sitting up on the side of the bed, his neck brace on the floor. Leilani approached slowly, her voice low and calm.

"Your X-rays were all negative. We're going to release you into police custody."

"Already told you," the patient said, teetering to his feet. "I ain't talking to no cops."

Time seemed to slow as Holden moved forward, his vision blurring with memories of the shooting. So much blood, so much chaos, so much wasted time and energy and life.

Breathe, man. Breathe.

The patient straightened, heading straight for Dr. Kim. The cops moved closer.

Her tone hardened. "I'd advise you to stay where you are for your own safety, sir."

"My safety?" The patient sneered. "You threatening me?"

"Not a threat." Leilani squared her shoulders. "Touching me would not be wise."

"Wise?" The guy snorted, his expression lascivious. "C'mon and gimme some sugar."

The cops placed their hands on their Tasers, saying in unison, "Stand down, sir."

Holden rushed toward the room, his cane creaking under the strain. He couldn't let this happen again, not on his watch. He couldn't fail, wouldn't fail.

Just as Holden shoved between the officers, the patient turned at the sudden commotion and swung. His fist collided hard with Holden's jaw and pain surged through his teeth. He stumbled backward. The cops pulled their Tasers as the patient grabbed Dr. Kim's ponytail. Fast as lightning, she swiveled to face Mr. Chambers, slamming her heel down on his instep until his grip on her hair loosened. Then, as he bent over and cursed, she kneed him twice in the groin. The guy crumbled to the ground and the cops took him into custody.

Over. It's over.

Holden slumped against the wall as time sped back to normal.

While the cops handcuffed Mr. Chambers and read him his rights, Leilani rushed to Holden's side. "You're bleeding."

Confused, he glanced down at his scrub shirt and saw a large splotch of scarlet. Then the ache in his jaw and teeth intensified, along with the taste of copper and salt in his mouth.

Damn.

"Here." Leilani snatched a few gauze pads from a canister on the counter and handed them to him. "Looks like there's a pretty deep gash on your lip and chin." She leaned past him to call out into the hall. "Pam, can you set up an open room for suturing, please?"

"No, no." He attempted to bat her hands away and straightened. "I can stitch myself up."

He was a board-certified trauma surgeon, for God's sake. Though as the adrenaline in his system burned away, it left him feeling a tad shaky. His lip pulsated with pain. At least it was a welcome distraction from the cramp in his thigh. "Seriously, I've got it."

"Don't be silly. It will be easier for someone else to stitch you up." She tugged him out the door and down the hall to the nurses' station once more. "Just let me sign off on Mr. Chambers first so they can get him out of here."

While he waited, he blotted his throbbing mouth with the gauze pads and admitted she was right, much as he hated to do so. He was in no fit state to treat anyone at the moment, including himself. Which brought another problem to mind. "What about the abdominal patient?"

"Let the residents take it. That's why they're here." Leilani finished her signing off on her discharge paperwork, then nudged Holden toward an empty exam room. Behind him, the cops hauled Mr. Chambers, still cursing and yelling, out to their waiting squad car.

Leilani led him into the room Pam had set up, then shut the door behind them. "Take a seat on the exam table and let me take a look at your lip."

He did as she asked, allowing her to brush his hand aside and peek beneath the gauze pad. This close, her warmth surrounded him, as did her scent—jasmine and lily. A strange tingle in his blood intensified. It was far more unsettling and dangerous than any punch to the face. She moved closer still to examine his cut lip and he jerked away, alarmed.

"Don't!" he said, then tried to backpedal at her concerned look. "I mean, *ow.*"

He turned away and she walked over to the suture kit set out along with a small vial of one percent lidocaine and a syringe on a wheeled metal tray. "The spilt is through the vermillion border, so no Dermabond or Steri-Strips. Sutures will give you the best result—otherwise it could pop open again."

Holden stared at his reflection in the mirror nearby to distract himself, frustration and embarrassment curdling within him. He already felt like an idiot after getting punched by her patient. Having her sew him up too added insult to injury. Pain surged through his leg and he gripped the edge of the table.

"Any dizziness?" Leilani asked. "He hit you pretty hard."

"No," Holden lied. He still felt a bit light-headed, but that was more from anxiety than the blow to his face. Needing to burn off some excess energy, he slid off the table and moved to the nearby sink to splash cold water on his face. The chill helped clear his head and after drying off his face with paper towels, he plucked at his soiled scrub shirt. "I should change."

"Hang on." Leilani ran back out into the hall and returned with a clean scrub shirt a few moments later. "Here."

"Thanks." He limped behind the screen in the corner and stripped, tossing the bloodstained shirt on the floor before slipping on the clean one. It was too big and the V-neck kept slipping to the side, revealing the scar from his second bullet wound through his left shoulder. He fiddled with the stupid thing, glancing up to find Leilani watching him in the mirror on the wall.

He attempted to play off the awkwardness of the situation with a joke. "Checking me out?"

"No." She looked away fast, but not before he spotted a flush of pink across her cheeks. His interest in her spiked again, despite his wishes to the contrary. She was his work colleague. Theirs was a professional relationship, pure and simple. Anything more was definitely off-limits. He made his way back to the exam table as she pulled on a pair of gloves, then filled a syringe with lidocaine.

"People can be unpredictable, can't they?" Leilani said, jarring him back to reality. "Like Mr. Chambers. You think they're going to do one thing, then they do something completely different. Lie down, please." Reluctantly, he did as she asked. The sooner they got this over with, the better.

Leilani moved in beside him again and he did his best to ignore the heat of her penetrating through his cotton scrub shirt, the soft brush of her bare wrist against his skin as she stabilized his jaw for the injection. "Hold still and try to relax. This may burn a bit."

"I know." He did his best to relax and met her intent stare. "Hard being on the receiving end of treatment."

She smiled and his pulse stumbled. "I understand, Dr. Ross. Doctors usually make the worst patients." She leaned back, her gaze darting from his eyes to his left shoulder, then back again. "But you've obviously had treatment before."

He swallowed hard and looked away, anxiety still shimmering like hot oil through his bloodstream. "Obviously."

"Sorry. I didn't mean to bring up a sore subject." Her hand slipped from his jaw to rest on his sternum, her smile falling. "You're tachycardic."

"I'm fine," he repeated, grasping her hand, intending to remove it from his person, but once her fingers were in his, he found himself unable to let go. Which was nuts. He didn't want entanglements, didn't want connections, and yet, here it was—in the last place he wanted to find one. Which only made his heart beat harder against his rib cage.

Get it together, man.

"Dr. Ross?" she asked, concern lighting her gaze. "Holden? Are you with me?"

The unfamiliar sound of his first name on her lips returned a modicum of his sanity. "Sorry. No, I'd rather not talk about my injuries. Bad memories."

"Okay. No problem. I understand completely. I have a few of those memories myself." Her calm tone, along with the understanding in her eyes, slowly brought his inner angst down to tolerable levels. She pulled her hand from his, then walked over to her tablet on the counter and tapped the screen. "How about some music? What kind do you like? Rock? Country? R & B?"

The change of subjects provided a welcome escape and he grabbed on to it with both hands. He stared up at the ceiling and couldn't care less what she played, as long as it distracted him from the past and her weird effect on him. "Uh...whatever you like is fine."

"Okay." Ukulele music filled the air as she moved in beside him again, a twinkle in her dark gaze as she raised the syringe once more. "I know this situation is uncomfortable for you, Dr. Ross, but the sooner you let me get started, the faster it will be over. I'll even make you a deal. Let me suture you up and I'll take you to a real luau."

"What?" He frowned up at her.

"A luau. You know, poi, Kalua pig, poke, *lomi* salmon, *opihi, haupia* and beer. The works. Plus, you might even get to see a genuine Don Ho impersonator."

"Um...a genuine impersonator?" He gave her a confused look.

She laughed. "Yep. He's the best on the island. Be a shame

for you not to get the full Hawaiian experience while you're here. Unless you've already been?"

No. He hadn't been to a luau yet. Hadn't really been anywhere on the island, other than the resort where he was staying and the hospital, to be honest. And sure, he'd planned to take in some sights while he was here, of course, including a luau, but he'd not really made any firm decisions. The fact she'd asked him now, both piqued his interest and set off all the warning bells in his head. "Are you asking me out on a date, Dr. Kim?"

"What?" She stepped back, looking nearly as alarmed as he felt. "No. I just felt bad because my patient punched you and wanted to make you more comfortable, that's all." That pretty pink color was back in her cheeks again, and damn if that unwanted interest in her didn't flare higher.

This was bad. So, so bad.

Luckily, she shrugged and turned away, her tone chilly now. "But I certainly don't want to give you the wrong impression. And I can see now that my asking was a mistake. Forget I mentioned it."

Holden wanted nothing more than to do that, but it seemed he couldn't. In fact, her invitation now buzzed inside his head like a bothersome fruit fly. He propped himself up on his elbows, feeling completely discombobulated. "I didn't mean to make you uncomfortable."

"Same." She glanced back at him over her shoulder. "I'm not even sure why I mentioned it, to be honest."

The sincerity in her tone helped ease the tension slithering inside him and he lay down flat again, blinking at the ceiling. Seemed they were both rusty at this whole social interaction thing. "I haven't really seen anything since I've been on the island."

"I can give you some suggestions, if you like, since Honolulu's my hometown. My parents own a hotel here," she said, returning to his side, her gaze narrowed as she took his chin again and lifted the syringe. "Okay, here comes the burn."

While the numbing medication took effect, Holden found himself reconsidering her offer. His therapist had told him during their last session back in Chicago that he needed to get out more. She could show him around, perhaps introduce him to some people, broaden his horizons. On a strictly professional basis, of course. Plus, spending more time with her should help lessen the strange heightened awareness he felt around her. Desensitization 101. Taken in those terms, accepting Leilani's invitation made good sense. He blurted out his response before he could second-guess himself. "Okay."

"Okay what?" She frowned down at him.

"Okay, we can go to a luau." His words started to slur as the medication took effect, making his bottom lip ineffective. "Show me some sights too, if you have the time."

Dr. Kim blinked down at him, looking as stunned as he felt. She seemed to consider it for a long moment before nodding. "Fine. But only as colleagues. Understood?"

He nodded, then exhaled slowly as he tapped his lip to make sure it was numb.

"Good." Her quick smile brightened the room far more than he wished. "Now, no more talking until I get this done. Otherwise, I can't guarantee this will heal symmetrical."

She got to work and he closed his eyes, the better to block her out. He still couldn't quite believe he'd said yes to her invitation. Part of him still wanted to get up and get the heck out of there, but the other part of him knew she was right. It was easier for someone else to stitch him up.

CHAPTER TWO

LEILANI STILL COULDN'T quite believe what had happened with Holden Ross. What had she been thinking, offering to take him sightseeing, let alone to a luau? Ugh. She didn't date coworkers. Didn't date anyone really these days, truth be told. Sure, she'd had relationships in the past, but nothing that had worked out long term. And the past six months or so, socializing had taken a back seat with the directorship position on the line.

But this wasn't really socializing, was it? He was new in town and she was being hospitable, that's all.

Like a good neighbor.

A neighbor you'd like to get to know a whole lot better.

Flustered, Leilani turned to face the counter.

This was so not like her to get all giddy over a man. Especially a potential rival for the job she wanted. Never mind there was something wildly compelling about him. Like the flash of panic in his eyes when she'd asked about his previous injuries.

Unfortunately, his reaction was all too relatable—the gut-wrenching terror, the uncertainty of being bruised and battered and broken and alone. If it hadn't been for the kindness and patience and fast thinking of the medical staff the night of the accident, she wouldn't be here today.

The old injury at the base of her neck ached again, reminding her of those who'd saved her, after the rest of her family had been lost. And that was probably exactly why she should be avoiding Holden Ross like the proverbial plague, instead of escorting him around her island as his tour guide. Maybe she could find some way out of it. Work usually gave ample excuses. There was bound to be a case or two requiring her assistance, right? Leilani ripped open the suture kit and pulled out a hemostat.

The music streaming from her tablet on the counter switched to a different song, this one slow and sweet and filled with yearning. Her own chest pinched slightly before she shoved the feeling away. She had nothing to yearn for. She had a great life. A good career. Adoptive parents who loved her and supported her decisions. A new house. A pet who adored her—U'i, her African gray parrot.

And sure, maybe sometimes she wished for someone special to share it all with. She'd get there when she was ready.

If you're ever ready...

She was taking her time, that was all. Being cautious. Never mind she still woke up with nightmares from the accident sometimes. She'd get over it. All of it.

Someday.

"No one told me you're a ninja," Holden said, his words wonky due to his numb lip.

"Those skills come in handy more often than you know." She opened a 6–0 suture and grabbed the curved needle with the hemostat to align the vermillion border with one stitch. Once that was done, she switched to a 5–0 absorbable suture for the rest. "Just four or five more then we're done."

"Internal?" he asked, though the word came out more like "ee-turtle."

"No damage to the orbicularis oris muscle that I can see, so all external." She tied off another stitch, then grabbed a couple more gauze strips off the tray, soaking them in saline before carefully pulling down his bottom lip. "Let me just check the inside to make sure there aren't more lacerations hidden in there."

The salt water dripped down his chin to the V-neck of his scrub shirt.

"Oops. Sorry." Leilani grabbed a tissue from the tray and dabbed at the wet spot, doing her best not to notice his tanned skin and well-defined muscles. Sudden, unwanted images of her kissing from his neck to collarbone, then down his chest, lower still, made her mouth go dry...

"Dr. Kim?" Holden said, yanking her back to reality.

Oh God.

Mortified, she tossed the tissue back on the tray then gave him a too-bright smile. "Almost finished."

He frowned, then looked away, the movement giving her another glimpse of the scar on his left shoulder. She gave herself a mental shake. His body and his wounds were none of her business. That was the exhaustion talking, making her nerves hum and her curiosity about him soar. She continued with the sutures, berating herself.

Focus, girl. Focus.

The song on her tablet switched again, this time to a sweeping, sexy guitar concerto.

Holden blinked up at the ceiling, looking anywhere but at her. "That's pretty."

"One of my favorites." Leilani tied off another stitch then started on the next.

He waited until she was finished before asking, "Where'd you learn to fight?"

It took her a minute to figure out his slurred question. "Oh. You mean with Mr. Chambers? I kickbox. I've taken classes since I was fifteen."

"Wow." Then, out of the blue, he reached up and cupped her face. Her pulse stumbled.

"What are you doing, Dr. Ross?" she managed to squeak out.

"That guy pulled your hair hard," Holden said, gently tilting her head to the side.

"I'm fine. Really." Her breath hitched at the intensity of his gaze.

Oh goodness.

The romantic music washed around them, and unexpected heat gathered in her core. Not good. Not good at all.

Holden Ross was the last man she should get involved with. He was her colleague. He was strictly off-limits. He was far too tempting for her own good. Any connection she felt to him needed to be severed, any awareness currently scorching her blood needed to be doused. End of story. She couldn't risk allowing him closer.

Can I?

Blood pounded in her ears and forbidden awareness zinged over her skin. She ignored the first and tamped down the last before forcing words past her suddenly dry throat. "Thank you, Dr. Ross. Now, let's finish these stitches and get you on your way."

"Holden," he said.

"I'm sorry?" She held the needle poised over his lip for the last stitch.

"Call me Holden."

"Okay." Leilani placed her thumb on his chin to pull slight tension and her finger along his chiseled jawline to steady her hand.

"So, you're native Hawaiian then?"

"Please try not to speak." She sat back. "And yes. Born and raised. My parents own a resort in town."

She could hear the sadness in her own voice and as perceptive as he was, she had no doubt he'd hear it too. Despite all the love and joy her adopted family had given her, part of her would always miss the ones who'd gone. The pain of the accident had never truly faded. Nor had the fear of losing someone else she cared for. She tied off the last stitch, then sat back with relief. "All done."

He sat up and looked in the mirror on the wall again. "Nice job, Dr. Kim."

"Thanks." She began cleaning up from the procedure. "There are more clean scrub shirts on the rack in the hall, if you want to grab a different size."

"Will do." He grabbed his cane and limped toward the door, then turned back to her once more. "Thanks again."

"No problem." Leilani watched him walk away, feeling that riptide of interest tugging at her again and knowing that if she gave in, it could pull her right under. And drowning in the mysteries of Dr. Holden Ross was not part of her plans.

The following morning, after his shift, Holden drove his rental car through the streets of Honolulu toward the Malu Huna Resort and Spa, the steady, hypnotic beat of the windshield wipers almost putting him to sleep. His current residence was only fifteen minutes outside of downtown but driving in the rain after work wasn't exactly his favorite thing.

He pulled into a handicapped parking spot near the entrance to the hotel then stared in through the front windows at the breakfast crowd filling the lobby of the resort. The unusual, crappy weather actually suited his mood far better than the cheerful tropical decor inside the place, but if he wanted to get to his room, he had to traverse the maze of tourists and guests filling the tables in the lobby.

After a deep breath, he cut the engine and grabbed his cane, before glancing at himself one last time in the mirror. The numbing medication in his lip had long since worn off and his lower jaw and into his teeth ached. Eating would be a joy for a while. Not that it mattered. He ate his meals alone in his room most of the time anyway, avoiding the other guests. No sense ruining everyone else's time in paradise with his gloomy attitude.

With a sigh, he got out of the car, then hobbled toward the entrance, his head down to keep the rain off his face. The automatic doors swished open and a gust of warm air swept around him, scented with maple and bacon from the food-laden coffers of the all-you-can-eat buffet in the dining room. His traitorous stomach growled, but Holden didn't stop to fill a plate. Just kept his eyes focused on the elevators ahead as he made a bee-line through the lobby. Since the shooting, he had a hard time spending long periods with large groups of strangers. He found himself too distracted, always scanning the room for danger.

His therapist back in Chicago had urged him to build up his tolerance slowly. So far, Holden hadn't tried that suggestion out, preferring his own company to constantly being on guard for the next attack.

Weaving through groups of tourists dressed in shorts and T-shirts and sandals, he felt more out of place than ever in his wrinkled scrubs, his name tag from work still pinned crookedly on the front pocket. He excused himself as he sidled by a quartet of women bedecked with leis and sun hats and nearly collided with a potted palm tree for his trouble.

The lobby of the Malu Huna looked like a cross between a *Fantasy Island* fever dream and a Disney movie in Holden's estimation—with its rattan furniture, gauzy white curtains and golden pineapple design inlaid in the shiny tile floor. There was even a parrot behind the front desk, squawking at the people passing by. Holden glanced over at the bird as he waited for his elevator. An African gray, if he wasn't mistaken. One of his roommates back in college had had one. Smart as a whip and quick learners. They'd had to be careful what they said around the bird because it picked up words like crazy, especially the bad ones.

Holden punched the up button again.

"Dr. Ross?" a voice called from across the lobby and his heart sank. The owner.

The elevator dinged and the doors whooshed open.

So close and yet so far.

He considered making a run for it but didn't want to be rude.

Forcing a weary smile, he turned to face the Asian man who bustled over to him from the dining room. The shorter guy beamed up at him now, his brightly colored Hawaiian shirt all but glowing beneath the recessed overhead lighting. "Won't you join us for breakfast?"

Holden glanced at the roomful of people and his stomach twisted hard. "Oh, I'm not really hungry."

Once more, his stomach growled loud, proving him a liar.

The hotel owner raised a skeptical brow, his grin widening. "Your body says otherwise. Please, Dr. Ross? We'd love to show you our hospitality during your stay." He gave Holden a quick once-over. "You look as if you could use a good meal. Come on."

Before he could protest, the man took his arm and guided him across the lobby. Familiar panic vibrated through his bloodstream and he looked over the man's head out the rain-streaked windows toward his car. It was only breakfast. He could do breakfast.

Sit. Eat. Talk.

Except the idea of making conversation with strangers made his spine kink.

Sure, he talked to patients all day long, but that was different. At the hospital, he had a plan, a specific purpose. Those things made it easier to shove his anxiety to the back of his mind. Small talk, however, required interest and energy, both of which Holden was running critically low on at the moment.

A year ago I could talk with anyone, party with the best of them.

But now, postattack, his social skills had vanished, leaving him feeling awkward and weak. He hated feeling weak. Weak meant vulnerable. And vulnerable was something Holden never wanted to be again.

He made one final valiant attempt at escape as the hotel owner dragged him thorough the dining room and a maze of packed tables. "Honestly, I can just order room service. I'm tired and grubby and probably won't make good company any-way, Mr....?"

"Kim," the man said, stopping before a table where two women sat. "Mr. Kim. But you can call me Joe. Please, sit down, Dr. Ross."

"Holden," he mumbled, staring at the woman across the table from him. Dr. Kim stared back, looking about as happy to see him as he was to see her. "Please, call me Holden."

She'd mentioned her parents owned a hotel in town while she'd stitched him up, but he'd been so focused on ignoring her and all the uncomfortable things she made him feel, that he'd let it go in one ear and out the other.

Now he felt like an even bigger idiot than before. "Uh, hello again."

"Hello," she said, fiddling with the napkin in her lap. "Are you going to sit down?"

Sit. Yes. That sounded like a marvelous idea, especially since his thigh was cramping again. With less grace than usual, he pulled out the empty chair and slid into it, stretching out his aching leg as he hooked his cane over the back of his seat.

Mr. Kim, Joe, was still smiling at him, as was the woman beside him, presumably Mrs. Kim.

Trying his best to not flub up again, Holden extended his hand to the older woman. "Dr. Holden Ross. Pleasure to meet you."

"Same." Mrs. Kim's dark gaze darted between Leilani and Holden. "You work with my daughter?"

"Yes. I'm filling in temporarily at Ohana Medical Center." He sat back as a waitress set a glass of water in front of him. "Trauma surgery."

"Excellent," Mrs. Kim said. "You and Leilani must work to-gether a lot then. Funny she's never mentioned you."

Leilani, who was quieter than he'd ever seen her before, stared down at her plate of food. "I'm sure I mentioned him, Mom."

"He'll have the buffet," Joe said to the waitress, ordering for Holden. "And it's on the house."

"Sure thing, Mr. Kim," the waitress said, walking away.

"No, no," Holden protested. "I can get this. My locum tenens position comes with a food allowance, so…"

"Locum tenens?" Mrs. Kim said, leaning closer to him. "Tell me more about that, Dr. Ross. Sounds fascinating."

"Holden, please," he said, eyeing the crowded buffet table nearby and longing for the peace and quiet of his hotel room. "I…uh…"

"Hey, guys." Leilani's calm voice sliced through his panic. "Leave the poor man alone. He's just worked a long shift. He needs coffee and a nap, not the third degree. Right, Dr. Ross?"

He swallowed hard and managed a nod.

Leilani poured him a cup of coffee from the carafe on the table and pushed it toward him. "Busy at the ER?"

"Yeah." Talking about work helped relax him and as he stirred cream and sugar into his cup, he told them about the cases he'd seen and the funny stories he'd heard from the staff and soon he'd even answered the questions the Kim's had asked him without locking up once. The whole time, he found himself meeting Leilani's gaze across the table and marveling at the sense of peace he found there.

Whoa. Don't get carried away there, cowboy.

His peace had nothing to do with Leilani Kim. That was absurd. They barely knew each other. It was the routine—talking about work—that calmed his nerves. Nothing else. Nope.

"Well, this has been fun," Mrs. Kim said once he'd finished, pushing to her feet. "But my husband and I need to get back to work at the front desk."

Joe looked confused for a minute before his wife gave him a pointed look. "Oh right. Yeah. We need to get to work. You kids stay and have fun. Lani, be sure to invite him to the luau next Friday." He shook Holden's hand again. "See you around the resort."

Holden watched them walk away, then turned back to Leilani. "So, this is the resort your family owns?"

"Yes." She gave him a flat look, then cocked her head toward the buffet. "Better get your food before they start tearing the buffet down."

CHAPTER THREE

LEILANI EXHALED SLOWLY as Holden hobbled away toward the food line. If she'd left five minutes earlier, she would've missed her parents trying to play matchmaker again, this time with the last man on earth she should be interested in.

They were colleagues, for goodness' sake. She didn't date people from work.

No matter how intrigued she might be by Holden's tall, dark and damaged persona.

Part of her wanted to get up and leave right then, but manners dictated she stay at least until he returned with his plate. They did have to work together, after all. She didn't want things to be awkward—or more awkward than they already were—between them.

So, she'd wait until he got back to the table, then make her polite excuses and skedaddle. For once, Leilani was grateful for the long shift ahead of her at work. Twenty-four hours to keep her busy and away from dwelling more on her encounter the day before with Holden. But first, she planned to hit the gym for a good martial arts workout.

She rolled her stiff neck, then sipped her water. Even tired as she'd been, her sleep had been restless, her dreams filled with images of dealing with combative, intoxicated Mark Chambers again. Those moments then had quickly blurred into memories of the long-ago accident that had taken the lives of her parents and brother. Mixed in were flashes of Holden, changing his scrub shirt, the scar on his shoulder, the wary look in his warm hazel eyes as she'd stitched up his lip. The rough scrap of stubble on his jaw that she'd felt even through her gloves as she'd held his chin, the clean smell of shampoo from his hair, the throb of his heart beneath her palm as she'd dabbed the saline solution from his chest...

"So," he said, shaking her from her thoughts as he straddled the chair across from her and set a plate of scrambled eggs, toast and bacon on the table in front of him. "You honestly don't have to stay if you don't want to. I can tell you'd like to leave."

Leilani did her best to play it off. "Don't be silly. I just have a busy day ahead."

He sat back as the waitress returned to fill a cup of coffee for him. The server gave Holden a slow smile filled with promise and a strange jab of something stabbed Leilani's chest. Not jealousy, because that would be insane. She had no reason to care if another woman flirted with Holden. He was a coworker, an acquaintance. That was it.

Holden continued to watch her as he stirred cream and sugar into his coffee, his gaze narrowed. His skeptical tone said he saw right through her flimsy excuse. "Well, don't let me keep you. I wouldn't be here either if your dad hadn't dragged me in."

She frowned at him. It was true she'd planned to leave soon enough, but that didn't mean he shouldn't want her to stay. A niggle of stubbornness bored into her gut, and she accepted a refill on her coffee from the waitress. At Holden's raised brow she said, "I've got a few minutes."

He took a huge bite of eggs and lowered his gaze. "Don't stay on my account."

"Are you always this jovial, Dr. Ross?" she snorted.

"No. Most of the time I eat alone in my room," he said, devouring half a piece of bacon before glancing at her again.

This time, his stoic expression cracked slightly into the hint of a smile. "Sorry. Out of practice with socializing."

A pang of sympathy went through her before she could tamp it down. Seemed they were in the same boat there. She sipped her coffee while he finished off his plate, then sat back in his seat. ER doctors learned to eat fast, at least in Leilani's experience, since you never knew when you'd be called out for the next emergency. Leilani wasn't sure where he put all that food, since there didn't appear to be an inch of spare flesh on him. A sudden, unwanted flash of him with his shirt off in the exam room flickered through her mind before she shook it off.

Nope. Not going there. Not at all.

With a sigh, she finished the rest of her coffee in one long swallow, then stood. "Right. Well, I really do need to go now. Have a nice rest of your day, Dr. Ross."

Holden wiped his mouth with a napkin, then gave a small nod. "Your shift at the hospital doesn't start until two. It's only 9:00 a.m. now."

"What?" Heat prickled her cheeks as he caught her in a lie. Outrage mixed with embarrassment inside her and came out in her blunt response. "I wasn't aware my schedule was your concern, Dr. Ross."

He downed another swig of coffee. "It's not. Helen mentioned it earlier."

At the reminder of Ohana's head administrator, Leilani's breath caught. Reason number one billion why she shouldn't be spending any more time than was necessary with this man. Not with Holden potentially vying for the same job she wanted. "Dr. King told you my schedule? That seems odd."

"Not really. She mentioned it in relation to some project she wants us both to work on." Leilani opened her mouth to respond, but he held up a hand. "Before you ask, she didn't give me any details yet. Said she wanted to discuss it with you first, as the acting director." He exhaled slowly, his broad shoulders slumping a bit, and he gestured toward her empty chair. "Look,

I'm sorry if I was grumpy before. Please, don't rush off on my account. It's actually kind of nice to have someone to talk to besides myself."

Much as she hated to admit it, Leilani felt the same. Sure, she had friends and her parents, but they weren't physicians. She couldn't talk shop with them like she could another doctor. Not that she really planned to discuss cases with Holden Ross, unless a trauma surgeon's skills were needed, but still. Torn between making her escape and being more enticed by his offer than she cared to admit, Leilani slowly took her seat again. "You don't get out much?"

"No. Not since..." Holden's voice trailed off, and that haunted expression ghosted over his face once more before he hid it behind his usual wall of stoicism. He cleared his throat. "Working locum tenens has a lot of advantages, but creating bonds and connections isn't one of them. Maybe that's why I like it so much."

"Wow. That sounds a bit standoffish."

"Not really." He shook his head and frowned down into his cup. "Just smart."

Huh. Leilani sat back and crossed her arms, studying him. Having been through a nightmare herself with the accident, she recognized the signs of past trauma all too well. Something horrible had definitely happened in his past—she just wasn't sure what. Given his limp and the wound she'd spied on his left shoulder, she'd bet money a bullet had been involved. That was certainly enough to ruin anyone's outlook on their fellow humans and relationships.

Before she could ask more though, he shifted his attention to the windows nearby and the gray, overcast day outside. "Does it rain a lot here?"

"Not really," she said, the change in subject throwing her for a second. "But it's March."

"And March means rain?"

"In Honolulu, yes. It's our rainiest month." Leilani held up her hand when a server came around with a coffeepot again. Too much caffeine would upset her stomach. "Why?"

"Just interested in the island." The same waitress from earlier stopped back to remove Holden's dishes and slid a small piece of paper onto the table beside his mug. From what Leilani could see, it had the woman's phone number on it. Holden seemed unfazed, taking the slip and tucking it into the pocket of his scrubs before reaching for the creamer again. The thought of him having a booty call with the server later made Leilani's gut tighten. Which was stupid. He was free to see anyone he liked, as was she. She wasn't a workaholic spinster, no matter what her parents might say to the contrary. Leilani had options when it came to men and dating. She was just picky, that's all. She had standards.

Holden must've caught her watching him because he said, "I promised to check on the waitress's son later. The kid's got what sounds like strep throat."

Uh-huh. Sure.

She managed not to roll her eyes through superhuman strength. His social life was of no concern to her. She flashed him a bland smile. "Nice of you."

He shrugged. "So, what are you rushing off to this morning? If you don't mind me asking."

Her first response was a snarky one that yeah, she did mind. But then she caught a hint of that lonely sadness and wariness in his eyes again and she bit back those words. She didn't want to get friendlier with Holden Ross, but darn if there wasn't something about him that kept her in her seat and coming back for more. She could lie and make up a story, but what was the point? So she went with the truth instead. "I was going to do my daily workout."

"Oh?" Holden perked up a little at that. "I've been meaning to try the hotel gym, but with my crazy schedule at work, haven't made it there yet. Mind if I tag along, just to see where it is? Then I'll leave you alone, I promise."

Alarm bells went off in Leilani's head. She already felt way more interested in this guy than was wise. Spending more time with him would only put her at risk of that interest boiling over into actually liking him and the last thing Leilani wanted was to open herself up to getting hurt again. Even the possibility of letting someone close to her heart, to be that vulnerable again, honestly filled her with abject terror.

"Let the man go with you, *keiki*," her father said from where he was helping clean up a nearby table, and Leilani tensed. Jeez, they were really on snooping patrol today. "Show our guest the gym."

She glanced over at her father and gave him a look. Her dad just shook his head and moved on to another section of tables to clean. They thought she was being ridiculous and maybe she was, but she needed to do things on her terms. Stay in control. Control was everything these days.

Holden chuckled and gulped more coffee. "Kiki?"

"Keiki," she corrected him. "It means child in Hawaiian."

Ever since they'd adopted her, the Kims had always called her that. First, because that's what she'd been. A scared four-teen-year-old kid with an uncertain future. Now it was more of a pet name than anything.

Leilani exhaled slowly before pushing to her feet again, her good manners too ingrained to refuse. "Fine. If you want to come with me, you can. Get changed and meet me in the lobby in fifteen minutes. Don't be late, Dr. Ross."

Holden's smile widened, his grateful tone chasing her from the restaurant. "Wouldn't dream of it, Dr. Kim."

The workout facilities at Malu Huna were much like the rest of the resort—clean, spacious and well-appointed—even if the decor was a bit much for his Midwestern sensibilities. More golden palm trees decorated the tile floor here and large murals of the famous Hawaiian sunsets bedecked the walls. There were neat rows of treadmills and stair-climbers, weight machines, stationary bikes and even a boxing area, complete with punching bags and thick mats on the floor.

Holden followed Leilani as she headed for those workout mats, her snug workout clothes clinging to her curves in all the right places. Not that he noticed. He was here to release some tension, not to ogle his colleague. No matter how pretty she was. It had been too long since he'd been with a woman, that was all. The slip of paper with the phone number the waitress had given him flashed in his mind. He hadn't lied to Leilani earlier, but he hadn't been entirely truthful either. He had spoken to the waitress a few days prior about her sick kid and offered to see him, but then the waitress had also asked him out. At the time, he'd declined because he'd been tired and busy and not up for company. But now, with loneliness gnawing at his gut again, maybe he should give the server's invitation second thoughts.

Leilani strapped on a pair of boxing gloves, then turned to face him once more.

Holden stopped short. "Are you going to hit me?"

"Not unless you provoke me." She raised a dark brow at him.

He snorted. "Remind me not to get on your bad side."

"Don't worry. I will." She grinned, then turned to face the heavy bag. "Well, this is the gym. Enjoy your workout."

Looking around, he considered his options. Treadmill was out, with his leg. So were the stair-climbers as they put too much pressure on his still-healing muscles. Stationary bike it was then. He hobbled over and climbed onto one, setting his course to the most difficult one, and began to pedal. Soon his heart was pumping fast, and sweat slicked his face and chest, and he felt the glorious rush of endorphins that always came with a hard workout. Near the end of his course, Holden glanced over to where he'd left Leilani on the mats and found her working through what looked like kickboxing moves with the punching bag.

Her long hair was piled up in a messy bun atop her head now and her face was flushed from exertion. Her toned arms and back glistened with perspiration beneath the overhead lights as she walloped the heavy bag over and over again. Jab, hook, cross, uppercut. Sweep, cross, kick. Jab, cross, slip. Front kick, back kick. Roundhouse kick. Repeat. Holden found himself entranced.

Once his bike program was done, he moved back over to where she was still dancing around the bag, her movements as coordinated and graceful as any prima ballerina. Even the hot pink boxing gloves didn't detract from Leilani's powerful stance. She looked ready to kick butt and take names. On second thought, just forget the names.

His gaze followed her fists driving hard into the bag. Then he couldn't help continuing to track down her torso to her waist and hips landing finally on her taut butt in those black leggings.

Whoa, boy.

Yep. Dr. Leilani Kim wasn't just pretty. She was gorgeous, no doubt about that. He glanced back up to find her staring at him, her expression flat.

Oops. Busted.

"You know how to fight," he said, for lack of anything better.

She steadied the swinging bag, then punched one glove into the other, blinking at him. "I do. Very well. Years of training, remember? I'm not afraid to use those skills either."

"I remember you taking down that patient. Don't worry. Point taken." Holden stepped back and chuckled. Back before the shooting he'd been into boxing himself, but he hadn't tried since his injury. He turned to head back to his bike but stopped at the sound of her voice.

"You box?"

"I used to," Holden said, looking back at her over his shoulder. He gestured to his right leg. "Haven't since this though."

"Want to give it a try now?" she asked, tapping the tips of her gloves together. "Be my sparring partner?" Her gaze dipped to his cane then back to his eyes. "I'll take it easy on you."

Whether or not she'd meant that as a challenge didn't matter.

He took it as one. The pair of black boxing gloves she tossed in his direction helped too. He caught them one-handed, then narrowed his gaze on her. For the first time in a long time, he wanted to take a chance and burn off a little steam. "Fine."

He strapped on the gloves, then moved back over, setting his cane aside before climbing atop the mat to stand beside Leilani.

"We can stick to bag work, if it's easier on your leg."

"Sparring's fine." He finished closing the Velcro straps around his wrists, then punched his fists together. "Unless you're scared to face off against me?" His tone was teasing. It felt easy to tease her. He didn't want to think about why.

Leilani snorted. "Right. You think you can take me?"

"I think you talk big, but you look pretty small."

"Them's fighting words, mister." She moved several feet away and faced him before bending her knees and holding her gloves up in front of her face. "All right, Dr. Ross. Show me what you got."

Holden smiled, a genuine one this time, enjoying himself more than he had in a long, long time. "My pleasure, Dr. Kim."

They moved in a small circle on the mat, dodging each other and assessing their opponent. Then, fast as lightning, Leilani struck, landing a solid punch to his chest. He gave her a stunned look and she laughed. "Figured you already had a split lip. Didn't want to damage that handsome face of yours any further."

That stopped him in his tracks.

She thinks I'm handsome?

The reality of her words must've struck Leilani too because the flush in her cheeks grew and she looked away from him. "I mean, I'm taking pity on you. That's all."

Pity. If there was one word sure to set Holden off, it was that one.

All thought of keeping away from Leilani Kim went out the window as he went in for the attack. Apparently still distracted by what she'd said, she didn't react fast enough when he charged toward her and swept his good leg out to knock her feet from under her. Of course, the movement unbalanced him as well, and before Holden knew it, they were both flat on the mat, panting as they tried to catch their breaths in a tangle of limbs.

He managed to recover first, rising on one arm to lean over her. "I don't need your pity, Dr. Kim."

She blinked up at him a moment, then gave a curt nod. "Understood."

"Good." He pushed away to remove one of his gloves and rake a hand through his sweat-damp hair. "Are you all right?"

"Other than my pride, yes." She sat up next to him and removed her gloves too, several strands of her long, dark hair loose now and curling around her flushed face. "I didn't mean to insult you with what I said, by the way. It was just trash-talking."

"I know." He released a pent-up breath, then wiped off his forehead with the edge of his gray Ohana Medical T-shirt. "The whole pity thing is still a touchy subject for me though, with my leg and all."

"Sorry. I should've realized." She got up and walked over to a small fridge against the wall to pull out two bottles of water, then returned to hand him one. Leilani sat back down on the mat and cracked open her water. "What exactly happened, if you don't mind me asking?"

He gulped down half his bottle of water before answering, hoping to wash away the lump of anxiety that still rose every time someone asked about his injury. He did mind, usually, but today felt different. Maybe because they were the only ones in the gym, and that lent a certain air of intimacy. Through the windows across the room, he could see a bit of the gloom outside had lifted and weak rays of sunshine beamed in. Maybe it was time to let some of his past out of the bag, at least a little. He shrugged and fiddled with his gloves once more. "I got shot. Shattered my femur."

"Yikes. That's awful." Leilani grabbed the white towel she'd tossed on the floor nearby when they'd first arrived and wiped off her face. He glanced sideways at her and did his best not to notice the small bead of sweat tickling down the side of her throat. Tried to stop the sudden thought of how salty that might taste, how warm her skin might be against his tongue.

Wait. What?

He looked away fast as she wrapped the towel around her neck, then faced him once more.

"So," she said, her clear tone cutting through the roar of blood pounding in his ears, not from anxiety this time, but from unexpected, unwanted lust. "Is that when you took the bullet to your shoulder as well?"

Holden nodded, not trusting his voice at present, then drank more water. He didn't want Leilani Kim. Not that way. She was his coworker. She was just being nice. She was drinking her water too, drawing his attention to the sleek muscles of her throat as they worked, the pound of the pulse point at the base of her neck, the curve of her breasts in that tight sports bra.

Oh God.

Move. He needed to move. He started to get to his feet, but Leilani stopped him with a hand on his arm. "I'm sorry that happened to you. I know what it's like to be in a situation where you feel helpless and alone."

The hint of pain in her tone stunned him into staying put. From what he could see, she'd had a fairy-tale life here in paradise, raised in this wedding cake of a hotel.

"How's that? And please, call me Holden," he said, more curious than ever about this enigmatic, beautiful woman. To try to lighten the mood, he cracked a joke. "You get hit by a pineapple on the way to surf the waves?"

Her small smile fell and it felt like the brightening room darkened. She shook her head and looked away. "No. More like hit by a truck and spent six months in the hospital."

"Oh." For a second, Holden just took that in, unsure what else to say. Of course, his analytical mind wanted to know more, demanded details, but he didn't feel comfortable enough to do so. Finally, he managed, "I had no idea."

"No. Most people don't." She sighed and rolled her neck, reaching back to rub her nape again, same as she had the other day in the ER with that combative patient. Then she stood and started gathering her things. "Well, I should go get ready for work."

Of all people, Holden knew a retreat when he saw one. He got up as well, reaching for his cane to take the weight off his now-aching leg. Doing that foot sweep on Leilani hadn't been the most genius move ever, even if his whole side now tingled from the feel of her body briefly pressed to his.

He grabbed his water bottle and limped after her toward the exit, pausing to hold the door for her. Before walking out himself, he looked over toward the windows across the gym one last time. "Hey, the sun's out again."

Leilani glanced in the same direction, then gave him a tiny grin. "Funny how that works, huh? Wait long enough and it always comes back out. See you around, Holden."

"Bye, Dr. Kim," he said, watching her walk away, then stop at the end of the hall and turn back to him.

"Leilani," she called. "Anyone who leg-sweeps me gets to be on a first-name basis."

CHAPTER FOUR

THE ER AT Ohana Medical Center was hopping the following Wednesday and Leilani was in her element. She was halfway through a twelve-hour shift, and so far she'd dealt with four broken limbs, one case of appendicitis that she'd passed on to a gastro surgeon for removal, and two box jellyfish stings that had required treatment beyond the normal vinegar rinse and ice. The full moon was Friday and that's when the jellyfish population tended to increase near the beaches to mate. There weren't any official warnings posted yet, according to the patient's husband, but that didn't mean there weren't jellyfish present. They were a year-round hazard in Hawaii.

So yeah, a typical day in the neighborhood.

Leilani liked being busy though. That's what made emergency medicine such a good fit for her. Kept her out of trouble, as her parents always said.

Trouble like thinking about that gym encounter with Holden Ross the week prior.

She suppressed a shiver that ran through her at the memory of his hard body pressed against hers on that mat, the heat of him going through her like a bolt of lightning, making her imagine things that were completely off-limits as far as her colleague was concerned.

Since that day, they'd passed each other a few times in the halls, both at the hospital and at the hotel, but hadn't really said more than a friendly greeting. Just as well, since time hadn't seemed to lessen the tingling that passed through her nerve endings whenever he was near. In fact, if anything, the fact they'd taken a tumble on that mat together only seemed to intensify her awareness of him. Which probably explained why she was still hung up on the whole thing. Leilani tried never to let her guard down but Holden had somehow managed to get around her usual barriers.

Boundaries were key to her maintaining control. And control required no distractions.

Distractions led to accidents and accidents led to...

Shaking off the unwanted stab of sorrow in her heart, she concentrated on the notes she was currently typing into her tablet computer at the nurses' station. The EMTs had just radioed in with another patient headed their way and she wanted to get caught up as much as possible before taking on another case.

As she documented her treatment for the latest jellyfish sting patient—visible tentacles removed from sting site, antihistamine for mild allergic reaction, hydrocortisone cream for itching and swelling, ice packs as needed—she half listened to the commotion around her for news of the EMTs arrival with her next patient. She'd just closed out the file she'd been working on when the voice of the sister of one of her earlier patients, a guy who'd broken his arm while hiking near the Diamond Head Crater, broke through her thoughts.

"Doctor?" the woman said, coming down the hall. "I need to ask you something."

Leilani glanced over, ready to answer whatever questions the woman had, then stopped short as the woman headed straight past her and made a beeline for Holden, who'd just come out of an exam room.

He glanced up at the buxom blonde and blinked several times. "How can I help you, ma'am?"

"My brother was in here earlier and I'm concerned he won't take the prescription they gave him correctly, even after the other doctor explained it to him. She was Hawaiian, I think, and—"

"Dr. Kim is the head of Emergency Medicine. I'm sure the instructions she gave him were clear." Holden searched the area and locked eyes with Leilani. "But if you still have concerns, let's go see if she has a few moments to talk to you again, Mrs....?"

"Darla," the woman said, batting her eyelashes and grinning wide.

Leilani bit back a snicker at her flagrant flirting.

"And it's Miss. I'm single. Besides, I'm old-fashioned and prefer a male doctor."

Holden's expression shifted from confused to cornered in about two seconds flat. Darla didn't want medical advice. She wanted a date. Leilani would've laughed out loud at his obvious discomfort if there wasn't a strange niggle eating into her core. Not jealousy because that would be stupid. She had no reason to care if anybody flirted with Holden. It was none of her business. And it wasn't like men hadn't tried to flirt with Leilani in the ER either. It was another occupational hazard. No, what should have bothered her more was the woman doubting her medical expertise. Shoulders squared, she raised a brow and waited for their approach.

Holden cleared his throat and stepped around Darla to head to the nurses' station and Leilani. "Dr. Kim is one of the best physicians I've worked with. She's the person to advise you and your brother on his medications, as she's familiar with his case." He stopped beside Leilani at the desk, tiny dots of crimson staining his high cheekbones. "Dr. Kim, this lady has more questions about her brother's prescription."

Leilani gave him a curt nod, then proceeded to go over the same information she'd given to Darla's brother an hour prior. Steroids weren't exactly rocket science, and from the way the woman continued to focus on Holden's backside and not Leilani, it seemed Darla could have cared less anyway. Finally, Darla went on her way and Leilani exhaled slowly as the EMTs radioed in their ETA of one minute.

Showtime.

Refocusing quickly, she grabbed a fresh gown and mask from the rack nearby and suited up, aware of Holden's gaze on her as she did so. Her skin prickled under the weight of his stare, but she shook it off. The incoming patient needed her undivided attention, not Dr. Ross.

"What's the new case?" Holden asked, handing his tablet back to the nurse behind the desk. "Need help?"

"Maybe," Leilani said, tying the mask around her neck. "Stick close by just in case."

"Will do." He took a gown and mask for himself, then followed her down the hall to the automatic doors leading in from the ambulance bay. His presence beside her felt oddly reassuring, which only rattled her more. She was used to handling things on her own. Safe, secure, solo. That's how she liked it.

Isn't it?

Too late to stew about it now. The doors swished open and the EMTs rushed in with a young man on a gurney. Leilani raced down the hall next to the patient as the EMT in charge gave her a rundown.

"Eighteen-year-old male surfer struck in the neck by his surfboard," the paramedic said. "Difficulty breathing that's worsened over time."

They raced into trauma bay two and Leilani moved in to examine the patient, who was gasping like a fish out of water. "Sir, can you speak? Does it feel like your throat is closing?"

The kid nodded, his eyes wide with panic.

"Okay," Leilani said, keeping her voice calm. "Is it hard to breathe right now?"

The patient nodded again.

"Are you nodding because it hurts to talk or because you

can't?" Holden asked, moving in on the other side of the bed once the EMTs got the patient moved from the gurney.

"I…" the kid rasped. "C-can't."

"No intubation, then," Holden said, holding up a hand to stop the nurse with the tracheal tube. "Dr. Kim, would you like me to consult?"

Nice. The other trauma surgeons on staff usually just commandeered a case, rarely asking for Leilani's permission to intercede. Having Holden do so now was refreshing, especially since she'd asked him to stick close by earlier. It showed a level of professional respect that she liked a lot. Plus, it would give her a chance to see firsthand how he handled himself with patients. For weeks now, the nurses had been praising his bedside manner and coolness under pressure. About time Leilani got to see what she was up against if they were both vying for the directorship.

"Yes, please, Dr. Ross." She grabbed an oxygen tube to insert into the kid's nose to help his respiration. "Okay, sir. Breathe in through your nose. Good. One more time."

The kid gasped again. "I c-can't."

Leilani placed her hand on his shoulder. "You're doing fine. I know it hurts."

Holden finished his exam then stepped back to speak to relay orders to the nurse taking the patient's vitals. "We need a CTA of his neck and X-rays, please. Depending on what those show, I may need to do a fiber-optic thoracoscopy. Call ENT for a consult as well, please."

"Where's my son?" a man's voice shouted from out in the hall. "Please let me see him!"

After signing off on the orders, Holden moved aside to let the techs roll the patient out of the trauma room, then grabbed Leilani to go speak to the father. "Sir, your son was injured while surfing," Holden said, after pulling down his mask. "He's getting the best care possible between myself and Dr. Kim. Can you tell me your son's name?"

"Tommy," the man said. "Tommy Schrader. I'm his father, Bill Schrader."

"Thank you, Mr. Schrader." Leilani led the man down the hall to a private waiting room while Holden headed off with the team to complete the tests on the patient. "Let's have a seat in here."

"Will my boy be all right?" Mr. Schrader asked. "What's happened to him?"

"From what the EMTs said when they brought your son in, Tommy was surfing and was struck in the throat by his surfboard. He's got some swelling in his neck and is having trouble breathing." It was obvious the man cared deeply for his son and it was always hard to give difficult news to loved ones. In her case, they'd had to sedate her after delivering the news about her family's deaths. At least Tommy was still alive and getting the treatment he needed.

"When I got the call from the police, I panicked. I told Tommy the surf was too rough today, but he didn't listen." Mr. Schrader scrubbed his hand over his haggard face. "All kinds of crazy things went through my mind. I've never been so scared in all my life."

"Completely understandable, Mr. Schrader. But please know we're doing all we can, and we'll keep you updated on his progress as soon as we know more. They're doing X-rays and a CT scan on him now to determine the extent of damage and the next steps for treatment." She patted the man's shoulder, then stood. "Can I get you anything to drink?"

"No, no. I'm good. I just want to know my son will be okay."

"He's in the best hands possible," Leilani said. "Let me go check on his status again and I'll be right back."

"Thank you," Mr. Schrader said. "I'm sorry I don't know your name."

"Dr. Kim." She gave him a kind smile. "Just sit tight and I'll be back in as soon as we know more."

"Thank you, Dr. Kim," Mr. Schrader said.

Leilani left him and headed up to radiology to check in with Holden. She'd no more than stepped off the elevators when he waved her over to look at the films.

"See how narrow this is?" Holden asked her, pointing at the films of the kid's trachea. "There's definite swelling in his airway. In fact, given that there's maybe only one or two millimeters open at most, it's starting to close off completely. There should be a finger's width all the way up."

Definitely not good, especially since the airway normally narrowed at that point anyway, right before the vocal cords. Which brought up the next issues.

"What about his voice box?" she asked.

"That's my concern," Holden said, the grayish light from the X-ray viewer casting deep shadows on the hollows of his cheeks and under his eyes. "Looks like the surfboard made a direct hit on that area. The voice box could've been broken from the impact. It's a high-risk injury in a high-risk area of the body." He shook his head and leaned in closer to the films. "At least this explains his trouble breathing."

"Are you going to operate?" Leilani asked.

Holden exhaled slowly. "No, not yet. Hate to do that to a kid so young. My advice would be to treat him with steroids first and see if the swelling goes down. Watch him like a hawk though. If conservative treatment doesn't work, then I'll go in with the thoracoscopy."

"Agreed." Leilani stepped back and smiled. Working with Holden felt natural, comfortable. Like they were a team. "Best to keep him in the ER then for the time being. That way if he needs emergency assistance, we're there."

"Yep. Let's do it."

She and Holden rode back down to the trauma bay with the medical team and Tommy, then called his father into the room.

Holden and Leilani exchanged looks, then she nodded. He stepped forward to take the lead. "Mr. Schrader, I'm sorry to tell you this is a very, very serious situation. Your son's airway is currently compromised due to swelling from the surfboard strike. It's possible his voice box had been damaged. If that's the case, it could have long-term effects on his speech."

"Oh God." Mr. Schrader moved in beside his son and took the kid's hand. "I told you not to go surfing today. I was so worried."

"I know," Tommy managed to croak out, clinging to his dad's hand. "Sorry."

"Our biggest concern though, at this point," Holden continued, "is that if his larynx—his voice box—is too badly damaged, your son runs the risk of losing his ability to breathe. We need to keep him here at the hospital, in the ER, for at least the next twelve hours for observation. That way if his condition worsens, we can rush him into surgery immediately, if needed. I'd also like to get a consult from one of the throat specialists on staff to get their opinion."

"Whatever you need to do," Mr. Schrader said. "I just want my son to be okay."

"Great. Thank you." Holden stepped back and glanced at Leilani again. "Both Dr. Kim and I will check on Tommy periodically through the night to keep an eye on him then."

"Yes, we will. You won't be alone." Leilani leaned in to place the call button in the kid's hand and give him a reassuring smile. Once upon a time, that had been her in a hospital bed—scared and unsure about the future. "And if you feel your breathing gets worse at any point, you just press that button and we'll rush back in right away, okay?"

Tommy gave a hesitant nod.

"Someone will always be here for you, Tommy," Holden said, meeting Leilani's gaze. "I promise. We're not going to let anything else happen to you."

The kid swallowed, then winced.

"Don't worry. We'll be in here checking on you so often you'll get sick of seeing us." Leilani winked, then headed toward the door with Holden. "Promise."

"And I'll be here too, son," his dad said, pulling up a chair to the beside.

She and Holden walked back to the nurses' station, discarding their masks and gowns in the biohazard bin and stopping to wash their hands at the sink nearby. His limp seemed less pronounced today, though he still used his cane to take the weight off his right leg.

She glanced over at him and smiled as she soaped up, then rinsed off. "You handled that case well."

"Thanks." He smiled, then winced, tossing his used paper towels in the trash and reaching up to touch the sutures in his lower lip.

"Stitches bothering you?" she asked, leaning a bit closer to inspect his wound. "Looks like it's healing well."

"I'm fine. It just stings a bit when I forget it's there," he said, holding up a tube of lip balm. "This helps though."

"Glad to hear it." Leilani turned away from the cherry flavored lip balm he held up. That was her favorite flavor. And now, for some reason, her mind kept wondering what his kisses would taste like with cherries in the mix. Ugh. Not good. Not good at all. She stepped back and looked anywhere but at him. "So, I should probably get back to work on another case then."

"Yeah, me too." He fiddled with the head of his cane, frowning slightly. "Hey, um, I meant to ask you about the luau."

"Luau?" she repeated, like she was channeling her pet parrot. Her pulse kicked up a notch. Damn. She'd been hoping he'd forget about all that. Apparently not. She forced a smile she didn't quite feel and flexed her fingers to relax them. Considering she'd just been having inappropriate thoughts about this man—her coworker—if she was wise, she'd get the heck out of there as soon as possible. Unfortunately, her feet seemed to have other ideas, because they stayed firmly planted where she was.

At least he seemed as awkward as she felt about it all, shuffling his feet and fumbling over his words. It was actually quite endearing… Leilani's heart pinched a little at the sweetness, before she stopped herself.

Keep it professional, girl.

"The other day, last week, uh," he said, keeping his gaze lowered like he was a nervous schoolkid and not a highly successful surgeon. "Anyway, I think your dad mentioned the luau at the hotel and I'd seen some flyers on it too, and I wondered if you still wanted to take me." He hazarded a glance up and caught her eye. "Not that I'll hold you to that. I just…" He exhaled slowly and ran his free hand through his hair, leaving the dark curls in adorable disarray.

No. Not adorable. No, no, no.

But even as she thought that, the simmering awareness bubbling inside her boiled over into blatant interest without her consent. Damn. This was beyond inconvenient. Of all the men for her to be interested in now, it had to be Holden Ross.

He huffed out a breath, then cursed quietly before straightening and meeting her gaze head-on as his words tumbled out in a rush. "Look. I don't get out much and I'd like to see some sights while I'm here, and since you offered the other day, I thought I'd take you up on that, if the offer…if it still stands. Not a date, because I don't do that. Just as two people, colleagues…" He hung his head. "I'm off tomorrow and Friday."

Leilani blinked at him a moment, stunned. Blood thundered in her ears and she turned away to grab her tablet from behind the desk, needing something, anything, to keep herself busy, to keep herself from agreeing to his invitation and more. Because for some crazy reason that's exactly what she wanted to do.

Think, girl. Think.

Saying yes could lead to a friendship between them beyond work, could lead to those uncomfortable tingles of like for this guy going a whole lot further into other *l* words. Not *love*, because that was off the table, but another one with a capital *L*. *Lust.* Because yeah, Holden really was just her type. Tall, dark, gorgeous. Smart, funny, sexy as all get out.

So, she should definitely say no. He was her coworker, her potential rival.

Except that would be rude. And she just couldn't bring herself to be rude to him. Maybe it was that haunted look in his eyes she spied sometimes. Maybe it was his obvious awkwardness around commitment.

I don't date.

Well, neither did she at present. Or maybe it was the air of brokenness about him that called to the same old wounded parts in her.

Whatever it was, she didn't want to turn him down, even though she should.

There was one problem though.

She looked back at him over her shoulder as she brought up the next patient's information on her screen. "Malu Huna's luaus are only on Friday nights. And I have to work tomorrow. If you wanted to see the sights on Friday," she said, taking a deep breath to calm her racing nerves, "then I guess we could. It will make for a long day though. Are you sure you're up to that?"

"I am if you are," he said, his cane clinking against the desk as he moved closer. "I'll double up on my pain pills so I'm ready for anything."

Ready for anything.

Damn if those words, spoken in that deep velvet voice of his, didn't conjure a whole new batch of inappropriate thoughts. The two of them on the beach, holding hands and running into the waves together, lying in the sand afterward, making out like two horny teens, the feel of that dark stubble on his jaw scraping her cheeks, her neck, her chest, lower still...

Oh boy. I'm in trouble here.

Heat stormed her cheeks and she swiveled to face him, not realizing how close they were until it was too late. Her hand brushed his solid, warm chest before she snatched it away. Holden's hazel eyes flared with the same awareness jolting through her, before he quickly hid it behind a frown.

"Look, if you don't want to—"

"No, it's fine. I promised you and I always keep my word." She focused on the file on her screen again, trying in vain to calm her whirling thoughts. This was so not like her. She never went gaga over men. Yet here she was, blushing and stammering and acting like an idiot over the last man on Earth she should be attracted to. And yet, she was. Much as she hated to admit it.

Gah! Images of them lying together on that mat in the hotel gym zoomed back fast and furious to her mind. No. If she was going to get through this with her sanity and her heart intact, she needed to think logically about it. She'd show him her island home, not just the tourist sights, but her favorite spots too. Besides, it might give her a chance to find out more about his relationship with Dr. King and his real motives for being here in Hawaii. Taken in that light, she'd be a fool not to take him up on his offer, right? She took a deep breath, then set her tablet aside. "Fine. We'll tour the town, then end with the luau. Meet me in the lobby at the hotel at 8:00 a.m. the day after tomorrow and don't be late."

Holden opened his mouth, closed it, then he smiled—the slow little one that made her toes curl in her comfy white running shoes. Ugh. No more of that. She turned away to head into her next exam room as his surprised tone revealed an equal amount of shock on his part. "Uh…okay. Eight o'clock on Friday it is."

Four hours later, Holden was finishing up his shift by checking for the last time with Tommy Schrader. The kid was lucky. The steroids had helped reduce the swelling in his larynx and it didn't look like the thoracoscopy would be necessary after all.

When Holden arrived upstairs to Tommy's room, several of the kid's surfer friends were there, along with Tommy's father. Tommy was holding court like a king on his throne from his hospital bed, sun-streaked shaggy blond hair hanging in his face and his voice like gravel in a blender. But the fact the kid was speaking at all was a minor miracle. His injury could've been so much worse, and Holden was glad such a young guy wouldn't carry lifelong scars from his accident.

Unlike Holden himself.

He cleared his throat at the door to the hospital room to announce his presence. "Sorry if this is a bad time. Just wanted to check in on my patient one more time before my shift is over." He limped into the room with his cane and smiled at Mr. Schrader and the new guests. "Tommy's very lucky."

"Dudes, you have no idea," Tommy rasped out, smiling at Holden, then his friends. "They were gonna stick a camera up my nose and down my throat and everything."

"Whoa," his friends said, both as shaggy and sunburned as Tommy. "Man, that's gnarly. You were gonna be awake for that?"

"Patients are usually awake for thoracoscopy, yes," Holden confirmed as he reached Tommy's beside and leaned closer to examine the kid's throat. The swelling was greatly reduced, even from the last time Holden had checked him about an hour prior. He'd be fine to discharge.

He straightened and turned to Mr. Schrader, who was sitting on a chair near the window. "Your son appears to be healing just fine now, though Dr. Kim will continue to check on him for the remainder of his stay. I don't imagine there'll be any lingering effects, but I'll leave orders to discharge him with another round of steroids and some anti-inflammatory meds too. Then have him check in with your family physician in two weeks."

"Sounds good." The father shook Holden's hand. "Thanks so much, Doc. Now that I know my son's gonna be all right, once I get him home I'll make sure his older brothers keep an eye on him too. And try to talk him out of surfing so close to a full moon again."

Holden grinned and turned back to Tommy. "Listen to your dad. Take care, Tommy."

"Thanks, Doc. *Mahalo*," the kid said, shaking Holden's hand too. "I'll be sure to thank the pretty lady doc too. You guys make a good team. She your girlfriend?"

"Son," Mr. Schrader said, his voice rife with warning. "Don't mind him, Dr. Ross. That's all him and his friends think about these days when they're not surfing. Girls."

"I'll pass along gratitude to Dr. Kim," Holden said, dodging the uncomfortable questions and ignoring the squeeze of anxiety in his chest it caused. "Take care, all."

"*Mahalo*, Doc!" Tommy called again as Holden walked from the room to the nurses' station down the hall.

He should feel relieved to have another successful patient outcome under his belt, but now all he could think about was Leilani and their upcoming date on Friday.

Wait. Scratch that. Not a date.

He hadn't lied when he'd told her he didn't do that. Life was too unpredictable for long-term commitments. The shooting had taught him that. Nothing was permanent, especially love. So now he chose short, sweet, no strings attached affairs. No deeper, messy, scary emotions involved, thanks. No connections beyond the physical. No chance to have his heart ripped out and shredded to pieces. Because that's what he wanted.

Isn't it?

Not that it mattered. He and Leilani Kim were work colleagues, nothing more. Best to keep his head down and focus on his work, then move on when this stint ended. That was the safest bet. And Holden was all about safety these days.

She'd show him around the city, then take him to the luau at the resort, as promised. That's all. Nothing more. And sure, he couldn't stop thinking about the feel of her beneath him on that stupid gym mat, the sweet jasmine and lemon scent of her hair, the warm brush of her skin against his and…

Oh God.

He was such an idiot. What the hell had he been thinking to bring up her invitation to the luau? He hadn't been thinking, that was the problem. Or more to the point, he'd been thinking with his libido and not his brain. Memories of her dressed in those formfitting leggings and tank top at the gym that day, how she might wrap those shapely legs of hers around him instead, and hold him close, kiss him, run her fingers through his hair. He shuddered.

No. No, no, no.

With more effort than should be necessary to concentrate, Holden finished electronically signing off on his notes on the Tommy Schrader case, then left instructions for his discharge for Leilani before handing it all over to the nurse waiting behind the desk.

"Dr. King asked to see you upstairs in her office when you have a moment, Dr. Ross," the nurse said.

"Thanks." Probably about that project she'd mentioned to him before. He took a deep breath, then headed for the elevators. The clock on the wall said it was nearly time for him to leave. Good. He'd see Helen, then head back to the ER to hand off his cases to the next physician on duty before going back to the hotel for some much-needed sleep.

Besides, talking to Helen should be a good distraction from his unwanted thoughts about Leilani. The elevator dinged and he stepped on board then pushed the button for the fifth floor, where the administrative offices were located.

He had to get his head on straight again before Friday. Hell, if he was really serious about keeping to himself, he'd cancel the whole day altogether. Given the surprised look on her face when she'd offered to show him around, she'd probably be glad to be rid of him as well. But then if he did cancel, she might take it the wrong way, and the last thing he wanted was to offend her. They still had to work together, after all.

You guys make a good team.

Tommy's words from earlier echoed through his head. The worst part was, they were true.

Working with Leilani on that case had felt seamless, effortless, *right.*

Which was just wrong, in Holden's estimation.

He didn't want partnerships anymore, professionally or personally. Getting too close to people only made you vulnerable and weak, especially when they could be taken from you so easily.

Ding!

The elevator doors swished open and Holden stepped out into the lobby on the administrative floor. Thick carpet padded his footsteps as he headed over to the receptionist's desk in the middle of the plush leather-and-glass sitting area.

"Hi. Holden Ross to see Helen King, please," he said, feeling out of place and underdressed in his shift-old scrubs and sneakers.

"Dr. King's been expecting you, Dr. Ross." She pointed down a hallway to her left. "Last door on the right."

"Thanks." He gave the woman a polite smile, then headed for the office she'd indicated. The other times he'd met with Helen here in Hawaii, it had been outside the hospital, either at her home near Waikiki or at the fancy restaurant she'd taken him to on his first night in the city. Other than that, he'd never been up here, since regular old human resources was in another building entirely, half a block down from the medical center. He made his way to the end of the hall and stopped to admire the amazing view from the floor-to-ceiling glass wall beside the office before knocking on the dark wood door.

"Come in," Helen called from inside, and Holden entered the office.

For a moment, he took in the understated elegance of the place. It was Helen to a T, no-nonsense yet comfortable. "Wow, this is a big step up from Chicago, huh?"

Helen chuckled, her husky voice helping to soothe his earlier anxiety. "It doesn't suck. Please come in, Holden. Have a seat."

He did so, in a large wingback leather chair in front of her desk that probably cost more than his rent back home. As always, Helen's desk was spotless, with stacks of files neatly placed in bins and every pen just so. "The nurse downstairs said you wanted to see me?"

"I wanted to see how you're settling in," she said, sitting back in her black leather executive chair that dwarfed her petite frame. With her short white hair and sparkling blue eyes, she'd always reminded Holden of a certain British actress of a certain age, who took no crap from anyone. "We haven't talked in a few weeks. How are you liking things here at Ohana?"

"Fine." He did his best to relax but found it difficult. He and Helen had been friends long enough for him to suspect this wasn't just a social call. They could've gone to the pub for that. "The facilities are top-notch and the staff is great."

Better than great, his mind chimed in as he recalled Leilani.

Not that he'd mention his unwanted attraction to his coworker to Helen. The woman had been trying to get him married off since they'd worked together back in Chicago. If she even suspected a hint of chemistry between him and Leilani, she'd be all over it worse than the Spanish Inquisition.

"Glad to hear you like it." Helen steepled her fingers, then watched him over the top of them, her gaze narrowed, like M getting ready to assign her best secret agent a new kill. "But do you like it enough to consider staying?"

"What?" Holden tore his gaze away from the stunning views of the ocean in the distance and focused on Helen once more, his chest tightening. He frowned. "No. I'm locum tenens."

"I know," she said, sitting forward to rest her arms atop her desk. "But what if you weren't."

The low-grade anxiety constantly swirling in his chest rose higher, constricting his vocal cords. "But I am. You know I don't want to get tied down to anywhere. Not yet."

Maybe not ever again.

Helen blinked at him several times before exhaling slowly, her expression morphing from confident to concerned. "I'm worried about you, Holden. You've been on your own since the shooting, jetting off to a new place every few months, no connections, no home."

"I'm fine," he said, forcing the words. "Look, I thought you called me here to talk about that project you mentioned, not dissect my personal life."

"Are you fine though?" Her blue gaze narrowed, far too perceptive for his tastes. She sighed and stood, coming around the desk and leaning her hips back against it as she changed the subject. "Well, all that aside... Fine, let's discuss the project then."

Holden released his pent-up breath, his lungs aching for oxygen, and stared at the floor beneath his feet. Helen had saved his life after the shooting. Stitching up his wounds and staunching his blood loss until the orthopedic surgeons could work their magic on his leg and shoulder. Without her, there was a good chance he would've ended up six feet under, just like David.

An unexpected pang of grief stabbed his chest. Even a year later, he still missed his best friend like it was yesterday. The funeral. The awful days afterward, walking around like a zombie, no emotions, no light, no hope.

Still, he was here. He was coming back to life slowly, painfully, whether he wanted to or not. Like a limb that had fallen asleep, pins and needles stabbed him relentlessly as the emotions he'd suppressed for so long returned. Maybe that was why he felt so drawn to Leilani—her vibrant spirit, the sense that perhaps in some weird way she understood what he'd been through, how she made him feel things he'd thought he'd never feel again.

Plus, he owed Helen a debt he could never repay. That's why he was here in Hawaii. Why he was here now. She'd saved his life and his leg. The least he could do was hear her out. He cleared his throat, then asked, "What kind of project is it?"

"Twofold, actually." Helen clasped her hands in front of her. "First, our national accreditation is coming up for renewal next year and we need to make sure all of our security policies are up-to-date for the ER. I'd like you to help with that."

Holden swallowed hard and forced his tense shoulders to relax. "I can do that."

"Good." Helen glanced out the windows then back to him again. "Secondly, you know I'm looking for a new director of emergency medicine, yes?"

"Yes," he said. "But I'm here as a trauma surgeon."

"True. But you've got the experience and the temperament to head a department, Holden." She crossed her arms. "You were on track to run the ER back in Chicago, before the shooting."

He had been. That was true. But those ambitions had died along with David that day. He didn't want to be responsible for all those people, for all those lives. What if he failed again?

"I don't want that anymore. I'm happy with the temporary stint." His response sounded flat to his own ears and his heart pinched slightly despite knowing he couldn't even consider taking on a more permanent role. "Besides, Dr. Kim is doing a great job as temporary director. Why not offer it to her?"

"She's in the running, to be sure," Helen said before pushing away from the desk and walking over to the windows nearby. "But I like to keep my options open. And it's been nice having you here, Holden. I won't lie. We're friends. I know you. Trust you. Dr. Kim seems more than competent and her record at Ohana is outstanding, but every time I try to get to know her better, she shuts me down. I'm not sure I can work with someone I don't know and trust implicitly."

Holden had noticed Leilani deftly skirting his questions around her past too. Then again, he had no room to talk. He hadn't told her anything about what had happened to him either.

He exhaled slowly and raked a hand through his hair. He didn't like the idea of spying for Helen, no matter how much he owed her. Maybe he should cancel Friday, just so it wouldn't come back to bite him later, one way or another. Shut down any semblance of something more between him and Leilani before it ever really started. The fact he seemed more drawn to her each time they were together scared him more than anything, to be honest, and Holden was no coward. But damn if he wanted to open himself up to a world of hurt again, and some hidden part of him sensed that getting closer to Leilani would bring heartbreak for sure.

"I don't feel comfortable spying for you," he said bluntly. "Not on a colleague."

"No," Helen said, giving him a small smile. "I didn't imagine you would. Well, that's fine. Just keep an eye out during the project. If you see anything you think I should know about, let me know. Oh, and I haven't talked to Dr. Kim about it yet, so keep it under your hat, until I do. Okay?"

"Okay." Seemed an odd request, but an innocent one. "No problem. Anything else?"

"Nope. That's it." Helen walked back around her desk and took a seat. "I've got work to do, so get out of my office."

He chuckled and stood, his cane sinking into the thick carpet as he leaned his weight on it. "Let me know when it's safe to mention the project to Leilani. I'll be out until the weekend."

Helen gave him a quizzical look at his use of Dr. Kim's first name, and he kicked himself mentally. Then she winked and grinned as he hobbled toward the door.

"Enjoy your days off," she called after him.

"Thanks," he said, gritting his teeth against the soreness in his thigh. He needed to finish up his shift, then get back to the hotel, take a shower, rest, recharge, decide whether to cancel on Friday or spend the day with the one woman who'd somehow gotten under his skin despite all his wishes to the contrary.

"Oh, and Holden?" Helen called when he was halfway into the hall.

"Yeah?" He peeked his head back inside the office.

"Don't stay cooped up your whole time here in Hawaii," she said, as if reading his thoughts. "Get out and live a little. Trust me—you'll be glad you did."

Holden headed back down the hall and over the elevators, unable to shake the sense of fate weighing heavy on his shoulders. Too bad he didn't believe in destiny anymore. One random act of violence had changed all that forever.

Still, as he headed back down to the ER his old friend's words kept running through his head, forcing him to reconsider canceling his Friday plans with Leilani.

Get out and live a little. Trust me—you'll be glad you did...

CHAPTER FIVE

AT SEVEN FIFTY-EIGHT ON Friday morning, Leilani stood behind the reception desk at her parents' resort, feeding her parrot, U'i, and wondering if it was too late to fake a stomach bug to get out of her day with Holden.

"Who's a pretty bird?" U'i squawked, followed by a string of curses in three languages—Mandarin, Hawaiian and English.

Leilani snorted and fed him another hunk of fresh pineapple. She'd had him as a pet since right after the accident and loved him with all her heart, even though he acted like a brat and swore like a sailor sometimes. Considering he was sixteen and African grays typically lived as long as humans, U'i was definitely in his terrible teen years.

"More," he screeched when she wasn't fast enough with the next hunk of fruit. He took it in his black beak, then held on to a slice of orange with one foot while cocking his head at her and blinking his dark eyes. "Thanks, baby."

"You're welcome, baby," she said in return, scratching his feathered head with her finger and grinning. "Mama loves you."

"Mama loves you," U'i repeated, before devouring his treat.

"Hey," a deep male voice said from behind her, causing her heart to flip.

Leilani set aside the cup of fruit she'd snagged from the

breakfast buffet in the dining room, then wiped her hands on the legs of her denim shorts before turning slowly to face Holden. *Too late to run now*, she supposed. She gave him a smile and prayed she didn't look as nervous as she felt. "Hey."

In truth, she'd spent the last twenty-four hours seriously questioning her sanity for offering to be Holden's tour guide today. Sure, she wanted to get to know him better, but that was a double-edged sword. Getting to know him better risked getting to like him better. And liking him even more than she did now was a definite no-no, considering she melted a little more inside each time she saw him.

Like now, when he was standing there, looking effortlessly gorgeous in a pair of navy board shorts and a yellow Hawaiian shirt that rivaled any of the loud numbers her dad wore. The open V of his collar beckoned her eyes to trail slowly down his tanned chest to his trim hips and strong, sexy, tanned calves. God. How was that even possible? Their schedules at the hospital were nuts. Who had time to soak up the sunshine? Apparently, Holden did, since he looked like he'd walked straight off a "hot hunks in paradise" poster.

He shuffled his feet and switched his cane from one side to the other, making her realize she'd been staring. Self-conscious now, she turned back to her pet and fed him another chunk of pineapple from the cup.

"Who's your friend?" Holden asked.

"This is U'i," she said, leaning in to kiss the bird's head.

"Huey?" Holden asked, stepping closer to look at the parrot, who was eyeballing him back.

"No. *U'i*," Leilani corrected him. "No *h*. It means *handsome* in Hawaiian."

"Ah." He reached up toward the bird, then hesitated. "Does he bite?"

"Only if he doesn't like you." She snorted at Holden's startled expression, then took pity on him, holding out the fruit cup toward him. "Here, feed him some of this. U'i's never met food he didn't like."

Sure enough, her traitorous pet snagged the hunk of melon from Holden's fingers, then gave him an infatuated coo that Leilani was lucky to hear even after a half hour of cuddles and tummy rubs. Seemed Holden's considerable charms worked on more than just her.

"African gray, right?" Holden asked, bravely stroking a finger over U'i's head.

"Correct." Leilani smiled despite herself. "You a bird fan?"

"A friend of mine back in med school had one. Smart as a whip and snarky too."

"Yep, that's my guy here." She gave her beloved pet one more kiss, then stepped away fast. Holden moved as well, causing his arm to brush hers, sending tingles of awareness through her already overtaxed nervous system. "So, are you, uh, ready to go?"

"Whenever you are," Holden said, stepping back and giving her a too-bright smile. "Doubled my pain meds, so lead onward."

For the second time since their conversation in the ER on Wednesday, the thought popped into her head that maybe he was as nervous about all this as she was. After all, he'd been stammering and shifting around as much as her, his frown still fresh in her mind. She'd assumed it was because he didn't really want to spend time with her, but now she wondered if it went deeper than that.

"Did you get Tommy Schrader released okay—the surfboard patient? He was doing much better the last time I checked. He told me *mahalo*."

"Yep. He was doing much better when I discharged him. Gave him your scripts too. I'm glad there wasn't any permanent damage to his voice box." She wiped her hands off again and tossed away the empty fruit cup before walking back around the desk and beckoning for Holden to follow her. Well, regardless of how he felt about things, they were both stuck together

for the day now. Correction, day and evening, since they had
the luau tonight after their day of sightseeing. Then they could
go back to their separate lives. Leilani glanced at the clock on
the wall again. Five after eight. Man, it was going to be a long
day at this rate.

Okay. At least she had a full itinerary to keep them busy. First
though, a few questions. She glanced at his cane, then back to
his eyes. "How are you with walking?"

"Fine, I think," he said, adjusting his weight. "Like I said, I
took my pain meds this morning and have another dose in my
pocket in case I need it later. Actually, I think the exercise might
do me good. My physical therapist back in Chicago is always
on me to move more. Says it's the only way I'm going to get
full function back and lose this someday." He waggled his cane
in front of him. "I may need to take breaks every so often, but
I'm looking forward to a day in the fresh air."

"Okay then. Great." She started toward the front entrance,
slowing her usual brisk pace to make it easier on Holden. "I
thought we could start at North Shore, since the beach there is a
bit less crowded than Waikiki and you can get to Diamond Head
easy enough on your own with it being so close to the hotel.

"We can maybe grab a quick breakfast at one of the stands
at North Shore too, then go see Honolulu's Chinatown markets,
stop by the Iolani Palace downtown and visit the USS *Arizona*
memorial, then end the day by hiking to Manoa Falls. It's short
and mostly shaded, so it shouldn't be too tough for you. That
should get you plenty hungry for the luau tonight when we get
back to the hotel."

"Sounds great. Let's roll," he said, climbing into the hotel
shuttle Leilani had commandeered just for their use today, then
holding his cane between his knees. He seemed more relaxed
now than she'd ever seen him, and Leilani had to admit she
found him more attractive by the minute. "I'm all yours."

At his words, that darned awareness simmering inside her
flared bright as the sun again, and she said a silent prayer of

thanks that she was sitting down, because she doubted her wobbly knees would've supported her. There was a part of her that wished more than anything that were true, that he was hers, and if that wasn't terrifying, she didn't know what was.

She turned out of the hotel parking lot and wound her way through town before merging onto the H1 highway heading north, allowing the warmth from the sunshine and fresh air breezing in through the open windows to ease some of her tension away. His comment had been innocent enough and the fact that she instantly took it as more spoke to her own loneliness and neglected libido than anything else. Traffic thinned as they left the city behind. For his part, Holden seemed content to just stare out the window at the passing scenery, dark sunglasses hiding his eyes from her view.

Good thing too, since they were passing right by the spot where the accident had happened years ago. Man, she hadn't even thought about that when she'd been planning the itinerary for today, which only went to show how torn and twisted she'd been about this whole excursion. Now though, as they neared the junction of H1 and H2 and she veered off toward the right and the H2 highway, Leilani spotted a sign for the outlet mall close by and gripped the steering wheel tighter. They'd been going there that day, shopping for back-to-school clothes for her and her brother, when the accident happened. Her mouth dried and her chest ached as she held her breath and sped past the spot where they'd skidded off the road after impact, their station wagon tumbling over and over down into the ravine until finally landing on its roof, the wheels still spinning and groaning, the smell of gasoline and hissing steam from the radiator as pungent now as they'd been that long-ago day when Leilani had been trapped in the back seat, upside down, gravely injured, screaming for help while her loved ones died around her...

"Uh, are we in a huge hurry?" Holden said from the passenger seat, drawing her back to the present. "Speedometer says we're pushing eighty."

Crap.

She forced herself to take a breath and eased her death grip on the steering wheel. Throat parched, her words emerged as little more than a croak. "Sorry. Lead foot."

Holden watched her closely, his gaze hidden behind those dark glasses of his, but all the same, Leilani could feel his stare burning. Her cheek prickled from it and she focused on easing her foot off the accelerator to avoid the unsettling panic still thrumming through her bloodstream. It was fine. Things were all fine now. She was safe. They were safe.

"Everything okay?" Holden asked after a moment. "You look a little pale."

"No. It's fine." She took a few deep breaths as a couple of cars passed them. "Driving on the freeway bothers me, that's all."

His full lips turned down at the corners. "You should've said something earlier. If this is making you uncomfortable, we can go somewhere else. I can see the beach myself another time."

"No, it's fine." She kept her eyes straight ahead, afraid that if she looked at him, he'd see all the turmoil inside her. "Look. There's a sign for the Dole Plantation."

Holden looked toward his window then back to her. "Should we go there instead?"

"Nah." She shrugged, releasing some of the knots between her shoulder blades. "It's pretty and all, but not very exciting."

"Not very exciting isn't always a bad thing," he said, shifting to face front again.

The hint of sadness in his voice made her want to ask him more about his injuries, but after her flashbacks a minute ago, now didn't seem like the best time. Instead, she drove on toward the beach and, hopefully, something to keep them busy and away from dangerous topics. The rest of the forty-minute trip passed without incident, thankfully.

Sure enough, the beach was lovely. Fewer people and beautiful stretches of sand and surf for miles. They grabbed acai bowls in Haleiwa Town, then headed over to Ehukai Beach Park and the Banzai Pipeline to watch the surfers shred some waves.

They snagged some seats atop a wooden table in one of the picnic areas lining the sandy beach and had excellent views of the massive waves crashing toward the rocks just offshore.

"Man, that's impressive," Holden said around a bite of granola, coconut and tangy acai berries. "Look at that. How big do the waves get here?"

"Up to twenty-five feet during the winter. We're at the tail end now, with it being March, but they can still get pretty big." She chuckled at a small boy running out into the surf. "Check him out. Can't be more than five and already fearless."

"Wow." Holden stared wide-eyed as the child held his own on the big waves right next to the adults. "That's amazing."

"Yeah. I remember being his age and coming here with my dad. I learned to swim not far from here at the Point." Sadness pushed closer around her heart before she shoved it away. "Those were good days."

"Really?" He blinked at her now, suitably impressed. "So, you can hang ten with these guys then?"

She laughed around another bite of food. "Back in the day, sure. It's been years since I surfed though, so probably not now. Though they say it's like riding a bike. You never really forget."

"Hmm." He finished his food, then tossed his trash in a nearby receptacle, scoring a perfect three-pointer. He swallowed some water from his bottle, the sleek muscles working in his throat entrancing her far more than they should. "Well, I certainly won't be doing much surfing these days with my leg."

He rubbed his right thigh again, tiny whitish scars bisecting his tanned skin. From a distance they weren't as visible, but this close she could see them all. The questions she'd been putting off rose once more, but before she could ask, he slid down off the table and toed off his walking shoes. "Think I'll take a gander down the beach, if you don't mind."

"No. Go for it." She watched him head off, then finished her breakfast before standing to throw her own trash away. It was a beautiful spring day, not too hot or too cold, the scent of salt and sand filling the air. Above her, seagulls cried and leaves of the nearby banyan trees rustled in the breeze. She'd used to love coming here as a kid, building sandcastles with her brother, or cuddling on her mom's lap beneath the blue sky. She wrapped her arms around herself and kicked off her sneakers, venturing down to the water's edge to dip her toes in the bracing Pacific waters.

Lost in thought, she didn't even hear Holden return until he was right next to her on the wet sand, his cane in one hand and his shoes dangling from the fingers of the other. His dark hair was tousled and the shadow of dark stubble on his chin made her want to run her tongue over it, then nuzzle her face into his neck. She swallowed hard and stared out at the horizon and the surfers balancing on the crests of the waves rolling in. "How was your walk?"

"Good. Needed to stretch my legs after the car ride." He took a deep breath in and glanced skyward. "Hard to imagine your dad out here though. Never thought of Joe Kim as a surfer."

"Oh, he's not," she said without thinking, then stopped herself. Too late.

Holden was looking at her again, reaching up to lower those sunglasses of his so his hazel eyes were visible over the tops of their rims. "I'm confused."

A few weeks ago, she would've walked away, shut down this conversation with him. But now, today, she felt tired. Tired of pushing him away, tired of keeping up her walls so high and strong, tired of running. Leilani sighed and shook her head. "The Kims aren't my real parents. They adopted me after my family was killed in a car accident twenty years ago."

"Oh," Holden said, his voice distant as he took that in. After a few moments, he seemed to collect himself and stepped closer to her to block the breeze. "I'm sorry. That must've been horrible."

"It's okay," she said out of habit. Years of distancing people took their toll. "I mean, it happened a long time ago, when I was fourteen. I've moved on." And she had, at least in most areas. Work. School. Anywhere that didn't require true intimacy. Speaking of intimacy, Holden's body heat penetrated the thin cotton of her pink tank top and made her crave all sorts of things that were best left alone. She moved away and headed back toward their car. "We should probably get going if we want to make our eleven-thirty ticket time at Pearl Harbor."

He lingered on the beach a moment before limping after her. "Right. Sure."

Three hours later, Holden sat on the hard bench seat in the Navy boat shuttle beside Leilani on their way to the USS *Arizona* Memorial, glad for a break to rest his sore leg. Not that he would've missed anything from their day. They'd already spent time at several of the other sites within the World War II Valor in the Pacific National Monument, including touring the USS *Bowfin* Submarine Park, the Pearl Harbor Aviation Museum, and the USS *Missouri* Battleship Memorial, as well as walking through the visitors center, the Road to War Museum, and the Aloha Court. Neither of them had said much since leaving the North Shore.

Holden had spent much of the time trying to wrap his head around what Leilani had shared with him. Being a teenager was hard enough without losing your entire family. He couldn't imagine what she must've gone through back then, the grief, the loss. That certainly explained the pain he saw flashing in her dark eyes sometimes though. Also explained why she'd known so much about that seat belt law in the ER that day.

He'd wanted to ask her more about what had happened, but then she'd not really seemed open to it on the ride to Pearl Harbor. Once they'd gotten inside the park there'd been films to watch and audio tours, and now Holden had no clue how to broach the subject with her again.

Of course, then there was the fact that coming here, to the

site where so many had lost their lives in another act of violence brought all of his own pain rushing back to the forefront. December 7, 1941, was a long time ago, and he hadn't expected it to affect him as much as it did, but there'd already been several times when he'd nearly lost it.

The first time had occurred when they'd toured the Attack museum, which followed the events from Pearl Harbor through the end of World War II, and he'd seen the delicate origami crane by Sadako Sasaki, a young girl of only two when the bomb had been dropped on Hiroshima. Her goal had been to fold a thousand cranes during her time in the hospital for her injuries, which according to Japanese legend meant she'd then be granted a wish, but she'd only made it to six hundred and forty-four before her death at the age of twelve. Holden's chest still squeezed with sadness over her loss. Her family had donated the sculpture to the museum in the hopes of peace and reconciliation.

The second time had been during the film they'd watched before boarding the shuttle to tour the USS *Arizona* Memorial. Hearing the servicemen and women and the eyewitnesses to the event talk about their fallen comrades and the horrific things they'd seen that day had taken Holden right back to the shooting in Chicago—the eerie quiet in the ER after the gunman had opened fire broken only by the squeak of the attacker's shoes on the tile floor, the metallic smell of the weapons firing, David's last desperate gasps for air as he'd bled out on the floor beside Holden, and the helpless feeling of knowing there was nothing he could do to stop it.

He forced himself to take a deep breath and focused out the open window on the gentle waves lapping the sides of the shuttle. The scent of sea and the light jasmine shampoo from Leilani's hair helped calm his racing pulse. This wasn't Chicago. They were safe here.

They docked a few minutes later and got out to traverse the new ramps that had been installed the previous year for visitors to the monument. The other passengers were quiet too, almost reverent at they stood before the iconic white stone structure. According the audio narration both he and Leilani were listening to through their headphones, it was built directly over the site of the sinking of the battleship *Arizona* in 1941 and to match the ship's length, to commemorate the lives lost that day.

Ahead of them in line was a group of six older men, dressed in hats and sashes from World War II. Some were in wheelchairs or walked with canes, like Holden. All of them were visibly shaken the moment they entered the memorial. Holden himself had goose bumps on his arms at the thought of the brave soldiers who'd perished that day with no warning, no chance to escape. He felt their panic, knew their fear, understood their need to protect others even at the cost of their own lives.

Lost in his thoughts, he barely noticed when the narration ended and Leilani put her hand on his arm. He leaned heavily on his cane, swallowing hard against the lump in his throat, and finally met her gaze. Her expression was both expectant and worried and he realized she must've asked him something. He removed his headphones and swiped a hand over his face. "I'm sorry?"

"I asked if you were all right," she whispered. "You look like you're going to pass out."

"I'm fine," he said, though he wasn't. Thankfully, a cool breeze was blowing in through the openings in the sides and ceiling of the stone monument, cooling him down a bit. At her dubious look, he gave her a wan smile. "Really. But could we just stand here a minute?"

"Sure." She moved them out of line and over to the railing, where the breeze was stronger, and the shade helped too. As the other patrons in their tour group made their way up toward the front of the memorial, where the names of all the people lost that day were etched into the stone, Leilani leaned her arms on the railing beside him and gazed out over the water. "Every time I come here it hits me. How fragile and precious life is.

How quickly it can be taken from you." She shook her head and looked at the horizon. "Not that I should need the reminder."

"True." He watched the group of veterans approach the wall of names, most of them openly crying now, and he blinked away the sting in his own eyes. He never talked about the shooting with people he didn't know. It was still too raw. But for some reason, Leilani didn't feel like a stranger anymore. In fact, today he felt closer to her than he had anyone in a long, long time. He rubbed the ache in his right thigh and exhaled slowly before saying, "I shouldn't need the reminder either. Not after what happened in Chicago."

She looked sideways at him then, her tone quiet. "Is that where you were injured?"

He nodded, absently fiddling with the head of his cane. "There was an attack in the ER where I worked."

Leilani frowned and shifted to face him, the warmth of her arm brushing his. "Someone attacked you?"

Holden took a deep breath then dived in, afraid that if he stopped he wouldn't get it all out, and right now it felt like if he didn't get it all out at once, he'd choke. "A shooting. Gunman looking for opioids. Guy needed his fix. Came in, got past the security guards and opened fire when we refused to give him anything."

"Oh God. Holden, I'm so so—" she started, but he held up a hand.

"I tried to stop the guy. Well, me and my best friend, David. We tried to take him down before he could hurt anyone, but we failed. I failed." He swallowed hard and forced himself to continue. "Took a bullet to my right thigh. Shattered my femur but missed my femoral artery, luckily. David was applying a tourniquet to my leg to stop the bleeding when the gunman shot him point-blank in the back. He died instantly. The bullet that pierced his heart tore through my left shoulder as it exited his body. I lay there, bleeding beneath my best friend's body, until help arrived. Longest hour of my life. I thought I would die too. For a long time, I wished I had."

Silence fell between them for a long moment. Leilani reached over and took his hand, lacing her fingers through his before giving them a reassuring squeeze. "How long ago did it happen?"

"Almost a year." The group of veterans at the stone wall turned to make their way out of the memorial arm in arm, a brotherhood forged by grief and remembrance. Holden used his free hand to swipe at the dampness on his own cheeks, not caring now what people thought about him crying in public. Hell, almost every person in the place had tears in their eyes it was that moving.

He took another deep breath, then hazarded a glance over at Leilani. "I don't tell many people about that."

She nodded, staring at the lines of people going in and out. "I understand. I don't talk about the accident much either."

Her hand was still covering his, soft and strong and steady, just like the woman herself. He had the crazy urge to put his arm around her and pull her into his side, bury his nose in her sweet-smelling hair, hold her close and never let her go.

Whoops. No.

He wasn't staying here in Hawaii. He never stayed anywhere long these days. Leilani deserved a relationship that would last forever, not a fling with a broken man like him. She deserved better than he could give. So he kept to himself and pulled his hand away before he couldn't anymore. They still had the rest of the day to get through and the luau tonight. Best to keep things light and not mess it up by bringing his libido into the mix.

They got back in line and saw the carved names of the people who'd perished, then they rode back to the shore on the shuttle before exiting the park and making their way back to their vehicle. A strange sense of intimacy, a heightened connection, had formed between them after their mutual confessions about their past, but Holden refused to make it into anything more than it was. No matter that his heart yearned to explore the undeniable chemistry between them. Leilani was off-limits, same as before. They could be friends, good friends even, but not friends with benefits.

Nope.

Now, if he could just get his traitorous body on board with that plan, he'd be all set.

"So, where are we going next?" he asked, once they were back in the car. He swallowed another pain pill, gritting his teeth against the lingering bitterness on his tongue, then forced a smile. They couldn't have a future together, but that didn't mean he couldn't savor the rest of the day.

"Figured we'd hit Honolulu Chinatown next, get some lunch, then head to the Iolani Place before hiking to Manoa Falls to round out the day." She grinned over at him before starting the engine and pulling out of their parking spot. "Sound good?"

"Sounds great," he said, ignoring the way his stomach somersaulted with need now every time he looked at her. He'd enjoy their time together, remember today and move on when it was over. No heartache, no emotions, no vulnerability. Because that's what he wanted.

Isn't it?

Except as they merged back onto the H1 highway toward Honolulu once more, the warmth in Holden's chest told him that quite possibly he'd already gotten far more attached to his lovely Hawaiian colleague than he'd ever intended, and the realization both thrilled and terrified him.

CHAPTER SIX

AFTER WANDERING AROUND the markets and arts district of Chinatown and enjoying a yummy late lunch of dim sum and noodles at the Maunakea Marketplace, they'd hit the Iolani Palace in downtown Honolulu before heading to a residential street just past Waakaua Street. Leilani parked near the curb and got out. It had been a while since she'd spent a day just enjoying all that her hometown of Honolulu had to offer, and she had Holden to thank.

She should also thank him for opening up to her about the shooting and for not pressing her about the car accident that had killed her family. In fact, she wanted to thank him for a lot of things, not the least of which was for helping her to relax and just breathe again.

Honestly, Leilani couldn't remember the last time she'd had such a fun, relaxing day.

No. Not relaxing. That wasn't the right word, given that her adrenaline spiked every time Holden brushed against her or leaned closer. More like exhilarating. She'd had an exhilarating day with him. Good thing the short hike to the falls would help to burn off some of her excess energy. Otherwise she just might tackle him and kiss him silly, which was unacceptable.

Leilani waited on the curb while Holden got out of the passenger side of the car, then hit the button on her key fob to lock the doors before they slowly started down the sidewalk toward the trailhead. He limped along beside her, looking better than he had back at the *Arizona* Memorial. When she first turned and saw him looking gray and desolate as a stormy sky, her immediate thought had been he was seasick. But then she'd seen the pain and panic in his eyes and feared an anxiety attack was on the way.

So she'd steered him over to the side of the space and heard his harrowing tale. Funny, but she'd always felt a bit isolated after the accident, as if she'd been the only person to experience such a violent and immediate loss. But hearing Holden speak about the attack in his ER made her realize that she wasn't as alone as she'd thought. Of course, she'd had twenty years to adjust to the past. For Holden it was still fresh, not even a year had passed.

Knowing what he'd been through made her want to reach out and hold him close, keep him safe from harm and soothe his wounded soul. Except she wasn't sure she could stop herself there, instead falling deeper into like or lust or whatever is was that sizzled between them.

She wasn't ready to go there, not now. Not with him.

Am I?

No. It would be beyond stupid to get involved with the guy. He was only there temporarily, and even if he wasn't, he was her biggest rival for the job of her dreams—which she needed to remember to ask him about too. Amidst all the fun they'd had, she'd forgotten earlier, but now she needed to remember her true purpose for today. Find out more about him and why he was here, so she'd know better how to handle the promotion competition at work.

The fact that he looked adorable and smelled like sunshine was beside the point.

"It's only about a half mile ahead to the start of the trail. Will you be okay?" she asked, giving him some side eye as they continued up the sidewalk.

"I'm good," he said, flashing her a quick crooked grin that did all sorts of naughty things inside her. "I took my other pain pill while we were in Chinatown, so I should be set for the next six hours at least."

"Great."

"Yeah."

They continued a while longer in companionable silence, dappled light through the palm fronds above creating patterns on the ground beneath their feet. The neighborhood was quiet and peaceful, just the occasional yap of a dog or the far-off rush of the ocean filling the air around them. The tang of freshly mowed grass tickled her nose and a pair of zebra doves waddled across the paths not far ahead of them.

"Did I ask you about Tommy Schrader?" Holden asked at last.

"Yeah, you did," she said, chuckling. "This morning back at the hotel."

"Right. Sorry." He looked away. "Thanks for today, by the way. All the places you've taken me to have been great."

"You're welcome." She pointed to the right and a sign for the trailhead. "There's so much more to see too. Besides Diamond Head, if you get the chance you should check out the snorkeling at Hanauma Bay. The zoo and aquarium in Waikiki are nice too. Oh, and Kualoa Ranch on the windward coast. It's beautiful, with a private nature reserve, working cattle ranch, as well as the most amazing zip line ever."

"Cool. I'd love to see it sometime." He closed his eyes and inhaled deep. "Maybe we can take another day trip together."

Her chest squeezed and she gulped. She'd like nothing better, so the answer was no.

When she didn't respond right away, he hurriedly said, "Or not. I'm sure I can find my way on my own. I didn't mean to—"

"No, no. It's fine." Liar. Leilani felt lots of things at the moment—excited, scared, nervous, aroused—but *fine* definitely wasn't one of them. Still, she'd gotten so used to blowing off people's concern over the years it was hard to shift gears now. "I mean, I appreciate the offer, but I'd have to check my schedule and things are a bit crazy right now at the hotel too, so my parents need my help sometimes in my off hours and..."

He gave her a curious look. "The Kims seem like good people. You were lucky to have them adopt you."

Glad for the change of subject, Leilani took the bait. "Yeah, they're awesome. They were friends of my parents, actually. It was easier for me to adjust to living with them than it might've been if they were strangers."

He nodded and continued beside her onto the wide, black, gravel-covered trail into the rain forest surrounding the waterfall. "Like I said before, I can't imagine how hard that must've been for you, losing your family. And at that age too. Being a teenager is hard enough as it is."

"True." The light was dimmer in here with the thick foliage and the temperature had dropped. Leilani shivered slightly and was surprised when Holden moved closer to share body heat. The scent of dirt and fresh growing things surrounded them, and the low hum of the waterfall ahead created a sense of privacy. She'd not gone into detail about the accident with Holden earlier at the beach, but with everything he'd shared with her about the shooting, she felt like, for the first time in a long time, she could open up with him too.

They crested a short hill and reached the falls. One hundred and fifty feet tall, the water cascaded down the granite walls behind it, shimmering with rainbows in the sun. She looked over at him, her pulse tripping a bit at his strong profile, his firm lips, so handsome, so kissable. He was almost as dazzling as the falls themselves. To distract herself she asked the most mundane thing she could think of. "Why'd you go into emergency medicine?"

Holden shrugged. "I always loved science as a kid and wanted to know how things worked, especially things inside the body.

I'm a natural problem solver and detail oriented. But I'm also restless and a bit hyperactive, so I needed to choose a specialty that took that into consideration. Trauma surgery ticked all the boxes for me." He smiled, his teeth white and even in the slight shadows from the trees around them, and the barriers around her heart crumbled a bit more. "What about you?"

"Well," she said, moving her ponytail aside to reveal the scar on her neck. "See this?"

He leaned in closer, his warm breath tickling her skin. She suppressed another shiver, this one having nothing to do with the temperature and everything to do with the man beside her. "Wow. Is that from the accident?"

"It is." Leilani took a deep breath, then exhaled slowly before diving in. "We were on our way to the outlet mall, of all places. It was a sunny day and hot. The sky was blue and cloudless. Weird how I remember that, right?"

"Nah." Holden took her arm to pull her aside to let another couple pass them on the trail. "I remember all the details about the shooting. What people wore, what the room smelled like, how the floor felt sticky under my cheek. It's what trauma does to people's memories."

She nodded, then continued down the trail once the other people had passed. "Anyway, our car was an older model. When the other driver T-boned us, it sent us through the guardrail and down into a ravine. Car flipped over three times before landing on the roof, from what the police report says." She blinked hard against the tears that threatened to fall. "My brother and parents died instantly." They stopped under a natural canopy of tree trunks entwined over the trail, and Leilani rested back against their solid weight for support. "I was the only one left alive."

"Oh God." Holden stepped closer and took her hand this time, holding it close to his chest. The steady *thump-thump* of his heart beneath her palm helped ground her and kept her from getting lost in the past again. "I'm so sorry, Leilani. How in the world did you survive?"

"Sheer luck, I'm pretty sure." She gave a sad little laugh. "Both my legs were broken, but I was awake the whole time. I still have nightmares about it sometimes."

"I bet."

After another deep breath, she continued. "The scar on my neck is from a chunk of glass that lodged there. It nicked the artery but kept enough pressure until help arrived. Otherwise I would've died like the rest of my family. The only reason I'm here now is the paramedics and the ER staff who helped me that day. So that's why I went into emergency medicine. Because of their compassion and to pay my debt to them."

"Wow." He slowly slid his arm around her and pulled her into a hug. She didn't resist, too drained from telling her story and, well, it just felt too darned good being this close to him at last. He rested his chin on the top of her head and said again, "Wow."

The stroke of his fingers against her scalp felt so good it nearly hypnotized her.

"That's why you knew about the seat belt laws, isn't it?" he asked after a moment, his voice ruffling the hair at her temple.

"Yeah," she said, pressing her cheek more firmly against his chest. "Seat belts and air bags would've made all the difference."

They stood there, wrapped in each other's arms and their own little world, until more people came down the trail and they had to step aside to allow them through. Once separated, neither seemed to know where to look or what to do with their hands.

For her part, it took all Leilani's willpower not to throw herself back into Holden's arms. But then, thankfully, her good old common sense kicked in, along with the warning bells in her head, telling her that no matter how tempting it might be to throw caution to the wind, she couldn't do that. Couldn't let him in because he'd either be leaving soon or possibly taking the job she wanted if he stayed. Both of which would only break her heart. And she'd had more than enough heartache for one lifetime.

Hoping for some time and space to get her head clear again,

she started back down the trail toward the car, then waited for him to follow. "We should get back to the hotel so we can shower and change before tonight."

Holden stared at his reflection in the full-length mirror in his room early that evening and hoped he was dressed appropriately for a luau. Honestly, he had no idea what you wore to a party on the beach. Swim trunks, maybe, but that seemed a bit too relaxed.

He'd opted instead for a fresh Hawaiian shirt, this one in a pale turquoise color with small palm trees and desert islands on it and a clean pair of jeans. Flip-flops on his feet, per Leilani's advice, since it was the beach after all, and sand was everywhere.

His mind still churned through everything that had happened that day, all he'd seen, and the things he and Leilani had told each other. He still couldn't quite believe he'd confided in her about the shooting. He never really talked about it with anyone, outside of his therapist back in Chicago and occasionally with Helen. But telling Leilani about what had happened had felt different today. Scary, yes, but also strangely cathartic and right.

Maybe it was because of what she'd gone through with that awful car accident, but she'd never once made him feel judged or forced him to go further with his story than he was willing. The fact that she'd also confided in him had made the exchange even more special. From working with her the past month, he knew she was almost as guarded as he was when it came to letting other people close, so for her to open up with him like that meant something.

Then, of course, there was that hug at the waterfall.

Couldn't deny that had been nice. Amazing, actually. And sure, it was ill-advised, given he had no business starting anything with Leilani. Holden never knew where he'd be from month to month, let alone year to year. Beginning a relationship only to move thousands of miles away wasn't fair to anyone.

Trouble was though, his heart seemed to have other yearnings where Leilani was concerned.

She was smart, sweet and made every nerve ending in his body stand at attention. But there was also a wealth of vulnerability lurking beneath her sleek, shiny exterior. Sort of like him. She'd been through things, dealt with pain most people never experienced, and yet she was still standing. That took guts. It also took a lot out of a person. Made them more resilient, yes, but at a cost. He absently rubbed the ache in his chest, then grabbed his cane.

Enough stewing over things that would never happen anyway.

He left his room and headed down to the lobby, where he was supposed to meet Leilani. Dinner was served at sunset, she'd said, but there were plenty of other things to see before then. It was going on seven now and the sun was just nearing the horizon. People milled about the lobby, most heading out toward the beach behind the hotel where the luau would take place. He'd chosen his outfit well, considering lots of other guys were wearing similar things. The ladies mainly had on casual dresses or skirts and a few had tropical flowers pinned in their hair. From somewhere outside the strains of ukulele music drifted through the air, and the general mood of the place was festive and fun.

Being taller than most people at six foot four did have its advantages, and over the tops of the people's heads, he spotted Leilani waiting for him against the wall near the exit to the beach. He started that way, only to find his path blocked by one of the hotel staff, a pretty Polynesian girl dressed in a traditional hula outfit.

"Aloha," she said, giving him a friendly, dimpled smile. She reached up and hung a lei made of black shiny shells around his neck, then kissed his cheek. *"Pōmakia'i."*

Blessings. He'd managed to pick up a few native words during his stay in Honolulu and he smiled down at the woman. Lord knew Holden and Leilani could use all the good fortune they could get.

"Pōmakia'I," he said in return.

He stepped around the woman and continued on toward the far wall, stopping short as he got his first full look at Leilani tonight.

Seeing her earlier today in shorts and a tank top or as she was usually dressed at work in scrubs was one thing. Seeing her tonight in a short, colorful sarong-style dress made of native tropical print purple and white fabric was, well... *Stunning.* Her sleek black hair was loose, streaming down her back like shimmering ink, and that strapless dress hugged her curves in all the right places, ending above her knee and revealing just enough of her tanned legs to give a guy all kinds of wicked fantasies.

She looked over and spotted him, then smiled, waving him over. He blinked hard, trying to clear his head of images of them hugging near the waterfall, of him pulling her closer, kissing her, holding her, unwinding that dress of hers and covering her naked body with his and driving her wild with passion until she was begging him for more...

Whoa, Nelly.

He ran a finger under his collar, wondering when the temperatures had gotten so warm. His pulse pounded and his blood thrummed with need, and man, oh, man—he was in serious trouble here.

"Holden," she called, "over here." The slight impatience edging her tone cut through his haze of lust, spurring him into action at last. He slowly limped through the people to where she stood near the open doorway. At least the spark of appreciation in her eyes as she took in his appearance made him feel a bit less awkward. She liked him too. That much was obvious. Too bad they couldn't explore it. If he'd had more time here, then maybe, just this once...

Helen's offer of the directorship position flashed back in his mind.

No. He couldn't take that job. Leilani wanted it. She'd be damned good at it too. Better than him, probably.

But if it gave me more time here in paradise...

"You look great," she said, her words a tad huskier than they'd been before. Or maybe that was just his imagination. Either way, the compliment headed straight southward through his body. "Like you belong here."

"Thanks," he managed, doing his best not to get lost in her eyes. "You look beautiful."

Pretty pink color suffused her cheeks before she looked away and gestured toward the outside. "Thanks. Shall we?"

He followed her out onto the cement patio, then down the stairs to the large grassy gardens spanning the distance between the hotel and the beach beyond. A line of palm trees designated the border between the two. Rows and rows of long tables and chairs had been set up for people to sit and eat, and along each side were buffet tables piled high with all sorts of food. Beyond those were other activities, like spear throwing and craft making. She led him through it all—the men weaving head wreaths out of coconut leaves, the women making leis, the young guys offering to paint temporary tattoos on the cute girls. All the hotel staff seemed to be participating, all dressed in native Hawaiian outfits—grass skirts for all with the women's being longer than the men's, elaborate neck pieces and headdresses, leis everywhere. It was walking into another world and Holden found himself completely enchanted.

"This is awesome," he said, accepting a leaf crown from one of the men weaving them. "I had no idea it would be so elaborate."

Leilani showed him a huge fire pit, where a whole pig was roasting beneath enormous banana leaves. The smell was so delicious, his stomach growled loudly. Lunch seemed way too far away at that point and he thought he could probably eat half that pig all by himself. "Don't worry," she said, as if reading his thoughts. "They've got more inside in the kitchen."

"Good, because I'm starving."

"Me too." She laughed, then took his arm, tugging him

toward the front of the area, where a stage had been set up and currently a quartet of local musicians played a variety of Hawaiian music. That explained the ukuleles he'd heard earlier. Holden spotted Leilani's dad behind the stage and waved to him. Joe waved back. Leilani pulled Holden out of the way of a racing toddler, then kept her hand on his bare forearm, the heat of her searing his skin and bringing his earlier X-rated thoughts back to mind. They stopped near the best table in the bunch, front row, center stage. "This is where we're sitting for dinner and the show."

"Really?" He raised his brows. "Pays to know people in high places, huh?"

"It does." She winked, then pointed back to where the pig was roasting. Two burly staffers in native costumes had pulled away the banana leaves and were raising the whole roast pig up in the air with a loud grunt. The crowd applauded and Leilani leaned in close to whisper, "C'mon. Let's eat."

Didn't have to ask him twice. After loading up their plates with Kalua pig and barbecue chicken and *lomi* salmon and poi and fresh pineapple, they made their way back to the table just as Leilani's father took the stage as MC for the evening.

"Aloha! Welcome to the weekly luau at the Malu Huna Resort. Please help yourselves to the wonderful food and enjoy our entertainment this evening. Mahalo!"

The band started up again, joined by hula dancers, and Holden dug into his food with gusto. "This. Is. Amazing," he said around a bite of tangy, salty *lomi* salmon. The cold fish mixed with ripe tomatoes and onions was just the right foil for the sweeter pork and chicken. "Thanks for inviting me tonight. And thanks again for today."

"You're welcome." She smiled at him over the rim of her mai tai glass. "I love my hometown and am always glad to share it with others."

"It's great here. Seriously." He swallowed another bite of food, this time devouring a spoonful of poi. It was a bit like eating a mouthful of purple cream of wheat mixed with fruit. Not bad at all. Next he tried more pork and nearly fainted from the goodness. "Man, why does food never taste this amazing back on the mainland?"

Leilani snorted. "Probably because you didn't hike all over an island back in Chicago."

"True." He continued munching away as the band played on and more dancers joined them onstage. They were picking tourists from the crowd as well, but he kept his head down to avoid eye contact and not be chosen for humiliation. Finally, he'd had enough to eat and sat back, rubbing his full stomach and smiling lazily. "I don't think I've felt this full in forever."

"There's still haupia for dessert, don't forget." Leilani said, still eating. "Can't miss that."

"Nope." He sat back as a server cleared his empty dishes, then hobbled over to grab himself a plate of said haupia. It looked a bit like cheesecake without the crust, served on top of more banana leaves. He brought back two slices, one for himself and one for Leilani, then took a bite. It was good—creamy like cheesecake, but a burst from the coconut milk that was pure Hawaii. "Wow, this is really good too."

"Told you." Leilani finished her food at last, then pushed her plate aside and pulled her dessert over. "Speaking of Chicago, how exactly to you know Helen King?"

Holden almost choked on his bite of haupia but managed to swallow just in time. "She was a visiting surgeon at the hospital where I worked. We got to know each other there."

She saved my life.

He kept that last bit to himself, figuring he'd already told her more than enough about the shooting and there was no need to ruin the night by bringing it up again. "Why?"

"Just wondered." She shrugged, then watched the dancers for a bit. "I'm interested in the directorship position, you know."

Ah. So that's where this was headed. He wanted to tell her she had nothing to worry about, but then he couldn't really. Could he? Even if he didn't take the offer Helen had made him, there was the other issue of Helen not feeling like she knew Leilani well enough to trust her with that much authority yet. Maybe her temporary stint as director would become a full-time gig, maybe it wouldn't. Either way, Holden planned to be gone before then anyway. He tried to play it off with humor instead. "I kind of figured, since you're doing the job already and all."

"Has she offered you the job?" Leilani asked bluntly.

Yes.

"No," he lied. Helen had brought the subject up, but he'd turned it down. No need to bring that up either, right? Leilani watched him closely, her dark gaze seeming to see through to his very soul and for a moment he felt like a deer in headlights. Maybe he shouldn't have lied. If he told her the truth now though, that might be the end of all this, and he really didn't want it to be over. Not yet. He looked away, toward the stage, without really seeing it. "Why do you ask?"

"No reason," she said, the weight of her gaze resting on him a bit longer before moving away. "I just…" She sighed, then faced the stage as well, her tone turning resigned. "Listen, Holden. About what happened at the waterfall earlier. I don't want you to get the wrong idea. I like you. You're a good doctor, but I'm not looking for anything more, okay? We can be friends, but that's it." She took another bite of her haupia then pushed the rest aside. "And as friends, I'd appreciate a heads-up if you decide to pursue the directorship, all right?"

"All right." He was still trying to wrap his head around the swift change of subjects and how she'd sneaked in the bit about the waterfall into the mix, like he wouldn't notice that way. Of course, his analytical mind took it one step further, making him doubt the connecting and chemistry he'd felt between them earlier. He shouldn't care and yet, he did. In fact, her words stung far more than he wanted. Which was silly because he didn't want that either.

No strings, no relationships. That was his deal.

Isn't it?

Holden hung his head, more confused now than ever. Maybe it was the fact she'd beat him to the punch that bothered him. Usually he was the one stressing that there'd be nothing long-term. Yep, that had to be it.

He shoved aside the lingering pang of want inside him and brushed his hands off on his jeans, doing his best to play it all off as no big deal—when inside it felt like a very big deal indeed. "If I decide to go after the directorship, I promise I'll let you know. And don't worry about earlier. Look, we shared some personal things, hugged. That was all," he said, trying to sound way more unaffected than he was. "No harm, no foul."

The band cleared the stage, replaced by a line of men with drums. Torches were lit around the area and the same big, burly guys who'd been weaving crowns and throwing spears earlier took the stage. A hush fell over the crowd as Leilani's father announced the fire dance. Much as Holden wanted to see it though, a strange restlessness had taken up inside him now and he needed to move, needed to get out of there and get some fresh air. Get his mind straight before he did something crazy like pull Leilani into his arms and prove to her that he didn't care about the job, to show her that their hug earlier really had meant something, no matter how much she denied it. Talk about fire. There was one raging inside him now that refused to be extinguished no matter how hard he tried.

Onstage, the male dancers stomped and grunted and beat their chests in a show of strength and dominance over the flames surrounding them. Holden pushed to his feet and grabbed his cane, feeling like he too was burning up from the emotions he'd tried so long to suppress after the shooting, but that Leilani had conjured back to life all too easily.

"I need to walk," he said to her before sidling away through the tables toward the beach beyond, one hand holding his cane and the other clenched at his side in frustration. "Be back in a bit."

CHAPTER SEVEN

LEILANI SAT AT the table for a few minutes, brain buzzing about what to do. He'd not really answered her question about the job, but she'd told him point-blank where she stood with that, so yeah. She'd put her cards on the table, careerwise. The next move there was up to him.

Emotionally though, there were still a lot of things she hadn't told him.

Things like if he'd have kissed her at the waterfall, she'd have let him. Would have allowed him a lot more than kisses too, if she were honest. An old, familiar lump of fear clogged her throat before she swallowed hard against it. Much as it terrified her to admit, she wanted Holden, plain and simple. If she were honest, she'd wanted him for a while now. That certainly explained the awareness sparking between them whenever he was around. She sipped her mai tai and tried to focus on the dancers onstage, but it was no use. All she could seem to think about now was him. About how well they'd worked together on the surfboard kid's case. About how adorable he'd looked that morning, awkward but adorable. About all the things he'd shared with her that day and how he'd made her feel less alone. About how he'd kept up with her, even though it had been hard with his leg. About how he'd not given up or given in.

He was kind and smart and more than competent as a surgeon. And truthfully, she'd always been a sucker for men with brains and brawn. Not to mention his dreamy hazel bedroom eyes.

Gah!

A waitress came by and replenished Leilani's drink, but she barely noticed now. All she could think about was the hug they'd shared earlier at the waterfall. The feel of him in her arms, the heat of his body warming her, the thud of his heart beneath her ear, steady, strong, solid.

The long-standing walls around her heart tumbled down even further.

Holden had lived through horrific events, just like her. He understood her in a way no other man ever had. And he didn't treat her differently because of what she'd been through either, whereas all the past men she'd been with had acted like she was made out of fragile china or something once they knew about the accident. Leilani wasn't breakable, well, not to that extent anyway.

She resisted the urge to rub the uncomfortable ache in her chest—yearning mixed with apprehension.

The trouble was Holden made her vulnerable in a whole new way. Part of her wanted to put as much distance as possible between them, let him go his way and stick to her own solitary path. But the other part of her longed to go after him, to find him on the beach and tell him that she didn't want forever, but she'd sure as hell take right now.

He made her want to take risks again. And that was perhaps the scariest thing of all.

Also, the most exhilarating. She couldn't remember the last time she'd felt so alive.

As the fire dancers reached a fevered pitch onstage, a volcano of feelings inside Leilani finally erupted as well, making her feel reckless and wild. She wasn't ready for a relationship with Holden, that was true. Relationships meant ties and connections and all sorts of other terrifying things that could rip out a person's heart and shatter it into a million pieces.

But a fling...

Well, flings were another beast entirely. If he agreed, a fling meant they could have their cake and eat it too. Given that Holden would most likely be moving on to another locum tenens position and the fact he'd flat out told her he wasn't interested in a relationship either, meant he might be game for an affair. He hadn't ruled that out at all.

She downed the rest of her mai tai in one gulp then stood. Desire vibrated through her like a tuning fork and adrenaline fizzed through her bloodstream. As the fire dancers' performance ended to thunderous applause and her dad took the mic again to introduce the Don Ho impersonator, Leilani weaved her way through the tables and headed for the beach in search of Holden.

Once she was past the light of the torches at the edge of gardens, it took her eyes a minute to adjust in the twilight. At first she didn't see him, then she spotted Holden near the shore, silhouetted by the full moon's light, his cane in one hand, his flip-flops in the other.

Heart racing in time with her steps, Leilani kicked off her own shoes, then rushed down toward the water, toward Holden, her mind still racing with discordant thoughts.

He wants you. He doesn't want you. It's all in your head. It's all in your heart.

Whatever the outcome, she had to try. Felt like she'd die if she didn't.

Leilani stopped a few feet behind Holden, hesitating before saying, "I lied."

For a moment he didn't turn, just stood there, staring out over the Pacific as the stars twinkled above. She lived and died in those few seconds. Then he turned to face her, his gaze dark in the shadows surrounding them. "About what?"

Feeling both brave and terrified at the same time, she stepped closer and forced herself to continue. She didn't do this, didn't run after men, didn't pursue her feelings. But tonight, with

Holden, she couldn't stop herself. She wanted him and she'd have him, if he wanted her too. "I lied, earlier." She fumbled for her words. "I mean not about long-term things. I don't do those either. Not after the accident. But I do want you. I mean I want to be with you."

Damn. This was harder than she'd imagined. She took a deep breath and forced the rest out before she couldn't say it at all, grateful the darkness hid her flaming cheeks. "Do you want to have an affair with me?"

Yikes. Way to be blunt, girl.

Holden blinked at her a minute, unmoving, looking a bit stunned. She couldn't really blame him. Her statement had been about as romantic as a foot fungus. But then he moved closer, tossing his shoes aside along with his cane, to cup her cheeks in his hands. His expression was unreadable in the shadows, but the catch in his breath made her own heart trip.

Then he bent and brushed his lips over hers, featherlight, before capturing her mouth in a kiss that rocked her to her very soul. Forget romantic. This was mind-blowing, astounding, too much yet not enough. Would never be enough.

Oh man, I'm in trouble here.

He broke the kiss first, the crash of the waves against the shore mixing with their ragged breaths and the far-off crooning of the Don Ho singer belting out *Tiny Bubbles*. For the first time in a long time, Leilani felt more than just a sense of duty, more than pressure to succeed, more than the low-grade sadness of loss and grief.

She felt needed and wanted, and it made her head spin with joy.

Before she could think better of it, she slid her arms around Holden's neck and pulled him in for a deeper kiss.

Holden got lost in Leilani—her warmth, the taste of sweet pineapple and sinful promise on her tongue, her soft mewls of need as she pulled him closer, so close he wasn't sure where she ended and he began. His lower lip stung where the stitches pulled, but not enough to make him stop kissing her. He pulled her closer still, if that were possible.

Then the doubt demons in his brain crept forward once more. He shouldn't be doing this, shouldn't be holding her like this. He was broken and battered, inside and out, and didn't deserve a woman like her, a woman who was as sunny and vibrant as the island around her. A woman who'd overcome the darkness in her past to forge a bright new future for herself.

A future he wouldn't be around to share.

He summoned the last remnants of his willpower and pulled away—only a few inches, enough to rest his forehead against hers as they both fought to catch their breath. His hands were still cupping her cheeks, her silky hair tangled between his fingers, and her skin felt like hot velvet to his touch. But he had to let her go. It was the right thing to do.

He wasn't staying. He couldn't stay. He'd been running so long—running from risk, from commitment, from the past—he didn't know how to stop. Leilani deserved so much more than he could give, even temporarily.

"I—" he started, only to be silenced by her fingers on his lips.

"An affair. That's all," she said, her voice hushed as the waves crashed nearby. "No strings, no pressure. I want you, Holden. For however long you'll be here."

The words made his pulse triple, sending a cascade of conflicting emotions through him—astonishment, excitement, want, sadness. That last one especially threw him for a loop. She was offering him exactly what he'd said he wanted. No strings attached. Just sex, fun, a fling. But for reasons he didn't want to examine too closely, the thought of a casual romp with Leilani made his chest pinch with loneliness.

She pulled back slightly, far enough to look up into his eyes, her own dark gaze as mysterious at the ocean beyond. "I know it's crazy. I just…" She hesitated, shaking her head. "I like you,

Holden. And this chemistry between us is amazing. Be a shame not to explore that, right? Especially if we both know the score."

Right, his libido screamed in response, but he needed time to sort all this through to make sure he made the best decision. Because the last thing he wanted to do was screw things up between them. They still had to work together during his time here. If things went south between the sheets, it could have direct impact on their professional relationship, if they weren't careful.

And Holden was nothing if not careful these days.

The reminder was like a bucket of cold water over his head. He took a deep breath and tried again to speak, "Listen, I—"

Her dad called out from the garden area in the distance. "Lani? If you're out there, Mom and I could use some help in the kitchen."

With a sigh, she stepped back, letting her hands slide from around his neck and down his chest before letting him go completely. His nerve endings sizzled in their wake and his fingertips itched to pull her close once more, but instead Holden forced himself to turn away and pick up his cane and shoes.

"Be right there," Leilani called back, staring at him in the pale moonlight. The question in her gaze prickled his skin. "Just think about it, okay? When's your next shift at the hospital?"

"Sunday," he said, shaking the sand from his flip-flops to avoid looking at her. Because if he looked at her now, there was every chance he'd throw caution to the wind entirely and carry her back to his room to make love right then and there.

"Good. That gives us a couple days to think this through. I'm working then too." After a curt nod, she started back toward the hotel. "We'll talk again then."

Holden stayed where he was, watching her walk away and wondering when in the hell he'd lost complete control of his senses because damn if he didn't want to say yes to an affair.

CHAPTER EIGHT

LEILANI SAT IN her tiny office at the hospital two days later, working her way through a backlog of paperwork that had stacked up over the last week or so while she'd been too busy in the ER. Today was slower, so she'd decided to tackle some of it while she could.

Well, that and she needed a distraction for the constant replays of her kiss with Holden on the beach and her brazen invitation for them to have an affair.

You shouldn't have done that, the commonsense portion of her brain warned.

The thing was though, Leilani had spent her whole life up to this point doing what she *should* do. For once, she was ready to go with what she *wanted* to do. And what she wanted was Holden Ross.

Even if the whole idea of opening up with him like that pushed every crazy button inside her.

A one-night stand was one thing but having to get up the next morning and see that person at work was entirely another. Of course, there wasn't any specific rule against dating coworker's in Ohana policies. She'd checked. But there was still the possibility that things could go wrong. And the last thing she wanted was to mess up her good reputation here by getting chewed up and spit out by the rumor mill. At least that's the excuse she was going with.

Truth was she was scared and looking for an opportunity to back out of the whole thing. Perhaps that explained why she'd been avoiding him since Friday night. Making heated suggestions in the moonlight was one thing. Looking that person in the eye again in broad daylight was quite another. So she'd kept her head down and her nose to the grindstone since their kiss. Because of that, she hadn't really seen Holden much at all since Friday night.

They'd passed each other in the lobby of the hotel twice, her on her way in, him on his way out. Between the crowds and her parents' watchful gazes behind the front desk, neither of them had said more than a basic greeting. And today, they'd both been so busy working and had barely had two seconds to say hello, let alone get into anything deeper.

So yeah. Pins and needles didn't begin to describe what she felt, trying to figure out what to do. Thus, she purposely put herself in paperwork hell to keep her mind off things best forgotten. She rubbed her temple and concentrated again on the requisition form nurse Pam had filled out for the monthly supply order in the ER.

She'd just ticked off the charge for two crates of gloves when a knock sounded on her door. Without looking up, she called, "Come in."

"Dr. Kim," Helen King said, "do you have a moment?"

Leilani's heart stumbled. She swiveled fast on her chair to face the hospital administrator, wincing inwardly at the mess her office was in at the moment. She stood and quickly cleared away a pile of folders and binders off the chair against the wall, then swallowed hard, forcing a polite smile. "Yes, of course. Please, have a seat."

"Thank you." The older woman, looking crisp and professional as always, shut the door behind her and sat on the chair Leilani had just cleared for her. Her short white hair practically glowed beneath the overhead florescent lights and her blue gaze was unreadable, which only made the knot of anxiety inside Leilani tighten further. Beneath her right arm was tucked a large black binder.

"I wanted to speak to you about a project that needs done here in the ER," Dr. King said. "I'd like you and Dr. Ross to work on it together."

Right.

Leilani nodded. She'd forgotten about Holden mentioning that with everything else going on. "Absolutely. Whatever you need, Dr. King."

"Good." The older woman sat forward and crossed her legs, placing the thick binder on her lap. "As you know, we're preparing for our JCAHO recertification next year and part of that is reviewing all the security protocols in the emergency medicine department. Since you've been with us for nearly a decade and are interested in moving into the directorship role for the department in the future, this would be a great opportunity to show me your leadership skills."

"Absolutely."

"Great. I'll send you more information on what needs be done and the deadlines. I've asked Dr. Ross to assist you because he handled a similar project at a different facility, and I believe he'll be able to provide good insight on the project. I've already spoken with him about it and he's on board with assisting you in any way he can. I'll need the project completed by the end of next month." She handed the heavy binder to Leilani, who needed both hands to support its weight. "The current protocols are in there."

"Okay. Wonderful." Leilani set the thing aside on her desk, then stood when the hospital administrator did. "Is that all?"

"Yes. That's all for now." Dr. King walked to the door and stepped out, then leaned her head back in. "And thank you, Dr. Kim. I look forward to your completed results. It will go a long way toward helping me decide the best candidate for the directorship position."

Leilani stood there a moment longer after Dr. King had left, wrapping her head around her new assignment. One month wasn't a long time for a project of that size, especially when both she and Holden had other job duties to attend to as well. But if it meant impressing Dr. King and potentially winning her the directorship, Leilani would get it done.

Of course, that meant another mark in the "Don't sleep with Holden column," since the last thing she wanted was for a potential drama between the sheets to jeopardize their new project together. And Holden and Dr. King were good friends too. Couldn't forget that. If things with their fling went south, then that could impact her chances at the new job as well.

Ugh. Things were getting way too complicated way too fast.

As she sank back into her chair, her chest squeezed with disappointment.

Her whole body still thrummed each time she pictured them together on the beach, the feel of his hard muscles pressing against her soft curves, the taste of salt and coconut in his kisses, the low growl of need he'd given when she'd clung to him tighter...

Sizzling connections like that didn't come along very often. Plus, she liked spending time with him, talking to him, just being around him. Their day sightseeing together had been one of the best she'd had in a long, long time. But was exploring that worth losing the future she'd planned for herself?

Feeling more on edge than ever, she pushed to her feet and headed for the door. She needed to move, to think, to organize the jumbled thoughts in her head before she and Holden spoke again.

But she barely made it through the door before she collided with six foot four inches of solid temptation, wearing soft green scrubs and a sexy smile on his handsome face.

"Hey," he said, his voice a tad hesitant. "I was just coming to talk to you. I'm on break."

Hands off, her brain whispered, even as her ovaries danced a happy jig.

"Good. Because I need to talk to you too. Dr. King came to see me about the project."

She gestured him into her office, then closed the door behind him. Perhaps discussing work would keep her errant brain on track. Except as he passed her, the smell of soap from his skin and his citrusy shampoo drifted around her and her chest squeezed with yearning before she tamped it down. He took a seat in the chair vacated by Dr. King, then set his cane aside.

"Well, on the bright side, the work should go faster with two of us working on it, at least," he said.

"True." She leaned her hips back against the edge of her desk and crossed her arms over her lab coat and stethoscope. "I want to do a good job, since she said this will help her decide who gets the directorship position." Her gaze narrowed on him, trying to read past his usual stoic expression. "Are you sure you're not considering the job yourself? Tell me the truth, Holden."

A muscle ticked near his tense jaw and he frowned down at the floor. "I'm not planning on taking the job, no."

Good. One less thing to worry about.

Then he stood and stepped toward her and the desire she'd tried so hard to keep on low simmer since Friday rolled over into full boil again.

"Can we talk about something else now?" he asked, his rough, quiet tone sending molten warmth through her traitorous body. "Like Friday night."

Leilani squeezed her eyes shut and took a deep breath. "Yes."

When he didn't answer right away, she squinted one eye open to find him watching her with a narrowed gaze, his expression quizzical now, as if he was trying to figure her out. Finally, he took one more step closer and slid his arm around her waist, his hand resting on her lower back as she placed her palms on his chest. That same spark of attraction, of need, flared to life inside her, urging her to throw caution aside and live again, to take what she wanted from Holden and enjoy the moment because it would all be over too soon. She inhaled deep and hazarded a look up into his eyes, noting the same heat there, feeling the pound of his heart under her palms.

"If we're doing a project of this size, it would mean a lot of hours, a lot of time spent together," he said, his words barely more than a whisper. His hold on her tightened, causing her to bump into his chest. Her eyes fluttered shut as he bent and brushed his lips across hers before trailing his mouth down her cheek and jaw to nuzzle her neck and earlobe. "I haven't been able to think about anything but you since Friday."

She shivered with sensual delight, craving his touch more than her next breath, but that small part of her brain that was terrified of getting too close demanded she set boundaries up front. "Me neither," she panted. "But whatever happens, we can't let it interfere with work."

"Never," he vowed, his breath hot against her throat. "I promise you this thing between us will stay between the sheets. I won't let it get out of hand."

"I won't either," she said, not knowing or caring if it was true or not. All she wanted right now was his mouth back on hers. That's when she noticed his stitches were gone. "You got them out?"

"I did. Removed them myself earlier today." He chuckled. "Good as new thanks to you, Doc."

He kissed her again then, deep and full of passion. When he finally pulled away, she felt bewitched and bewildered and all kinds of bothered. Holden straightened his scrub shirt, then gave her a sexy smile before grabbing his cane. "What time does your shift end?"

"Four," she managed to say past the tightness in her throat. "You?"

"Six." He headed for the door, then turned back to her with a wink. "Come to my room for dinner. Number 1402. Eight o'clock. Don't be late."

Holden stood before the doors leading out to his room's balcony later that evening, wondering exactly what had possessed him to be so bold earlier in Leilani's office. Maybe it was the fact he hadn't been able to stop thinking about her since their kiss on the beach. Maybe it was the fact that after that day they'd spent together and sharing their most traumatic moments in life, he felt the bond between them even more strongly than before.

Whatever it was, he was now on a collision course of his own making.

He turned slightly to look back over his shoulder at the small table set for two in the corner of his junior suite, set up by room service and complete with a white linen tablecloth and a bottle of champagne chilling in the ice bucket. The lights were lowered and the single candle at the center of the table flickered in the slight breeze drifting through the open doors, casting a soft glow around the room. The scent of surf and sea surrounded him, as did the occasional notes of music floating in from a party somewhere on the shore. All of it should've soothed him.

But Leilani was due to arrive any minute and Holden felt ready to jump out of his skin from a mix of nerves and excitement. Now he'd made the decision to pursue an affair with her, he was second-guessing himself. Was this the right choice? Yes, he wanted her more than he'd wanted any woman in a long, long time, perhaps ever. And yes, she'd already made it clear that this was only a temporary thing, that she didn't do forever. Usually he was the one saying those words, and honestly, he wasn't sure how he felt about that. His analytical brain said he should be relieved. Leilani had taken the guesswork out of it all, taken the burden off him by offering a no-strings-attached affair.

Instead though, he felt torn.

Which was stupid, because a guy like him who was too

scarred both inside and out to settle down for long had no business wanting more than a few nights in paradise. He should be
happy with what he got because it could all disappear in the
blink of an eye anyway.

Then there was the fact they'd now be working on that project for Helen together. And while he'd agreed days ago to do it,
even before Leilani knew about it, now he was feeling a bit off-
kilter about it. The fact he should've thought it through better
in the first place bugged him. Going over security measures in
the ER would be triggering for him, regardless of whether they
addressed a mass shooting scenario. But really, how could they
not, since that type of violence was on the rise nationwide. Not
to address it would be wrong.

But at the time of the meeting with Helen, he'd been eager
to please and wanted to help in any way he could to repay her
for saving his life back in Chicago. The fact she'd tried to pressure him about the directorship position didn't help either. Now
he had firm proof from Leilani that she wanted the job, and he
wouldn't go near it, even if Helen wanted otherwise. Leilani deserved the position. He scrubbed a hand over his face, then fiddled with the hem of his black T-shirt. No sense getting worked
up about it now. He had bigger things to deal with at present.

Get out and live a little. Trust me—you'll be glad you did...

Helen's words echoed through his head again and made him
wonder if perhaps his old friend had assigned them both to this
security project as a way of bringing him and Leilani together.

He snorted and shook his head. Nah. He was just being paranoid now. Helen knew how squirrelly he was about commitment after the shooting, how he didn't want to stay in one place
too long or form deep attachments. She wouldn't try to play
matchmaker now to get him to stay in Hawaii.

Would she?

A knock sounded on his door while that thought was still
stewing in his mind, making his heart nosedive to his knees. His
pulse kicked into overdrive and his mouth dried from adrena-

line, like he was some randy teen before the prom. No. Honestly, it didn't matter what Helen may or may not have intended. Both he and Leilani were consenting adults and they'd both made the choice to be here tonight. They were the engineers of their fates, at least in this room.

After a deep breath, he wiped his damp palms on the legs of his jeans, then limped barefoot over to the door to answer, his trusty cane by his side.

Leilani stood in the hall, shuffling her feet and fiddling with her hair, looking as wary and wired as he felt. She'd worn jeans too, soft faded ones that hugged her curves and made his fingertips itch to unzip them. Her emerald green top highlighted her dark hair and eyes to perfection and contrasted with the pink flushing her cheeks. The V-neck of her shirt also gave him a tantalizing glimpse of her cleavage beneath and suddenly it seemed far too warm for comfort.

Holden resisted the urge to run a finger beneath the crewneck of his T-shirt and instead stepped back to allow her inside. "Hey. Come on in."

"Thanks." She gave him a tentative smile as she brushed past him, the graze of her arm against his sending a shower of sparks through his already-overtaxed nervous system and notching the want inside him higher. Leilani stopped at the end of the short entry hall and stared at the table set up in the corner. "Are we eating here?"

"Yeah," he said, limping up to stand behind her, close enough to catch a hint of her sweet jasmine scent. Her heat and fragrance lit him up like neon inside, and his body tightened against his wishes. To distract himself, he concentrated on dinner. "Uh, I thought after a busy day, it might be nice to just chill and relax. Is that okay?"

She exhaled slowly, then turned to face him with a smile as dazzling as the stars filling the cloudless night above. "It's perfect, actually. Thank you for thinking of it."

"My pleasure." Holden grinned back, imagining all the ways

he'd like to pleasure her, with his mouth and hands and body. He cleared his throat and gestured toward the love seat against one wall. "Make yourself comfortable. There's champagne I can open if you want some."

"What are we having for dinner?" She walked over to the table and lifted one of the silver domes covering their plates, then the other before turning back to him. "Salads?"

"I figured it would be healthy and—"

And would keep for a while in case we didn't eat right away and ended up in bed first.

He didn't say that last part out loud, but then, it turned out he didn't have to, because next thing he knew, Leilani had kicked off her sandals and was heading back toward him, the heat in her eyes heading straight to his groin.

"Good. Because there's something else I'm hungry for right now..." She reached out and traced a finger down his cheek, his neck, his chest, lower still. "And it isn't food or booze."

Before he could rethink his actions, he let his cane fall to the floor and pulled her into his arms, kissing her again like he'd been wanting to since their encounter in her office earlier, since the night at the beach, since eternity. It started out as a light meeting of their lips, but soon morphed into something deeper and more intense. Leilani sighed and ran her hands up his pecs to his shoulders, then threaded her fingers through his hair, making him shiver as she pulled his body flush to hers. "How's your lip?"

"Never better." He whispered the words against the side of her neck, licking that special spot where throat met earlobe—the one that made her sigh and mewl with need. Holding her felt like the most natural thing in the world. Even when she slipped her hands beneath his T-shirt and tugged it off over his head, exposing the scar on his left shoulder from the shooting. Usually, he kept it hidden, a dark reminder of a dark day, but now with Leilani, he wanted her to see it all, every part of him, the good, the bad, the damaged and the whole. In fact, the only thing he was thinking about now was getting Leilani naked too, and into his bed—over him, under him, any way he could have her.

She leaned back slightly to meet his gaze. "Sure you don't want to eat now?"

"Oh, I want to eat all right," he growled, grinding his hips against hers and allowing her to feel the full extent of his arousal. "I plan to lick and taste every inch of you, sweetheart."

She snorted, then wriggled out of his arms to take off her shirt and toss it aside, revealing a pretty pink lace bra that served her breasts up to him like a sacred offering. He reached out a shaky hand to run the backs of his fingers across the tops of their soft curves.

Then Leilani undid the clasp, letting the straps fall down her arms before allowing the bra to fall to the floor, where she kicked it away with her toe.

Oh man.

His mouth watered in anticipation. Man, he couldn't wait to find out if she tasted as delectable as she looked, all soft and pink, with darker taut nipples.

Unable to resist feeling her skin against his any longer, Holden slipped one arm around her waist, tugging her close so her breasts grazed his bare chest.

Exquisite.

Then he went one step further, cupping one breast in the palm of his hand, his thumb teasing her nipple as he nuzzled the pulse point at the base of her neck, sliding his tongue along her collarbone. Her moan and answering shudder was nearly his undoing. He smiled, savoring the moment. "You like that?"

Her response emerged as more of a breathy sigh. "Yes."

"Good." Holden dropped to his knees, ignoring the protests from the muscles in his right thigh, and kissed her belly button, her stomach, the valley between her breasts, before taking one pretty pink nipple into his mouth.

"Holden," Leilani groaned, her nails scraping his scalp. "Please, don't stop."

"Never," he murmured, kissing his way over to her other nipple to lavish it with the same attention, his fingers tweaking it as he licked and nipped and sucked until she writhed against him, her head back and her expression pure bliss. Normally, he'd be unable to stay in such a position long, given his leg, but there was something about being with her that made his pain disappear.

The only thing that mattered now was this night, this moment, this woman.

Steering her by the hips, Holden managed to get them to the bed. His leg would protest the effort tomorrow, he was sure, but for now all he wanted was to get them both naked and to bury himself deep inside her. He'd stocked up on condoms in the nightstand, just in case.

Once Leilani's knees hit the edge of the mattress, she tipped back onto the bed, and he crawled atop the mattress over her. She ran her fingers up and down his spine, making him shudder again. It had been so long, too long, since anyone had touched him like this, since he'd allowed anyone close enough to try. And now that he had, he couldn't get enough.

Before he took his pleasure, however, he wanted to bring Leilani there first. Needed to see her come apart in his arms as he licked and kissed and suckled every square inch of her amazing body. To that end, he worked his way downward from her breasts, his fingers caressing her sides, her hips, before slipping between her parted thighs to cup the heat of her through her jeans.

"Holden," Leilani gasped, arching beneath him. "Please."

"Please what, sweetheart?" he whispered, nuzzling the sensitive skin above her waistband. "Tell me what you want."

"You. I want you," she panted, unzipping and pushing down her own jeans before kicking them off, leaving her in just panties. "Please. You're killing me."

He chuckled, ignoring the throb of his erection pressed against the mattress. He was determined to make all this last as long as possible. He parted her thighs even more and positioned himself between them, then slowly lowered her panties, inch by torturous inch, until she was completely exposed to him. The scent of her arousal nearly sent him over the edge again, but Holden forced himself to go slow.

After kissing his way up her inner thighs, he leaned forward and traced his tongue over her slick folds. Leilani bucked beneath him and would've thrown him off the bed if he hadn't been holding on so tight. Tenderly, reverently, he nuzzled her flesh, using his lips and tongue and fingers to bring her to the heights of ecstasy over and over again. When he inserted first one, then two fingers inside her, preparing her for him, she called out his name and he didn't think he'd ever heard a sweeter sound in his life.

"Holden! Holden, I…" Her breath caught and her body tightened around his finger as she climaxed in his arms. This was what he'd been imagining for days, weeks. Hearing her call out for him and knowing that he was responsible for that dreamy look on her gorgeous face.

Once her pleasure subsided, he kissed his way up her body, stopping to pay homage to her breasts again before leaning above her and smiling at the sated expression on her face. She gave him a sleepy grin, then pulled him down for another deep kiss. Her hand slid down his chest to the waistband of his jeans, then beneath to take his hard length in hand.

He could have orgasmed just from her touch, but he wanted more. Tonight, he wanted to be inside her. Tonight, he wanted everything with Leilani.

Summoning his last shreds of willpower, he captured her wrist, pulling her hand away from him and kissing her palm before letting her go. "If you touch me now, sweetheart, it'll all be over and I want this to last as long as possible."

"Me too," she said, touching his lips. "Make love to me, Holden."

No need for her to ask twice. He grabbed a small foil packet out of the nightstand drawer while kissing her again, then climbed off the bed to remove his jeans and boxer briefs, putting the condom on before returning to her side. Supporting his weight on his forearms, he leaned above her once more, positioning himself at her wet entrance, then hesitating. "You're sure about this?"

"Absolutely," she said, pulling him down for an openmouthed kiss.

Holden entered her in one long thrust, holding still then to allow her body to adjust to his size. Leilani began to move beneath him, her hips rocking up into his and he withdrew nearly to his tip before thrusting into her once more. She was so hot and tight and wet, everything he'd imagined and so much more.

Pain jolted from his leg all too soon however, and he couldn't hide his wince.

She must have seen it because, before he knew what was happening, she rolled them, putting him flat on his back with her over him. He'd thought having her beneath him was hot. Having her above him like that though, with the moonlight streaming over her beautiful face as she rode them both to ecstasy drove his desire beyond anything he'd ever imagined. Soon they developed a rhythm that had them both teetering on the brink of orgasm again far too soon.

"Oh," Leilani cried. Her slick walls tightened around him, her nails scratched his pecs and her heels dug into the side of his hips, holding him so close, like she'd never let him go.

Then she cried out his name once more, her body squeezing his, milking him toward a climax that left Holden stunned, breathless and boneless and completely drained in the best possible way.

He might've blacked out from the incandescent pleasure, because the next time he blinked open his eyes, it was to find Leilani laying atop his chest, drawing tiny circles with her fingers through the smattering of hair on his pecs. He stroked his fingers through her silky hair and for those brief seconds, all seemed right with the world. In fact, Holden never wanted to move again.

Finally though, Leilani raised her head slightly to meet his gaze, her chin resting over his heart as she flashed him a weary smile. "That was incredible."

"It really was," he said, the remnants of his earlier excitement dissolving into warm sweetness and affection. Then his stomach rumbled, reminding him of the dinner they'd neglected. She giggled and he raised a brow at her. "How about a picnic in bed?"

She rolled off him before he could stop her and rushed across the hotel room naked to grab one of the giant Caesar salads topped with crab and lobster before rushing back to bed. They got situated against the headboard, under the covers, then she handed him a fork and napkin before digging into their feast first. "My favorite kind of picnic."

CHAPTER NINE

THE NEXT MORNING Leilani blinked her eyes open and squinted at the sunshine streaming in through the open doors to the balcony. It took her a minute to realize that she wasn't in her own room. The warm weight around her waist tightened and a nose pressed into the nape of her neck, close to the scar there.

Holden.

She yawned, then snuggled deeper into his embrace, not wanting to get up just yet, even though she was scheduled for another shift later that day. Her body ached in all the right ways and sleepy memories of the night before drifted back. Honestly, after their first round of lovemaking, she'd expected to have been worn out. But man, there was something about Holden that kept her engine revved on high. The guy definitely knew what he was doing between the sheets.

Not to mention his stamina. They'd ended up having sex twice more. Once in the bed and again in the bathtub, just before dawn. Afterward, they'd finally fallen asleep together, wrapped in each other arms.

Being with him had been amazing. Awesome. Enlightening.

She'd expected his past and injuries to maybe cause issues, but they'd found ways to make it work. In fact, some of the new positions they'd tried were better than she'd ever imagined. Plus, it was as if telling each other about their worst moments in life had opened them both up to just be present now and enjoy the moment. It was refreshing. It was energizing. It was addictive.

A girl could get used to that.

Except she really couldn't. Leilani sighed and slowly turned over to face a still-snoozing Holden. He would be gone soon, no matter how easy it might be to picture him now as a steady fixture in her life. Besides, she'd been the one to lay the ground rules between them at the start of all this. She couldn't be the one to change them now.

Could I?

She reached out and carefully ran her fingers along the strong line of his jaw, smiling at the feel of rough stubble against her skin. His long, dark lashes fanned over his high cheekbones and the usual tension around his full lips was gone. He looked so relaxed and peaceful in sleep she didn't want to wake him. Then she spotted the scar on his left shoulder and couldn't stop herself from touching that too. The thought that he might have died that day, been taken away before she'd ever had a chance to work with him, to know him, to...

Whoa, girl.

She stopped that last word before it fully formed, her chest constricting.

Nope. Not going there at all. No ties, no strings. That was their deal.

The happiness bubbling up inside her wasn't the *l* word. It was satisfaction.

Yeah. That was it. And sure, she liked Holden. Liked talking to him, liked working through cases with him. Liked the way he looked, the way he smiled, the way he smelled and tasted and...

"Hey." His rough, groggy voice wrapped around her like velvet, nudging her out of her head and back to the present. "What time is it?"

"Early," she said. From the angle of the early-morning sun

streaming in, it couldn't have been much past six, she'd guessed. "You've got time before your shift. We both do."

"Good." He stretched, giving her a glorious view of his toned, tanned chest before propping himself up on one elbow to smile over at her, all lithe sinew and sexy male confidence. "How do you feel this morning?"

"Fine." The understatement of the century. Heat prickled her cheeks despite her wishes. "And you?"

"Leg's a bit sore after the workout last night, but otherwise, I'm excellent." He pulled her closer and she snuggled into his arms, tucking her head under his chin.

"We should try and get some more sleep while we can," she said against the pulse point at the base of his neck.

"Hmm." He kissed the top of her head and her whole body tingled, remembering how he'd felt moving against her last night, moving within her. The feel of his lips on hers, the taste of him on her tongue. If he hadn't mentioned his leg hurting, she might've climbed atop him again for round four and give him something nice to dream about.

As it was, she lay there until his soft snores filled the air, letting her mind race through what was becoming more undeniable to her by the second. Somewhere between the hospital and their day touring the island and their post-luau beach kiss, she'd gone way past *like* with this guy. In truth, she'd fallen head over heels for Holden.

Her muscles tensed and she took a few deep breaths to force herself to relax.

Love was a four-letter word where Leilani was concerned. Yes, she loved her adopted parents and U'i. But what she felt for Holden was different—deeper, bigger, stronger. And so much scarier.

She didn't want to love him. He'd be gone soon, and she'd be left to pick up the pieces, the same as she had after her family had died.

Unfortunately, it seemed her heart hadn't gotten that memo though, dammit.

She fell into a restless sleep, dreaming she was back on the highway heading for North Shore, then down in a ditch with Holden trapped and with her having no way to help him. She'd woken with a start, thankful to find him still asleep.

Leilani eased out of bed to shower before heading back to her room to have breakfast alone and get ready for her day. She'd hoped time and space would help her forget about her foolish thoughts of things with Holden being about anything more than mutual lust, but that pesky *l* word continued to dog her later as she started her shift at the hospital as well.

At least the ER was busy, so there was that.

"I haven't gone for a week and a half," the middle-aged black woman said, perched on the end of the table in trauma room three. "Tried mineral oil, bran cereal, even suppositories my family doc recommended. Nothing."

Leilani scrolled through the woman's file, frowning. "Well, I see here you're on a couple of different pain medications. Constipation is a common side effect with those. Are you drinking lots of water?"

"I'm trying," the woman said. "But my stomach's cramping and it hurts."

"Yes, it can cause a lot of pain. We can do an enema here today and see if that helps." She made a few notes on her tablet, then walked over to a drawer and pulled out a gown to hand to the woman. "Put that on and I'll be back in shortly to do an abdominal exam, Mrs. Nettles."

Leilani stepped back out into the hall and closed the door before walking over to the nurses' station. Pam was there, typing something into the computer behind the desk. She glanced up at Leilani, her gaze far too perceptive.

"Hey, Doc." Pam smiled. "You look awfully refreshed for a Monday. What'd you do over the weekend? Have a hot date or something?"

"What? No." Leilani frowned down at her tablet screen. "I'm probably going to need an enema for the patient in Room Three."

Pam snorted. "Way to change the subject. Dr. Ross seemed to have a bounce in his step too when I saw him a few minutes ago."

Leilani prayed her cheeks didn't look as hot as they felt. "Well, good for him. That has nothing to do with me."

"Uh-huh." Pam sounded entirely unconvinced. "Well, I think two people as great as you guys deserve happiness where you can find it."

"Thanks so much," Leilani said, her tone snarky. "But can we focus on patients, please?"

"Sure thing, Doc." Pam finished on the computer then came around the counter. "Heard you and Dr. Ross are going over the security protocols. That's good, since your loudmouth MVA patient showed up here again last night. We've all been a bit on edge since."

Her gaze flew to Pam's. "Mr. Chambers came back?"

"Yep," Pam said, gathering supplies for the enema patient onto a tray. "Claimed he still had pain and wanted more drugs."

"Did you call the police?" Leilani asked, concerned.

"No. One of the guards got him out of here." Pam snorted and shook her head. "But the guy was shouting the whole time about how we hadn't heard the last of him."

Damn. That wasn't good news. She had a bad feeling about that guy.

"If he shows up again, please text me right away, okay?" Leilani said, heading back toward room three with Pam by her side. "Let's finish examining Mrs. Nettles."

Hours later, Holden sat in Leilani's office, going over the safety polices for the ER. So far it hadn't been triggering at all, he was happy to say. In fact, it had all been about as exciting as watching paint dry. If it hadn't been for her nearness and the enchanting way she blushed each time their gazes caught, he probably would've dozed off a while ago. As it was, he couldn't stop thinking about their night together. Or the fact she'd been gone when he'd woken up again.

Usually, he would've been fine with that. Save them both the morning-after awkwardness. But being with Leilani last night had felt different. Seemed the more time he had with Leilani, the more he wanted. Which was not good.

He'd agreed to her terms. A fling, nothing more. He wouldn't go back on that promise now.

She didn't do relationships and he was the last guy in the world anyone should get involved with. There were too many shadows still lurking from his past, too many demons he still had to conquer from the shooting before he'd be good company long-term for anyone. Some days he wondered if he'd ever be victorious over them and get back to the man he was before the shooting. Not physically—since his physical therapist assured him his mobility would only improve with enough time and hard work—but emotionally. When he was with Leilani though, she made him feel like he could heal the darkness inside him, could open his heart and love again. Truthfully, after being with her, getting to know her better, he felt pretty invincible all around. But that was just the endorphins talking. He knew better than anyone what a lie that false sense of security was, that false high of connection that made you believe in rainbows and miracles and love…

Whoa, Nelly.

This wasn't love. They'd had one night together. Things didn't happen that fast.

Do they?

"Okay," she said, glancing over at him. "We've knocked out most of the updates, and I put this one off until the end, but it's probably the most important. I understand if you'd like me to handle this one on my own."

"The active shooter protocol." He raked his hand through

his hair and shook his head, hoping to expel the sudden jolt of anxiety bolting through him. He'd been expecting this, and still it took his breath away. He pushed to his feet to pace. He could do this. It was important. It could save lives. "No. I can handle it. What's the current protocol?"

"It's pretty basic," she said, her expression concerned as she looked away from him and back to the black binder in front of her. "The last time this was revised was three years ago and the problem has only gotten worse since then. This only lists sheltering in place and calling the police."

"Both of those are good, but it's not enough." Holden walked from one side of the ten-by-ten office to the other, then back again. His therapist back in Chicago had told him talking about what happened was good for him, better than keeping it all bottled up inside. Didn't mean it was easy though. Especially now, when he was still trying to process all his feelings from last night with Leilani. Still, this was a chance to create some good out of the tragedy he'd suffered. It's what David would've wanted. Perhaps he could find some closure too. Helen's suggestion that he help Leilani with the project made more sense taken in that light.

He took a deep breath, then began to talk his way through the problem while Leilani took notes. "We need to check out the Homeland Security website. They've got lots of good information and videos there to help us get the staff trained properly." He'd watched them all hundreds of times since the incident in Chicago, searching for reasons to explain why the shooting had happened and how to make sure it never happened again.

"Run, hide, fight are the three options basically. In the ER we've got both soft targets and crowded spaces to contend with." As he went over the whole "see something suspicious, say something" issue, Leilani gave him a worried look. He stopped his pacing and frowned. "What?"

"Nothing." She shook her head and scowled down at the paper again. "Pam mentioned that my patient from a few weeks ago, Greg Chambers, showed up here again last night asking for more pain meds."

"Did he make threats?" Holden asked, tension knotting between his shoulder blades.

"No." Leilani sighed. "Just lots of shouting and being generally disruptive. I told Pam to let me know immediately if he shows up again."

"Make sure to tell her to phone the cops too." He clenched his fist around the head of his cane. "The shooter in Chicago was after drugs. All the staff need to be trained on how to handle those situations, so they don't escalate into something much worse. If we'd had the proper training back in Chicago, then..." His pulse stumbled at that and he leaned his hand against the wall for support. Dammit. The last thing he needed was a panic attack. Not now.

"Okay," Leilani said, getting up and guiding him back into his seat. She stayed close, crouching beside him, stroking his hair and murmuring comforting words near his ear to keep the anxiety at bay. Slowly, his breathing returned to normal and his vision cleared. The ache in his chest warmed, transforming from fear to affection to something deeper still...

No. No, no, no.

He didn't love Leilani. They'd only known each other a few weeks, hadn't spent more than a few days together, had only had one incredible night. None of that equaled a lifelong partnership. It was just the stress of this moment, wasn't it?

Except...

Holden took another deep inhale to calm his raging pulse and caught the sweet jasmine scent of her shampoo. Damn if his heart didn't tug a little bit further toward wanting forever with her.

"Hey," Leilani said, standing at last and moving back to her seat. "I think I can find enough information on the internet to handle this section of the protocol from here. How about I put it together and then you can go over it all later to make sure I didn't miss anything?"

He appreciated her concern, but needed to keep going, if for no other reason than if he didn't, he'd have nothing else to think about other than the fact he'd gone and done the last thing in the world he ever wanted to do—fall in love with Leilani Kim. And if that wasn't a disaster waiting to happen, he didn't know what was. He swallowed hard, then shook his head. "No. Let's keep going."

"Are you sure?" She cocked her head to the side, her ponytail swinging behind her.

"I'm sure."

They spent the next few hours watching videos online and reading PDF manuals, coming up with training programs and protocols for the staff. It would take a while to implement everything, but at least they knew what needed to be done and that was half the battle.

The knots that had formed between Holden's shoulder blades eased slightly and he sat back as a knock sounded on the door to Leilani's office.

Pam stuck her head inside. "Sorry to interrupt, guys, but the EMTs called. They've got a new case coming in. Toddler caught in the midst of a gang incident."

"Be right there," Holden said. "What's the ETA?"

"Five minutes out," Pam said before closing the door once more.

"I'll help," Leilani said. "I could use a break from all this stuff too."

They moved out into the bustling ER again, and Holden tugged on a fresh gown over his scrubs and grabbed his stethoscope from behind the nurses' station while Leilani did the same. They met up again near the ambulance bay doors to wait.

The knots inside Holden returned, but in his gut this time. Hurt kids were always the worst. Plus, there was also the unresolved, underlying tension of the situation with Leilani. He cared for her, far more than he should. Love made you vulnerable, and that led to heartache and pain in his experience.

An ambulance screeched to a halt outside and the EMTs rushed in with the new patient.

"Two-year-old girl, bullet fragments in left lower leg from a drive-by shooting," the paramedics said as they raced down the hallway toward the open trauma bay at the end. The little girl was wailing and squirming on the gurney.

"Please, help my daughter," the mother cried, holding on to her daughter's hand. "I tried to take cover, but it all happened so quick."

"She's in good hands, ma'am. I promise," Leilani said, glancing from the woman to Holden then back again. "Can you tell me your daughter's name?"

"Mari," the mother said. "Mari Hale."

Holden helped the EMTs transfer the child to the bed in the room, then moved in to take her vitals. "Pulse 125. BP 102 over 58. Respirations clear and normal." The little girl gave an angry wail and reached for her mom, who was fretting nearby as the cops arrived to take her statement. Holden placed a hand gently in the center of the little girl's chest and smiled down at her. "It's okay, sweetie. I promise we're going to take care of you."

Leilani moved in beside him to examine the wound to the little girl's leg. "One four-centimeter laceration to the left inner calf. On exam, her reflexes are normal and there doesn't appear to be any nerve damage or broken bones."

"Okay." Holden stepped back and slung his stethoscope around his neck once more as the nurses moved in to get an IV started. "Let's get X-rays of that left leg to be sure there's no internal damage and to visualize the foreign material lodged in there." He called over to the mother, who was speaking to the cops near the entrance to the trauma bay. "Ma'am, does your daughter have any allergies or underlying conditions we need to know about?"

The mother shook her head. "Will she be okay?"

"We'll do everything we can to make sure she is." Holden typed orders into his tablet for fluids and pain medications for the child, then waited while the techs wheeled the table out of the room and down the hall to the X-ray room. The mother went along, taking her daughter's hand again and singing to her to keep her calm.

Depending on how deeply the bullet fragments were embedded in the child's leg and where, would determine whether he could do a simple removal here in the ER of if she'd need more extensive surgery upstairs in the OR.

"You okay?" Leilani asked, her voice low.

"Yes," he said. Shooting cases always brought up painful memories, but he was a professional. He pushed past that to do his job and save lives. The fact that Leilani thought maybe he wasn't all right chafed. He turned away to talk to the cops instead. "What happened?"

"According to the mother, it was two rival gangs settling a dispute," one officer said.

"Gangs?" Holden scrunched his nose. "They have those in Hawaii?"

"Yep," the second officer said. "Not as bad as they were back in the nineties, but a few are still here. The mom and kid live in Halawa. Lots of the gang activity centered there these days."

Holden glanced sideways at Leilani for confirmation.

"The tourism board likes to keep it under wraps as much as possible, but unfortunately, it's true," she said. "The housing projects in Halawa are filled with low-income families looking for a way out. Gangs exploit that and use it to their advantage. And every once in a while there are turf wars."

"And this poor kid got caught up in one," the first officer said.

"Is the mother involved with the gangs?" Holden asked.

"No," the second officer said. "Just in the wrong place at the wrong time."

Holden knew all about that. "Did you catch the people who did this?"

"Not yet," the second officer said. "Neighbors generally don't want to get involved for fear of retaliation. The mother gave us descriptions of the men who opened fire though, so at least we've got that to go on."

"What about her and her daughter then?" Leilani asked, frowning. "Will they be safe when they go home?"

"Hard to say," the first officer said. "We'll add extra patrols for the next week or so, but that's about all we can do, since we're understaffed as it is at the moment."

Deep in thought, Holden exhaled slowly to calm the adrenaline thundering through his blood. The last thing he wanted to do was patch the kid up only to send her and her mother right back into a war zone.

The radiology techs wheeled the little girl back in a few minutes later. Both she and her mother were a bit calmer now, which was good. Holden pulled the films up on his tablet and assessed the situation. None of the fragments were too deeply embedded. He could remove them in the ER and send them on their way. Good for the little girl, bad for their situation at home.

Leilani peeked around his arm to see the images. "Thank goodness the damage is only superficial."

"Yes," he said quietly. "But I hate to discharge them until the guys who did this are caught."

"Then don't." She shrugged. "Say we need to keep her overnight for observation. I can make arrangements upstairs for a room with a foldout bed so the mom can stay with her."

"Are you sure?" He gazed down into her warm brown eyes and his heart swelled with emotion. The fact that they were on the same wavelength with the kid's case only reinforced the connection he felt for her elsewhere too. Which filled him with both happiness and trepidation.

Leilani nodded, and Holden turned back to the patient and her mother. "Right. I'll need to perform a minor surgery here in the ER to remove the bullet fragments still lodged in your daughter's leg, then we'll want to keep her at least overnight to make sure she doesn't develop any clots from the injury. Pam, can you get the procedure room set up for me?"

"Sure thing, Doc," Pam called, walking out into the hall.

"And I'll walk you through all the forms to sign and answer any questions you might have," Leilani said, guiding the mother toward the door. She glanced back once at Holden and gave him a small wink, then led the woman from the room.

Holden smiled down at the little girl. He couldn't do anything about the gangs out there, but he could keep her safe in the hospital, at least for tonight. Plus, helping his young patient and her mother gave him a break from stewing over the mess in his personal life. He took the little girl's hand and rested his arms on the bedside rail. "Don't worry, sweetie. We're going to take good care of you and your mom."

CHAPTER TEN

THE NEXT MORNING Holden was at the nurses' station, working through documentation on the charts from the patients he'd treated through the night. His mind wasn't fully on the task though, with part of it upstairs with little Mari Hale and her mother on the third floor. The two-year-old had come through the procedure to remove the bullet fragments from her leg nicely and there shouldn't be any lasting effects. He hoped that both the patient and her mother had gotten a good night's sleep in the peace and safety of the hospital.

Another part of his brain was still lingering on thoughts of Leilani. He'd missed sleeping with her last night, holding her close and kissing her awake so they could make love again. His body tightened at the memories of how amazing she'd felt in his arms, under him, around him, her soft cries filling his ears and the scent of her arousal driving his own passion to new heights.

But he shoved those thoughts aside. He was at work now. People needed him here. He needed to clear his head and get himself straightened out on this whole affair. No matter what his feelings were for Leilani, the thing between them was temporary because that's what she said she wanted. He refused to pressure her into anything she didn't want.

Period. Amen.

In fact, it was probably a good thing she'd been busy too since last night, dealing with her own cases and the security paperwork in her office, for them to have seen much of each other after dealing with the little girl. Images of her from their day on the town popped into his head. She'd been so happy, so relaxed and in her element as she'd showed him around the island. He honestly couldn't remember when he'd had a better day, or better company. It was almost enough to make him want to stick around Hawaii for a while…

"Hey, Doc," Pam called to him from her desk nearby. "Dr. King wants to see you again."

With a sigh, he finished the chart he was working on, then shut down his tablet and stood. Helen probably wanted to check in on their progress on the project. "Be right back then."

"Happy Monday, Doc," Pam said, chuckling as he headed for the elevators.

The ride to the fifth floor was fast, and the receptionist waved him into Helen's office even faster. She looked perfectly polished, as usual, which only made Holden feel more unkempt. He patted his hair to make sure it wasn't sticking up where it shouldn't, then took a seat, setting his cane aside and folding his hands atop his well-worn scrubs. "Good morning."

"Morning," Helen said from behind her desk, watching him over the rims of her reading glasses. She set aside the papers in her hands, then leaned forward, resting her weight on her forearms atop the desk. "So, Holden. Have you given any more thought to staying here in Honolulu?"

He had, yeah. But not for the reason Helen hoped, so he fibbed a bit. "Not really. I've been busy."

"Hmm. Working with Dr. Kim, I suspect," she said. Well, it was due to Leilani, but not because of the project. "I've heard gossip that you two have been spending more time together."

He took a deep breath and stared at the beige carpet beneath his feet. Damn the rumor mill around this place. "I'm staying at the resort her parents own. We're bound to run into each other on occasion."

"Uh-huh." His old friend's tone suggested she didn't buy that for a minute. Helen sat back and crossed her arms, her gaze narrowing. "After everything you've been through, you deserve to be happy."

He hid his eye roll, barely. "Is this going to be some kind of pep talk? Because I really don't have time for it this morning. I need to get back to work."

"You know me better than that." Helen laughed. "I'm not a rainbows and sunshine kind of person."

Nah, she really wasn't. That's probably why they were such good friends. Helen told it like it was. A trait Holden appreciated even more after the shooting, when people treated him like he'd shatter at the slightest bump. Still, the last thing Holden wanted was relationship advice. "So, what is it you needed to see me about then?"

"I want you to think seriously about taking a permanent trauma surgeon position, Holden. That's what I want." When he didn't say anything, she continued. "Look, you turned down the directorship job, and I respect that. Having had a chance to go over Dr. Kim's credentials again, I think you're right. She is a better fit for the job. But that doesn't mean I can't use your skills elsewhere. You could stay in Honolulu, build a new life for yourself here. I can already see a change in you for the better since you arrived. You're more relaxed, less burdened by the past."

Holden took a deep breath and stared out the windows at the bright blue sky. Helen was right—he did feel better. Even his leg wasn't bothering him so much—well except for after his night with Leilani...

"Here," Helen said, handing him a job description. "At least look at what the job entails before you turn it down. I've added the salary I'm willing to pay in the corner there too, as an enticement."

Shaking off those forbidden thoughts, he focused on the paperwork. It was a good offer, with way more money than what he was making now, higher even than what he'd made back in Chicago. Plus, the benefits were great too. And it would allow him to put down roots again, if he wanted. Allow him to continue exploring this thing with Leilani too, if they both agreed.

But he wasn't quite ready to take the plunge yet. "Can I think about it for a few days?"

"Of course," Helen said, smiling. "Take as long as you need. I'm just glad you didn't flat out say no again. Now, get back to work. My next appointment should be here soon."

"Thanks." He hobbled to the door and opened it, stepping out into the hall before turning back. "I really do appreciate the offer and you're right. Staying in Honolulu would be nice."

He'd just closed the door and turned toward the elevators when he nearly collided with Leilani. He put his hand on her arm to steady her, then dropped it fast when he took in her stiff posture and remote expression. Not sure how to react, he fumbled his words. "Oh...uh...hi."

She blinked at him a moment before sidling around him, her tone quiet. "I have an appointment with Dr. King. Excuse me."

Leilani walked into Dr. King's office with her heart in her throat, Holden's words still ringing in her ears.

I really do appreciate the job offer and you're right. Staying in Honolulu would be nice...

Thoughts crashed through her brain at tsunami speed. When she'd first seen him in the hall, before he'd spotted her, she'd been happy, smiling, excited to be near him again. Then her brain processed his words to Dr. King. What job offer? The directorship? Did he want to stay in Honolulu? Did he want the same job she did? He'd said he didn't, but maybe he'd lied. Maybe he wanted to keep her off balance. Maybe he'd only slept with her as a distraction.

Wait. What?

No. Her heart didn't want to believe that, refused to believe that. But damn if those good old doubt demons from her past didn't resurface and refuse to be quiet. She ignored Holden's befuddled stare and fumbled her way past him and into Dr. King's office, closing the door behind her. She flexed her stiff fingers, more nervous now than her initial interview for the directorship position.

"Dr. Kim, please sit down." Dr. King gestured to a chair in front of her desk. "I wanted to ask you for an update on the security protocols for the ER."

Right. Okay. So, it wasn't about the job.

Why would it be, if she's already offered it to someone else? her mean mind supplied unhelpfully.

Leilani forced a smile she didn't feel and concentrated on explaining the pertinent details of the plans she and Holden had been working on downstairs earlier. "They're coming along well. We've worked through most of them already. The only one with substantial changes is the active shooter policy and I'm working on coming up with a substantial training protocol for the staff we can implement soon."

"Excellent," Dr. King said, fiddling with some paperwork on her desk, not looking at Leilani. "We'll need the details solidified by the end of the month to add to the rest of our recertification packet."

"I'll make sure it's completed." She swallowed hard, wondering if she should just come right out and ask about the directorship. Torn as she was about her feelings for Holden anyway, it would be better to know the truth up front so she could nurse her wounds in private. Her heart, her future, everything seemed to be on the line. If he'd lied, then she needed to know. Hurt stung her chest, but she shoved it aside. This was business. She had no right to be upset with Holden for taking the position out from under her. They were technically still rivals, after all. And the fact that she'd fallen for him anyway was entirely on her. Her heart pinched, but she pushed those feelings down deep. Personal feelings had no business in professional life. Honestly, if she'd been faced with the same choice, she would've made the same decision as Holden, wouldn't she?

Except no, she wouldn't have. Because she loved him, even though she shouldn't. It was so stupid. He'd never once said he wanted anything more than sex from her. She'd gone into their fling with her eyes wide-open and set the rules herself. No strings attached. The fact she wanted more now was her problem, not his.

Doing her best to stay pragmatic despite the monsoon of sadness inside her, Leilani cleared her throat and raised her chin. "Have you made a decision on the directorship position?"

"What?" Helen King looked up and seemed distracted. "Yes, I have, actually, Dr. Kim." Before she could say more, however, the phone on her desk jangled loudly, cutting her off. She held up a finger for Leilani to wait as she answered. "Yes, Dr. King speaking. What? Hang on." She covered the receiver and said to Leilani, "I'm sorry, I need to take this. Can we continue this later, Dr. Kim?" At Leilani's reluctant nod, Dr. King smiled. "Good. Have the receptionist pencil you in for another slot on your way out. Excuse me."

Right. Leilani left the office and headed back out to schedule her appointment then down to the ER, still stewing over things in her mind. She hadn't gotten the answers she needed from Dr. King, so it was time to be a big girl and confront Holden directly.

Determined, as soon as the doors opened and she stepped off into her department, Leilani made a beeline toward the nurses' station, her adrenaline pumping hotter with each step. "Where's Dr. Ross?"

Pam glanced up at her, her gaze a bit startled, and she took in Leilani's serious expression. "Exam room two. Stomach flu case. Everything okay, Doc?"

"Peachy," she said over her shoulder as she headed down the hall toward where Holden was working. She knocked on the door, then opened it to find him performing an abdominal exam on a middle-aged man. "Dr. Ross, can I speak with you a moment, please?"

"Uh, sure. Let me just finish with this patient first."

"I'll be waiting outside," she said, ignoring the curious look the nurse working with Holden gave her.

"It won't take long," he said.

Several minutes passed before he limped out of the room and followed Leilani down the hall to a quiet, deserted waiting area. "Is something wrong? Is it the little girl from last night?"

"No. The last time I checked in on her, Mari was fine." Leilani crossed her arms, her toe tapping on the linoleum floor to burn off some excess energy. "Want to tell me about your meeting with Dr. King?"

His stoic expression grew more remote, telling her everything she needed to know. "Uh, no, Not really. Why?"

"Because it would have been nice to have a heads-up that you were taking the directorship job I wanted." Her anger piqued at his audacity, standing there looking shocked and innocent when he'd gone behind her back to swipe the job out from under her. She should've known better than to trust him. Letting people into your heart only caused you pain in the end. And yet Holden Ross had gotten past all her barriers. Dammit. She wasn't sure who she was more furious with—him or herself. "That's the offer you were thanking her for, wasn't it?"

"No." The confusion in his eyes quickly morphed to understanding. "Leilani, that's not what happened."

"So, she didn't offer you the directorship?"

"No, she did, but I turned it down."

She couldn't stop her derisive snort. "You turned it down? I don't believe you."

A small muscle ticked near his tight jaw. "Well, it's the truth. She asked me weeks ago about it and I told her I didn't want it. Told her I thought you should have it. She agreed."

"Excuse me?" she said, battling to keep her voice down to

avoid feeding the rumor mills any further. "Then what offer were you thanking her for upstairs? And why would she ask for your opinion anyway?" Then a new thought occurred, as bad as the previous ones. "Wait a minute. Have you been spying on me for her?"

The more she thought about it, the more it made sense. All that time they'd spent together, the day touring the island, the cases they'd worked together, their night in each other's arms. All of it was a lie.

He cursed under his breath, crimson dotting his high cheekbones now. "No." He raked his hand through his hair again, something he did when he was stressed, she'd noticed. Well, she'd be stressed too if she'd been caught in a lie. "I mean, originally Helen did ask me about you because she said she knew so little about you, but all I told her was that you were more qualified for the directorship than me."

"Damn straight I am," she said, on a roll now, hurt driving her onward, completely ignoring the fact he'd all but said Leilani was getting the job. This was about far more than work now, as evidenced by the crushing ache in her heart. She'd loved him, dammit. Opened up to him. Trusted him. And look what it got her, more pain and sorrow, just like she'd feared. "So, I'm just supposed to believe you now, that everything that happened between us wasn't just some ploy to keep tabs on me for your friend?"

"Is that what you think? The kind of guy you think I am?" That knocked him back a step and pain flashed in his hazel eyes before being masked behind a flare of indignation. He turned away, swore again, then shook his head, his expression a blend of resignation and regret. "Well, I guess that works out just fine then, doesn't it? I'm glad to know the truth because that makes my decision a hell of a lot easier." He wasn't trying to keep his voice down now, and the other staff started noticing them at the end of the hall.

"You want to know about my meeting with Helen King? Fine.

For your information, Leilani, the job I was referring to upstairs wasn't the directorship. It was a permanent trauma surgeon position. Not that it's any of your business. And if you don't believe me then there's nothing else I can say. I thought what we shared together the past few weeks, the connection between us, spoke for itself, but I guess I was wrong. I was so stupid to think this would work, to think there might be something more between us than a fling. You said you don't do relationships? Well, neither do I. Especially with a woman who's so afraid to let anyone in that she pushes everyone away."

"Me?" She stepped closer to him, her broken heart raging inside her. "You're the one who's always running. Always hiding from your past. Don't talk to me about trust when you flat out lied to me."

"I have never lied to you, Leilani," he said, the words bitten out. "I—"

Whatever he'd been about to say was silenced by what sounded like a firecracker going off near the front entrance to the ER. The loud bang was followed in short order by screaming and people running everywhere.

Leilani started down the hall toward the nurses' station. "What's happening?"

Holden grabbed her arm and hauled her back. "I don't know, but I do recognize that sound. It's gunfire."

CHAPTER ELEVEN

TIME SEEMED TO slow and speed up at the same time as Holden's mind raced and his blood froze. Shooting. Screams. Sinister flashbacks nearly drove him to his knees. Another ER, another gunman. David, bleeding out on the tile floor as Holden lay beside him, too injured himself to help.

Oh God. Not again. Please not again.

"Holden!" Leilani shouted, struggling to break his hold on her arm. "Let me go! We've got to help those people!"

He wasn't expecting the punch of her elbow to his stomach and he doubled over, releasing her as he struggled to catch his breath.

"Wait!" he called as she ran off toward the front entrance, toward danger. "Leilani!"

"Use the emergency phone to call the police," she shouted to him before disappearing around the corner.

Damn.

Blood pounded loud in his ears, making it hard to hear as he dialed 911. After relaying the info to the dispatcher, he hung up, then swallowed hard and hobbled toward the corner, his breathing labored from the anxiety squeezing his chest. If anything happened to Leilani, he'd never forgive himself. Regardless of what she thought of him now, he couldn't lose her, not like he'd lost David. He couldn't fail this time.

But what if you do...?

Teeth gritted, he pressed his back to the wall, the coolness shocking to his heated skin. He feared the shooter might be one of the gang members who'd shot the little girl upstairs, come to finish off the job. But as a male voice yelled, he realized it wasn't a gangbanger at all. He recognized that voice. Greg Chambers, the guy who'd punched him a few weeks back. The man Leilani had warned him about the day before in her office.

"Give me my opioids and no one gets hurt," the guy snarled. "Or don't and die."

Reality blurred again, between the ER in Chicago and now. The other shooter had wanted drugs too and he'd made the same threat. Made good on that threat too. Dammit. Holden cursed under his breath. The police were on their way, but what if they didn't make it in time? They hadn't been able to save David. No. It was up to him.

His analytical mind kicked in at last, slicing through the panic like a scalpel. Berating himself and "what if" thinking wouldn't help anyone now. Action. He needed to move, needed to find a way to take down Greg Chambers before he hurt anyone else.

Run. Hide. Fight.

Those were the words Homeland Security drilled into the heads of everyone who encountered an active shooter situation. Running was out, since the gunman was already here. Hiding would be good for those in the lobby, but not for Holden. He was the one person here who'd been through this before. He was outside the current hot zone and in the best position to surprise the attacker and possibly take him down and disarm him before the cops arrived.

More shots rang out, followed by screams and crying.

The unbearable tension inside Holden ratcheted higher as precious seconds ticked by.

Think, Holden. Think.

Eyes closed he rested his head back against the wall and thought through what he knew. Greg Chambers was an addict. He liked alcohol and drugs. Chances were good he'd be intoxicated now, since no sober person would attack an ER. If he was lucky, the guy's reflexes and reaction time would be affected by whatever substances were in his system. Holden could use that, if he could sneak up on the other man. He glanced down at his cane and winced. Hard to be stealthy with that thing. Which meant he needed to leave it behind.

Okay. Fine.

He set the cane aside, then took another deep breath, listening. Greg Chambers was still talking, but Holden was too far away to understand what he was saying. Then another voice, clear and bright, halted his heart midbeat. Leilani. As fast as his pulse stopped, it kicked back into overdrive again. If the bastard harmed one hair on her head…

Move. Now!

Holden hazarded a peek around the corner and spotted the shooter with his back toward the hallway. Saw Leilani near the nurses' station, hands up as she faced down the gunman while the people behind her cowered on the floor. She was so brave, so good, so beautiful and honest and true and he realized in that moment he'd do anything to keep her safe.

Even risk his own life.

After one more deep breath for courage, Holden inched his way toward the front entrance, doing his best to stay as silent as possible. His right leg protested with each step, but he pressed onward, knowing that if he didn't act now, it might be too late.

"Shut up, bitch!" Greg shouted, aiming his gun at Leilani again. "Sick of your talking. Give me my damned drugs before I blow your head off!"

"I can't do that, sir," she responded, her voice calm and level. Her dark gaze flicked over to Holden then back to the shooter, faster than a blink, but he felt that look like a lifeline. She'd seen him, knew he was coming to help. Leilani continued. "The police are on their way. Let these people go and put your gun down. You can't win here."

"Shut up!" Chambers yelled, his tone more frantic now as he looked around wildly. "I ain't going to jail again. I can't."

In the far distance, the wail of sirens cut through the eerie quiet in the ER. Holden spotted the two security guards near the automatic doors. One was down and bleeding. Holden couldn't see how badly. The other guard was kneeling beside him, trying to help his wounded comrade. Both guards' guns were at Chambers's feet, probably kicked there as the gunman had ordered.

"Give me the opioids and let me the hell out of here," Greg screamed again, waving his weapon around. "Do it, or I'll open fire. I swear I will. Ain't got nothing left to live for anyway."

He took aim at Leilani, at point-blank range.

"Bye, Lady Doc," Greg Chambers said. "You had your chance."

The snick of the trigger cocking echoed through Holden's head like a cannon blast. Adrenaline and desperation electrified his blood and he forgot about planning, forgot about strategy. Forgot about everything except saving the woman he loved.

Holden charged, wrapping his arm around Chambers's neck from behind and jerking him backward along with his weapon, sending the bullets skyward. He wasn't sure what was louder, the bullets firing from the semiautomatic or the screams from the people crouched in the lobby. Florescent bulbs shattered and chunks of ceiling tile rained down.

The muscles in his right thigh shrieked from the strain, but Holden held on, knocking the gun from Greg Chambers's hands, then flipping the smaller man over his shoulder and tossing him flat on his back on the floor. Tires screeched outside the front entrance and sirens screamed inside as the Honolulu PD SWAT team raced inside and took control of the gunman.

"Get off me!" the guy screamed, fighting and wrestling to get free as the cops handcuffed him and hauled him to his feet, reading him his Miranda rights as they walked him out the door. "I ain't going to jail!"

The adrenaline and shock wore off, and Holden slumped back onto his butt on the floor, breathing fast as he started to crawl toward the injured security guard near the door.

"Doc, we need help over here!" Pam called from behind him. "She's been hit."

His chest constricted and his heart dropped to his toes.

Holden swiveled fast, his leg cramping with pain, to see Leilani slumped on the floor against the front of the reception desk, a blotch of crimson blooming on the left arm of her pristine white lab coat. She looked pale. Too pale.

No. Please God, no!

"Leilani," he said, reaching her. She frowned and mumbled something but didn't open her eyes. David had looked like that too, just before he'd lost consciousness. He'd never woken up again.

No. No, no, no. I won't fail this time. I can't fail this time. Please don't let me fail this time.

His hands shook as he carefully slipped her arm from the lab coat then pushed up the sleeve of her shirt. From the looks of it, the bullet had passed clean through. It had also passed perilously close to her brachial artery. Years of medical training drowned out his anxiety and emotional turmoil and spurred him into action once more. "Check her vitals. Order six units of blood on standby, in case she's hypotensive. We need an O2 Sat and X-rays to see the damage. Let's move, people."

While the residents dealt with the wounded guard and the other patients, Holden stuck by Leilani's side. He held her hand as they raced toward trauma bay one, refusing to let go, even as Helen King ran into the room and took over.

"Holden, tell me what we've got," she said as she did her own exam of Leilani's wounds. He recited back what he knew and what he'd ordered, all the while still clutching her too-cold fingers. When he was done, Helen came over and put her hands on his shoulders, shaking him slightly. "You're in shock, Dr. Ross. I've got her. Go and sit in the waiting room. You look like you're ready to pass out. You saved the lives of a lot of people today. You're a hero. Now go rest and talk to the cops."

Pam took Holden's arm and led him back toward the front entrance and helped him into a chair. He couldn't seem to stop shaking. "I can't lose her," he said to Pam. "I can't."

"She's in the best care possible, Doc. You know that." Pam shoved a cup of water into his hands before heading back toward the trauma bay. "I'll keep you posted on her condition."

A while later the cops took his statement, then left him alone with his thoughts. Holden tipped his head back to stare at the bullet holes in the ceiling and swallowed hard against the lump in his throat.

You saved the lives of a lot of people today. You're a hero.

Helen's words looped in his head but rang hollow in his aching heart.

He didn't want to be a hero. He just wanted Leilani alive and well again.

Leilani blinked her eyes open slowly, squinting into the too-bright sunshine streaming in through the windows of her room at the hotel. Except...

She frowned. The windows were on the wrong side of the room. And where were the curtains? And what was that smell? Sharp, antiseptic. Not floor cleaner or bleach, but familiar, like...

Oh God!

Head fuzzy from pain meds, memories slowly began to re-surface.

Gunshots, Holden tackling the shooter, shouting, screams, a sharp burst of pain then darkness...

She moaned and tried to sit up only to be held down by the IV, tubes and wires connecting her to the monitors beside her bed. Her left arm ached like hell and her mouth felt dry as cotton.

"Welcome back, Dr. Kim," a woman's voice said from nearby. Leilani blinked hard and turned her head on the pillow to see Dr. King at the counter across the room. "How are you feeling?"

"Like crap," she mumbled, trying to scoot up farther in her hospital bed and failing. The whole scenario brought back too many memories from after the car accident for her comfort. "What's going on? Where's Holden?"

"He's fine. Should be returning to your bedside shortly," Dr. King said, moving to check the monitors attached to the blood pressure cuff and the pulse ox on Leilani's finger. "I made him go home to sleep and shower. Otherwise he hasn't left your side since the surgery."

"Surgery?" The beginnings of a headache throbbed behind Leilani's temples as she tried to recall more about what had occurred in the ER. "I had surgery?" She glanced down at the bandages wrapping her left bicep. "Who operated?"

"Yours truly." Dr. King smiled, then adjusted the IV drip settings on the machine. "Holden was a bit too close to the situation to handle it. And he was exhausted after taking down that gunman."

That much Leilani did remember. Considering what he'd been through, his actions had taken a tremendous amount of courage. He'd been a hero, saving her and countless other people. She ached to hold him and thank him for all he'd done, to beg him to forgive her for accusing him of stealing her job. He hadn't stolen anything. Except her heart.

"Anyway, I had to make sure you healed up nicely. Can't have

my new Director of Emergency Medicine less than healthy."
Dr. King stood near the end of the bed as Leilani took that in.
"If you still want the position, that is."

"I..." She swallowed hard. "Yes, I want it. But what about
Holden?"

"What about him?" Holden said from the doorway. Limping in, he set his cane aside, then took a seat in the chair at her
bedside. "You look better now. Not so pale."

"Her vitals are good," Dr. King said. "And her wound is healing nicely. I'm just going to pop out for a minute. Dr. Kim, we
can discuss your new position further once you're back to work."

An awkward silence descended once the door closed behind
Dr. King, leaving Leilani and Holden alone in the room.

"So, I guess I should thank you," Leilani said at last.

"For what?" Holden frowned.

"For saving my life."

He gave a derisive snort. "I didn't save anything. In fact, I'm
the reason you got shot in the first place. After all the research
I did into active shooter situations, I should've known better
than to tackle a man with a weapon."

"What?" Now it was her turn to scowl. "You're kidding,
right? I don't remember everything that happened in the ER,
but I do remember you taking that guy down. If anyone's at fault
for me getting shot, it's Greg Chambers. You were a her—"

Holden help up a hand to stop her. "Please don't say hero.
That's the last thing I am."

Leilani ignored the pain in her left arm this time and shoved
higher in her bed to put them closer to eye level. "Well, whatever you want to call yourself, you saved a lot of lives down
there and I'm grateful to you." She exhaled slowly and fiddled
with the edge of the sheet with her right hand. "And I'm sorry."

"Sorry?" His expression turned confused. "What do you
have to be sorry for?"

"For accusing you of stealing the directorship job. That was stupid of me. I should have believed you." She shook her head and gave a sad little chuckle. "I don't know why I didn't, except that I've been a mess emotionally since the luau and then that night we spent together and I took it out on you, and…" She shrugged, looking anywhere but at him. "I'm sorry."

"It's okay. I haven't exactly been thinking clearly myself since that night." He sighed and glanced toward the windows, giving her a view of his handsome profile. His hair was still damp from his shower and his navy blue polo shirt clung to his muscled torso like a second skin. Leilani bit her lip. He really was the most gorgeous man she'd ever seen, even with the dark circles under his eyes and the lines of tension around his mouth. She longed to trace her fingers down his cheek and kiss away his stress but didn't dare. Not until they hashed this out between them.

"Look, Leilani." His deep voice did way more than the meds to ease her aches and pains. "I know we agreed to just a fling, but the thing is, I don't think I can do that anymore."

"Oh." Her pulse stumbled and the monitor beeped loud. Apparently, she'd misread the situation entirely. Just because she'd fallen head over heels for the guy didn't mean he felt the same for her. She should have kept her barriers up, should have known better. "Don't worry about it," she said, doing her best to act like it wasn't a big deal and failing miserably as tears stung the back of her eyes. Leilani blinked hard to keep them at bay, but her vision clouded despite her wishes. "We can go back to just being colleagues. Probably better that way since we'll be working together permanently."

"Yeah," he said absently. Then his attention snapped to her and his scowl deepened. "No. That's not what I meant."

"You mean you're not taking the trauma surgeon job?" she asked, confused.

"No. I am. I just… I don't want to be your friend, Leilani." Holden reached through the bedrail to take her hand, careful of her injuries. "What I mean to say is that I want to be way more than just your friend." He sighed and stared down at their entwined fingers. "I know I promised to just have a fling, no strings attached, but I can't do that anymore because I fell in love with you."

Stunned, she took a deep breath, her pulse accelerating once more. "Uh…"

"No. Let me finish, please." He exhaled slowly, his broad shoulders slumping. "You were right. I was running. I've been running since I left Chicago. Too afraid of getting hurt again to settle down anywhere. I never wanted to get that close to anyone again. Losing my best friend, David, nearly killed me, even more than the bullets did." He gave her fingers a gentle squeeze. "But then I met you. You were so full of life, so vibrant and smart and funny and kind. You were everything I didn't know I needed. You healed me, from the inside out. Showed me I could laugh again, love again. So no, I can't go back to just having a fling with you, Leilani Kim. Because I want more. So much more. If you'll have me."

She sniffled, her tears flowing freely now. "You're the one who healed me, Holden. I thought I'd gotten over the accident that took my family all those years ago, but I'd just walled myself off, thinking that not caring too deeply would keep me safe. All that did though was make me lonely. You opened my heart again." She laughed, then winced when the movement hurt her arm. "I love you too, Holden Ross."

"You do?" His sweet, hesitant smile made her breath catch. "I do."

He leaned closer to brush his lips across hers, and she let go of his hand to slip her fingers behind his neck to keep him close.

"I'm glad you're staying in Hawaii," she said at last, after he'd pulled back slightly.

"Me too." He nuzzled his nose against hers. "Does this mean we're officially dating?"

"I believe it does, Dr. Ross," Leilani said, winking. "The rumor mill will be all abuzz."

"Good, Dr. Kim." Holden kissed her again. "Give them something new to talk about."

CHAPTER TWELVE

One year later...

"WHAT DO WE have coming in?" Leilani asked, tugging on a fresh gown and heading toward the ambulance bay entrance.

Nurse Pam was waiting there for her, already geared up. "Per the EMTs, it was a rollover accident on the H1. Family of five. ETA two minutes."

Not exactly how she'd expected to spend the morning of her wedding day, but the ER had been short-staffed and as Director of Emergency Medicine, it was her duty to fill in when needed. Besides, it helped her stress levels to keep busy, since all the planning was done and all she had left to do was show up and marry the man of her dreams.

First though, it seemed like an ironic twist of fate that the last case she worked as a single woman was a rollover. Her biological family hadn't survived their similar accident, but today, she planned to do all she could to ensure history did not repeat itself.

Two ambulances screeched to a halt outside and soon the automatic doors whooshed open as five gurneys were wheeled in by three sets of paramedics. The trauma surgeon on call—not Holden, thank goodness—and a resident took the mother and son and the son's girlfriend. Leilani and another resident took the father and the daughter.

"You're in good hands, sir. Just lie still and let us do all the work, okay?" she said to the father as they raced for an open trauma bay. Then she focused on the EMT racing along on the other side of the gurney. "Rundown, please."

"Car rolled five times. Wife was driving," the EMT said.

"I just remember coming around the bend and that other car slammed into us. Then rolling and rolling."

"It was so scary," the daughter said as they transferred her to a bed adjacent to the one her father was on, her voice shaky with tears. "My first car accident. With the four people I love most."

Leilani's heart squeezed with sympathy. Twenty-one years ago, she'd experienced her first car accident too. Worst day of her life. Funny how life worked, because now—today—would be the best day ever. Once her shift was over, of course. She rolled her left shoulder to ease the ache in her bicep, then began taking the father's vitals while the resident working alongside her in the trauma bay did the same with the daughter.

"Do you remember what happened, sir?" Leilani asked the father.

"I remember my life flashing before my eyes," he said, his voice husky with emotion. "I remember glass flying and people screaming, then everything stopped. I'm just glad we're all still alive."

"Me too, sir," she said, swallowing against an unexpected lump of gratitude in her throat. "Me too."

"Patient is complaining of abdominal pain," the resident called over to Leilani. "I'd like to get an ultrasound to rule out internal injuries or bleeding."

"Do it," Leilani said before continuing her own exam on the father. "Where are you experiencing pain, sir?"

"My neck is killing me." He lifted his arm to point at his throat, then winced. "My chest hurts too. How are my wife and son? His girlfriend?"

"As far as I know, they're doing fine, but I'll be sure to check on that for you as soon as we get you set up here." She finished checking his vitals and rattled them off to Pam to enter into the computer, then carefully removed the plastic neck brace the EMTs had applied and examined the man's neck while a tech wheeled in an ultrasound machine for the daughter. "After you finish with that patient, I'll need a cardiac ultrasound over here too for the father, please. He's complaining of chest pain and has a history of high blood pressure and arteriosclerosis. Rule out any issues there, please. While we wait, let's see if CT can work him in for an emergency C-spine. I'm concerned about intracranial bleeding or neck fractures."

"Sure thing, Doc," Pam said, setting the tablet aside. "Keep an eye on your time too, Dr. Kim. Don't want to be late for your big day."

"I will. Thanks." She smiled at the nurse, then turned back to her patient. "Sir, we're going to get some tests done on you to make sure there are no underlying conditions going on I can't see on exam. Some films of your neck and head and also an ultrasound of your heart." She looked up as two techs came in to wheel her patient to radiology for his CT scan. "While you're doing that, I'll check in on the status of your family members, okay?"

"Okay." The father reached out and grasped Leilani's hand. "Thank you, Doctor."

"You're most welcome," she said, smiling.

The EMTs were still hanging out in the hall when she headed toward the other trauma bay to check on the mother and son and his girlfriend. One of the EMTs stopped her and showed her a picture he'd snapped at the accident scene of the mashed-up SUV lying on its side in a ditch. "The way that car looked, I'm surprised they all walked away. It's a miracle," the EMT said.

"It is." Leilani nodded, then headed for trauma bay two. "But miracles are what we specialize in around here."

She was living proof of that. She was also proof that you

could not only survive the worst thing possible, you could thrive after it. Thanks to her wonderful adopted family, and Holden, who'd taught her how to love again. Her heart swelled with joy as she walked into the room where the son and his girlfriend were now sitting up and chatting while his mother gave her statement to a police officer. They appeared bruised and a bit rattled, but nothing too serious.

"I drive that route every day from our house," the mother said to the cop. "We were on our way home to watch a football game. That didn't work out so well." She sniffled. "When I saw that other car coming at us, I didn't know what to do. I didn't want him to hit us head-on, so I swerved to the left and my poor husband took the brunt." She looked up and spotted Leilani, her expression frantic. "Is he okay? Is my husband okay? I never wanted our day to end like this."

"He's fine, ma'am," she reassured the woman. "We're running a few tests to rule out any broken bones or bleeding internally."

The woman bit back a sob and reached over to take her son's hand. "Oh thank God. I'm so grateful we're all okay."

"Me too, ma'am. Me too." Leilani pulled the resident aside and got the scoop on the three patients in the room before they wheeled the father past the door of the room heading back to trauma bay one, and she excused herself to check in on her patient once more.

While Leilani went over the images, the ultrasound tech performed a cardiac ultrasound and Pam cleaned and bandaged up the lacerations on the man's hand. Of the five passengers in the car, the father seemed to be the one most badly hurt, but the CT had ruled out any fractures in his neck or bleeding in his head, which was great. The man would be sore for sure for a few days, but otherwise should make a full recovery, barring anything abnormal on the cardiac ultrasound.

"Everything looks fine, Doc," the tech said a few minutes

later, wiping the gel off the patient's chest. "No abnormalities seen."

"Perfect." Leilani moved aside so they could wheel her portable machine back out of the room. "All right, sir. Looks like you're banged up a bit, but otherwise you'll be fine. I checked on the rest of your family as well, and they're all doing fine too. You all are very lucky."

The daughter, who'd been cleared to move about freely, jumped down and walked over to take her father's hand. Soon, the rest of the family entered to join them in the trauma bay.

"How are you, honey?" the mother asked her husband, kissing his cheek.

"My neck still hurts," he said, then held up his other hand. "And this got messed up a bit. But otherwise, I'm fine." He chuckled. "Remind me never to ride with you again though."

The mother promptly burst into tears and he pulled her down closer to kiss her again.

"I'm kidding," the father said. "You handled that situation better than I would have. I love you so much. It's fine. We're all fine, thanks to you."

Leilani checked the time, then backed out of the room while the family gathered around each other, hugging and laughing and saying prayers of thanks. Tears stung the backs of her eyes, as an unexpected feeling of completeness filled her soul. That's how it should have been for her family all those years ago. It hadn't been, but now at least she'd been able to give that gift of a future to another family. Circle of life indeed.

After finishing up the discharge paperwork for her patients, she checked the time, then discarded her gown and mask into a nearby biohazard bin.

Speaking of futures, it was time to get on with hers.

Holden stood on the beach in front of the Malu Huna Resort as a warm breeze blew and the waves lapped the shore behind him. Joe Kim stood beneath an arbor adorned with palm fronds, tropical flowers and white gauzy fabric that flowed in the wind, ready to marry off his adopted daughter. He'd gotten ordained just for the ceremony. Leilani's mother was passing out leis to the guests as they took their seats. Now all Holden needed was his bride.

He shifted his weight slightly, his bare toes sinking deeper into the sand. His leg hurt less and less these days, thanks to all the outdoor activities available in and around Honolulu. He loved hiking and swimming and had even tried his hand at surfing. The warmer temperatures helped too. And of course, having the woman he loved by his side while he did all those things was the biggest benefit of all. In fact, he'd left his cane inside the hotel today—as he was doing more and more often now. He'd stop and get it though, before the reception, since there would be dancing involved later.

They'd decided on a casual, traditional Hawaiian wedding and he was not upset with it. His white linen pants and shirt were certainly more comfortable than some tuxedo monkey suit, that was for sure. Especially with the great weather. Blue skies, sunshine, a perfect day in paradise.

Hard to believe that a year ago he couldn't wait to get out of this place. Now he couldn't ever imagine calling anywhere else home ever again. He and Leilani had moved into her—now *their*—newly remodeled house three months prior, and things were pretty magical all around as they started their new life together. But even with the great beachfront abode, it wasn't the location so much as the people.

Once they'd told the Kims about their relationship, they had taken him in like a prodigal son. Family like that was something to appreciate and Holden didn't take one day of it for granted.

Same with Leilani. They'd both wanted to go slow, explore their relationship before diving into anything permanent too fast. Given their collective past, it was understandable. But now they were both ready to take the leap.

Holden glanced over and caught sight of his own parents sitting in the first row and flashed them a smile. They'd flown in from Chicago and were loving all Hawaii had to offer. Maybe someday they'd move down here too. He'd like that. As the guests' chairs filled in and the ukulele band they'd hired to play for the ceremony finished a sweet rendition of "Somewhere Over the Rainbow," a hush fell over the crowd. Holden looked up to see his bride at last at the end of the white satin runner covering the aisle of sand between the rows of bow-bedecked folding chairs.

He couldn't stop staring at her, his heart in his throat and his chest swelling with so much love he thought he might burst from the joy of it. She looked amazingly beautiful in a strapless white gown that was fitted on top, then flowed into a silken cloud around her legs, the breeze gently rustling the fabric. Like an angel. His angel, who'd been heaven-sent to teach him how to live and love again, who'd filled his life with so much purpose and meaning and emotion.

The band began "Here Comes the Bride" and the guests stood as Leilani slowly made her way toward Holden, her long dark hair loose beneath the woven crown of flowers on her head and her eyes sparkling with happiness.

She was everything he'd ever dreamed of and nothing he deserved, and his life was infinitely better because she was in it. He planned to tell her as much in his vows. They'd each written their own, but no matter what she said today, it would never mean as much to him as the moment she'd told him she loved him for the first time that day in her hospital room.

Music floated on the jasmine-scented breeze and Leilani reached his side at last.

Before the ceremony began, while the guests were settling into their seats again, Holden leaned closer and whispered for her ears only, "You look spectacular and I'm the luckiest man in the world. I love you, Leilani Kim."

Her smile brightened his entire universe as she beamed up at him. "I'm pretty lucky myself, Holden Ross. I love you too."

He leaned in to kiss her, but Leilani's father cleared his throat. Chuckles erupted from the assembled guests. Holden winked down at his wife-to-be instead, unable to keep the silly, love-sick grin off his face. "Ready to do this thing, Doc?"

"So, so ready," she said, slipping her hand in his as they turned to face her father.

* * * * *

It Happened One Night

Sharon Sala

HEART

Home is where the heart is.

CHAPTER ONE

HARLEY JUNE BEAUMONT had been awake for at least five minutes and still didn't have the guts to move, not even an eyelid. Her head was pounding, her stomach wanted to heave and the taste in her mouth was disgusting.

The last thing she remembered was being in Las Vegas, toasting her best friend Susan and her new husband, Mike, as they cut their wedding cake. There were a few vague images of a champagne glass that never seemed to empty, throwing streamers and rice, then dancing on a table and looking down at the bald spot on a waiter's head. After that, everything else was a blur.

What she did know was that she needed to go to the bathroom, which meant getting out of bed, which meant she would have to move. And, because she hadn't wet the bed since the age of three, it also meant she was going to have to get up.

Opening her eyelids in minuscule increments, she took a slow, shallow breath. So far, so good. The room looked vaguely familiar. Oh yes, the Las Vegas Motel.

From where she was lying, she could see a sheer mauve dress that had been tossed casually on the back of a chair. One matching shoe was on the table beside it, the other nowhere in sight.

My maid of honor dress... I think.

With a groan, she began to inch toward the side of the bed, wincing as the movement increased the pounding in her temples. When she felt space, she stopped, convinced she had come to the edge. Now it was sit up or die. Her bladder won out. Unwilling to be found dead in a puddle of pee, she got up, consoling herself with the notion that she could always die later.

There was a large pile of bedclothes on the floor at the foot of the bed. She frowned as she sidestepped them, thinking to herself that was why she'd woken up cold, and was halfway to the bathroom before it dawned on her that she was naked. She glanced around the room, wondering where her nightgown had gone, then saw her bra draped over a lampshade and her panties hanging on the doorknob. She winced again. At least she could be thankful her mother was not present to give her hell.

Harley June's mother, Marcie Lee Beaumont, was a direct descendant of General Robert E. Lee, and according to Marcie, genteel Southern ladies did not sleep in the altogether. But right now, Harley June was sick and a missing nightgown was the least of her worries.

The bathroom tiles were cold beneath her feet and she shivered as she hurried to the commode. As she lifted the lid to sit down, she gasped. There were flowers growing in the water in her toilet!

She leaned a little bit closer, then snorted lightly and fished Susan's bridal bouquet out of the commode before tossing it in the trash. Talk about a lost weekend. All she wanted was to get cleaned up, pack her things and catch the plane back home to Savannah. Later, when she could think without wanting to throw up, she might be willing to pursue the vagaries of her memory, but for now, survival depended on minimal thought and motion.

A couple of minutes later, she stepped into the shower, relishing the warm jets of water sluicing her face and body. Later, as she began to dry off, she glanced toward the full-length mirror on the back of the door and frowned. What little she could see of herself was just like she felt—wet and foggy. Impulsively, she gave the mirror a swipe with her towel, then as she started to turn, caught a glimpse of something red on the left side of her hip. Frowning even more, she dried a larger spot on the mirror and then turned sideways, angling for a better view of her backside.

What came out of her throat was little more than a squeak and was nothing to describe the shock she was feeling at seeing something red and heart-shaped on the left side of her rear.

She stepped closer, peering intently into the mirror only to realize there were words inside the heart. Unable to believe her eyes, she began scrubbing at the spot and then winced and quickly stopped. It was tender! Dropping the towel, she traced the shape with her fingers as her mind accepted the only obvious conclusion.

'Oh. My. God. A tattoo. I have a tattoo.'

She moved closer, squinting at the heart. The words were backward in the mirror and it took her a few moments to spell them out and then reverse the order of letters.

Junie Loves Sam.

'Sam? Who, in the name of all that's holy, is Sam?'

The tone of her voice rose several decibels as reality hit. It didn't matter as much that she didn't know a Sam as it did that the name was on there.

'Sweet Lord… I have a man's name tattooed on my butt.'

She moaned and began rubbing harder at the tattoo, praying that if she scrubbed it enough, it would come off, which of course, it didn't.

'This can't be happening,' she moaned, and at that moment, heard the distinct but horrifying sound of someone moving around in her bedroom.

Grabbing the towel she'd discarded, she yanked it up in front of her and started to lock the door when it began to open.

With heart thundering and a scream hovering on her lips, she gasped. Too stunned to cut loose with the scream, she found herself face-to-face with the biggest man she'd ever seen. His

shoulders spanned the width of the doorway, his long, mus-
cular legs were firmly planted as he ran a hand through his
short, spiky hair. His eyes were a sleepy blue, his smile slightly
crooked and apologetic and his hair was black as coal. His features were strong and regular, although his nose looked as if it
had been broken at least once. But it was none of the above that
brought the impending scream she'd been holding into fruition
as quickly as the fact that he was naked.

Harley cut loose with the scream she'd been saving, then
started to beg.

'Oh God…oh God…don't hurt me! Please don't hurt me! My
purse is in there…somewhere. Take it! Take everything I've got,
just please don't hurt me!'

The man smiled and glanced over his shoulder to the bed
she'd recently vacated.

'Honey, you already gave me everything you had…and then
some…last night.'

Harley yanked the towel a little further beneath her chin
and glared.

'What are you talking about?'

He looked back at her and grinned.

Unaware that the pupils of her eyes had just doubled in size,
she grabbed a hairbrush, aiming it at him like a gun.

'You're lying. You stay away from me, you pervert.'

He swooped her up into his arms and planted a slow, sexy
kiss in the middle of her mouth. The moment their lips met,
Harley knew it had happened before. Her lips had curved to fit
his mouth as if they had a mind of their own, and even while her
good sense told her to stop, there was a part of her that didn't
ever want to let go. To her chagrin, the man was the first to
pull back. He set her back down on her feet and then grabbed
a fresh towel and began drying her backside as if he'd done it
a thousand times before.

Harley spun out of his grasp, taking the towel with her.

'Who are you?' she asked.

His smile faltered, but only slightly as he gently tucked a damp strand of her hair behind her ear.

'I'm not a pervert, honey. I'm your husband…and you're my wife.'

'Wife? I'm not your wife! I'm not anyone's wife!' she shrieked, and then winced at the sound of her own shriek. Her headache was getting worse, not better.

He reached for her, gently fingering the gold band on the third finger of her left hand.

'How quickly she forgets,' he said softly. He lifted her hand to his lips and kissed the ring, then turned her hand palm-side up and kissed it too.

Something close to electricity coiled deep in her belly before settling between her legs. She took a slow breath, startled by the sudden lethargy of her limbs. But even the sexual tension between them did not blind her to the fact that there *was* a ring on her finger that had not been there the night before.

'Who?' she mumbled.

He looked at her and then shook his head.

'Junie, darlin'…please don't tell me you've already forgotten my name, too?'

Junie? She flashed on the tattoo on her hip. Junie Loves Sam.

'Sam?'

'That's my girl,' he said slowly, and took the towel out of her hands and dropped it on the floor between them.

Harley saw the want in his eyes and shuddered. At that moment, she couldn't have moved to save her life.

'No one calls me Junie.'

His blue eyes darkened. 'I do,' he said, and picked her up.

'What are you going to do?'

'Make love to my wife.'

'I'm not… I can't—'

He covered her mouth with a kiss, stifling her answer, laid her down in the middle of the bed and then crawled in beside her, levering himself above her still-damp body.

'Yes, you are, and yes, you can,' Sam said. 'And very nicely, if I say so myself.'

If there was a thought in Harley's mind about arguing, the enigmatic Sam's kisses wiped it away. And when she felt the weight of his body settling down on hers, she knew she'd been here before. God help her, but for everything wrong about what they had done, making love with Sam seemed so right.

It was ten minutes after 11:00 a.m. when Harley awoke again, only this time she was under no illusions as to where she was. Her headache was still present, and only a degree or so less intimidating than the man in whose arms she was lying.

Sam. He'd called himself Sam.

Fighting panic, she closed her eyes, refusing to contemplate how much she liked the weight of his arm across her belly, or the fact that for the first time since she'd left the comfort of her parents' home, she felt safe.

And the sex.

Dear Lord, they were combustible. Twice since he'd taken her back to bed, she thought she would go up in flames. But that had to be lust, and according to her mother, decent Southern girls made their marriage beds based on good bloodlines and money, not lust.

She took a deep breath to steady her nerves and then began to worm her way out from under his arm. She needed to put space between her and this man, however devastating he might be. She wasn't sure how to go about it, but this marriage had to go away. This was Las Vegas. Surely a marriage could end as simply as it had begun.

Carefully, she inched her way out of his grasp and then, holding her breath, got out of bed. Once on her feet, she looked back at the man. Without thinking, she touched her tattoo and at the still-tender sensation, yanked her hand away in embarrassment. The tattoo was another problem altogether, although something told her it was going to be easier to get rid of the marriage than it would that red heart.

She kept staring, her gaze fixed on the sensuousness of his mouth and the shading of dark lashes on his cheeks. She had to admit he was gorgeous. She sighed. So he was handsome. That only meant liquor did not drown her good taste—just her good sense.

But she was awake now and painfully sober. The way she saw it, her only recourse was to disappear. As quietly as she could, she dressed and packed, stuffing her clothing into her bag without snapping or zipping a single compartment. When she moved to the dresser to retrieve her watch, her gaze fell on a Polaroid picture and the paper beneath.

Oh Lord.

It was their wedding picture—and the license. She picked up the picture, tilting it toward the light for a closer look. When she saw the expressions on their faces, she wanted to cry. They looked so happy. She focused on her own image and had a small moment of satisfaction that even though she must have been drunk out of her mind, she looked normal. Another Marcie teaching was that decent women did not make spectacles of themselves.

Harley sighed and laid the picture down, only to find another peeking out from beneath the license. She picked it up and then stifled a groan. The man standing between them couldn't possibly be the preacher, but then who else could he be? There was an altar behind them and she was holding her friend Susan's bridal bouquet. She looked closer, trying to find another reason why an Elvis reject would be in a picture with them. His black pompadour hairstyle, complete with sideburns all the way to his chin, looked slick and greasy, and the white, rhinestone-bedecked jumpsuit he was wearing was nothing like her pastor's somber black robes. She glanced down at the marriage certificate and then rolled her eyes in disbelief. She hadn't been married in her mother's Southern Baptist church as she'd planned to all her life. She'd gone and gotten married in the Love Me Tender wedding chapel by a man who looked like Elvis.

What in hell had she been thinking?

Her shoulders slumped. Therein lay the problem. She hadn't been thinking, and obviously, neither had Sam. She glanced again toward the bed, thankful that he was still asleep, then back at the paper.

Samuel Francis Clay. His name was Samuel Francis Clay.

My mother was a huge Sinatra fan.

She shivered, suddenly remembering the sound of his voice explaining the significance of his middle name as he leaned over her shoulder to write his name.

Harley's chin quivered. My name is now Harley June Clay.

She turned again, this time staring long and hard at the man still in her bed, then slipped the wedding ring off her finger. Seconds passed as her heart grew heavy. Something inside her kept saying this would be a mistake even bigger than the marriage had been, but she could see no other way out of what they'd done. Slowly, she looked away, laid the ring on top of the dresser beside the pictures, then picked up her bag and slipped out of the room. It wasn't until later when her plane finally took off for Savannah that she let herself cry. And even then, she wasn't sure if she was crying for the mess she'd made of her life by getting married, or the fact that she'd walked out on the best thing she'd ever done.

Savannah, Georgia—Four days later

The phone on Harley June's desk rang abruptly, breaking her train of thought.

'Turner Insurance Agency, how may I help you? Oh…hello, Mrs. Peabody. Yes, I gave Mr. Turner your message. No, I'm sorry, but he's still not back from his meeting. Yes, I will certainly tell him you have called again. No, ma'am, I am not giving you the runaround. Yes, ma'am, I know you are a busy woman.

No, ma'am, it isn't polite to lie. Yes, Mrs. Peabody, I will give my mother your regards. Thank you for calling.'

'Mrs. Peabody still got her panties in a twist?'

Harley looked at one of the other insurance agents and resisted the urge to sigh.

'What do you think?'

Jennifer Brownlee laughed.

'Oh, I almost forgot. Your mother called while you were out to lunch.'

Harley rolled her eyes, wondering what her mother could possibly want now. Ever since Harley had come back from Susan's wedding in Las Vegas, her mother had been grilling her like a sergeant. First on what everything looked like and then who attended, always curling her lip just the least little bit as she asked. Even though Harley loved her mother dearly, she also knew and accepted the fact that Marcie Lee Beaumont was a bit of a snob.

She picked up the phone and called her parents' number. Her father answered on the second ring and Harley smiled at the familiar sound.

'Hi, Daddy, it's me. Jennifer said Mama called earlier. Is she home?'

'Yes, she's in the kitchen ironing aluminum foil,' Dewey Beaumont said. 'Want me to get her?'

Harley stifled a giggle. Her mother's penury was well-known among friends and family. Dewey Beaumont had plenty of money. The Beaumont family home and their lifestyle reflected it, and yet Marcie pinched pennies as if they were about to be evicted. The fact that she washed and ironed used aluminum foil over and over until it completely lost the ability to fold was one of her more quirky habits. It was something Harley had long ago accepted about her mother and something her father prayed had not been passed on to his only child.

'It can wait. Do you have any idea what she wanted?' Harley asked. Then she heard her daddy chuckle.

'No, but I know she made the call right after she talked to Susan's mother, Betty Jean.'

Harley's heart skipped a beat, then settled back into its normal rhythm. There was no reason to panic. Susan was long gone by the time Harley must have taken off with Sam Clay. Her fingers tightened around the receiver. If only she could remember the details of that night, she would feel a lot safer.

As her daddy droned on, talking about this and that, Harley let her thoughts drift, and as they did, they headed straight for Sam Clay. The last time she'd seen him he'd been bare naked and barely covered, lying on her motel bed like a sleeping Adonis. In weaker moments, she let herself wonder what might have happened if she'd stayed and faced the music, so to speak. But then reason always seemed to return and Harley accepted the fact that she'd done the right thing by leaving. Somewhere down the road when she could face the truth of what she'd done, she would see a lawyer about getting the marriage set aside. Surely she couldn't be held to something she didn't even remember.

Then she sighed. What she did remember was making slow, sweet love to a most magnificent man. That, she told her errant conscience, was something she *needed* to forget.

'…and so I told her it was none of her business, but you know your mother.'

Harley blinked, realizing she hadn't been paying any attention to what her daddy had been saying.

'Hmmm… Oh…yes, I think I do,' Harley said.

Dewey hesitated. It wasn't like him to broach tender subjects that he considered 'woman business' with his own daughter, but he considered her the best thing he'd ever done in his life, and didn't want to see her waste her life. She was twenty-seven years old and had yet to be engaged. In Savannah, an eligible young lady quite often went through a couple of suitors before settling on the proper one. Harley didn't seem interested in the things that most young women her age focused on and it bothered him greatly. He wanted to see her happy and wanted her children playing around his knees before he was too old to enjoy them, so he cleared his throat and said what was on his mind.

'Harley June, did you have a good time in Las Vegas?'

Again, Harley's heart skipped a beat. Guilt settled heavy on her heart. She hated lying, but how could she tell what she'd done without making herself appear a total fool.

'Why, yes, Daddy, I had a good time. Susan and Mike made such a wonderful couple and the wedding was beautiful.'

Dewey frowned. 'But what about you? Did *you* have a good time?' He chuckled. 'If that had been me at your age, I would have at least hit the gaming tables—gone to a few shows—you know... lived it up a bit before I settled back into the same old routine.'

Harley thought about telling him, but how do you say, *Oh sure, Daddy, I cut loose like you wouldn't believe. I not only partied all night, I let Elvis marry me to a total stranger.* Instead, she heard herself saying...

'The wedding was marvelous. I had a very nice time dancing. I even had champagne, Daddy, okay?'

Dewey sighed. 'Now, honey girl, I just worry about you, that's all. It's a daddy's job. Don't take this wrong, but I would hate to see you wind up exactly like your mama, God bless her. I love her with all my heart, but I do not want to know that I sired a daughter who saves buttons and aluminum foil.'

Harley burst out laughing. 'I know, Daddy, and I promise, I won't. I've got to get back to work now. Tell Mama I'll call her tonight, all right?'

'Yes, I will. I love you, Harley June.'

'I love you, too, Daddy.'

Harley was still smiling as she hung up the phone. She glanced across the aisle at Jennifer as she started to swivel her chair back to the computer when Jennifer's eyes suddenly widened and then she let out a fake moan.

'Oh my lord! I think I'm in love.'

'What are you talking about?' Harley asked.

Jennifer pointed.

Harley turned around.

'Oh God.'

The smile died on her face just as Sam Clay leaned across her desk and planted a kiss square in the middle of her lips, then whispered softly.

'Junie, darlin', I'm not God, I'm Sam. How can you keep forgetting when it's tattooed on your butt?'

Harley June jumped to her feet, poised to bolt. Reading her body language, Sam put himself between her and the door.

'What are you doing here?' Harley asked.

'I came to take you home,' Sam said, and then lifted her jacket from the back of her chair. 'Where's your purse?'

She began to sputter. 'I can't go yet. I'm at work. Besides, you have no business—'

'You are my wife, therefore you are my business,' he said calmly, then looked beneath her desk, spied a handbag and picked it up.

But he hadn't counted on the stir his words would cause. Before Harley could argue, the other two insurance agents, their secretaries and the mail clerk all had to have their say. Shouts of surprise were followed by cries of congratulations. Sam suddenly felt like a bug under glass, but he held his ground. He hadn't had two solid hours of consecutive sleep since he woke up in Las Vegas to find Harley gone. Added to that, his stomach had been in knots ever since he'd found her ring on their picture. He knew what they'd done had been crazy and impulsive, and there had been a brief moment when he'd picked up that ring and thought about following her lead—of going home and never looking back. But that notion had lasted all of a minute until he looked at the bed. Remembering the magic they made together when they made love was all the impetus he'd needed. He'd taken the next flight home to Oklahoma City, worked his shift until he'd had his next four-day hiatus, then had taken a plane straight to Savannah.

And the moment he'd walked into the insurance office and seen her sitting behind that desk and laughing into the phone, he knew he'd done the right thing. All he had to do was convince Harley.

Jennifer was the first to reach Harley's side. She winked at Sam and then hugged Harley.

'Harley June! I can't believe you didn't tell us you were married. When did this happen? Aren't you going to introduce us to your new husband?'

Harley's mouth was moving, but nothing was coming out. Sam figured if anyone was talking, it would have to be him.

'We got married four...almost five days ago,' Sam said. 'In Las Vegas.'

Unknowingly, he flashed Jennifer a smile that made her wish she was fifteen years younger and single.

'And my name is Sam Clay,' he added, extending his hand.

Jennifer giggled. 'Pleased to meet you, Sam Clay. I'm Jennifer.'

Before anyone could answer, Waymon Turner, of Turner Insurance, came in the door.

'What's going on here?' he said.

Harley groaned. The boss was back, and it looked like they were having a party.

'Uh... Mr. Turner, Mrs. Peabody has called four times for you. She's very upset and—'

Sam held out his hand. 'Mr. Turner, I'm Sam Clay. Pleased to meet you. I know this is a big imposition, but Junie is turning in her resignation.'

'Who's Junie?' he asked, then eyed Sam closely. 'Am I supposed to know you, son?'

Harley rolled her eyes and elbowed Sam. 'I told you no one calls me that.' Then she tried to smile, knowing that her explanation was only going to make everything worse, but it had to be said.

'He's talking about me, Mr. Turner, and uh... Sam is my... well, when I was in Las Vegas we...you see I—'

'I'm her husband,' Sam said. 'I came to take Junie home.'

Now Waymon Turner was thoroughly confused. He eyed Harley June, trying to gauge the mood of the moment by the expression on her face and saw nothing but panic and confusion. He knew just how she felt.

'I didn't know you were married, Harley June. When did this event take place?' he asked.

'Almost five days ago at four-fifteen in the morning at the Love Me Tender chapel in Las Vegas, Nevada,' Sam said.

Jennifer squealed. For a woman her age, it was hard to pull off, but somehow she made it work.

'Oh my Gawd! How romantic! I can't wait to tell Johnson.'

Harley groaned.

Sam smiled. 'Hold out your arms, darlin',' Sam said, and held out the jacket that he'd taken from the back of her chair. He slipped it on her while she was trying to argue.

'Here's your purse, too.'

Harley snatched it to her chest like a shield.

'You can't just—'

'Here you go,' he said, slipping the long strap over her shoulder and then taking her by the elbow and guiding her to the door. 'Everyone, it's been nice meeting you,' he said. 'If you're ever in Oklahoma City, give us a call.'

Harley's heart dropped.

'I'm not going to—'

She found herself outside and standing in the street.

'Listen here, Sam Clay, you can't just—'

Sam cupped her face with his hands and kissed her.

Harley's arguments died along with the last of her good sense. There was nothing in the world that seemed to matter but the feel of his hands on her face, the sensual tug of his mouth against her lips and the scent of his cologne. She'd dreamed about the way he smelled.

When he lifted his head, she moaned aloud.

Sam hid a smile. He didn't have a damn thing going for him

except the fact that they were good together in bed. He knew she was afraid. Dang it all, so was he. But the moment he'd walked into that hotel bar and seen her dancing on a table in the middle of a pile of poker chips, he'd been lost. She'd been holding a handful of flowers that looked suspiciously like a bridal bouquet, and had done a neat pivot on the tabletop to the beat of the music playing in the background before giving the flowers a toss. He'd caught them in reflex and then caught her as she started to fall. She didn't look like the kind of girl a serious man took home to Mother. She didn't appear to be the homemaker, baby-loving type—and he was. But she'd gasped when he caught her and then looked up at him with those dark brown eyes and laughed. After that, he was lost. Hours later they'd gotten married and he wasn't going to give up—at least not until they'd given the marriage a serious try.

'What are you really doing here?' Harley asked. 'If you've come to make trouble, I can assure you that I don't—'

Sam put his finger in the middle of her lips and then shook his head.

'Sssh, darlin'. I don't make trouble. I make love. Don't you remember?'

Harley's knees went weak. She didn't remember a lot of things, but she well remembered the feel of his weight on her body and sweat-slick hammer of his hips between her thighs.

'Have mercy,' she mumbled.

He slipped his arm around her shoulders and began leading her toward a waiting cab.

'I'll give you mercy and anything else your little heart desires,' he whispered, as he opened the door.

'Where are we going?' she asked.

'Well…for starters, our flight leaves day after tomorrow morning. That doesn't give us much time.'

Flight. The word made her stomach turn. Day after tomorrow. Surely she could come up with something between now and then that would get her out of this mess.

'Time for what?' she asked.

He scooted into the cab beside her.

'To meet your parents. Pack your things. You know. Stuff.'

Parents! Lord have mercy, no! Harley opened her mouth to object when Sam leaned over the seat and gave the driver the address to her parents' home.

She stared at him in disbelief, thinking that she must have married herself to a handsome but dangerous stalker. How else would he have known her parents' address? She pulled away from him, shrinking into the corner of the cab and eyed him with something close to panic.

'How do you know where they live?' she whispered.

'You told me,' he said.

'I didn't!'

Sam grinned. He was starting to enjoy her discomfiture. She'd put him through four days of hell. It was good for her to be a little bit nervous.

'Oh yes, you did. You told me lots of things,' he said, as the cab started to move. 'Like...' He hesitated, then leaned over and whispered in her ear.

Harley's eyes widened. Her face flushed and her mouth went slack.

'I did no such thing,' she whispered, glancing nervously at the driver who, thankfully, was paying them no attention.

Sam grinned. 'Oh, but you did.'

Harley felt the blood draining from her face. He had to be telling the truth, because she'd never told anyone that fantasy. Ever.

'Oh no.'

'Oh yes,' Sam said. 'And we did it the night we got married. Twice.'

Harley closed her eyes and leaned back against the seat. Her life was seriously out of control.

CHAPTER TWO

HARLEY WAS TRAPPED—both by Sam's proximity and the stupidity of her actions. She wanted to be mad at him, but in all fairness, it seemed as if he had married her in good faith. If he'd had any other ulterior motive, it would have been evident the 'morning after.' All he would have had to do was walk away from what they'd done just as she had. Instead, he'd come after her—like some knight in shining armor come to rescue the fair damsel in distress.

However, distress was a mild word for the trouble Harley considered herself in, and he wasn't exactly a knight in shining armor. She kept eyeing his profile as the cab sped through the streets of Savannah, and as she did, it occurred to her that she had no idea where he lived or what he did for a living. Following that revelation came the thought of what kind of man would marry a woman he'd just met? What was wrong with him that he would settle for a drunk-out-of-her-mind female he'd only just laid eyes on a few hours before?

She shivered in spite of the warmth of the day.

'Sam?'

He turned toward her. 'Yeah?'

'Do you have a job?'

He laughed. 'You could say that.'

Harley frowned. 'What do you mean?'

'I'm a fireman for the Oklahoma City Fire Department.'

'Oh.'

'That wasn't a very enthusiastic 'oh,'' Sam said. 'What's the matter, don't I look like the kind of man who could put out fires?'

Harley thought of the sexual chemistry between them and resisted the unladylike urge to snort beneath her breath. From the way they made love, she could have more easily believed he started fires, instead of extinguishing them. There had been a time or two back in the motel after they'd made love, if she could have moved, where she would have gotten up to see if she was smoking.

'I don't know. I was just curious, that's all.' Then she added, 'Why did you marry me?'

He stared at her, letting his gaze linger longer on the fan of eyelashes partially shading her soft brown eyes and then on the sensuous curve of her lower lip. It was a good question. One he'd asked himself a thousand times since. He sighed.

'Do you remember our first kiss?'

She flushed, looked away briefly, then made herself face him when she answered.

'I'm ashamed to say I do not.'

A wry smile turned up one corner of his mouth. 'If you did, I don't think you'd be asking the question.'

Her eyes widened. She knew they were volatile together in bed, but surely it hadn't been that sudden.

'You mean—'

'I thought the top of my head was going to come off,' Sam said softly, and then threaded his fingers through her hand. 'Honey, I'm thirty-seven years old and I've seen the dark side of the moon more than once and lived to tell the tale, but I have never...with any woman...felt the earth tilt beneath my feet like it did at that moment.'

'What did I do?' Harley asked and then blushed. 'I mean, when we kissed.'

'You stared at me like you'd seen a ghost and, truth be told, I knew just how you felt. I'd been thinking about settling down for more than five years but had never met the right woman... until you.'

Harley pulled her hand away from Sam and curled it around her purse instead. Her voice was shaking, her heartbeat pounding against her eardrums so loudly she could barely hear herself speak.

'But surely you can see my position. How can you say I'm the right woman? You don't know me, and God knows I'm ashamed to say I don't remember that much of what happened.'

'I know a lot about you,' Sam said.

Again the thought came to Harley that she might be the victim of a handsome stalker.

'How so?' she asked.

He smiled. 'You told me. I know your great-great-Granny Devane personally slapped General Sherman's face when his men rode their horses up the steps of her plantation house. I know that when you were little you were afraid of clowns and that every time your mother fixed fried chicken livers for dinner, you fed yours to the family cat. I know you're afraid of spiders but once rescued your younger cousin from a flooded creek without any thought of your own safety. I know—'

'Stop! Stop!' Harley moaned, and then buried her face in her hands. 'My God, how could I turn loose so much of myself and not remember it?'

Sam wanted to hold her, but this wasn't the time. He'd come this far to prove to her he was serious about making their sham of a marriage work. But Harley June was going to have to come the rest of the way to him on her own or it would never work.

'I don't know,' Sam said. 'All I know is that I want to give this...give us...a chance. I need it, Junie, and I think deep down you do too, or you would never have said, I do.'

'Not Junie,' she muttered.

'That's not what it says on your butt,' Sam countered.

Her eyes narrowed angrily. 'A gentleman would not remind me of such an indiscretion.'

Fed up with her constant referral to Southern gentility, Sam's eyes narrowed sharply.

'Gentleman be damned, Harley June. I told you once before, I never claimed to be anything but your husband.'

The cab came to a sudden stop.

Both Sam and Harley June looked up, slightly surprised that they had reached their destination so quickly.

'Looks like we're here,' Sam said. Tossing a handful of bills across the seat to the driver, he grabbed his suitcase as he got out and pulled a reluctant Harley out of the cab.

The cab drove away from the curb, leaving them on the sidewalk with nowhere to go but up the front steps of Harley's childhood home.

'You ready?' Sam asked.

'I can't do this,' Harley said, and grabbed Sam by the arm. 'Please! Isn't there anything I can say to make you stop? You don't understand what this news will do to my family!'

'Damn it, Junie, you're twenty-seven years old. Are you trying to tell me you still let your parents tell you what to do?'

'Of course not, but—'

'Fine then,' Sam said, and took her by the hand, pulling her none too gently up the walk toward the house, his suitcase bouncing against his leg as they went.

Harley's feet were moving but her mind had gone numb. She kept thinking at any moment she would wake up only to find this was all a bad dream. But when she heard her father's voice, she knew the nightmare was only beginning.

'Why, Harley! I didn't expect to see you today! Come look at my Sister Ruth!'

Both Sam and Harley turned. Harley felt a muscle jerk in

Sam's hand, but it was the only indication she had that he might be dreading this as much as she.

'Who's Sister Ruth?' Sam asked, as they started across the lawn.

'One of Daddy's rosebushes,' Harley said. 'Roses are his hobby.'

'Oh, yeah, I remember you saying he won a blue ribbon at the Savannah Garden Show last year.'

Harley shook her head as they started across the lawn, wondering what else she had told this man that she didn't remember.

Dewey Beaumont was on his knees beside a massive rosebush bursting with blossoms in all stages of bloom. The flower's apricot color was almost as stunning as the scent. Dewey pushed himself up with a grunt, brushing off the knees of his pants as he stood. He eyed the tall man beside his daughter, noted the suitcase he was carrying and the strained expression on Harley's face and wondered what was up.

'Your mother will have a fit if she sees what I've done to the knees of these pants,' he said, then smiled at Sam and extended his hand. 'I don't believe I've had the pleasure.'

Harley jumped, quickly remembering her manners.

'Daddy, this is Samuel Clay. Sam, this is my father, Dewey Beaumont.'

Sam smiled. 'Mr. Beaumont, it's a pleasure to finally meet you. Harley speaks highly of you, sir.'

Dewey beamed. 'Harley June is my finest achievement in life.'

Harley groaned.

Sam gave her fingers a gentle squeeze.

Dewey frowned.

'Harley...is something wrong? You are pale as one of your mama's sheets.'

One glance at Harley and Sam knew if any explanations were forthcoming, they would have to come from him.

'Mr. Beaumont, Harley's a little nervous right now.'

'Yes, I can see that,' Dewey said, not for the first time eyeing the fact that Sam Clay was still holding his only child's hand. 'Might you be able to explain that for me?'

'Yes, sir. Junie and I got married while she was in Las Vegas. I've come to meet the family and then take her home.'

Dewey was lost. 'Who's Junie? And what does that have to do with—'

'Your daughter, sir. It's what I call her.'

Dewey's mouth dropped. 'My daughter? You married my daughter?' He stared at Harley. 'Harley June Beaumont! Have you nothing to say to me?'

Harley's stomach was rolling, but she surprised herself by answering in a rather calm voice.

'It's true, Daddy. I did marry this man in Las Vegas.'

'Lord have mercy,' Dewey muttered. 'What will your mother say?'

Sam already had a notion that Marcie Beaumont was a true steel magnolia, but he was willing to face anything and anyone for Harley June. He tightened his grip on Harley's hand and smiled.

'Well now, honey, let's just go find out for ourselves, what do you say?'

Without giving her a chance to answer, Sam took off for the house. Harley found herself running to keep up with his stride with Dewey not far behind. They were on the second step of the front verandah when the door opened and Marcie Beaumont came out, her round, cherub-shaped face framed in skillfully dyed, auburn curls. Sam had a moment to notice that her pink, flowing dress was almost the shade of her cheeks and then she was coming toward them.

'Why, Harley June! How sweet of you to surprise your daddy and me like this!' Then she batted her eyelashes at Sam as she must have done since her childhood when she realized that conquering the opposite sex was part of the Southern rite of womanhood. 'And who is this good-lookin' man you have on your arm?'

Sam glanced at Harley. Her teeth were clenched so tight there was a white line around her lips and Sam figured that today the introductions were all on him.

'I'm Sam Clay, Mrs. Beaumont, and may I say it's a real pleasure to meet you. I can certainly see where Harley gets her good looks.'

Marcie beamed as she tilted her head, having to look up to meet Sam's gaze.

'Now aren't you sweet?' she murmured, and cast Harley a flirtatious grin. 'Honey, where on earth have you been keepin' this sweet boy?'

'Under wraps,' Harley muttered.

Sam heard her and stifled a grin. Poor Junie. This wasn't her day, but he was feeling better by the minute.

'Five days ago Junie and I were married in Las Vegas.'

Marcie's expression fell as the possible suitor she'd envisioned for her daughter just faded away.

'I'm sorry, Harley, I don't remember you having a friend named Junie.'

Sam laughed. 'This is Junie,' he said, and slid his arm around Harley, then gave her a quick kiss on the lips.

While Harley's toes were curling from the contact, her mother's breathing had started to sound as if she was strangling.

Marcie grabbed Harley by the arm, all but yanking her out of Sam's arms.

'Harley June, you better tell me this—'

Sam calmly unwound Marcie's grip from Harley's arm and then tucked her hand beneath his elbow.

'It's Clay, Mrs. Beaumont. She's now Harley June Clay. You know, it's hot as blazes out here in the sun. Do you think you might have something tall and cold for us to drink?'

Without waiting for her to answer, he led Marcie into the

house, leaving Harley and her father momentarily alone on the verandah.

Harley looked at her father, almost afraid to speak.

'Daddy?'

Dewey was still a little shell-shocked, but he was starting to grin.

'I don't know where you found him, sugar, but damned if he isn't the first man I've ever seen who got the upper hand on your mama and made her like it.'

Harley blinked back tears and tried to smile, although she felt like laying her head on her daddy's shoulder and bawling. This was so messed up.

'Do you love him?' Dewey asked.

Harley shrugged. 'I'm not sure, Daddy.'

He frowned. 'What do you mean?'

She swallowed nervously, but wasn't going to lie. Not to her Daddy, and not about something as serious as this.

'I don't remember a thing about the wedding…only waking up the next morning with that man in my bed and a heart-shaped tattoo on my hip.'

Dewey's eyes bugged. 'Good Lord! Are you saying you were drugged? If so, then—'

Harley sighed. 'No, Daddy. I wasn't drugged. I was drunk.'

Dewey stared in disbelief, but the longer he looked at his only child, the more his mouth began to twitch. Harley was twenty-seven, almost twenty-eight, and truth be told, he'd been afraid she was going to turn into an old maid like his oldest sister, Mavis. This stunt was the first truly daring thing that Harley had done since her eleventh birthday when she'd announced to her teacher that she was going to be a stripper when she grew up.

He chuckled.

Harley stared.

'You think this is funny?'

'I just didn't think you had it in you,' Dewey said. 'At least you can sleep easy now, knowing you will never succumb to the ordinary things in life.' Then he took her by the hand and started inside. 'We'd better hurry. I wouldn't miss the rest of this show for another year added onto my life.'

They walked in just as Sam was taking a long sealed envelope from inside his jacket pocket. Sam turned, smiling at Harley. She shivered. His smile was almost as devastating as his kisses.

'Mr. Beaumont, I realize you must have a thousand questions you'd like to ask and certainly have concerns as to your daughter's safety.' He handed the envelope to Dewey. 'Inside are the names and phone numbers of my banker, my boss and my pastor. My parents are dead, but I have a brother and two sisters who all live in Oklahoma. Their names and numbers are also listed, although I'd appreciate it if you'd not take everything they say about me to heart. I'm the oldest and growing up, they didn't much like my bossy nature.'

Once again, Dewey was taken aback by the man's ingenuous nature.

'Yes, well...thank you. Of course we have concerns. I will make some calls later.' Then Dewey looked at his wife, whose face was two shades of pink deeper than normal. 'Marcie, I think we'd like some of your fine lemonade.'

Marcie sputtered then squeaked. 'Lemonade! You want my fine lemonade? Dewey George Beaumont, have you no sense of decorum? Our daughter has gone and married herself to a total stranger and all you want is lemonade?'

'I'd take something stronger, if you have it,' Sam said.

Marcie's lips went slack. Harley stifled a grin. Dewey headed for the sideboard in the library where he kept a decanter of sippin' whiskey for occasions out of the ordinary. Dewey was of the mind that this was one of those times.

'You'll be stayin' for supper?' Dewey said, as he poured liberal shots of the amber-colored liquid into glasses for himself and for Sam.

Marcie moaned. 'Dewey! I can't believe you are just standing there letting this happen.'

'Oh, it's already happened,' Sam said, and grinned at Harley. 'Several times now. Right, darlin'?'

Harley wanted to throttle him. How dare he even hint about their lovemaking to her own mother and father?

When Harley didn't answer, Sam just winked and grinned. 'We'd be happy to stay for supper, wouldn't we, Junie?'

'I do not answer to that name,' she muttered, and then pointed at the whiskey.

'Aren't you pouring one for me, too, Daddy?'

Dewey hesitated. 'Daughter, after what you told me, I don't think you have the head for drink.'

Sam handed Harley his glass and poured himself another, ignoring Dewey's sputter of disapproval.

'On the contrary, Mr. Beaumont. Junie's about as centered a woman as I've ever met. For me, it was love at first sight.'

Marcie's shoulders slumped as she glanced at her daughter, her voice just shy of a whine.

'I can't believe you're married.'

Harley tossed back the whiskey as if it were water, blinking back tears as she choked. When she could breathe without fearing fire would come out her nose, she answered.

'Well, Mama, neither can I, but I've got a tattoo on my butt and a ring on my finger that says different.' She set her glass down with a thump. 'Now I am going to peel potatoes, and if I'm real lucky, my knife will slip and slit my wrist and everyone's misery and disappointments will be over.'

She stomped out of the library, knowing that her mother wouldn't be far behind.

'Tattoo? You have a tattoo?' Marcie yelped, and put a hand to her throat in disbelief. 'Dewey, did you hear her? Harley June has gone and gotten herself tattooed.'

Dewey was feeling pretty good about things so far and chose to pour himself another shot of liquor.

'Marcie, you go help Harley finish up supper now, you hear? I don't know about Sam, but I'm feeling mighty peckish.'

Marcie threw up her hands and bolted after her daughter, muttering beneath her breath about morals and traditions.

Sam felt sorry for what Harley was having to face, but there was nothing he was willing to do to change it. He wasn't giving her up for anything or anyone, and the sooner that became evident to all parties concerned, the better off they would be.

'Mrs. Beaumont, this fried chicken is delicious. You soaked it in buttermilk before you battered it, didn't you?'

To say Marcie was surprised by his question would have been putting it mildly. She had alternated between the certainty that her social standing in the community was forever ruined and the knowledge that her daughter was tattooed. Now, to hear this man—the man who had so smilingly announced himself as her son-in-law—ask if she used buttermilk to soak her chicken was almost ludicrous.

'Why, yes, I did,' she muttered.

Sam nodded. 'I thought so. My Grannie did the very same thing. Said chicken wasn't worth frying without it.'

Marcie was interested in spite of herself. The mention of ancestry in any form was of grave importance to her.

'My grandmother didn't cook,' Marcie said.

Sam frowned. 'Wow. I'll bet her husband had a fine time with that. How on earth did her family get fed?'

Marcie's nose tilted upward to snooty and Harley winced. She knew what was coming, but figured Sam had asked for it.

Marcie's mouth pursed primly. 'Why, they hired a cook, just like every genteel family did in those days.' Then she sighed. 'Oh, for the good old days.'

Dewey snorted. 'You don't clean your own house and you haven't cooked a meal like this since last Easter, Marcie Lee, so don't go all pitiful on us now.'

Sam laughed, which insulted Marcie highly.

Personally, Harley just wanted the night to be over.

'I come from people who did their own cooking and cleaning,' Sam said. 'I do my own, between shifts at the firehouse, of course.'

Dewey leaned forward, resting his elbows on the table as he fixed Sam with a curious gaze.

'Sam, what made you want to be a fireman?'

Sam shrugged. 'I don't know. Just always thought I'd like it.' Then he looked at Harley, wishing he could say something that would take that 'shoot me and get it over with' look off her face. 'And I do…like it, I mean.'

'But it's so dangerous,' Dewey said. 'I know this isn't a topic for supper conversation, but were you working in Oklahoma City when that federal building was bombed?'

The animation went out of Sam's face, and when it did, Harley felt as if something inside of her had twisted and cracked. She had a sudden urge to put her arms around his neck and cradle him to her breasts. He looked so—stricken.

'Yes. I was there.'

'Daddy, would you care for another piece of chicken?'

Dewey blinked. Harley was passing him the platter of chicken, and the look in her eyes ended whatever else he might have asked.

'Well, uh, yes, don't mind if I do.'

Marcie wasn't interested in jobs as much as she was his past. If only he had some ancestors of which she could brag, maybe then this wouldn't be a total fiasco.

'So…have your people always lived in Oklahoma?' she asked.

Sam shook his head, glad that the subject had changed. The hell that he and all the other rescuers had seen was still there in the back of his mind, ready to slip out in the quiet of the night.

'No, ma'am. My great-grandfather was originally from Boston. He came to Oklahoma when it was still a territory.'

Harley felt obligated to add her bit to the lagging conversation.

'My friend Susan's family was originally from Boston,' Harley said. 'Of course, that was several generations ago. They've long since become true Southerners.'

Marcie snorted delicately. 'Oh no, Harley June. Susan Mowry's family were carpetbaggers. They didn't come here until after The War of Northern Aggression.'

'Mother! For goodness sake.'

Marcie sniffed delicately, her nose rising a bit higher in the air.

'It's true, Harley June. Carpetbaggers. The lot of them.'

Sam laughed. 'If that's the kind of stuff that matters to you, ma'am, then my ancestral family will probably turn your hair gray. The first Clay to hit Oklahoma, the one I said was from Boston, was running from the law. He married a Kiowa Indian woman and had four children with her before his legal wife caught up with him and ran her off.'

Marcie gasped, her voice just above a whisper. 'And which woman would your lineage be tied to?'

'That would be the Kiowa with the four half-breed bastards.'

Harley hid a grin as her father laughed aloud.

Marcie paled. So much for bragging rights on the son-in-law.

'Anyone for strawberry shortcake?' Harley asked.

Sam cut his gaze toward her, his eyes suddenly dark with promise.

'We had strawberries and champagne on our wedding night. Do you remember, darlin'?'

Harley started to deny it when she flashed on Sam leaning over her, pouring champagne in the valley between her breasts and then licking it off with his tongue. She looked at him then, unaware of the want in her eyes.

'Yes. I remember,' she said softly.

Sam's heart skipped a beat. Glory hallelujah. It was her first moment of honesty.

Marcie scooted her chair back abruptly and stalked into the kitchen in disgust. Dewey stood.

'I'll just go help your mama with the dessert,' he said.

Sam was still staring at Harley and she felt pinned beneath that dark gaze, unable to breathe.

'Do you really?' Sam asked.

'Really what?' Harley whispered.

'Remember.'

She shuddered, letting her eyelids drop for just a moment to shutter the intensity of her emotions. When she looked up, Sam was leaning across the table. She had just enough time to catch her breath before their lips met. The kiss was brief and hot, like heat lightning in a storm.

'Harley, darlin'.'

'Hmmm?'

'When we get back to your apartment, we are going to make love. You know that, don't you?'

It was a warning and a promise and Harley shivered, both from fear and longing. Longing for this evening with her parents to be over and fear that making love to Samuel Clay would never be enough to make up for the rest of what was lacking in this marriage. It was a sham, and she suddenly wasn't so sure that she wanted it to be over.

'You didn't answer me, sweetheart,' Sam said.

'I didn't have to,' Harley said. 'Some things you just know.'

CHAPTER THREE

EVEN BEFORE SAM and Harley left her parents' house to go to her apartment, she'd made up her mind to give their marriage a real try. She wasn't clear on when the notion had settled, but it was somewhere between the time he'd stifled Marcie's continual whine and made her like it, and the joke he'd told that had her father laughing aloud. She couldn't remember the last time she'd seen her father that way—his eyes sparkling and slapping his leg in glee from the punch line of Sam's stupid joke. Something told her that if he could do that to her parents' staid, cocoon-like existence, then she needed to think about what their life might be like.

God knew hers was in a rut. At least it had been until she'd gotten on that plane to Las Vegas. All too aware of the man in the seat beside her, she gave him a nervous smile and clasped her hands a little tighter in her lap, trying desperately to calm down. By the time their cab reached her apartment, she was trembling, but from anticipation rather than fear.

Sam knew Harley was in a panic. He'd seen it set in the moment they'd said their goodbyes to her parents. By the time they'd shut themselves inside the cab, she'd been a mess.

Now that they'd arrived at her apartment, it was up to him to put her at ease, and he knew just how to do it.

He got out of the cab, and as the driver took his bag out of the trunk and set it down on the sidewalk, Sam reached in his pocket for money to pay.

Harley felt as if she was coming down with the flu. Her teeth were chattering and her stomach was turning somersaults. Every muscle in her body was straining to run, and yet the only place she really wanted to go was into Samuel Clay's arms.

The faint light from the streetlight on the corner exaggerated the size of his shoulders, making him seem broader, almost menacing, as he straightened, then turned to face her. He looked at her and smiled and Harley exhaled softly. It was going to be all right.

Sam picked up his bag, took Harley by the hand and together, they started toward the door to her apartment building. A few steps from the door, she stumbled. His grip quickly tightened as he pulled her close against his side.

'Honey…are you okay?'

She sighed. 'I will be.'

He gave her hand a squeeze. Moments later they were inside the building and climbing the stairs to the second floor. Harley opened the door and then looked at Sam.

'Welcome to my home,' she said softly.

Sam set his bag down just inside the door and gave it a small kick as he took her in his arms. Harley sighed again, only this time it was from the inevitability of this moment.

'The door…lock the—'

Sam reached behind him and turned the dead bolt without looking, unwilling to take his gaze from Harley's face.

'I've dreamed about this nonstop for days.'

Harley's knees went weak. 'I'm a little bit scared.'

'June Bug, the last thing I would ever do is hurt you.'

'June Bug?'

'Yeah. We've got a lot of them back in Oklahoma. They're persistent little things, too. They come out at night and spend the biggest part of their lives trying to assassinate themselves against the brightest lights that they can find.'

Harley almost smiled. 'So, are you saying I have a death wish, too?'

Sam shook his head and cupped the palms of his hands against her cheeks.

'No, but you're damned persistent in claiming you don't remember anything about us, and I can't accept that. I *won't* accept that. I think the more time we spend together, the more you're going to remember.'

He brushed her lips with his mouth, letting the sound of her soft moan feed his soul.

'I know you remembered the strawberries and champagne. I saw it in your eyes.'

Sam's hands were underneath her jacket and unbuttoning her skirt. When he pulled her close against him, Harley felt the hard ridge of him against her belly and shuddered with sudden longing.

'Yes, I remembered.'

He was pulling off her clothes now, piece by piece. His voice was tugging at her senses, his touch making her ache for so much more.

'Then make some more memories with me, Harley June. Make them now, before you forget how much you cared.'

Harley reached for his belt buckle.

'First door down the hall on your right.'

It was all Sam needed to know.

Harley's bedsprings squeaked. The rhythm matched the hard body sound of flesh against flesh. Sam was sprawled on top of Harley, his long arms holding the upper half of his weight from her body as he drove home the point he'd been trying to make ever since that day in Las Vegas when she'd come to in a blue fog. No matter what else was lacking between them, it wasn't sexual chemistry.

Harley's heart was pounding, her eyes were closed. Every fiber of her being was focused on the body-to-body contact between her and Sam. With her fingernails digging into his forearms, her legs wrapped around his waist, she was lost in the ride, chasing elusive and mindless pleasure with the stranger who was her husband. The feeling continued to build, pushing them to a frantic need for completion.

The end came suddenly. One second it was just a good feeling and the next thing it was there, ripping through her body and up her throat in a husky, guttural groan.

For Sam, it was the trigger that made him lose his control. In the space of a heartbeat, he was helpless. The climax was upon him, washing over him in waves. One thrust. Another thrust—and another and his mind went blank. Only afterward did he think to raise his weight from Harley as he gathered her in his arms and rolled so that she was on top, resting on him.

He tangled his hands in the dark lengths of her hair as the aftershocks still reminded him of what they'd done.

'Dear Lord,' Sam whispered, and pressed a kiss on Harley's brow.

She was quiet. Too quiet. Lying silently in his arms.

He lifted his head.

'Junie…are you okay?'

'No,' she mumbled.

His heart jerked. In his selfish need for completion, had he hurt her? The thought horrified him.

He scooted her off his chest onto her side, then rose up on one elbow to stare down at her face. Even in the shadows of her bedroom, he could see tears running down her face.

'Baby…what's wrong? Please tell me I didn't hurt you.'

Harley shook her head and then covered her face with her hands.

He had to strain to hear her answer.

'No, you didn't hurt me,' she said.

'Then what's wrong? Why are you crying?'

She looked at him then, her heart in her eyes.

'I didn't know I could feel like this—be like this. I don't know who I am anymore.'

Sam reached for her, encircling her shoulder, then sliding his hand across her back as he pulled her close.

'I do,' he whispered.' I know who you are. You're my wife.'

Harley shuddered on a sigh.

'But that's just it. Don't you see? How can I be a wife when I don't even know my husband?'

Sam felt her confusion, and if he'd been honest, he would have admitted to some worries of his own. But his greatest hurdle had already been passed when he'd found her again.

'Look at it this way, darlin'. We've got this making love stuff down to a science and the rest of our lives to get acquainted.'

'You're a crazy man, you know that?' Harley whispered.

Sam grinned. 'Yeah. Crazy for you. Now come here to me, woman, and close your sweet eyes. We've got a big day ahead of us tomorrow and we'd better get some rest.'

Harley stiffened. 'What's happening tomorrow?'

'For starters, packing what you want to take with you when we fly home. The rest we can have shipped.'

'Home?'

'Yes, baby. Home. To Oklahoma City. I've got to be on duty in two days.'

'Duty.'

Sam smiled. 'If you keep repeating everything I say, we're never going to get any sleep.'

'You mean being a fireman.'

He chuckled. 'It's what I do, remember?'

'You fight fires.'

Sam sensed where this was going.

'Yes, just like I've been doing for the past fourteen years.'

'Have you ever... I mean...were you—'

'June Bug, I was in more danger in Las Vegas when I pulled

you off that poker table than I've been in any fire. I knew the moment your arms went around my neck that I was in too deep.'

'Really?'

'Yes, really.'

He heard her sigh. 'I wish I could remember that.'

This time, it was Sam whose voice was tinged with regret.

'Yes, well, so do I, June Bug, so do I.'

The trip to Oklahoma was anticlimactic compared to the scene Harley's mother had made at the airport in Savannah. She'd cried and she'd begged and then resorted to threats, at which time Sam's patience had run thin. He could tell that Harley was already nervous, and her mother's behavior was adding to her guilt. Despite the fact that he didn't want to incur his new in-law's wrath, he was too afraid of losing Harley to stay quiet any longer. When Marcie grabbed Harley's arm and threatened to disinherit her, Sam lost his cool.

He stepped between Marcie and his wife, his voice low and angry.

'Mrs. Beaumont, I do not appreciate listening to you threaten my wife.'

'She's my daughter!' Marcie cried.

'Then quit acting like a bad version of *Mommie Dearest.*'

Marcie gasped in anger and would have said more but Dewey hushed her instead.

Sam shoved a hand through his hair in frustration and glanced at Harley, who was struggling not to cry.

'Look, I understand your reluctance to see your daughter leave, but no one's forcing her. Don't you want to see her happy?'

'Yes, but—'

Harley took a deep breath and interrupted.

'Then, Mama, you're going to have to trust me to make my own decisions.'

Marcie glared, still unwilling to back down.

'I always dreamed of watching you walk down the aisle in

our church in Great-Grandmother's wedding dress. The vestibule would be filled with lilies and forsythia and I'd be dressed in pink. It's my best color, you know.'

Harley sighed. 'Mama, that's your dream, not mine. Besides, lilies are for funerals and I'm thirty pounds heavier and six inches taller than Great-Grandmother was. I could never wear her wedding dress, even if I waited another forty years to get married.'

'Hush, Marcie,' Dewey said. 'It's Harley June's life, not ours.' Then he looked at Sam. 'I made those calls. According to your boss, you're one of the best firemen on the squad. Your pastor speaks highly of your whole family, and your banker was assuring as well. I am trusting you to care for my daughter, and...' He looked at Harley June. 'I am trusting my daughter has enough sense to take care of herself. If things aren't right, she knows how to get home.'

Sam sighed. 'Fair enough.' He glanced at Marcie one last time. 'Mrs. Beaumont, it's been a pleasure meeting you, and I've promised Junie that we'll come back to Savannah for Christmas, okay?'

Marcie's anger shifted slightly. 'Really?'

Harley nodded and smiled. 'Yes, Mama, really.'

'Well, then,' Marcie said. 'I suppose that's that.'

Within a few minutes of the cease-fire, the plane started to board. No one was more relieved than Sam when Harley allowed him to take her by the hand and lead her down the walkway toward the plane.

A few hours later, the flight attendant had the passengers making preparations for landing at Will Rogers Airport in Oklahoma City. For Sam, it was none too soon.

'This is it,' Sam said, turning into the driveway.

Harley leaned forward in the car, her gaze fixed on the sprawling, single-story brick home.

'It's really nice,' she said.

Sam smiled. 'Don't sound so surprised.'

Harley blushed. 'I didn't mean that—'

'I was teasing,' Sam said, then he pointed toward the front porch as he killed the engine. 'I inherited it from my grandfather. It's a nice neighborhood. You won't be afraid here, I promise.'

'It's not the house I'm afraid of.'

'I hope you're not referring to me.'

There was both shock and hurt in Sam's question and Harley heard it. She looked at him then, still unaccustomed to the fact that this big gorgeous man was actually her husband.

'Just the situation in general,' she said.

Sam hesitated then nodded. 'I can accept that…at least for now.' He leaned across the seat and brushed a kiss across her lips. 'It's going to be all right, June Bug.'

Harley made herself smile. 'So give me the cook's tour, okay?'

They got out and started toward the front porch when someone called out Sam's name. They turned to see an elderly woman across the street, waving at them.

Sam waved back.

She came off her porch and headed for the street before Sam could stop her.

'Sorry,' he told Harley. 'That's Mrs. Matthews. She's nosey but nice.'

'I have survived my mother's raising. I can take anything, remember?'

Sam chuckled. 'Your mother's okay.'

'She's spoiled and controlling and living in the past. Other than that, I'm sure she's no different from anyone else's mother.'

Sam squeezed her hand in warning as Edna Matthews crossed the curb and started up the walk.

'Prepare to be grilled.'

'Yes, well, since you're still smoking from what my mother did to you, I'm sure I will survive.'

Sam grinned. Harley's tongue-in-cheek comment spoken in her slow, Georgia drawl was priceless.

'Sammy, I'm so glad I caught you,' Edna Matthews said, as she huffed and puffed her way to where they were standing, then handed him a small box. 'The UPS man left this on your doorstep day before yesterday morning, but Henry's dog got to it before I could stop him. It's a little chewed up. I hope nothing is damaged inside.'

Sam took the box. 'Thanks a lot, Mrs. Matthews. It's a part that I ordered for my lawn mower, so it should be okay. I really appreciate you being so observant on my behalf.'

She beamed. 'That's what good neighbors are for.' Then she gave Harley a pointed look.

Sam winked at Harley before introducing her to his neighbor.

'Mrs. Matthews, I'd like for you to meet my wife. Her name is Harley June and she's all the way from Savannah, Georgia, so I'm counting on you to make her feel welcome to the neighborhood.'

Edna Matthews's mouth dropped. Sam Clay was considered a prime catch. To hear he'd been taken off the marriage market was quite a coup. She couldn't wait to spread the word. She eyed Harley up and down as if imprinting the image for future use and then smiled and held out her hand.

'Harley June? An unusual name to be sure.'

'It's my mother's maiden name,' Harley said. 'It's not uncommon to do that where I grew up.'

'I see,' Edna said. 'Savannah, you said?'

'Yes, ma'am. It's a beautiful city. Have you ever been there?'

'No. My late husband and I preferred the western part of the States. He was partial to Las Vegas and Reno. Have you ever been there?'

Harley wouldn't look at Sam and resisted the urge to roll her eyes.

'Yes, ma'am. I have been to Las Vegas.'

Edna beamed. 'Well, then. We have something in common

already. As for our Sammy, here, you are to be congratulated. He's considered quite a catch.'

'I consider myself the lucky one,' Sam said, and took the opportunity to end the conversation before Edna invited herself inside as she'd been known to do. 'Thank you again for rescuing my package. Next time I have a cookout, you're invited, okay?'

'Why, thank you, Sammy, I'd be honored. I'll bring my Italian cream cake.' Then she looked at Harley. 'Everyone loves my Italian cream cake.'

'Sounds good,' Harley said.

'Oh, it's marvelous,' Edna answered. 'Do you cook, dear?'

'Yes, ma'am. All Southern girls are brought up to take care of their men, and you know what they say. The way to a man's heart is through his stomach.'

The moment she said it, she eyed Sam nervously, all too aware that the way to his heart had nothing to do with food.

'We're pretty tired now,' Sam said quickly. 'Thanks again, Mrs. Matthews. I'll be in touch.'

He headed Harley toward the door, hoping that Edna Matthews was going in the opposite direction. He turned to look just as he put the key in the lock and was pleased to see her disappearing into her own house. Then he opened the door, picked Harley up in his arms, and carried her across the threshold.

Harley was unprepared for the symbolic moment and caught herself choking back tears.

'Welcome home, Harley June,' Sam said softly, then set her down in the hallway and kissed her.

Harley's heart was pounding when he lifted his head, but Sam wasn't through. He reached in his pants pocket and pulled out a small, gold band, then slipped it on the third finger of Harley's left hand.

'I've been saving this for the right time. Is this okay?'

She stared at her hand, remembering the mixed emotions she'd had the first time she'd taken it off, and then looked up at him, unaware that her thoughts could be so easily read on her face.

'Yes, it's okay.'

Sam lifted her hand to his lips and pressed a soft kiss on the band itself, then gave her a hug.

'The guest bathroom is the second door down the hall on the left. As soon as I get our bags out of the car, I'll give you a tour of your new home.'

He was gone before Harley could think, but instead of moving around, she found herself staring at the small circle of gold on her finger and wondering how something so fragile could make her feel so bound.

Twenty-four on. Twenty-four off. Twenty-four on. Twenty-four off. Twenty-four on. Twenty-four off, then home four days.

After three weeks of marriage, Sam's work schedule at the Oklahoma City Fire Department was, metaphorically speaking, burned into her brain. On the days that he was gone, she cooked and cleaned and worked outside in the yard like a woman possessed. On the days that he was home, she was a little uneasy, still unable to believe that she was living with a man she hardly knew. She knew Sam was doing his best to make her feel at ease, but it was difficult. His brothers and their families had all come calling just long enough to give her the once-over, express real interest in the fact that she'd been named after the father of all motorcycles, tease her about getting married in Las Vegas and let their children stain the living room carpet with Kool-Aid. Even though she'd tried to explain that Harley was her mother's maiden name, they hadn't wanted to listen.

Sam had taken them to task in a jesting manner, telling them to quit picking on the love of his life, and then treated them all to barbecued ribs at a local restaurant. Harley had been overwhelmed by their boisterous manner and more than a little intimidated by the monumental platters of ribs and the amount of beer that flowed with them.

One of Sam's brothers had passed her a freshly topped mug of the brew, which she quickly refused.

'Hey, Sam,' his brother said. 'What did you go and do—marry a little Southern teetotaler?'

Harley had turned instantly, giving Sam an 'I'll kill you if you tell' look, which made him grin.

To her relief, Sam's answer was less than revealing.

'You just worry about your own wife and leave Harley to me,' he drawled, then to her surprise, he leaned over and planted a hard kiss right on the middle of her slightly parted lips.

He'd tasted of barbecue sauce and beer. The swift shaft of want that she'd felt at that moment had pierced clear through to her gut.

He'd seen her expression and whispered in her ear.

'Hold the thought.'

She'd held on for dear life. That night after everyone had gone home, he'd made the thought well worth her while.

There were still the occasional days when she was certain she'd made a big mistake in coming with Sam to Oklahoma, but they were becoming few and far between. Most of the time she was going through the motions until he wheeled into the driveway and then came striding through the front door yelling, 'Hey, Junie, I'm home.'

Life was good. Sex was great. And just when she was getting the hang of being married, she tried to pull a hero routine that would have been better left to Sam.

There was a cat up the tree in their front yard.

Harley had heard it meowing when she'd gone outside to get the morning paper. Thinking little of it at the time, she'd gone back inside. Later, when she'd gone out again to drop some letters in the mailbox, she'd heard it again and took the time to stop under the tree.

She looked up into the foliage and, at first, didn't see it. But then it spied Harley and the meow turned into a loud, plaintive squall.

'Poor kitty,' Harley muttered, and shifted her stance just enough that she could see a fuzzy orange cat face peering down at her through the branches and leaves.

The cat meowed again, this time adding a warble to the squall.

'I'll bet you're hungry, aren't you, baby? If you come down from there now I'll get you a big dish of milk. Come on…here kitty, kitty. Come on, kitty. Come on. Come on.'

'Waarrrooowww.'

Harley dashed back into the house, returning moments later with a piece of bread, thinking that the scent of food might coax the cat down. All she got for her troubles was another squalling wail.

Five minutes and a bowl of milk on the ground later, the cat was still up the tree and Harley's empathy for the situation had gotten completely out of hand. Instead of going back into the house and leaving the cat to come down after the food on its own time, she was convinced that it couldn't come down. Of course the logic that it had gotten up by itself was now completely lost on Harley June. She wanted to help poor kitty out of the tree, at which point, she had another idea—equally as bad as her first one.

There was a ladder in the garage. It hung on the wall above an old bicycle and a pair of Sam's boots that had seen better days. As she dragged the ladder down from the wall, she kept telling herself she could do this. All she had to do was go up the ladder, brace herself carefully as she climbed up through the branches, get poor kitty and then down they'd come.

The first part was simple. The tree was large. The ladder was tall. She went up the steps carefully, and by the time she was halfway up, could already reach the lowest branches of the tree. It didn't occur to her to be worried that the moment the cat had seen her coming up, it had climbed higher, rather than coming down to meet her.

When she looked up to gauge her position and saw the cat still several branches above her, she frowned, thinking that the cat must have been higher up than she'd imagined. Bracing herself by holding on to the closest branches, she swung a leg out around the ladder and put a foot on the branch. Within moments she was off the ladder and in the tree.

'Here, kitty, kitty,' she called. 'Come on, kitty.'

'Maaarrroooww.'

She hefted herself to another branch, automatically elevating her position higher up into the tree, at which point the cat began to hiss.

Harley frowned.

'Look, kitty, don't you want to come down and get some nice warm milk? Come on, kitty, kitty. Here, kitty.'

Harley stretched out her hand. The cat extended its neck, sniffing in the direction of her fingers.

'That's a good kitty. Come on, kitty.'

All she needed was another six inches and she'd have the cat by the nape of the neck. Confident that this could be done, Harley moved just a little bit higher, only slightly aware of the sound of a truck engine coming to a stop beneath the curb.

The door opened—the driver emerging to the tune of country music blasting from the interior of the cab at earsplitting decibels. Harley looked down, saw the top of a baseball cap on a fat man's head and then to her horror, watched her ladder being dragged away from the tree and loaded onto the top of the truck.

'Hey!' she shouted. 'That's my ladder! You can't take my ladder!'

The man gave no sign of having heard her above the din of music as he proceeded to tie the ladder down. To Harley's horror, he got into the truck and drove away.

'Stop! Thief!' Harley shouted.

The driver didn't stop and the cat moved up another two branches, this time completely out of sight.

'Oh fine,' Harley moaned, got a sudden burst of vertigo and

grabbed on to the branches as the ground beneath began to waver and roll.

For several minutes she clung to the tree without moving or speaking while the cat, having tired of something else occupying what had once been its private domain, climbed down on the opposite side of the tree from Harley and proceeded to eat the bread and drink the milk that she'd brought before ambling off down the street in search of quieter quarters.

Harley stared in disbelief, and was then forced to close her eyes again as, once more, vertigo threatened to unseat her.

'Ingrate,' she muttered, and then sniffed as a few errant tears blurred her vision.

Sam wouldn't be home until sometime tomorrow and it was too far to the ground to just climb down to the lowest branches and let go. The last thing she wanted was to break a leg or an ankle. Added to that, not knowing anyone in the neighborhood but Edna Matthews pretty much limited the people who would even know she was missing. The thought of being caught up a tree was only less embarrassing than the fact that she'd torn her shorts. Although she was afraid to check the damage, she suspected it was severe because she could feel breeze on her backside where her shorts pocket was supposed to be.

Time passed.

Enough that her legs were beginning to cramp and her fingers were getting numb. Added to that, she needed to pee. It was, except for that morning when she'd come to in Las Vegas and found herself married, the worst day of her life. The way she figured, she had two choices. She could pee her pants and hope they dried before someone actually found her, or she could forget her embarrassment and start yelling for help.

She opted for the latter.

'Help! Help! Somebody help.'

On the seventh call, she heard the blessed sound of someone calling back.

'Who's calling for help?'

'Me,' Harley answered, and ventured a look down. Edna Matthews was standing on Harley's front lawn looking around in complete confusion.

Edna turned. 'Harley, dear, is that you?'

'Yes,' Harley shouted.

'Where are you?' Edna shouted back.

'Up the tree,' Harley answered.

Edna's mouth made a small *o* as she looked up in disbelief. 'My goodness, dear. How on earth did you get up there?'

'I climbed a ladder and then someone stole it.'

'Oh my,' Edna said. 'Are you all right?'

'No,' Harley said, trying hard not to cry. 'I can't get down.'

'Yes, I can see that,' Edna said. 'Don't you worry, though. I'll go call for help right now. You wait right there.'

She bolted before Harley could answer. Harley laid her cheek against her arm, resisting the urge to laugh. Where the hell did Edna think she could go?

A few moments later, Edna was back. 'I called the fire department, honey. They'll be right here.'

Harley moaned. Sam. Oh Lord. Something told her she'd never hear the end of this.

'Honey?'

'What?' Harley muttered.

'Not that it's any of my business, but why did you go up that tree to begin with?'

'There was a cat up the tree and I thought he couldn't get down.'

'But, honey...how did you think it got up there?'

Harley stifled an expletive. 'I guess I didn't think, did I, Edna, or else I wouldn't be in the predicament.'

To Harley's relief, Edna did not laugh.

'I think I hear a siren,' Edna offered.

'Great,' Harley mumbled and closed her eyes.

CHAPTER FOUR

WHEN THE CALL went out for Sam's company to roll, he donned his gear without thought, concentrating only on the impending job and wondering what they would find upon arrival. It wasn't until he'd jumped onto the ladder truck that the captain had come running out, yelling that the call had come from his residence. Within moments, every fireman on the rig knew where they were going, and although they cast the occasional nervous glance in his direction as the big red engine raced through the Oklahoma City streets, no one spoke. To a man, they were all empathizing with Sam's shock and fear.

For Sam, the ride was a blur. All he could think was that Harley was in trouble. He'd been anxiously scanning the horizon for smoke, but as they neared his home, he'd come to the conclusion that whatever had happened to Harley, it didn't involve a fire—at least not anymore.

As they turned the corner, he saw Edna Matthews standing in his yard and gesturing wildly. Sam was off and running before the truck came to a complete halt.

'What happened?' he yelled, grabbing Edna by the shoulders. 'Where's Harley? Where's my wife?'

'Up the tree,' Edna said, pointing up and over Sam's head.

'Up the what?'

'The tree! The tree!' Edna cried. 'Someone stole your ladder and she can't get down.'

By now, it was evident to all the firemen that no one was in mortal danger. Relief swelled through the crew as they gathered around Sam and looked up the tree.

Sam squinted. He could see a familiar length of bare leg and shoe, but he couldn't see Harley's face.

'Junie. Are you all right?'

Harley rolled her eyes. God, but this was humiliating.

'Someone stole your ladder. I only saw the top of his head but he was driving a big black truck.'

'Why did you climb up the tree?'

Harley resisted the urge to scream.

'It's a long story,' she said. 'Suffice it to say, I want down. Would you please make that happen?'

One of the firemen slapped Sam on the back as another placed a ladder under the tree.

'Sounds to me like she's running out of patience, old buddy. If I were you, I'd save the questions for after she's down.'

'Yeah…right,' Sam said, and started shedding his bunker gear. He dropped the coat, hat and gloves on the ground and readjusted the suspenders on his pants to make sure they would not get hung up on the limbs. The less he took up the ladder, the easier it would be to help get Harley down.

Another one of the firemen waited with Sam, making no attempt to hide his glee.

'Been wanting to meet your new missus,' he said. 'Now's as good a time as any, I suppose.'

Sam glared. 'If you're smart, you will not tick her off.'

The fireman grinned. 'Hell on wheels, is she?'

'Just steady the ladder and shut up,' Sam muttered, and started climbing. 'Hang on, honey. Here I come.'

'Don't hurry on my account. I've been hanging for the better part of an hour now with no immediate plans to turn loose.'

A round of laughter from the men below followed her terse

remark. Sam heard her mutter something unsavory beneath her breath and began climbing a little faster. When he could finally see her arms and then her face, his heart skipped a beat. He could see the tear tracks on her face. Whatever he'd been going to say was forgotten in his need to comfort.

'I'm here, now, darlin'. Can you scoot backward toward me about six inches?'

'Yes,' Harley said, and did as he'd asked.

When his fingers curled around her ankle and then slid up the curve of her leg to steady her, she resisted the urge to cheer. So she looked like a fool to about a dozen men. So what. She was still going to be down from this tree.

'Easy does it,' Sam said. 'Now put your foot here.'

He placed her foot on the top rung of the ladder.

'Okay…good…good. Now the other foot. It's okay. I've got you. You're not going to fall.'

Finally Harley was standing upright, sandwiched between Sam and the ladder that was leaning against the trunk of the tree.

'Thank God…and Edna Matthews,' she said, and rested her forehead against a rung of the ladder.

Sam's nose was against the back of her head, his arms encircling her as she stood. Her hair smelled as if she'd washed it this morning, although there were bits of leaves stuck in the curls. He kissed the back of her neck behind her ear and then gave her a quick hug.

'Ready to go down now?'

'Yes, you go on ahead,' she said. 'I'll follow.'

'We'll go together,' Sam said.

Harley sighed. 'Sam. Please. I'm not hurt. Just stupid. You go first and I'll be right behind you.'

He could tell she was embarrassed and figured that arguing with her wouldn't help.

'Okay, if you're sure.'

'I'm sure.'

He came down the ladder as quickly as he'd gone up. It wasn't until he got down to the ground and looked up that he realized there was a large tear in the seat of her shorts.

'Uh, honey, maybe I'd—'

'Sam! For pity's sake. Allow me the dignity of disembarking from this tree on my own.'

'But your—'

It was too late. She was already halfway down before he could warn her that everyone was going to have a pocket-size view of her backside, and in a most unfortunate place.

Harley was halfway down when she heard the first whistle then a couple of men's chuckles. She heard Sam mutter something beneath his breath and the chuckles stopped, but only momentarily. By the time she got to the ground, every man there except Sam had a big silly grin on his face.

'Well,' she said, pasting a smile on her face. 'I've been wanting to meet the men Sam works with for weeks now, but didn't intend for it to be quite this way.'

'Yes, it's real nice to meet you, too, Junie,' they chorused.

'Harley,' she said. 'I'd really rather be called Harley. Now if you'll excuse me, I'm going into the house and call the police to report a stolen ladder.' Her cheeks were pink with embarrassment as she glanced at Sam, but her shoulders were straight and her chin was held high. 'Sam, we must have the men and their families over for a backyard picnic. We'll grill hamburgers and hot dogs and whoever wants can swim in the pool. You set up a date with the men and just let me know.'

'Hey, thanks, Junie... I mean Harley. We'll look forward to it,' one of them said.

Harley glanced at Sam and smiled primly. 'Now that the emergency is over, I suppose you'll need to get back to the station. I'll let you know what the police have to say about the ladder.'

With that, she pivoted sharply and headed for the house, resisting the urge to run.

Five steps later, a slow wolf whistle sounded, then someone called out in a slow, Okie drawl.

'Hey, Harley...nice tattoo.'

She froze in mid-step and reached behind her, felt the dangling remnants of her hip pocket and gasped. Without missing a beat, she pulled it up over the bare spot, pasted a smile on her face and turned.

'Thank you,' she said primly, then strode into the house as if it was of no consequence that a covey of men she did not know had just seen her bare ass.

'Dang it, guys, you are not helping matters any,' Sam said.

The men laughed among themselves as they began returning their gear to the fire truck and tying down the ladder that they'd used. Just as they were about to pull out, a big black pickup truck came around the corner and then screeched to a halt in front of the house.

The driver bolted from the truck cab, then pulled a ladder from the back of the truck.

Sam frowned. That looked like his ladder. Thinking of what Harley had been forced to endure, he jumped off the fire truck and headed toward the man with single-minded intent.

'What in blazes do you—'

'Look, I am real sorry,' the driver said, still dragging the ladder behind him. 'My boss sent me to pick up a ladder they'd left behind on a paint job yesterday, but they gave me the wrong address. When I got back to the shop, I got chewed out big time for going to 904 instead of 409 Carolyn Lane. I hope I didn't cause any trouble. You got any idea where the owner is? I'd like to apologize.'

'I'm the owner,' Sam said, and took the ladder out of the man's hands. 'You left my wife stranded up a tree. If I were you, I'd get myself back in the truck and get out while the getting is good.'

The driver groaned. 'Oh man, I am so sorry. So I guess she's pretty ticked, huh?'

'That doesn't come close.'

When the front door slammed, they turned. Harley was coming out of the house on the run.

'That her?' the man said.

'Yep,' Sam said.

'Tell her I'm sorry,' the man said, and bolted for his truck.

By the time Harley reached the curb he was almost out of sight.

'Why didn't you stop him?' she yelled.

'He brought it back,' Sam said. 'It was all just a mistake.'

Harley stared at Sam as if he'd lost his mind and then put her hands on her hips and gave him a cold, angry glare.

'Fine, then you can be the one to call the police and tell them that the ladder is back. I've had all the humiliation I can stand for one day.'

Then she fixed the grinning men with a look that wiped the smiles from their faces.

'Don't you people have someplace to be?'

'Load up,' Sam told them. 'I'll hang the ladder in the garage and be right with you.'

Glad to be out of the line of Harley's fire, the men headed for the truck.

'Don't bother,' Harley told Sam, yanking at the ladder he was holding. 'I got it down. I can put it up.'

Sam held on tight, refusing to relinquish the ladder and resisting the urge to turn her over his knee.

'I will put it up and you will take a deep breath before you say another word to me,' he muttered, then turned and headed for the garage.

It was the first sign of anger she'd ever seen in Sam, and it stunned her. Suddenly, she realized she was standing alone in the yard and Sam was already at the house. By the time she got to the garage, the ladder was on the wall and Sam was turning around.

'You over your hissy fit, yet?' Sam asked.

'I do not have fits,' Harley said. 'They aren't ladylike.'

Sam snorted beneath his breath and then grabbed her by the shoulders and hauled her into his arms.

'Honey, my first impression of you was anything but lady-like, and it was enough to make me want to spend the rest of my life with you, so climb off your high horse just like you climbed down out of that tree and get over it. You were the victim of circumstances and you're okay. If the worst you got was embarrassed, then so be it. You don't know how scared I was when we got the call to this address. I don't ever want to feel that sick and empty again, do you understand me?'

Overwhelmed with shame, Harley could barely meet his gaze. She hadn't thought about the call from his point of view.

'I'm sorry,' she said.

Sam shook his head and pulled her close against his chest, holding her so close she could barely breathe.

'God, woman, I would have thought you'd figured out by now that I love you so much I ache.'

He kissed her then, taking what was left of her breath with his words.

'I've got to go,' he said quickly, kissing her again, only this time harder and swifter, groaning softly when he had to let her go. 'I'll be home this time tomorrow and then we'll have four days together. Don't climb any more trees until I'm here to catch you, okay?'

Too stunned to do more than nod, she watched him jog toward the truck, then watched as they drove away. Only after the big red rig was gone did she turn and go back into the house.

The rooms were cool, quiet and empty. It occurred to her then that without Sam's presence, the house was not a home. He made everything come alive—especially her.

She touched her mouth where his lips had been.

I love you so much I ache.

The room blurred before her eyes. The words had never been said before—by either of them. And now the truth was out in the open and Harley had to think about what she felt for him. Was it possible that in this short period of time that she, too, was falling in love? She'd been attracted to him sexually. That was a given. And with passing time, she'd come to realize that her husband was a man whom people trusted and admired. But she'd been so busy trying to cope with the chaos of an unplanned marriage that she hadn't allowed herself to feel. She took a deep breath and closed her eyes, remembering her relief as she'd heard Sam's voice beneath the tree, then knowing as he helped her onto the ladder that he would never let her fall. That was trust. But did she love him, like a woman was supposed to love her man? She wasn't sure. What she was sure of was that Sam was light and laughter and kept her safe.

And he loved her so much it made him ache.

The doorbell rang again, as it had off and on for the last thirty minutes. Harley raced to answer it, sidestepping two firefighters' wives and a half-dozen kids and wondering as she did what on earth had made her invite all these people to their home for a cookout.

She opened the door, recognized the man holding the cake as the firefighter who'd complimented her on her tattoo and tried not to blush.

'I'm Charlie Sterling,' he said quickly. 'This is my wife, Tisha.'

'Come in,' Harley said. 'Sam's out back cooking hamburgers and if you all brought your swimsuits, feel free to jump in the pool.'

'Love your accent,' Tisha said, and took her cake from Charlie's hands. 'You can go outside and play, but be nice, you hear?'

'Real cute, honey,' Charlie said, and patted his wife on the rear as he headed for the kitchen and the patio beyond.

Tisha rolled her eyes and then grinned at Harley.

'He's not quite housebroke yet,' she said. 'Can't take him anywhere.'

Harley laughed. It was the first time since this whole day started that she thought she might have found a friend.

'According to my mama, the best ones are always like that,' Harley said. 'I've got some beans baking in the oven, so follow me.'

'Oooh, you cook, too,' Tisha drawled, then spied the other wives and had to stop for a hug and a hello. It was a couple of minutes later before she made her way into the kitchen where Harley was taking a large pan of baked beans from the oven.

'Those smell heavenly,' she said.

Harley smiled. 'Grannie's recipe, but it makes so much that I never make them unless I have company.'

Tisha gazed around the kitchen, noting the changes that had taken place since Harley's arrival.

'We were all here about three years ago for a party, but that was when Sam had the pool put in. Haven't been here since, but it looks like you've fixed the place up a lot.'

'Mostly just new curtains and paint. Have to do something while Sam's gone to occupy my time. I'm thinking about looking for a job, but haven't decided what I want to do.'

'Did you work before you and Sam got married?' Tisha asked.

'Yes, for an insurance agency. Very boring. I'm not doing that again.'

Tisha filched a handful of potato chips from a big plastic bowl and started munching as she watched Harley flit about the room. First impressions were usually her strong suit, but she couldn't quite put her finger on who Sam's wife really was. Being the nosey person that she was, she pressed on for answers to satisfy her curiosity.

'You sure pulled a good one,' Tisha said.

Harley looked up from the boiled eggs she was peeling.

'What do you mean?'

'Snagging Sam. Taking him off the marriage market, so to speak.'

'Oh, that,' Harley said, and reached for another egg. She had to get them peeled and deviled before the hamburgers were done or the cookout just wouldn't be right.

Tisha frowned. It wasn't exactly the giggle she'd expected from a newlywed.

'Don't tell me the bloom is already off the rose,' she said.

Harley paused and looked up, a slight grin on her face.

'Do you always speak in analogies?'

This time it was Tisha who'd gotten lost in the conversation. 'I don't know what you mean.'

Harley's smile widened. 'Well, first you tell me I pulled a good one and now you're asking if the bloom is off the rose. Why don't you just come out and say what you mean?'

Tisha swallowed the last chip she'd been chewing and dusted off her hands.

'All righty then, since you asked, how long have you and Sam known each other? He never mentioned you until he came back from Las Vegas and then, according to Charlie, you were all he talked about. As for the bloomin' rose, you aren't as gooney-eyed as I expected a newlywed to be.'

'Oh. That,' Harley said, and began cutting the eggs in half and dumping the yolks into a bowl.

She didn't know Sam had come into the kitchen until he slid his arms around her waist and kissed the back of her neck.

'Tisha, are you grilling my ever-loving wife about our love life, because if you are, you're gonna be sorry.'

'Why?' Tisha asked.

'Because ours is so good it'll make you mad at Charlie, and don't tell me it won't. I know the man. He bunks next to me at the station, remember? Ten minutes after a meal, he's asleep.'

Tisha laughed. 'You've got that right. The moon has long since set on the honey part of our life.' Then she sighed. 'But I have to keep him around. Lord knows no one else would have him.'

Harley laughed, more than a little surprised at herself for being so at ease with Sam's public affections.

'What are you making now?' he asked, as he watched Harley mashing a bowl full of boiled egg yolks.

'Deviled eggs,' she said. 'Do you like them?'

There was a glitter in his eyes as he whispered against her ear.

'June Bug, I like everything you do.'

Tisha grinned. 'Obviously, you don't know all of his likes and dislikes yet, but that will come.'

Sam bit the edge of Harley's ear, well aware that she was struggling not to go limp in his arms.

'Shoot, Tisha. We don't know fudge about each other yet, but we're learning, aren't we, honey?'

Harley blushed, but she was one to give back as good as she got.

'Oh yes, and it helps that I'm such a quick study.'

This time it was Sam who was caught by surprise. His eyes widened suddenly and then he burst into laughter.

'And a damned good dancer, too,' he said.

Tisha's interest piqued again.

'You were a dancer? I thought you said you worked in an insurance agency.'

Harley glared at Sam. 'I'm not a dancer and I do…rather, I did, work in an insurance agency.'

Tisha leaned across the counter, her eyes alight with interest.

'So, exactly how long did you two know each other before Sam popped the question?'

Harley knew from the look on Sam's face that he was going to tell the story and while it was inevitable that they would eventually find out, she would have preferred they got to know her better first. However, never one to let a man tell something that she knew she could tell better, she blurted out the truth.

'Beats me,' she said. 'I was drunk at the time.'

The expression on Sam's face was priceless, and then he started to grin.

'Let's see,' Sam added. 'If I remember right, it was about

two hours after I pulled you off the poker table where you were dancing and right before you went swimming in the nude in the waterfall at the Mirage.'

Harley's face fell. 'I didn't.'

'Well...actually, you did,' Sam said. 'But I hauled you out before the cops got there and hid you in the bushes. In fact, that's where I proposed.'

Tisha whooped with laughter, which promptly brought the other wives into the kitchen.

'What's going on?' they chimed, but Harley was too horrified by what Sam was telling her to care.

'I was naked in the bushes?' Harley mumbled.

'No, I had your panties and your bra back on by then.'

She looked down at the egg yolks and groaned, unaware of the rapt attention of their audience.

'I can never go back to Las Vegas again,' she said.

Sam gave her a quick hug. 'Naw, it'll be all right. I can assure you that the few people who saw you in the water weren't looking at your face.'

'Why didn't you tell me?' she moaned.

He shrugged. 'The subject never came up.' Then he dug his finger into the egg yolks and took a quick taste. 'I think this needs some salt.'

'Don't put your fingers in the food,' she muttered, almost as an afterthought, and reached for the saltshaker. 'Was that before or after I got the tattoo?'

'You have a tattoo?' Tisha squealed. 'Where? Can we see? I've always wanted a tattoo but you can't get them done in Oklahoma. Charlie keeps telling me that he'll take me across the border into Dallas, but he hasn't done it yet. What does it look like, Harley?'

Harley looked up, all too suddenly aware that she and Sam had captured quite an audience.

'You must think I'm awful,' she said, and bit her lower lip to keep from crying.

'Oh no,' Sam said. 'You're not awful, darlin'. You're the best... I mean, the best thing that ever happened to me.'

'Well, whoop-de-doo,' Tisha said, and then came around the island where Harley was working and gave her a quick hug. 'Honey, the only thing on my mind right now is how to get through the rest of this day with good manners, because right now I'm so jealous of you I can't stand myself.'

'Yeah, me, too,' another woman said, and several more chimed in.

'Jealous? I made a complete fool of myself.'

Tisha winked at Sam and then blew him a kiss. 'Yeah, but look what you wound up with.'

When Harley realized the women weren't going to turn her into some kind of pariah, she started to relax.

Tisha sidled up close to Sam and tickled him under the chin.

'Sam, honey, did you get a tattoo, too?'

A dark flush suddenly appeared on his cheeks as he swatted at her hand.

'You're a menace to society,' he muttered. 'And I gotta go flip the burgers. We'll eat in five, Junie. Will you be ready?'

'Aren't I always?' Harley said sweetly, reached for the mayonnaise and mustard to finish the filling for her eggs, plopped in a couple of spoonfuls and then blasted him with a smile.

Sam exited the house to the sound of women's laughter. He was all the way out to the grill before he realized he'd forgotten what he'd gone in the house for.

'Did you find the ketchup?' Charlie yelled.

'It's on the way,' Sam said.

Even though it was a lie, it was better than admitting that he'd gotten caught in a trap of his own teasing.

CHAPTER FIVE

SOMETHING BEGAN TO change between Sam and Harley after the barbecue. For Harley, it had been her baptism of fire and one that she'd survived quite nicely. When she realized that Sam's friends and co-workers had not judged her harshly for the manner in which they met and married, she quit judging herself. She began to see Sam, not as a mistake, but as her friend and husband. On the days when he was home, there were times when she forgot that she hadn't known him all her life. Occasionally, she was reminded of the strangeness of her situation, but even then was leaning toward the theory that marrying Sam was the best mistake she'd ever made. He was a tender lover and a fair and just husband. But it was the day she broke down in tears after a phone call from her mother that she learned Sam also considered himself her guardian angel.

She was in the bathroom washing her face and blowing her nose when Sam found her.

'Junie! What's wrong, honey? Are you sick?'

Harley took one look at the sympathy on his face and burst into tears all over again.

'No,' she sobbed, burying her nose against his chest as he took her in his arms.

When Harley cried, Sam got physically sick. It was a phenomenon he had yet to get used to. His stomach was churning as she wrapped her arms around his waist.

'Then talk to me, darlin'. Why are you crying?'

'Mama,' Harley mumbled.

Sam frowned. 'You're missing your mama?'

Harley shook her head and pulled back.

'No! Nothing like that,' she said. 'She called and—'

Her chin quivered again and she shook her head, unable to finish. But Sam saw enough to read between the lines.

'Your mother made you cry?'

Harley sighed and then nodded.

'What the hell did she say?'

Harley shrugged. 'That I've embarrassed her forever…that her reputation is ruined.'

'Bull.'

Harley's tears ceased. In all the time she'd known Sam Clay, she'd never heard him curse. And when he handed her a washcloth and told her to wash her face, she was so stunned by the anger in his voice that she did as she'd been told. While she was washing her face, Sam stalked out of the bathroom and headed toward the living room.

His hands were shaking in anger as he dug through the desk drawer for the number to Dewey Beaumont's home. He found it and dialed, punching in the numbers with short, angry jerks, unaware that Harley had followed him into the room. Two rings later, Harley's father answered the phone.

'Hello, Dewey, this is Sam. Is Marcie there?'

The delight in Dewey's voice was obvious.

'Sam! Great to hear from you, son. How are things in Oklahoma?'

'They're fine, thank you. At least they were until a short while ago when your wife called and made your daughter cry.'

There was a brief moment of silence and then Sam heard Dewey curse beneath his breath.

'I'd like to speak with Marcie if she's home,' Sam said.

'She'll be right here,' Dewey said. 'And for what it's worth, when you get through with her, I'll be batting cleanup, if you know what I mean.'

'Thank you, sir. I would appreciate it.'

'You tell Harley that her daddy loves her and is proud of her, too, you hear?'

'Yes, sir. Now may I please speak to Marcie?'

'Hang on.'

There was a brief moment of silence, after which Sam heard a series of short steps, then an absolute bellow as Dewey shouted out Marcie's name. If he hadn't been so angry, he would have grinned, imagining the look of shock on Marcie's face from being shouted at by her husband.

Back in Savannah, Marcie Lee was so stunned by her husband's behavior that she came running out of the library, convinced that a calamity was about to occur.

'What on earth!' she gasped, as Dewey took her by the arm.

'Sam is on the phone,' Dewey said. 'He wants to talk to you.'

Marcie's mouth pursed in abject disapproval at the tension in her husband's fingers.

'You're hurting my arm,' she said primly. 'And you didn't have to shout. It's so uncouth.'

'Oh, I think maybe I did,' Dewey muttered. 'And when you're finished speaking with Sam, come into the library. You and I are going to have a talk.'

'Dewey, I will not be ordered about in my own—'

'Sam's waiting,' Dewey said, 'but I won't be so patient.'

He strode off toward the library without waiting to see Marcie's reaction.

Marcie, on the other hand, was so stunned by Dewey's unusual behavior that she found herself hurrying to the phone.

'Hello? Sam? Is something wrong with Harley June?'

'Yes, ma'am, there is, actually.'

Marcie gasped. 'I knew it. I just knew it. There she is so far away from all who love her and—'

'Marcie… Ma'am…pardon me for being so blunt, but I need you to shut up now.'

Marcie gasped. 'You can't talk to—'

'Yes, ma'am, I can. I can when it comes to protecting my wife.'

'Protecting? What on—'

'You made her cry.'

Four little words. But they had the effect of a bucket of cold water on Marcie's bruised senses.

'I don't know what you mean,' she said, and knew he could tell she was lying.

'Yes, ma'am, I think you do. I don't know what you said to your daughter, but I would suggest you not say it again. Harley is a wonderful woman and a damn good wife, so it stands to reason that she is a good daughter, as well. Therefore, I cannot understand why a mother would purposefully say hurtful things to someone they're supposed to love. Can you?'

Marcie started to tear. She cried real pretty and knew it. But as the first tears started to fall, she realized that they weren't going to do her any good. No one was there to see them.

'I didn't mean for—'

'But that's just it,' Sam said. 'I think you did. And I'm telling you right now to stop it. Harley is your daughter, not the means to your social calendar. If our getting married has cheated you out of some big social event that you've always dreamed of, then I suggest you invite all your friends to an absentee reception, play that video we sent you last week as part of the night's entertainment, eat, drink and be merry on our behalf and let them see that your daughter is still in one piece and relatively happy. At least she was until you called. Do I make myself clear?'

Marcie was unswervingly single-minded, but part of her upbringing had been to acknowledge a true 'head of the house' and from the tone in her new son-in-law's voice, she had far overstepped her bounds.

'Yes, dear, you do. Please accept my apologies and then put Harley on the phone. I'll tell her the same.'

'No, ma'am. I don't think so, at least not today. Harley's heard the sweet sound of her mother's voice just once too often today. You call next week when we're all in a better frame of mind, okay?'

Marcie sniffed appropriately and then delicately blew her nose, wanting Sam to know that she was crying.

'Yes, I will do that. You tell Harley I'm sorry, though. Will you do that for me?'

Marcie rolled her eyes as she hung up the phone. That hadn't gone well at all. And then she remembered Dewey was in the library waiting and stuffed the handkerchief back in her pocket. Something told her that the more tears on her cheeks, the better off she would be when she faced him.

Sam's anger was still simmering as he hung up the phone. He turned around and saw Harley standing in the door. Unable to read the expression on her face, he caught himself holding his breath. Would she be mad at him for talking to her mother that way, or would it be okay?

'June Bug, I—'

'Sam.'

'What?'

'You are forever my hero.'

Tension slid out of him all at once.

'You aren't mad at me?'

'Hardly.'

Then she crossed the room, wrapped her arms around his neck and kissed him soundly.

Sam's body responded with instant need.

'Yes,' Harley said.

Sam lifted his head and grinned.

'I didn't say anything…yet.'

Harley's eyelids lowered as she leaned against the hard ridge behind his zipper.

'Oh, yes, you did.' She swayed her hips slowly from side to side, knowing how quickly they could give each other pleasure.

Sam groaned. 'Damn… Harley…let me get us to the bed.'

'Too far,' Harley whispered, and slid her hand between their bodies.

Seconds later, they were tearing off their clothes and sliding to the floor.

Harley had a brief moment of lucidity as Sam rolled her on her back and she looked up at the light fixture in the hall. There was a long thin strand of spider-web dangling from the ceiling. She tried to make a mental note to clean it later, and then felt Sam's tongue dipping into her belly button and lost her train of thought. All she remembered was that she'd been right all along. It *was* too far to the bed.

Harley was stretched out on a chaise lounge by the pool, watching a pair of robins in the shade tree overhead, barely aware of the condensation from the ice-cold lemonade in her glass running between her fingers. Tiny bits of sunlight filtered through the canopy of leaves forming her shade, glittering like tiny diamonds against the green. She adjusted her sunglasses on her nose and then sighed.

Today was September 1st. Labor Day weekend. Three months ago today she'd come to in that Las Vegas motel and found herself married. Who could have known how much difference the ensuing ninety-two days would have made in her life?

Sam would be home tonight and then would be off for four days. She could hardly wait. There was so much she had to tell him. She closed her eyes, picturing his face—the way his eyes crinkled up at the corners when he smiled, the way his muscles bunched and rippled as he walked, the way his mouth felt on her lips when he was kissing her good-night.

She shuddered on a sigh. Yes. She had fallen in love. Head over proverbial heels in love. And it was about time. After all, a woman should be in love with the man who was going to be the father of her child.

A faint breeze shuffled the hair against her forehead and she stifled a soft moan. It reminded her of Sam's breath on her face as they made love.

Goodness. Making love. If she'd had half a brain, she should have known that chemistry like that had to come from something other than lust. They'd been made for each other. Sam had seen it from the start. It had just taken her longer to get past the shock of what she'd done to see the man with whom she'd done it.

Now, they were going to have a baby.

Sam's family would be happy for them and her parents would be beyond excited. After the dressing-down Sam had given her mother a month ago, things had been absolutely perfect. Marcie and Dewey called regularly once a week but always had positive things to talk about. Without knowing the details, Harley could tell that the level of power within her childhood home had shifted, but she didn't care how it had happened. All she knew was that her parents seemed happier.

Of course some things would never change. Marcie still saved aluminum foil and took home packets of salt and pepper from fast-food restaurants, insisting that Dewey use them on his morning breakfast while saving the salt and pepper in her fine crystal shakers for company.

As she lay in the lounge chair contemplating the impending changes in her body and her life, she heard the faint but unmistakable sound of sirens in the distance. Her stomach clenched and she sat up with a jerk.

Fire sirens.

She'd long since learned to distinguish them from police or ambulance. And while she knew this was a part of Sam's life that he truly loved, it took everything she had not to show how much she feared his chosen work.

'Hello, dear. Having yourself a nice morning, I see?'

Harley turned and tossed her sunglasses aside. Edna Matthews was waving at her over the backyard fence.

'I rang your doorbell. When you didn't answer, I thought you might be out here,' Edna said. 'I hope you don't mind the intrusion, but I brought you that recipe you've been wanting.'

Thankful for a reason to think of something besides fires, Harley hurried to the backyard gate to let Edna in.

'You know we never mind a visit from you,' Harley said, and held up her half-empty glass. 'Would you like to join me in some lemonade?'

'Thank you, dear, but not this time. My sister is on her way over to pick me up. We're going to the mall. There's a giant Labor Day sidewalk sale. Want to come?'

Harley thought of all the crowds and the heat and quickly declined.

'No, but thanks anyway. Maybe another time.'

'Can't say as I blame you. It'll be a mad crush, that's for sure, but I've always been a sucker for sales. Anyway, here's the recipe. It's quite easy, although you don't need to worry about details like that. You're such a marvelous little cook.'

Harley grinned as she took the recipe. 'Only one of the useful things my mother taught me. It's right up there with knowing how to pick ripe watermelons and keep the curl in my hair on rainy days.'

It wasn't the first time Edna had heard Harley speak of her mother and her unique requirements for being a proper Southern lady. She chuckled.

'I can't wait to meet your mother. She sounds like quite a girl.'

'That she is,' Harley said. 'Have fun with your sister and remember to use sunblock. It's very hot outside today.'

'Already applied it,' Edna said, patting the lines and wrinkles in her pudgy face. 'Well, I'm off. Take care, dear. I'll talk to you later.'

Harley was still smiling as she entered the house. She laid

the recipe card on the cabinet and put her sweating lemonade glass in the sink. Surprised that it was almost noon, she set out a bowl of tuna salad that she'd made the day before and decided to have a sandwich. While she was eating, she began mentally planning the meal she would make for tonight. It had to be special. All of Sam's favorites. He would know when he saw what she fixed that something was up, but she wasn't going to tell him until after they'd eaten. She knew exactly what she was going to say and the way she would say it. I love you, Sam Clay, more than I ever believed it possible to love, and we are going to have a baby. And the moment she thought it, something skittered through her mind that took the smile off her face and sent shivers up her spine.

Harley jumped up from the table and spun around as if someone had just tapped her on the shoulder, but there was no one there. Hugging herself against the sudden dread in her heart, she strode to the patio door. The serenity of their backyard was still in place. The clear, crystal blue water in the pool sparkled brightly in the noonday heat. The pair of robins that had been in the shade tree earlier were now hopping about on the lawn and there were a pair of butterflies in the flower bed having a meal of their own. Nothing had changed, but Harley knew something was wrong.

And then her gaze slid up beyond the treetops where a large black column of smoke was quickly spreading against the sky. Her heart skipped a beat. Something very large was on fire. Remembering the sirens that she'd heard earlier, she clutched her hands against the middle of her stomach and closed her eyes in prayer. Seconds later, the phone rang. She dashed to answer.

'Hello.'

'Harley, it's me, Tisha. Turn on your TV.'

'Why?'

'Just do it.'

'What channel?' Harley asked.

'Any local channel. It doesn't matter. They're all there.'

Harley ran for the living room, carrying the phone as she went. Seconds later she had the remote in hand. The picture came on just as she sat down. The image was a mesmerizing hell. Flames as tall as a three-story building were eating through the roof of a massive, single-story structure. Firefighters were silhouetted between the camera and the fire while long columns of water crisscrossed in the air in a dubious effort to put out the flames.

'Oh my God,' Harley whispered. 'Is it Red company?' referring to the crew on which Sam worked.

'They're there, but so are a bunch of others,' Tisha said. 'It's a four-alarm, honey, but try not to worry too much. The guys have been together for years without coming to any harm. I know this is your first big one, so I thought I'd better call you and tell you not to panic, okay?'

Suddenly Harley's hands were shaking too hard to hold the phone to her ear.

'I don't feel so good,' Harley said. 'I can't talk anymore.'

She disconnected before Tisha could say anything more and then sat in front of the television without moving, glued to the unfolding drama of the fire. That it had occurred at a very large supermarket during business hours had also complicated the firemen's ability to proceed in an orderly fashion. Because of the holiday weekend, a large number of people had to be evacuated from the building, and the parking lot had been packed with an unusual number of vehicles. Everyone had been shopping for Labor Day celebrations. It couldn't have happened at a worse time.

Harley watched, wanting to cry and knowing it would solve nothing. She kept telling herself this was part of Sam's life. It was something she had to get used to. Finally, after more than an hour, programming resumed with only the occasional bulletin updating the viewing area on the disaster. She told herself that the lack of coverage had to mean that everything was going okay, but there was that knot in the pit of her stomach that had nothing to do with fear. It was a helpless knowing that someone she loved was in danger.

The parking lot was a mess. Police had cordoned off the area directly around the building to give emergency vehicles easier access, but the people who'd been in the store were still stuck at the perimeter of the area, unable to get to their vehicles and leave while others were being treated for smoke inhalation and hysteria. The temperature of the day was in the high nineties. Coupled with the intense heat from the fire, many firefighters were being treated for heat exhaustion, as well.

Sam and Charlie had been part of the evac-crew and were nearly blind from heat and exhaustion. Sam had stripped off bunker gear, and was bent nearly double, holding on to his knees to keep from falling while Charlie downed a bottle of Gatorade. The wind was strong, giving power to flames already out of control, but as it blew, it also caught spray from nearby hoses, sending a welcoming drift of mist onto their overheated bodies.

Sam straightened with a groan and took the bottle of Gatorade someone handed him. It was his second, but the much-needed electrolytes in the drink were replenishing fluids and minerals he badly needed. As he turned around, two more units from nearby station houses were arriving. He breathed a sigh of relief, knowing they could use all the help they could get.

Suddenly, a woman pushed her way past the roped-off area and began running toward the firemen, screaming as she ran.

'My son! My son! I can't find my son.'

Sam's heart stopped. A trapped victim was one of a fireman's worst fears. Their captain caught her before she had gone too far, and as Sam watched, saw her gesturing wildly toward the engulfed building, then saw her fall to her knees, screaming as she went.

Tossing aside his drink, he retrieved his bunker gear and headed for their captain. Charlie was right behind him.

'Sir?'

Captain Reed turned, his expression grim.

'She says her son was in the bathroom when they began evacuating the store. She says that when she tried to go after him, they wouldn't let her go, but assured her that store personnel were checking all the offices and bathrooms and that she could find him outside.'

'But she didn't find him, did she, sir?'

Reed glanced down at the prostrate woman and then back up at Sam.

'No.'

'How old is he?'

'Twelve.'

A muscle jerked in Sam's jaw as he gazed back toward the burning building.

'Where are the bathrooms located?' Sam asked.

Captain Reed shook his head. 'Oh, no, you don't. The front of the building is already engulfed.'

'Yeah, but maybe we can get in from the back,' Charlie said. 'I was there only a couple of minutes ago. There's a lot of smoke, but I didn't see any flames.'

The mother heard what they were saying and clutched at Sam's pant legs in deep despair.

'Please! Please let them try. He's my only child.'

'Captain?'

Captain Reed hesitated briefly, then yelled for the manager of the store who'd been standing nearby. When he heard his name being called, he came running.

'Where are the bathrooms located?' Reed asked.

The manager looked panicked. 'In the back of the store. Why?'

'We think we've got someone trapped.'

'Oh, I don't think so. My assistant manager checked. He assured me that all the rooms were empty.'

'Where is he?' Reed asked.

The manager turned, quickly surveying the area, then shouted. A short, stocky man of about forty came running.

'Henry, did you check all of the offices and bathrooms before you left?'

Sam could tell by the look in the man's eyes that he had not.

'I tried,' Henry said. 'But the smoke was so thick I—'

'Dear Lord,' the manager muttered, then gave Captain Reed a horrified look. 'I didn't know! I swear I didn't know!'

'Ma'am, what's your son's name?' Sam asked.

'Johnny. His name is Johnny.'

Sam looked at Charlie and then grabbed the manager by the arm.

'Come with us,' he said. 'Show us the back door closest to the bathrooms and give us a layout of what's inside as we go in.'

The man hurried to keep up with Sam and Charlie, shouting as they ran.

'Two in! Two out!' Captain Reed shouted, and two firemen quickly moved with them, dragging hose lines as they went. Within seconds they were at the back of the building and hooking up to another hydrant while Sam and Charlie put their bunker gear back on. Sam checked his SCBA, making sure that the Self-Contained Breathing Apparatus had the full thirty minutes of compressed air, then settled the visored-helmet on his head.

'Take these,' Captain Reed said, handing Sam and Charlie two-way radios. 'I want to know what's happening at every turn.'

Sam nodded and thrust the radio in one of his voluminous pockets. He knew where he had to go to reach the bathrooms. If God was with him, and if the boy was still inside—

Then he stopped. He wouldn't let himself think past those two ifs. He couldn't think of Harley, or let himself panic at the thought of never seeing her again. All his focus was on the direction he had to go and the boy who might still be inside.

'Ready!' he shouted, and then he and Charlie raced toward

the back door as a spray of water began raining down upon their heads.

As they opened the back door, billowing clouds of black smoke emerged from the opening along with flesh-searing heat. Sam paused inside and looked back for Charlie. He was right beside him, as were the two firemen outside the door with the hoses. The two out would follow with the water for as long as the hand lines would reach. After that, Sam and Charlie were on their own.

Ignoring everything but the task at hand, Sam said a quick prayer and felt for the wall.

CHAPTER SIX

RELYING ON WHAT the manager had told him and the constant spray of water at their backs, Sam put his hand flat against the wall. Using it as a boundary, he began a mental countdown of the distance they needed to go.

Charlie tapped him on the shoulder to let him know he was there beside him. At that point, Sam keyed the hand radio.

'We're in,' he said.

Reed's voice bounced back, giving Sam and Charlie the illusion that they were not alone.

'Good, but don't take any chances. You don't have any time to waste. Do one thorough sweep of what's not burning and get the hell out.'

'Yes, sir,' Sam said, then he and Charlie dropped to their knees and began crawling through the smoke with the imprint of the layout stuck fast in their minds. Two firefighters just inside the doorway continued to man the hand lines, keeping water on Sam and Charlie's backs.

According to the manager, the first two doors they would pass were offices. They would be locked. Then there would be a space set back from the straight line of the wall where the box crusher sat. The opening was ten feet in length and about twenty feet deep. They had to bypass that to reach the next section of wall and the first thing they would come to would be the store's walk-in freezer. Next door on the right would be the men's bathroom. If the boy was where his mother said he would be, he'd be in there, or at the least, close by.

Sam crawled with his flashlight in one hand while keeping the other one on the wall as a guide. Water from the hoses aimed at their backs kept raining down around them, but the effort did little to dilute the smoke. At any moment, Sam knew the whole back of the building could erupt just as the front had already done, and when it did, their chances of getting out safely lessened drastically. Charlie was still with him, holding on to Sam, while following along behind.

Again, Sam shouted out the boy's name, and again his words were muffled by the mask of his SCBA as well as the roar of the fire. He didn't hold out hope of being heard. A few seconds later, he felt a doorknob against the wall and tried to turn it. It didn't give.

The first locked office.

This was good. It meant they were on theright track. He paused momentarily, tapping Charlie on the shoulder and pointing to the door so that Charlie also understood where they were at.

Charlie tapped him on the arm and nodded. They resumed their trek.

A few feet farther Sam felt the second knob. It, too, was locked. But, while they were proceeding according to plan, they had crawled out of the range of the water's spray which had intensified the heat. Before Sam had time to adjust to that fact, he suddenly ran out of wall. He stopped, replaying the instructions he'd been given.

This had to be the space where the box crusher was. It should be about twenty feet deep and at least ten feet in length before he'd find any more wall. Trusting instinct and the manager's directions, he started to crawl, well aware that the farther they went, the closer they got to hell.

A few feet more and once again he felt wall to his right. Charlie tapped him on the leg, indicating that he'd felt it, too. Sam kept on moving, the flashlight's beam little more than a wink in the dense, acrid smoke.

Sam tried to slow his breathing, knowing that at the rate he was going, the compressed air in his self-contained breathing apparatus wouldn't last more than fifteen minutes. They couldn't be far from reaching their goal. All they had to do was keep moving. But the distance from the wall to the next landmark was farther than he imagined. Just when he feared they might be lost, he felt a long, metal handle. Adrenaline spiked.

The freezer. This had to be the walk-in freezer. Only a few more steps and he should be at the door to the men's bathroom. Please, God, let the kid still be inside.

'Johnny! Johnny! It's the Oklahoma City Fire Department. Can you hear me?'

Even as he called out, he knew hearing any answer would now be impossible. The hiss and roar of the fire was like an oncoming storm, and the constant explosions of aerosol cans and cleaning supplies in the front of the store sounded like ground warfare. He swept his hand along the wall, expecting at any moment to feel the doorknob to the men's bathroom, but there was nothing but smooth surface beneath his glove. The muscles in the backs of his legs had started to jerk from the tension of crawling and his gut was in knots. So if he was still on the right track, then where the hell was that door?

One second he was questioning their path and the next he was clutching a doorknob. The men's bathroom! It had to be the men's bathroom! Rocking back on his heels, he grabbed Charlie's shoulder and then slapped the wall. Charlie nodded to indicate he'd seen it too.

Sam made a motion, then he and Charlie stood abruptly. Yanking the door open, they moved inside, quickly sweeping the flashlight beams in every corner. Almost instantly the room filled with smoke, but they had visibility long enough to know that there were two stalls besides the urinal, and they were both empty.

Ah God.

Charlie pointed toward the door. Sam nodded and they immediately turned, retracing their steps out of the bathroom. Either the manager had told him the wrong door, or the boy had tried to make a run for it and failed.

They dropped back to their knees, seeking respite from the thick and boiling smoke. The heat was intense now, seeping through their bunker gear. Everything inside Sam told him to run, to get the hell out while there was still time. His gloves were so hot, he imagined them melting into his skin. Staying any longer was going to be suicide, but oh God, he wanted to find the kid.

He thought of the mother—picturing her waiting—picturing her expression if they came out alone. Just one more sweep. They'd go back the way they came, but down the other side of the wall. Maybe they'd get lucky.

'Let's get out of here!' Charlie yelled.

Sam nodded, but took Charlie by the arm as he pointed.

'Down the other side as we go out!'

'Yeah!' Charlie shouted.

Sam grabbed the hand mike to tell their captain.

'Captain! It's Sam! We can't find the boy. We're coming out down the opposite side of the wall.'

A spate of static cut through the noise inside the building. Sam knew Captain Reed was answering, but couldn't make out anything except the words 'now.' Then he heard Reed shout 'breaking through' and his blood ran cold. The fire must have gone through the ceiling in back.

He pocketed the radio and shouted at Charlie.

'We gotta get out now!'

Charlie nodded and together they began to move. Seconds later, Sam realized he was no longer crawling on concrete. Even through the thickness of his gloves, he could feel the outline of a body on the floor.

'Charlie! We've got him!' Sam shouted.

Charlie crawled up beside Sam.

'You take his legs. I'll get his shoulders,' Charlie shouted.

But before they could move, a fireball exploded. Sam looked up just as a wall of flame came billowing toward them. Slapping Charlie's headgear, he screamed.

'Fireball! Get down!' then threw himself on top of the unprotected boy, pulling him under just as the fireball roared overhead.

The horror of what was above him was equal to the fear of the too-still child beneath him. His mind was reeling. Was the kid already dead, and if he wasn't, how could they keep him alive? They couldn't go out the way they'd come in and there was no other exit except through the fire, which now was no option at all.

And then the answer came as suddenly and clearly as if someone had spoken right in his ear.

The freezer. Get inside the walk-in freezer.

He looked up, reaching for Charlie as he did and then his heart almost stopped. There was a large chunk of smoking metal on the floor that hadn't been there moments before—and Charlie wasn't moving.

'Charlie! Charlie!' he shouted, but Charlie didn't respond. Now Sam had two victims to worry about besides himself.

He scanned the area frantically as burning debris began to rain down on their heads. The freezer couldn't be more than four or five feet behind them. He grabbed his hand mike.

'Mayday! Mayday! We're trapped near the middle. I found the boy but Charlie's down. Repeat! I found the boy and Charlie's down!'

Another loud explosion rocked the building. Sam looked up. The ceiling was awash with flames, beautiful, deadly curls of orange and yellow rolling along the surface of the ceiling, like surf upon the shore—defying gravity while consuming everything combustible in its path.

Rollover—and it was out of control.

He keyed the hand mike again.

'Captain, we're going into the freezer!' he shouted. 'In the walk-in freezer.'

Then he stuffed the mike back in his pocket, grabbed the back of Charlie's coat and one of the boy's legs and started scooting himself backward, dragging the bodies as he went.

The muscles in his back were on fire, he didn't know whether from strain or heat. Although he kept on pulling, progress was slow and he felt that too much time had passed. Certain that he'd veered off course, he let out a shout of relief when he suddenly hit solid wall. He turned loose of Charlie and the boy long enough to feel behind him, and when his fingers curled around the handle on the freezer, he said a quick prayer of thanksgiving. Someone was guiding more than his thoughts.

The freezer opened easily. Sam slid the boy in first, his inert body moving easily and lifelessly along the smooth, cold surface, then he reached for Charlie and dragged him in, too, quickly slamming the door behind him.

Still on his hands and knees, he took off his headgear, lowered his head and fell face forward onto the floor, his heart hammering inside his chest.

The cold against his cheek was like water to a man dying of thirst. Relief from the intense heat of the fire outside was coupled with the knowledge that the power was off inside the freezer, which meant no new air would be circulating. If things didn't go right, they could just as easily suffocate before they were found, but that was a worry for another time.

Sam struggled to get up. He had to know if the boy was breathing. He had to check on Charlie's injuries. But the silence inside the freezer was almost mesmerizing. Only the faintest of sounds penetrated the thick walls. If they died, then so be it.

At least their families would have something to bury besides a couple of bones and some ashes.

Finally, he got to his feet and began feeling along the floor, wishing he hadn't dropped his flashlight. Sweeping his arms out in front of him, he found the first body. It was Charlie. Removing his gloves, he ran his fingers along Charlie's neck, searching for a pulse. It was there, strong and steady. He ran his hands all over Charlie's body but couldn't feel any blood. What he did feel was a definite dent in Charlie's helmet that hadn't been there before. All he could do was hope that Charlie had only been knocked out.

His next concern was the boy. He found him quickly, and tested him for a pulse. Unlike Charlie's, the boy's life was hardly there. The pulse was weak and thready and he could barely detect any signs of breathing. He felt along the floor for his SCBA and quickly slipped it over the boy's head. Whatever air was left in the pack was better used for the kid than for him. With a weary groan, he sat down with a thump. Without light or first-aid equipment, there was nothing more he could do but wait.

Within seconds, Sam began to feel the cold. Confident that Charlie was protected by his gear, his focus shifted to the boy. He opened his coat, gathered the boy up in his arms and pulled him tight against his chest.

'Johnny, can you hear me? You're safe now, but you've got to stay with me. Your mother's outside and she's real worried about you. You're gonna have to be tough, son. Tougher than you've ever been before.'

Knowing there was nothing more he could do, Sam clutched the boy close against his chest. As he sat, he thought of Harley, remembering the laughter in her eyes and the way they made love. Knowing that her life would go on if he died and resenting the hell out of the fact that his might end before they'd had a chance to make this marriage thing right.

* * *

Outside, Captain Reed had gotten just enough of Sam's last message to know they were in trouble. He spun, shouting as he ran.

'I want the Rapid Intervention Team in here now.'

Firefighters sprang into action, stringing new hose lines and grabbing SCBAs as they moved toward the back of the building.

'What's happening?' Johnny's mother screamed. 'Did they find my boy?'

Captain Reed shouted at a nearby policeman.

'Get this woman out of here now! The area is too dangerous for civilians.'

The woman grabbed hold of Reed's arm, her eyes dark with fear and shock.

'I don't move until you tell me what you know,' she said. 'That's my son. I have a right.'

Reed hesitated and then covered her hand with his.

'Ma'am, it's not good. All I heard my firefighters say was that they'd found him but they're trapped. I don't know what his condition is. I don't know if he's alive or dead, but unless I can get my men out, they're all going to die. Please go with the officer. He'll take you to a safer place and I swear that when I know something definite, I'll tell you first.'

'Dear God,' she whispered, and dropped her head as the officer led her away.

Reed resisted a shudder. He had no time to give in to his own emotions. Lives depended on rational decisions. He moved toward the fire, giving orders as he ran.

Harley had known for almost an hour that something was wrong with Sam. Every breath she drew was painful and every second that ticked away was time lost with the man she loved. She sat without moving, staring blankly at a phone that didn't ring. Sam couldn't die because she hadn't told him that she loved him. Life couldn't be that unfair.

Sometime later the doorbell rang, but she couldn't bring herself to answer. Then knocking sounded and she heard the familiar sound of Tisha Sterling's voice.

'Harley! Harley! It's me, Tisha. Are you in there?'

Harley shuddered. Her body was weak with fear, but her need to know was strong. Slowly, she made her way to the door and then opened it.

Tisha grabbed Harley by the shoulders.

'We've got to go! I got a call,' she said. 'It's—'

'Sam's in trouble,' Harley said.

Tisha frowned. 'Who called you?'

'No one,' Harley said, staring blankly at a space over Tisha's shoulders.

'Then how did you know?' Tisha asked.

Although she was unaware of moving, Harley's hand drifted toward her heart.

'I feel it.'

'Get your purse and come with me. I'm not waiting for a call from Captain Reed. Charlie's in danger, too, and I've got to know what's going on.'

Harley shuddered again and then turned around, staring blankly at the room.

Tisha screamed with frustration and bolted for the hall table where Harley usually kept her purse. Sure enough it was there. She grabbed it on the run and then headed for the door, yanking Harley with her as she ran.

The Rapid Intervention Team was fighting a losing battle. Walls had already collapsed on the north side of the building and the steel arches of the long, metal roof had long since caved in.

Franklin Reed was sick to his stomach. He was forty-seven years old and wanted to cry. Ever since the rollover, he'd been second-guessing his decision to let Sam and Charlie go in. If he hadn't they'd still be alive. And they were dead, of that he had no doubt. They would have long since run out of air in their SCBAs. He kept telling himself that they had probably succumbed to smoke before the fire had gotten them, but he didn't know that for sure. Media vans from local television stations were lined up a good four blocks away, but he could feel the long-range lenses trained on him. For that reason and for that reason only, he kept his emotions masked. When he grieved, it would not be in front of a camera.

As he looked away, he saw movement from the corner of his eye and then started to frown. The cops had let two women under the blockade and they were coming toward him. He recognized Charlie Sterling's wife but not the woman she had in tow.

'Damn it,' he said to no one in particular. He didn't want to have to tell Patricia Sterling that her husband was most likely dead.

The air was full of smoke and noise and the moment Tisha and Harley crossed the police barrier they found themselves walking in water.

Harley let herself be dragged along, but she wasn't looking at the tall, stern-faced man in uniform waiting for them at the end of the block. Her focus was on the flames silhouetting him against the sky.

'Oh God,' she whispered, then stumbled.

Tisha caught her by the elbow.

'Don't stop,' she said, her eyes bright with unshed tears. 'And don't look at the fire. Captain Reed will tell us what we need to know.'

Reed came to meet them.

'Patricia, isn't it?' he said, touching Tisha on the arm.

Tisha's chin wobbled, but she made herself smile.

'Yes, sir, and this is Sam's wife, Harley.'

'You shouldn't be here, you know.'

'Where else would we be?' Tisha asked.

Reed shrugged and then glanced at Harley. He took her hand and knew immediately that she was unaware she'd even been touched. Her eyes were wide, her pupils fixed and dilated as she stared in disbelief.

'Mrs. Clay. I'm sorry we have to meet under these circumstances. I tried to make the cookout you and Sam had last month, but my youngest son broke his leg that day playing baseball. My wife and I spent the afternoon and most of that evening in the emergency room. You know how it is.'

Harley blinked. 'I'm sorry,' she muttered. 'What did you say?'

Reed sighed and shifted his gaze to Tisha.

'I'm assuming someone called you or you wouldn't be here.'

'What can you tell us?' Tisha asked.

A muscle jerked in Reed's jaw. Unconsciously, his grip tightened on her arm.

'Sam and Charlie went in after a kid who'd gotten trapped.'

Tisha moaned and then pressed a finger to her lips to keep from screaming.

'And?'

'They found the boy but didn't make it out,' he said. 'Last message we had was a Mayday from Sam. He said something about being trapped and then most of the other words were too garbled to understand. We sent the RIT team in immediately, but they were unsuccessful.' He took a deep, shuddering breath. 'I'm so sorry.'

Tisha covered her face and then went to her knees. Almost immediately, Harley's hand was on Tisha's head.

Reed saw Harley's eyelids drop as she swayed on her feet. Thinking she was going to faint, he caught her by the shoulders, then found himself caught in the undertow of a blank stare.

'They're cold,' Harley said.

'Ma'am… Harley, is it?'

Harley nodded, then smiled. 'But Sam likes to call me Junie.'

Reed sighed.

'Harley, let me help you to a—'

'No, I'll wait here for Sam,' Harley said. 'He's just cold. Somebody needs to get him a blanket.'

Reed's eyes filled with tears. 'Mrs. Clay, please. You and Patricia need to come with me.'

A frown creased the surface of Harley's forehead as she abruptly pulled out of his grasp.

'You're not listening to me,' she said, her voice rising with each word. 'They're not dead. They're cold.'

The store manager had been nearby, listening to what they'd been saying, and then suddenly, a thought occurred to him.

'Captain Reed. Captain Reed!'

Reed turned. 'What?'

'What if she's right? We couldn't make out the last part of the fireman's message, but remember you thought he was shouting for someone to free them. What if he was saying freezer? The walk-in freezer is right beside the bathrooms. What if they took shelter in there?'

For the first time since the roof went in, Captain Reed felt a glimmer of hope. It wasn't based on anything but a young wife's refusal to give up hope and the small bit of truth in what the manager was saying. It wasn't much, but he'd seen miracles before with far less reasons. He pointed to Tisha and Harley.

'Stay with them,' he said, and started toward the fire at a lope.

They were sitting in water, which didn't surprise Sam because the world had surely melted from all the heat. Once he thought he'd heard Charlie groan, and he'd called out to him, letting him know that he was there. But Charlie hadn't responded and so he'd opted to save his breath.

The boy was breathing. Sam knew because he could feel the faint rise and fall of his chest. He also knew that the kid had certainly suffered from smoke inhalation and was in dire need of medical attention, and yet all he could do was hold him in his lap. Frustration coupled with acceptance. They'd come so close. It was damned unfair that it would end like this.

He took a slow, even breath, inhaling the smell of thawing meat and wet paper along with badly needed oxygen. Their headgear was empty of compressed air and the oxygen inside the freezer was depleting fast. He was getting sleepy—so sleepy. Once he thought of getting up and trying the door, just to see if the fire was over. But if it wasn't, fire would be the last thing he saw and he didn't want to die that way, knowing the thing he'd given his life to fight had won out in the end. So he'd stayed inside the freezer with the boy cradled in his arms, listening for the moment when breathing would finally cease, wondering if his would be the first to go.

Don't forget me, Junie. I sure won't be forgetting you.

The boy was so heavy in his arms and he was tired—so tired. He let his head fall back against the wall and closed his eyes. They burned some, but itched even more. His mind wandered again and he had to focus on why his eyes were bothering him. Oh yes. Just a hazard of the smoke. He needed to rest—but just for a minute.

Seconds ticked by and ever so slowly, the boy slid out of Sam's arms and down into his lap as his arms went limp. Except for the constant drip of melting ice, it was quiet—deathly quiet.

Captain Reed's hand mike crackled with static and then he heard a fireman shout.

'We found them!'

He keyed his own mike.

'In the freezer?'

'That's a positive, Captain. We're bringing them out right now.'

'Are they alive?'

'They've got pulses.'

Reed's knees went weak.

'Thank you, Lord.' When he turned around, Harley Clay was there. 'They found them, Mrs. Clay. They're alive.'

'Yes,' Harley said.

Reed stared at her for a moment, and then took her by the hand.

'Harley?'

'What?'

'How did you know?'

'That Sam was alive?' she asked.

He nodded.

'I could feel him…here,' she said, and put her hand on her heart.

Reed shook his head. 'Excuse my language, but I'm thinking that's a sign of a damned good marriage. You two are to be congratulated on making such a good choice.'

Harley nodded, her chin quivering as the Captain walked away. The longer she stood waiting for the men to be evacuated, the lighter her heart became.

Choice?

Maybe. But it wasn't good sense or choice that had first led her to Sam, it had been the champagne. After that crazy ceremony she didn't really remember, then yes, it had been about choices. She'd certainly chosen to stay with him when every instinct she'd had told her it was a mistake. Now they had the beginnings of a wonderful marriage and a baby on the way. Thank God Sam was alive to hear the news.

Suddenly, there was a stirring of people near the doorway and she knew they were bringing them out. She started moving toward the waiting ambulances, desperate to see Sam's face. He would be all right. She knew that just as she'd known he was still alive.

Tisha was there, too. Still crying, but now with tears of relief. Harley moved past her toward the first stretcher.

It was the boy. She looked down, staring past the oxygen mask to the thin, smoke-streaked features of a man/child's face. Pride for what Sam and Charlie had done brought tears to her eyes. No matter how the boy's fate ended, they'd given him another chance at life.

The second stretcher was coming now. She ran to meet it. It was Charlie, his head swathed in bandages.

'Is he going to be all right?' she asked.

'Yes, ma'am,' a paramedic said.

She clutched her hands against her middle and turned toward the smoking building, waiting for them to bring out the man who'd claimed her heart.

Seconds passed. Long, interminable seconds in which her breath caught and started a dozen times, and then she saw them coming with the last stretcher and started to run.

'Sam.'

He heard her voice and opened his eyes. Harley was running beside him, trying to keep up.

'Junie?'

'I love you, Sam. I almost waited too long to tell you, but I'm telling you now.'

Peace settled within Sam in a way he'd never known. He reached for her hand and she caught it, still moving with the men who'd brought him out.

'Thank you, June Bug.'

She started to cry, hiccuping on sobs as she trotted to keep up with the men's longer strides.

'Don't cry, honey,' Sam said. 'I'm not hurt. Just got a little smoke.'

'I'm not crying,' Harley said.

Sam wanted to laugh, but his chest was too sore and tight.

'Then you're leaking,' he said.

Moments later, the firemen lowered him to the ground beside a waiting ambulance. One of the men patted him on the shoulder.

'I need to get another gurney, then we'll load you up in a couple of seconds, Sam.'

'Take your time,' Sam said. 'I've got all I need right here beside me.'

Harley dropped to her knees. Ignoring the streaks of soot and smoke, she laid her cheek against Sam's grimy face.

It took all the strength Sam had, but he got his arms around her neck. His voice was quiet, but the truth of what he said told Harley far more about what he'd gone through than she wanted to know.

'I wasn't sure I'd ever get to do this again,' he said.

Harley started to cry.

'Ah, God, Junie, don't cry. You'll have me bawling, too.'

She kissed him then, tasting fire and smoke and the man who was her husband.

'Sam?'

'What, honey?'

'I'm going to have your baby.'

Shock rocked Sam where he lay. He stared at her in disbelief, gazing at the familiar curves of her mouth, at two very small freckles on the bridge of her nose that she continually denied existed, remembering the way she sighed when he slid inside her, knowing he'd given her all he'd had to give.

He thought of how close he'd come to not hearing this news. Her face blurred, but he quickly blinked away tears.

Ah God.

'Sam?'

He grabbed her hand and pulled it to his lips, almost too moved to speak.

'Thank you, Harley, for giving us a chance.'

'Thank me? I should be the one thanking you,' she said. 'You came after me when I got scared and ran. You loved me when I was afraid to love myself. You're my hero, Sam Clay, now and forever.'

He shook his head. 'I'm no hero. I'm just a man, and only God in heaven knows how much I love you.'

Harley wanted to hug him but was afraid she'd squeeze a part of his body that was hurt, so she settled for another brief kiss.

'I'm getting you all dirty,' Sam said, and pointed to the streak of black that was now on her chin.

Harley shivered. She wanted to strip him naked just to make sure he was unharmed and he was worrying about getting her dirty? If he only knew. Not wanting him to see how close she'd come to coming undone, she made herself smile.

'I've been dirty before. I seem to remember you telling me something about our wedding night and strawberries and champagne.'

'That wasn't dirt. That was good, messy sex.'

Harley wanted to laugh. The fear she'd lived with all afternoon was almost gone, but it was still too fresh to allow much room for joy.

'Sam?'

'What, honey?'

'When you're well, there's something I want to do.'

'Anything,' he said.

'I want to marry you again. I don't want to go through life without remembering our vows.'

Sam's eyes filled with tears. With a few simple words, Harley had shattered what was left of his control.

'It would be my pleasure,' he said.

Harley grinned.

'Oh, yes, Sam, I promise you it most certainly will.'

EPILOGUE

HARLEY JUNE, are you sure you want to do this?'

Harley smiled at her mother and patted her cheek as they waited for the minister to appear.

'Yes, Mama, I'm sure.'

Marcie made herself smile when she wanted to scream.

'It's just so…so…'

'Tacky. The word is tacky, Mama.'

Marcie sighed. 'Yes. Well. I'm sure you know what's best.'

Harley grinned. Mama had come a long way in the past five months just as they all had. Charlie had suffered a concussion from the fire but had quickly recovered. The boy Sam and Charlie had rescued was alive and on the road to complete recovery. The baby she was carrying was healthy and due the day before Valentine's Day. The way she figured it, she could afford to cut her Mama some slack.

And she had to admit, the Love Me Tender wedding chapel left a lot to be desired. It was a cross culture of architectural nightmares, somewhere between *Little House on the Prairie* and *The Best Little Whorehouse in Texas*. Fake flowers hung from rustic beams inside the small chapel, interspersed among what appeared to be chasing Christmas lights wound around two fake pillars near the pulpit. There was a flashing neon cross over the pulpit, while the pulpit, itself, was draped in purple satin with a picture of Elvis embroidered on the front.

Sam stood nearby, his hands in his pockets, deep in conversation with Harley's dad. The two men had taken to each other like ducks to water and the coming attraction of a grandchild had cemented their bond even more. Ever since the day Sam had taken Marcie to task for making Harley cry, she deferred to him with batting eyes and homemade pound cakes, betting on the philosophy on which she'd been raised to see her through. If feminine wiles didn't work on a man, feeding him would.

The baby kicked and Harley laid her hand on her tummy.

'Patience, sweet thing,' she said softly. 'We're waiting on the preacher man.'

No sooner had she spoken when music began to play. The familiar strains of 'Love Me Tender' filled every tiny space inside the room.

'Here we go,' Harley said, and patted her mother on the back.

In the midst of the chorus, there was a loud popping sound at the altar and then a large puff of smoke, through which the preacher appeared; complete with black hair and sideburns, and wearing a white satin jumpsuit. He gave his embroidered cape a dramatic flourish, not unlike that of a cast-off vampire and began to sing along with the song.

'Good Lord!' Marcie muttered, and cast a nervous eye at Harley.

'Mother,' Harley said warningly.

'I'm just startled, that's all,' Marcie said, trying not to glare back at her only child.

Sam caught Harley's eye and winked. Harley stifled a laugh and winked back. So this was what she couldn't remember. No wonder.

'Mother, it's time,' Harley said.

Marcie gathered her matron of honor bouquet tightly against her middle and lifted her chin. In that moment, Harley got a glimpse of her great-great-grandmother Devane standing on the steps of her plantation home and slapping General Sherman for riding through her yard. There was something to be said for Southern women besides their gentle speech and impeccable manners. They had backbones made of steel.

Marcie started down the aisle toward the hip-hunching preacher, thinking she should be carrying a gun for protection, not a handful of daisies. To her relief, the song ended and the preacher stilled before she reached the altar. She caught Sam's gaze and then looked at Dewey and sighed. They were actually smiling. It figured. Men had no sense when it came to decorum.

More music swelled within the room as a taped version of 'The Wedding March' rocked the walls. They all turned to look up the aisle.

Harley was coming toward them carrying a bouquet of white roses in front of her burgeoning belly. The hem of her pink maternity dress brushed gently against her knees as she walked and Sam's heart swelled inside his throat. At this moment, nothing else mattered. He had it all.

And then Harley was holding his hand and smiling at him as they turned to face the preacher.

The words came and went, the same as they had before, and Harley would later realize she still didn't remember saying her vows to Sam. All she'd seen was the love in his eyes—and all she'd heard was the beating of her heart.

Suddenly, the preacher slapped the Bible down on the pulpit and lifted his arms up to the ceiling.

'I now pronounce you husband and wife,' he shouted. 'Thank you ver' much.'

Suddenly, 'You Ain't Nothin' but a Hound Dog,' blasted from the loudspeakers. The preacher looked wild-eyed and bolted for the back where the sound equipment was housed.

Dewey snorted.

Marcie gasped and dropped her bouquet.

Harley laughed out loud.

Sam took her in his arms and kissed the laughter, trying hard not to cry.

It was the best damned day of his life.

* * * * *

Keep reading for an excerpt of
The Troublemaker
by Maisey Yates.
Find it in
The Troublemaker anthology,
out now!

CHAPTER ONE

HE WAS THE very image of the Wild West, backlit by the setting sun, walking across the field that led directly to her house. He was wearing a black cowboy hat and a T-shirt that emphasized his broad shoulders; waist narrow and hips lean. His jaw square, his nose straight like a blade and his mouth set in a firm, uncompromising manner.

Lachlan McCloud was the epitome of a cowboy. She was proud to call him her best friend. He was loyal; he was—in spite of questionable behavior at times—an extremely good man, even if sometimes you had to look down deep to see it.

He was...

He was bleeding.

Charity sighed.

She had lost track of the amount of times that she had stitched Lachlan McCloud back together.

"I'll just get my kit, then," she muttered, digging around for it.

Not that there was any other reason Lachlan would be coming by unannounced. Usually now she went to his house for cards or for dinner; he didn't come here. Not since her dad had died.

She found her medical bag and opened up the front door, propping her hip against the door frame, holding the bag aloft.

He stopped. "How did you know?"

"I recognize your *I cut myself open and need to be sewn back together* walk."

"I have a...*need to be sewn back together* walk?"

"You do," she said, nodding.

"Thank you kindly."

She lived just on the other side of the property line from McCloud's Landing. One of the ranches that made up the vast spread that was Four Corners Ranch.

Thirty thousand acres, divided by four, amongst the original founding families.

Her father had been the large-animal vet in town and for the surrounding areas for years. With a mobile unit and all the supplies—granted, they were antiquated.

Charity had taken over a couple of years ago.

Her dad had always understood animals better than he did people. He'd told her people simply didn't speak his language, or he didn't speak theirs, but it didn't really matter which.

Charity had known how to speak her dad's language. He liked chamomile tea and *All Creatures Great and Small. Masterpiece Theatre* and movies made in the 1950s. Argyle socks—which she also loved—and cardigans. Again, something she loved, too.

He'd smoked a pipe and read from the paper every morning. He liked to do the crossword.

And just last month, he'd died. Without him the house seemed colder, emptier and just a whole lot less.

It was another reason she was thankful for Lachlan.

But then they'd both had a lot of changes recently. It wasn't just her. It wasn't just the loss of her father.

Lachlan was the last McCloud standing.

His brothers, resolute bachelors all—at least at one time—were now settled and having children. His brother Brody was an instant father, since he had just married Elizabeth, a single mother who had come to work at the equestrian center on McCloud's Landing a couple of months back.

But Lachlan was Lachlan. And if the changes had thrown him off, he certainly didn't show it.

He was still his hard-drinking, risk-taking, womanizing self.

But he'd always been that way. It was one reason she'd been so immediately drawn to him when they'd first met. He was nothing like her.

He was something so separate from her, something so different than she could ever be, that sometimes being friends with him was like being friends with someone from a totally different culture.

Sometimes she went with him and observed his native customs. She'd gone to Smokey's Tavern with the group of Mc-Clouds quite a few times, but she'd always found it noisy and the booze smelled bad. It gave her a headache.

And she didn't dance.

Lachlan had women fighting to dance with him, and she thought it was such a funny thing. Watching those women compete for his attention, for just a few moments of his time. They would probably never see him again.

She would see him again the next day and the day after that, and the day after that.

"What did you do?" she asked, looking at the nasty gash.

"I had a little run-in with some barbed wire."

He was at the door now, filling up the space. He did that. He wasn't the kind of person you could ignore. And given that she was the kind of person *all too* easy to ignore, she admired that about him.

"We've gotta stop meeting like this," he said, grinning.

She'd seen him turn that grin on women in the bar and they fell apart. She'd always been proud of herself for not behaving that way.

"I wish we could, Lachlan. But you insist on choosing violence."

"Every day."

"You could stop being in a fight with the world," she pointed out.

"I could. But you know the thing about that is it sounds boring."

"Well… A bored Lachlan McCloud is not anything I want to see." She jerked her head back toward the living room. "Come on in."

He did, and the air seemed to rush right out of her lungs as he entered the small, homey sitting room in her little house.

She still had everything of her father's sitting out, like he might come back any day.

His science-fiction novels and his medical journals. His field guides to different animals and the crocheted afghan that he had sat with, draped over his lap, in his burnt orange recliner, when at the end of his days he hadn't been able to do much.

She had been a very late-in-life surprise for her father.

She'd been born when he was in his fifties. And he had raised her alone, because that had been the agreement, so the story went. Amicable and easy. Which made sense. Because her father had been like that. Steady and calm. A nice man. Old-fashioned. But then… He had been in his eighties when he'd passed. He wasn't really old-fashioned so much as of his time.

He'd homeschooled her, brought her on all his veterinary calls. Her life had been simple. And it had been good.

She'd had her dad. And then… She'd had Lachlan.

And there was no reason at all that suddenly this room should feel tiny with Lachlan standing in it. Because he had been in here any number of times.

Especially in the end, visiting her dad and talking to him about baseball.

She sometimes thought her dad was the closest thing that Lachlan had to a father figure. His own dad had been a monster.

Of course, the unfairness of that was that Lachlan's dad was still alive out there somewhere. While her sweet dad was gone.

"It's quiet in here," Lachlan said, picking up on her train of thought.

"It would've been quiet in here if Dad was alive. Until you two started shouting about sports." She grinned just thinking about it. "You do know how to get him riled up." Then her smile fell slightly. "*Did.* You did know."

"I could still rile him up, I bet. But I don't know that we want séance levels of trouble."

She laughed, because she knew the joke came from a place of affection, and that was something she prized about her relationship with Lachlan. They just *knew* each other.

She hadn't really known anyone but adults before she'd met Lachlan. She'd known the people they'd done veterinary work for; she'd known the old men her dad had sat outside and smoked pipes with on summer evenings.

Lachlan had been her first friend.

He was her only friend. Still.

He'd taught her sarcasm. He'd introduced her to pop culture.

He'd once given her a sip of beer when she'd been eighteen.

He'd laughed at the face she'd made.

"I do not want that level of trouble. I also don't want *your* level of trouble," she said. "But here you are. Sit down and bite on something."

"I don't need to bite on anything to get a few stitches, Charity. Settle down. I know what I'm about."

"You can't flinch, Lachlan, and sometimes you're a bad patient. So brace yourself."

"You could numb me."

"I could," she said. "But I'm not just letting you use all my supplies. I'm stitching you for no cost."

"Considering you normally stitch up horses, you should pay me to let you do this."

"Please. Working on animals is more complicated than working on people. People all have the same set of organs right in the same places. Animals... It's all arranged differently. I have to know way more to take care of animals."

"Yes. I've heard the lecture before."

"But you've never taken it on board."

"All right," he said, resting his hand on the coffee table in front of her and revealing the big gash in his forearm.

She winced.

"Hardass doctor, wincing at this old thing," he said.

"It's different when it's on a person," she said.

Except it really was different when it was on him. Because he was hers.

He was special.

Seeing him injured in any capacity made her heart feel raw, even if she'd seen it a hundred times.

"All right, Doc."

"Okay," she said.

She took her curved needle out of her kit, along with the thread, and she poked it right through his skin.

He growled.

"I told you," she said.

She thought back to how they'd met. He'd been bruised and battered, and in bad need of medical attention.

His had been the first set of stitches she'd ever given.

She swallowed hard.

He winced and shifted when she pushed her needle through his skin again.

"I can't guarantee you that you're not going to have a scar," she said, her tone filled with warning.

"Just one to add to my collection of many."

"Yes. You're very tough."

"Oh, hell, sweetheart, I know that."

"Don't *sweetheart* me." He called every woman sweetheart. And she didn't like being lumped together with all that. She liked *their* things. Baseball and jokes about séances and *Doc*. "How is everything going at the facility?"

She had a hands-on role in the veterinary care of the animals at the new therapy center on McCloud's Landing. But everything had taken a backseat when her dad had declined, then passed. She was working her way back up to it all, but it was slow.

"It's going well. Of course, I am tripping over all the happy couples. Tag and Nelly, Alaina and Gus, Hunter and Elsie, Brody and Elizabeth. It's ridiculous. It's like a Disney cartoon where it's spring and all the animals are hooking up and having babies."

"The domesticity must appall you," she said. But she wasn't even really joking.

She continued to work slowly on the stitches, taking her time and trying to get them small and straight to leave the least amount of damage, because whatever he said about scars, she was determined to stitch her friend back together as neatly as possible.

"I'm glad they're happy," she said.

"Yeah. Me, too. It's a good thing. It's a damn good thing."

But he sounded a bit gruff and a bit not like himself. She had to wonder if all the changes were getting to him. It was tough to tell with Lachlan, because his whole thing was to put on a brave face and pretend that things were all right.

He'd tried that when they'd first met.

She had been playing in the woods. By herself. She was always by herself. Even though she'd been fifteen, she'd been a young fifteen. She'd never really gotten to be around other children. So she was both vastly older and vastly younger in many different ways. She liked to wander the woods and imagine herself in a fairy tale. That she might encounter Prince Charming out there.

Then one day she'd been walking down a path, and there he'd been. Tall and rangy—even at sixteen—with messy brown hair and bright blue eyes.

But he'd been hurt.

Suddenly, he'd put his hand on his ribs and gone down onto his knees.

She could still remember the way she'd run over to him.

"ARE YOU ALL RIGHT?"

"Fine," he said, looking up at her, his lip split, a cut over his eye bleeding profusely.

"That's a lie," she said.

"Yeah." He wheezed out a cough. "No shit."

She'd never heard anyone say that word in real life before. Just overheard in movies and read in books.

Her father was against swearing. He thought that it was vulgar and common. He said that people ought to have more imagination than that.

"That is shocking language," she said.

"Shocking language... Okay. Look, you can just... Head on out. Don't worry about me. This is hardly the first time I've had my ribs broken."

He winced again.

"You need stitches," she said, looking at his forehead.

"I'm not going to be able to get them."

"Why not?"

"No insurance. Anyway, my dad's not gonna pay for me to go to the doctor."

"I... I can help," she said.

She could only hope that her dad was still at home.

He had a call to go out on later, but there was a chance he hadn't left yet.

"Can you stand up?"

"I can try."

She found herself taking hold of his hand, which was big and rough and masculine in comparison to hers.

Like he was a different thing altogether.

She'd seen the boys on the ranch from a distance before, but she'd never met one of them.

He might even be a *man*, he was so tall already.

He made her feel very small. Suddenly, her heart gave a great jump, like she'd been frightened. He made her feel like a rabbit, standing in front of a fox, and she couldn't say why.

But he wasn't a fox. And she wasn't a rabbit.

He was just a boy who needed help.

"Lean on me," she said.

He looked down at her. "I don't want to hurt you. You're a tiny little thing."

"I'm sturdy," she said. "Come on."

"All right."

He put his arm around her, and the two of them walked back to the house. Her father was gone. But his bag was still there.

"I've watched my dad do this a lot of times. I think I can do it."

"Your dad's a doctor?"

The best thing would be to lie. It was to make him feel better, not for nefarious reasons. It wasn't *really* a lie. But of course what this boy meant was a doctor for humans…and she was going to let him believe it.

"Yes. I've been on lots of calls with him. I can do this."

"Good."

She found a topical numbing cream in the bag and gingerly applied it around the wound on his forehead.

His breath hissed through his teeth.

She waited a few minutes before taking out a needle and thread. Beads of sweat formed on his forehead, his teeth gritted.

But when she finished, he looked up at her and smiled.

"Thanks, Doc."

SHE LOOKED DOWN at the stitches she was giving now.

"That ought to do it," she said.

"Thanks. Hey, Doc," he said and he lifted his head up so that they were practically sharing the same air.

His face was so close to hers; close enough she could see the bristles of his stubble, the blue of his eyes, that they were a darker ring of blue around the outside, and lighter toward the center.

What is happening?

Her throat felt scratchy, and her heart felt…sore.

"Yes?" It came out a near whisper.

"I need a favor."

"What?"

"I need you to reform me."

NEW NEXT MONTH!

There's much more than land at stake for two rival Montana ranching families in this exciting new book in the Powder River series from *New York Times* bestselling author B.J. Daniels.

RIVER STRONG

In-store and online January 2024.

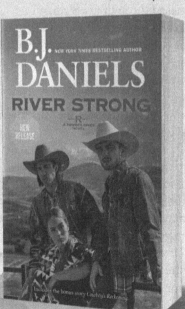

BONUS STORY INCLUDED

MILLS & BOON

millsandboon.com.au